THE
BECKONING HILL

THE

BECKONING HILL

James Playsted Wood

LONGMANS, GREEN AND COMPANY

New York   London   Toronto

1954

LONGMANS, GREEN AND CO., INC.
55 FIFTH AVENUE, NEW YORK 3

LONGMANS, GREEN AND CO. LTD.
6 & 7 CLIFFORD STREET, LONDON W I

LONGMANS, GREEN AND CO.
215 VICTORIA STREET, TORONTO I

PUBLISHED SIMULTANEOUSLY IN THE DOMINION OF CANADA BY
LONGMANS, GREEN AND CO., TORONTO

LIBRARY OF CONGRESS CATALOG CARD NUMBER: 54-7677

Printed in the United States of America

for

E. C. W.

Contents

WHERE WORLDS COLLIDE

1885-1890

He had no sight for pale and twilit pearl
Or thirst for the slow fragrances that swirl
Deliciously about the evening's time,
Nor could he answer sweet bells' wistful chime
With tone-matched wistfulness. He dreamt no dreams
Of longing in that soothing mist which seems
To rise sometimes rose-shadowed in the soul.
He lived when glory came where worlds collide,
And systems smash and formulas abide
But till the lightning spits its vivid gleam
Across the livid sky. Beam racked from beam,
The house of pretense falls. White flashes sear
Truth into darting ruin with the laugh
And twisted lips of earth's essential sneer.
Then the trembling ground was holy ground,
And he was sane, and God's scheme still life-sound.

Chapter 1

THE LOW KITCHEN in the sturdy frame house, standing alone high above the south end of the city and the river, was warm and cheerful. Thomas Stapely, a broad, square-shouldered man of almost sixty, looked a little anxiously at his wife as he shoved himself into his heavy overcoat.

Mary was moving briskly between the black stone sink and the polished black range where steam hissed softly from the curved spout of an iron kettle. The light from the coal fire in the big range glowed through the four holes of a partly opened damper over the firebox. It threw four dancing spots of fiery red and gold on the dark-painted wood floor. Two oil lamps, one on the pine table which was covered with a patterned red cloth and one on the shelf over the sink, gave steady light. Their wicks were evenly trimmed and their chimneys burnished.

It was a point of honor with Thomas Stapely that there be no untrimmed lamps in his house. Agnes, their oldest daughter, had been made to see to the lamps while she was growing up. Now it was Emily's chore. Thomas Stapely knew what the Bible said about untrimmed lamps. He knew what the Bible said about most things.

"I'll not be late, Mary," he said. His accent was of the English Midlands. His tone was slightly defensive.

Mary, tall, slender and straight, her fair hair precisely parted and so arranged that three tight curls lay each side of her oval head, put down the dish she had been drying with a tea cloth, and the lamplight caught its shining surface. Ten or eleven years younger than her husband, Mary had features that were delicate and proud. Her quick-moving blue eyes often showed a gayety at variance with the dignity she could assume when she wished.

She held her husband away from her.

"Are you washed?" she asked with mock disdain.

It was a familiar jest between them. In the old days Mary had never let him kiss her when he came in from work until he had scrubbed his hands and face.

3

The square face with the strong cleft chin relaxed as Thomas smiled. He was freshly shaved and pink from washing in the cold back kitchen. His large, square hands, heavy with blue veins, and showing brown kidney spots looked very white against his dark clothes.

"Yes," he said almost shyly. His clear gray eyes and well-shaped mouth were as strong as the forceful chin and the powerful body. His whitening gray hair was thick and had been vigorously brushed.

Mary inspected his black broadcloth suit, dark overcoat, and the white shirt she had sent to Mrs. O'Rourke to be starched and ironed.

Thomas watched her anxiously.

"You'll do," she decided, flicking what might have been a speck from his coat lapel. She kissed him firmly. "Enjoy yourself."

"You know it's choir practice," Thomas protested, hurt at her light tone. "It's not a social. We have to work on the Easter music as well as the music for tomorrow."

"Enjoy yourself anyway," said Mary dryly. She smoothed down her starched white apron as she picked up her tea cloth. Her blue eyes were touched with mischief and light irony. "You look fine."

On the point of further defending himself, Thomas hesitated. After all the years, he could never be quite sure when Mary was teasing him, but he was pleased. He knew he was a handsome man. He was Tom Stapely, and he liked to look his best when he went to the church.

"Yes, yes," he said impatiently.

Mary laughed. "Go on now. You'll be late."

A yellowish, oak-grained door in a dark corner of the kitchen opened an inch slowly and silently.

" 'Night, Pa," called a muffled voice.

Thomas swung heavily about. His voice roughened.

"Isn't that boy in bed? He ought to be asleep."

"I *am* asleep!" the voice protested. There was a muted child's laugh.

"Willy, you'll wake Emily!" warned Mary. She waved Thomas aside.

His face had showed quick anger. Mary spoiled the boy. Even if he was so much the youngest of the four children, it was wicked to spoil him as she did. It was a Christian's duty to instill the fear of the Lord into the young. The boy had enough of the imp in him. He was not at all like James. It was time he learned a few things. Thomas went out the back steps into the night.

There was still a trace of snow on the ground, but the sharp air was springlike. It had thawed during the day and was only now

4

beginning to freeze again. As he turned the dark corner of his house, and felt his way for a few steps, Thomas Stapely forgot his youngest son and felt again the deep satisfaction that sometimes welled up in him as, a good week's work behind him, he started for Saturday night choir practice at St. Mark's.

Below him as he started down the steep hill were the dim clustered lights of the city stretching far to the north and the scattered nearer lights in the houses and buildings of the South End. A straight line of gas-lighted street lamps showed where South Avenue, which ran into Ilium, cut through South End, almost touching the bottom of the hill. For a moment Thomas Stapely stood still.

The night was very quiet. Few noises from South Avenue, even during the busiest part of the day, reached to the hilltop. He recognized a light here and there. There was Harvey's house, next to Jenkins', which was dark. Beyond was drunken Mike Fuller's and Fred Armstrong's barn of a place. He could make out the lights in the upstairs window of Mrs. Jackson's beyond a flat line of darkness which would be the roofs of the shops on the west side of South Avenue.

That house he had built almost two years ago, and it was one of his best. There were nearly forty houses now in South Ilium that he had built into the ground and from the ground up, and he had made additions or repairs to many another. If any man had built South Ilium, he had done it, and done it all with God's help but without fear or favor from any man, in the twelve years since he and Mary had first left England.

Twelve years? It was almost fourteen! This was 1885, and they had left the Forest of Dean in 1872—almost fourteen years since they had sailed from Liverpool for Ilium, State of New York, "the Birmingham of America."

People had shaken their heads when he had dared lift his eyes to one of the Miss Powitts. Mary Powitt, tall and fair, daughter of James Powitt, mineowner and landowner, would never lower herself to a forester's son, Stapely or no. But Mary had known her own mind and heart, and they'd lived in the cottage at Beechenford with Mary proud as a queen, having her mother and her father to tea, using her best china and treating the rector himself in a way that said plainly she thought her husband as good as he or her father, or any man.

Thomas Stapely had worked hard at his trade in Beechenford and all the towns about the Forest, and first he'd worked hard in London by himself to give Mary all the things he had sworn she was to have. It was many a year, not until the blight of work in the sixties when

5

he'd found himself hard put to earn as much as a pound a week, before he would admit failure.

He had always wanted to go to America, but when the time came it was different. They had thought and talked about it for almost two years before they could bring themselves to the wrench. The same people had shaken their heads again. Mary's father had threatened when he found he could neither dictate nor coax. At the last minute her brother almost decided to go with them, but he was too soft, too weak—and there was no need. He had not so much as to work to live; just ride about overseeing at the iron works and the colliery when it so pleased him. They'd come alone, and he had fought alone. Now he was a master builder, and a landlord who owned tenements and collected rents.

He wished fiercely, as he had many times wished before, that they could see him now. Mary and he had twice been back, but that was not the same thing. Letters were not the same. Suddenly he was terribly homesick for England and the Forest of Dean. For an instant he gave in to a pervading softness of longing, happiness, and dull grief. Angrily he shook it off. Thomas Stapely had no patience with weakness.

He started so rapidly down the hill that he almost lost his footing in a shallow puddle of crusting slush. This was Ilium, and he had helped make it, at least that part of it dominated by the great iron works at the South End. Ilium made iron and steel; Ilium rails, Ilium stoves, Ilium steel plates for ships and railroad cars went everywhere. The city had sixty thousand now. It would have twice that in another few years. All up and down the east bank of the river were the mills with their puddling and heating furnaces. Clear nights you could hear the thudding of the forge hammer even up on the hill, and any night you were apt to see the whole sky lighted when one of the great Bessemers was blowing off.

They had machines down at the iron works which could turn out sixty horseshoes a minute and did—a whole keg full of them before you could turn away. There were eighteen hundred men working at the iron works now and the steel plants. The bell foundries and the stove factories were thriving too, and the collar and shirt factories the other side of Ilium. But that was women's work. Thousands of Ilium women did piecework at home for the collar factories. Not the women of his household.

Now he could even make out the red lantern before the fire house on South Avenue where right now he was building a twenty- by thirty-foot extension. The brick work was done, and Fred and his helper were laying the floor. They would be ready to start the plastering as soon as he could be sure of a night without frost. His bid for the job had been fifty dollars higher than the lowest, but the city had still given him the job. The commissioner himself, he remembered proudly, had said it was because they knew they would get an honest job of work from Tom Stapely.

He was on South Avenue now, on the level, and he could look back up the hill to his own house. It stood above and apart from the row houses of brick and wood along South Avenue and the tightly spaced square workmen's cottages that started up the hill on both sides of every street that climbed from the Avenue. That too he had built, and on the spot, high above everyone else, that he had determined to have from the day he first saw it. Unlike the houses at the bottom of the hill, it had a wide bay window and a porch. The cellar was deep, and the sills were oak. Every nail of that house he had driven himself, with James, a small boy then, eagerly fetching and carrying tools and lumber for him. A frown deepened on Thomas Stapely's forehead for an instant.

All except the roof. He'd had to get August's help with that. He was not good with roofs. He could frame a window or lay a floor with anyone. No one could match him getting up a house frame as sound and true as a level itself, but he could never get the flashing around the chimney. It would look all right, but a bad storm and the roof would leak. He felt resentful about it for a moment. It wasn't as if he hadn't worked hard at roofing.

But it was a good house, a wonderful house. He'd wanted it and he'd made it for himself and Mary and the children. From it they could see down over the city and across the river. Behind it the fields stretched away into the hills. Emily had been born in that house and then Willy. Agnes and James had been born in England. James! His heart warmed as he thought of his eldest son.

He was passing row houses now, narrow and flat-roofed, uneven in height. Some of them sagged. The brickwork at the corners of one was crumbling. They were shabby, unpainted houses, and none of his building. Mostly they were inhabited by Irish workmen, their families and their mongrel dogs.

St. Mark's was in sight now, and that too he had helped build. It was not St. Paul's at which he had used to marvel in his London years, nor Gloucester itself; but it was bigger than All Saints at Great Dean or Calvary at Gray's Field. It could stand next to many a church he knew in the villages about the Forest.

Dim light shone through one of the Gothic windows so he knew that Stephen Binder, the organist, was already there. Probably others had arrived before him. Thomas Stapely was senior warden of St. Mark's now. At home in England, Mr. Olmstead, owner of the Tread-holm Mines, of one colliery at Wakeney and another at Ironford, had been senior warden of Christ Church. Even Mary's father had never been senior warden. He refused to admit the idea that James Powitt, hardly a religious man, had never wished to be.

Warmth flooded Thomas Stapely as he turned into the brick-paved walk to the church. A saloon down the street was brightly lighted, but it did not disturb him at the moment. Horses pulling a big dray that was returning from a late delivery in downtown Ilium, were jogging easily through the dirty snow toward the barn at the coal and lumber-yards down the Avenue. A sudden bright flare against the black sky told him that the great iron works down by the river was busy again. As he opened the heavy oak door of the church, a door that he had fashioned and hung himself, notes of the softly played organ came to him deep and clear. Installing that organ, building its frame and the oaken casing of the console had been one of the accomplishments of his life, a labor of joy and love.

Thomas Stapely felt humble, but he rejoiced and was strong. Nothing of what he had accomplished could he have done without help from Above, but a man can take an honest pride without offending God.

Chapter 2

SHORTLY after eleven o'clock the next morning the big oak door of St. Mark's slowly opened ten or twelve inches. A late winter sun shone brightly on the brick and the stained glass window of which its parishioners were so proud. The sounds of the organ and of voices chanting their praise of God swelled louder. They grew muffled as a boy slipped swiftly through the narrow opening and, after a quick look about the almost deserted Sunday morning street, closed the door gently behind him.

The boy jerked a blue wool stocking cap over his bright, blond head and raced up the street, struggling into a short overcoat as he ran. Halfway down the first block he was joined by another boy who had been hiding behind the scarred bole of a big maple which stood near the curb before a vacant lot between a shabby cottage and a one-story shop.

Their eyes darted greeting, but they did not speak. Side by side they raced until they had turned a corner out of sight of the church.

"Old man see you, Willy? Is he after us?" panted the second boy. He was taller and perhaps a year older than Will. He had a tough, wizened Irish face, and scrabbly black hair fell from under his torn cap.

Will's blue eyes flashed with excitement.

"No. He can't see from the choir. They were doing the responses. Emily knows, but she won't tell. Got it?" he demanded breathlessly.

The other boy's lips twisted. He spoke through clenched teeth as his eyes darted up and down the empty side street.

"Hid it in the barn," he hissed. "C'mon."

They raced off again, three blocks down South Avenue, around several corners, then dodged into an alley between McGraw's foul-smelling saloon and a dirty grocery. Mickey's enormous family lived in what was little more than a shack behind the saloon. Ostentation was less important to Mike Cassidy than convenience to plenty of whisky.

Will, his heart pounding, drew back as they neared the unpainted house with its rotting roof and crazily leaning sides.

" 's all right," encouraged Mickey in a hoarse whisper, though under the freckles and the ingrained dirt he was white-faced himself. "They ain't come back from Mass yet, and the old man's sleepin' it off. Frankie ain't been home all night."

"Where is he?"

Mickey, as befitted the brother of a hero and one who was even now proving his own power and daring, was elaborately casual.

"Think he has to come home every night if he don' wanna? Maybe he's over to Albany. He might even be in Noo York doin' a job for McGraw or somebody. Maybe the cops picked him up again. Probably he's down to River Street right now. They don't dare do anything to him, though. Know why?"

"Why?" begged Will, trembling deliciously.

"Cause the other guy'd kill 'em, that's why. I might even kill Stupe Harrigan myself. C'mon."

"Stupe's all right."

"He's a cop, ain't he?"

Carefully, Mickey opened the broken door of an outbuilding hardly distinguishable from the house itself. He had to be careful, for the door hung on one broken hinge. Inside, Mickey rummaged feverishly under the heaped rubbish in what had once been a horse stall. A

9

finger to his lips, he glared dramatically over his shoulder. With a jerk he pulled out a rusty .22 rifle.

"Jeez!" gasped Will, his blue eyes wide. "Jeez!"

"Shut up!" hissed Mickey. "Wanna wake the old man?" But he was trembling himself.

"How'd you get it? Let me hold it! Let me hold it!" According to Mickey, two men had already been shot with this very gun. One had never been seen again.

"Gimme the knife first."

Will did not take his eyes from the .22 as recklessly he passed over the jackknife he had been holding in the fist in his pocket. The bone handle was broken, but one long blade was still intact, and he had sharpened it to a fine edge in his father's shop. He had a better knife anyway. This one he had got in a swap.

He gazed fascinated at the gun. Frankie Cassidy, Mickey's oldest brother, was one of the leaders of the famous South Avenues. The South Avenues, who had their headquarters at McGraw's, terrorized South Ilium. Victors in many a street brawl with the River Rats and the Third Street gang, they had even put the Ilium Boys to bloody rout when the city's leading gang had rashly decided to invade South Ilium.

On his way home from school that day, Will had witnessed part of that famous battle. Torn between elation and fear, he had picked up a small boulder himself and was waiting his chance as the cursing and shouting gangs had skirmished back and forth on South Avenue, but the sight of one Ilium fighter sprawled across the cobblestones with blood spilling from a nasty cut on his head and of Big Tom Kirk with his face all bloody and one arm hanging limp had sickened him.

Frankie and his pals, armed with pick handles and blackjacks made out of lead pipe or window weights, had driven the foreigners back a full block when two clanging paddy wagons with helmeted cops hanging on ready to jump in with their night sticks had scattered the armies. Will had dropped his rock and run all the way home.

Will knew most of the South Avenues. Fat Grogan always grinned when he saw him and said, "Hello, kid." Once in a while, if they were hanging around outside McGraw's when he went by, Slats Moriarty would say something, but most of them just looked. Tight-lipped, Frankie, who was smaller than Connie Connors or Happy Jones, never said anything, except once he had sworn at Will and Mickey and told them to get the hell home.

Unless there was a paddy wagon full of them, the cops didn't bother the South Avenues. It wasn't safe. Everybody knew they had burned down Bill Moore's house when the foundryman had made them sore;

and they'd smashed his shop and stolen all his stock when a Jew dared open a jewelry and watch repair store on South Avenue. They'd beaten the Jew so badly he never dared come back. In a corner of the school yard, Mickey had shown them the big gold watch and chain Frankie always wore on Sundays after that. Mickey had filched it when Frankie and some of his friends were briefly in jail.

"And I got three bullets out of Frankie's coat the other night," hissed Mickey proudly. He displayed them in a dirty palm.

"Hurry up," urged Will. "You know I have to get back!"

Mickey shoved the .22, which had a short octagonal barrel, under his coat and they sneaked out of the barn, skirted along one side until they had it between them and the house, and headed for fields that were patches of snow and tussocks of coarse brown grass with puddles of mud between. Beyond the fields were woods. Through the trees slivers of silver river mottled with chunks of ice gleamed in bright, wintry sunlight.

Joy in illicit adventure, triumph at his escape from the church, possession of the forbidden firearm, fear of detection and punishment, had Will gasping as they hugged a wire fence, then crossed into a second field.

Mickey, dressed in the worn and torn hand-me-downs he always wore, had little to fear. His black ribbed stockings, one almost green, were already torn at the knees. Will in his Sunday knickerbocker suit of blue serge had to be more careful. A rip in his pants or stockings would mean certain detection. His tight black shoes were already soaked through, as he had not dared hunt for his rubbers under the pew before fleeing the church.

"It's my gun. I shoot first!" warned Mickey.

"Hurry up!"

They were almost far enough from any houses so that the sound would not carry too loudly.

"Put in the bullet!" Will begged.

Mickey's hands were red and chapped. They were wet from snow. He fumbled clumsily with the small copper cartridges. Will, who did not know how to load the gun, watched with helpless impatience.

"What'll we shoot at?"

" 'Providence?' " answered Will.

Far across the field a lone cow lumbered slowly into view. Mickey's eyes lighted wickedly. His lips tightened and his eyes narrowed in imitation of Frankie. He jammed in the cartridge and fumbled at the breech of the rifle.

"No!" cried Will. "No! We can't! Don't!"

Face tight with fear and frenzied pleasure, Mickey pointed the rifle at the distant Holstein and jerked on the trigger. There was what seemed to both boys a deafening report. Black smoke squirted from the gun barrel, then drifted slowly back and up. Undisturbed, the cow went on nuzzling hungrily into a patch of dead grass.

Both boys were running, but they had separated. Mickey was running back toward McGraw's. Will, moaning with fear, afraid to look around toward the cow which he was convinced lay dead or dying, had cut across at an angle and was skipping from tussock to tussock in desperate eagerness to rejoin the safety of South Avenue and St. Mark's.

The empty street and the sight of a half-dozen sleepy horses tethered with their buggies in the long shed behind the church, showed him that he was in time.

His side pained and he had no more breath as he slid into an empty pew in the dimness at the back of the church. The final hymn was about to begin. He dared not squirm down the empty aisle to their own pew. Emily looked anxiously around, and, gasping, he nodded at her. He knew that the recessional would bring the vested choir, followed by the rector in surplice and stole, up the aisle past where he sat.

As the first notes of the organ sang out and the voices of the choir rose above those of the congregation, Will dived under the seat in front of him, bruising his arms on a kneeling stool. There he hid smelling the dust of the carpet, the silk of Mrs. Dunwoodie's Sunday dress and the blacking on Mr. Dunwoodie's Sunday boots. His head whirled with pictures of dead black and white cows, of the accusing faces of ferociously moustached cops, and of his father with his face contorted with rage and his black belt raised to strike.

The choir was passing now where he lay crouched. He saw his father's feet and the lowest inches of his trouser legs as he marched by with firm, heavy tread and heard his deep bass drowning out the others in the choir as Thomas Stapely devoutly and confidently sang the praises of his Lord.

Two minutes later, he had joined his mother, Emily, and Agnes in their own pew. The final phrases of the benediction were still echoing through the church. Will's blue eyes were innocent and clear. His well-shaped face, almost girlishly pretty, was without guile. His fearsomely impressive brother, James, who had sat one pew to the front, scowled at him suspiciously, but Will met his glance evenly.

His mother, tall and stately, engaged immediately in hurried talk with neighboring Mrs. Humphrey, whose rustling silk elegance matched her own. Agnes, stiff in her Sunday best, was being overly gracious to another young woman of her own age who had stepped across the aisle crowded now with people murmuring polite remarks as they left the church. Both girls knew that they were being watched by William Stickman who stood with his mill superintendent father further up the aisle. A half-dozen men were trying to draw Mr. Stickman's attention to them, but they were handicapped by having to maintain expressions of piety and dignity befitting their surroundings.

James, dark bearded and moustached, in black broadcloth and starched white linen like his father, whom he closely resembled, stood waiting for their mother. With all the aloofness and importance of one who would soon be a young doctor, he looked scornfully at nothing in particular over the bobbing heads of those about him.

"One of these times you'll get caught!" scolded Emily fiercely. Her wide forehead wrinkled with anxiety.

At fourteen, Emily already showed certain promise of beauty. Her eyes as blue as Will's were larger and bolder. Her features were handsome, her expression was vividly alive. Though she wore the flounced skirts of a young girl, ending inches above the tops of her high boots to show white cotton stockings, her dress could not repress the budding figure. The round, schoolgirl hat clamped down on her golden blonde head did not hide the thick braids hanging over each shoulder. She had been Will's protector since the day she first took him to school, defending him from the other children, hiding his lapses from their parents, fighting for and with him when it was necessary. She was still his active ally in everything he undertook.

"Keep still!"

"Pa looked right down twice. I was sure he'd see you were gone, so I tried to take up all the room I could." Mary was beckoning, smiling. Emily's voice changed. "Yes, Mother," she answered obediently.

"Get along, you little idiot," growled James, giving Will a jolting nudge.

Will scurried past him. His mother and father, he knew, were going to visit their Aunt Simpson. Agnes was to serve their dinner, which had been put into the oven before they all left for church. Outside he waited for Emily. Ignoring others about them, they hurried off.

"See any cops?" he asked anxiously.

"What? Will, what did you do?"

"Nothing," he boasted darkly.

As soon as they reached the house on the hilltop, he hurriedly changed his shoes, shoving the wet ones far back under his bed in the dark room off the kitchen. By this time Agnes was calling for him to bring in wood for the kitchen stove.

"I'm coming! I'm coming!" he shouted back. "Have to change my shoes, don't I?"

"Never knew you to be so careful before," snapped Agnes. "Emily, get your apron on and mind you don't spill anything."

Proud to be mistress of the house, yet impatient at interference with her plans for the afternoon, Agnes bustled importantly about. James was posed at the bay window in the front room looking down toward the river.

The tall chimneys at the big iron works poked up into the sky like black sticks. In summer they were partly hidden by trees, and less of the curving river's length was visible. James grunted. The grunt signified nothing. It was a practice grunt, an imitation of the mannerism of a professor at the medical college whom he admired.

Agnes, who was twenty-four and James, who was twenty-two, were both dark-haired, as their father had been. Emily and Will looked on their much older brother and sister as alien adults to whom they owed no allegiance. James and Agnes inspired some awe, but could exact neither respect nor obedience.

There was more than a mere difference in age between James and Agnes, and Emily and Will. There was energy which approached the possibility of violence in all of them. But where it was controlled and purposeful in Thomas, sharp and hard in James, stifled by prudery and religiosity in Agnes, it was gay and quick in Mary, wild and reckless in Emily and Will.

Will and Emily, most like their mother in temperament, were quick, lighthearted, and restless. James and Agnes were sober, but the soberness in James was a smothered fire. The violence thudded beneath his cold control. Already he felt scorn for most of his fellows, even for some of his teachers. He looked on the working people of South Ilium with the eyes of a man who was in college and not only knew Albany, but also had twice seen New York.

The older children were their father's pride. Agnes, now at work in a factory office and fearful that because of it her social standing had suffered, had inherited her father's musical tastes and ability. Already she sang Sunday evenings in the paid choir of the big Presbyterian church in Ilium, and at two services had been the soprano soloist.

James, home for the Sunday, as usually he was, was in his third year at the medical college in Albany. Thomas, who could hardly believe that a son of his would soon be a doctor, saw in James the fruition of all his own genius. A doctor was a man apart from other men, a man dedicated, like a minister. He was educated, important.

He drove his own carriage. Already Thomas stood somewhat in awe of his first-born son.

Emily was singing as she set the table in the low-ceilinged dining room. An apt mimic, she had picked up vocal mannerisms from both her father and from Agnes. Thomas thought, and had told Mary privately, that Emily might some day have a better voice than Agnes. He had not told Emily. His younger children would never have the same stature in Thomas' eyes as his older son and daughter.

Emily sang more loudly.

> *Over the garden wall, the sweetest girl of all—*

"Emily! That is *not* a proper song for Sunday! If you *must* sing, sing a hymn."

"But I don't like hymns. I like this song." Waltzing around the table, Emily swung again into the popular refrain.

> *And you may bet, I'll never forget*
> *The night our lips in kisses met*
> *Over the garden wall.*

James wheeled about. "Emily! You heard your sister!" he thundered.

"She can sing what she wants to," said Willy, coming in from the back yard and dropping his armful of wood with a crash into the box behind the stove.

"You keep your mouth shut, you little fool!" advised James.

"The Bible," said Emily maliciously, "says that whosoever shall call his brother a fool shall be in danger of hell fire."

Agnes turned an angry red. "Emily! Cursing and swearing as soon as Pa and Ma go out of the house. And on a Sunday! Set the table as I told you."

"I was only saying what the minister says."

"*He's* the minister," said Agnes.

"Well," said Emily, who was arranging the napkins in their rings by each place, "I don't see—"

"Stop your arguing," ordered James. "You little idiots don't know what you're talking about. I want some quiet here."

"Trying to act like Pa again," taunted Will. As James, enraged, started for him, he fled through the back door into the yard.

Will was elated. He had done it again! None of them except Emily suspected he had not been at church. Mickey would tell the rest of their gang at school what he had done. It would add to the reputation he had achieved by playing hooky again most of the week past. A sudden vision of a dead cow sent a thrill of fear through him, but he was getting very hungry. Cautiously he opened the kitchen door and looked in. James was not in sight. Dinner, he could see, was almost ready.

A few minutes later James, standing at the head of the table in their father's place, carved as importantly as though he were dissecting a cadaver. Agnes, seated in their mother's place, was fussing placidly with the knitted pink and blue and ribboned tea cosy. Emily and Will, sitting together at one side of the table had been sternly told to be still.

The dinner was good, the fare hot and substantial. The Stapelys ate well, just as, in most ways, they lived a little better than their neighbors. They had a finer home, and more and finer furniture. Thomas might have left the plastering rough as it had been in the forest lodge where he had been born, and contented himself with oak benches to sit on, but he had sworn that Mary would have as good in America as she had had at her home in England. She did not, but there were oak, mahogany, and walnut pieces in the Stapely house, good Brussels carpeting, and really fine china. South Ilium, even the envious and derisive, was impressed, as Thomas intended it should be.

"Stop shoveling your food," ordered James irritably, though not as irritably as he would have spoken before dinner. He chewed noisily on another piece of well-done beef.

"I'm only eating," protested Will indignantly. "Can't I eat? More Yorkshire pudding, please, and more gravy." He held out his plate to Agnes.

"He's a growing boy," said Agnes firmly, and dipped deep into the pudding.

Even though it was Sunday, she was planning to baste the seam of her new blue silk so she could wear it to choir at the Presbyterian church that evening. She had been forced to forego morning service there in order to free her mother for the promised visit to Aunt Simpson's. Resentful at first, she no longer was.

Richard had come to St. Mark's that morning instead of going to his own church. That might mean only that he wanted to attend church with his sister and brother-in-law. She hoped it meant more. And he would be at the Presbyterian church that night.

"Thank you," said Will dutifully, as Agnes handed back his plate. He broke off a huge piece of the pudding and sloshed it in the beef gravy.

But Emily was nudging him violently. She whispered something and seemed about to choke.

"What is it now?" demanded James, his carefully trimmed black whiskers bristling. But his face was growing red.

All of them stared at him.

"What *is* it?" shouted James more loudly.

"He's—he's—" Emily swallowed hard and tried again but could get no further. Gagging with repressed laughter, she could only point.

It was then that Will, till then intent on his dinner, saw. His eyes widened in unbelief.

"It's spikes," he said earnestly. "He's got spikes on his moustache."

He and Emily burst into uncontrollable laughter. Even Agnes first looked amused, then laughed in ladylike fashion.

James swelled dangerously. He had, indeed, while awaiting dinner surreptitiously waxed the ends of the moustache he had been carefully tending for months.

"He looks—" began Emily. "He looks—" She gestured expressively. Rocking back and forth in her chair, her face suffused with derisive merriment, she gave up.

But Will had understood. With his pointed beard and waxed moustache James looked like the devil—like the pictures of Mephistopheles in the Sunday school books. It was what he meant when he shouted, "Like the devil! He looks like the devil!"

James leaped to his feet, almost overturning his chair.

"Shut up!" he roared. "Shut up or I'll kill you."

His beard stuck out almost straight. His waxed moustache did incredible maneuvers as his face grew contorted with wrath. It was too much for Emily and Will. The angrier James grew, the funnier he looked. They were so completely overcome that they could only clutch at each other for support while the tears streamed down Emily's face and Will gagged and choked.

"Shut up, I say!" cried James, his face going white. Without further warning he flung the dinner knife in his hand straight at Will's face. It chipped the plaster behind Will, a foot above his head, clung for an instant to the wall, then·clattered to the floor.

Agnes jumped up, overturning her teacup and catching her shirtwaist on the table edge.

For seconds they all stared at each other in horrified silence. Fear had expelled the anger from James's eyes, although his face was still baleful. Will was white. Agnes had begun to cry.

"Mother will see the tablecloth all stained!"

Will jumped up, grasped Emily's hand, and they ran into the kitchen and out into the yard. He pulled her after him toward the big workshop and shed that stood back from the house. They rushed inside and Will barricaded the door with saw horses and some timbers he lugged hurriedly across the floor. Emily added a broken crate and an almost empty keg of sixpenny nails.

They were breathing hard.

"He'll kill us!" whispered Will. "Gimme that pickax. I'll show him. Thinks he's as good as Pa. *Doctor* Stapely! Old pill swiller!"

Emily began to giggle again.

"His moustache looked like the cat's did when he got stuck up with honey out of that old bottle!"

Will laughed, but he was watching the house anxiously out of a window that was clogged with dirt, sawdust, and cobwebs.

"He isn't coming yet. He better not!"

"There's Agnes. She's calling us. Bet she wants us to do the dishes. Let her do them herself."

"*Em*-ly, *Wil*-ly!" screamed Agnes from the back steps. She was looking exasperatedly in every direction. Her angry shriek penetrated the thin walls of the shop. "*Em*-ly, *Wil*-ly!" Then her voice changed and she began to sing their names coaxingly. Her listeners knew it was because she had suddenly realized that their neighbors down the hill might hear her, and Agnes had her character as a sweet and talented young lady to uphold. "Emily," she trilled. "Willy! Willy, dear!"

"Listen to her," said Will disgustedly.

"And look at her," Emily added.

Head cocked slightly, Agnes was listening to her voice carry in the clear, hill air.

"Thinks she can sing!" Emily muttered, brushing a cobweb off her smudged nose.

"I think she sings all right," said Will critically. "So does Pa."

"I can sing just as well as she can. Better."

"When you're older, maybe," said Will doubtfully.

"I can now. Listen—"

"No! They'll hear us. We've got to keep still." Will paused impressively, but he could keep the glorious and frightening secret no longer. "Oh, I shot a cow this morning," he said, as though he had just remembered it.

"You *what?*"

The confession had all the effect Will wished. Emily'e eyes rounded to a blueness of amazed disbelief. Her expressive mouth curled back to show her white, perfectly formed teeth. There was sawdust in her bright hair and there were smudges on her cheeks.

"It was really Mickey shot it," Will admitted honestly. He never lied to Emily.

"Is it dead?" Emily screwed her face up with dread and distaste.

"I don't know. But if Pa or James finds out they'll kill me." Will paled as his ready imagination took over.

"Oh, Will!" Admiration and apprehension were mixed in Emily's cry.

"It'll be all right unless Pa finds out," said Will carelessly. "Him and God—they think they're a lot!"

The moment he had said it he felt frightened. He hadn't really meant to say it. He hoped God knew that and would not strike him dead. It was just sometimes Pa acted as though he thought he and God were the same. He even thought he looked like God. That was the way he had looked in church that morning. Will looked around for something he could touch three times to take the curse off what he had said. He was glad he'd said it low so that Emily might not have heard. That way she couldn't be blamed too.

He kept watching the house for signs of pursuit. Emily had leaned back to sit against the rungs of a paint-stained ladder leading up to the rafters where Thomas Stapely stored his choicest mahogany, oak, and walnut trim.

"It's nice in here," she said comfortably. The afternoon had warmed. There was no wind, and the sun beat through the dusty windows of the shop. "I'm getting sleepy. Let's just stay here."

"Was Old Man Watson at church?" asked Will suddenly.

"I didn't see him. Will, did you play hooky again Friday?"

"Only in the afternoon." Will was matter of fact.

"Pa's going to find out even if Mr. Watson doesn't tell him, and you know what happened last time."

"It didn't hurt," said Will with bravado. "What good's all that stuff in school, anyway—except the history and geography. Some of the gang wanted me to hop freights with them Friday. We went all the way to Schenectady and back."

"To Schenectady!"

"Tom Sullivan almost got caught by a yard cop. Some day I'm going all the way to New York."

"You'd better not!" Suddenly Emily looked alarmed. "Agnes'll tell Ma if I don't help with the dishes."

"Let her."

"No, I promised, Will. I've got to go in."

"You can't!" exclaimed Will, fearful of being left alone.

Emily looked miserable.

"I've got to," she repeated stubbornly.

Will was still watching the back door of the house. No one had come out after Agnes gave up calling and went inside. Perhaps James had gone out the front door to call on one of the neighbors. He liked to show off when he was home and had his good clothes on. Some of the neighbors already called him "Dr. Stapely."

"What was for dessert?" he asked suddenly.

"Fig pudding. I made the hard sauce. I'm still hungry, too."

"I'll go with you." Will began dragging the saw horses and boards away from the door before his courage could ebb. What could James do anyway? Maybe he was as big and strong as he thought he was, but he could fix him.

He'd give him a knee in the stomach. That's what Fat O'Connor said the guys in the big gang did when they caught one of the other guys down on South Avenue. It squeezed the gizzards out of them. Pieces popped out of their ears. Sometimes they got his neck in their elbow from behind and choked his head back while another guy socked him. Will saw himself towering over James who had been knocked down by a single blow and cowered with an arm held before his face while he pled for mercy.

He flung the door wide open.

"Let him try," he said darkly. "Let him try, that's all."

"What?"

"Never mind," retorted Will, "and don't you be scared either. I could lick 'em both if I wanted to."

"You come here this instant!" screamed Agnes as they tiptoed into the house. "Help me with these dishes. I've a good mind to box your ears. I'll certainly tell Pa about this." She pushed a tea cloth at Emily. "Willy, stir yourself."

"Yes, ma'am," answered Emily pertly.

Agnes seemed not to hear her. She was "her father's daughter," a phrase she was proud to hear him use, for she worshipped her father. She contrived to have her father's features without his handsomeness. Her body was large and heavy, deep-bosomed and bulging in her tight clothes. Her nose was broad in an otherwise rather pretty face. Her pale eyes were usually either clouded with dullness or sharp with scheming.

Agnes had inherited or acquired all of Thomas' piety without either his energy or common sense. She wanted to be good, to be sweet, to be saved. She also wished intently to be married. Sometimes in the darkness her face went livid at the warmth of her thoughts.

She began to sing again, forming her lips carefully in the oval prescribed by her voice teacher. Her tones were full and rounded.

Greatly daring, for she and Will knew when they could safely venture, Emily raised her voice and joined her much older sister in *Nearer My God to Thee*.

They had begun on a second verse when Agnes rapped sharply on the dishpan with the kitchen spoon she was scouring.

"No, no! Try again. It goes *la*—la—la!"

Eagerly Emily imitated her.

"That's better. Now—"

They began again.

Will had returned to the shop where they could hear the muffled sound of his hammering. He was making a wall rack of slender plate shelves for his mother's birthday. Only Emily knew that he had been working at it off and on for weeks, hoarding scraps of hardwood, planing and sanding them carefully, working with infinite care over the joints. He liked to make things.

"That's the way I like to hear my little nieces sing!" approved a new voice. "Their voices raised in praise. Is that Willy hammering and sawing in the shop? His father will not like his working on the Sabbath."

"Auntie!" trilled Agnes.

"Hello," said Emily without enthusiasm. "Ma and Pa are at Aunt Simpson's."

"I know, child," Maria assured them, untying the silk strings of her black bonnet. "Now help me off with my cape. *There* we are."

Maria, plump, rosy-cheeked and sharp-eyed, was Thomas Stapely's widowed sister whom he and Mary had brought back from Trewsted Village in the Forest on their last trip home to England. For a time she and her son, Arthur, had lived with the Stapelys, further crowding their already crowded house, for James had been at home then. Then Thomas had built a small cottage for them only a stone's throw from their own house. He had got Arthur a job at the iron works, then another in a lumberyard, then a third elsewhere when Arthur lost that one too. Maria came over every day.

Emily disliked her aunt. Maria was the ally of Thomas or of Mary, of Agnes or James, as the occasion or chances of success dictated. She certainly was not the ally of Will and Emily. Her continual praise of Agnes and James was too transparent an attempt to curry favor with their father, and they suspected rightly that Aunt Maria carried tales.

Maria was also a worker. It was her help with the washing, ironing, and housecleaning which enabled Mary to spend as much time as she did away from home. She seemed actually to enjoy tasks which Mary faced only because she had to and worsted only through strategem or, when stratagem failed, through sheer desperation.

"They'll all be back for tea soon," announced Maria briskly. "I'll see if I can't tidy things up a bit. We must look our best for Aunt and Uncle Simpson, you know. Now, where's a clean dust cloth?"

"Ma doesn't like people to touch her best china," said Emily spitefully, as her aunt moved toward the dining room and the parlor.

Her aunt looked at her coldly.

"I am the best judge of that. You, young lady, had better put on a clean dress. How do you manage to get yourself so dirty? I do believe there is sawdust in your hair. I often tell your mother that with Agnes as neat and ladylike as she is, it's a pity—"

Emily escaped to Will in the shop.

"Aunt Maria's here!"

"Oh, her!"

Will was so intent on his work that his tongue stuck out between his teeth, and his forehead was wrinkled in painful concentration. Fine sawdust powdered his clothing. He wiped his face on his sleeve. He unlocked a slender strip of mahogany from a wood vise, twirling the lock with a fine professional flourish.

Emily shot a glance at the house, her young face hardening.

"Is stinky Arthur with her?" asked Will. "Even Pa says he's lazy."

"I hate her," announced Emily. "Sometimes I hate them all."

Chapter 3

IT WAS LATE afternoon when the others returned.

They were all slightly out of breath as they reached the top of the hill after getting off the horse-drawn streetcar at the corner of South Avenue, but they were all happy and in good spirits. Mary's eyes were alight with pleasure, for she loved to visit and to entertain; and even Thomas' stern face was relaxed in a smile. He liked people to see his home and that he provided handsomely for his family.

Aunt Simpson looked a little envious as they approached the gate, and the two men, Walter Simpson and John Armstead, the mason, a broad-shouldered bravely moustached bachelor who lived with them, seemed a little abashed as Thomas led them into the house. All were scrubbed and in their Sunday best.

Maria fussed and bustled about. Aunt Simpson, who was not an aunt at all but a distant cousin of some kind from Bristol, too old for the children to address by her Christian name, seated herself a little stiffly in the walnut lady's chair in the parlor. Mary, rustling pleasantly in her silk, moved proudly and graciously about her domain.

They had met James somewhere near the foot of the hill and, as by adult right, he had taken his place in the parlor with its plush and tapestried chairs and antimacassars and doilies, and the wide bay window filled with Mary's flowering plants. The women exclaimed over the plants.

"You are so good with flowers!" said Aunt Simpson brightly. "I don't know how you do it. And no one else in all Ilium has a view of the river like this."

The sun was dropping, darkness graying into the cold blueness of the sky, but the icy river still showed white and clear beyond the houses at the foot of the hill and the plain of trees and factory chimneys.

James stood posed by the mantel next to the shining coal stove. He looked slightly bored. The men had seated themselves carefully in the highly polished walnut chairs with their elaborately carved backs. Thomas looked sharply at his oldest son.

"More important," said Maria grimly to Aunt Simpson, "Mary has the best tea in South Ilium. It will be ready in a minute. I had the kettle on the boil when I saw you coming."

"Fire all right?" Thomas asked James.

James opened the stove door with its isinglass panels to show his father the bed of red coals evenly spread and alive with dancing blue flames. Thomas nodded abruptly.

"A fine home you have here, Mr. Stapely," said John Armstead. "Very fine." He coughed, covering his wide mouth politely with a huge, work-scarred hand which had been scrubbed nearly raw.

Thomas frowned. "It will do," he admitted. There was a touch of Christian condescension in his voice. "Willy, run down cellar and get a scuttle of coal, and be quick about it."

Will and Emily had been hanging about the edges of things, trying to share in the excitement without being noticed. Will, fearful that his absence from school and church might have been reported or that somehow his father might have heard of the slaughtered cow, jumped to obey.

"Mary, where is Agnes?" Aunt Simpson inquired. "She must be such a comfort to you!"

"Gone into Ilium to meet Blanche Jones before they go to the Presbyterian choir," answered Maria before Emily could speak.

"And what a big girl Emily's getting to be!" cried Aunt Simpson, looking significantly at the curves beginning to show under the tight bodice of Emily's Sunday dress.

"Yes," said Maria dryly.

Mary smiled apologetically to Aunt Simpson.

"Yes, that's it. Agnes had to leave for choir. I know she was worried to leave before you came." With a smile she slipped toward the kitchen to aid in the preparation for tea.

"You bidding on the new machinery shed at Wilson's, Thomas?" asked Walter Simpson interestedly. There was no use Thomas Stapely's trying to come it over him. He'd known him when they were both boys in the Forest of Dean.

Walter was short and fat with shrewd eyes. His serge vest was tight over a comfortably rounded stomach, and his heavy gold watch chain gleamed in the after-light pouring in a west window. It went dull as Maria lighted the lamp with its ball shade of frosted pink glass on which a border of blue flowers had been painted. It stood on a marble-topped table. She gestured James aside so that she could also light the tall mantel lamp. The lamps cast new shadows into the corners as the center of the room grew bright.

"I may," said Thomas shortly.

He did not wish to acknowledge to Walter Simpson that his bid, over which he had spent several evenings of close figuring, was already in. He had plenty of work on hand to carry him well into the summer, but the Wilson job would be a plum. He would have to hire additional men and contract for added cartage, but he had carefully allowed for all that. The shed was a big job.

"That job," said John Armstead unexpectedly, "will go to O'Brien, no matter who the low bidder is. His brother-in-law is top foreman at Wilson's. He'll get a percentage for putting it O'Brien's way."

Thomas Stapely might be a hard man and successful, but Armstead was, after all, a master mason himself. He stood to get part of the work no matter who got the contract.

Aunt Simpson, quick to see the anger in Thomas' face, swiftly changed the subject.

"We'll soon have to be calling you 'Dr. Stapely,'" she said loudly to James who had been carefully watching his father's face.

"Yes," James answered firmly and seriously. "I've been thinking of that. I think people should begin to get accustomed to calling me 'Doctor.' Even"—he avoided looking at Thomas now—"my own family."

"What?" exploded Thomas. "What? Did I hear you aright, boy? I'll call you 'Doctor' when I've made up my mind to, and that won't be for some time." John Armstead's insolence had infuriated him.

James was instantly deflated.

"Well, the children should anyway," he said defensively.

"Tell us, Doctor," said Aunt Simpson too quickly, "about your work now. We'll be needing you soon if your Uncle Simpson's leg keeps bothering him."

"Had me real doubled up lately," Walter told the angry Thomas. "I—"

"We're dissecting cadavers," said James bluntly, sure they would not know what he was talking about.

"Cadavers? What are they, boy?" asked his father sternly.

"Corpses, dead bodies," said James clearly. "It's an important part of our work."

Aunt Simpson squealed in horror. The mason looked uneasy. Thomas squared his wide shoulders.

"Had a nice one in yesterday," said James briskly. "Almost still warm. Rigor hardly started. One of our surgeons was in attendance on the case, and he notified our morgue two days ahead of time he expected to have a nice case of inflammation of the bowels for us up at the hospital, so they were right there to pick him up."

"Oh," said the mason, blinking nervously. He had slightly bulging eyes which were always bloodshot from stone dust and mortar.

Willy, who had threaded the room as inconspicuously as he could with his scuttle of coal and placed it next to the stove, listened fascinated from the doorway.

James leaned negligently against the mantel and surveyed his audience coolly. There was an evil gleam in his eye.

"We gave a leg to two of the first year men and the head to a postgraduate who is going to specialize in brain surgery. It was the intestines we were after—a beautiful morbid specimen we found when we'd got them snaked out."

In the doorway Will twitched involuntarily.

"Snakes?" he gasped.

"Quiet, boy!" thundered his father.

"What did you do with the rest of him?" asked Walter Simpson. His fat face was pale, but his eyes were blazing.

A savage humor showed around James's lips.

"Gave the kidneys to the lab dog. He likes them. Can't tell them from beef kidneys if the cadaver's fresh and was drained right away. We got rid of the rest." He looked unpleasantly secretive.

A bony hand grasped Willy's shoulder, and he jerked upright.

"Down cellar with you," ordered his Aunt Maria, "and bring up a bottle of your mother's catsup. Your father likes it with his tea."

Will raced for the door in the kitchen which led into the cellar. Eager to miss none of his brother's story, he did not bother to light a candle, but grasped in the darkness for the shelf of preserves, pickles, and fruit which his mother and aunt had put down the previous autumn. He selected a bottle of catsup by feel and raced upstairs again.

"Open it!" snapped his Aunt Maria as he hurried through the kitchen. His mother, a starched white apron covering all of her gown, was carefully placing a padded and embroidered cosy over her best Staffordshire teapot.

Willy fumbled with the cork as he slipped back into the doorway of the parlor. Aunt Simpson looked feverishly interested. Walter Simpson had his mouth open and was breathing heavily, his stomach rising and falling with excitement. John Armstead was trying not to be sick.

"Not always," James was saying learnedly. "Sometimes post-mortem findings simply verify a diagnosis. Take post-operative gangrene. There is a distinct and characteristic smell—unmistakable. Just the other—"

"Wup!" choked Will.

The cork, which had resisted at first, flew bulletlike out of his hand. It splatted bloodily against the middle of James's starched shirt front, and a thin stream of catsup squirted across the room before Will could get his thumb over the bottle top.

James leaped as though shot. He had been. Aunt Simpson squealed shrilly. Uncle Simpson flailed his pudgy arms against further attack.

"Willy!" roared his father. "Come here this instant!"

"He needs a thorough thrashing!" shouted James, mopping at his ruined shirt front. "He's needed it all day. Look at the carpet!"

"Gee!" protested Willy, stupefied. "Gee—I didn't—"

"This minute!" roared Thomas again. He started for Will with powerful hands ready to grasp.

"Here! Here!" cried Mary gaily. "What's all this?" She laid a protecting hand on Will's shoulder as she called to the others. "Tea's all ready on the table in the dining room, and we don't want it cold. Come!"

Aunt Simpson, who after hasty examination could find no trace of the catsup on her billowing skirts, beamed tactfully.

"Just a little accident, Mary. Willy couldn't help it."

"Oh, that catsup! I knew some of it was heady. Too bad, James, but you'll live." She gave Will a gentle shove. "Tea's set for you and Emily in the kitchen," she whispered.

In the protection of his mother's person, Will, harassed as he was, managed a smile for his wild-eyed brother.

"Doctor Stapely!" he mimicked scornfully and fled.

Emily, who had seen it all was choking back her laughter in the kitchen. Her eyes were filled with tears.

"Will, you did it on purpose."

"Of course I did it on purpose!" lied Will stoutly. "Threw a knife at me before, didn't he? *Doctor* Stapely! Boy, I'm hungry!"

He grabbled up a snow-white piece of homemade bread fresh from the baking of the day before, and slathered it with gooseberry jam out of a stone jar. He chewed ravenously, then washed it down with a gulp of weak tea, first dipping his finger into the cup to make sure it was not too hot.

Emily, more decorously, began to eat. They were both listening to the polite prattle of their elders in the other room. Their mother's clear, crisp voice came easily through the rumble of the men's voices and the sharper sounds of Maria's unctuous comments and Aunt Simpson's almost girlish laughter.

Suddenly Thomas' voice rose angrily.

"I'll have no union men working for me," he made clear. "I drove the fellow off the job before he could get his breath. I'll pay an honest wage for an honest day's work. I'll have no union loafers on a job of mine."

Emily began to gag again.

"James—he—it bounced right off the front of his shirt, and—and —and one drop hit—hit right—on the end of his nose!"

Will grabbed a bottle of vinegar out of the cruet on the kitchen table, shook it, and pretended to shoot his sister between the eyes.

"Pop!" he said, remembering happily. He dropped his voice. "I'm Doctor Stapely," he growled. "Like to have a leg cut off?" He twirled his moustache. "M'mm," he grunted thoughtfully. "H'mm. Give me another tart, please."

Chapter 4

ILIUM was dirty, devout, tough, purposeful, and confident. It was dignified, pious, sedate, but pulsing with energy and charged with determination. Since the beginning of the nineteenth century it had, by sheer force, pushed itself up from the handful of cornfields and riverside meadows of a Dutch patroon to be the fourth city of New York State. It meant soon to be at least the second.

Ilium was the steel city of the country. Ore was riding the Lakes from Superior, through the Erie Canal to feed its blast furnaces. The busy iron works was turning out a horseshoe every second. Great piles of coal, fed by strings of blackened barges, stood next the tall, smoke-belching chimneys along the river. All day long and through the night there was a clank, clank, and thud of steam hammers, the whir of machinery, the slapping of leather belts. Fire hissed into the sky, and sparks fell in showers that scorched the earth. Ilium had provisioned troops for the War of 1812. It had made the plates for the *Monitor* during the Civil War. Ilium had profited well by the Civil War. Now the great arsenal just across the river was turning out shells and ammunition for any new enemy foolhardy enough to bother Uncle Sam.

Lumber schooners, coal barges, tugs and loading cranes, excursion boats, passenger boats, and pleasure craft jammed Ilium's harbor, from April to November, for Ilium was the head of steam navigation on the Hudson. Canals which Ilium had planned and dug ran north and west. The river itself was Ilium's broad highway to New York, the coast, and the rest of the world. Forging the rails, a new type, and building the cars, the best yet made, it had thrown its own railroad to tap the rich agricultural country of the Mohawk Valley. It had dynamited the world's largest tunnel through rock mountains to the east to open commerce with Yankee Boston and New England.

Ilium's mills and factories were thriving. Its churches were busy with good works. Its Sunday schools were noisy and enthusiastic. Its saloons were crowded. Ilium was proud of them all. It was proud of its fine engineering school, its pioneer woman's college, its musical societies, its imposing banks and well-stocked stores, and of the mansions of its wealthy families on the heights above the river where the kills tumbled, rushing through their rock channels into the river,

turning mill wheels on the way. It was proud of its old strain of
Dutch sobriety and thrift, its Yankee ingenuity, the famous soldiers
and evangelists it had produced, and of its paraded preference for
hard common sense over either the frivolous or the aesthetic.

Ilium's capitalists had or could produce the funds for any enterprise that promised growth and profit. Its industrialists could turn
out the goods in quality and quantity and at the price demanded.
It could pour the finest bell or make the strongest steel plate, build
the best coaches, forge the best rails. All these things it did. It
boasted that it could make shirts for the backs and collars for the
necks of all the men in the country and half the men in Christen-
dom; and it was doing almost that too.

Its leading citizens were the few remaining descendants of the old
Dutch families and the more numerous and vigorous descendants of
the Yankees who had seized upon and developed the commercial pos-
sibilities of the village just after the Revolution. These were the
hardheaded men in beards, broadcloth, and linen who drove their own
horses and ran Ilium's business and industry while their wives ran
its churches and established the city's standards of decorum. Under
them, aping them, were the skilled workers, the Yankees, the English, and the Welsh. Many of the straw bosses and gaffers in the
mills were experienced hands imported from the collieries of Wales
and the factories of Sheffield and Birmingham. Others, like Thomas
Stapely, had been drawn by reports of earlier adventurers, by the
promise of enterprise and betterment which Ilium, State of New York,
America, offered. Some of them had realized their dreams and ambitions.

Ilium's laborers were the hordes of Irish immigrants who had
poured in to work on the canals and the railroads, then stayed on
to man the steel mills and the iron works or work about the port.
A rabble followed. Some of the older men were tamed and their offspring were diluted and, on the surface, subdued, but most were
roaring bog-trotters and shanty Irish whom it took cool and efficient
priests to keep under nominal control.

Fast-growing South Ilium was dirtier, tougher, more pious, and
more joyfully unrepentant than even Ilium. It had the biggest Sunday schools and the busiest saloons. Here were the men who could
work in the heat that melted steel and could shrivel human flesh in
a fraction of a second—and the women who could handle such men.
South Ilium could outwork, outdrink, outpray, outbrawl, and out-
produce Ilium itself. It had naked energy and intensity enough to
run twenty more blast furnaces and a dozen more churches than it
had; and it didn't care who heard it say so, whether it was Ilium,

aged and decaying Albany, or wicked and wonderful New York itself.

Life was hard and demanding in South Ilium, a fit match for a man. It had material and spiritual rewards for the strong. For the weak it had nothing. Thomas Stapely, who believed in God and hard work, found it satisfying and good.

Life was the simplest thing Thomas Stapely had to cope with. It was made simple by God's master plan which showed birth and death, heaven and hell, and the way a man in his short life on earth should walk among them. Thomas knew the plan and had no slightest doubt of his knowledge.

Thomas Stapely lived with certainties. He was pained when God was pained; happy when He was pleased. All else was weakness and vanity. Disobedience of him was a flouting of the will of God. It enraged him and confused him because he could not comprehend it. Life was simple. Other things constituted the problem—recalcitrant workmen, the wickedness of the sinful, the perverse wilfulness of children.

He was at the height of his powers. He worked hard and long, for the submerged fury of his nature demanded the solid satisfactions of visible achievement. He knew sternly his duty to God. Yet he did not always work now with the joyous strength of his youth. Ambition was still strong, but there was no longer the drive of hard necessity or the need to prove himself to himself. In spite of himself, he welcomed every occasional half-hour of relaxation, half-hours which he also resented unless he could spend them homehow happily and gratefully in the service of the Lord at church, in Sunday school, or with his music.

Mary's energy had increased. She had been brought up to move through the life of her English village as one who had a right. She looked forward to callers for tea and to calling on her friends. She had never allowed her household, even when Agnes and James were children, to absorb her. When Emily and then Will were born, forming almost a second family, she had fully decided that neither they nor her home would take all of her time. Pleasure was a necessity of her nature that was not without its vanity.

There was a restlessness in Mary, imagination, a need for excitement. She wore with cool grace the poise and dignity she had been taught. They befitted one who had been a daughter of the big house in Wakeney and had long been the wife of strong Thomas Stapely. She wore even a touch of imperiousness sometimes, but underneath danced a rebellious uneasiness and a capriciousness that were essential parts of her. This was what had made her dare America with

Thomas, what made her invite risks which sometimes puzzled and frightened him.

Mary knew her position in the English community of South Ilium, and her quiet assurance of it brought tacit acknowledgment from others. Her china was the best. What she served at tea became the proper thing to serve at tea. The flowers Mrs. Stapely raised in her garden were the best kind to raise. The Stapelys might be head-strong and highhanded, as many thought them, but they were *the* Stapelys. Tom Stapely was a hard-driving successful builder. His wife was a lady. It was right that they did as they wished.

Though careful not to overdo it, Mary took full advantage of the situation and of her ascendency over Thomas. She had done so when she opened the furniture store on South Avenue. Thomas had been horrified when she broached the idea, though not as horrified as he would have been had she not carefully prepared him for the news. Some of their neighbors along the hilly streets professed to be shocked, then quickly forgot their shock as curiosity overcame them. There were storekeepers along South Avenue who audibly resented the likes of Mrs. Stapely's intruding on the likes of them, but they too succumbed and soon were offering professional advice and shar-ing their tradesmen's lore.

To Mary it was all so simple she could not understand why she had not thought of it before.

A scoundrelly tenant had left one of their Third Street houses owing three months' rent. He had abandoned his furniture which had to be cleared out before the cottage could be re-rented. The only place to put it was in the loft of the home workshop with the furniture of an earlier tenant who had done much the same thing. Only the first family had absconded with six months' rent, Thomas having softheartedly believed their tale of woe.

Thomas' main office and shop was in a building on South Avenue with a large brick and lumber storage yard and rows of tool sheds behind it. Next to it a narrow little store was vacant, and its owner had long owed Thomas a bill for repairs to it and other property. It needed only a little paint and freshening to convert it from the greengrocers which it had been to a secondhand furniture shop. The laboring families, which were continually moving in and out of South Ilium as they took or left jobs in the iron works and other manu-factories, offered a ready market. The furniture abandoned by the tenants, together with discards from their own household, was the nucleus of a stock which Mary quickly added to by attending auction sales in Ilium and nearby villages. The children, she told herself, were old enough to look after themselves when they came home from school, and Maria was ready to help with chores at the house. Mary had dived delightedly into her new enterprise.

Will and Emily were delighted from the first.

Will was kept home from school for a week to help ready the shop. He hauled and tugged, swept and dusted, hammered loose chair rungs into place, mended broken bed slats and sawed table legs to evenness with joyous abandon. Mary praised him, and even Thomas admitted that he had worked hard. Will felt adult and important. He managed to avoid school for half the next week by continuing the same excuse.

Mary kept shop hours only when it pleased her or a prospective customer had sent word that he could be at the store at a certain time. Still, she was away from the house, either at an auction or in the store, most days when Emily and Will came home from school. Unless their Aunt Maria was there, the house was empty, and they were free to do as they pleased. They made the most of their new freedom. If they were neglected, as some unkindly critics said they were, they thoroughly enjoyed the neglect. They had only to make sure Maria was not about.

From Will's viewpoint, the store was perfect. If Maria ordered him to do chores about the house, he could always plead that his mother needed him at the store. If Mary wanted him at the store, he could point out earnestly that there were jobs at the house he had to get done before tea. This left him free to attend to his own affairs with a clear conscience.

It was the store that gave Will his chance to play marbles, spin tops, follow the leader, smash a few windows, in company with kindred souls to learn to smoke expertly, and generally to foregather with those whom Thomas considered the ragamuffin offspring of slatterns and loafers. Thomas, who knew that the devil finds work for idle hands and, despite a fervent belief in the magical powers of education, vaguely resented Will's idling away his time in school all week, kept him busy on Saturdays. He had him work at the house, sweeping out the shop and office on South Avenue, or shining the rust off shovels in the tool shed.

He knew and was pleased that Will and Emily were favorites with the sober Welsh and English of the neighborhood, who saw the quick-witted and handsome children as the best of their own kind and pointed out their industry and politeness as examples to their own offspring. He had no idea that Will was likewise the darling of many an Irish household where James was detested for his superior ways and where Thomas himself was the natural enemy of the men who, when no easier job offered, worked for him as laborers or carried the hod on one of his jobs. Will was the accepted intimate and ally of the Raffertys, the Murphys, the O'Tooles, and the Connellys. More than once he had run down to McGraw's—"that's the darlin' boy" —for Maggie O'Toole when she needed a quart of beer against her Mike's coming home dry as a bone from the mill for his supper. Maggie did not dare trust any of her own thirsty offspring.

It was a busy, active, and satisfying life for Will and for Emily, who shared as much of it as her sex allowed, and the partial homelessness which afforded them the opportunity hastened their education. They learned to rely on their own efforts both for entertainment and to get what they wanted without collision with Thomas or bothering their mother who was so busy with her outside enterprises. They developed the sharpness and wary instincts of street gamins at the same time that they enjoyed the security of a warm home and good food. Outwitting their parents and the detested Maria became a game which the conspirators learned to play with finesse.

Without knowing that he did so, Will learned to use his boy's charm to full advantage. Sober, thoughtful, and industrious before his father, he was quick and playful with his mother. He smoked more and swore more roundly with the gang to make up for his unfortunate and suspect background and to hide his sick hatred of the cruelty they enjoyed in stoning stray dogs, and tormenting captured cats or new boys.

Will found out that one kind of a smile was effective with Mrs. Whitehead, whom his mother met at church and worked with on committees of church societies, another on old Mrs. Wright, and still another on the Maggie O'Tooles. The same charm worked on his teachers at school. Though he stayed away as much as he could and seldom studied, his quickness at memorizing and ability at reciting in Friday afternoon contests won their approval and even their tacit connivance at some of his other known shortcomings. When caught out, as occasionally he was, he could hang his head and look repentant with an air of convincingness and blundering innocence. He felt neither fright nor remorse. Simply he had learned that hanging his head and looking appealing was a good thing to do. Miraculously, it sometimes worked with his mother too, though he had the uneasy suspicion that she saw through the sham and forebore punishment because she enjoyed the performance.

Emily too learned to use her powers. Once Will's formidable protector, she was his partner now, sometimes even his follower. Instinctively she had learned what she could do with her appearance, her smile, a lift of her head. She was quick to catch a glance, a gesture, a manner of talking or walking she saw older girls and even some of her mother's friends use, and to practice them at the first opportunity. Fear of Will's ridicule made her keep some things to herself. She even felt pangs of disloyalty when some days she found herself willing to heed Aunt Maria's teachings about the preparation of dinner or the proper way to do this or that stitch. She managed to keep out of his sight sometimes now when he had looked on her coldly after seeing her laughing with some of the older girls in the school yard. One of the girls was Mamie O'Keefe, black-haired, blue-eyed, flirtatious. Will could not tell Emily the things that Mickey had told him about Mamie and Frankie Moriarty and about Mamie and some others. He avoided his sister for a day or two, and both of them were miserable.

Emily had even begun to like church. It was the music which had first attracted her. Now she could not have said what else it was that drew her, but something did. Soon she would be putting up her hair and wearing long skirts. She dreaded and resented this, and looked forward to it with delicious anticipation. Without urging, she joined the Girls' Guild, and went uncomfortably the first time with Will glowering after her.

There was something else that Will did not know. One day she had met Francis O'Connor as he walked along South Avenue on his way home from high school in Ilium. Francie was dark and quiet, with fine, thick black hair neatly combed and a pale, thoughtful face. Francie was seventeen, and everyone knew that he was going to be a priest. He was an acolyte at big St. Joseph's. Emily had been frightened to walk with him, but he had talked quietly about what they did in the high school and seemed glad to talk to her. She had hurried along with flushed cheeks after Francie turned off at his street.

One windy April day white clouds scudded fast across an early spring sky. The sun flashed on the fields beyond their hilltop as the clouds threw shadow and then brilliance on the earth. The warm air smelled of wet soil and drying leaves. Green buds were starting on some of the shrubs Mary had planted about the back door, and there were even tiny red leaves, folded into scrolls, coming out on the swamp maple Thomas permitted to grow until an oak he had planted a few years before gave sufficient summer shade.

Will was just emerging from the shop door, carefully easing through the big kite he had been working on before he started the shelf for his mother's birthday.

"Will, wait for me. Wait! Wait!"

"Hurry your horses then!" cried Will joyfully. "It's perfect wind!"

They had been saving string and cord all winter, adding each piece carefully to the sizable ball they already had. Mary had given Will an old petticoat to tear up for a tail, and Emily had stripped and knotted it for him.

She threw her schoolbooks on the kitchen table, grabbed a thick crust out of the bread box, and smeared on bacon dripping from the can that always stood at the back of the stove. Will, she could see, had already been eating.

A moment later they were scurrying across the brown fields that lay between their house and a steeper hill beyond which the distant Berkshires sparkled in the sun, the dun browns and cold grays of the winter warmed by the early spring afternoon, the pines and hemlocks shimmering like massed emeralds.

"We'll sail it to China!" cried Will exultantly.

"China's the other way," said Emily. "It's down under. If you could dig straight through the earth—"

"I know! I know! Africa then or the 'Far Antipodes'—wherever they are." He screwed up his mouth as one of their teachers always did in reciting poetry. "Don't let the tail drag in that puddle. Here, hand it to me after I get over the fence. You can slide under."

They raced across another field, panted up the steep hill. A startled cow that had been basking comfortably in the sun, climbed stiffly to her feet and lumbered off. Another standing nearby gave out an offended "moo."

Soon they were atop a stony pasture from which they could look down on their own house. It was small and, even on its comparative height, far below them here. They examined the pasture with expert eyes. It was long and wide, free of the scrub trees which are the enemies of kite flyers. A cornfield crisscrossed with the deep furrows of autumn plowing, lay on one side of the pasture; a woodlot of maple, ash, and chestnut lay on the other. It was here Will and Emily gathered chestnuts in the autumn.

Emily knew her part. Halfway up the hill they stopped. She took the kite, holding it upright near the tail and backed off as Will paid out the line.

"Wait a minute! Wait a minute!" he cried as he hit a tangle in the cord.

The kite tugged impatiently in Emily's hands. Once a gust of wind almost tore it loose.

"Hurry up, Will!"

"Got it!" he waved her on. "Stand still! When I say three, go—one—two—three!"

At "three" Emily tossed the kite in the air at the same instant that Will started to run.

The kite, a sail which Emily had stitched out of worn sheeting, a blouse which had already done duty as a duster, and pieces of feed bags, took one wide, heart-stopping swoop, then, as Will ran, paying out line as he moved, righted itself. Will was standing still now, almost at the crest of the hill. He played the kite like a skilled angler striving to net a salmon, controlling, urging, checking, and coaxing with his right hand as he let out more line from the ball held in his left.

Emily raced toward him, slipped in a blob of cow dropping, regained her footing after grazing one knee on a sharp stalk, and was breathless at his side.

Will's hat had fallen off. His blond hair, always in need of cutting, blew in the wind. His eyes were shining and his lips tight with concentration.

"Let me, Will!" cried Emily excitedly. "Let me!"

He did not answer. The cord was alive in his hands, tugging steadily. He let out five feet more, and the kite took up the slack. A deft maneuver, and he had sent it ten feet higher, straight into the sun which came out just then to blind him and throw a wide spotlight of gold around the boy and girl.

"There you are, Em!" said Will, his face radiant with triumph and happiness. "Just hold her steady, let out more line a little at a time."

"I know as well as you!" retorted Emily, but without rancor. The kite moved sideways across the sky in a majestic sweep. "Oh, Will, look at it go!"

Too satisfied to speak, they contemplated their handiwork in silent ecstasy. They took turns holding the kite, shouting with delight as new currents caught it and tossed it higher or dashed it down and the kite, truly built, fought back, pulling hard on its moorings. They let out more cord and more until the kite was far off over the woods.

There was a thrashing in the leaves and branches behind them. They turned to find the two cows they had disturbed and a dozen others which had joined them all watching the kite. Necks outstretched, they swung their heads from side to side as the kite veered and jibed, tacked, and came back on course again.

Will and Emily burst out laughing at their absurd antics. They tried to make the kite do tricks to see what the cows would do.

"That one!" cried Emily. "No, not that one, *that* one—looks just like Tommy Anderson trying to do his arithmetic. And there"—she pointed to a brindled beast chewing reflectively as it contemplated the kite with the detached reflectiveness of a philosopher weighing problems of conduct and metaphysics—"is Mrs. Hawson asleep in church—only she has a moustache."

Will caught on. He found an important-looking small Jersey mongrel that was Aunt Maria and a fat, heavily-uddered, frowsty-looking reddish beast with drooping, bloodshot eyes that was Mrs. McLaughlin, who beerily surveyed her own brood of ragged and howling urchins and those of her equally prolific neighbors from a window on South Avenue where she seemed to lean, her arms folded on the window sill, all day long.

"And there's Pa," Will decided as one cow looked away from the kite and dropped what seemed a baleful glare toward them. Unlike the others, it had horns. It took a threatening step in their direction.

"It couldn't be Pa!" objected Emily, looking about for a stick or a stone in case the cow meant to attack.

"Why not?" demanded Will, ready for argument. "Looks like him, doesn't it?" He addressed the cow in a deep growl. "Here, here, boy! That will be enough of that. You'll do better to listen to your elders and have less to say. Get on to bed. Go on to bed without your supper!"

Emily laughed. "It still couldn't be Pa, though," she insisted.

"Why not?" demanded Will again.

Emily flushed.

Suddenly one cow decided that it was frightened. It waved its tail in a circle, kicked up its heels like a clumsy schoolgirl, and galloped off. The rest of the herd, cued by their leader, performed the same maneuver and disappeared.

Somehow the antics of the cows added almost unbearable pleasure to what was already perfection. Will pulled up two flat stones. Though they were wet, they sat down on them, and Will anchored the end of the kite cord to another. They breathed the air and felt the warm wind. They were alive in the silence. They looked down through the sunshine over Ilium with its tall church towers and its high buildings, over their own home and all of South Ilium which lay small and unimportant in the sun. Across the river were other brown fields and hillsides with here and there the dot of a farmhouse. Miles away from them a windowpane glinted like gold. Smoke coiled and wreathed out of tall black chimneys, then was whisked away as it met higher and colder air. Branches that near at hand were hard, cold, and still winter-black flashed in lacelike traceries as the breeze moved them.

Will touched his sister and winked broadly. He touched his forehead humbly and bowed. There was a leering slyness about his mouth, amusement in his eyes. The acting demanded a larger audience, but some kind of fitting ceremony was needed. He produced two cigarettes from his pocket and gave her one.

"Will! Whole ones! Where'd you get them?"

"Never you mind, m'girl," said Will in Aunt Maria's tones. His head disappeared into his coat as he lighted his own, not daring to trust Emily lest she put out one of his few matches. Emily closed her eyes and screwed up her mouth as he lighted hers.

Will threw himself on the ground to look up at the sky and let the whole sky look at him. He gulped in a whole mouthful of smoke, then blew it out at the pale daylight moon just beginning to show under the tail of the distant kite.

"Ah!" he said. He rubbed his stomach and contemplated the long droop of their cord through the sky until it disappeared in the blueness. Then he looked at the thin gray wafer of moon sharing the sky with his kite. He thought for a moment that if he pulled the cord, it might be the moon that dived, then rose, dived, then came steadily in.

He looked at Emily who was concentrating fully on her cigarette, frowning as though she was puzzling over something. "Ah!" he said again.

"Will," said Emily suddenly, "let's never go home. Let's never go anywhere. Let's just stay here always."

"All right," he agreed. "Sure. Suits me. Say, you better clean your shoe before Ma sees it. It's all cow flop."

Chapter 5

EVEN AS WILL took his ease on a spring hilltop his enemies were accomplishing his downfall.

Mary was triumphant that afternoon. She had sold a set of dining room furniture, with the leg of the table needing only minor repairs and two of the chairs in perfect condition, for six dollars to a foundryman and his wife. It was a set for which she had paid only three dollars. One hundred per cent profit! She had had to sell it to make up for the chair and bed she had the day before given poor Mrs. Stelling, whose husband drank so, and whose son was a bad boy.

She moved about the little shop with the air of a conqueror and thought that soon she would lock the door and go home. Agnes would be leaving work. Maria had stopped in, as she did some shopping for food, to say that she had already done the ironing and was now going to pare the vegetables for the night meal. There had been a certain acidity in the way she said it, and then Maria had stopped next door to chat for a moment with Thomas.

She knew that Maria did not approve her business venture and suspected that she sometimes said as much to Thomas, pointing out, in her sweet-sharp way that she had better be at home caring for the house he had struggled so—that would be Maria's phrase—to build for them and looking out for Willy and Emily instead of letting them run wild about the streets. Mary was glad to have Maria for company and she was really such a help, but she knew that Maria sometimes saw herself as the defender of her brother, and was not above insinuating to him that he was injured and neglected.

Mary smiled. She knew Thomas. And he had been having a bad day. Several times she had heard his voice raised in anger in the shop, once ordering one of the carpenters to get some flooring laid and be quick about it, and another time storming out at Mr. Grady, the plumber. Thomas was worried. He was behindhand on one of the two houses he was currently building on the extension at the fire house and was going to lose money he said; at least, he was not going to make as much as he had hoped. That he realized now he had made a mistake in his estimate did not make matters better. It made them worse. Thomas did not like to be caught in an error.

It would soon be getting dark. She decided that she would lock the door and go home so as to be in good time with tea, for Agnes would have to be off early for choir practice at the Presbyterian church, and Thomas had a vestry meeting at St. Mark's. Everything was in order, and it would save lighting the lamps. She had had such a nice day. In the morning, taking the streetcar in, she had shopped in Illium and at Lewis's big store found just the material she wanted for a new skirt. She would have Mrs. Curtin, the dressmaker, make it up as soon as she could. She had made her big sale to the foundryman—a great hulking fellow, like some of the Forest woodmen—and his wife, and Mrs. McCurley had dropped in. They had had such a nice chat.

Mary arranged a row of battered chairs more neatly, decided she would have Willy pile two commodes, one oak-grained, the other painted pine, atop two others in order to save space, and started for her coat. Mrs. Walter Morgan thought she would buy the oak commode for their upstairs bedroom, for she was expecting to have a new boarder soon, and some woman new to South Ilium seemed to want one of the others and several chairs. They were moving into one of the older cottages by the livery stable on Van Vorst Lane.

In passing to get her coat and bonnet Emily touched the red plush cunningly inserted in the exquisitely veneered top of the library table. She had bought it when the effects were auctioned off at one of the big houses in Ilium when rich old Mr. Manning had died. He had been a fine old man, and everyone said he had done so much for Ilium, giving work to hundreds of men and then giving so much money to the library and to his church. He had been a Baptist.

Mary had not been able to resist the table, though she knew it was too expensive and far too fine for anyone in their part of town. She had bid it in at a price which she had not dared tell Thomas.

The table was long, its top elaborately cut and beveled; its legs, encrusted with scrollwork and carving, dipped and curved to the floor. Two shallow drawers, without handles, slid cunningly out when a hand was pressed beneath them, and the whole shined with oil and wax so that its mahogany surfaces reflected the light from every direction. The table was intricate, extravagant, and Mary loved it. She had told Thomas she was sure to find a buyer for it, but from the first she had envisioned it in her front room with an embroidered white doily of fine linen covering a part of the plush and on it, perhaps, the big Bible with its golden brass hasp and its gold-edged pages.

Mary was just about to put on her coat when the door opened. It was Professor Watson, the principal of the South Ilium Grammar School.

Edwin Watson was not as tall as Mary, but a Williams College education and his position as one of the few men of learning in South Ilium held him very erect. A frock coat with food stains on its satin lapel covered his meager figure as he advanced with his tall hat in his hand. Its weight had plastered the thin white hair to the forehead of his small, pinched face.

"How do you do, Mrs. Stapely," he said in formal but pleasant tones. It hurt Edwin Watson that the men of South Ilium regarded him with ill-concealed contempt or good-humored toleration as a mere pen-pusher. He was important only in the eyes of their wives or the ministers and priests. He looked on Mrs. Stapely as one of the few who really understood his mission and his trials.

"Why, Mr. Watson," said Mary. "How nice of you to call!"

The principal bowed. It was a pleasure to talk to such a woman as Mrs. Stapely. James and Agnes had been fine pupils, a credit to their parents and their good upbringing. He only wished the two younger children were more like them. Fine children, of course, of good family and distinctive, but—

"It's about William," said Mr. Watson precisely.

Mary's heart started. She wanted no more trouble between Thomas and Willy.

"We were all so proud of his winning the declamation contest at our exercises last year, even with the older boys competing, that we have decided he shall have a fine part in our school play this year. I thought you'd like to know."

"Oh," said Mary relieved, "that's very nice. I'm sure his father will be very pleased." She could hear Thomas moving next door. He had been talking to someone who had left. She had heard the outer door close. "We must tell him. Thomas!" she called. It was so seldom she had a chance to bring him pleasant news of Willy.

Mr. Watson beamed and waited.

Thomas entered through the connecting door.

"How do you do, Mr. Stapely."

"Mr. Watson." Thomas was polite but a little impatient. He was trying to finish up for the day. A teamster had not yet returned from Ilium with a load of pine boards.

"Mr. Watson has been telling me, Thomas, how well Will is doing. He's to have a big part in the school play."

"Yes," said Mr. Watson, pursing his thin lips. "And I thought as William has not been at school the last few days you would like to know."

Thomas' jaw set. He looked at Mary, whose eyes widened involuntarily.

"Hasn't been at school?" he repeated slowly.

"I thought of course you knew," said Mr. Watson with affected surprise. His eyes showed his pleasure. He had not been mistaken then. "I thought perhaps he was helping Mrs. Stapely here or that you had him busy about your work." There was bitterness in his tone. These people, even the best of them, would never learn that the lessons of grammar and history were more important than their work-a-day affairs.

"I have had him helping me a great deal," said Mary quickly. "Today—"

"I think, Professor," said Thomas slowly, "you had better put some other scholar into the part in the play."

Mr. Watson pretended alarm he did not feel.

"I hope—" he began. His voice squeaked in triumph.

41

Thomas ignored him. His face was tight with fury. His hands were clenched into hammerlike fists. As though he had not had enough trouble that day!

"We'll go home, Mary," he ordered. "We'll go home now."

"Well, I—" said Mr. Watson.

Mary too ignored the schoolmaster. The sight of the petty-minded little jackanapes filled her with loathing which for once overcame her manners.

Mr. Watson backed to the door, opened it and fled.

It was almost dark in the store as Mary and Thomas faced each other.

"It's as Maria says," said Thomas heavily. "The boy—"

"Maria has no part in this," said Mary acidly. "Willy is a good boy. He's young. He'll learn."

"He'll learn!" snapped Thomas, struggling to maintain his self-control. "Indeed, he'll learn! You know what I said last time. The boy has run off from school for the last time. He's spent his last day in school. Tomorrow he goes to work."

Mary started to protest, then stopped. It was not the time to talk. When Thomas was quieter, they'd discuss it. Yet, it was long since she had seen him so angry. This was not the vexation which caused him to explode. "We'll see," she said quietly. "Come now. We'll go home."

"James," said Thomas, his face violent, "appreciated the chance we gave him. At this rate Will will land in the reformatory. Some of his friends are there now. I've stood it long enough." His voice grew colder and more set as they climbed the hill past the lesser houses that lined the way. "If I'd his chances as a boy—"

Thomas was building to a fury, thought of which frightened Mary. She put her hand on his arm, as though for assistance up the steep grade. Thomas did not respond. He strode doggedly, tensely, purposefully.

When Will entered the house through the back door he was greeted by a blow to the side of the head which sent him reeling through the dimness of the back kitchen. Before he could recover a second blow across the other side of his head knocked him down. Thomas pulled the inner door to behind him and pulled off his heavy belt.

Inside the kitchen Mary and Emily heard Will's whimpering cries, the scuffling, then his screams. Mary was white. Emily, sobbing convulsively, dashed at the door. Mary grasped and held her. She winced as a louder scream came from Will. Emily knew what it was. The sharp belt buckle had cut into her brother.

She struggled to free herself.

"I'll kill him! I'll kill him!"

Agnes came downstairs smiling. She was dressed to leave for choir rehearsal. "I hope," she said happily, "Pa is giving Willy what he deserves."

Emily broke loose, kicked her sister viciously in the shins, and ran upstairs holding her hands over her ears.

Agnes, all her ladylike dignity gone, howled.

"Mother! That child—"

"You got what you deserve," said Mary.

The door was flung open, and Thomas pulled Will in by the ear, twisting it for the added pleasure. He hurled the boy against the door of the bedroom off the kitchen. There was blood and dirt on Will's face. He was moaning and sobbing as he clawed blindly for the latch of the door.

"You'll have no supper! In the morning you'll go to work with me!"

Thomas was breathing hard. His cheeks were white. His eyes shone like a madman's. "Now," he said, his voice trembling, "I'll have my tea."

"If you do have your tea," said Mary, "you will get it yourself."

"My tea!" roared Thomas, looking frightened.

Mary swept past him and went up the stairs to comfort Emily.

"I'll get your tea for you, Pa," cooed Agnes.

"Thank ye, m'girl," said Thomas heavily. "Thank ye."

Later that evening at the meeting of the St. Mark's vestry, Thomas was white-faced, stern, and silent. The rector, a slender, scholarly man from Devon who knew the Stapely's part of England, looked at Thomas Stapely's handsome head and wondered but did not comment. He admired the man.

For centuries the Forest of Dean had produced strong, determined men who knew their own minds and set squarely about getting what they wanted. Once in a while some Forest family produced one who was just a little stronger and more determined, had a little more courage and vision than the rest, and he broke loose to cut new paths for himself. Often there was a strain of mysticism in Forest men like Thomas Stapely, but it was counterbalanced by a hard-headed stubbornness that sometimes made life hard for them and for those about them.

The rector did not pry. He knew that there are depths and struggles in any man's mind that are not for others to peer into. Yet he managed to linger with his senior warden after the others had tramped out.

"I didn't leave the Forest because I did not love the place," said

Thomas, his voice trembling. "I worked in London as a young man, helping to build the houses out along Oxford Street. London was a busy place in the 'Fifties. Houses going up everywhere, and shops. I used to go to St. Paul's now and then, and I've heard Spurgeon in the Gardens. But it was always the Forest with me. I know every foot of it—Wakeney and Millstone Green, the Roman scowles, the mines at Beechenford and on the Lydney road, the collieries all about, and the Acorn Plot."

"I know," murmured the rector, wondering what Thomas Stapely was trying to say. "I think the Forest is one of the most beautiful spots in all England. 'Happy is the Eye,' you know."

" 'Twixt the Severn and the Wye'." Brightening a little, Thomas finished for him. "Many's the time I've heard my father say that. He was Keeper. I used to walk the beats with him or with one of his woodmen early in the morning guarding the King's trees, when I was just a little tyke, before I was put to learn my trade over in Broadley with my uncle. He was a joiner there."

"I know Broadley, too," said the rector quietly. "There's a little inn there. I used to come down from Cambridge in the spring."

"I left to better myself," said Thomas, almost mechanically, "to be my own man in a new and faster moving place, to give my wife and children the things I could not give them in the Forest."

"And you've done it," said the rector firmly. "You've accomplished much for yourself and for St. Mark's too."

"With God's help," said Thomas. "Now, today I've been shown that I have been too proud. My youngest boy is worthless and an ingrate." He told the rector the story.

"You don't think you were too hasty?" asked the priest, watching Thomas' face.

"He'll work," said Thomas stubbornly. "He's had his chance."

"He's of a different generation."

"James is of the same."

"But James's character was formed in England. William has known only Ilium and the ways here. Mischievous, perhaps, but not bad. He's sensitive and of a different temperament from James."

"He'll work," repeated Thomas, coldly now that he was opposed. "He'll learn as I learned."

The rector looked at him quietly. The man had been injured badly, hurt in his hopes. What he thought of as his sacrifice, though he had been indulging an equally strong or perhaps stronger part of his nature, had been held at nought, or he thought it had. The taste was bitter in his mouth.

44

"Perhaps it may not hurt him to miss school—for a time," he said.

Neither Mary nor the rector really understood, thought Thomas as he walked heavily home. They came of a different class, of an easier life. They did not know, even Mary, the full depths of joy in the Lord and trust in Him, or the law that said that a man and a man's children should walk uprightly and joyfully in the way of the Lord.

He walked on down the gas-lighted street that was dark except for the pools of light around the lamp posts themselves. It was that kind of night, and colder, to make up for the warmth of the false spring day. Men carrying lunch boxes and tools passed him on the way to work on one of the night shifts. Some of them spoke to him. The thudding of the big hammer at the forge came clearly from down by the river. A streetcar passed, the driver, his coat collar up about his ears, chirping to his horses. A woman cried out in one of the crowded tenements.

Thomas walked past the corner that led up to his own house and down South Avenue toward Ilium. Gradually the brittle armor of self-righteousness, which he had assumed as first defense and which had been choking him, began to melt away. He loved his son who had Mary's eyes and Mary's hair and something of Mary's way. He loved God, and he loved Mary, and he loved his son.

James would be a physician and a healer of men. Perhaps he could make Will a carpenter as he had been and was, a fine carpenter with skilled, sure hands and a steady eye. Christ had been a carpenter. A timid joy began to seep back warming the edges of his heart that had seemed a frozen weight within his chest.

It was God who had planned the miracle of his life and Who had walked by his side and watched over him at every step. He was watching over him and guiding him now. He loved God as he loved the house that he had built on the hill and the land on which it stood, and the oaks in the Forest of Dean. God was from everlasting to everlasting.

The spirit of Thomas Stapely was soothed and made glad. He turned and went back to the turning of his own street. His heart was full as he entered his home and, hesitating, held out his hands to his wife.

Mary looked at him.

"Your feet are wet, Thomas. You had better get off your shoes."

"Mary—" He was afraid.

"I gave Will his tea and put arnica on his bruises," she said without looking at him. "There was one cut on his leg I had to bandage."

"I did what I thought was right," said Thomas hoarsely. His joy was gone. The iron bitterness returned. "He goes to work with me in the morning. He'll learn."

Mary's heart ached for the confused hurt of the man and the wounded body and spirit of the boy. She moved quietly away.

Upstairs, Emily, who had heard her father come in, prayed that she might grow up quickly so that she could be twice as strong as her father. She would beat him as he had beaten Will.

Earlier she had crept down to comfort Will, knowing that her mother heard but would not interfere. Now she sobbed quietly with choking rage, the desire to kill her father, and the helpless knowledge that there was nothing she could do. They could run away, she and Will, but they could not do it that night. Besides that would not hurt her father enough. It would only grieve her mother. The streak of light, coming in at the side of the blind in the room she shared with Agnes, waved and twisted as blurring tears streamed down her face.

Will had been at work two days, leaving Emily's life desolate and empty at school and at home, before there was anything she could do to help.

She was waiting by the gate in the side street that ended with the path going into their yard when James came home from Albany late Saturday afternoon. She smiled brightly at him when he was halfway up the hill and, surprised, her older brother started grudgingly to smile back.

Emily waited until he was nearer. Not for nothing had she traveled the streets of South Ilium with Will.

"You dirty bastard!" she said. "You dirty, stinking bastard!" She turned and ran.

Chapter 6

THERE WERE MUTTERINGS among the men when Thomas Stapely brought his son, who carried a cut on his forehead and a bruise on one cheek, with him at half past seven in the morning and roughly ordered him to work. Alongside Thomas's shop and sheds was part of the builder's yard opening directly on South Avenue and separated from it only by a low fence of wooden palings. Into it Thomas had had dumped two great drayloads of used brick, ten thousand of them, which he had foresightedly bought from a wrecker who was tearing down a number of old houses in Ilium to make way for business structures.

He gave Will a battered trowel and an old file and put him to work cleaning the hardened blobs and streaks of old lime and mortar from the bricks. He wanted, he said, each brick, even each half-brick, clean enough for laying without the mason or his helper's having to waste their good time on them. He ordered Will brusquely to see that they were just that clean.

Will did not answer but slowly and sullenly went to work, squatting down on his heels among the rubble. He wore old overalls over the oldest of his school clothes, and a worn sweater. He pulled his cap down over his eyes so that no one could see that he had been crying and dragged off the clumsy mittens his mother had insisted that he wear. Every part of his body ached, though he would admit it to no one.

Tom Stapely was going a little too far this time, the men agreed. They put their own sons to work as soon as they could, but that was different. Will was a general favorite with them all, at least with all those steadily employed by the contractor and not the drifting laborers who worked only until they had enough money for more gin. The Stapelys were supposed to be better than mere workingmen and their families. A fact which they could resent at other times, the men put forward inconsistently now as another reason why "Honest Tom"—and they used the term with anger and contempt this time—should have kept his boy in school and made an educated man of him. This wasn't the way he had treated his prig of a James, whom most of them could not abide.

They felt admiration for Will for standing up to the old man, as rumor said he had done; and they felt sorry for him and wanted to show that they were on his side. Thomas gave them no opportunity. As a prisoner is put in solitary confinement during the first days of his sentence, Will was isolated from the other and older workers, but instead of being hidden from sight he was forced into a conspicuous place where his humiliation would be the more painful.

No one could get in or out of Tom Stapely's place without seeing him. Painters, carpenters, masons, plasterers, teamsters, and all the others—for Stapely's was busy these days—made it a point to wave and call their greetings, but Will only said "hello" almost under his breath and looked away when some of those he knew best and liked most spoke. The men understood and did not press their attentions.

Some of his erstwhile fellows on their way to school stared dumbfounded.

"Hey, Willy, watcha doin'? Geez! Lookit Willy!"

Fiery red, Will tried to grin at the first lot. As another batch stopped and one of the girls giggled, he went doggedly on with his chipping and filing, afraid to slow up lest Thomas be watching him from the window. When three of his cronies who courted rather than feared lateness at school, stood on the bottom board of the fence and hurled good-natured insults, he made as if to throw one of the bricks, and they ran laughing to tell the good news of his downfall and misery.

August, his father's carpenter and cabinetmaker who did most of the fine work Thomas had to have done, came out and drove away the last lot.

"Git avay!" he shouted at them. "Loafers and good vor nothings!" He walked over to Will. "Slow up, Villy. You gonna haf plenty of time to do all dem bricks. Look, I show you how."

With two deft strokes August had a brick cleaner than the one Will had gnawed and filed at for five minutes. August cleaned off another.

"I get you a block of vood to sit on," said August. "You get all stiff dat vay. Your fadder crazy man vit dat temper of his."

"He's all right," muttered Will.

He was getting used to his task, though his chapped hands were getting raw from handling the coarse bricks, when his Aunt Maria tripped by on her way to the butchers. She carried her empty shopping basket and moved smartly along.

"That's the boy," she said, nodding her head in approval. She had decided not to rub in what she saw as her triumph. She had not known until that morning how icily haughty and cutting her sister-in-law could be. Mary had really frightened her. "That's how Auntie likes to see her little man work."

"Get out of here, you old bitch!" warned Will under his breath.

"What did you say?" asked Maria suspiciously.

"I said 'good morning,'" lied Will. He looked the other way, and hammered so viciously with the edge of his trowel that a brick broke in his torn hands.

He was so tired that night he could hardly eat his supper. Little was said at the table, though Thomas was trying to act as though nothing had happened and Emily was bursting to tell Will how their friends at school had taken the news and what their teachers had said. Everyone was full of his praise now, and Old Man Watson was even saying he might call and try to get Mr. Stapely to reconsider. Agnes had not come home. She was having her tea with one of her friends in Ilium and was to take the streetcar home before nine o'clock.

Will worked on the brick pile the rest of that week. All of South Ilium knew of his downfall. "Jest like what convicts does," the boys assured each other loudly from the other side of the fence.

A few men who dared spoke quietly to Thomas Stapely. Opposition increased his determination, and his brow blackened with a forbidding frown when the subject was mentioned. Early the next week he called Will into the shop.

There were several clean new sheets of official-looking paper on top of the jumble of small tools, notebooks, and bits of wood littering his battered roll-top desk.

"I've had your apprenticeship papers made out," he told Will. "You'll learn your trade as I did."

Will knew what that meant—years! He knew what happened to apprentices who tried to run away or to cheat their masters. At least he had many times heard his father and other men tell of their apprentice days in England, and he supposed it was the same now in Ilium.

He soon learned that though he had been apprenticed to his father as a master carpenter, he was to work with the various carpenters in his father's employ. It was his good fortune that he was first handed over to August.

The middle-aged German had worked for his father before Will had been born. It was August who had let Will play in the curling and sweet smelling wood shavings when his father had brought the small child to work. It was August from whom Will had begged bits of wood for whatever he was trying to contrive, even the pieces with which he had been making the plate rack for his mother's birthday.

Fat, bald, with a drooping brown and yellow moustache, August was an artist. A hard-working perfectionist squinting through his half-moon eyeglasses, which were always so smeared with fine dust from his handsaw that it was a wonder he could see through them at all, he worked at what he loved and could have considered no other existence. August was independent. He brooked interference from no one, and grunted away suggestions as though he had not heard them. Even Thomas had learned not to interfere too much with August. There was not a workman in Ilium to match him.

August would ready trim for insertion in one of Thomas's houses, and put it in, build steps, panel doors, do any of the finishing. He would do none of the rough carpentering. That, as he made clear, was for butchers. Though he was a carpenter and joiner, as Will was to be, August was a cabinetmaker at heart. At home at night, in the

49

small and scoured house where he lived with his comfortable wife and their half-dozen children, he relaxed by continuing the work he did during the day. The house was full of fine chairs and delicate tables which August had made. Planing, sanding to the smooth finish of polished marble, contriving joints so fine that they were almost imperceptible, working carefully in fine veneers and inlays were August's joy. Patiently he would spend days of undiluted happiness finishing the wood, staining it, oiling it, rubbing it, until the mahogany glowed with a deep luster and all the perfect grain in a quartered-oak surface was brought out.

August was glad to have Will work with him. The boy's hands were good and his eyes were sharp. He himself had long ago taught him how to square up a joint, how to lock one board against another, to tap a finishing chisel with a mallet just so.

"You vork hard," he told Will, "and August show you all he knows. Ve do good vork. Ve do everything right as ve can. Ve hurry up vor nobody, no matter vat de old man say."

It was the beginning of happy days for Will. He could not admit it. He had to keep up his front as a wronged and resentful victim of his father's harshness and stupidity and, when he was with Emily, to mouth dire threats of horrible vengeance. To maintain his mother's added tenderness he found it useful to appear hurt and suffering but trying to do his best.

August would not let him near the wood lathes. Not yet, he said. But Will was happy even to be handing August the tools he called for. He had always, it seemed to him, known the difference between a crosscut and a ripsaw. Now he learned the uses of all the others, the compass saw, the coping saw, the keyhole, and the rest. He learned to saw a straight line, cutting down the waste side of the piece to avoid the kerf. August taught him how to set a saw, keeping him at it with the files for days before he pronounced his work satisfactory.

The methodical German, pleased with his apt pupil, taught Will one tool at a time, how to care for it and keep it sharp, before he let him try the simplest work by himself. When he assigned Will the job of planing the edge of a board to be fitted into a structure he was making, every dimension had to measure perfectly before he would accept the finished piece. More than once tears of vexation sprang to Will's eyes when August rejected an attempt he had thought perfect, and bade him try again.

As he respected his tools, August loved the stuff with which he worked and transmitted both his knowledge and appreciation to Will. He drilled him until he could recognize a piece of maple, oak, cherry, walnut, and the other northern hardwoods at a glance. He taught him to distinguish quickly between native and southern pine and spruce. When Will, reacting to the man's contagious admiration for one noble wood, expressed his contempt for another, August would have none of it. All wood, he explained to him, was good; only some wood, when it was properly seasoned, yet not too dry and brittle, was better for some things than some other kinds.

Will surreptitiously extracted from the house workshop and carried to work with him the almost finished plate rack he had been making for his mother's birthday. August inspected it and approved. He showed Will how to hide the necessary holes for the wall hanging so cunningly that they would scarcely be noticed, and with boiled linseed oil and turpentine stolen from the shop's store and some powdered pumice, which August brought from home, helped him to finish the wood.

Mary was delighted with the gift, and together she and Will hung it on the dining room wall. Without so much as a "by your leave," thought Thomas bitterly, or, as his own father would have said, a "damn your eyes." His own gift of a fine pair of long kid gloves, which he and Maria had gone for to the big Ilium department store one night, was received merely with polite thanks.

Then August put Will to work making a tool box for himself. It was a necessary article and a sound lesson in woodworking. A tool box had to be sturdy enough to take hard usage. It had to be strong and to show that the man who had made and used it knew his craft. They picked out good straight-grained boards. August sketched out the box and copied the dimensions of his own. As his other duties allowed, Will worked at his box with absorption and growing delight. He was anxious to please August, but more anxious to please himself. This August noted with an artist's approval. It was a good sign. Tom Stapely was a big fool!

Freedom from school gave Will an inner elation he could hardly disguise. Except where it had touched his imagination, school had bored him. He had been impressed mostly by the pointlessness of his painful lessons in grammar, and arithmetic. Now he was learning facts that mattered in a man's world. He was a man doing man's work.

He was being initiated into the mysteries of an ancient and honorable craft. He was both vain of his new knowledge and humbled. He was amazed at the lore and skills which a good carpenter had to have. It stupefied him that all his years he had watched his father and his father's men hammering and sawing without once suspecting that locked in them were the secrets of japping, fishing, scarving, housing, dovetailing, doweling, and morticing. Unwillingly he began to have a new admiration for his father whom he had so often watched handling with force and sureness the tools of his trade.

His father was a good carpenter, August solemnly assured him one day when they were eating lunch. He had learned his trade well in the Old Country. His father was not a good cabinetmaker, August had to admit in strict accuracy, as he gnawed off another huge and satisfying bite of his knockwurst and rye bread sandwich, but he built strong and sound. Joists his father had notched stood up to strain and weather. Will, eating the last of the delicious lard cake Emily had put into his lunch box and savoring the caraway seeds between his teeth, listened intently.

"Vork vat is all right," he told Will, "vill last a lifetime. Better vork vill last ein hundred years. Good carpenter vork vill last till the vood rots!"

If Will quickly accustomed himself to the new order of his life, Thomas showed no signs of relenting. Perhaps it was the uneasy consciousness that he had been wrong, perhaps the dawning realization that he had succeeded in giving Will just what he wanted, that kept his severity from relaxing.

Emily had gone downtown to Ilium by herself and squandered all of her savings, money given her as presents on Christmas and at her birthday, to buy Will a lunch pail like the other men's. He had been overjoyed with the gift. It not only served its useful purpose, but was also symbol of his new stature. He knew too well what it had cost Emily.

Thomas had never given them any allowance, holding that money in the hands of children was open invitation to sinfulness. This, instead of preventing wrongdoing, had led to crime. More than once Emily and Will had pilfered bits of change they had found about the house, once even stolen a half dollar from their mother's pocketbook. They had taken no joy in the crime, not even in helping Mary hunt for the half dollar she was sure she must have lost in the house. It had been the only way they could attend a school treat for which they knew their father would have refused the money.

It had been one of Will's chief consolations in his first days at work that now he would earn money of his own.

Thomas paid off his men on Saturday afternoons, taking their wages to those out on jobs, handing the others theirs at a line-up at his desk. Will wondered how much he would get. Jimmy Michaels, a fourteen-year-old machinist's apprentice in one of the shops, got three dollars. He knew an older boy who got six, and even one Croesus who after three years was getting eight dollars and sometimes more a week at piecework in the stove factory. He gave his mother six dollars and kept two for himself.

Perhaps his father would give him two dollars. He had it all planned that he would give his mother a dollar and a half, and give a quarter to Emily and keep the other for himself. Hopefully he followed August, whose dubious look he did not see, into the place where his father was.

Thomas was just paying off two of the carpenters who were not working that day because of rain. A bricklayer and a mason's helper were waiting. There were other men whom Will did not know.

Thomas handed August his money, then looked up and saw Will. All the smothered bitterness of his defeat broke out. His hard eyes went malevolent.

"What do you want, boy?"

"I—" Embarrassed and taken by surprise, Will stammered.

"Is it money you want?" taunted Thomas, safe in his own world where there were no Marys or rectors to make him feel inferior. "You'll get your board and room as you always have. Only now you'll earn them."

Anxious to toady favor, two men laughed. One of the other carpenters looked hard at Thomas and spat tobacco juice deliberately on the floor. Will fled. When August found him in the shop he lay with his head in his arms and his fists clenched in a pile of sawdust and shavings.

August said nothing, but the next week, when it could seem to have no connection with the incident, he brought Will a small pipe with a curved stem and a cunningly carved bowl and a tobacco pouch of cowhide which closed with a drawstring.

"You smoke, so you smoke," he told Will. "I vasn't using dese." He had smoked the pipe once so that it would not look new. "Just don't let no one else find dem."

If anything was needed to complete Will's worship of the man, it was this gift. He was able to buy more tobacco when that in the pouch ran out by palming the money Thomas gave him on Sunday to put in the collection plate. Emily did the same with hers. And one week he got an unexpected windfall.

His new status did not free Will entirely from work in the store. When Mary was visiting or shopping and yet wanted the store open, she would borrow Will to take care of it. She always had candy or some treat for him when she returned.

One afternoon when he was on duty in the store, he sold three chamber pots for a dollar, but returned Mary only seventy-five cents of the amount. Encouraged by the success of his first attempt, he sold a small table for four dollars and gave her only three. He had to be careful not to sell to anyone who might know his mother and innocently give away the details of the transactions. Luck played into his hands by sending an occasional stranger into the store. This became a dependable source of income.

He had worked with August for several months when Thomas took him out of the shop and turned him over to Hank Edwards, straw boss on a new cottage Thomas was starting a half-mile down South Avenue toward Ilium, in a busier part of town. Though reluctant to leave August, Will was glad to get outdoors. The weather was fine now, and he was anxious to prove his heroism further by doing heavier work.

Foul-mouthed, loud talking Hank Edwards was very different from August. A lanky, energetic man of middle age, he had other fish to fry, as he told everybody, than working for Honest Tom Stapely. Politics was the thing. That was where the money was. And he wasn't paid to be no nursemaid. Stapely's kid or not, he'd have Willy hauling two-by-fours, yeah, *and* four-by-eights till his arms pulled out of his sockets.

Yet Edwards was a good rough carpenter who could get the framework of a house up in a hurry and whose work, though it might not stand inspection by the fastidious, was fundamentally sound. August would grunt disapproval when he came to lay the floors and frame the doors and windows, but Edwards was also a useful man.

Despite his loud talk, he was careful of Will. A man had to look which side his bread was buttered. He was careful to praise the father to the boy and the boy to the father.

"Kid's a good worker, boss," he announced loudly after Will had been working with him for several weeks. "Be a real builder like yourself."

"What's that lumber doing there?" demanded Thomas, pointing to a pile of finishing board that had not yet been put under shelter. He disliked being called "boss." Yet he was pleased. All the reports he had got of Willy from the men were good. There wasn't a lazy bone in the boy's body he told himself with sour satisfaction as he drove away.

He would have liked to express his approval but did not know how. The best he could do was to give Mary, with instructions that she could give it to Willy, the worn calf-bound copy of Treadway's *Pocket Carpenter's Assistant and Practical Instructor in Joining* that he had bought in his London days and used on many a job there and in the Forest. It was one of his prized possessions.

Will took the book proudly and every day carried it in the hip

54

pocket of his work breeches as Thomas carried his rule. He said nothing to his father about the book and Thomas, glancing sidelong when he thought Will was not looking, was never able to catch him reading it.

Yet things were easier between them after that. Some mornings, when Thomas was going first to the shop, they walked to work together. Now and again Thomas explained a point of construction, and Will listened attentively.

Thomas was busier than ever with the affairs of St. Mark's and with his other religious activities. He went with the rector to a diocesan convention in Albany, attending some of the lay meetings. His talk to Mary at dinner was full of bishops and dignitaries he had seen and even talked with. He was inspired by the address of a missionary bishop from India. He and the rector had new plans and ideas for the parish. He was to talk at a mission in the downtown slums of what he had seen and heard and attempt to rouse the hearts of the sodden unfortun es there to a knowledge of the blessedness of our Lord Jesus.

Agnes went with him as she usually did. There was seldom an evangelist of any persuasion who came to Ilium that Agnes did not go to hear speak, and she always went to hear her father. Mary was to visit that evening with old friends from England who lived on the other side of Ilium.

Will went to bed before his parents and Agnes left the house. Five minutes afterward, with Emily's assurance that all was safe, he was out of the house and headed for South Avenue.

He witnessed at least part of the traditional yearly battle between the Orangemen and their bitter enemies, the Loyal Sons of St. Patrick of South Ilium. It was a ferocious battle, men with mayhem in their hearts and whisky in their blood striving to break each other's heads for the greater glory of whichever side they espoused. Street lamps were broken. The night was loud with shouts and curses. Coats were ripped from backs and sleeves out of coats. Women using the windows of their tenements as box seats, screamed imprecations and encouragement. The police arrived with bells clanging, the horses on the paddy wagon pawing the air as they were brought up short after a headlong gallop.

It was glorious stuff. Surprisingly, though there were a few cuts and bruises, no one was really hurt. Both sides, making black threats of what they would do the next year, retired with their honor intact. Will saw several of his father's men in the Orange ranks. One of them saw him and winked. Gravely Will winked back and emitted an extra large puff of smoke from the little curved pipe August had given him and which that night he was smoking openly in the street. The man would not tell his father. They were fellow workmen.

Chapter 7

WHEN THE RECTOR fell ill of *la grippe,* Thomas was in his glory. He became lay preacher of St. Mark's as well as senior warden. For two consecutive Sundays he delivered the sermon from the aisle before the altar. The parish listened as intently as it did to the rector himself. Thomas moved through those weeks as a man consecrated, poring over his Bible, carefully writing his sermon on lined yellow foolscap with one of the flat carpenter's pencils—a lumber company supplied them, and Will himself would handle no other now—which he always used. Thomas' lips moved silently as he went abstracted about his work during the week, and Will knew that he was memorizing his sermon.

On Sunday they all sat in the family pew to listen. Mary looked dignified, a little removed. She regarded her husband almost curiously. Agnes was bursting with pride. James, whose graduation neared, looked attentive and inscrutable when he felt his father's eyes were on him. Emily, whose prettiness and maturity had increased noticeably in the past months, looked almost as dignified as her mother and as completely self-possessed. Will, though he did not wish to be, was slightly awed.

Of them all, it was he who knew his father at work as well as at home. He was seeing him in still a different role. That the white-haired man whose real nobility of expression was marked as he stood talking simply in his choir gown was the same man who, drunk with rage and lusting in his cruelty—it was that which had really frightened Will —had struck him with all his force again and again, intent to lacerate and wound, did not seem possible.

Thomas, standing there before God's altar in a church he had helped build, convinced his listeners with the intensity that informed his whole figure and trembled in his voice. His simple words, clothed in the Biblical and traditional language from which he could not disassociate his love of God, carried meanings that lay in sound as well as in sense to his devout hearers.

He felt humble that he could stand and speak where for centuries men like him and better men had stood and spoken in the churches of England. He thought, as he faced the west, of St. Paul's in London, of the rose window in Gloucester, of the simple church of St. Stephen's in the Forest where he had been confirmed, and of Calvary where he had been a communicant when he and Mary, before any of the children were born, lived in Beechenford. He was humble and grateful but charged with such fullness of spirit that he had the strength of ten, the power of a host. His words faltered as a sense of the fullness of life choked his heart and knowledge of the nearness of God, yea, of His very Presence, made him afraid.

Will had recovered and was looking around.

"Old hypocrite," he thought.

He tried to catch Emily's eye. She was thinking her own thoughts. He wondered what they were. He felt, uneasily, that she had changed, though she still watched out for him as much as she could. Since his going to work she was spending more time with girls she knew at school, particularly Blanche Stebbins, a dark girl with searching eyes and a nervous giggle whom Will did not like. Once she had even got her mother's permission to stay at the Stebbinses for tea, though the Stebbinses did not go to St. Mark's. They were Methodists. Emily never told him where she and Blanche went or what they did.

Mary felt pity for her husband. He'd tried so hard. He had accomplished so much. He might have been a clergyman had life been differently ordered. She began to make her plans for tea. Mr. and Mrs. Jenkins were to call that afternoon. Maria and Arthur would be there, as every Sunday, for tea. She would have to return with Thomas for evensong, otherwise his feelings would be hurt and he would sulk. Maria was trimming her new bonnet that she had bought to wear to James's graduation. Of course, Maria could not touch it on a Sunday, still, if just this once—she was anxious to see what it looked like.

They need have no fear for James after his graduation. James would succeed. He would get what he wanted. He was not like Willy. He was selfish, if the truth were told. He was not like her, or even like Thomas, though he looked so much like him. He was more like his great-uncle George in Bristol, who was said to be getting rich from his factories. But, of course, he was like them all.

"Emily," she whispered. "Pull down your skirts."

James's graduation was a great event. It threw other things that had happened into the past and unimportance. Will's working, with occasional time off to help his mother, occasional days at home when his work was outside and the weather was too bad, or he was ill, as everyone was often ill in those days, was now an accepted part of the order of things. Mary's hostility to Thomas had disappeared, as, in time, it always did. Thomas' severity and militant righteousness had lapsed into merely his normal sternness.

The graduation was as good as a wedding or a funeral. There were preparations about the house for weeks ahead. Letters came from aunts and uncles in England whom Emily and Will had never seen. The dressmaker was there for almost a week, making new dresses for the occasion for both Mary and Maria. There were bits of cloth and half-finished sleeves or flounces all over the living room and thread and lint on the floor even in the parlor. Thomas bought a new suit. Emily and Will were told to behave themselves or they would not be allowed to go to the graduation, just as though it were a Sunday-school picnic or a holiday treat.

There were other mysterious preparations having to do with James's entrance into the world as a physician. Thomas went several times to one of the Ilium banks on work afternoons, and he called twice to see Dr. Samuels, their family doctor, and one evening Dr. Samuels came to the house. He and Mary and Thomas talked a long time in the parlor with the door shut.

All of them enjoyed the general excitement, and Will shared in some of his brother's reflected glory, answering the questions of neighbors who waylaid him on the way to and from work. South Ilium had produced several young men who went off to study for the ministry, and one was even a missionary in Japan or Kentucky, Will was not sure which, but James would be the first doctor to spring from the English community. There were none, of course, from the Irish element, though some of their sons had become policemen or bartenders or well-known street fighters in New York itself.

As he did only on great and state occasions, Thomas hired a livery stable carryall when the great day came. He took Will with him to the stables and watched sharply while the liveryman harnessed a sound looking beast with a bright eye who seemed as glad to get out as Will was to take him. Because he was in high good humor, Thomas let Will handle the reins part of the way up South Avenue to their corner.

This put Will into a state of fine excitement. He held the reins taut and high in his left hand, as the best coachmen did, chirped in the approved manner, and nodded to awed acquaintances as the horse broke into an easy trot in passing a long dray loaded with pig iron on its way to the furnaces.

They did not attempt the hill, which few horses could negotiate except with the lightest buggy and the driver, if he were careful, walking alongside. Will was as well pleased. There were a score of neighbors waiting to see them embark at the corner. He sat holding the reins while his mother and aunt and his two sisters, all anxiously handling their skirts and calling warnings to each other, stepped into the carryall. He hoped his father would forget to take the reins, but perhaps Thomas, too, was conscious of the scene and what was fitting. He motioned Will aside, sat himself very upright in the driver's seat, smiled at their friends, and they started for Albany.

Will turned and looked covertly at Emily. Her hair was up, and she wore the long skirts of a young woman for the first time. There were pink rosebuds about her bonnet, ribbons of light blue silk matching the color of her eyes knotted loosely under her firm young chin. Will thought she looked beautiful, and he was almost afraid. For a moment he felt lonely and resentful and small alongside his father. But when he looked again, Emily made a face and silently stuck out the tip of her tongue at Thomas' broad back.

Will laughed happily. They had crossed the bridge over the Hudson below South Ilium. They were in the country now, and it was one of the rarest of late June days, bright, sweet-smelling, radiant. They would be driving most of the morning. Will hoped they would never get there.

Chapter 8

THOMAS WAS very happy one winter a few years later. Looking back, he could contemplate the past with satisfaction. The present was good, and the future was safely in God's hands.

Events had vindicated his judgments and his actions. Willy was a different lad. At home he was willing and industrious. Already he was as good a carpenter, in Thomas' private opinion, as some of the men he had working for him, and at far less cost. Will could lay a floor or frame a window as well as anyone. At Christmas he had bought him a fine new set of tools, and it warmed him to remember how pleased the boy had been. Then, just before Easter, his mother had taken him into one of the big stores in Ilium and bought him his first long trousers suit and a new outfit from head to toe. The two of them had had a fine time of it, and the boy looked well. It pleased Thomas to recall his generosity.

Emily was in high school. Mary had insisted that the girl have the schooling denied Will and he had given in, grudgingly at first, for keeping a girl in school seemed a waste. But she was smart at her books, and people kept telling him that she was pretty as a picture. It was clear that Emily was to be the real beauty of the family, though Thomas always answered stoutly, "Handsome is as handsome does."

It was still James and Agnes who were his real pride. Dr. Samuels and some of the professors at the college had arranged for James to work for a time with a fine doctor in Brooklyn. He had been there more than a year and a half now in the handsome brownstone house on DeKalb Avenue where he had his office with Dr. Moses and lived almost as one of the family with Dr. Moses and his wife. He had done well. Dr. Moses himself, a distinguished-looking, bearded, elegantly dressed practitioner, had told him so, for Thomas had been down once to visit James, and Mary had gone several times.

With his own eyes he had seen the neat sign, lettered discreetly in gold on a small black board, which read: ROGER T. MOSES, M.D., and right beneath it in letters the same size, JAMES T. STAPELY, M.D. Thomas had walked three times past the house just to see it before he knocked.

Dr. Moses was urging James to stay, saying there was practice enough for two, and some day James would have it all, but James was anxious to set up for himself. He was on the lookout for a place where he could begin practice on his own. Thomas had humbly suggested Ilium or even Albany, but James had shaken his head. He wanted to stay in the city, and Thomas could understand.

On a Sunday afternoon they had taken the ferry over to Manhattan and he and James, who looked so much like him—they were so unmistakably handsome father and handsome son that people had turned to look—had walked about the Battery and up lower Broadway. It was a warm day, and at Fulton Street they had stopped and eaten some ice cream even though it was Sunday, and later they had gone to vespers in Trinity at Broadway and Wall Street.

He missed James. He had not realized how it would be after he had finished medical college and was no longer near at hand. It made Thomas turn more and more to Agnes, who revelled in the attention. It was Agnes who went with him to hear visiting ministers in Ilium, Agnes who sang with him when he got out his cello in the evening and Walter Ambridge brought his violin over to join them in the parlor. She had sung a solo part when the oratorio was put on in the gray stone Presbyterian church with its commanding spire where

60

some of Ilium's richest families attended. The newspaper had listed her name along with that of the choirmaster and the other solists, not just mentioned her in the program. Thomas had sent a clipping to his brother in England.

"Agnes certainly is her father's daughter," Mary remarked dryly one afternoon when she had just a few of her closest friends in for afternoon tea. There were Mrs. Ambridge, Mrs. Glover, the apothecary's wife, Mrs. Stillwait, a widow whose husband had been for years a foreman at the carriage factory, and Miss Loren, who had never married but kept house for her brother who was with the railroad and said to have a very fine position. Mrs. Glover—tiny, bright-eyed, quick—understood. She smiled, raising her well-shaped eyebrows slightly, and Mary smiled back at her. Aunt Simpson had been unable to come as Walter was not feeling very well. They were all very sorry.

More than ever, it was an honor to have tea at Mrs. Stapely's. James and Agnes reflected great credit on the family. Thomas's prestige in the English community was even stronger. Men came in the evenings to discuss problems of St. Mark's and problems of their own. They were proud to tell people the next day, Tom Stapely said this and Tom Stapely that, but none of them called him Tom to his face. They liked to talk over their affairs with him. It was like talking to the rector, like, only easierlike, they said.

The rector himself came often to see Thomas Stapely. His worth to the parish and his own good fortune in having such a layman he well knew and valued, but that was another thing. A thoughtful, imaginative man who, had life gone differently for him, had he been a little wiser perhaps in his youth than in middle age, might well have lived out his life as a don in some college of his own university— a don more after the manner of a Gray or a Carroll than a Pusey or a Newman—he saw the man as a stalwart specimen of the best type of English workman, and a man as native to his part of Gloucestershire as one of its oaks. Transplanted to America, he had come to substance and authority he could never have commanded at home.

Mary he always enjoyed seeing. Her casual graciousness and humor were a relief after the mumbling diffidence he often met with in some of his parishioners or the artificial overpoliteness, which so often masked a resentfulness of class distinction which those who displayed it would not have known in England. All did not transplant as well as Thomas and Mary Stapely.

His own wife, pretty, thin, pale, was lonely away from England and her own kind. She tried bravely sometimes, but she was too finely made. She could never quite face Ilium and America. He had promised her that when the experiment seemed over, they would return. He knew they would have to some day.

The rector's own relaxed manner sometimes perplexed Thomas, who wanted to look up to the clergy as ordained by God and by His Ordinance made different from other men. Yet he succumbed to it as did the others.

The rector had attempted to approach Will at the time of Will's disgrace, and been sullenly rebuffed for his pains. He knew immediately that he had been clumsy and that the boy was right. He was annoyed with himself for his stupid attempt to comfort.

From time to time he had noticed Will in church. He had spoken to him in passing on the street. The boy's mouth was sensitive. His smile was ready. The eyes which lighted his young face were intelligent and curious. His features were fine like his mother's rather than strong like Thomas Stapely's. Cap pulled down to one side, hands in his pockets, he was getting the mannerisms of the young workman, but he wore them as a jacket he could strip off as easily as he had donned it.

One day when they were not busy, Thomas sent Will down to make some repairs at the rectory, which he had promised for some time to attend to.

The rectory, which stood next to the church, was an ample, square frame house well back from the street. It had generous windows and wide, gently sloping roofs. The foundation was of granite blocks rather than brick. It looked more like a country than a city house. It actually had once been the farm home of some member of one of the great Dutch families who had held original grants to that portion of the Hudson valley. It had long been boarded up and in disuse when St. Mark's was built and an absent descendant of the family had been prevailed upon to deed it to the parish. Thomas Stapely had done most of the work of putting it into livable condition again, working whenever he had free time, often late at night.

A cleaning woman whom Will knew let him in at the back door, urging him to make no more noise than he had to as the rector's wife was taking a nap upstairs.

Will nodded and thought derisively, how does she expect me to saw and hammer without making any noise?

He knew the house well, as he had played in it as his father worked, and he knew that it was in the library that the repairs had to be made. He walked through to the room.

One window sill was rotted, as was the bottom member of the sash. Another sill was in bad shape. Will had cut and shaped the needed replacements in the shop and now had to tear out the old pieces and put in the new. He put down his tools and looked about him.

He had never seen so many books. His mother and father had a glass-fronted bookcase full of them in the living room at home, but there were many times that number here. They filled the low shelves that ran all around the square room.

At the wide fireplace of fine dull brick, real eighteenth century English brick, was the set of iron poker, shovel, and tongs which Sandy McGracken had wrought for the rector down at the forge. The inside of the fireplace was smoke blacked and there were inches of gray ash from the winter's fires. A full wood box stood handy. There were oil paintings, one on each wall, in heavy gold frames.

Will went to work, carefully prying loose some of the rotted woodwork. He had trouble extracting some of the old hand-wrought square nails. The claws of his hammer, though he had recently sharpened them, would not catch them easily, and some of the nails broke off as he tugged at them. He worked patiently so as not to destroy the parts to which he had to join the new pieces and not to mar the finished work that was still in good condition. The rotted sash pieces would be the worst. He thought his father should have sent a whole new frame.

He was working intently when the rector, evidently just home from some errand for his face was fresh as though he had been outdoors, walked into the room.

"Hello, Will!"

Will looked up and grinned, his hands still busy.

"Hello."

"Hard at it, I see."

Will could not answer immediately. He had, after some difficulty, just got the first sill board into place. He gave it the tap which would send it home and straightened up. He had grown considerably taller, but he was still slight. He was getting the workman's square, big-knuckled hands, but his frame was light and boyishly supple.

"This should have been done before," he said seriously. "The rain's been coming in. The floor's marked."

"I'm afraid I've been careless about it," the rector admitted.

"Oh, I didn't mean that," said Will quickly, afraid he had seemed to be finding fault. He bent to go on with his work.

The rector, smiling at the boy's back, watched him for a few minutes. He wondered if it made Will nervous. It annoyed him to have someone watch when he was attempting some manual task or even writing a sermon. It did not seem to bother Will. Perhaps it pleased him to have someone see how skillful he was at his work.

"Why not stop and rest for a bit," suggested the rector. "I shall be glad of someone to talk with."

Will hesitated.

"Your father is very proud of you these days, Will. Everyone says how well you do at your work, and now I can see it for myself."

Will flushed with pleasure, his fair cheeks burning. He tried to think of something to say. With someone else he might have made a flippant rejoinder or a rude disclaimer to hide the fact that he was pleased.

"I think that if you wanted to he would let you go back to school. I could speak to him about it, if you wanted me to."

"No!" exclaimed Will quickly. "I don't want to go to school any more."

The rector looked at him thoughtfully for a moment. The boy's rejection of the idea had been vehement.

"It doesn't hurt in the long run to have stayed at school as long as possible."

"I'm too old now," said Will earnestly. "I couldn't go back. The other fellows would be ahead of me. I'd be laughed at."

"Perhaps, but—"

"Besides I like what I'm doing. I would not like to give it up. I have to finish my time," said Will proudly.

"I see."

"If I had stayed right along," Will explained, answering the doubt he saw in the rector's face rather than his words, "it would be all right. But you can't go back and do what maybe you should have done."

"What did you say?"

"I said you can't go back and do what perhaps you should have done."

Out of the mouths of babes!

When he reached home, he found the whole family there and in a state of excitement. A letter had come that afternoon, and Mary had taken it right down to Thomas who had come home with her. Agnes had come home early from work just by chance.

"James has got his own practice!" Emily called to him before anyone else could spoil it. "It's in Brooklyn but a different part. Ma's going down to help him find a house and get settled. Pa's going to buy him a horse!"

"Emily!" scolded Agnes, who saw no reason why matters of importance should be talked of by either of the children, or even why they should be told.

Will looked at his mother, who nodded, smiling brightly. She was glad of the excuse for another trip to New York. South Ilium had seemed dull and her life in it gray and monotonous the last few weeks. She had not been feeling herself, as she put it, though she was not ill. It was difficult to explain. Already at the idea of the journey and new activity at the other end of it, she felt better.

"Pa says that he has to get the horse because James would be cheated by those traders down there. He says they'd be too sharp for him."

"Pa is getting him the horse for a present. All doctors have to have them. James is too smart to be cheated!" contradicted Agnes.

Emily made a face at her. "Pa said—" she began.

"Here, here now!" cried Thomas, as excited as any of them. "We'll see about that all in good time."

"Pa, can I go with you!" Will cried. He cared nothing for James or his affairs, but the idea of going down to Travers with his father to buy a horse was thrilling.

They had never been able to prevail upon Thomas to get a horse and buggy of their own. Thomas held that having their own horse would be extravagance, putting on airs, and a nuisance. At home in England only the gentry had their own horses and he saw no reason for doing differently here.

"Is tea ready, Mary?" Thomas asked by way of answer. "I think we'd all be the better for a good cup of hot tea. Sit you down, children."

James with his own practice! He'd be a rich man, an important man, and a good man doing Christ's work of healing the sick. He wanted to signalize the occasion, and he wanted to share in his son's new life. Nothing less than the gift of a horse seemed called for. He had not put forward the idea on a sudden. He had thought about it for long, ever since, in fact, he had been to Brooklyn and seen how city doctors like Dr. Moses comported themselves.

Harry Travers, who owned the biggest and busiest livery on South Avenue and bought and sold horses throughout the whole of Ilium and the surrounding country, was delighted to see them the next morning. He was of only medium height, but thin so that he looked taller, and smartly dressed in a tight-fitting dark suit, a Tattersall waistcoat, and a jeweled pin in his wide cravat.

He was particularly delighted to see Mr. Stapely, he said, because just that day he had in one of the finest pieces of horseflesh he had ever handled. It had not been there the day before. It would not be there the next, not at the price he was asking, for—confidentially— he had got the animal at a bargain and he was willing to turn it over quickly at a bargain.

Seven years old, sound in wind and limb, steady as you please but good for a fast trot. He was a beauty, and just the type a rising young doctor should have. If Dr. Jenkins on Morgan Street knew there was such a horse in his stalls he'd be there before you could say Jack Robinson, and Dr. Dyson, to whom he'd just sold a pair of spanking grays for his wife's carriage would be green with envy. Yes, green was what he'd said, doctor or no doctor. He, Harry Travers, knew the horse a young man like Dr. Stapely should have, and this horse was it.

Before Mr. Travers was halfway through, Will was dancing with impatience and fear lest this paragon of a horse should somehow have disappeared. Thomas, who knew even less about horses than Will, was also agog with eagerness, though from habit he was attempting rumbles of caution.

"Wanna see him?" Mr. Travers sounded surprised. He seemed reluctant. "I did kinda promise—" he began. "Well, you're here and he ain't. It'll be his loss."

Carefully he donned leather gloves and tied a short leather blacksmith's apron about his small waist. He placed a hard black hat over his pasted down black hair with the curl glued to his narrow forehead. He walked at a horseman's gait down between the long rows of stalls. Will kept well to the middle for fear of flying hooves. The stables smelled deliciously of horse, hay, oats. They were clean, and two stablemen were cleaning droppings out of the long trenches behind the stalls and flushing them out with buckets of water.

Harry patted a broad rump here and there as he passed. "Fine work horses, those two," he said, indicating great Percherons with gleaming brown coats in adjacent stalls. He went into one stall, nudging the horse aside. "Cribber," he explained. "Have to keep him muzzled. Good horse otherwise."

Thomas nodded sagely, though he did not know what a cribber was. He waited as humbly as Will on the livery man's pleasure. Mr. Travers was humming now. He seemed to have forgotten why they had come into the stables. "Now there's a sweet little mare for you. Just the piece for a lady's carriage."

Thomas cleared his throat. Mr. Travers came back from his abstraction.

"Oh, yes," he remembered, looking surprised. "Right behind you. Beauty, ain't he?"

Black with white stockings and, when a stableman whom Mr. Travers called over had backed him out, a white star on his forehead, the horse was handsome. He looked balefully at the stableman, and stretched his neck to bite a stanchion or the man's arm, whichever he could first reach. The man stepped back and jerked the halter sharply.

"Playful," observed Mr. Travers easily. "Full of life."

"What's his name?" cried Will. "What's his name?"

"Never christened," said Mr. Travers, winking at Will. "Name him yourself." He lowered his voice. "I ought to get two hundred at least for him."

"Not from me you won't," said Thomas firmly. Fellow think he was born yesterday?

Will thought Mr. Travers was wonderful. He believed now none of the stories repeated by all the boys on South Avenue, about his lying and cheating. Anyone could see he was kind and fair. He trembled for fear his father decide not to buy the horse, though he could see he was impressed.

"Nor a hundred and fifty, either," he heard his father say.

Mr. Travers voice went even lower. He was speaking with utter confidence telling things he would never in the world tell to anyone but a gentleman like Mr. Stapely who really knew a horse when he saw one.

Blackie was too common. Will didn't like Joe or Harry or names like those. Roger, that was it. The name came to him in a flash. Black, pirates, the jolly roger. Roger would be a fine name. "Hello, Roger," he whispered, stroking the horse's neck. It was warm and firm. Roger suffered his attention, looking at him with mild eyes, though he had been moving his feet uneasily and twice reared back forcing the stableman to give ground.

"We'll take him!" said Thomas finally.

"Good!" cried Will. "Oh, Pa!"

If only the horse were not going to James. A lot James needed a horse like this. He wouldn't even know how to treat him! Still, it was better James should have him and the horse be part of the family, really, than not to have him at all.

Thomas arranged to have the horse kept at Travers' for the next night or two. Then either James would come up and take the horse back with him by freight or on the night boat down the Hudson, or he would have to take the horse down.

"Can't we take him home now, Pa," begged Will. "We could put him in the shed. I could carry up the oats and we could get some hay from the Robbins. I know they'd let us have some."

The men smiled at his enthusiasm.

"Tomorrow night, perhaps," said Thomas, "so that we'll have him there to take to the station."

Will could hardly wait until the next afternoon after work. Then he and his father returned to the stables. Thomas paid his money and they came out with Roger, Will holding the horse's halter as he and his father walked along beside the beast. It was a triumphal procession. Roger, quiet now, walked along with them like a great dog. Twice he shied at sudden movements of other animals pulling wagons in the street and once tried to break into a trot, but held back when Will pulled firmly on the halter rope. His hooves clattered briskly on the cobblestones of South Avenue, sliding forward an inch or two after each step. He seemed nervous but docile.

"Whose horse, Willy? Whose horse?" cried some of his friends who failed to notice Thomas walking a little to the rear.

"Ours!" Will shouted proudly back. He wished he could make Roger arch his neck like horses in pictures he had seen.

Men were streaming home from work in the iron works and factories on the river side of South Avenue. Will was conscious of their curious glances and pleased when he overheard admiring remarks. He could see his mother and Emily and Agnes waiting on the side porch as soon as they turned the corner and started up the hill. Roger stepped along, picking his way neatly up the steep slope as though he had done it every day of his life.

Will handed the halter rope to his father and went to open the footgate into the yard, as his mother and the girls exclaimed over the animal.

"All right, Pa!" cried Will, holding open the gate.

Awkwardly Thomas tugged on the halter to start the horse through the narrow opening. Roger tugged back. He jerked free, reared back, spun on his hind legs, and took off downhill, turning the corner into South Avenue at a gallop and heading for Ilium. He neighed warning as he rounded the corner, his hooves striking sparks from the cobblestones.

Thomas, shouting and waving his arms, was halfway down the hill before Will could get out of the yard. Attracted by the clamor, men and boys came running from their houses. Most of them had finished or were just finishing their suppers. Women ran to the windows.

A runaway horse was nothing new on South Avenue. When they had nothing better to do, the boys at McGraw's often amused themselves by flinging stones at some horse moving sedately by, especially if he drew the buggy of anyone too well dressed to be a resident of South Ilium. They had caused some splendid crashes and provided the whole section with Fourth of July excitement.

Usually, though, a wagon or carriage, empty or with its helpless passengers hanging on for support and screaming for help, clattered after the free-running horse. It was seldom that South Ilium could enjoy the spectacle of a horse encumbered only by a halter and dangling length of rope galloping down its main thoroughfare with a respectable citizen in full and futile pursuit.

Terrified that Roger might get away and either escape into the open country or return to his home in Arabia, Will passed his father soon after he turned the corner. He was glad that his father and not he had let the animal escape, but mostly fearful of losing their prize.

"Roger! Roger!" he shouted, racing at full speed. Only a few steps behind him was Emily, with her long skirts hiked up and her legs flailing.

"Head him off! Head him off!" Thomas ordered the universe.

"Head him off yourself, you old jackass!" advised a workman, who did not even know who Thomas was but all of whose sympathies were with the horse.

Roger was on the sidewalk now, dodging trees and being dodged by men and women who leaped into doorways or ran up side streets. He veered and streaked down the middle of the road, his tail waving high, his head tossing happily. He neighed loudly. He stopped and looked back challenging.

"I'll run past! We'll drive him the other way!" cried Emily.

"All right!" Will's eyes were on the horse.

A man, braver than his fellows, walked quietly up and grabbed for the halter rope. Roger jerked his head away, and the man jumped back. Tenement dwellers on both sides of South Avenue had flung up their windows. Some shouted encouragement to the pursuers. Most shouted encouragement to Roger.

"Roger! Roger!" Will was almost sobbing now. He was within a half block of the horse and slowed to consider tactics. Suddenly he dived into an alley to knock down a boy who stood aiming a slingshot. It was Emily, her gold hair tumbled down about her shoulders, who got behind and alongside Roger, waved her apron at him, and started Roger back.

Roger cut through Thomas and his other pursuers like a sharp knife through cheese. Alf Clockman fell and cut one knee. Thomas himself scratched both hands as he hugged the rough bole of a maple that he wanted between him and Roger's threatening hooves.

Roger took to the alley this time, thundering along at high speed between the outhouses, sheds, and rubbish heaps. That was his mistake. A quarter-mile past St. Mark's he found himself boxed by a high board fence, a barn, and a litter of wagons, broken shafts, and wagon wheels with rusting hubs. Will and Emily were there almost as soon as he was. Others had given up far back. After all it was not their horse, though they were full of admiration for the beast who had enlivened what might have been a dull evening.

The breath was spurting from Will in gasps. Emily was in no better condition. She had torn her skirt and Will had lost his cap. They could not speak as they stood holding their sides. Roger, nibbling at some grass that grew between the spokes of an old carriage wheel which lay on the ground, regarded them curiously. He seemed not even winded by his exertions. He swung his head around and looked with mild interest at Will as, walking boldly forward, he grasped the halter rope.

Will proudly patted the horse's neck and Emily, encouraged, stroked his mane.

"I'll bet he's a race horse!" exclaimed Will, his eyes blazing. "I could ride him on the track over in Albany. I'll ride him home. No, you ride, and I'll lead."

Emily, still panting, had been brushing twigs and dirt from the hem of her skirt. "I can't! Ma would say it wasn't ladylike, and Pa would be mad again."

"C'mon!" urged Will excitely. "You can get off before we reach the house."

Emily clambered up on some boards and boxes that tilted dangerously and slid on to the horse's back. Roger did not protest.

"Don't let him run!" begged Emily, aghast at the distance to the ground. She gripped handfuls of Roger's mane as they started back.

"Pa better not try to beat him," said Will. "I'll kill him if he does."

"He can't beat him and make him be a carpenter," said Emily, gazing fearfully at the ground, but having to be brave before Will. "Besides, he hasn't a whip."

They need not have worried. Thomas Stapely ignored the horse that had so affronted his dignity. He did not as much as come out of the house as Will and Emily put the horse into an empty shed and happily gave him a pail of oats.

There was no talk now of his escorting the horse to Brooklyn. James would have to come and get the ugly brute off their hands. Thomas took the streetcar to Ilium and sent a telegram that night. Two days later James arrived—two days during which Will and Emily adored Roger and let him run on a long rope about the field behind the house, taking turns riding him bareback within the fences of the field.

Busy and important, he was soon deep in talk with his excited parents, and they laid plans for the ordering of his house and for his mother's arrival in Brooklyn as soon as she could get packed to come. His father would come for her after a few weeks. James was condescending with Maria and Arthur, who regarded him shiftily and sourly. He seemed hardly to notice Emily and Will. Roger he inspected with a professional eye as though hunting for hidden symptoms. He looked at his teeth, even rolled back the lids to look in his eyes.

"Wonder he doesn't try to count his pulse," said Will disgustedly. The idea of James's making off with Roger was pain enough without seeing Roger subjected to such indignities.

James, of course, could not lead Roger to the freight station himself. Bearded and frock-coated, he sat inside the streetcar while Will stood on the back platform holding the halter as Roger followed the car. Roger offered no objections, except at one downtown corner when he decided to take himself, Will, and the streetcar up a side street. Will and the conductor tussled to hold him. James surveyed the scene with the other passengers as though he had no part in it.

At the freight yard, heavyhearted, Will watched Roger being led up a ramp into the open doors of a horsecar that stood waiting. Other horses, already in place for the trip, were stamping inside. Roger disappeared with a swish of his magnificent tail. He and Emily had combed it out as they brushed his coat the night before, finishing the job by lantern light.

Will waited until the man reappeared to make certain that Roger would have plenty of water and hay.

"Sure, bub," the man told him. "And nights we tuck 'em in."

His eyes blinded by tears, Will turned to go. James was somewhere buying his ticket and getting papers for Roger. He did not care where James was. But James was watching.

"Willy!" he called.

Will turned. "What!" he shouted. "What do you want?"

"Come here!" ordered James.

With jaw set Will walked slowly toward him. He did not have to, he told himself. James could not make him do anything.

James's voice was so different from usual that Will looked at him in surprise.

"Thanks, Will," said James. "Here." He handed Will a silver dollar he had held cupped in his hand. "You don't have to tell Pa, either," said James. "I won't."

Chapter 9

THE CHANGE in James's fortunes brought change to the whole household in South Ilium. After Mary had been two weeks away, Thomas went down to see for himself the kind of house James had rented and to fetch Mary home.

Mary returned with presents for them all, mittens for Will, a silk scarf for Agnes, a ribbon for Emily, a lace collar for Maria. She was full of plans for furnishing the new house. She and James had already bought what was immediately necessary for his office and his bedroom. The rest of the house was still largely unfurnished.

She decided to close the store. It had served its purpose. It had been amusing but for some time she had been tired of it. Whether she had made or lost money she had no accurate idea. She had more important things to do now. There were plenty of pieces which would be just the thing for James's house, a few—including the elaborate walnut table with the red plush inset—which she would use herself. The rest she would dispose of as quickly as she could. Will was taken off the job for a few days to help dismantle the place he had helped refurbish a few years before. It seemed a long time before to him. He had been just a boy at that time, he thought, as once more he lugged and carted, and crated chairs and tables and chests of drawers that were to be shipped to Brooklyn.

Thomas, too, was well pleased. James had a house that was fit for an up-and-coming young doctor. He had surveyed it with an expert's eye and, though it needed a bit of fixing here and there, it was sound. The house was one of a row of frame three-story, parlor-floor and basement houses which stretched for the length of both sides of the street between South Brooklyn's Third and Fourth Avenues. At First Avenue were the Narrows of the New York harbor. On Third Avenue was the steam-propelled Third Avenue Railway which was helping to fill up that part of Brooklyn at a great rate.

The air was raw and damp. It seemed properly unhealthy to Thomas. There was a large shipyard with one of the only dry docks large enough to take ocean-going vessels in the New York harbor. There'd be accidents there. The section was already crowded with clerks, dock workers, commuters to offices and factories in Manhattan, shopkeepers and their families living over their shops which lined

Third Avenue. Be plenty of sickness among them. James should have a good practice in no time, thought Thomas shrewdly. Fourth Avenue was a pretty boulevard. On it and stretching up the side streets toward Fifth Avenue were the homes of the better class. There were other and older doctors well established along Fourth Avenue, but there was no reason why James, if he minded his *P*'s and *Q*'s, shouldn't find patients among those people too.

Mary assured Will that Roger was established and happy in a livery stable on Fourth Avenue. James had bought a secondhand carriage, and Roger was waiting ready harnessed for him in the mornings. Already he had attended several patients at their homes, and one night there had been three people at his evening office hours. The next thing she had to do was find a suitable housekeeper for James, some sensible hard-working woman who would not charge too much and who would know what was expected of her with no other woman around to see to things. It would not be easy to find just the right one.

She was off again to Brooklyn in two weeks' time, and Thomas decided that he himself would do the repairs he had seen were necessary in the kitchen of the new house. There was no use James's paying city prices for work. He decided he would see the renting agent about redecorating the living room where the paper was faded and stained. He might even get the front of the house painted. He took the night boat down, carrying with him the small tool chest he had brought with him from the Forest.

Will and Emily made the most of the new turn of events. Maria and Agnes took over management of the household while Mary was away, but they stood in awe of neither. As befitted a man doing man's work, Will ignored them as much as he could, doing the chores grudgingly. Emily, gay and derisive, could be as independent as she pleased. It did no good for her aunt to threaten to tell her father of her "impudence" or for Agnes, exclaiming that she did not know where Emily could have learned to be so bold, to mouth the same threat. Emily listened demurely to Maria, and laughed at Agnes.

Several evenings Emily went off to parties given by classmates. She came home so late one night that Maria, who had been lying in wait before going to her cottage, was triumphant.

"This time, young lady, you've overdone it!" she said triumphantly. "After half past ten. Your father will hear about this."

"He won't care. He wants me to go to the Girls' Guild. *He* thinks it is a good thing for us to sew things for the poor."

Maria, who realized too late that it had been Guild night, was defeated. She did not know that the Guild had been over for an hour, and that a strange boy had slipped down the hill after seeing Emily home.

But Will had seen the boy and was perturbed. It was quiet, fine-featured, dark-haired Francie O'Connor. "Gee, if Pa ever finds out!" he warned.

"He won't," said Emily blushing, "and I don't care what you say, Francie is a nice boy. He—he's not half as fresh as some of the boys at school, even if he's not a Protestant."

Agnes was too intent just then on affairs of her own to be watchful. She had a new beau, a clerk at the big Ilium department store, Richard having treacherously taken a job in New York and moved away. Already he had asked Agnes to a church social and for permission to call some Sunday after her parents returned. Will and Emily heard her discussing him with her Aunt Maria.

Emily made a face at Will and tried not to laugh for fear the others should hear her.

"A damned ribbon clerk," said Will, using a phrase he had heard men use at work. "Serve her right if he married her. Do you suppose anyone ever *will* marry her?"

"Of course," said Emily, ready to spring to the defense of even Agnes on that point. "Some man will be glad to marry her, and he'll be lucky too!"

"Stop rolling your eyes!" exclaimed Will disgustedly.

That day Emily was Beatrice out of *Henry Esmond*. Emily read every book she could lay her hands on, delighting in the novels she had found in the high school library, and she was the heroine of every novel or play she read. She was Portia in *The Merchant of Venice*, Rowena of *Ivanhoe*, or sometimes Rebecca. She could be Laura of *Pendennis*, Nausicaä, Jo of *Little Women*, and she had no difficulty in shifting from role to role or being all of her heroines the same day.

Emily laughed and slipped out of the house, touching her hair daintily at a mirror in the hall as she went by.

All that spring and summer there was a great running back and forth between Ilium and South Brooklyn. Whether she went by boat or train, Mary was happy. She had always loved to travel, to be going somewhere. Motion itself was exciting. The train trip reminded her of going down from the Forest to London as she had used to years ago. Whether on the train or the boat, her fellow travelers were attentive to the tall, graceful woman, her features composed but animation and intelligence showing in her eyes, amusement about her lips, who was so manifestly a lady. Conductors and pursers were polite and friendly. Maria could look after Thomas and the younger children. Mary felt herself again, an individual, active and effective about affairs of importance.

On one trip during the summer school vacation she even took Emily with her for several days. She was pleasantly aware that people looked and commented on mother and daughter. Emily, lithe, young, both demureness and assurance in her mobile face, her turquoise blue eyes candid, innocent, or mischievous as she wished, attracted attention everywhere. She knew it but knew also and as if by instinct, as her mother approvingly observed, how to appear unconscious of it. Emily's gold-blonde hair glinted beneath the wide brim of the hat she had fashioned herself. She wore her clothes with an air, carried herself with a self-possession that made her seem twenty instead of sixteen.

When she was home again on the hill in South Ilium, the lady vanished and the gamin returned. She was pleasant even to grim-visaged Aunt Maria and told Will excitedly of Brighton Beach and Fort Hamilton.

"James drove us and Roger passed everything else on the road!" she told Will. "We went down Fourth Avenue. It's wide with grass and trees in the middle. There are beautiful houses all along, horses and carriages, then country, and then the ocean. You can smell it before you see it. James was nice all the time." Her tone was wondering. "And he's busy too. There were patients at the house every day. Some of the women were going to have babies. His housekeeper's no good though. She's a frump. I should think she'd scare people away. I could do better than her myself."

"When I go," said Will, frowning intently, "I'm going to the race track at Brighton or maybe Sheepshead Bay or Jamaica."

From men at work he had discovered betting. Twice he had lost a quarter on horses running at some distant track. Then he had won a half dollar and last time a dollar. At first Mike Blueman, a plasterer, had taken his bets with the other men's. Then he'd discovered the poolroom itself and fat Al Redder who carried the slips in the pocket of one side of his coat and his big roll of bills in the other. Will sneaked off to the poolroom now as often as he could. There was some point now in going to New York where he could actually see the horses run at one of the crowded tracks. He had seen pictures and heard men talk. He could imagine the crowd in the grandstands and infield, the horses flashing past, the bright silks of the jockeys, and the golden fortune he would win.

Emily, who knew all about his betting, laughed.

"Pa wouldn't let you!"

"Ma would! I bet a quarter for her once. We won too."

"You did!"

"Sure, but don't tell. She doesn't want anyone to know."

"Suppose," said their Aunt Maria dryly to Emily, "you forget your fine city ways and help me with the dishes."

What Thomas was thinking of letting his wife run all over the country she didn't know.

"I thought your father told you," she said to Will, "to clean the ashes out of the stove and fix the grates. The oven hasn't been right for weeks. But I suppose he knows that talking to you is of no use."

"Have to go down to St. Mark's. Rehearsal for the Guild entertainment," said Will, winking at Emily as he escaped.

"That boy will get into real trouble one of these days," Maria warned Emily as she gave the meat platter a vicious swipe with the dishcloth.

Emily rolled her eyes ceilingward but did not answer. She was resolved that Maria could make no complaint about her this time. She wanted to begin taking piano lessons from a new teacher in downtown Ilium where several of her school friends went. Her mother, to whom she had broached the idea while they were away, had given her consent depending on her father's approval.

New York had decided Emily. She would be a singer, a famous soprano, perhaps even sing in opera. She would never marry, but would scorn the crowds of handsome gentlemen, all in frock coats and tall silk hats, who begged her to marry them. She and Will would live together in a brownstone house in the most fashionable part of Manhattan. She did not know just where it was, but she had passed it as she and her mother went by trolley from Grand Central Station to South Ferry. She began to hum, testing her voice.

"Pay attention to what you are doing!" snapped Maria.

Thomas and Agnes were closer than ever. With no help from his sister's words, Thomas had begun to feel neglected and resentful that Mary spent so much of her time with James in Brooklyn. Though he knew the importance of his son and his son's affairs, he had not intended that the boy demand so much of his mother's time and attention. He felt affronted.

He was careful to let Mary see none of this. Out of pride, he could speak of it to no one, certainly to none of his family. His sense of injury made him even more brusque and harsh at work. He became more forthright and dictatorial in the counsels of St. Mark's. Because jealousy was sinful, he knew that he felt no jealousy. Nor would he admit that Mary was doing anything but her duty. Twice he peremptorily silenced Maria, who retired bitterly to her cottage to meditate on the thanklessness of her life.

Hypocritically, Thomas was glad that Agnes understood. Her increased solicitude for his comfort, her sympathetic tones, her heightened expression of Christian forbearance made it manifest that she shared a burden which neither could mention. She went with him to midweek prayer meetings at other churches, once to hear a famous Edinburgh preacher who visited Ilium that year, and then to the Water Street Mission when Thomas was asked to speak to the sodden unfortunates there. She welcomed the chance for there was something she wanted to say to her father.

It was such a district as Agnes could not have visited alone, especially at night. She gloried in feeling helpless but stalwartly protected as they got off the streetcar in a dark section of gloomy warehouses and factories. She wanted to speak but dared not then, for Thomas was preoccupied with his message as they walked ill-lighted, narrow streets which ran down to the river where the black water lapped dismally at dock pilings and about the hulls of ships tied alongside. They went inside what had once been a store but was now a gas-lighted hall with rows of collapsible wooden seats facing a wooden platform which carried a simple pulpit on which a large Bible lay open.

Agnes, seated in the first row facing her father, could smell the unwashed bodies and alcoholic breaths of the derelicts who, herded by the gentle-faced old mission head, shuffled in and seated themselves behind her. She dared not turn to look. She shrank a little but glowed with the thought that her presence that evening enabled these men to feel the purity and gentleness of womanhood even as they listened to her father's words.

Only she, she felt, of all the family truly shared the inner light with her father. She thirsted to drink of the Blood of the Lamb, to repent and be saved. She wanted to swoon before the mesmerizing evangelist and be transported by the fervor in her soul. At the same time she wanted to be properly corseted, to honor her mother and worship her father, but not to forget Howard Jones, who was being more and more attentive. It was right she should tell her father, warn him of what she had discovered. She tried to as they left the mission.

"Those poor men!" she murmured. "Father, I—"

"Yes, yes!" said Thomas, a little impatiently. The fresh, cool spring air had dissipated a little of his sympathy. Most of his audience had been able-bodied. They should be put to work.

They made their way back through the dark, empty streets where only dim lights showed behind drawn blinds, to brighter South Avenue to wait for a return streetcar. A few people moved about on the Avenue. A few shops were open. Night softened the squalor. A gas-lighted saloon on the corner where they waited showed more life than any other place nearby. Voices were raised in argument inside. Gaslight and beer smells leaked out over patches of the sidewalk. Thomas peered irritably for the car.

This was her chance. Agnes opened her mouth to speak, but there was a new interruption. The saloon doors burst open and a burly figure, hat cocked rakishly, tieless, collar torn open, rolled out and leaned against the outside wall of the building. He looked interestedly but without recognition at Thomas and Agnes. Then a great light dawned in his face. He knew them, and he was pleased. It was a plasterer Thomas had discharged for drunkenness.

"Hones' Tom Stapely!" he said, smiling pleasantly and choosing his words with extreme care. "Hones' Tom Stapely! Hones' Tom Slave Driver!" He considered a moment. "Hell with him!" he decided.

Thomas tensed as anger sent the blood rushing to his face. Agnes clung frightened to his arm. She felt it necessary to seem more frightened than she really was, for drunken men were no novelty in South Ilium.

The plasterer watched them with distinct curiosity, then decided to re-enter the saloon. He wheeled, flailed his arms in all directions as he lost his balance, and crashed to the sidewalk. A partly filled bottle in the side pocket of his dirty coat, splintered, and raw whiskey flowed dark over the stone slabs of the walk which showed in the light from under the half-doors of the saloon. Its fumes boiled into the air.

"Sorry, Mr. Stapely," apologized the bartender, who had been watching surreptitiously over the top of the black-painted window and now came bustling out. He wiped the beer foam off his hands on the white apron that bulged over his broad belly before reaching down to grasp the coat collar of his prostrate customer. "Had a drop too much."

"A drop!" snorted Thomas.

The car was coming. He signalled the driver to stop his horses.

The incident had ruined the evening. He had been serene. The unfairness of it enraged him. He sat silent in the jolting car, his jaw set, his eyes narrowed and grim. Agnes spoke quickly.

"Emily is seeing that Francie O'Connor again," she said virtuously. "You told her before that she mustn't."

Though he heard, Thomas neither looked at his daughter nor replied.

Mary should come home. He needed her help with the accounts. There were bills to be sent out and notes due at the bank, matters to which Mary always attended. Thomas' bitterness grew.

It did not wholly dissolve even after Mary's return. She soon took care of the accounts and pitched into household affairs with a burst of efficiency and determination, but her evident happiness and the pleasure she had manifestly taken in being away kept the resentment smoldering in Thomas.

It faded as spring came on again. It came late that year, but when it came, it struck with brilliance and extravagance. One week the ground was wet and muddy, the air chill, the wind sharp, the sky sullen. The next South Ilium was flooded with caressing warmth. Leaves had burst out on the trees. Green grass sprang through the matted dead blades of the year before to sparkle in vivid sunlight. Windows were flung open, and the grime and grayness of the winter vanished as though it had never been. Men and women walked with lifted hearts, and the cries of children at play rang out with vibrant happiness. It seemed impossible to stay indoors.

Spring seemed to strike on the hill with peculiar recklessness. The brilliant yellow crocuses had sprung up overnight in the bed at the south side of the house. The forsythia were about to bloom. There were tiny leaves unfurling to the sun along the hedge. The tulips Mary had planted in the autumn would soon be up. It was time to rake the leaves away from under the lilac bushes and to uncover the roots of the shrubs they had buried in leaves for the winter.

Thomas and Will came home early from work and the family hurried through tea, though Emily had not yet returned from her music lesson in Ilium. Agnes stayed inside to help Maria clear away the meal, but Thomas and Will got rakes from the workshop and Mary grasped her trowel and gardening gloves from the shelf in the back entry. Laughing and calling to each other, they went to work, Will raking the lawn and hedge, Thomas tackling the tall white lilac that grew at one corner of the yard, and Mary happy to get her hands into the warm earth, transplanting geraniums out of the pots in which they had been kept in the house all winter into the border along the path from the gate.

The sun was setting, but the hill was bathed in soft blue light shot with shafts of gold from the afterglow. There would be light for an hour. Thomas had dropped his rake to unfold his razor-sharp pocket-knife and prune dead branches and shoots from the lilac. It was badly overgrown. The ground at his feet grew littered with boughs that he let fall.

"Not too much, Thomas!" Mary called from where she knelt.

"Never you fret yourself, m'girl," Thomas answered in broad Gloucestershire accents. "Oi knows what Oi'm abaout!"

Will laughed. It was a good sign when his father mimicked the accents of old men he had known in the Forest.

Agnes, walking back and forth in the kitchen and talking to her aunt as they worked, watched enviously from the window. Only her sense of duty had kept her inside. She felt unappreciated. Then, as she was hanging the pots and pans on the proper hooks in the pantry cupboard, she happened to look out of a side window that gave out on the road up the hill. What she saw made her face tighten and her eyes light.

Emily and Francie O'Connor were coming happily up the hill. Emily was laughing and the boy, carrying his cap and Emily's music roll, was smiling quietly. Agnes could see that Emily, the sly minx, was guiding him toward the seldom-used front of the house where it was unlikely they would be seen. She put down the baking tin she held in her hand and, without a word to her aunt, hurried out to her father, who was busy now raking up the twigs and branches he had cut from the lilacs.

Francie, still destined for the priesthood, was to enter St. Michael's Seminary the next autumn. The sunlight caught his smooth black hair. His fine-lipped, studious face was composed but alight. His dark, thoughtful eyes were intent on Emily's face. Emily was aglow with the spring, with consciousness of the boy's admiration, with happiness at being alive and being near him. Her lips were slightly parted, her eyes shone. They lingered at the gate before the steep steps to the front veranda.

Something in the way they stood, quiet but expectant, eager but not impatient, happy as though they shared mysteries he could not fathom, frightened Thomas Stapely and added to his fury. Rake in hand, he strode around the side of the house, roaring as he descended upon them. Agnes, hands clasped at her waist, face tightened with righteousness, eyes glinting with expectation, hovered in his wake.

"Be off!" Thomas shouted at the boy. "Be off with you! I'll have none of your dirty Irish kind about!"

Startled, Francie dropped the music roll he had been about to hand to Emily. He bent, wincing involuntarily, to pick it up but without removing his eyes from Thomas, whose face was nearly purple with rage as he stormed and waved his rake about.

"Pa!" cried Emily, horror-stricken.

Will came running. He went white-faced as he saw at a glance what had happened. He had an instant's wild impulse to run at his father and strike him down. He knew that he could not and hung hesitant, his hands twitching.

Thomas had wrested one child from sin! With God's help he had driven off the devil who had tempted and almost won. He would worst him again.

"Be off! Be off!" he cried, advancing on Francie in an insane fury.

Bewildered rather than afraid, Francie was transformed on the instant from a graceful youth to an awkward boy. Thomas swung his rake, narrowly missing the boy's head. Trembling, Francie stood his ground. Then he looked pleadingly at Will, turned and started down the hill without uttering a word.

"Francie!" screamed Emily. She started to run after him.

This time Thomas did not miss. His rake caught Emily hard on one thigh. With a cry of pain she fell to the ground.

"Slut!" roared Thomas. "I'll have no child of mine acting like a common slut! Get into the house!" He grabbed savagely and jerked Emily upright by her hair.

Agnes, properly, covered her ears. Yet she knew that God would forgive her father such language because He understood.

"I knew this was coming," said Maria triumphantly.

Will gave her a glance of hatred and rushed to his sister who had crouched away from their father.

Tall and erect, her face expressionless, Mary had watched from a corner of the house. She did not look at her husband or speak to him as, breathing heavily, he passed her on his way back to the garden.

Upstairs Emily was sobbing and groaning. Will could hear the soothing murmur of his mother's voice. She had gone up carrying a white cloth and a basin of warm water. Thomas and Agnes had gone over to Maria's. Will sat at the kitchen table with his head in his arms and his fists clenched. The light from the lamp over the black sink shone dully on the red cloth of the kitchen table and across the back of his blond head and his slender neck with the too long hair curling about the nape.

He did not know what to do. He knew he could not go upstairs. Through clenched teeth he swore vengeance on his father.

"But I didn't *do* anything!" he heard Emily cry again. She had been saying it over and over. "Honest I didn't, Ma. I didn't do *anything*."

Emily was hurt. He had seen the blow their father had struck her. He wanted to beat him with the same rake, to beat him and beat him until he begged for mercy. Everybody knew that Francie O'Connor was all right. He was different from the others. He was the best scholar in the whole high school. Everybody knew that. His father was a—

"We—just—walked home," Emily was sobbing again. "Honest, Ma—oh!—oh!"

"Try to quiet yourself, Emily," he heard his mother say. "Just lie still, that's the good girl. Just let me wipe your face—"

"And Mr. George," Emily was sobbing, "said I had a good lesson. He said I'm the best of all his pupils. Oh, I hate him, I hate him, I hate him!"

"You musn't say that, Emily!"

Why mustn't she say it? Why shouldn't he say it, or anyone? Everyone knew it was wrong to strike a girl. Even Mickey and the others with the way they talked wouldn't hit a girl. Only cowards struck girls. Why could his father, who was supposed to be good, hurt anyone he liked? The Sunday-school teachers were always saying the strong should take care of the weak, that it was wrong to be a bully. His father was worse than a bully.

Shocked as well as hurt, Emily was whimpering harshly. It did not even sound like her voice. Will could not make out what she was saying. He brushed angrily at his own tears, and his heart pounded with impotent anger. He opened his eyes though he did not move his head. The white pattern in the dark tablecloth was only inches from his eyes. It was so close he could not tell whether it was a bunch of flowers or some acorns. He stared at it in the darkness made by his encircling arms. He heard a coal fall on the grate in the range which, as soon as tea had been readied, had been banked so as not to heat the kitchen.

Emily was quieter now. The murmur of his mother's voice, quiet, soothing, steadying, began again. He had a sudden strange memory of hearing her talk so when he was a little child and she held him on her lap. He had never remembered that before. Then he remembered falling down the stairs, the same stairs his mother had gone up to Emily, and crying with fear until his mother had come and picked him up. The next thing he could remember was crawling under the bed to hide, and listening to them all look for him. He had fallen asleep under the bed. Now he was falling asleep again. It was good to creep into sleep when you were hurt. Perhaps Emily would fall asleep soon. It was an effort to raise his head. He jerked it up with an effort of will, then settled back again.

"You'd better go to bed, Willy," his mother was saying softly. He had not heard her come down the stairs. "You're almost asleep now. You've had a long day."

He looked at her through blurred eyes, remembered, and shook his head sharply. He waited until she had gone into the living room, then hurried quietly up the kitchen stairs.

It was dark. He felt his way along the wall. He could hear Emily breathing. He was his father's apprentice, his father's slave. He was helpless. Emily must be asleep. He started to tiptoe back down the stairs.

"Will!"

He felt his way into the room and sat on the edge of the bed. It was soft. The blinds had been drawn. It was very dark. He groped to feel for her hand but could not find it, and he was afraid to reach for fear of hurting her leg. There was no movement from the bed. Evidently Emily had not stirred.

Emily's voice came in a tense low whisper.

"I'm going to run away."

"You can't!" he whispered back.

"I'm going to, Will."

"Where will you go?"

"I don't know, but I won't stay. I knew what I was going to do all the time Ma was up here."

"Em, you can't!"

"He struck me. You saw him."

"Did it hurt much?"

"Yes. I thought my leg was broken, but it wasn't. There wasn't much blood—a little, though. It's all swollen, and black and blue."

"I'll *kill* him!"

"No, you have to stay. In a few years you'll have your carpenter's papers. Then you can go. I'm going now."

"Please don't, Em. I don't want you to go."

Emily's voice came hard through the blackness.

"I don't mind his hitting me. But he called me names, horrible names! They aren't true. He can't call me things like that. Nobody can—ever. I'll pretend to go to school tomorrow, but I won't go. And I won't come back. I have almost ten dollars. I'll go somewhere. I can get a job."

Will's imagination caught fire. It would serve his father right. He had been lucky at the races again and he had been paid two dollars for helping lay a floor after working hours.

"I have four dollars and sixteen cents. You can take that too."

"I'll pay you back," swore Emily. "I have it all planned. I'll wear an extra dress underneath when I leave in the morning. I'll carry my coat. I can pack a few things. They'll think it's my lunch. I'm going to take the prayer book you gave me for my birthday."

A step outside made Will spring up. There was no time for more talk. He got downstairs just as his father came in.

Thomas looked drawn and tired. His eyes searched Will's. He did not speak for a moment.

"Go to bed, Willy," he suggested humbly.

"Go to hell," answered Will under his breath.

"What? What was that?" asked Thomas dully.

"Yes, sir," said Will. He went into his own room off the kitchen, and lifted the pile of shirts and underwear in the drawer of the chest. He found his money, opened the door to make sure Thomas could not see him, and slipped upstairs again. This time he found Emily's hand. It was hot and dry. He slipped the money into it but begged, "Don't go, Emily. He'll be sorry, and things will be all right."

"He called me those names," said Emily stubbornly, her voice still hard. "You'll be at work when I go. Kiss me, Will."

Ashamed, afraid for her, afraid for himself, Will hesitated. Not since he felt that he was grown up had he kissed his sister, except when she had gone with her mother to visit in South Brooklyn. He kissed her warm lips, tasted the salt tears, stifled sobs of his own. They could hear their mother talking downstairs to their father. Blindly Will made his way back to the kitchen.

Will avoided going to work with his father the next day. He managed to avoid him at work. Half-convinced that Emily had changed her mind, he hurried home to look for her. She was not there. The others refused to acknowledge their uneasiness as it grew later and she failed to appear. The atmosphere at tea was strained and silent. It did not break until Thomas put down his tea cup and inquired harshly of Will, "Where's your sister?"

"How should I know?" asked Will blandly. He was worried. He did not know where Emily might go or what might happen, only that she was sure to let him know somehow as soon as she could.

"Sulking somewhere, no doubt," said Maria tartly.

"Hold your tongue, Maria," said Thomas sharply.

"Well, I declare!" Maria started up and minced righteously from the room. She came back with her bonnet on. "Thomas," she began, "I have never been so—"

"I said hold your tongue!" roared Thomas.

Agnes paled. Mary, her forehead wrinkled, looked curiously at her husband. Finding no help in her face, Thomas got his hat and hurried out.

Fear and suspicion gripped them all at once. Soon Mary followed her husband. Even Agnes was alarmed.

"Perhaps," she said, seeking comfort of Will, "she has just stopped at one of her friends."

"A lot you care," retorted Will bitterly. "I think she may have gone down to the Hudson and drowned herself. Or maybe she got run over by a train. She could have been kidnapped by some of those —you know what. That's what should happen to you."

Agnes began to cry, her face crumpling horribly.

"I just did—"

"—what you thought was right!" mocked Will. "You and Pa!"

He had frightened himself with his imaginings. People did drown or get run over. The newspapers told mysteriously of young women being lured from their homes. He felt glad he had given Emily all his money to help her escape and afraid of what might have happened to her.

Thomas was back now. Emily had not been at school. None of the neighbors had seen her. Mary had gone downtown to ask at the music teacher's and at the railroad station.

Fear deepened into panic as the time went on. For the first time, Will saw his father suffering, his face white, perspiration on his broad forehead, hurt and puzzlement in his eyes. Thomas knew he had done only what was right. The Lord would not punish him for keeping the feet of his children set in the straight path.

"I'm sure everything will be all right, Pa," comforted Agnes.

Thomas turned on her treacherously.

"If you had minded your own affairs," he said, "none of this might have happened."

"Now, now, Thomas. Agnes is not to blame," interposed Mary. "Emily is safe, I'm sure. If you just sit quietly, I'm sure she will be home by bedtime."

But Emily was not, nor was there word of her the next day. Will saw his mother's fear mount. Thomas stayed home from work. Should they, he asked his wife timidly, notify the police?

The whole neighborhood was agog now. Everyone knew that Emily Stapely had run away from home. Some said she had run off with a strange man. Thomas Stapely was out of his mind, and it served him well. Poor Mrs. Stapely was going into a decline. They had always said that Emily was coming to no good end, or that she was too good for a man like Tom Stapely to have for a daughter, or that she would come home famous and with a fortune, or that she was too good-looking for her own good.

Aunt Simpson and Mrs. Glover and Mrs. Morgan came hurriedly. Men tried to question Will at work. He shook his head and stayed in the shop with August who said nothing.

It was not until the second evening that the wire came from James. It said only: "Emily with me." Thomas and Mary packed a bag and took the night train for New York.

Two days later they returned together but without Emily. Thomas, though he held his head high and his shoulders square, looked dazed. Mary was silent. If she felt a certain sense of victory, she did not show it. She told Will and Agnes quietly that it had all been arranged. It had been, in fact, fortunate the way things turned out. Emily was to stay and keep house for James who would let his housekeeper go. She had been unsatisfactory anyway. James would pay her wages, though not, of course, as much as he had paid the older woman, and Emily could go on with her musical studies. There were better teachers of voice and piano in New York than in Ilium. They would all miss Emily, of course, but it was for the best, and they would get used to it in time.

Inwardly she marveled at the courage and determination with which Emily had faced her father. She had coldly refused to return home. She had accepted his clumsy attempts at amends with dignity but without softening or changing her mind. She was sorry, she said, that she had disturbed him, but she would not return to the place where she had been humiliated before a stranger nor to the chance of being treated so again.

Thomas had gone to make his peace with his sister Maria. He walked slowly back to the house. His head ached dully. What had completely confounded him was that James had not joined him in ordering Emily home. James had not taken Emily's side, but neither had he supported his father. Thomas' awe of his son and his son's growing strength had in it now a touch of fear. If it was God's will that he should suffer through Emily the pain of having an ungrateful child, he could bow his head and bear the pain, but James's attitude hurt and puzzled him.

Mary knew that James was shrewd enough to see in his young sister someone who could manage efficiently both his home and his office and whom, in addition, his patients and friends would find attractive. It was a relief that Emily had gone to James when she might have run off anywhere. She could keep an eye on both of them. She was gentle now to Thomas, whose hurt she understood, and tried to comfort him.

Agnes was indignant. James had never suggested that she come to South Brooklyn and keep his house. It was she whose voice could profit by training in New York. It looked, she told Maria, as if those who abandoned their parents were the ones who were rewarded.

Will laughed derisively when he heard her. He was on his way down to bet a half dollar his mother had given him. He had a tip on Blackbonnet in the fourth at Belmont.

"Want me to ask Pa to wallop you a few times with the rake handle? Be glad to do it myself if you like."

BOOK 2

ONLY THE SUN

891-1893

The hill is never mountain,
No other: eyes are eyes.
There is no other wisdom;
Only you re wise....

No other love is love;
Only the sun is sun.
No other life is life;
Life's one. There's one you. One.

Chapter 10

ONE AFTERNOON in 1891 James was out on a call that had come in after his crowded office hours. The cleaning woman had just gone after doing the upstairs rooms. Emily had made preparations for dinner while James was seeing his patients. The potatoes were pared and in a pot of water on the back of the stove ready to be shoved forward. There were fresh bluefish ready in the pan for broiling. She had bought them that morning from the fish peddler who came up their street every day from the docks.

Everything was in good order. She had just freshened up. She had been busy all day, but had not nearly expended her pent-up energy. She could practice for an hour; she could always practice for as much time as there was, but she was tired of singing scales and working at the keyboard. Unconsciously Emily flexed her long fingers as she moved restlessly from the shining kitchen through the dining room and waiting room into James's empty office to look out into the street.

As in every other house on both sides of their street, the two front-room basement windows were latticed with long ornamentally wrought-iron bars painted black. The basement rooms were just three stone steps below the level of the sidewalk, and the windows looked out on a small areaway of grass and concrete to the iron fence and gate matching the ironwork at the windows.

Three children were playing about the stoop of one of the houses across the way. On another stoop which, as in every house, led up to the double doors of the parlor floor entrance, a small girl was quietly playing jacks all by herself. Emily smiled as she saw her carefully bounce the small rubber ball, scoop up the jacks, bounce the ball again, miss, and start over. The child was studiously determined, practicing as carefully as she practiced the lessons laid out for her by Mrs. Angerson.

There was little else on the street to attract her attention. In another hour the men would come swarming up from the dry docks on their way home from work. It was just like the men's coming home from the iron works, the steel furnaces, and the factories in

South Ilium, only these men wore greasy caps pulled down over blackened faces and worn sailor's jerseys or old coats spattered with paint or tar instead of the ironworker's rust-stained overalls. There were dark-skinned foreigners among them.

Emily was about to turn from the window when good fortune offered a chance to ease her restlessness. Down the middle of the street, came a vegetable peddler's wagon, the reins dragging along the asphalt as the horse stepped smartly. She knew whose horse and wagon it was. Tony, the peddler, had told her just the other morning of Jerry's habit of starting for the barn when he was delivering at somebody's house in late afternoon.

Emily hesitated a few seconds. She was no longer a child. She had a certain dignity to keep up. James would not like her running into the street after strange horses. Then without stopping for a covering to throw over the white nurse's uniform she found practical—and becoming—to wear during the day, she jerked open the door, cleared the three steps, flung open the gate, and started after the horse and wagon which were moving at a quicker pace well down the street.

The air was warm and soft on her face, the exercise exhilarated her. There was no one to see except a few children who did not matter. Gathering her skirts in one hand she ran hard after her quarry, wishing she did not have on high heels.

"Jerry! Jerry!"

In mid-road she grasped the greasy leather of the black reins near his bit. Surprised, the horse stopped immediately, looked at her doubtfully, but offered no resistance. Emily stroked his soft nose.

"You know better, silly!" she told him. Then, not knowing where the peddler was, she did not know whether to try to turn the rig around, back it up, or simply lead the horse to the curb and hold him until Tony came.

"I'll have a peck of potatoes, and are the onions nice today?" said a level voice at her shoulder. "Or can I help you control this unruly beast?" A hand moved out and smoothed down Jerry's tangled mane.

Emily saw the hand, a man's hand, small, white, and well-formed before she could turn.

"Oh!" she said. Then she explained. "He's not mine."

It was a man of middle age, slight, hardly taller than she, who stood watching her with an amused smile on his clever face. He was clean shaven except for a closely trimmed dark moustache, and expensively tailored.

"Then you're not a peddler? Never mind about the potatoes and onions then." He spoke gravely.

Emily blushed and held tight to the reins. Her other hand flew to her hair. Its blonde wealth was swept back and up in a smooth pompadour.

"I don't do this all the time," she explained further.

"I'm sure you don't. I know it's the first time today I have seen Miss Lillian Russell leading a horse and cart."

"Don't tease me!" laughed Emily. "Help me put him somewhere." But she was pleased. Others had commented on her resemblance to the singer. She wanted to think she looked like Miss Russell and the pompadour, tried for the first time only a few days before, was part of the attempt. James had made fun of it.

The man laughed too, took the reins from her and led the horse to the curb. Tony, who had emerged from a house up the street bearing an empty basket, came running.

"Tanka you! Tanka you!" he said, puffing, to them both. "Dat Jerry bad again. You bad boy, Jerry. You lika da apple?" He snatched two from a basket in the cart, rubbed them hastily against his sleeve, and proffered one to each.

"No thank you," said Emily quickly. "But you won't forget to bring me some nice peaches in the morning, Tony?" She did not need them, but it would show this stranger that she was mistress of her house and not, as he might suspect—what could he think she was? Her cheeks were still burning.

"I bring," Tony assured very earnestly. "Nice peaches," he promised. "Verra nice!" He chirruped to Jerry and they moved off, Tony gallantly doffing his hat to Emily.

Emily, still embarrassed, smiled in flustered fashion and started to move.

"Perhaps you can help me," the gentleman suggested quietly. "I'm looking for Dr. Stapely's house."

"Oh," said Emily. "It's right here. I—I'll show you."

"I'm so seldom introduced to young ladies by a horse," said the man as they walked the few steps, "that I'm not sure how it is properly done. My name is Andrew Gray."

"This is it," said Emily, swinging open the iron gate. "Dr. Stapely is out, but he should be back soon. If you'll just wait—"

He was looking at the outside of the house.

"So this is it. Thank you." He looked surprised as Emily led the way in.

Emily had recovered from her confusion. She was all dignity and poise. The contrast with her youth amused the visitor who was careful not to show it. But it was her beauty that had startled him when he first saw her.

"I am Emily Stapely," she told him proudly, "Dr. Stapely's sister. If you will just have a seat here, he will attend to you as soon as he returns. I'll light the gas."

"But I'm not sick," the visitor explained. "I've not a single pain. I'll be glad to try to think one up if I can't stay otherwise, but I honestly feel quite well."

Emily looked puzzled. A tiny frown spoiled the effect of her dignity.

"Then why," she asked curiously, "do you want to see the doctor?"

"I don't particularly, though I'd rather like to. You see," he said humbly, "I'm your new landlord." He stood still, hat in hand. He watched her curiously, enjoying the changes of expression on her face and in her eyes. They were beautiful eyes, he thought. One seldom saw such eyes.

Emily laughed outright. Then stopped. "You're not going to make us move, or—"

"No, I'm not going to raise the rent either. You see I'd never actually seen the house. I bought it as an investment along with some other property. I had an errand in Brooklyn today so I thought I'd satisfy my curiosity."

Emily laughed again, then decided it was improper and tried to stop.

"Oh!" Andrew Gray laughed too. "You thought I had the measles or the mumps, or perhaps colic!"

"I thought maybe *la grippe*. There's been an epidemic, you know. But you sounded all right, and you don't look as if you have a temperature."

"So you're a doctor too," Gray asked as he took one of the upholstered chairs in the waiting room. Emily hung his hat on the hall rack and, busied herself lighting a green-shaded gas student lamp on the table.

"No," said Emily seriously, "but, of course, I see so many patients come in and out that I get used to looking for symptoms."

She felt elated. This was better than a horse.

Mr. Gray—she now remembered hearing his name when the agent told James there had been a change of owners—was markedly different from the men she saw about. There was a quiet distinction about his appearance and his speech. With his hat off he was even better looking. The brown hair, cut short, lay close to a well-shaped small head. There were touches of gray at the temples, but his intelligent finely-cut face was unlined and firm. He had gray eyes that were wise and kind but clear and shrewd. They showed admiration which warmed and excited her.

She sat down across from him. Then she got quickly to her feet. "You want to see the house, don't you?"

"Why—why yes, if you don't mind."

He had not intended to inspect the premises, merely to locate the place and get a general idea of where it was and in what condition, but he was in no hurry. The unusual girl had aroused his curiosity. He had not connected women like her with South Brooklyn. In fact, he had connected little with South Brooklyn except his broker's advice that it was fast growing and might be a good place to buy up some property.

Emily, pleased to be seen and appreciated in her role as mistress of the house, led him into the kitchen which, she knew, Lillian, the cleaning woman, had left spotless, the floor freshly scrubbed and the stove blacked. She had hung newly laundered curtains the week before and put clean white paper on the shelves.

Gray noted each detail with a casual glance. Obediently he looked out into the back yard at Emily's bidding, saw the backs of other similar houses on the next street and all the rectangles of bits of lawn and garden crisscrossed by clothes lines.

"No complaints?" he asked Emily. "No sagging floors or creaking doors, no leaks in the roof, no rotted sills?"

"My father took care of everything," said Emily. "He's a builder upstate, and my brother has come down several times and made repairs. He works for my father."

She showed him the front room which had been made into James's office with his roll-top desk, the dispensing cabinet which smelled of iodoform and all the varied and mysterious medicaments in bottles and tubes, the long chair which could be tipped back and opened into an emergency operating table. For a resident practitioner's office, Gray noted approvingly, it was well equipped. He saw James's diploma and medical certificates on the wall. "Albany," he said aloud, reading from the diploma.

"Do you know Albany?" asked Emily eagerly. "Then you must know Ilium too. That's where we are from. Our home is there."

"I know it quite well." He did not tell her then that what he knew in Albany was not the medical college but the legislative rooms at the state capitol and, better yet, the bars and hotel rooms, where lobbying, flagrant or discreet, went forward to the greater glory and profit of many a company and equally to the benefit of many a wise politician. He had successfully completed an errand there just the week before.

Emily looked at him with renewed interest.

"We live on a hill a little way south of the city. It's a beautiful spot. My father built our house there almost as soon as he came from England."

"So you're English." Perhaps that explained what had seemed familiar in the girl, why she had seemed foreign to Brooklyn. "So am I."

"You are!" Emily was as pleased as though she had herself been responsible for his origin. "That may be why—" She stopped.

"Why what?"

Emily flushed again, the color mounting to her high cheekbones. "Why it seemed as if I knew you," she said boldly.

So the girl too had noticed! Her transitions from hauteur to youthful awkwardness, then to bright, gaminlike daring, fascinated him. It was all done with a certain unconscious artistry, as though there were a touch of the actress in her.

"Being English at least makes us both superior to everybody else," he said.

Emily laughed once more as she led the way upstairs.

"That's what my brother—the doctor, I mean—always makes fun of. Yet he certainly thinks he's superior."

"Perhaps he is."

Emily shrugged and showed him the top floor bedrooms, her own, James's, and the guest room in which her mother or Will, sometimes her father too, slept when they came down. Mary had furnished and arranged them all, even to the carpets and the curtains. They were comfortable with touches of Mary's elegance and taste in each.

Purposely, Emily had saved the parlor floor for the last. It was the best. The living room held their choicest furniture and rugs. There were two oil paintings of the French romantic school, landscapes which somehow had found their way into Mary's store on South Avenue and which she had sent to South Brooklyn on its closing. Other parlors held ornate pianos, closed and glistening with furniture polish whose odor choked the room. This instrument was of a good make and obviously it was used. There were two stacks of music on top of it where usually there were an embroidered runner of imitation Chinese brocade hung with colored tassels and a pair of painted crockery vases. On the keyboard was a piece of unfinished music manuscript, as though someone had been composing or studying harmony. More music was stacked neatly in a nearby cabinet which Will had made.

"You *are* Miss Russell after all," said Gray reproachfully. It was

94

getting late and time that he returned to Murray Hill. "Surely you'll sing just one song for me before I go."

"Of course," said Emily recklessly. She indicated a chair with an easy gesture that burlesqued all such gestures, bowed with ludicrous gravity, slipped onto the piano bench, and let her fingers run fluidly down the keyboard in a scale which she transposed swiftly into the opening bars of *Un bel di vedremo*. She began to sing softly, easily.

Then, as her left hand strengthened the accompaniment and her right picked out the melody cleanly, almost teasingly, she let her voice out. It grew in volume and in tone until it soared through the small rooms, then for one instant crashed and echoed as the piano accompaniment softened. She sang more softly, her voice hovering over a note, caressing it almost, then rising again to full volume. The aria stopped on a high full-throated note held after she had ceased to play. It vibrated about the room, softened, faded, died.

Emily swung around. Her face was as laughing and unafraid, as defenseless with pleasure as when she and Will had sailed their kite on the hills behind the house in South Ilium.

Andrew Gray had been taken completely by surprise. Volume, timbre, control, they were all there. The music had struck through to his emotions as well as to his mind. His body had tensed and then relaxed as the girl sang, but all he said, with mock protest in his voice and expression, was, "And I thought I was jesting!"

"I've been studying it for months," Emily confessed. "It's the only operatic aria I know, really. Oh, there's James." A little alarmed at what she had done, she was glad when she heard the downstairs door open.

Gray followed her down the stairs. She introduced the two men, and explained Gray's mission. "He's English too," she added to her own surprise.

James, after shaking hands, looked at Gray curiously, his heavily bearded face showing little expression. His eyes were tired and Emily, though she could not smell it on his breath, suspected that he had stopped for a drink before coming home.

He bit tentatively at his thumb, a habit which had become fixed. "Sit down, sit down!" he suggested gruffly. It might have been his father speaking.

"I shouldn't really," Gray demurred. "Miss Stapely has been more than kind showing me about." Actually, he had no wish to go. He had still not recovered from the surprise of hearing Emily sing. His ready curiosity had been sharply aroused. "I know you are busy too."

James, after grunting off his hat and gloves, had sat himself in the swivel chair at his desk to make a note on a prescription pad.

"The next patient that comes in here, I'm going to shoot." He opened the top drawer of his desk and shut it again, picked up a paper knife and felt of its edge. "I may cut his head off."

"Sounds like a strenuous cure," said Gray. "It might be effective though."

"It's what a lot of them need," said James. Emily saw that James, shrewd always beneath his assumed rudeness, recognized their visitor as a different kind of man and was somehow impressed. Yet she was amazed when James said, "It's getting late. We'll be having dinner soon. Like to have you stay."

"Certainly you are hospitable," said Gray quickly. He was about to refuse. Then he looked at Emily who was watching him eagerly. She nodded quickly. "Thank you, I will," he said. "I'll be glad to stay—that is, if I may use your telephone."

"Of course." James gestured at it. Suddenly his eyes gleamed. "Don't by any chance play checkers, do you? I got in the habit in medical school. No one to play with around here."

"I got in the same habit in newspaper offices," smiled Gray.

"Get the board while you're telephoning," said James. He moved off in better spirits than Emily had seen him in in months.

She had already started upstairs to change her dress. She reversed her direction and headed for the kitchen, deciding to start the dinner before she changed. Then she dashed up the steps two at a time.

There were the two new dresses which Mrs. McGuire had just finished, the green silk and the brown. But she chose the old aqua silk with the bit of real lace at the collar which so nearly matched her eyes. She had worn it many times, but she knew that it became her—and to her visitor it would be new. She took down part of her carefully built coiffure and brushed vigorously at it before she combed it through and wound it into place again. She changed into high black shoes with higher heels and even more pointed toes, before she hurried downstairs and grasped an apron and tied it around her waist before she opened the oven door.

She looked into the other room. James, chin in his elbows, was intent on the board. Mr. Gray, thinking himself unseen, was looking at James, as though studying him. James grunted, and moved a king. Mr. Gray jumped two of his kings immediately. James, Emily knew, would be furious.

The doorbell rang. She had hoped no patients would interrupt, and James had no office hours that evening. She answered it and was relieved that it was only a man with a heavily bandaged hand who came in early each night to have James change the dressing. The man had crushed two fingers at the docks, but James had said the wound was coming along nicely and was almost healed.

When James put on his coat and went into the office, closing the door behind him, she went into the waiting room to entertain their visitor. Gray had got up from the table with the checkerboard on it and was wandering about the room.

"Who's winning?" Emily asked.

"There's a man in New York I'd like to have hear you sing," said Gray. "He's a music critic. Not a very pleasant gentleman, but he knows what he is about. He could tell you whether you are practicing correctly. Perhaps you should have different teachers. What do you want to do?"

"Sing!" said Emily quickly.

"Opera? Concert? Another Jenny Lind? Another Lillian Russell?"

"Oh, better than them!" she laughed. "James will be through quickly. Dinner will be ready then."

It was after dinner that they fell into easy, cheerful talk. At first there had been some constraint as they ate. Gray had found himself wondering what he was doing in such a place in such company. He was surprised at his own action in accepting their invitation to stay. James, smarting under losing three out of five games of checkers, and losing the three so quickly, had tried unusually hard to be congenial but had only succeeded in sounding morose. Emily, conscious that the men were not completely at ease, had become nervous about how her table was set and fearful lest she spill something in passing it. She had taken pains that morning with a dessert which James particularly liked and which, fortunately, was simple. She had made fresh tea as she cleared away the dishes after the main part of the meal. James accepted a cigar from Gray who, looking first to Emily for permission, lighted both James's and his own.

"M'mm," murmured James appreciatively, savoring the smoke.

"As long as Miss Stapely doesn't mind," Gray smiled.

Emily wondered what he would say if he knew that she and Will had more than once shared a cheap cigar filched from a South Avenue tobacconist.

They talked then of Brooklyn and James's practice, of Ilium and South Ilium, of England, and of New York about which Gray seemed to know everything. He spoke pleasantly but vaguely of his own activities. His eyes, often on Emily, sparkled as he described amusing

97

incidents. He urged on them the necessity of visiting parts of New York he seemed surprised they did not know.

Emily was fascinated and James, though he tried not to show it, was impressed with the intelligence and charm of their guest.

"Then you're a reporter really!" cried Emily at one point.

"Not exactly," Gray answered, "though I'm still concerned with the press in one way or another." He mentioned the household name of a great insurance company and explained that he handled what he called its "literary work." He said that there was property of his wife's and a few parcels of his own which required occasional attention, and that he had in addition some other small business interests.

"It must keep you pretty busy," James observed, a trifle enviously.

"Either too busy or not busy enough," Gray said lightly, "that is, at the kind of things one likes to do. Either there is not time enough in life to live it fully, or we are not strong enough to live all of it that we can."

"That's what I think!" Emily cried.

"H'umm!" James grunted, not sure he knew what either of them meant.

Gray switched the conversation back to South Ilium. He seemed interested in the whole family. They came from much the same part of the western English Midlands as he, though he did not know the Forest of Dean itself. He asked about Will.

"A young scamp if ever I saw one," said James.

"He's not. He's not at all. James just means he isn't like him, and I'm glad he isn't!" James grinned under his beard while Gray smiled at the girl's quick defense. "He's more like you," she told Gray earnestly.

James guffawed while Gray laughed lightly, saying, "I hope he's pleasanter than that."

"But he *is* like you," Emily insisted, struck now by the likeness she had discovered. "He's slight and he laughs a lot. He's not serious and dull like James. He works hard at what he likes to do—"

"And loafs as much as he can and only stays out of jail by God's grace and Pa's watching him!"

"Then he really must be like me in some ways," Gray agreed. "And you said there is a sister?"

"Agnes, and I'll be damned," James told him, "if she didn't get married last year."

"James! She's older than all of us," said Emily. "And last year she married a young doctor James knows. They live in Mott Haven in the Bronx."

"I know where that is."

"Fellow saw her at my graduation," said James, as though he still could not believe it. "Said nothing. Turned up last year and after a couple of weeks asked her to marry him. Said he'd made up his mind when he saw her that day but didn't want to say anything until he was established. Queer stick all around. A fair doctor though, or will be," he added grudgingly. "Works hard."

When, perhaps an hour later, Gray was getting ready to leave, he spoke seriously to Emily.

"Willard will know right away about your voice and he'll tell the truth. Will you go with me if I can persuade him to hear you? He's not that important, but he likes to pretend he is by being difficult sometimes."

"Oh, yes!" breathed Emily, looking at James.

"Can't see any harm in it," he said. "And I'll try to keep the rent paid," he said turning to Gray. "If I could just be sure some fool wouldn't talk people into taking care of themselves sensibly and put us doctors out of business, I'd be certain of it."

"I'll risk that," said Gray gravely. To Emily he looked as he stood there like some elegant and fastidious visitor from what must be almost another world. She was almost afraid lest he disappear forever into the night.

"What did you mean a while ago," asked James suddenly, just before they bade their guest good-night, "that one life isn't enough?"

"Something like that—not just that perhaps."

"Sometimes I think," said James slowly, "that one life is too much."

Gray looked at him more sharply.

"There's that too," he politely agreed.

Chapter 11

THERE WERE SOCIAL and political idealists in New York who considered urbane Andrew Gray a brilliant and dangerously capable man who might as easily have been on their side. At times he had been. There were very rich and powerful men who considered him eminently useful. With seemingly no effort except the quiet exercise of his skill and charm, he had accomplished some very practical miracles for them and a few for himself.

There were those who thought him too coldly purposeful. There were others who knew that he was unselfish and kind. Under his wit and gentleness of manner he was astute, cynical, compassionate, and wise.

That he had been one of the cleverest and most successful newspapermen of the city was acknowledged even by his critical fellows. For a time after first coming to New York, he had been one of Dana's bright young men on the *Sun*. He had never quite belonged, though, with that group of earnest young Americans. Mature even then, though actually he had been younger than some of the others, he had watched them sometimes with amused surprise. His mind moved fast and, though he kept it discreetly hidden, his ambition was sharp.

He had left the *Sun*, moving on as opportunity offered. At one time or another he had worked in almost every city room in Manhattan, taking from each sheet the knowledge and experience he wished. He was city editor of one, managing editor and chief editorial writer for several years of another. He was suspect by some of the cautious and slower-witted, but even they admired him. Underneath his civilized exterior, they complained, Gray had a mind like a knife, and, they said with envy, he could *write*. He was surefooted, and he could make the complex simple or the devious seem straight.

Like all newspapermen of the time, he knew everyone who was important, famous or notorious in the city: politicians, criminals, artists, financiers, industrialists. He could, when he wished, talk the language of each. It had long been his job to get from each the facts he wanted and use them or file them away for possible use later.

What Gray's early-day fellows could not understand was his financial success. It was not in character. It was not in the newspaper tradition. Of course, his marriage to the daughter of a wealthy and influential family of Manhattan's Murray Hill had brought him money and connections which did not come the way of most press men. For years now he had not been on the staff of any daily. He had jumped from leader writer to editor and then publisher of a Sunday paper. He had founded and owned outright one of the established and conservative weeklies of the insurance trade press. But he had strategically placed real estate holdings in Manhattan and Brooklyn, and he was an active partner in an oriental importing house whose Fifth Avenue showrooms were well known.

There were rumors, still repeated now and again by old-timers at the Press Club on Williams Street or at Dr. Perry's Pharmacy in the new World Building on Park Row, that certain political connections almost twenty years before had done Andrew Gray no harm.

He had been managing editor then of one of the few newspapers in New York which supported the Tweed Ring when it was under attack by *Harper's Weekly* and the *Times*. Tweed had been more than generous in buying support with money he had stolen by the ton from other people, and not all newspapermen had turned down the bribes offered, as had George Jones of the *Times* and Thomas Nast of *Harper's*. Nothing had ever been proved. The matter had never come up for inquiry after Tweed's downfall and the dissolution of the Ring.

Of course, many of them admitted, it might not be true, but Gray under his controlled and fastidious manner had always been capable of any action, no matter how reckless, once he had been convinced or something had appealed to his fancy. Soon after Tweed's death in the Raymond Street jail, Gray had seemed to have plenty of money. It was about that time he had founded the *Insurance Tribune* and gone into several other things. He had a way of attracting success, a sure ability at anything he undertook. He could work like a fool when he wanted to, without sleep, even without food. Once, they remembered—there were many stories about Andrew Gray.

If at any time Andrew Gray had veered slightly from the ways of unimaginative rectitude, he had no compunctions. Neither did he regret the energies he had expended in what seemed like lost causes. He would have regretted only what was stupid, what might have blurred his cool insight, his sometimes cynical delight in life.

As a young man fresh from a newspaper in staid Bristol where the limitations of a man's life had been set for generations, and an unimaginative family added their own restrictions, he had been intoxicated at what was to be done and what was to be got in New York. It was not long after the Civil War. New York, like the rest of the country, was bursting with energy it was wild to expend. Scoundrels, and even a few honest men, were amassing fortunes. It had been fascinating to watch and record and to stir about in that atmosphere. There were no limits for a man with imagination and enterprise, if, without showing it, he was just a little sharper, worked just a little harder, had just a little more talent than the others, and if now and again he dared accept a risk—or seek one out.

At nearly fifty, he found it as stimulating as he had found it at twenty-five. The energy, the rawness, and the crudeness of teeming

New York still fascinated. Activity edged with danger still attracted. Work which he could shape and form to near perfection still delighted. Art was joy. Beauty tantalized and allured.

He had, he felt, gained a certain material success, known the satisfaction of certain small achievements. He could look more dispassionately now on himself and others. The spectator's amused detachment had always been natural to him, but so had the intense concentration of the artist which he knew as the perfect freedom. He had never tried to reconcile the two forces in himself, but to realize them both and, at the same time, know the relief and excitement of practical action for material or emotional gain.

Andrew Gray's was not a simple nature. Under his urbane manner, under the geniality which yet warned of an essential aloofness, there was a dissatisfaction which demanded expression in many directions. There were painters who knew him only as a talented amateur in water color and, with more hesitation, in oil. A volume of humorous tales and a book of whimsical essays published under the same initials had been good enough to make some writers glad that he had not made writing, other than journalism, a serious career.

Which of his many selves was the real Andrew Gray he did not know. Few men know this of themselves. He had only laughed when a critic friend had scolded him for dissipation of his talents.

Had his private life been different, he sometimes thought, some of his hunger might have been appeased. He might have channeled his efforts, co-ordinated his forces and desires toward some single and perhaps admirable end—and probably have disliked doing so even if he were capable of the integration. His marriage had brought him tenderness and affection as well as financial security when he was young and best able to use that useful asset. When tragedy, it deserved the name, he thought, had struck after the first few years he had perforce made the best of it. Fortunately there had been no children.

Never strong, his wife had very nearly succumbed all those years ago to the sudden, crippling onslaught of rheumatic fever. Only expert medical attention and skilled nursing had kept her alive. The long ordeal had left her with a badly weakened heart, frail, anemic, a semi-invalid. Then her worn body and shattered nerves had begun to give way. Fatigue, as much of the mind and spirit as of the body, had become a settled depression, a wan apathy from which she emerged with less and less frequency.

"Neurasthenia complicated by anxiety and a valvular condition of the heart," was how one very modern doctor had triumphantly diagnosed it. Gray remembered because the specialist had acted as though giving it a name had exorcised the evil, as though a phrase solved.

It was the cardiac involvement that had brought his wife close to death so many times from recurring bouts of near heart failure. It seemed as though every time she brightened, it struck. Each time the life flame flickered lower, but did not go out. Sometimes she seemed to emerge a little stronger in wracked body and tormented spirit.

Few, even of those who passed for Gray's intimates at work or in his clubs, knew much about it. Those few knew better than to ask facts that he did not volunteer.

Incessant activity, the pleasures of subtle business, financial, and political maneuvering, writing, and enjoyment of the minor art forms had filled Gray's days and nights. Neither they nor his moderate club life, masculine and gastronomic, had quite stilled his loneliness. He had not always recognized his unease as loneliness or as springing from loneliness. All of it had not but, especially of late, he had been conscious of his continual and sometimes depressing solitude. He was always aware of it when for a day or two the sensation disappeared.

He knew the morning after his visit in South Brooklyn that it had left him the night before, and he was grateful.

The girl's beauty had excited, still excited. It would excite any man. Her voice had amazed him, though he could not remember now whether it had seemed truly musical or had hypnotized through its power and vitality. Her brother unlike most doctors was intelligent, if rude about the edges. His strong face showed a capacity for ruthlessness. His square hands were powerful. He was in his early thirties, Gray imagined, and the girl perhaps ten years younger. Actually, Emily was not yet twenty.

They were young, strong, confident. The girl was fearless. She could be willful. Either would strike hard for what he wanted. Ignorant of much, they knew much by instinct or sound English heredity. Gray smiled at his own prejudice as he walked steadily down Madison Avenue. The morning was bright and clear with the sun warm but not yet hot. Leaving his brownstone house on a quiet side street, he had turned into the avenue, deciding to walk as far as Twenty-third Street before turning off to take the Elevated at Third Avenue.

He was eager to see them again. He would get in touch with Willard and arrange an audition as soon as possible. He was curious as to its outcome. Last night he had been certain that he had heard an unusual, even a rare voice. But he had been taken by surprise and could not be sure.

It was mid-morning. The El was not as crowded as it would have been an hour earlier. He watched the tenements go by, looking into the open windows at unmade beds in dingy rooms where women unconcernedly brushed their hair or men in undershirts stared dully at the train.

He stayed on past his old haunts about City Hall—where the grass in the park showed a vivid green that morning—and Printing House Square. Sunlight slanted sharply across the faded red brick of the square Tribune Tower and blazed on the gold dome of the great new World Building on Park Row. St. Paul's spire showed for an instant in an opening between tall buildings. He got off in the Wall Street district and started up Wall Street toward Trinity before turning off through the ornate portals of an imposing office building. A uniformed doorman touched his hat as he passed through the marble lobby.

"Mr. Ventnor has been asking for you," said his typist as soon as he had reached his office. "I didn't know whether you were coming in today."

The Apex Life Insurance Company, greatly daring, had worriedly employed a few of these modern young women.

"I think I know what he wants." He looked at a pile of papers on his desk. "You've been busy."

"I've got it all ready for you," said the girl proudly. "And Mr. Smith and Mr. O'Connor have the new copy and releases all ready for you to approve."

"I can see I could just as well have stayed home!"

The girl smiled happily and went back to her typewriter. She made no secret of the fact that she considered Mr. Gray all perfect as well as all powerful.

Gray went on to see what the president of Apex wanted. He passed long offices filled with busy clerks, others where actuaries worked interminably over their tables. The sight always pleased him. Gambling life against death. That was all life insurance was, really. You bet you'd die. The company bet you'd live. Thanks to these little men and their mathematics, the company usually won and pocketed the winnings, though there were other ways too of making a profit, and the company, all the life insurance companies, made profits. Little men in spectacles gambling with God's prerogatives. He thought that sometimes God must feel surprised.

The great Charles Ventnor looked up ready to scowl as he entered the spacious office with its deep rug and walnut-paneled walls. Ruddy-faced, bull-necked and heavy-stomached from the years of good dinners he had eaten, Charles Ventnor in his frock coat, winged collar, and rich silk cravat, was an impressive figure. His Fifth Avenue mansion, his Long Island estate, his yacht, had many times made good Sunday newspaper copy for the awestruck masses, many of whom had his name on their policies—if they had not foolishly let them lapse.

Ventnor's face relaxed when he saw who it was, though his darting eyes lost none of their intentness.

"Sit down, Andrew, sit down!" he said, motioning to a chair near his desk.

Andrew Gray seated himself easily and looked inquiringly at the other. Ventnor was neither the rapacious monster cartoonists pictured him nor the philanthropic humanitarian described in company reports. He was neither insensitive nor sentimental. He was simply a hard-working, hard-driving successful man who loved power, money, and the prestige they brought him. In a way Gray liked him. They passed, after a fashion, for friends.

"You spiked it? That crazy idea isn't going to go over?"

Gray shook his head.

"It's finished."

"Why some damned fools who can't do simple arithmetic think they can tell us how to run our business," Ventnor exploded in his relief, "is beyond me! And it would have been just like that crazy pack upstate to put it into law. What this—what are you grinning at?"

"What this administration is trying to do you don't know," Gray finished for him.

For an instant Ventnor did not know whether or not to be angered by the effrontery. He decided against it and grinned himself. He lifted a half-dozen sheets of typed paper from the top of his enormous flat-topped desk with its gleaming mahogany surface.

"This is all right," he said. "How much are you going to charge us this time to run it in your damned paper."

"As much as I possibly can, possibly a little more."

"There was a time—and this time don't interrupt—when we didn't have to give a damn for public opinion, as you call it."

"But you do now, and there'll never be a time again when you won't," smiled Gray. He took the papers. "I'll take these up and have them set this afternoon. This week's issue goes to press tonight." He nodded and started out.

"Come to dinner Thursday night. My son-in-law and his wife will be there, that crowd. Some others, I don't remember. Need somebody there I can talk sense to."

"Will you excuse me this time," said Gray quickly. "Unfortunately,

I've already made another engagement. Sounds silly, I know, but it happens to be true."

It wasn't, but if he could get Willard to agree to hear her, he would have Emily Stapely and perhaps her brother as his own guests, perhaps at Delmonico's. It was unlikely they had ever been there. If they had, he'd take them to a place he preferred and considered better.

Chapter 12

THE POSTMAN had just been, puffing a little, as he always did from the climb up the hill and keeping a wary eye on Carlo who was sniffing at his heels and gave him a tentative nip on one trouser's leg just as he closed the gate behind him.

"Carlo!" called Mary, waving the letters at him threateningly. "Carlo, you bad boy!" She smiled apologetically at the back of the retreating postman. He did not turn around.

There were four letters, two from England which would give them all the news of home, one from Agnes, and one from Emily. Mary read Agnes' letter standing in the kitchen. She went into the sitting room and sat down in the Morris chair before opening Emily's. Emily's last letters had been all happy excitement. This one was the same.

She and James had been to New York and dined again with Mr. Gray at a wonderful restaurant where there was an orchestra and wine. All the men had been in evening dress and the women in beautiful gowns. She had worn her light blue. Mr. Gray was so handsome and kind and thoughtful. Next week she was to have her last lesson with Madame Danford and then begin with a Professor Risviglio, a funny little Italian man on East Seventeenth Street in New York. Mr. Willard, one of Mr. Gray's friends but not nearly as nice, had arranged it. Professor Risviglio took only a few pupils, only those he considered most promising, but he had said he would take her. She had been very nervous, and at first after hearing her he had said nothing, but he had told Mr. Gray he would take her. Mr. Gray had arranged it all, and James thought it was all right.

Mary quickly refolded the letter and placed it in its envelope for

Thomas. She was excited too, and pleased for Emily. This Mr. Gray must be a fine man. As soon as Emily had mentioned him, Maria had said she should go right down to New York and see what was going on. Emily was still a very young girl, and James was too busy to look after her properly. Mary looked thoughtful, then smiled.

Maria lived in the house now. She had moved in after Agnes and Emily were both gone, leaving their room vacant. Maria's tiny cottage was rented to a Mr. and Mrs. Betsworth, who had just come over from England. He was a machinist and had got work right away at the iron works.

The iron works was thriving. All the factories were busy. St. Mark's was filled every Sunday, and the Parish School was crowded. The whole of South Ilium was vibrating with life. Thomas was very busy. The day before he had signed a note for twenty-five dollars for Walter Armstrong, and Walter had stayed to tea. He'd signed a note for fifty dollars for three months for Edward Budd, but that was different. Edward Budd was a hard-working foreman who would pay promptly. Thomas had been home almost all day, for a man had come to discuss a barn he wanted built, and Thomas had been dickering with Mr. Gorram over the contract for a new house. He had bid on three houses the stove factory wanted to put up for their workers and expected to get the job.

Now he was annoyed that Will, who claimed a headache, had stayed home that morning. Thomas had started to pay Will six dollars a week when he got to be sixteen; now he was paying him eight. He said he was sorry he'd started to pay him at all.

Mary was glad Will had stayed home because that morning he had put a good solid door on the preserve closet in the cellar. The rats had got into it during the winter and eaten a part of all seventeen jars of the green grape jelly she and Maria had put up. They had even eaten the string over the covers. One had got into the house, scaring Maria and her half to death; but Carlo had caught it when it ran from the sideboard cupboard in the dining room into the shoe closet in the back kitchen. The cornered rat, a big one, had bitten Carlo in the nose, but the dog had held on and killed it.

. It was this had persuaded Thomas to let them keep the stray that had come shivering to the back door one cold night and refused to go away. She and Will had fed him and rolled an old blanket on the floor of the shop for him to sleep on. Now he slept in the house. He was a good dog, though he had bitten Mr. Roberts a little when he came to pay his rent and had chewed up a pair of Will's old shoes. She had bought him another pair, and they had not told Thomas.

Will, his headache gone, was off now to look at the fire which they said was still smoldering. The night before a house had caught fire in the congested district a mile nearer Ilium and down near the river. There had been a strong wind and, though three fire companies had galloped out and the men pumped till they were exhausted, the next house had caught and then the next. Willy had bought a new suit, a brown plaid that looked well on him, for fifteen dollars at Macaulay's store in Ilium.

Intending to show Emily's letter to Maria, Mary had forgetfully gone into the yard to walk across to the cottage. It was early October and the weather, after several days of rain and raw wind, was warm and pleasant. Carlo followed at Mary's heels. He was mostly spaniel with a thick body covered by brown and white curly hair, but there was enough terrier in him to give him a sharp, worried face. When Mary stopped, he stopped and sat down to scratch himself.

Mary noticed with surprise that the raspberry bushes were in bloom. It was said in the Forest of Dean to be a sign of death when berry bushes bloomed in autumn. Not in her family, she hoped. A cry and a shout, then a scream drifted up the hill from one of the tenements on South Avenue. Poor Mrs. Rafferty! This was the second beating she had got today. Mike Rafferty had been out of work and drunk for a week.

It was so pleasant outside, with the year's declining sun still warming the earth, though the leaves were beginning to turn on the big maple and had already started to fall from the elms, that Mary lingered. She looked affectionately at the small peach tree she and Thomas had planted and nursed for several years. This year for the first time it had yielded bountifully. The geraniums along the border would soon have to be potted and taken indoors for the winter. The tall hollyhocks alongside the house were still in bloom. Goldenrod nodded and waved in the field behind the house.

How old, she wondered, was Mr. Gray? Emily had not said. If he had held positions of such importance, he could not be very young. Mary tried to visualize him. It was easy to see that Emily was attracted. It would be hard to imagine any man's not being attracted to Emily. Perhaps Emily, too, would soon be married!

Mary came alive with the idea. She picked a dead branch off a flowering plant, straightened quickly as she reached a decision, and started for the house.

Then she saw Maria toiling up the hill. With her were Cousin Harriet and her daughter, Blanche. Mary smiled with pleasure and hurried in to change her dress and get the tea things ready.

Cousin Harriet, a tiny little lady in her eighties, with bright eyes and round, red cheeks, talked brightly and cheerfully. Lily, she said, was going to have another baby, and Harry was pleased as Punch. And how were dear Thomas and Willy?

Blanche and Maria were having a serious conversation under cover of Cousin Harriet's prattle. Blanche had found a new and better way of putting up greengages and damsons, though she had scalded her hand dreadfully with steam from the kettle. There was so much to do now that her mother could do nothing about the house. And how did poor Arthur like his new work? She hoped they'd not try to put upon him as they had in the last place. Some people would work a willing horse to death!

"A jackass is too smart to let them do it!" broke in Cousin Harriet, who had a disconcerting way of hearing more than she seemed to hear, and an even more disconcerting habit of saying what she thought.

"Mother!"

Maria, furious at the comment on her son, who even Thomas admitted was lazy, rustled her silk petticoats as she moved her fat legs in irritation.

"How's my girl?" Cousin Harriet demanded of Mary.

"Agnes," said Maria maliciously, "is very well. Doctor Richards could not have chosen a better helpmeet. She may be expect—"

"Maria!" cried Mary warningly.

"Expecting!" exclaimed Blanche. "How wonderful! When—?"

"Agnes is not even sure," said Mary firmly.

"I did not mean Agnes at all," said Cousin Harriet triumphantly. "I mean Emily. Now there's a girl has some get-up and gumption."

"I had a letter just today," Mary, who had been waiting her chance, announced quickly to them all. "She wants me to visit her very soon. I think I shall go down by boat tomorrow night. Perhaps I'll take Will with me—if Thomas can spare him."

Maria sniffed.

"Hello, Cousin Harriet. Hello, Blanche," said a cheerful voice from the doorway. Cousin Harriet was a favorite of Will's. She had fed him apples and cookies when he was a child and stood up for him often when he needed it.

"Willy!" she called happily. "Was it a good fire?"

"Gutted! Some of the people were back poking around, but the South Avenue boys got anything that was any good last night."

"Poor souls!" murmured Blanche.

"Needed burning down, those places," said Cousin Harriet. "Ought to burn more of them. Let's you and I set some tonight, Willy."

"Soon as it gets dark!"

"But the people!" protested Blanche piously.

"Somebody always takes care of them. They come out better off than they ever were. Not that I want any of them roasted, and I don't want you," Cousin Harriet warned Blanche and Maria, "saying I did."

"You said *toasted,* not *roasted,*" laughed Will.

Cousin Harriet's eyes snapped. "Now, who said I said toasted *either.* If I'd said some of the men were *fried* every night—" She winked at Will.

"Mother! I don't know where you pick up such talk!"

"Have a good time in New York, Willy!" Cousin Harriet called, as he turned to look in the kitchen for a piece of caraway seed or lard cake.

"New York? Are we going to New York?" Will swung eagerly around to question Mary.

"We'll see what your father says when he comes home," said Mary demurely.

Will laughed again. His father would not object if his mother insisted.

New York! That would be all right. It would be just fine! He had to be back for the Guild entertainment, but that was still two weeks off, and he already knew his part. He found lard cake in the tin and broke off a large chunk.

He was hungry. He was always hungry. Slight still, but taller, well-muscled, he was in fine health and spirits. His eyes were bright, and his fair cheeks showed color from his afternoon in the air. His bright hair, blown by the wind, waved and curled about his head.

When Mary showed Thomas Emily's letter that evening and said she thought she had better go down to James's to see how things were and perhaps take Will for company, he not only offered no objections but also gave her readily more money than they would need for the trip.

Emily's good fortune was but vindication again of his God-guided conduct. Had he not chastised her, Emily would never have gone to James and would not now be getting along so well. He got out his books to study a Parish School lesson but could not settle his mind on it. He took the green cloth case off his cello, tuned it, and began softly to play. He played his favorite hymns, then songs of the English countryside he had learned as a boy. Mary sat with some sewing in her hand and listened. Maria had gone to bed. Will, dressed in his new suit, and a new hat he had bought, had gone off to a fair the Girls' Guild was putting on.

Will had promised three different girls that he would come. He had also promised his parents that he would be home early, knowing as he promised that he would be as late as Kate Harrison or Nancy Greencastle allowed. He'd take one of them home, which one didn't much matter. He knew he could get his choice. Or he might take the pretty cousin Fred White had visiting from Schenectady. They might all go somewhere.

During the summer Will had spent almost three weeks working at one of the mansions above Mt. Olympus Park in Ilium itself. Such jobs seldom came Thomas' way, but Mr. Garver, who owned the big mills across the Hudson in West Ilium, was one of the chief supporters of the mission where Thomas sometimes preached, and he had met him there.

Will had done odd carpentry jobs of all kinds, built new shelves in the pantry, repaired a damaged cornice on the stables, replaced scarred wainscoting in a conservatory filled with flowering plants—most of which he had never seen before—and hung a new door in a sewing room cut out of a wide upstairs hall. Will had never before seen the inside of such a house or surveyed its lawns and gardens from near at hand. It was a house all towers and gables with wrought-iron trimwork and a Japanese summer house on the lawn.

Several servants were on the place, a groom in the stables where there were saddle horses as well as a carriage pair of matched grays, and there was a Scotch gardener. Will had not known that anyone lived in such splendor. It both awed him and seemed somehow wicked. He did not know why.

He had quickly got used to the place and enjoyed being there on the pleasant summer days. Often Mrs. Garver had sent him tea and sandwiches by one of the maids and even come herself to watch him work and talk cheerfully for a few moments. Young Jim Garver, a quiet youth of about his own age, had been home on vacation from Yale, and they had become very friendly. Jim, who had been away on Cape Cod and was all bronzed from swimming and sailing, seemed not to know what to do with himself until he could pack for New Haven again.

He had spent many mornings and several full days with Will, fetching and carrying for him as Will had done for August when he was an apprentice, and seeming to enjoy the work. He had told Will stories of college life which Will, with his ready imagination, had been able to visualize and enjoy.

One evening he and Will had gone together to see the sights of an amusement park near the city and enjoyed themselves hugely, returning later than either of their fathers liked, though each thought his son safe because he was in the company of the other.

Jim Garver was going to be a lawyer because his parents wished him to, though probably he would go into the family business. It would be the same, he said, with him as with Will, who would probably take over his father's building business some day.

Will appreciated the courteous fiction that their fathers, as members of the employer class, were comparable in stature and that his own fortunes would thus be laid along lines similar to Jim's. Yet the idea that he would succeed his father surprised him. It had not occurred to him that his stalwart father would age, perhaps retire, some day die like other men. He was too formidable a figure, had loomed too large and threatening in life. For a day or two he fancied himself gravely as Will Stapely, Builder, South Ilium, N.Y. Then he forgot the fancy.

Observant and imitative, Will patterned his dress and manner after Jim Garver's. He remembered how the mansion had been furnished. It changed some of his standards of taste. He picked up bits of college slang for use in South Ilium, buttoned his jacket and wore his gloves at St. Mark's on Sundays as he had seen Jim Garver wear his jackets and gloves.

Mr. Garver had complimented him highly on his work and asked whether he would care for work at his mills where he kept three carpenters in steady employ. Will was surprised and pleased but had hardly considered the offer before refusing. The idea of leaving his father was startling. The best part of it was that Thomas was impressed by Mr. Garver's praise of him. Will's freedom, seldom seriously questioned now, grew wider.

Now Will was delighted with the idea of going to New York and South Brooklyn. He would have been equally delighted to remain in South Ilium. Life anywhere was a delight for Will just then.

He revelled in being no longer a boy but a young man and regarded as such. He was a skilled artisan and an accepted member of the adult community, while the boys he had left in school were still boys, some of them just getting started on jobs as messengers, apprentices, or clerks. They admired him, and he knew pleasurably that the pretty girls of South Ilium looked on him with favor. At St. Mark's he was still the son of prominent and feared Thomas Stapely, brother of Dr. Stapely of Brooklyn and of stunning Emily Stapely, whose adventures in fleeing South Ilium for fashionable New York where she was studying music were the envy of all the girls who knew her. Even Jim Garver had been impressed when Will told him about Emily and showed him her picture.

Quick, laughing, gay, Will, had he had time to look at it, would have known his life was good. He knew it anyway.

Chapter 13

"MA!" CRIED EMILY. "Ma. And Will!"

She had come to the door of the Brooklyn house with an inquiring look on her face. It had vanished and her eyes widened in amazement.

She hugged her mother tightly with Mary, relishing the surprise she had created, holding herself stiffly so that Emily would not disarrange her bonnet or her cape.

Will, carrying the one bag in which they had packed their things, stood back grinning.

"We missed one ferry and had to wait a half hour for the next," he explained, "or we'd have been here before. Where's Bones?"

"Out on a call. Oh, come on in, come on in, come on in! I was just getting dinner ready. Oh, this is wonderful!"

Satisfied with her reception, Mary looked about her in the hall as Emily helped her off with her cloak and stood by breathlessly as she unfastened the silk strings of her bonnet. She moved deliberately, looking carefully about her.

Things seemed clean and in good order. There were fresh curtains up in the front room. She noticed that they had moved a chair from one corner of the waiting room to another and decided it looked better there.

"James will be surprised!" breathed Emily, "and Mr. Gray is coming tonight. I'm so glad you've come."

"I shall want my tea," Mary announced. "We're both tired. Willy, don't put the bag on that chair. Take it right upstairs."

"How's Pa? And Aunt Maria? Is Carlo's paw better? I'll get the tea right away. The kettle's boiling now. Will, you're taller. And you have a new suit."

Will laughed and curtsied solemnly. He went off upstairs.

The two women went through to the kitchen.

"Mr. Gray has been away," said Emily, as she opened the tea canister and weighed the right amount in her fingers and dropped it into a fat brown teapot. "He's been in Washington this time. He does so many things!"

She added another pinch of the tea, and was about to close the canister and replace it on the shelf over the polished stove, when her mother reached out and took it from her. She inspected its contents sharply.

"It looks a little green to me." She sniffed it. "I'm surprised James likes it."

"Oh, but he does and I do too." Emily poured steaming water from the kettle into the pot and put the lid in place. "Mr. Gray has his own newspaper, an insurance paper. He also works for the Apex Life and—"

"Let me get my breath, Emily," her mother interrupted. She had seated herself at the kitchen table to wait for the tea to steep. "We shall have to go shopping to New York one day. I want a gray serge skirt to go with the shirtwaist I had Mrs. Curtin make. And I'd like to call on Mrs. Baker too. Cousin Harriet asked me to be sure to see her. Willy has the address. That is," she added, "if you and James are willing to keep us that long."

"Mother!" cried Emily reproachfully. "James had better be pleased or we'll poison him. No, we'll poison his patients—that would be worse."

"And we'll have to see Agnes one day, of course," planned Mary. "Then—"

Emily was hurrying back from the dining room where she had gone for bone china cups and saucers. She knew her mother would not use the thick kitchenware which contented her for an occasional cup of tea.

"I haven't seen Agnes in months," she confessed. "I think she's angry with me again. And, of course, she won't come here. She's furious with James."

"What about?" asked Mary, sipping her tea gratefully. It was still steaming hot.

Emily shrugged. "I don't remember. I honestly don't. It's always something." She sat back, deciding to let her tea cool. She cast a quick look at the stove where dinner was simmering. Perhaps she should pare more potatoes, but she decided there were enough. There would be more than enough of the roast.

"It is not right," said Mary conscientiously, "that brothers and sisters don't get along better, especially when they are away from home like this."

Emily laughed, and even Mary smiled faintly, though she tried not to.

"Mr. Gray does so many things," said Emily eagerly, "yet he never *seems* to be busy. Oh, you'll like him."

Mary watched her intently as she sprang up to move something on the stove.

"What's for dinner? When's it going to be ready?" demanded Will from the door.

He had washed his face and combed his hair in an upstairs bathroom, looking carefully to see whether he might not need to shave again though he had shaved the day before. Thomas had given him a straight razor at Christmas, and one of his savored pleasures was keeping it sharp.

"As soon as James comes. And we'll have ice cream for dessert," promised Emily, her eyes glad.

"Ah!" Will rubbed his slender middle. " 'Tis foine oi'll be likin' that!" he assured her.

"An' how's me friend, Mrs. Cassidy?" inquired Emily in as rich a brogue. "An' is himself hearty enough to be dippin' inter the can what keeps his insides from curlin' up loike?"

"He is an' all," said Will, "and make it quick will you! All we had was a coal-dust sandwich on the train. They were so bad I had to eat Ma's too."

They heard James come in and go into his office.

"He never noticed your hat and cloak," whispered Emily. "We'll surprise him. James," she called. "Can you help me here a minute?"

There was no answer. They looked at each other with their eyes dancing.

"James!"

A grunt came back and in a moment James's hard tread through the hall.

Being James, he was as determined to show no surprise as his mother was to surprise him. Being his mother, Mary knew this.

She offered her cheek for him to kiss and stifled an impulse to rub it where his beard had tickled her. For a startled instant she thought she smelled liquor on his breath, then decided immediately that it was medicine. James always smelled of the pills he carried in his pocket.

Broad-shouldered and upright in his dark serge suit, he sat down to let her look at him. A half-smile played about the full lips, dark red in contrast to his black beard.

"You're looking well," he told his mother after scrutiny that might have been directed at an ailing patient. "Very well. How's Pa?"

"We've both been very well," said Mary with great dignity that hid real pleasure. James looked so distinguished.

James looked around to where Will was grinning impudently.

"Don't you ever work?" he asked wryly.

"Not when I can help it," answered Will cheerfully. "Do you?"

James was grave and profound at dinner. He talked about his practice and his patients, about his plans. They'd made one mistake. He should have settled the other side of Fourth Avenue. That was where the money was. People there had no more illness than this side, but they could afford to pay for it, and they did pay. They were building more houses up that way, too.

Emily was radiant. She and Will quipped back and forth as though they were children again. She mimicked Professor Risviglio whom she pictured as a peppery and impatient little Neapolitan, but Mr. Gray said he was the best singing teacher in the city. She mimicked some of the other pupils she had seen. One was a tall coloratura soprano with a vinegar face. The cords stood out on her scrawny neck when she reached for a high note. She had sung once at Carnegie Hall and never got over it. She was supercilious and affected. Will, delighted, stretched his neck and looked down his nose at his mother.

"Will, you're at the table," Mary reminded him from habit.

"Better stay here," James advised, in good humor himself. "I could pay you to scare patients into convulsions or out of *delirium tremens.*"

Emily laughed more loudly.

"He tried that himself, Ma. Frowns and grunts and looks sober. Calls blood poisoning a 'septic condition' and a stomach-ache an 'intestinal disturbance' just to frighten them. Is Pa's knee better?"

Thomas had wrenched it climbing over a pile of lumber in a partly finished house.

"Much better. Dr. Samuels thinks it will soon be all right. He sent his love to you both."

"Samuels! Is that old fraud still practicing?" scowled James.

"Old fraud, indeed. He brought both Emily and Will into the world," his mother chided.

"Exactly what I meant. Exactly what I meant," said James, closing his lips tightly so that his beard stuck out.

"You'll have to come more often, Ma!" cried Emily. "The dignified Dr. Stapely is joking. It's wonderful!"

How much of her radiance was due to her coming, Mary wondered. She noticed that Emily grew more nervous and excited as the time passed. She kept looking at the clock on the dining-room mantel—one

Mary had salvaged from the store and had repaired—as they ate their dessert.

James dragged out the checkerboard and bullied Will into the office almost before they were finished eating. Mary remained to help clear away the table and do the dishes. Emily went at them with a fierce energy, tying big aprons around them both, splashing hot water into the dishpan out of the kettle, and throwing in a chunk of Maria's homemade soap.

Andrew Gray came at about eight o'clock. He carried a pound box of chocolates for Emily and cigars for James.

"But you are so much nicer than I've been told!" he said quietly to Mary, with an accusing glance at Emily, an intimate glance which Mary did not miss.

"And I'd no idea what you looked like," said Mary, taking to the man instantly. "Are you nice too? You've been very nice to my children."

Gray bowed. "Not as nice as they are to me, or as I hope to be. You," he told Will, who was standing to one side wearing a self-conscious smile, "look enough like Miss Emily to be her brother."

"I am," Will started to say, then flushed as he realized that Gray was jesting. But the man's eyes were warm and friendly, including him in the jest. He shook hands gladly.

He and James went on with their game. James beat him badly and crowed gleefully. They started another.

They had gathered, without thinking, in the waiting room, free that evening of patients. James twisted his whiskers and gnawed on his cigar. Will, intent on winning this time, was jiggling one foot nervously. On the other side of the room in chairs drawn closely together, Mary, Emily, and Andrew Gray chatted easily. The laughter of the women rose musically as Gray talked humorously of Washington from which he had just returned.

Then they went upstairs, and Emily sang for them. Will was proud. James was frankly bored. He could never see all the to-do about people's singing. The human animal, male and female, had been given a voice for making its wants known. There was point to a baby's crying or a man's roaring with pain. Tacked to a mind, the voice could be used for communication with other animals. Using it as a toy, playing with it for effect, was silly. James was glad when the ringing of the telephone called him away.

It was a young mother calling from a corner grocery to say that her child's fever had gone up again. James had told her to watch it, and she was frightened. Could he come right away? James went upstairs to make his excuses, and left.

Emily was concluding a third song. She was breathless. Her face glowed with triumph. Mary was trying to hide her pride and surprise at the way in which Emily's voice had developed. Gray watched them both.

"I wish your father were here to hear you," said Mary.

"He'll hear her some day," said Gray. "We all will. Emily, will you—?"

Emily shook her head. "That's all this time," she said with finality.

Will was getting sleepy. Mary too was beginning to feel the fatigue of their journey from South Ilium.

Gray was quick to notice. He pleaded the long trip he had facing him back to New York. It was already past eleven o'clock.

"I'll go with you to the El," said Emily quickly. "Will will go with us so I'll have company home. I'll get a wrap."

She tucked her hand under Gray's arm as they started up the sidewalk toward Third Avenue with Will walking on the other side of her.

"Oh, it's a wonderful night out!" she cried. "Smell the sea?"

A fresh breeze was driving up the still, dimly lighted street. The sky was high and of deepest midnight-blue except where a young moon lighted a path of soft radiance through clusters of glinting stars.

"You're like your mother, Emily," Gray answered. "You look like her and you are like her. It's the same, Will, with you."

"But there is father in us too, just as there is in James," Emily warned, a laughing threat in her gay voice. "We shall get what we want."

"Yes, yes, m'girl," growled Will deeply.

"I hope you will," said Gray quietly. Unseen by Will, he pressed the girl's light hand warmly to his side.

Third Avenue, Will decided, was like South Avenue in South Ilium. There were just more shops with brick flats on top of each of them and the El high over the street, which was darkened by the tracks and the great iron supports. Some of the shops were in darkness, but most were dimly lighted. A chinaman was ironing busily in the window of one, a dim gaslight outlining him against the dirty window which bore the name Sing Loo in gold letters. There were saloons all along. All of them were open, and noisy singing came from one. There were still a few horses and wagons banging along over the cobblestones and the trolley tracks, for the streetcars were electric here. Will had seen them before. The Bay and the Narrows were down where the Hudson River would be if he were at home. The streets, all alike, were hilly, too, though nothing like as steep as their hill at home.

"Thursday?" whispered the girl eagerly, as they stopped at the foot of the long iron stairs leading up to the lighted El station at one corner.

"I shall be there if I can," Gray answered. He pressed her hand. "Good night, Will," he said and Will swung around from watching the people on the avenue. Some of them, he thought, were sailors by the look of them. They shook hands. "I'll show you some of New York before you go back," Gray promised him and started up the stairs.

"Isn't he wonderful?" asked Emily, waving and gazing after him.

"He's all right," said Will. "What kind of a store is that?"

"A pawnshop. They always have those three gold balls over the door. There are several along here. . . . There are no men like that in Ilium."

"The rector is like him a little," said Will. "Mr. Garver is too, though not much."

"The rector!" scoffed Emily, then added, "yes, perhaps he is just a little. Mr. Gray has been everywhere. He's so wise and kind and good. Can't you see how different he looks from—from everybody—everybody in the world."

Will had never heard his sister talk this way. He looked at her, surprised. They had turned and started back, Emily taking long, free strides, as though glad to be out. Her head was tossed back and she was breathing deeply.

"Are you going to marry him?" he asked curiously.

Her white teeth flashed and her hair caught the light from a shop window.

"Marry him!" Emily laughed. "Don't you remember we said we'd never get married, just stay in South Ilium always and fly kites and smoke cigarettes."

Will laughed too. It was wonderful to be with Emily again. It was wonderful to be in New York. It was wonderful to be alive.

"But are you?" he persisted.

"Let's not go home yet. Let's go this way and walk around the block first. I never get out at night. I can't go alone and James is always busy. He'd not walk anyway. I get so tired of being in the house all day. Oh, Will, I'm glad you're here. I wish you and Ma were here all the time!"

"We can't do that," said Will reasonably. "She has to take care of Pa, and we're busy as anything. He depends on me too now, some. I really have charge of the repairs down at the Parish House—practically."

They were going up the gentle slope now toward Fourth Avenue. Each house had its basement and the stoop running to the parlor floor. In some, light showed behind the drawn blinds. The house roofs were a single line slanting toward the top of the hill. Only the chimneys, dark against the sky, some thin and tall, some short and squat, a few covered with protective tin domes, were different.

"You couldn't marry him anyway. You have to look after James's place." The idea had become an obsession. He was afraid.

"He *is* married," said Emily, a trifle wildly. "He's been married a long time."

"He *is* married! Then how—"

"I don't know, I don't know, I don't know! Don't tell Ma, not now anyway."

Chapter 14

WILL HURRIED OFF to the livery stable right after breakfast the next morning for Roger. The black horse knew him, he was sure. He drove back slowly and carefully, holding the reins tightly as they crossed Third Avenue just as an El train roared by overhead. An older and sedater horse, Roger seemed bothered not at all. He moved on and from habit stopped before the house. Will tethered him, patted him, and went in to get James.

His mother, in a housedress borrowed from her daughter, was helping Emily in the kitchen. They were laughing and talking like two girls. James was inspecting the contents of his little black bag. He put in a small bottle and instruments from his desk. Then he drew on his gloves, and he and Will started off on the doctor's rounds with Will driving.

The weather was still fair but brisk. In South Brooklyn as in Ilium, the autumn was coming on. There were brilliant leaves on the soft maples, some of them mere saplings but others of a good size, along the tree belts. The youngest were surrounded by tall iron railguards to keep horses from nibbling at them. Fortified by James's presence, Will dared try getting a little more speed out of Roger. They trotted smartly down the street.

"Not too fast. We have a lot of calls to make. Eight of 'em," James warned. He had lighted one of the cigars Andrew Gray had brought him and blew smoke thoughtfully.

James was in genial and pleasant humor as he told Will where to turn, where to stop. He pointed out various landmarks. Their first call was down near the docks. James, cigar clenched between his teeth, disappeared upstairs over a dirty store.

The wide street was busy and noisy, with great horses straining as they tugged at heavily loaded drays whose wheels clattered over the cobblestones. Their drivers shouted and cursed. Machinery clanked and whirred in sheds on the dock side of the street. A derrick lifted large crates and boxes, swinging them aboard the deck of a tramp steamer where men pushed and strained to lower them into the hold. Other men, on scaffolds lowered from the deck, were scraping away at the steamer's rusty sides. Alongside were tied up other steamers and tall-masted sailing vessels. They were lumber schooners, James had told him. The water lapping around the scarred hulls was dirty, almost black. Garbage and broken lumber rocked back and forth in the water. The air smelled of tar, brine, rope. It was a heavy, heady smell.

Will, standing near Roger's head lest he be startled by the noise of some wagon flashing by too near him, breathed deep and stared curiously. Men lounged about a corner watching him for lack of anything more interesting to watch. They were tough looking men and Will remembered nervously stories he had heard of shanghaiing. He moved a step nearer the carriage weight, resolving to sell his life dearly.

James, looking angry, came down the creaking stairs, relighted his cigar, and climbed into the carriage.

"Take the next right," he told Will, who started Roger with some relief. "Fellow is faking. He's a dockworker. Fell the other day. Claims he hurt his back and wants to sue the company. Nothing the matter with his back. I'll sign no paper for him."

He stopped Will the next time before a row house in a street almost indistinguishable from his own. There were few signs of life about as it was mid-morning. Men were at work and the children at school. Here and there a housewife was sweeping down the stoop or emerging from the basement entry with a shopping bag on her arm. The houses were all neat and well painted. To Will's experienced eye they looked sound and in good condition.

"Won't be long. Confinement case." James slewed his eyes around to see if Will understood. Will, who thought that he did but was not sure, blushed faintly. Then he blushed hotly as he tried not to. James, already out of the carriage, did not notice.

They stopped before a block of unkempt flats in an unsavory neighborhood along the El line. Slatternly women leaned out of windows calling to one another or staring idly down into the street. Strings of drying peppers, bed linen, and lines of washing were hung out on the fire escapes. Several small boys came running to stare at Roger. Will warned them away importantly.

They stopped at a discreet brownstone several streets away on the better side of Fourth Avenue. A Negro girl in a housemaid's uniform was polishing the brass around the door knob. She said "Good mawning" and flashed white teeth in a smile as James entered the house.

They drove a long distance then to a hospital where James had performed a tonsillectomy on a child a few days before. It was a grim-looking place where a white ambulance, horses fully harnessed, stood ready. The white-jacketed driver smoked a corncob pipe as he waited for a call.

Other doctors came out of the hospital, got into their carriages and drove off. Old men and women shuffled through the door to the out-patients' clinic. A thin, shabbily dressed young woman held the hand of a boy inching along on twisted, pipe-stem legs. His every move made Will wince. The head and face of one old man was swathed in bandages. Only one eye showed. The bandages were dirty and stained over one cheek with a large yellow spot.

A black hearse pulled out of a court. Its unshaven driver wearing a torn sweater and a greasy cap was smoking a clay pipe. He winked at Will as he went by with the hand holding the reins propped easily on his knee.

Will shuddered inwardly though he tried to look unperturbed. Obviously the man had called for a newly made corpse. James found him looking pale when he finally came out.

"Don't like it, eh?" he jeered. "It's a fine hospital. Best in Brooklyn."

He took the reins himself this time and clucked sharply at Roger. It was almost time for office hours. They found Mary and Emily already dressed to go to New York shopping. A child howled lustily in the waiting room, his mother trying to quiet him. A dignified old gentleman was trying to ignore the disturbance. A small girl looked superciliously at the howling child, and her mother, though trying to look sympathetic, let it be seen she was thankful her children were better behaved. Without speaking to his mother or Emily, James bustled into his office, called in the woman with the child she was try-ing desperately to quiet, and shut the door. The frightened boy's screams came muffled but violent.

Mary, excited over the idea of going in to New York shopping, was moving briskly about attending to this and that. She had had to press the dress which had got wrinkled in the gladstone, and her hair, now precisely parted and curled, had needed hard brushing out after their train ride. It framed the delicate oval of her face.

She flashed Will what was almost a conspiratorial smile. This was a younger and more vital Mary than the one who presided over the tea table in South Ilium. She was well pleased. That morning she and Emily had had a long talk. There was nothing wrong. She had seen Mr. Gray and approved him. It was obvious both that Emily was fascinated and that Mr. Gray admired her, but he was a friend of both Emily and James. He would be a friend of the family. After all Emily was only nineteen. Mr. Gray, she imagined, was somewhere in his forties. She was certain everything was all right because she wanted to feel it was.

"Did you have a good ride, Will?" she asked. "Tomorrow I shall go with James perhaps. You'll want a fresh collar before we start out, and dust off your shoes. Emily wants you to fix the trap under the sink before we go home. It's clogged, and I notice there's some paper loose in the back bedroom upstairs."

The dining-room table had been set for him and James. The women had already eaten. Will drank soup and ate bread and a cold slice of beef with some of his mother's mustard pickle sent down from South Ilium and listened to the sound of smothered voices from the front of the house. Will tried to eat without making any noise. He ate almost surreptitiously as though he were in a public place.

Soon James came in, loosening his collar and stripping off his tie. He sat on the edge of a leather sofa in the dining room and kicked off his shoes, grunting and grimacing. Will grinned at him a little self-consciously as he chewed on a piece of beef that had a knot of gristle in it. An unwilling respect for his much older brother had caught him.

Emily and his mother, dressed in all their finery. Emily, with a large hat with a flopping brim that hid part of her face, rustled in.

"James—" Emily began.

The doorbell banged noisily. Its noise was followed by an impatient hard knocking.

Emily exclaimed in vexation. With a *moue* at Will and a humorously resigned look, Mary seated herself carefully in a straight-backed dining-room chair. Muttering, James began to put on his shoes again while Emily hurried to the door.

"Doctor!" she called sharply.

A deep gruff voice was saying something. A feminine voice squealed. James was struggling to replace his collar and tie. The gruff voice grew louder and sounded angry. There was a groan.

"Doctor will be right here," they heard Emily say in reassuring, artificial tones. "Doctor Stapely!"

"Doctor will always be right there," muttered James bitterly. He grabbed up a slice of beef and chewed down on it, his beard bobbing. Then he hurried off.

A powerful, white-bearded man, half-a-head taller than James and broader of shoulder, was lowering a young woman into one of the chairs in the waiting room. Another woman fussed around her.

They were obviously a father and his two daughters, both girls fashionably dressed. They took over the waiting room, all of them talking at once and talking fast.

"It was those damned El stairs!" boomed the old man. "A disgrace. Whole fool contraption is a disgrace. Ought to sue them."

"A shame!" Emily was murmuring. She had hurried for a pillow to put under the foot of the young woman in the chair.

"We were just getting off the El to make a call on the Johnsons on 52nd Street—perhaps you know them—when Laura slipped and almost fainted. She went right down. Papa picked her up, but she couldn't walk. They told us this was the nearest doctor."

The lips of the thin, intense young woman in the chair were tight with pain. "Oh!" she cried. "Oh!" as Emily slipped the pillow deftly under her foot. She attempted a brave smile.

"So you're the doctor," accused the old man loudly as James entered. He glared at him. "I hope you know your business, young man. Hazard to life and limb that Elevated. Shouldn't be allowed, by God!"

James ignored him.

"No, leave her here," he said to Emily as she looked questioningly at him and indicated the open door of the office. "Take the rest of them away." He knelt and touched the injured girl's foot.

She winced and cried out, then bit her lip impatiently.

"It's twisted and probably sprained," she told James practically. "I'm sure there is nothing broken. You will probably have to cut my shoe away. That is all right. Janet, take Papa with you. Papa, don't go on so! Nothing serious has happened."

"By God!" said the old man. "That El—"

"It was *not* the fault of the Elevated," contradicted his daughter from her seat. "We were hurrying and I—Oh, oh!" she broke off, tensing her thin shoulders. "Perhaps you need not cut the shoe," she told James, as she recovered. "They are new ones."

Emily was shepherding the reluctant old man and the prettier of the two girls down the hall.

"A shame," she murmured sympathetically. "It's really too bad."

Now she and her mother would miss the half-past one boat from 39th Street, but it could not be helped.

"We were so looking forward to this afternoon," complained the other daughter. "Papa's ship is tied up at Erie Basin. He and Laura have just come back from South America. I've been staying with friends on Brooklyn Heights."

"Mother," said Emily, "this is Miss—"

"Gravet," said the old man, staring at Mary and then at Will, who had got up from the table and was standing uncertainly out of the way. "One *t*. I'm not a damned Frenchman—excuse me, ma'am. This daughter is Janet. The older one's Laura. Fool thing, twisting her ankle that way. Girl ought to have some sense."

"Papa! It wasn't Laura's fault any more than it was the El steps. She caught her heel. She could not help that."

"She could help wearing such fool heels!" retorted her father. "If your mother was alive, she'd not allow it. I won't allow it when she's aboard ship."

"Well, we're not aboard ship now," said the girl. She looked helplessly toward Mary.

"Sooner we're back there, better pleased I'll be," said the old man. He had sat himself on the sofa where James had been, the springs giving under his considerable weight. He held a master's blue cap with gold insignia in great, blue-veined hands. He wore a sharply pressed dark blue suit. He stared at Will as though he had not seen him before.

"How do you do?" said Mary with great dignity.

"What?" he asked truculently.

"Papa gets so upset," said the pretty girl apologetically.

"We'll be delayed a little, Mother," said Emily, ice edging her voice.

"Oh, you were just going out! This is too bad!"

"It's nothing unusual," said Emily too sweetly. She disliked the way these people had taken over the household. "We have these minor accident cases every day."

"Minor!" exploded the captain. "Girl's probably broken her leg. May be crippled the rest of her life, hobbling around on a cane. Won't be able to marry and have children." He was roaring as his imagination led him on. "Might affect her brain. Wouldn't take much to affect the brains of both of these two. What's minor about that?"

"Papa!"

"Emily!" James was calling. "Emily!" He met her halfway down the hall. "Get a basin of hot water," he ordered, "and that roll of wide bandage out of the cupboard in my office."

Emily, her face twisted in vexation, looked at him a second, but he turned and hurried back to his patient. With a shrug she turned back to the kitchen. She might as well, she thought, have kept her white uniform dress on. Certainly she didn't wish to ruin her gown. She tied an apron around her waist before she went to the stove.

"Had a seaman broke his leg once down in the Caribbean," Captain Gravet was telling the others. "Some kind of nigger I signed on in Haiti. Thing was hanging loose from here." He pounded a massive thigh. "It was hot as Hades down there. He went out of his head. Had to tie him in his bunk."

Mary was carefully stripping off her long gloves which she had already put on.

"What became of the man?" asked Will anxiously.

"The man?" asked Captain Gravet, looking hard at Will. He had a big square face, ruddy and seamed, and faded blue eyes deep under shaggy white brows. His neck was red and strong.

"The sailor—the black one."

"Oh, he died. Threw him overboard. Didn't last long in those waters. Sharks. Some of the men didn't like it much."

Suddenly Mary relented. The girl was a pretty girl. It was not her fault.

"Would you like a cup of tea?" she asked. "Let me get you a cup. It won't take a moment."

"Please don't bother, Oh, please don't. Well, then, I *could* drink—"

"Had no lunch," grunted her father. "Spent the whole morning getting dressed and the rest of the time falling downstairs. Why a grown woman can't walk down a simple flight of steps without breaking her neck, I don't know."

Mary, glad of the excuse to move, went to the kitchen.

"We're going to New York, I don't care what," hissed Emily. "These people—"

"S-sh. I'm going to get them some tea."

"Tea? That's silly, Ma! They're just patients."

"They've had nothing to eat," said Mary firmly. "The other girl was probably feeling faint when she fell." She counted. "We'll need two more cups."

The captain had lapsed into surly silence. The girl, waiting anxiously, smiled timidly at Will, who abashed by her prettiness and the splendor of her costume, did not know whether or not to smile back. He was bored and uneasy. Besides he wanted to go to the bathroom. As soon as Mary returned with spoons and napkins to set at the table, he slipped out.

"You can come in now," James told Captain Gravet and Janet. "The ankle is sprained, badly. She'll have to stay off it for a while."

"I'm just getting some tea," said Mary. "Can't you bring Miss Gravet into the dining room?"

James looked surprised, then annoyed, then laughed. The big old man and his younger daughter had hurried down the hall into the waiting room.

"Think I feed my patients as well as patch 'em up?" he asked his mother. "But I guess we can this once. I'm hungry enough myself. I'll see if we can bring her in."

"The doctor was so gentle!" Laura was exclaiming to Emily as the others hovered about. "He has such skillful hands!" Her bright, sharp eyes were looking Emily up and down. "He's told me you are his sister. You don't seem at all alike."

"Oh, I'm brutal and clumsy enough, if that's what you mean," Emily agreed. It was no use their trying to get to New York now. That decision made, she relaxed a little. They could start early the next morning. "The family can only support one genius."

A hard, practical piece, she thought, but Laura had put up a minimum of fuss, and her ankle must have hurt like the devil. She was clearing away the basin and bandages. She put the bottle of iodine back in the dispensary.

One arm around her father, the other about James, the patient hobbled down the hall to the dining room. Mary, very self-possessed now that she was in charge, had sliced more beef and was buttering thin slices of bread and placing them nicely on a dinner plate.

"I'm famished!" cried Laura gratefully as James arranged a stool and a pillow. Everything about her thin face was sharp, chin, nose, gray eyes. Yet, animated and intelligent, it was not unattractive. "Does spraining one's ankle always make one this hungry, doctor?"

"It usually teaches 'em to be more careful the next time," said James.

Captain Gravet grunted agreement.

Mary and Emily sipped their tea while the others ate hungrily, the captain champing enthusiastically, the girls trying for manners' sake to go slowly. James looked at Laura as he ate and drank.

"Don't try walking on that foot at all for a while. It should clear up in a few weeks if you give it proper attention. We'll have to retape it in a day or two. I'll look in on you tomorrow."

"I'll do just as you say, Doctor Stapely," she answered meekly.

"Keep it propped up and sit still."

"How's she going to do that," demanded Captain Gravet. "We haven't even begun to load yet. Nobody aboard but a watchman."

"You're living on your ship?" Will, who had returned, exclaimed.

"We'll manage," said Laura quickly. "Papa and I always manage." She looked at him in a friendly way, and Will liked her at once. He offered her the bread.

Mary poured her more tea. "Your house is so attractive," she said to Emily. "Wouldn't it be more convenient, though, if you had the doctor's office and waiting room upstairs? I should think he would like it better."

"No it wouldn't," said Emily shortly.

Captain Gravet wiped his drooping white mustache on the back of his hand and looked about him curiously.

"Any money in this?" he asked James bluntly. Then he answered himself.

"Can't be much," he said contemptuously.

"Papa!" cried Janet shocked.

Laura only laughed. "This isn't buying by the cargo and selling by the ounce, Papa. A doctor is different. And, I think," she said, looking directly at James, "that it is about the finest thing a man can be."

Emily arched her eyebrows at her mother.

"There's enough money," said James with surprising equableness. "Overcharge some patients. Sprained ankles come high. Make a lot of calls on a sprained ankle."

Captain Gravet looked hard at him, then roared with laughter.

"By God," he said, "that's good! That's a good one!"

"He thinks I'm joking," said James. To his mother's surprise, he winked gravely at Laura.

"How pretty you are," said Laura directly to Emily. "You'll be getting married one of these days. Then what will the doctor do?" She looked thoughtful.

"Hire a more efficient housekeeper and a regular nurse, I imagine," Emily answered, pleased in spite of herself.

James sent Will off to Third Avenue to find a cab. He came back riding with the driver.

"You've been so good to us," said Laura prettily. "We've taken your whole afternoon and upset all your plans."

"We've enjoyed it," said Mary honestly, "and tomorrow's another day."

James and Captain Gravet helped Laura into the carriage as Mary and Emily watched from the doorway, and Laura made a point of thanking Will for going for the cab.

At the last moment James decided to go with them. They would need his help at the other end. He could take the surface car back.

"Well!" said his mother as the cab pulled away. "Well, just what is James about? But they are very nice people," she added.

"Whew!" commented Emily. "Oh, well."

But she was thinking of something else. Thoughtfully she watched the cab out of sight.

Chapter 15

MARY SAT on a formal chair in the stiff front parlor of a brownstone house on East 18th Street and looked contentedly out of the window at passers-by. Her legs ached, her feet were tired, and the hem of her skirt was dusty, but she and Emily had had a glorious morning in the big stores, eaten a hasty lunch, and had time to do still two more of the smaller stores before Emily had to go for her vocal lesson.

Mary had bought gloves for Maria, a cravat for Thomas of just the type—dark blue with tiny white dots—he liked, and even a new scarf pin for Will. They had been such a bargain, she had been unable to resist them in the biggest store of them all on Sixth Avenue just off Fourteenth. The pin was a tiny fleur-de-lis set with garnet chips and imitation pearls. Thus far he had only an old one of his father's. She intended to save the new pin for his birthday.

For the sixth time Emily's voice rose in an ascending scale from another room.

For the sixth time Professor Risviglio's shrill voice screamed, "No! No! Do like dis!" He let out a falsetto note that jerked Mary upright in her chair. It was like the vicious rasp of a file against a vibrating sliver of rusty iron.

Emily tried again, and the round notes pealed golden through the room where Mary sat. She listened critically, having learned now that it did not do just to admire.

It was a street of quiet brownstones. Now and again a gentleman passed alone or with a lady. Delivery boys pushed carts along the sidewalk and disappeared into basement entries, opening their carts for a package and letting the lids fall with a thump. Two very fashionably dressed young women came out of a house and stood waiting for a carriage. Mary's sharp eye took in every detail of their costumes, from their great hats with flopping brims and their wide, padded shoulders, to their tiny waists emphasized by bright encircling ribbons, and their flowing skirts held daintily in white-gloved hands from trailing on the walk.

Emily looked as well. Emily looked finer, for she had beauty which these girls lacked, though, Mary admitted, they were pretty enough. They were joined by a gentleman in a frock coat and winged collar. He lifted his shining tall hat in greeting, then raised his stick to the driver of a polished carriage which pulled up before them at the kerb. They all got in. Mary craned to watch.

Professor Risviglio was accompanying Emily at the piano now, as tentatively she began on a soprano aria. They stopped and tried again. They stopped and tried again. They stopped and tried again. Professor Risviglio's annoyance expressed itself through his fingers. The piano crashed and thundered, drowning Emily's voice.

Adjusting her bonnet once more and smoothing her skirts again, Mary looked about her at the square parlor. To her mind, the room was bare, and it was dusty. A plaster bust stood on the white marble mantel over a blackened cast-iron register which was thickly decorated with leaves, flowers, and birds. A small statue of a woman, naked except for the veil tossing about her body, stood on a carved teakwood table in one corner. Mary was not sure she liked it. There was a stiff settee upholstered in faded red silk, and there were two tapestried chairs besides her own. A worn oriental with geometric patterns in reds and yellows covered most of the floor. The white plaster ceiling was ornately decorated with chubby angels circling about the pendant gas chandelier. Another angel, cast iron but gilded, wings outspread, stood tiptoe on the wall holding a candle in each chubby fist. He needed a fresh coat of gilt, and the ceiling needed a fresh coat of calsomine, Mary decided. It was unlikely, however, than an Italian like Professor Risviglio would realize it.

She was startled when a fat woman with frizzed hair carelessly dressed and an incredibly deep bosom swept into the room. She glanced imperiously at Mary who stared coldly back as soon as she could collect her wits. She was too late. By this time the woman was not looking at her. The woman thumped herself down on the settee which creaked under the sudden strain and looked impatiently at the closed door into the other room.

She moved her small feet quickly, careless of her skirts, and Mary was astonished to see that her fat legs were incased in bright red stockings. Mary's lips came tightly together, and she looked again into the street. The window was not clean either.

When Mary dared look back, the woman was staring at her out of great dark eyes but, no longer impatient, listening intently to the music. She kept time with a thick forefinger as she held Mary's glance, first shaking her head as though Mary had been about to interrupt.

Hypnotized, Mary watched her.

The forefinger stopped, and the woman frowned.

"Not good!" she said distinctly.

Mary reddened and was on the verge of angry retort when, with a warning shake of her head, the woman bent her head to listen and began keeping time again to Emily's singing. The frown vanished. She broke into a broad smile and nodded energetically at Mary. "Better," she said. "Good. Better." Mary haughtily ignored her and looked pointedly out of the window again.

Suddenly Emily's voice rose. Notes pealed golden through the room. The fat woman jumped to her feet. "That is good, good—good!" she exclaimed. "That," she flung at Mary as though Mary had denied it, "is a *voice!*"

Mary was staring at her fascinated as the sound stopped. There was a moment of confusion as the door of Risviglio's studio opened and Emily, flushed, her eyes lighted, emerged almost at the same instant as Andrew Gray, who had entered unnoticed from the street, advanced toward her, his lips parted and his own eyes warm.

They saw only each other, noticing neither Mary nor Professor Risviglio and the fat woman who were embracing and squealing in Italian as they bustled into the room Emily had just left.

It was Emily who recovered first and turned toward Mary.

"Andrew!" she said swiftly. "Mother is—" She gestured toward Mary with her music.

Gray spun about. "I hoped you would come with Emily," he said very quickly. "I thought if I could catch you both here, we might have tea or some ice cream."

Mary glowed with pleasure. She knew as they descended the stoop, Emily on one side of her, Gray gently guiding her elbow, that they looked far finer than the two young ladies and the gentleman who had gone off in the carriage. Thomas would be so pleased with the way Emily was getting on. She wished the whole of South Ilium might see them now.

"I *knew* you were coming," Emily whispered to Gray as they turned toward Fifth Avenue. "I was so excited I could not keep my mind on the lesson, and Professor Risviglio was getting more and more cross!"

"You must pay attention to Risviglio," Gray whispered back laughing, "but I'm glad you thought of me a little too."

Fifth Avenue was thronged with a well-dressed crowd. The roadway was crowded with carriages with here and there one of the new hansom cabs, its driver perched high above his passengers and the reins, caught in gracefully curved iron uprights, coming down across the shining roof of the cab. It always looked to Mary as though the weight of the driver would tip the hansom backwards tossing the horse into the air. Most of the carriages were rubber-tired. There was only a clip-clop of the horses' hooves on the smooth Belgian block pavements. Helmeted policemen directed the traffic so that people could pass at the intersections.

There were fine shops, great homes in gray and brown stone silent and discreet behind iron railings and heavy doors with polished hardware. A gorgeously uniformed doorman stood haughtily before the expensive pile of New York's largest and finest hotel while two underlings in less striking uniforms directed the flow of carriage traffic at the kerb. Bell boys hurried across the sidewalk with luggage.

Gray guided them into a beautifully decorated tea room and confectionary next door to the hotel itself. It was, he explained, under the hotel's management. They ordered tea and muffins and, at Gray's insistance, ice cream. It was the most delicious Mary had ever tasted.

Gray directed his conversation with friendly warmth to Mary, but his eyes sought Emily's.

"I'm learning Italian fast!" Emily laughed as she tasted her pale-green and pale-yellow ice cream. "Oh, this is good! *Uno, due, tre, quattro—uno, due, tre, quattro—buono*. Bah! Ah!" she mimicked Risviglio.

Her white teeth flashed. The color was high in her cheeks. The gold of her hair shone in the light sparkling from an electric globe overhead.

Gray watched and listened with fast-beating heart. His emotions were absurd, ridiculous, and wonderful. He had waited all day for these moments. The girl's youth and beauty delighted him. His own feelings fascinated and appalled. They had interfered with the article he had been trying to write, with his planning of a page for the *Tribune,* with an idea which Ventnor had turned over to him for refining and advice as to action.

It was twenty years since he had experienced such pure and unthinking joy. He had never expected to experience such emotions and sensations again. Perhaps he had never really known them before. They would have to be stopped, to be stamped out and forgotten. He was cynical, worn and soiled. The girl had not yet touched life. He would have to stop before he made a fool of himself and perhaps hurt others. But not yet—not today. Under his elation there was warmth and peace he had almost forgotten existed. He could not discard what forgetful gods had let slip. He credited them with no generosity.

They would snatch back quickly enough if he let them suspect his pleasure.

He forced his eyes away from Emily's, forced repose and politeness back into his face.

"But all New York isn't like this," he said, responding to a remark of Mary's. "Some of it is vicious and filthy. Not a quarter-mile away are some of the worst slums in any city in the world. Then there is Riverside Drive and there is Gramercy Park, not very far from here. Very different from the Bowery, Hell's Kitchen, or the Five Points. The next time you come we'll see as much of it as we can—Coney Island, Chinatown, the mansions along Fifth Avenue, Central Park, all the rest."

Mary's eyes sparkled.

"I do want to see them."

"Ma!" cried Emily, though she had not been listening. Her eyes, wide and alight, were still on Gray's face. Their meaning was unmistakable. It was that and the sudden, perverse wish to hurt himself that stung Gray to harsh speech.

"I'm sorry," he said to Mary, his words distinct, "that I cannot ask you to call at my home. My wife has been a partial invalid—a nervous disorder—for many years. She does not leave the house when she is in the city. She has a nurse with her always. I try to spend a part of each day with her when I can, but even my own life is largely outside of my home."

Emily had paled. Her full lower lip was caught between her white, even teeth.

"I'm very sorry," said Mary softly, but the expression on her face did not change. "It must be very hard on you." Emily had never told her this!

He had started out to cut cleanly, to disillusion, to destroy his own absurd happiness. His insistent cunning, as of its own volition, had painted a sympathetic picture of himself.

"Harder on her, I'm afraid," he said quietly. "It is not something I speak of often. It is unlikely I shall again." His face, which had tightened, relaxed.

"Ma," said Emily tensely. "We should go. James's dinner will not be ready. I left directions with Mrs. Spanner, but you know how she is."

Mary smiled at Gray.

"James can make shift," she assured Emily lightly. "Your father has had to do the same sometimes. I never believed in ruining anyone's independence entirely."

It was Gray who caught his breath this time. Both he and Emily had caught the deliberate approval in Mary's tone. He looked steadily at Emily whose color had returned.

"You mean you have kept your own independence!" he laughed to Mary.

"I didn't say so," she smiled back, knowing they had understood her, "but isn't that the principle of this country? I hear it shouted about sometimes."

She talked on easily, watching them, watching graceful women and quietly gallant men at the other small tables near them. The electric bulbs glowed prettily in what had been cut-glass and crystal gas fixtures. The waitresses serving rich looking confections glided swiftly between the tables, serving deftly. Mary enjoyed it all. She ate the last of her ice cream, deciding that the odd flavor she had caught with the lemon and pistachio was almond. She wondered what terrible price it had cost.

Emily said little. She was too happy to talk, too happy even to notice the admiring and curious glances sent their way. Once or twice Gray bowed politely to someone he knew. People seemed to know him wherever they went. Her eyes took in every detail of his face, every detail of his clothes. He wore a tightly buttoned dark suit which, like all his clothes, fitted perfectly. His fresh and spotless white collar was low with its opening broad. In the wide knot of his dull silk checked cravat gleamed a tiny blue stone in a Tiffany setting.

"You're coming back with us?" implored Emily as they got up from their table.

Gray shook his head. "Only as far as the ferry. We go to press tonight. I always like to look in. I shall be busy till midnight, but I shall see you soon."

They lagged behind as Mary walked firmly ahead.

"Very soon!" whispered the girl. "Oh, please!"

Again Andrew Gray tried to compose himself, to withdraw a little, but accidentally or through Emily's intention, their hands touched. His blood leaped and what seemed almost a physical pain constricted his chest. His eyes contradicted the aloofness of his kindly smile, and it was his eyes that Emily saw.

Chapter 16

ONE AFTERNOON several weeks later Emily darted breathless out of Professor Risviglio's room again. Her eyes flashed about the parlor.

Gray smiled at her from where he stood near a window.

"I didn't hear you come in! I was afraid you had not come! I've not been able to keep my mind on what Professor Risviglio was saying for the past ten minutes!"

"I've been here a long time. I came early to listen. It was beautiful. It's not everyone can have a private concert as I do. *Merci, Mam'selle Stapelie!*"

The girl's eyes were very bright, her lips were slightly parted as Gray held her coat for her. She stripped on her gloves excitedly, smoothing the tight kid back over her strong fingers. "Oh!" she breathed.

"Where shall we go?" Gray asked. "It's too late for a matinee, and it's too early for Peacock Alley, though that is where all beautiful ladies should be seen. The Fifth Avenue? The Brevoort?"

"Oh, anywhere, Andrew! Anywhere! It's been four days since I saw you, four whole days!"

Gray smiled teasingly.

"That long!" he mocked. "Have I aged greatly? It must be a little time, for you have grown more beautiful than ever. I think I have been a pretty frequent visitor at your house."

"But that is to see James as much as to see me," said Emily jealously. "That doesn't count."

"It's really," Gray confessed, as they left Risviglio's, "to see that you haven't broken any of my windows or marred my walls."

"Couldn't we," breathed Emily, "go to your *Insurance Tribune?* I've never seen a newspaper office. I want to see what your world is like—part of it anyway."

"It's just a print shop and very dirty, some type and some printers, a press, the stones, ink smells. It would be squandering what is left of your day, and we mustn't do that."

Emily laughed unsteadily. "But I want to, and we've lots of time today. I'm not going home until late, until very late."

"Then we can have dinner too?" Gray asked, trying to keep the eagerness from his voice.

Emily nodded, still laughing. They were walking toward Broadway, but she hardly knew it. She was aware of no one else on the street. She did not know whether the day was cold or warm, whether the sky was bright or dull.

"Excellent!" Gray's hand tightened lightly on her arm.

"James tried to tell me to be home early. I told him I'd do as I liked. He was furious!"

Gray looked thoughtfully ahead. "Perhaps he was right," he said gravely.

"James?" asked Emily scornfully. "I may never go home. I may just stay right here!" She wanted to add "with you," but she did not dare. The man heard what she left unuttered. "If I stayed in New York," Emily explained, "I could sing and practice all the time. I could live in my own place instead of cooking and dusting and nursing for James."

Gray guided her across the street without answering.

"We must take a car here," he said. "That is if you really must see the *Tribune*."

"Oh, yes!"

All week she had been living for this hour. When he had last been at the house, she had ached to be with him alone. She could hardly believe that Gray was here with her now. She wanted to savor every instant of their being together so that later she could remember every expression of his face, every word he spoke.

The Broadway car was crowded. They found a seat for Emily, and Gray stood before her, bending slightly as they talked. Their knees touched as the car jolted and swayed.

"Would you come to see me every day?" asked Emily in a low voice.

"Every day?" he asked, his face questioning.

Gray, too, seemed under a spell. He had to concentrate to speak. Words seemed unnecessary, and he was aware that they both knew it. He was frighteningly happy.

"I mean if I moved to New York to a place of my own."

"Well," he managed, "not *every* day perhaps."

"But *almost* every day!"

Emily, her beautiful eyes deeper than he had ever seen them, and the rapt smile still on her face as she looked up at him, was satisfied.

"Then I *will* move to New York," she decided as though she were jesting.

Gray smiled as though he were jesting too. His fingers curled tightly about the leather strap suspended from the car's ceiling. He bent to look out of the smeared window to see where they were. The movement brought their faces close, and the faint scent Emily wore reached his nostrils. Gray dared hardly breathe. He forced himself erect.

"Almost Chambers Street," he said.

They alighted at the Broadway and Chambers Street corner of City Hall Plaza, Emily gathering her skirts for the step down from the car, Gray taking her arm as they stood to let carriages and laden drays pass before they could reach the safety of the crowded sidewalk.

The late afternoon was clear; the air cold but crisp so that the city's building stood sharp against the sky, and the noises of the traffic and the shouts of drivers to their horses rang with musical distinctness.

Emily breathed deeply. "It's wonderful," she said, looking quickly about her at the busy, congested downtown district, seeing everything, seeing nothing.

"Very wonderful," said Gray quietly, his eyes on the girl.

She seemed not to notice.

"It *is* the center of the world, isn't it? Your world, I mean."

"The center of the world changes sometimes."

Emily looked at him quickly as, almost unconsciously, they started across City Hall Park to get away from the crowds and noise of the streets.

"What do you mean?"

What did he mean? Movement in the fresh air had brought him back to actuality—or should have. He looked across the brown lawns behind their iron railings to Park Row.

"Mean? I don't know. Now there's a brave new *World*," he evaded, gesturing toward the golden dome, shining in the sun, of the World Building. He began to talk rapidly. He touched his hat merrily, obsequiously as if he were a professional guide. "That's newspaper row over there. That, of course, is the Tribune Tower. There's the *Press,* the *Globe.* The *Times* put up that new building just a few years ago, but it is not doing too well. You can't see it from here, but the old *Star* is trying to pull itself together with pictures and gossip. Other gossip has it that the *Herald*—that's the *Herald*—is going to risk moving away up to Thirty-fourth Street. But it's the *Sun*—"

They had stopped walking and stood close together at one side of the walk out of the way of hurrying passers-by.

"Did you work on all of them?" marveled Emily.

"You interrupted," said Gray severely. "I did not. What I was about to say was that it is still the *Tribune* and the *Sun* that matter. Reid has done a good job with the *Tribune,* so now he's running for vice-president, though why a good editor should want to be vice-president I don't know. If you could see through City Hall and around a corner or two you might be able to see Horace Greeley himself. He's been dead nearly twenty years, but I'm sure he's still about." He looked intently at Emily and shook his head. "But you don't look like Margaret Fuller at all."

"Should I? Who was she?"

"You should not. She was a terrifying woman. I saw her once or twice. But I think she made life a little pleasanter for Uncle Horace, and I liked her for that."

"Then I like her too!"

"And if you could see through the wall of that old building there—it was Tammany Hall once, but it's the *Sun* now—you might see old Dana himself." Gray looked at his watch. "Yes, he should be there now. He was the first edior I worked for in New York. Chet Lord and Boss Clarke run the paper now, but the old man with the gray beard sits in a little room wearing his black skullcap and seeing everything that goes on through those thick lenses of his. The *Sun* is still the 'newspaperman's newspaper,' and it always will be while Dana lives."

Gray kept on talking. He did not dare stop. He knew he was talking so that he would not say what he felt. They passed close to the steps of City Hall.

"It's so small!" Emily protested. "The city hall in Ilium is bigger."

"It's large enough. New York is not run from City Hall. It's run by Dick Croker from Tammany, just as New York State is run from Tom Platt's 'Amen Corner' of the Fifth Avenue Hotel on Twenty-third Street."

"Are they?" murmured Emily happily.

"They are. Men don't like to be governed. The human race abhors being policed and taxed. Men have as little to do with it as they can. So government here has become the preserve of scoundrels and the unscrupulous, of the stupid, the avaricious, the cruel. I think it was always that way."

"I see."

"Do you? I'm not sure I do." Once more they waited at a kerbing for a chance to cross the street and started down Broadway toward the thin spire of Trinity.

"Religion on the right. Wall Street ahead." Gray's voice was mocking as he burlesqued his role of guide again. "We're leaving politics for money. They are always close together, and whether politics or finance is the greater confusion, the larger fiction, I don't know. There's been money lying everywhere for the earning or the stealing.

138

Suddenly, I'm told, there isn't any. Not gold enough, anyway, to pay all the outstanding railroad and industrial paper. There is just as much real value in land and in what men can do with their hands and with their minds, but we are toppling into another panic."

"I could get piano pupils and voice pupils, too. I know I could!" cried Emily. "If I could do that, I'd have all the money I need to live in Manhattan. I would, wouldn't I?"

They stood still on the pavement again. A telegraph boy scurrying behind them almost collided with them. Other people on the sidewalk flowed around them. Gray forced himself to look directly into Emily's face, as he had not dared do since they got off the street car.

"I—I don't know," he said in a low voice.

"But I *could!*"

"If—perhaps there will be some way I can help. Financially, I mean. I'll be near you. I want to help! I want to be near; I—" Startled, Gray looked quickly away from Emily's excited face. Almost awkwardly he took a quick step in the direction they had been going. Emily, who had been standing very still, one gloved hand half raised, jerked into movement.

"There, young lady," said Gray swiftly, "is Apex Life, scene of my present labors or part of them."

"Where? Where? I want to see!" cried Emily. Her face was flushed, and she breathed rapidly. "Tell me! Tell me *everything!*"

"Down that street,"—Gray's tone was mocking still, but his voice was unsteady—"I write, I edit. I issue magazines, articles, and news despatches by the ton. I urge the agents of Apex Life to greater and greater efforts. I cajole, wheedle, threaten, persuade. I try to convince the entire population of this and other continents that life insurance is as necessary as daily bread, as important as breathing, as miraculous as winning the sweepstakes, and that Apex's is the best kind of life insurance ever concocted—and I do various other little things for Mr. Charles Ventnor, a very different man from Mr. Charles A. Dana."

"It sounds—oh, wonderful. Everything is wonderful today! Why?"

"It's exciting sometimes." The man's face and voice went unguarded for an instant. "There's an element of risk, an edge of danger—just as there always is where life is quick and sweet and free. Intelligence and wisdom are good, but there is wit to be kept sharp. There are emotions to know, to know through and through and to hold to. Wonderful, did you say? Yes, it is."

"Don't stop! Don't!"

Gray's quiet smile was back. His eyes were gentle and humorous again.

"I started merely to explain the world. I've explained the universe. Isn't that enough?"

"No! No!"

"It's almost dark. It *is* dark. Did you know? All these people are on their way home, and here we stand in the middle of Broadway like Hansel and Gretel lost in the forest. I'm hungry. You're hungry, or didn't you know that either? Where shall we go? Gardner's? No. The Brevoort? Perhaps. No, I know just the place. Come, we'll have a cab." Moving with a boy's eager grace, Gray stepped to the kerb.

It was quiet in the deeply-carpeted dining room of the small, almost London-like hotel. Men and women dined decorously and well at nearby tables, and black-coated waiters moved unobtrusively about with dishes and silver. Gray saw only Emily's face, young and beautiful, her eyes deep in the candlelight that threw soft shadows on her cheek. With one long-fingered hand she was slowly turning her thin-stemmed glass, still half filled with amber sherry, but her eyes were on his face.

To Gray his wife had become more and more a shadowy figure flitting with her nurse companion from one sanatorium to another, from Hot Springs to the Adirondacks, from Vermont to Georgia. In recent years she seemed to have spent only a few weeks now and again in the Murray Hill house as she moved south with the sun or north for the summer. She touched only his deep sympathy and tender affection.

The girl across from him was vibrant and immediate. She was life. Suddenly she had become *his* life. The two things, at this moment anyway, were distinct and whole in themselves. The afternoon had been a dream, or it had been so real that he was not yet aware of its full significance.

He took Emily home through the late winter darkness. No light showed in the Brooklyn house and, despite himself, Gray felt relieved. He would *not* feel like a small boy or like a clandestine lover.

"James must be out on a case."

"I think he's in bed," whispered Emily. Sated with happiness, she felt sleepy.

"I'll come in just until you get a light on. I shan't stay," said Gray in low tones.

They entered through the basement door, and Emily felt for the taper in its long metal stick with which the lamp hanging from the hall ceiling was always lighted. Gray struck a match and lighted the end for her.

"James isn't in bed," said Emily suddenly. "He has gone to see

Laura Gravet again. He's been there a lot lately, and he's been irritable as a bear. I'd not be surprised if they—that is—"

"Oh!"

"So I *can* move to New York, you see." Emily's words came in a rush. "James wouldn't need me if he marries. Oh, I hope they do! They'll object to my going, but I'll go anyway. Oh, Andrew, it will be wonderful!"

"Yes, Emily," he said gently. As gently he kissed her and slipped quickly out into the night.

The taper still in her hand, Emily stood trembling in the dimly lighted, deeply shadowed hall.

Chapter 17

IN SOUTH ILIUM that winter, life was busy for seventeen-year-old Will. It was long after midnight this time as he struggled over the snow and ice up the hill and tumbled sleepily into bed. Once more he was safe. His father had been asleep when he slipped out of the house, and he was still asleep; and the wake for Paddy Boylan was the best South Ilium had had since Mike Gleason fell drunk into his well and was not found until his companions slept off their stupor the next day and remembered where they had last seen him. That time hardly an Irishman in South Ilium had been sober for two days, and Thomas, fuming but helpless, had been held up on two jobs for lack of laborers and hod carriers.

Instead of warming and thawing between spells of intense cold, it seemed to stay cold all the time that year. One snow followed another, piling up deep and dirty in the streets, deep and white on the hills. It got so cold that for the first time in years the plank bridge was laid down across the ice from Ilium to West Ilium. Even Thomas had gone down and walked across the Hudson. The cold stopped his outdoor work, slowed the work indoors. There were many days when Will could not work, and he made the most of them, skating, bobsledding, and keeping out of Thomas' sight.

He went to a round of church socials and entertainments, of parties and dances. When there was no social at St. Mark's, there was one at South Ilium Baptist or at little St. Martin's, the missionary church in the River Parish. There were lectures and shows at Mechanics Hall. Will missed few of them. When his mother was home, she aided and abetted, despite Thomas' grumbling; when she was away, as she was now, Will expanded his activities generously.

Almost every morning Thomas complained of his son's late hours, but Will, as long as he was sure his father did not know of some of his escapades, grew more and more indifferent. There was not much his father could do now, and he was not even sure he meant all of his complaints.

Will was enamored of himself, enamored of every girl he saw, enamored of being alive. He gave careful attention to his clothes, painstaking care to his hair and the polish on his shoes, then forgot clothes, hair, and polished shoes as he rushed headlong into whatever the day offered. If his father frowned, he did so without animus. With the other children all away, Will seemed to him now a picture of his own youthful exuberance and popularity. The vanity he had retained through life, despite his piety and his stern visage and conduct, made him approve deep inside of him what he could not countenance without show of complaint. Mary either regarded Will with an indulgent smile or urged him on. His old Irish friends said, "Ah, that Willy!"

Maria and Arthur were back in the cottage now, for Mary's older sister had come over from England on a long, and long-deferred, visit. The oldest of the Powitt sisters, she had never married. An unfortunate love affair or a sense of duty to her parents—among the adults it was told either way as suited the occasion—had kept her at home. As tall as Mary but thinner, she was pale and delicate. It was understood that Aunt Julia was unwell and it was hoped that her visit to America would help her. Unlike the practical, hard-working Maria, she attempted little about the house, but gently and sweetly accepted the attentions due a visitor. Will liked her. She was company for Mary and delightful excuse for tea after tea so that their friends and all the relatives and connections who had settled about Ilium could see her. Even Thomas was glad to have one more friend of his youth in the Forest to talk with.

With one distant cousin brought by her mother and aunt to call on Aunt Julia, Will promptly fell in love. Of about his own age, Edith was dark, vivacious, flirtatious, laughing, and agile. She lived to the north of Ilium, as far one way the other side of the city as they were in the other. Will soon found out where, and he was off to Edith's as often as he could manage.

Mary made one trip to New York in midwinter and stayed three weeks. A few weeks later Thomas, after receiving a letter from James, went off with a face as black as thunder. He returned in a few days' time looking mollified and even pleased. It had something to do with James and Emily and Andrew Gray, Will gathered from what he overheard of the muffled conversation of his elders, but he was too busy with his own affairs to be curious. One thing he did learn was that this time Agnes was not mistaken. Agnes and her husband were expecting a little stranger some time in—Mary broke off as she saw Will come in. His Aunt Julia murmured that she thought it was lovely, and Thomas wore an odd grin.

Will grinned himself, a farewell grin, and tore out of the house and down the hill. It was five above zero with a moon shining cold on the snow and ice but he walked, nearly ran, with his coat open, his muffler that his Aunt Maria had knit him for Christmas flying, and his hat in his hand. The air was too good, the night was too good, to put on his hat or button his coat. Besides, he was in too much of a hurry.

The Guild entertainment that year was to be a regular vaudeville show, a series of music hall turns such as many of the older people had seen in London or Birmingham or Manchester. They had been rehearsing for weeks. There was a clown act, a Negro act, a rendition of popular songs with the audience joining in, a comedy playlet, and four other turns. Will had the center spot all by himself with a humorous recitation in Irish dialogue. He had practiced it before the mirror. He had practiced it for August. Better yet, he had done it for old Mrs. Rooney and Mike Garrity and got their expert criticism and uproarious Irish laughter.

He was a little late when he reached the Parish House. Ned and Al Harrison were hammering away at the stage they had all erected. Freddy Atkins with his face already blackened was banging his tambourine. Skinny Davis and Mugs Moore were banging around making noise and doing little else. A half-dozen girls from the Girls' Guild had come to help with decorating the hall and with them was Edith whose close friend was Gladys Hardman, a St. Mark's girl. They all shouted at him as he came in. Will tore off his coat and took charge as one who had a right.

"Edith, begorra!" he said to the girl, pretending to reach out and pull her hair.

"Behave yourself!" she scolded. "I came with Gladys to see if I could help. You needn't think I came just because you were here."

"I don't care why you came as long as you came. Will you kiss me now or when I take you home?"

"Oh, now," said the girl. "It will save time later." Promptly she kissed him full on the mouth while the others shouted encouragement.

Taken aback, Will blushed violently. He could only cover his embarrassment and the desire to grab the girl and kiss her again and again by making more noise than all the others.

"We're cousins," he shouted. "So it's all right."

"Yah!" called Ned Harrison with a knowing leer which Will appreciated. He squared his shoulders.

Another girl brushed his shoulders as she went by with an armful of colored streamers which were to be tacked about the rafters. Sadie worked at one of the collar factories.

"I could be your cousin if you liked," she offered, but then she ran coyly to the foot of the tall ladder and stood safely in the shadow of loutish Mugs Moore who, for no particular reason, was banging away at a ceiling beam with a large hammer.

It took hours to see Edith home that night. They were fortunate enough to miss one streetcar in South Ilium and then another when they had to change in Ilium. The streets were dark and deserted. The silence awed and kept them talking in whispers. Whispering brought them closer together in an intimacy which thrilled and frightened them both. They stood outside her house where one lamp had been left burning low on a hall table, its light showing pale through the glass of the front door. The house was silent. The street was silent. Their breath rose like smoke in the clear air, and they laughed about it.

Edith blew hers lightly in Will's face, forming her lips prettily from a few inches away.

"I feel like a teakettle," she laughed. "S'sh!" she warned, with a gloved finger to her lips though Will had uttered no sound. "You'll wake them."

The girl wanted him to kiss her, and he knew that she did. Desire tingled his skin like fire. She was daring him, yet denying the dare.

"I—" stammered Will, inching away from her.

The girl moved closer, making a question of her face. "What?" she pretended. "I couldn't hear." She put her hand on his arm.

He stood stock-still, not daring to move.

It began to snow again lightly. Three flakes shone on her beaver hat, a few others on the high fur collar which framed her face and dancing eyes.

"So I better be goin', I guess I better, so Clancy says to him!" Failing miserably, awkward and ashamed, Will took refuge in a burlesque of his Irish dialogue.

The girl changed swiftly.

"You'll be wonderful tomorrow night, Will," she said. "You'll be the best there."

"You're coming?" he asked anxiously.

"Both nights. We all are!"

"Well," said Will, courage returned. He stepped toward her, his hands starting up.

Edith turned swiftly, her eyes laughing.

" 'Night, Will," she teased and slipped into the house.

Blood singing and dancing within him, Will moved swiftly off. He shared the last late streetcar into Ilium with a drunk and two foundrymen going to work on the night shift. There was no car to South Ilium. He walked the three or four miles without noticing that he walked or anything that he passed.

Three times he was called back the next night. He was the hit of the show. The Parish House was packed. Thomas, Mary, Julia, and Maria all were there. So was everyone else. Will, clay pipe clamped between his teeth, his faded blue smock covered with brick dust, a ragged straw hat tilted over his blond head, was as Irish as Paddy's Pig and as accurate in his brogue as any shanty Irishman of South Ilium, and they all knew scores of them.

The audience clapped and laughed until the tears came, and Will showed off to his heart's content. It was a triumph, and he loved it.

The Guild had taken in over a hundred and fifty dollars. They expected to do as well the next night. Everyone was jubilant.

They all went to the house on the hill for a bite to eat after the performance was over and all the hearty congratulations had been showered on all the performers, but especially on Will. Aunt Simpson was there and Cousin Harriet and Blanche and Edith and her parents. Her mother was a fat and happy soul, her father a thin machinist with a worried expression on his lined, narrow face.

Fifteen or eighteen people were crowded into the dining room and living room, and Will was no longer the boy to be suffered, but, for that evening, the hero to be universally admired. What puzzled him was that Edith had so changed from the night before. Staying close to her mother and aunt, she was more ladylike than any of the others. She was such a perfect little lady that her mother received numerous compliments on her pretty daughter's behavior. Edith smiled on Will and complimented him prettily on his performance, but acted as though the night before had never been. Will could not understand it. He laughed and joked and displayed his Irish brogue extravagantly to ease his discomfiture. Even his father laughed. Will flaunted his brilliance until he grew tired of himself.

Chapter 18

THE NEXT DAY the letter came from James. It was a warmer day, and Will was at work with several other men finishing up the framework for a new house. He made good progress, hammering lustily to work off his high spirits, but it was not work he much enjoyed. Any butcher, as he told his intimates scornfully, could do that kind of thing. Privately he knew that they could not, and knew they knew it too. His scorn for the work increased his stature in their eyes. It was not until he came home from work a little early to prepare for the second and final performance of the Guild entertainment that night that he found out what had happened.

His mother and father were talking seriously in low tones in the kitchen. In the living room Maria and Julia were exclaiming.

"James is going to be married," Mary told him immediately.

"Married? Old Bones? Who in the world would marry him?" Somehow it had never occurred to him that James might marry.

"That's no way to talk of your brother," said Thomas mechanically. He seemed abstracted.

"Laura Gravet," said Mary happily. "Isn't that fine. You remember—the girl who hurt her ankle on the El and came with her father and sister that day."

"That skinny girl!" exclaimed Will.

"She's a very nice girl," said Mary firmly. "Her father and Miss Janet went off on another voyage, but Laura stayed with friends in Brooklyn so her ankle could mend properly. She and James have seen a lot of each other, and Emily has had her to dinner several times. Though I never expected this," she added thoughtfully.

"Girl knows what she's about," said Thomas bitterly. James had no business to desert him.

It was seldom Will found himself sharing an attitude with his father. He made the most of it.

"Guess she knew a good thing when she saw one," he said wisely. "James being a doctor."

Thomas nodded absently. He accepted Will into the conversation.

"The trouble is Emily," he explained. "What's to become of her? James wants to know what to do about Emily."

"Why can't she just stay?" asked Will surprised.

146

"This Laura has ideas of her own, it seems," said Thomas darkly.

"James is right," said Mary significantly. "Two women in one house does not do. And I would not wish Emily to be ordered about like a servant by an outsider."

"And I," flared Thomas, resenting the implied reference to Maria, "won't have her going off by herself. She sees too much of this Gray fellow as it is."

"Andrew Gray is one of the best friends this family has ever had," said Mary firmly. "He got Emily the best music teachers in New York and see how well she is doing? And now he has lent James this money toward his new house. James," she explained to Will, "is going to buy a fine new brownstone house on the other side of Fourth Avenue. It will be better for his work."

"Gee!" was all Will could think of. Perhaps Emily would come home now. That would be the best.

"I think I should go right down, Thomas," said Mary happily.

Thomas nodded grimly.

"I didn't think," Maria was saying in the other room, "that James would be fool enough to be taken in by some designing woman."

"But after all," Julia was objecting mildly, "he is thirty-three and time he married some nice girl."

"Nice girl!" echoed Maria, who had never seen Laura, who, in fact, had never been to New York except on landing from England. "Nice girl! H'mph!"

"Julia, you'll help me pack my box after tea, won't you?" said Mary. "I hate to leave you, but I feel I must—"

"Of course, Mary," said her sister. "Oh, dear, this is exciting, isn't it?" She looked girlish and happy, showing more life than Will had seen in her before.

"Poor, poor Emily," Maria was saying dolorously at dinner. "I knew, of course, things could not last the way they were."

"Speak of the devil," suggested a new voice dryly.

Emily, smiling, but looking pale and tired, stood in the doorway.

Her mother rushed to greet her, throwing her arms about her and kissing her. Emily kissed them all dutifully as soon as she could remove her hat and gloves. She kissed Will hard.

"Em! You can come to the show tonight! You can see me do my act!"

"It's why I came," she assured him. "We'll be off as soon as I've had my tea. I'm famished."

"You'll stay here, m'girl, and we'll talk this over," said her father harshly. "Mary, there's no need now for you to pack your box." There was a touch of irony in his voice.

"There will be plenty of time for that tomorrow," Emily answered him evenly. "People have got married before. James and Laura haven't invented the idea. I want to see if Will is as good as he thinks he is."

"Far, far better," said Will theatrically.

A half-hour later they went off together down the hill. Emily with her sealskin muff and the matching sealskin collar and cuffs of her coat, a white silk scarf about her neck looked like visiting royalty on shabby South Avenue. She wore no hat, having assured her mother that it was not necessary in the evening, that even respect to St. Mark's did not require it. Her gold hair gleamed. Her clothes, poise, manner almost awed Will, but Emily had not changed.

"It's *my* life," she told Will, "and I am going to live it. James is not going to tell me what to do. Neither is Pa."

"What do they want you to do?" asked Will puzzled.

"I don't know. It's what they don't want me to do. James and I had a real quarrel. Oh, I suppose he thinks he has to look after me or something. He means all right, but no one has to look after me. Besides, that girl has him right under her thumb. I can't stand her."

"I liked her all right," said Will stubbornly.

"So do I sometimes, but it's the things James said. Imagine accepting a loan from Andrew for his new house and then talking about him that way."

"But what way? What did he say?"

"It doesn't matter," said Emily, her mouth tightening. "It doesn't matter what anyone says or does or tries to do. Don't let them try to run you either, Will!"

"Never fear! But I'm glad you came. Honest, Em, it went great last night. I had to come out on the stage three times. Look, Em, will you sing? Yes, you sing! We'll bring down the house!"

Emily laughed and grasped his arm tight. "Pa and Ma'll be there, won't they?"

"I think so. They have tickets anyway."

"All right, Will! We'll bring down the house! Come on, I'll race you." Emily darted off.

Mr. Emmett, the Sunday-school teacher would have liked to announce Emily, and Will saw that he wanted to. He didn't give him a chance. The South Ilium Trio had just given their second encore and the twang of their banjos and mandolins was still vibrating through the Parish House hall when Will slithered out on to the stage again.

"Don't go, ladies and gentlemen," he urged, waving his hands high. "Tonight the Boys' Guild of St. Mark's Church in South Ilium is honored to present an extra added attraction. Straight from the concert stage of New York City—Miss Emily Stapely!"

Emily came on in pretty, laughing, protesting confusion, acknowledging the new burst of enthusiastic applause. She knew almost everyone in the crowded parish hall. Over the crude footlights, she saw face after familiar face. She searched until she saw her own people in a center row halfway back. Her mother looked pleased and happy, her father forbidding.

Emily had sung at weddings and at funerals in New York. She had sung at Professor Risviglio's recital in Carnegie Hall. Three times she had sung at a fashionable Fifth Avenue church. Most of the engagements had come through Risviglio and her piano instructor, Mr. Hamilton, who was also organist at St. Andrew's on 21st Street. She had been taught poise and stage presence, how to breathe, how to smile, how to form her mouth, how to gesture. What she had been taught she had learned, and she had qualities of her own which no one had had to teach her.

She now chose a simple ballad, one her audience knew and would understand. Adoring Katie Anderson accompanied her at the scarred square piano in the corner down off the stage. She sang simply and sweetly, her face relaxed, her eyes moving easily about the hall, but she stood erect, stood inches taller than she was, pouring lyric music through the place. She sang another simple song, but this time she let her voice out and though she stood very still, her hair shone in the light and her eyes flashed.

She was singing to Thomas, singing at Thomas. He knew music, not as she knew it, but through his love for it. It was the one place where they could meet and understand each other, and where she could vanquish him. She knew before she had finished the song that she had won. He did not move as she held the last note softly and clear, none of them moved.

Her audience sat in wonderment for seconds, then clapped or shouted their applause.

Emily danced down the three wooden steps and sat herself at the piano. This time she burst into an operatic aria that was one of Andrew Gray's favorites, Puccini's *Mi Chiamano Mimi* from *La Bohème*.

Emily made no concessions to her audience. She sang it as she would have sung it for Andrew, with full-throated power but dramatic restraint, with passion but with subtlety, then with the glory of her triumph over Thomas. Beauty and violence and danger rocked the parish hall. Her listeners were transported and frightened. Thomas felt numbed. Mary was aware of emotions she could not understand.

"Phew!" said Will as Emily joined him in the impromptu "back stage." "I didn't know you could!"

"I can't really," breathed Emily. "I just did."

She was offhand and casual with those who crowded about her, not bothering to be either deprecating or coyly modest. Those who tried to gush retreated in discomfiture. Young men hung back abashed. Only the rector seemed to know what to do, and he said little. Simply he and Emily seemed to speak the same language in an understanding smile that passed between them.

Edith, without her parents, had been out front with Gladys Hardman. She had applauded Will without restraint, and he had seen her. She would be expecting him to take her home. She had been watching him all evening. Will ducked out of sight. With Emily at hand, he had no wish to waste his time with a silly girl like Edith.

Most of the crowd had gone.

"Get me an apron someone!" cried Emily. "I'll help take down the decorations. I love to tear things down! Will, where's your hammer?"

But everyone had not gone. "Haven't you done enough damage for tonight?" Cousin Harriet called out to Emily. "Did my wicked old heart good!" In tow of shocked Blanche she waved her stick gaily at the rector who laughed back at her.

Chapter 19

JAMES WAS SAFELY out one evening shortly after Emily's return from triumph in South Ilium. He would not be back for hours. He had several calls to make, then he would have to see Laura, and, if Emily knew her brother, he would stop in for a drink or two before coming home. She wondered if he thought her too stupid to suspect. She looked across at Andrew Gray. They were alone together in the living room of the Brooklyn house.

"I love you," she said softly.

"Emily—" he began. The beginning of a slight frown creased his forehead.

"No, don't stop me. Whether you want to hear me or not, I want to say it. I love you, I love you, I love you!"

"James is right, you know. I *am* old enough to be your father."

"But not his," said Emily quickly. "You're not old enough for that. Besides you couldn't be his father, not with that beard of his, not with the way he is. Besides he has a father. So have I—the same one!"

"All right!" laughed Andrew. "Still, Emily, I want you to be serious. Even my approaching senility is not the real difficulty, as you well know."

"I love you, I love you, I love you! And you love me, you know you do. Aren't you ashamed that I have to say it instead of you?"

The girl was radiant with happiness. The man looked at her and feared for her. A woman in love was so helpless, so utterly lost, so defenceless. His compassion was moved as well as his passion and tenderness.

"Perhaps I'm ashamed of many things," he said quietly.

Emily sprang up, anger flashing in her eyes.

"Ashamed! Why should you be ashamed?" But when she sat again it was on the settee next to him. Her shoulder touched his shoulder, though she kept her hands still in her lap.

"Because I am the one who should be a little wiser, who should have realized—many things."

"I realize everything, Andrew," she said quietly. "I know everything. I know you. I know myself. Though I no longer know where you end and I begin. Does that make sense? I don't care whether or not it does. I'm so sure, so certain, so very sure."

"Yes, Emily," he said gently. "It makes sense. I understand. That way I am sure too. But there are other things."

"What people say? What people think? I don't care what they think, what they say, or what they can do."

"You think that now, because you are beautiful and young and strong. I don't want you hurt."

"I've been hurt. Pa and his rake. Remember, I told you. The bruise didn't last long."

"There are worst hurts," he said desperately. "You must believe me, Emily. I want to be your friend, the friend of all of you—"

Emily laughed harshly and Gray flushed.

"I'm afraid I did sound stuffy and hypocritical."

"You could not sound stuffy or hypocritical if you tried. You could not sound like anybody but yourself, and there is no one in the world like you."

"Or like you, Emily. I think you are the most beautiful—"

"Kiss me, Andrew! Put your arm around me. Don't fight me or yourself. That's what you're doing, you know." She snuggled into his arms.

But Gray was resolute. He stroked her forehead and her hair as she lay still, but went on relentlessly.

"Do you know why there are conventions?" he asked her. "Because the world crucifies you if you break them. It makes you suffer—from loneliness and hurt, from being misunderstood and avoided, from—"

"Lady Hamilton survived."

"Don't say it, Emily, please don't," he begged. "Anyway, I'm not Lord Nelson. Understand me, Emily. I've few scruples. I've little moral sense, as the term is generally used. But I don't want to hurt. I certainly don't want to hurt the one I love most in all the world."

"You've said it!" she cried triumphantly.

"Yes, I've said it," Gray admitted. Perhaps he had only been arguing so as to lose, attempting as a gesture to dam a torrent with pebbles, excusing himself on the grounds that he had uttered a warning which he hoped she would not take.

"Emily, we must not! Probably it would be best if I never saw you again."

"Perhaps," she smiled, "but you see, you won't do that. Even if you could, I wouldn't let you. You need me as much as I need you."

"The difference in years doesn't seem so important now, but it will become so."

"And some day you'll be *free*."

Gray did not answer for a moment. Anxiously Emily watched his eyes.

"Perhaps," he said finally. "We can't know that."

She spoke now as though she were the older and the wiser.

"We can't know anything ever, Andrew, not really. About anything. We only know what is—what is, and what is good, and what is true."

It was her youth and her proud certainty rather than her words that reached him.

"Oh, my dear," he murmured brokenly. "My dear, my dear, my dear!"

Laura was knife-thin. Her brown hair was scanty and she had drawn it back for convenience tightly about her head. She was talking rapidly as she and James drove along Fourth Avenue at a good pace.

"You've told Emily," she said to James.

"I told her."

"James, you understand that I like Emily, but it simply would not do for her to stay."

"I understand."

"I shall always appreciate everything Emily and all your family have done for you," said Laura formally. "Besides," she added in different tone, "this will give Emily more time to spend with her music. That always came first, your house second."

"She did all right," said James briefly.

"We'll do better," said Laura enthusiastically. She placed her thin, firm hand over his that held the reins. "Oh, James, I can hardly believe it."

"Neither can I," said James. He told the truth. He was not at all sure how it had happened. Still, Laura was a game one. Nothing much was going to stop her. She'd take a lot of worries off his shoulders. His mother and father had both seemed pleased. At least their letters made it seem they were pleased. He wondered if they were.

"Have to stop here," he told Laura. "Shouldn't be long. Measles."

"All right, dear," said Laura briskly. "I'll wait. No, I shan't. I'll hurry over and see how the painters are coming along. The man should be there to lay the tile in the front hall in the morning. I made the plumber change the line of his pipes through the kitchen. Imagine his telling me it couldn't be done."

"Showed 'em, didn't you?" grinned James.

"I certainly did," said Laura briskly. "I'll come back for you. Then we have to stop at the dressmaker's."

"But I've two more calls, then office hours."

"It won't take a minute, but you needn't wait for me. Wouldn't you like to have seen my father's face when he got the cable?"

"Not particularly," said James. "See it when he comes back anyway. He'll have it with him, I imagine."

"He'll what? Oh, you! Go along about your measles. How many calls have you made here? Have you kept a record? I'll bet you haven't. You will after we get married, or rather, I will. I'll attend to the books."

"And welcome to 'em," said James. "Do I have to kiss you now?"

"And why shouldn't you?"

"Not hygienic."

"Nonsense," said Laura. She looked both ways. Then she looked at the horse. Then she blushed. "Of course you have to kiss me, doctor or no doctor."

James shook his head. "Haven't time. When you come back, perhaps. And you better be here." He picked up his bag, stepped out of the buggy, and chirped at the horse to start before Laura could grasp the reins.

"Damn you!" called Laura.

James tipped his hat to her gravely as she scrambled for the reins. Horse and buggy were already in the middle of the road. Then he went into the patient's house.

Thomas got up and sharpened his flat pencil for the third time, using a scarred knife with a sharp blade and cutting the shavings toward the fire in the kitchen stove. He had already removed the lid. He swept the stray shavings in and they blazed briskly. He went back to the table and his figuring. He turned up the lamp and wished that Mary would go into another room so that he could put on his spectacles.

He had had difficulty seeing at close hand for some time, but would not admit it. Finally he had bought a pair from the department store. Surreptitious examination of his spectacled face in a mirror had showed him that they did nothing for his appearance. They made him look like an old man, like a half-blind old man beginning to decay.

The figures blurred before his eyes. He decided it was because he had stared at them too long. Then he could not remember whether or not he had allowed for the mortar and cement. Painfully he went back over two columns of figures. He'd counted everything now, he was sure. Still he hesitated. Too high an estimate would lose him the job; too low an estimate would lose him money on the finished job. It was always that way.

And he was tired, too tired tonight to bother with the eternal figuring. He wished he could get out his cello. He would, as soon as he had the estimate done. The *A* string had snapped but he had a new one. He looked forward to the pleasure of replacing it, then of playing softly by himself. Now was when he missed Agnes most. Had she been home, she would have sung with him as he played. Emily never did that. The others seldom came to play any more. John Armstead was too old; Frank Sewdley had moved away.

Emily and this man Gray . . . James and his marriage! He could make head or tail of nothing.

"Better run a little piece on lapsed policies again," said Charles Ventnor. "The busybodies are at it again. You saw that piece in the *Transcript?*"

"And one in the *Courier* and another in the *Morning News*. It's a perennial, of course."

"What do they expect us to do, carry policies for people who won't pay their premiums? We wouldn't be in business long. Why, we couldn't pay off legitimate death claims!"

"I'll do something," Gray promised. "And I'll have those pamphlet proofs ready for you in a day or two. Young Michaels did a good job on them."

Ventnor was looking at him curiously. "How you can look so pleased with yourself in a world like this I don't know. I wish I did. I've been feeling like the devil. Don't know what's the matter with me."

Did his love show so clearly?

"It must be the spring?"

"You mean United has gone up ten points," said Ventnor shrewdly. It was always a relief to talk to Andrew Gray. It wasn't necessary to put up a front of any kind. Gray made you uneasy if you did.

"That could be part of it," Andrew smiled.

Ventnor lowered his voice. "The company is going rather heavily into steel. The board passed it yesterday. You might see Jenkins about it."

Andrew raised his eyebrows. "Thanks," he said, "I shall."

Later that day he walked across City Hall Park to Broadway. Spring *was* in the air. A fresh breeze was blowing up from the Battery. The grass was very green and the sparrows were noisy and busy. Horses moved along with zest in their step. People's faces were bright and pleased. It was a noisy, busy, crowded, cheerful scene. He saw newsmen hurrying across to Chambers Street and Park Row, evening paper men trying to make deadlines for the last edition. Some district men off the morning papers were smoking cigarettes and sunning themselves on the City Hall steps. Probably they were waiting pronouncements from the mayor or some other Tammany politician. Gray threw up his hand at them and two of the older men waved back. One of them called something he did not hear.

Though it was not necessary, he stopped in at the office of the *Insurance Tribune*. It was two stories up rickety wooden stairs in a dim hall that reeked of printers' ink, a smell that meant home to Andrew Gray. Both the editor and his assistant were out but he knew where they were; one in Albany to pick up some late trade news, the other at a convention of insurance salesmen in one of the uptown hotels. They should provide his lead stories for the week's edition. His own editorial and the column of whimsy and humor that it pleased him to write were already in type.

A pressman and two compositors were busily at work. He wondered which of them had been at the window and seen him coming. It didn't matter. They were good boys who always came through in a pinch. He inspected the frames tied up on the slab, reading the type upside down with the skill of long practice.

"Everything all right, Jack?" he asked the aproned compositor with the cockade of newsprint on his head.

"Yes, sir. All hunky-dory, Mr. Gray." The man, face lined and grimy, watched him anxiously.

Gray saw the half-consumed quart pail of beer not quite out of sight on a shelf of dusty slugs and pied type. He looked again at one page frame.

He pointed. "Let's shift those two stories. You can make it if we drop that one to a fourteen-point head. Need to space it out, won't we?" He thought a minute. "Here." He wrote a new head on the back of a proof he drew toward him. "Can you read it?"

"Yep. Right away, Mr. Gray. Tommy!" Jack called an apprentice who was putting type back into a case.

Gray took a streetcar this time, alighting after a twenty-minute ride on Madison Avenue in midtown Manhattan. He walked west to Fifth Avenue. Spring was even more pronounced here. There were women about in light costumes and flowered hats. Some had their carriages waiting while they shopped. There were two before Oriental Importers, Inc. They had made no mistake in moving this far uptown.

The place soothed with cool elegance. Jade, ivory, rich silks, porcelains, blue and buff Tientsin and Peking rugs on the floors, intricately carved teakwood tables and smooth, subtly polished yellow rosewood. The store was uncrowded, as he had insisted. One fine piece showed off the beauty of the next. He looked at the apricot gold of a Chien Lung rug from the northern provinces and at a tall, beautifully slender and swelling Ming vase in peacock blue as he walked through the cool dimness to the office at the back.

One suave clerk was talking quietly with a pretty woman. They were looking at a necklace of amethyst quartz. The woman's face showed longing but indecision. Gray hoped she would buy it, for she was pretty and it was spring and it was a lovely piece.

The short, white-haired old man who rose quietly to greet him might have been the curator of a museum rather than the manager of a very profitable business.

Gray smiled at him quietly. He was fond of the old man and knew his sensitive taste.

"The new shipment come?" he asked.

The old man's gentle face lighted and he threw up his hands.

"The one from Shanghai, not the Peking. Some beautiful things. Mr. Schwartz and Mr. Ling were in, and they were delighted. And the price—disgraceful!"

"Not from our point of view though?"

"No, oh, no. No indeed! Look."

There were some cloisonné and lacquer pieces, neither very good. The old man pushed them impatiently aside to display a fluted agate bowl. It was perfect. Wordlessly he brought out a table screen of deeply carved nephrite framed in dull black teak. The carving showed the Eight Immortals in a garden scene. It was exquisitely done; Chinese lapidaries working for love of their own skill and the beauty of the material they worked on. Time did not exist for them. It slowed for the beholder of their work.

Gray nodded agreement. He touched the screen, tracing the smoothness. He looked at other things. A small pendant of spinach green jade with floral carving lay on the table. It was perfect in color and delicately cut. He picked it up, and it lay cool in his hand. It was set in a simple oval of plain gold and hung on a chain of links so small he could hardly see them. Its value was not great, but it was finely made.

"I think I'll take this with me," he said slowly. "Have it charged to my account, will you." He slipped it into an upper pocket of his waistcoat.

"Of course, Mr. Gray. I noticed it myself. It's very nice."

Had he been looking deliberately, he might have chosen turquoise because of Emily's eyes, but Gray disliked turquoise. It was opaque and lumpy. The jade would contrast with her bright hair and fair coloring. He took the pendant from his pocket and looked at it again. The quartz traces streamed cool and liquid behind the light-vivid cold green. He loved the piece. He loved Emily.

Chapter 20

IT WAS RIOTOUS at the house in South Brooklyn when Mary and Will arrived for James's wedding, Will carrying not only their big gladstone but also a box holding the dress his mother was to wear.

It had been a nuisance trying to hold it flat and keep it from getting crushed ever since they left Ilium on the boat the night before. Will didn't see what all the fuss was about anyway, but the others did.

Not only was a wedding imminent, but a move into James's new home and office and a resettling of Emily in quarters and circumstances not yet decided on. Laura, already in charge, was briskly ordering about a cleaning woman and a man brought in for the heavier work. She wore an enveloping apron, and her soft brown hair was pinned back out of her way.

She put down her broom long enough to embrace Mary and laugh and cry and exclaim, then shot off to correct the overalled man who was rolling up a carpet the wrong way. Mary and Will edged their way through unpacked wedding gifts which had just arrived and boxes of James's medical books packed ready to go to the new house. Some curtains were down; others were up. Captain Gravet's schooner had been reported from Sandy Hook, but he and his younger daughter had not yet landed. At least, no one was certain that they had. A strange woman was screaming a question from the kitchen.

Upstairs Emily was addressing last-minute wedding invitations that somehow had been overlooked. James was so busy with his practice that she had even had to buy the wedding ring for him, and Laura had been so busy overseeing work at the new house that she had begged Emily to attend to the writing. Emily was already in trouble. In her hurry she had addressed the outer envelope "Dr. and Mrs. Richards," but the inside one to Dr. Richards alone. Agnes, outraged, insulted, spoiling for a fight, had immediately made a special trip to Brooklyn to tell Emily and James that now she would not come to the wedding under any conditions. She hinted at deeper and darker reasons too.

"I shall go right over and talk to her," said Mary instantly. "No, I can't go. There's too much to do here. Will, you will have to go and talk to Agnes."

"But James is waiting for Will to lay the floors at the new house!" Emily exclaimed. "The living room and dining room furniture are all piled in the hall waiting until they are down."

"I don't want to go to Agnes' now," complained Will. "Has the flooring come? Did James get the kind I wrote for? Where is his house anyway?"

"Oh, dear, I don't know!" said Emily. "I mean, I know where the house is, or where it was before everything got so mixed up, but I don't know about the rest of it. And the dressmaker hasn't come, and my dress is only half done, and James won't pay any attention to anything!"

"Now, now!" comforted her mother. "It's a good thing I came. I'll see to everything."

"It's two blocks up and two—no, three—over," Emily told Will. "I think the number is four-something. You can't miss it."

"How could I with directions like that?"

There was louder noise from downstairs and the sound of new voices.

"It's Captain Gravet and Janet! That's good. I was afraid he wouldn't be here to give the bride away—though Laura's perfectly capable of doing it herself."

"Or has already done it. Is that what you mean?" asked Will.

"Oh, Will, I don't mean anything, and you know I don't." Emily quieted. "Andrew, you know, is to be best man."

It was no place for him. Will escaped to look for the new house. He found it and was impressed. It was a spacious, three-story brownstone front, the end of a row in a finer neighborhood. Old Bones must be doing well. He certainly was doing himself well. Will looked over the job. The flooring was there ready to be laid. A painter at work upstairs helped him find the nails, a half-keg hidden by packing cases of newly bought furniture, rolls of carpet, and packages of kitchenware.

At the old house, the telephone was ringing. James was wanted on an emergency case, and no one could find him. He had said he was going to the barber's to get his hair cut and his beard trimmed, but no one knew which barber's he had gone to. Laura had stopped all her work to open more wedding presents which had just been delivered. It was the set of Wedgwood china from Andrew Gray which Emily knew had been sent. Laura, exclaiming over them, decided to examine each piece to make sure nothing had been cracked or broken. Bits of excelsior spilled everywhere over the floor which Emily had had newly scrubbed.

Captain Gravet was trying to tell everyone of the voyage from which they had just returned, and was sulking because no one would sit still to listen. Janet, too prettily dressed to help, was flitting happily about. Mary declared she could not do one more thing until she had had her tea. Emily, more distracted than ever, had gone to see that the kettle was boiling.

It made her blood boil, as she told Will, who had come back to change into overalls, the way Laura had taken over before she was actually mistress. She was glad their mother was there to say which of the furnishings James was to take with him to the new house and what was to be left for her use, either there or wherever she went.

"But where *are* you going, Em?" Will was gobbling a sandwich he had made for himself with bread and a jar of meat paste he had found in the ice chest.

"Oh, I don't know—that is—I can't tell you now," said Emily hurriedly as someone came in. "Oh, there's James. James—excuse me, Captain Gravet—you're to go to—wait a minute. I wrote it on a slip in the office." She hurried through to him.

"Care to have me start a fire?" asked James coldly. "Might help to clear out the place."

"Captain Gravet and Janet are here," whispered Emily, as she gave him the slip. "You'll have to come and speak to them."

"Can't," said James. "This is urgent." He waved the slip with the address and sniffed at himself. "Confounded fellow put on too much bay rum. How's Ma?"

"James, you'll *have* to come in!"

"Haven't time. Be back in three-quarters of an hour."

"It's a wonder you have time to get married."

"May not have," grinned James, showing his teeth through his beard. "You and Ma may have to do it for me." He disappeared.

"Really, Captain Gravet!" Emily heard her mother saying. "Really?"

The captain rumbled and blustered on.

Thank heavens, the dressmaker had come anyway. She was in a top-floor bedroom tacking the second sleeve of her gown into place. As soon as that was done, she wanted Laura for a final fitting.

"Laura!" Emily called. Her voice took on an edge of anger and exasperation. "Laura! Laura!"

"Coming," Laura answered calmly.

Somehow things quieted down and a semblance of order emerged by late afternoon. Captain Gravet and Janet retreated, dragging a protesting Laura with them, for Laura still had a dozen matters to attend to. Emily sighed and set about getting tea. Perhaps she could stand one more day of it.

That evening James and Will played checkers while Mary and Emily, both of them tired out, talked quietly upstairs. James was catching a cold. He sneezed and rubbed his nose.

"Found a place to sleep?" he asked Will.

"On the sofa in the dining room—if I can squeeze in beside the boxes and barrels. Your move."

"H'mph. How about that floor?"

"I'll take care of the floor," said Will coolly. "Move, will you?" He was sure he had James in a trap. In two moves he would be able to jump two kings and a single man.

James saw it.

"Needn't think I'm losing my wits just because I'm getting married," he taunted. He jumped three of Will's men, picked them up and clicked them down hard at his edge of the board. He lighted a fresh cigar and offered Will one. Will held up his cigarettes to show he preferred them.

"Pa's not coming down," he said suddenly. "Did you know it? Says he can't get away. I think he just doesn't want to come. He could get away if he wanted to."

James looked at him. A half-smile, gentler than his usual clenched-tooth grimace, showed behind his beard.

"M'mm." He jumped two men. "Perhaps that will teach you to pay attention to your game," was all he said.

James, his mother thought the next morning, looked more as if he were going to be buried than married. The cold had got into his chest. His face was white though his nose was red and sore. He had been out most of the night on a confinement case. There would be another on Friday. The Johnson boy's arm was not mending properly. The flesh was red and angry, and there was still pus. The little fool had got himself an ugly compound fracture falling off a shed roof in a game of follow the leader. Old Mrs. Jennings was demanding attention. There was nothing the matter with the old witch that he or any other medico could do anything about, but she was money in the bank, a steady income. A few soda pills and some more drops would keep her quiet for another week or so.

He needed a drink. The new mare—for Roger, middle-aged and a little weary, could not make all the calls now; at least it was so James justified his extravagance in adding the new animal—had broken into an easy jog. She jerked her head up in surprise as he yanked her to a stop. He clipped the heavy sidewalk curb to her bit, picked up his little black bag, and strode briskly into a corner saloon. To the passer-by it would look like a professional call.

"Whiskey," he told the bartender sharply.

"Sure, Doc," said the man, noting the black bag. He wiped his hands down the front of his stained white apron.

James glared, resenting the familiarity.

He gulped the whiskey. It was raw and fiery. James's eyes watered as he strained not to cough. He cleared his throat brusquely, paid for his drink and left. Throwing the curb weight into the buggy where it thudded on the floor, he chirped at the mare and left smartly for home.

Laura was waiting outside for him. Her eyes were bright. "Two patients waiting for you," she whispered excitedly. "Just think, James, one more day!"

He tried to force an equally enthusiastic smile, but failed.

"Is your cold worse, James?" she inquired anxiously.

"Better, much better," he said hurriedly.

He glanced into the waiting room as he took off his coat and hurried into his office.

"Doctor will see you now," said Laura sweetly in the other room.

Emily went by through the hall, and he saw the look of light sarcasm on her face as she heard Laura speaking.

James frowned and laid his stethoscope and thermometer on his desk.

An old man shuffled in. He looked doubtful.

"Doctor—" he began in querulous tones.

James looked at him with distaste.

"H'mm," he observed. The habit was fixed now. "H'mm. Sit down, sit down."

He jerked his thumb at the straight chair facing the swivel chair at his desk. Then the thought struck him anew, startling and frightening. Tomorrow he was going to be married. He, Dr. James Stapely, was going to be married to Laura Gravet. It was happening to him. And he'd be married a long time.

"It hurts here, doctor," the old man was saying eagerly. He poked his abdomen with a shaking finger. "Especially mornings, and—" he lowered his voice—"after—"

James looked at him blankly. In the other room he could hear Laura chatting with the second patient. Her voice was too bright and purposeful. She was always too damned purposeful. She knew what she wanted, that one, and she'd spend her life getting it. How was he going to spend his?

"What?" he asked the old man loudly. "What?" he accused.

That evening James drove his mother out Fourth Avenue toward Fort Hamilton to show off the mare's paces. Mary was all dignity in a new coat and bonnet. She thought it was a nice little horse and exclaimed over the rubber tires which made the brightly varnished rig ride so quietly and comfortably.

"How much?" she demanded shrewdly.

"Two hundred for the beast, seventy-five for the carriage, fifty for the harness," James told her.

Mary was impressed and a little shocked, but she was not going to let James see it.

"That seems about right," she said sagely.

They rode along silently for a quarter-mile, the mare's hooves beating a steady tattoo on the smooth asphalt. Carriages passed the other way on the far side of the narrow grassplot which made Fourth Avenue a boulevard. Mary noted each rig and the costumes of its occupants.

"Tomorrow will be one of the milestones in your life, James," she said firmly. "I shall be proud to see my oldest son married and set up in a home of his own, especially to such a fine girl as Laura. I know you are going to be very happy. You've made a fine start in your practice, and this will be——." She could not find just the phrase she wanted or seem to say exactly what she meant. "Be very good, indeed," she ended even more firmly to hide her unexpected confusion.

"Get along there," snapped James, though the mare was moving beautifully. He put out his hand as though to reach for the whip.

For one horrible moment he wanted to grasp his mother about the knees, as he had long years ago when he was a child, and blurt out that he didn't want to be married at all. He didn't even want to be a doctor very much now. He just wanted to be back home safe in Ilium. He didn't know how it all had happened.

Mary patted his knee with her gloved hand.

"There, there!" she said comfortingly. Then fearful he might know she had understood, she added, "I want you to get rid of that cold. Tonight we'll use some of the goose grease I had Emily put by and wrap your chest in red flannel."

James could not sleep. Laura had left for her home early that evening, gone off in a flurry of excitement. Her sister and some strange woman had whisked her away, making a great play of mystery and excitement and titillated modesty. Fools! Laura had been busy till the last moment ordering this rug taken to the new house, deciding to leave that chair, demanding to know whether the new curtains had arrived. If she were not so damned practical! Her goodnight kisses had failed to excite him at all.

He was all right by the middle of the next day. Coat off, cuffs off, sleeves rolled up, angry at death and at the foulness of life, he was in a slum tenement down by the water fighting to save an eight-months'-old child that was in convulsions. By three o'clock he knew he had won. Cursing the man who would keep his wife and child in such a hole, he instructed the frightened young mother on what to do, told her gruffly not to call him again that day unless it was absolutely necessary, and went for a drink he knew he had earned. Then he went home to get ready to be married.

Will had been despatched to persuade Agnes. There was no sign of anything to eat. The door of his office was shut, and the sign had been turned to read: "Doctor is out." Upstairs the house was in an uproar. Laura was in the corner third-floor bedroom, where she was being dressed by Mrs. Hermans, the dressmaker, and the rest of the women were rushing in and out.

"You mustn't come up, James!" Janet called down gaily. "It's bad luck to see the bride before the wedding." Why didn't she get dressed in her own place? He supposed there was no room there. He knew there was not.

He grunted a reply. He had no wish to go up. He went to the icebox to look for cold meat and to the breadbox. He could find no butter. The servant wasn't worth her keep.

Soon his mother came down. He could see that she was partly dressed for the wedding, though three curlers were still twisted in her hair.

"I put your dress clothes in your office, James. I thought you could dress more easily there."

"Thank you," he said gratefully.

"Laura will look beautiful," she told him. "Her dress is white silk trimmed with orange blossoms. She has a prayer book bound in white velvet the Captain brought for her. Mr. Gray and two of the ushers came, but they went on to be out of the way. They said they'd be at the church."

Across the street a stray dog was rummaging through the contents of a garbage pail he had overturned. James watched him through the window. He was not listening.

"You'd better begin to dress, James," said his mother sharply.

The servant girl slipped in to check the fire in the stove. It was chilly that May morning. Apologetically, she put in a shovelful of coal from the scuttle, trying not to make any noise, trying to hide the fact that she shared in the general excitement. Mary smiled at her.

"Oh, Doctor Stapely!" exclaimed the girl, thus encouraged, "I— we hope you will be very happy!" She fled with hand covering her mouth as though she had frightened herself.

"And so we all do, James," said Mary firmly. "Now get into your things. You must look handsome tonight. Oh dear, why isn't Will back? I wonder if Agnes is coming. Hurry now!" She disappeared.

James continued watching the dog. Poor beast! A fat meal he'd get out of the Wallace's garbage can! They threw nothing away. He saw Will, walking swiftly, push open the gate and take three steps through the areaway toward the basement front door. Then he heard his steps in the hall.

He was delighted to have someone he could safely abuse.

Young, alive, alert, his cheeks flushed with health, Will pushed open the door. His bright hair shone.

"Where've you been, you young scoundrel?" James shouted before the door was fairly open. "Ma's been worried. Where're your clothes? Get into 'em."

Will grinned.

"Nervous?" he inquired politely. He was far too good-looking. "I've been to see Agnes. She's coming. Come right down to it, she wouldn't miss it! But what's she so sore about? It's not just the invitation. She kept raving something about the way Em's behaving, and she's mad at you for having Mr. Gray for best man. What's the matter with her anyway?"

"Oh, Agnes!" James spoke contemptuously.

"Here, here's some cigars I bought you—they're good ones. Have to find my studs. Ma's got 'em in her bag." Will, too, disappeared.

James looked at the cigars. They *were* good ones. He felt surprised.

"Thanks," he said grudgingly, though Will was no longer there.

He blundered into the living room. It was all disarranged to display the presents. There was the huge soup tureen from Captain Gravet's ship's company, the splendid set of dinnerware from Andrew Gray, the silver from this one and that, all the rest of the stuff.

So Agnes was trying to be difficult! He was sorry now he'd tried to be pleasant to her and her stupid little husband the last time they'd met. Call himself a doctor! H'mph! The shrill laughter upstairs angered him. He wondered about the baby he'd worked on earlier. He'd a good mind to go back and find out. Then he remembered that the horse had been put up. It was too late to back out now. Even if someone telephoned, they couldn't get him now. The servant had been instructed to turn away all callers. "Doctor was busy."

Busy!

"James, you must get into your things. We can't be late, you know."

His mother had come quietly into the room.

"I was just going to," he said defensively.

She smiled.

The church was crowded. James, backed against the altar with Andrew Gray and the four ushers, felt bewildered. Laura, all white, on the arm of her upright and stern-looking father at the back of the church, was suddenly lovely and desirable. The rector and the curate were smiling smugly. They didn't often get a chance to go through the full ceremony of the Church of England. The organ, which had been playing low, swelled to full diapason as the procession started down the aisle.

The blood began to throb in James. Andrew Gray, perfection in his evening dress, passed him the ring deftly at just the proper instant. James put it firmly on Laura's finger, noting approvingly as he did so that her hands were cool. Captain Gravet loomed mountainous and threatening behind his daughter. Next to Laura, Janet, all in bridesmaid's white, looked dainty and fragile, eyes luminous with happy tears.

Suddenly James began to enjoy himself. He stopped listening to the droning rector. He looked at his mother in a near pew and was proud of her. Emily in a modest bonnet with tiny pink roses and a black and gold lace dress was the handsomest woman in the church, though he would never have told her so. Even Will, in evening dress and gleaming shirt front for the first time in his life, looked a credit to the family. He glanced contemptuously at the rest of the crowd. Always people staring—at animals in the zoo, at accidents, at a fallen horse, at a wedding. They'd stare at anything.

Laura, radiant, held tightly to his arm when it was over. Women were crying and exclaiming, men shaking his hand. None dared slap him on the back.

Andrew Gray, smiling warmly, gripped his hands.

"Thanks," James said to his best man, "for taking my side!"

He was surprised to see tears in Emily's eyes as she kissed him. Then he saw that her hand slipped into Gray's as they backed away into the crowd. Well, he was no longer responsible for Emily.

Laura nudged him when they approached the fat rector whom they found just free of one group, and James remembered to slip him one of the envelops they had prepared beforehand. There was ten dollars in it, ten in another envelop for the curate, five for the organist, five for the sexton.

The sexton opened his before they could get away, and James thought he looked disappointed.

"What'd he want?" he growled. "Those fellows make more burying them than I do keeping them alive."

"Never mind, James," Laura whispered. "We're going to do things you and I. We're going to show them all." She had caught a signal from someone. "The carriages to take us to the reception are waiting. I must get my cloak." Captain Gravet was giving the wedding party at Fort Hamilton. There would be no wedding trip. Not now.

Patients wouldn't allow it. Neither would Laura. Still plenty to do at the new house.

Infused with at least momentary confidence, James went proudly for his coat and his tall hat. His mother had brushed it carefully that afternoon. He saw her across the crowd, but there was no chance to speak. He would see her later.

"Congratulations, doctor!"

"Your bride looked lovely, Dr. Stapely!"

"Such a lovely gown, and the bridesmaids were charming!"

Outside a crowd of urchins cheered and would have enjoyed throwing a brick or two as the bride and groom broke for their carriage, but there was also a policeman. He touched his helmet to the happy couple.

Suddenly expansive, James returned the salute. By God, maybe things were going to be all right!

Chapter 21

WILL, his forehead wrinkled in concentration and the tip of his tongue caught between his teeth, sawed and hammered, and nudged and tamped away at the dining-room floor in James's new house. He had a blueprint pattern tacked on the wall. This was the most elaborate parquet job he had ever undertaken. It was demanding, soul-satisfying work.

The weather continued fair and fine. He had all the windows open, and sun poured into the generous-sized room. Elsewhere in the brownstone house Laura and the servant girl she and James had hired were sweeping, scrubbing, hanging curtains, and laying rugs. Laura was a perfectionist, and she had a furious energy. She and Will called back and forth, laughing, driving happily at their work.

James dodged in and out between calls, inspecting, ordering, instructing. He took off his coat and his starched cuffs and carried lumber for Will and helped Laura hang oak-framed chrome etchings of the Parthenon and the Colosseum in the downstairs front hall. Laura had bought them to impress patients with the culture and dignity of their surroundings. That done, James donned coat and cuffs again as though with great effort he had accomplished wonders. He began telling Will what size brads to use and how to hold his hammer and to instruct Laura on how to clean the place. He ran his finger along a high ledge and pretended to discover dust. Indignantly Laura and Will drove him off and went back to their work.

There was a great deal of laughter and of happy confusion. They were all still sleeping at the old house, as it had been agreed there was no need for Laura and James to go to the new place until the house was settled. The old house was still in a state of upset. It remained that way until a decision could be reached as to what to do with Emily.

There were family conclaves, conferences, and crises as Will went happily along hammering on James's new dining-room floor. James discussed the matter with Mary. Mary wrote long letters to Thomas. Thomas replied. Emily, it seemed, would listen to no one, though she would not say what she would do. At one point, Laura broke down and wept that it was all her fault. If she had not come along and upset things—but she could not help falling in love with James! Mary cried too, and even Emily, after which they all kissed each other and liked each other better.

James said it was all nonsense. Emily could stay where she was and take boarders or she could take a job of some kind somewhere and room in the new house with them. Mary would not hear of Emily's taking boarders as though she were an Irish housewife. Emily said that if she were going to take a job, she'd get one in one of the New York stores and room and board in Manhattan. James declared a doctor could not have his sister working as a common shopgirl.

There was a great running back and forth to New York to look at rooms and flats advertised in the *Tribune*. Three days after the wedding Andrew Gray appeared with a bouquet of roses each for Mary and Emily, and to say that he, too, was worried about getting Emily settled and had found a flat which he thought might do. Mary wrote Thomas another letter, and they set off to look at it.

Before they left, the postman brought Emily a letter from Thomas which made her angry and had her almost in tears again. She would not show the letter to her mother. Mary, who did not intend to waste all her time in New York, thought they would all feel better if they went to a show, so they sent James for Will; and Mary, Emily, and Will went to see the play *Yon Yonson*. They came back to Brooklyn with Mary declaring she had never in her life seen anything funnier, and with Will talking in a Swedish dialect he intended to add to his repertoire.

Emily had talked with Andrew Gray while they were in New York, and the next day she and her mother returned there to look at the flat on West 19th Street which he had described. Emily did not tell her mother that she and Andrew had already inspected the premises and that she fully intended taking the flat whether or not any of the rest of the family approved.

The apartment house, old but in good repair and evidently well kept, was near the city's chief shopping district along Sixth Avenue but still in a quiet and respectable residential neighborhood. The street was mostly private houses of brick with brownstone stoops and sills, and here and there a doctor's or a dentist's sign. There was a neighborhood grocery and a vegetable stand and a drug store. It would be convenient both to Professor Risviglio's, and to Mr. Hamilton's, Emily's piano teacher. The vacant flat was on the fourth floor, high enough above the street to be quiet and cool in summer. From the one side window in the small dining room it was just possible to glimpse the shipping in the Hudson.

There were six rooms strung along a narrow hall, two of the rooms separated by folding doors which squeaked and stuck when Mary attempted to close them. Will, she said, would soon fix that. The living room was quite large for a flat, and the small kitchen was convenient, though the gas stove badly needed cleaning and blacking. The bedrooms would certainly have to be repapered and painted. She chose the smaller immediately for herself.

"I think this will do fine," she said, trying to appear thoughtful. The idea that Emily, too, would have her own place in New York elated her. With Emily alone in the city she would have to visit her frequently as well as spend a few days now and then with James and with Agnes.

"Oh, Ma, I want it!" cried Emily. "It will be my place, not James's or Agnes' or anybody else's. We can have fine times here."

Mary's imagination leaped ahead.

"We'll see what your father says," she said judiciously.

"He'll say 'no.'"

"But he doesn't always mean what he says," smiled Mary. "I think he'll see that this is just the thing."

"Then you approve?" asked Andrew Gray quietly. He had come in soon after they arrived.

"I think so. I think it will do very nicely," said Mary primly. "Was there a closet in the second bedroom? I don't remember." She hurried off to see.

"Oh, Andrew!" whispered the girl, slipping into the man's arms.

"I don't enjoy deceiving your mother this way," he murmured after he had kissed her. "You look lovely."

"I'm not too sure we are deceiving her," Emily answered with an odd smile. "I've an idea—"

Gray looked thoughtful.

"Oh, no, she's said nothing, but—"

"There's a good-sized closet," announced Mary triumphantly, as Emily and Gray slipped quickly apart. "The windows are terribly dirty. We will have to get Will over right away and perhaps we can get the colored girl to come over from Brooklyn. Emily, you can put the sideboard there, but the rest of the dining-room furniture isn't worth moving. We'll get new. I saw a sale advertised in yesterday's paper—"

Andrew Gray and Emily both laughed as Mary went rapidly on with her plans.

"Ma's in her element!"

"And I seem to be in mine," said Gray, smiling.

They all went back to Brooklyn, missing one ferry with the result that a half-hour later they traveled on a Hamilton Street boat loaded with workers returning from New York to sleep in Brooklyn before they ferried back to New York and their shops and offices the next day. Bootblacks scurried through the crowds on deck. A beggar with empty sleeves whined professionally. An Italian organ-grinder and his wizened monkey dressed in scarlet coat and red fez were reaping a harvest. Delightedly Mary extracted a penny from her purse and put it into the monkey's paw. He ran the length of his chain to give it to his master, jumped up on the Italian's shoulder and stared back at Mary.

"Look, Emily, I do believe he knows me!"

"Ma! People are watching you."

Mary, fishing for another penny to bait the monkey with, ignored her. The grim brick buildings of Ellis Island sailed by, and they saw the flash as the sunset gun went off on Governor's Island. Dray horses stamped restlessly, their harness creaking. The engines thudded and a bell rang from the ferry bridge. Snorting tugs were urging a great liner out on the late tide. They could see the people waving on the liner's deck high above them. A grinning crewman stuck his head out of a porthole. The Union Jack waved from the liner's stern as it slid by.

"I wish we were aboard," said Emily, breathing deep of the salt air.

"Some day, perhaps," said Andrew Gray.

They were all at dinner when Thomas, his face black with suspicion, thumped into the Brooklyn house, surprising them all as he had intended to. Emily's heart leaped with dismay and her face fell.

Thomas was tired after his trip. He was angry at having had to leave South Ilium, but he had got too worked up over their unsatisfactory letters to stay still. He had come down to settle this business of Emily's moving once and for all. He saw no reason, and he had written so, why she should not return to Ilium. She could teach music there, if that was what she had determined to do. If she didn't want to do that—

"Thomas!" cried Mary. She kissed him placidly.

Emily rushed out to bring a heaping plateful of meat and vegetables. James, his face alight, greeted his father with warmth unusual for him. Laura shrilled her pleasure that he had come, and was immediately the sweet and dutiful daughter-in-law. As soon as they had finished dinner she said she wanted to take him to the new house. They had been waiting to get his ideas on several things. Andrew Gray, his face a mask of friendly interest, was deferential as he acknowledged Emily's breathless introduction to the older man.

Gray, to Thomas' astonishment, seemed like an English gentleman. He felt abashed where he had meant to be stern and outspoken.

" 'Lo, Pa," said Will carelessly. He went on eating.

"We're all here, all together for the first time. I think it is the nicest thing that has happened!" cried Laura, and Emily looked at her gratefully.

All the obstinacy and anger melted out of Thomas before he had a chance to put them to use.

"You'll like the new mare," James was saying. "Give you a run tomorrow."

"How are Julia and Maria getting along?" asked Mary anxiously. "I do hope poor Julia is feeling better."

"But when did you come?" Emily demanded. "We must just have missed you on the ferry."

"Give Father a chance to eat his dinner!" Laura cried, and Thomas heard the 'Father' with pleasure. He might have known James would pick a fine woman. Laura ran to get the fresh tea she had made for him.

Thomas' face was uncompromising. His white hair was plastered to his scalp in front where he had been perspiring. His linen was dusty, and there were black rims under the fingernails of his huge, calloused hands. Andrew Gray noticed every detail. So all of Emily's appearance had not come from her mother. The grace was from Mary, but some of the strength, the squareness of feature, the occasional flash of power in the blue eyes, had come from this handsome old man.

Yet Thomas did not give up without a struggle.

"Agnes wrote me," he said, after he had cut himself a piece of meat, tasted and approved it and then swallowed it. He did the same with his tea, though it was scalding. "Agnes wrote me that she does not think it is proper for a young lady like Emily to live alone in a flat in New York." He stared at Emily as his jaws champed hungrily on his food.

They all laughed, even James who earlier had expressed much the same sentiments.

Laura laughed loudest of all.

"That *is* the old-fashioned idea!" she exclaimed. "But times have changed. Plenty of young ladies do just that now. Women are not the sheltered creatures they used to be." She owed Agnes one for the way she had behaved about the wedding invitation. "Why in London when I was there with Papa it was quite the thing, and even in Paris it's done."

Thomas listened with surprise and respect. He knew that Laura was world-traveled.

"I never heard such nonsense," said Mary firmly, now that she had such unexpected backing. "Agnes should have known better than to upset you that way."

"Well, that's what she said," replied Thomas. Then, treacherously and somewhat ashamed, he smiled himself.

The absent Agnes became the butt of their attack.

"If Agnes would pay more attention to her own business," said Emily indignantly, "and spend more time cleaning up that untidy house of hers—"

"Emily, that will be enough," said Mary firmly.

When his father was not looking, Will put a thumb in his ear and wiggled his fingers triumphantly at Emily. Laura looked significantly at James and shook her head slightly to warn him against getting into the discussion. The sooner Emily was settled, the better off they'd all be.

Unexpectedly Andrew Gray spoke.

"It really isn't good for any young person to be absolutely alone in New York. Perhaps I can help there a little. Emily will have to have housekeeping help, of course. There is a young colored girl, some vague sort of a cousin of one of our maids," he smiled, "who has come up from South Carolina and would like to stay on. She seems a nice respectable girl. She is untrained so the wages would

be very small. She could sleep in that little room off the kitchen."
He turned to Mary.

"That would be fine," said Mary quickly. "If Emily gets many
scholars, she won't be able to do the dusting and the other things.
And there're her own lessons and her practicing."

"We'll talk about it later," Andrew Gray said conspiratorially to
Mary. He tried to keep from looking at Emily.

The next morning Thomas inspected the flat with Mary and
Emily. He pointed out flaws that they had overlooked. He brought
up considerations that two women might not have been expected to
realize. Once he had done this and made it clear that the decision
and accomplishment were his, he astounded them by paying the first
month's rent—which he was surprised to find so reasonable. Leaving
Emily in New York to take her weekly piano lesson, he hustled
Mary back to Brooklyn and started the moving with the air of a
man who intended to get things done.

"A dozen of them standing around trying to make up their minds,"
he boasted to Will, "and nothing done. We'll clear this up in no
time. Now, shake a leg there, you young loafer."

He was in high good humor. Everyone was in high good humor. Will
was incredulous. Usually someone was out of sorts. An opportunist,
he made the most of the situation. Whenever anybody wanted him
to do one thing, he was earnestly busy doing another. One day he
and his father took up the rest of the carpets and together they beat
them lustily in the back yard; but Will managed to keep on the
road most of the time, running up to James's to finish the floor, hurrying over to New York where Mary reported that the plumbing
in the water closet needed attention, racing back to go to downtown Brooklyn with James to bring back a new sign he had had
made.

It was a discreet sign in gold letters on a black board sanded
and varnished, as the old one had been, but this one under the legend
JAMES T. STAPELY, M.D. listed afternoon and evening office hours.
Thomas helped Will and James hang the new sign, though it was
Will who actually bolted it to the hooks sunk into the cement joints
over the basement door, which in this house was at street level in-
side a cement court instead of down three steps to a dark basement.
Thomas was as impressed by the ceremony as he had been when
James hung out his first shingle. Then they went in to look again
at the floor which Will had laid.

The floor was of narrow boards of well-seasoned hard maple.
Around the outer edge, a foot from the walls, Will had inserted a

border of darker wood. Then came a chain pattern of diamond-shaped links, then an inner border.

"I could not have done as well myself," said Thomas slowly, after he had inspected every nail.

James and Will looked at each other in genuine surprise. Will tried to hide his pleasure.

"Why don't you let me look you over before you go home, Pa?" suggested James casually. Unobserved, he had been scrutinizing his father. He looked sound as an oak but there was his age. His color was a little too high, he looked a little tired, but probably there was nothing really wrong with the older man yet. There might not be for years. Naturally, whether he knew it himself or not, he *was* slowing up a little.

"There's nothing the matter with me," said Thomas sharply. He'd be pawed over by no boy, son or no son. "Not had a doctor in years and don't need one now." Anger glinted in his eyes. So they thought he was getting old, did they! He'd live to die at home in the Forest yet.

James shrugged and, when their father's back was turned, winked at Will.

He and Laura were to sleep in the new house for the first time that night. That is, he'd sleep if some fool didn't wake up with a belly-ache and get into a panic about it. It wouldn't occur to the fools to get their aches and pains done with at civilized hours.

Two days later the movers loaded all the furniture from the old house into two vans and headed for the ferry. Mary and Emily and the new colored girl were there when they arrived at 19th Street. Will got pails of hot water and a sponge and began scraping the old wallpaper off the bedrooms with a wide-bladed putty knife. He sang happily at his work while he listened to his father directing the movers. There was a great shuffling and scraping. The men grunted and complained as they tried to bend the piano around the turns in the stairs. Thomas roared directions, and, quailed by the authority in his tone and manner, they quieted, strained, and got it up and into place.

"No beer here, boys," one growled as he passed another grunting under the weight of a sofa.

"I'll take the blonde," said the plug-ugly who was loading at the van. "You can have the black piece."

"Good to me, aintcha?"

But Thomas had been handling men too long. It was a hot day. He sent Will around for a pail of ale at what seemed the halfway mark and sampled a glass himself. It was vile stuff. He watched the men swill it down with disgust. It was only in the Forest they knew how to brew an ale with flavor and body. He looked into a gray airshaft and choked. James could keep his house, and Agnes hers, and Emily have her flat. A man needed room around him. It was worse than London. He'd be back in Ilium the morrow. He'd not change the house on the hill for another in the world, unless it was the Lodge at Far Walk Ledge where he'd been born.

The movers were gone. Emily came into the room where Will was working. Her hair was askew, she had a smudge on one cheek and another on her chin, but her face was radiant. Without a word she grabbed him and hugged him hard, almost upsetting the pail he held in one hand.

"I'm damned!" cried Will, looking after her. But he understood what Emily meant. He splashed more water on the wall and scraped vigorously. The paper, two layers of it, one pink and the other of faded blue rosebuds on a sickly yellow background, came off in strips and sticky gobs. He began to sing again at the top of his voice:

> *Onward, Christian soldiers*
> *Marching as to war.*
> *With the cross of Jesus—*

"Here, take this," Thomas broke in, handing him some folded currency. "Buy the paper and paint you need for these rooms. Your mother can pick it out. I shan't have time. Been too long away now. Don't know what kind of a mess they're making at the house on Whipple Street or with the Wilson job."

"All right," said Will. They weren't making any kind of a mess probably. Hank and August knew what they were doing, though his father ought to fire Donovan and either make Harry Denis smarten up or get rid of him too. He'd have told him long ago, only it was understood by the men and himself that he didn't carry tales.

A strip of the blue rosebuds three feet long and two inches wide came off beautifully. Will tried carefully for a longer and wider piece and took up where he had left off:

> *—Going on before!*
> *Da da da da di-di-um*
> *Da da di da da—*

His mother joined in from the other room and then his father. Suddenly Emily's voice rose full and almost overpowering in the small rooms. The squealing of one of the heavier pieces being rolled on its casters stopped. Suddenly the tears sprang to Will's eyes, though he did not know why. He could not help it.

By mid-afternoon the living room and the dining room were fairly comfortable, and there was a bed ready for Emily to sleep in. A cot had been put up in the kitchen for Will. Mary was to sleep at Agnes' where she was expected for a visit of several days, and Thomas intended to catch the quarter-of-seven train from Grand Central Station for his return home.

Will awoke with a start the next morning, banging his head on the kitchen sink in Emily's apartment. It was already mid-morning, for he, Emily, and Andrew Gray had stayed up very late the night before. Emily and Gray, laughing and talking, then going silent, had worked away at rugs, curtains, and pictures, though Will could not see that they had accomplished much. He himself had kept at his wall-scraping and had all of the old paper off the first room. At almost one in the morning they had had hot chocolate and cookies, the only refreshment they had been able to find in the larder, which had not yet been stocked.

Will scrambled into his clothes, damp and rumpled where he had tossed them on a chair. "Emily!" he called, struggling with his collar and tie as he hurried through the hall. "Emily!"

He found her fully dressed but not yet fully awake in the living room, where she was smiling at nothing he could see.

"Will! I was going to let you sleep. We'll get some breakfast."

"Got ten dollars?"

"Why, I suppose so. Look in my purse. It's on the sideboard. What do you want it for?"

"See you later," said Will, waving the ten dollars at her to show he had found it. "Pay you back this afternoon."

"Will, you've not had your breakfast!"

"Get that this afternoon too!"

Will had not wasted all of his time in Brooklyn. On Third Avenue in a likely-looking saloon he had found just the man he was looking for. Will's South Ilium training had stood him in good stead. The Brooklyn bookmaker wore a derby, a cigar, and a diamond stickpin. He did business on a larger scale than McGraw, or any other South Avenue sportsman. He even had his own telephone.

The track was offering four to one, but he would give Will only three to one on Sir Richard to win in the third.

Will gave him the ten he had borrowed from Emily, five which James had given him for laying the dining-room floor in the new house, and the twenty Thomas had left with him for wallpaper and paint. He spent the intervening hours gaily helping Laura about her house, but he kept one eye on the clock.

It was Sir Richard by a length and a half. Sourly the bookie paid off late that afternoon.

"Where you gettin' your tips, bub?" he wanted to know.

"Dreamt it! Dreamt it last night!"

Will paid Emily back her ten dollars before dinner time.

"O Death," he asked her happily, "where is thy Sting; O Grave, thy Victory?"

Chapter 22

IT WOULD BE warm later that June day, but the morning was cool and clear. As always, Andrew Gray enjoyed his walk. The mass of New York's workers had gone off to their factories and offices a half-hour earlier, crushed into streetcars and El trains. The Second, Third, and Sixth Avenue Elevated were said to be carrying a quarter-million people a day. Too many for comfort. Still, his El shares should hold up whether or not rails went down, as they seemed to be doing. Several large roads had gone into receivership. More were expected to fall.

There were even more disturbing signs on the financial horizon and unpleasant rumors about Wall Street, but, Gray decided, whether Harrison was re-elected or Cleveland came in again would make little real difference. Gray had just returned from Washington and Albany where, as instructed, he had turned over considerable sums of money. Isaacs in Washington and Plater in Albany knew how to dispose such funds most usefully. It was only good sense for Apex, like its rivals, to insure the good will of strategically placed politicians of both parties.

The real rulers of the country were not the politicians anyway, but the industrialists, the steel kings, railway magnates, coal barons, and the manipulators of finance. Gray had nothing against the Carnegies and the Vanderbilts, the Morgans, Hills, Harrimans, the Fricks, and the Flaglers. They were no better and no worse than all the others. He had seen them all in his newspaper days and talked with most of them. They got things done. Gould and Fisk had undoubtedly been scoundrels, but you could get on a train and ride almost anywhere you wished at any time you wished. There was that to be said for them. And there was always the Central's Chauncey Depew.

Gray's lips formed into a half-smile as he remembered a characteristic Depew witticism he had heard when Depew had been the after-dinner speaker at a Press Club banquet a few nights before. He waited until the helmeted bluecoat stopped the traffic, then crossed a cobblestoned street, and kept evenly on his way down Madison Avenue.

Halfway along the next block a carriage passed him. Its lone occupant was a large man in a panama hat who stared straight ahead, his heavy shoulders hunched. Looking quickly, Gray glimpsed the great red nose, the penetrating eyes. The carriage passed so near he could have reached out and touched it. Morgan himself! He and J. P., who was not far from his 36th Street house, often went off to work at about the same time, Gray thought, and smiled at his conceit.

Few people on the street seemed to notice the great man, and certainly Morgan was paying no attention to them. Gray admired Morgan. Morgan did as he pleased and did it magnificently. He commanded, and smaller financiers and large industrialists leaped to obey. Morgan was not quite like the others. He spent almost as much time in London as in New York. He bought books and pictures. One of his agents, without so much as asking the cost, had bought entire an especially fine collection of lacquer from his Fifth Avenue oriental house. Gray still did not know how Morgan knew it had been received.

The gold and silver controversy was no nearer useful solution. Foreign investors were calling in their loans and demanding payment in gold. The country's gold reserve was getting dangerously low. It could all add up to an unpleasant business condition, even another panic. Still, he had made a neat little profit, no, a really handsome profit, on the last tip Ventnor had given him. There was always a profit to be made somewhere if you knew when and where, and he knew those who did. Ventnor and a few others always knew. They saw to it that his salary was not the whole of his stipend for favors received.

Ventnor himself probably did not understand all the ramifications and complexities of the great and powerful company he headed, any more than the presidents and directors of the other big insurance companies understood theirs. The Big Five with a few smaller companies had millions on millions of policy holders. Money poured in fast in the millions of dollars and went out much more slowly and in much smaller amounts. There were millions to invest. There were always more large sums around for further investment or shrewd expenditure. There was so much money that the insurance companies, almost without trying, controlled investment syndicates, brokerage houses, and banks. They could dictate financial policy to manufacturing corporations. They could push a security up or down by the mere act of purchase or sale or refusal to buy.

Under such conditions—Gray's brow wrinkled a little as he walked steadily and pleasantly along, enjoying the morning and the activity of the Avenue, the splendor of houses he passed, the bright objects in shop windows, the movements of the horse-drawn traffic—favoritism and extravagance were almost inevitable. Privileged company officers and officials could always borrow at little or no interest, invest without risk in indicated stocks or bonds, and haul in a staggering profit—with a little extra for a European tour or a Mediterranean cruise.

He had still to make a trip to Boston, for Apex had extensive interests there too. He did not look forward to it. Boston, with its artificial Englishness, always seemed like an overgrown provincial town based solidly on a foundation of its own priggishness. Even corrupt legislators about the gold-domed State House looked like small town deacons or puritanical country squires. They might at least have the decency to look the sly and capable schemers they were.

What, Gray wondered, would happen if some of the sharper New York editors got facts about certain already suspect practices of the big life insurance companies? There were a few about who'd risk anything in the battle for circulation and journalistic power, and they'd about worn out the beef trust, the sugar trust, the whiskey ring, the New York Central, and their other favorite targets.

Pulitzer had lost Cockerill and George Turner, but the new men were eager to show themselves as good. Madison Square Garden was in sight. The *World's* last big stunt had been the strawberry festival there for ten thousand poor children.

Well, Anthony Comstock would be happy! The undraped St. Gauden's Diana which Stanford White had poised atop his great pile was down. Comstock had been having fits about the poor girl! She was in Chicago for the Columbian Exposition. Well, everybody else was going.

Gray had walked further than he intended. Instead of taking the El at Twenty-third, as usually he did, he found himself nearing Union Square. He had walked himself into an even, thoughtful mood which he was reluctant to jar with practical matters at the office. Things were well in hand there. He could see Washington Square far ahead of him. He kept on going.

The city shone golden and smelled sweet. Horse-drawn streetcars, bells jangling, moved leisurely across town. He watched the driver of one skillfully shake his car out of the tracks to pass a truck which was backed up against a building to unload. Seemingly another victim of the pleasant morning, the driver did not even bother to curse out the offending truck driver but waved his whip in salute as he passed. Riders in the car seemed not to notice that they were off soundings, though they must have felt the jolting as the car left the tracks and, further on, dropped back into them again.

Tiffany had a few sparkling diamonds on display in his window, but it was a large star sapphire which caught Gray's eye. He stopped for a moment to delight in its perfection. The Union League and the Century looked dignified and mellow in the sunlight of the Square.

Soon, Gray thought, he would have to go to England. He had not yet told Emily. Parts of his father's estate were still unsettled, though his father had been dead for several years, and for months his London barrister brother had been demanding his presence. Gray thought for a moment of his dignified, and often horrified, elder brother and smiled. It would be good to see him and Margaret, good to be home for a time.

Be a good idea to have his English affairs in order. If bad times were coming, he was glad most of his holdings about New York were in real estate. He had retained the Englishman's belief in land and houses. They might depreciate, but they always held value of some kind. Even if there were a panic, little permanent damage would be done. A few banks and business houses would fail, but not the sound ones. There was enough, almost too much, of everything in the United States. Only a fraction of the country's wealth had been touched. There was a clamoring market for everything which could be produced.

The United States, rude and half-civilized, was only now going through stages which older countries had experienced long ago. European and Asiatic cultures had been formed out of just such uprisings of human energy, but so long ago that most of them had forgotten it.

Men like Thomas Stapely came from countries which had met and faced such situations as the United States was just impinging upon. Implicit in them was the stored experience which made what was strange and often frightening to the native American familiar and simple. The German shopkeeper whose ancestors had kept shop in a side street of Hamburg, the Norwegian sailor whose Viking ancestors had built and sailed ships for centuries, the Belgian artisan, and the English worker had accrued advantages far beyond their skills at their trades. Even the criminals and congenital paupers who had scurried from the sewers and ratholes of European cities to contrive new dives in the underworld of New York, had subtleties and refinements of depravity which made the native product seem innocent and helpless.

American vice would catch up in time, just as the shrewd American businessman, revelling in his acuteness, might in a generation or two match his French counterpart. The United States might some day catch up with England in inventiveness, industrial skill, and the capacity to govern itself. It had the desire to learn and the eagerness to compete. It was impatient only of time. Like a child, it wished everything now. It demanded everything not tomorrow, not next year, not in the next century, but now.

Gray reached Washington Square. He eschewed the El and turned east a few blocks to take a streetcar. It went slowly along under the shadows of the El into the filth and squalor of the crowded Bowery. He looked out of the car's smeared window. The spectacle of New York was still there. This was only a different part of the same scene.

He was to call for Emily at Professor Risviglio's at four o'clock. Then they were to have tea at her flat with the giggling colored maid, Ellen, for chaperon. Emily was as proud of her flat as a small girl playing at keeping house. The sight touched his heart and his imagination.

He had not the right to refuse any beauty life offered. He might, in his wisdom, set himself up as God and decide that abnegation would be better finally for the girl—and he might well be wrong. He usually was when he tried to play the part of God.

Chapter 23

By MIDSUMMER Mary was in New York again. Andrew Gray, they all knew now, would be leaving shortly for England. Mary had little difficulty convincing herself that Emily would be lonely and need her for company. To Thomas she sagely explained that she agreed with him that it was best all around if she were in New York to keep an eye on Emily for a time.

She was all animation as Emily and Andrew Gray met her at Grand Central Station and led her to a carriage.

Ellen, the Negro maid, had evidently been watching from the window of the flat, for she had the door open by the time they came up the stairs. She was a dainty, comely girl, and she had arrayed herself in a fresh white apron and tied a pink ribbon in her frizzly black hair for the occasion. Her perfect teeth flashed in an excited, welcoming smile.

"Ah got everything all ready, Miz Emily!" she gasped. "Jes' lak Mistah Gray said."

Mary exclaimed with pleasure while she removed her bonnet. Then, Emily and Gray smiling after her, she hurried through the rooms to inspect everything at once.

There were new chairs, fresh, light summer curtains at the windows, pictures and ornaments she had not seen before. Fresh flowers —tea roses of a delicate yellow, deep-red carnations, and maidenhair fern—were arranged in a slender vase of sparkling cut glass.

"Yes'm," said Ellen, who was excitedly following Mary about, "Mr. Gray he brought 'em this afternoon. He said they was for you and Miz Emily both."

"They're very nice, Ellen," said Mary primly.

The flat seemed to her like a doll's house. She saw quickly that there was a blue Wedgwood urn with a frieze of Grecian figures chased around the border on the mantel. A pair of Chinese rugs in pale blue and buff, the patterns elegant and subdued, had been arranged on the plain Brussels carpet. A photograph of Andrew Gray stood on the piano next to Emily's neatly stacked music. The keyboard was open, the ivory keys looking white and cool, and a piece of vocal music stood open on the rack.

Andrew Gray had made all kinds of plans for them. That very night they were going to the Madison Square roof garden where it would be cool and they could look down and see all the lights of the city. A few nights later they all went to see *A Trip to Chinatown,* and then to McGard's for their famous ice cream. Gray, deferential and solicitous, seemed to be enjoying it all as much as they, and Mary was delighted with everything but the heat, which continued oppressive.

The thermometer reached 98 degrees and stayed there, the city steaming and sizzling in a humid heat which kept people sitting on the stoops of their brownstone houses until midnight, with thousands sleeping on the sands at Coney Island, and the parks filled with gasping tenement dwellers whom the police watched sharply but, out of humanity, did not disturb.

Dead and dying horses littered the streets. Swarms of flies gathered about those which the police shot to put out of their misery. The dead animals, stripped of harness and straw hats, lay in pools of dark blood partly soaked up by the sawdust spread around them until their carcasses could be carted off.

Lightning flashed across the skies one night and thunder echoed back from the Palisades, but still it would not rain. Almost panic-stricken now at being walled in by the city while the smothering heat continued, Mary decided that she would have to see James sooner than she had planned. She was too unwell, she told Emily, to go on.

Emily advised against the trip to Brooklyn in the heat, and her heart leaped. She and Andrew had had hardly a chance to speak apart from her mother's presence. Mary, pale and pressing the knuckles of her right hand hard against her forehead to ease her aching head, insisted she would have to go. The animation had gone from her face which was drawn and haggard.

Emily turned away to hide her smile. She did not doubt that her mother felt poorly, but she knew that she also liked to dramatize her passing illnesses now and again when things were dull.

While her mother was dressing, she slipped out to a drugstore and called Andrew Gray at his office to tell him that they would be alone that evening. To her disappointment he was not in, and she dared not leave a message.

When they reached James's new house, they found that both James and Laura were out, the servant girl explaining that Laura had gone with him on his rounds. She brought them a drink of lemonade when they went upstairs to wait in the darkened parlor which was cool and pleasant. Mary closed her eyes and rested. Emily got up and moved restlessly about the house. Laura was an immaculate housekeeper. The house shone upstairs and down. She went out into the street in front of the house.

It seemed cooler in Brooklyn. The sun was bright, but there was more open space to let breezes flow unimpeded. She thought of walking down toward the old house just to look at it once more. It had been rented to people she did not know. Then she decided that she might go and see their dressmaker who had made their gowns at the time of James's wedding and order new dresses she wanted for the autumn. She went back in and told her mother where she was going and started out lightly, careless of the heat, her imagination leaping ahead to the evening. She was certain her mother would stay in Brooklyn for a time, though they had brought none of her belongings. She could send them over the next day by Ellen or she and Andrew might even bring them in the evening.

Mary heard the telephone ring downstairs and the maid answer. Then came the maid's footsteps on the stairs. It had rung several times before and the girl had answered.

"It's de dactah," the girl said. "He wants to know does anybody want him. Ah tol' him 'yes' a lady call twice her little boy sick. Shall ah tell him youah heah!"

"Yes, please. Tell him his mother, Mrs. Stapely, is waiting and that I am not well."

"Youah mothah is waitin' and she sick," repeated the girl as she hurried back down the stairs. "Youah mothah is waitin' and she sick. Youah . . ."

Mary smiled and closed her eyes again. She would be glad when James came. Surely he could give her something which would make her feel better. She began to feel better at the very thought of it. She wished she had gone with Emily. She needed a new dress too.

The girl came back.

"Ah tol' 'im," she said doubtfully. "Ah tol' 'im that lady call two times, too. Says her li'l boy got 'vulsions. Then man call too about li'l boy. They all upset."

"That's too bad," said Mary sympathetically. "In this hot weather too."

It was less than a half-hour before James and Laura returned, and Mary from her seat at the front window, where she had moved to watch for them, saw that they were in a great state. The horse was in a lather of sweat, foam frothing at its nostrils. James dashed inside and Laura after him. He emerged with a pail of water which he threw over the horse's head while Laura held his bridle. They ran in again, and this time Laura hurried out with another pail full of water which she dashed over the heaving animal's back. The maid was talking volubly from the doorway, though Mary could not make out what she was saying. James came out with a sponge now and stood there sponging the horse's head while Laura ran inside again.

Evidently the girl was telling him that she was there for James looked up and waved at her briefly, then went on with what he was doing.

Mary stood up smiling expectantly as she heard Laura hurrying up the stairs. But, Laura, instead of stopping, ran up the next flight and Mary heard her opening and closing drawers in one of the dressers. She realized now that her new daughter-in-law wanted to be freshly dressed to greet her for her first real visit to their new home, and she approved. The horse seemed easier now, and James had gone. She supposed he had gone into his office. She could hear Laura rushing about overhead. Mary reseated herself and adjusted her dress and the brooch at her throat so as to be in proper dignity to receive her son's wife.

Within a few moments Mary heard Laura's quick steps descending the stairs, and the welcoming smile began again on her lips.

Laura hurried through the hall, stuck her head inside the door, said, "Hello!" in a surprised, impatient voice. More meaningfully she added, "Isn't Emily with you—and, of course, Andrew?" Then she raced downstairs.

Mary heard her call to James and turned to the window just in time to see James and Laura jump into the buggy and dash off.

Astonishment, chagrin, and anger clouded Mary's face. Her eyes flashed. The affront to herself was as nothing compared with the implications of Laura's question about Andrew!

"You may tell the doctor when he returns," she said distinctly to the maid, "that I came over here feeling quite ill, but that I shall not put up with such treatment from him or from anyone else. You may tell him that I have gone back to New York and shall not return."

"Yes'm," said the girl doubtfully.

"Good-bye," said Mary sweetly. "You have been most kind."

Laura's remark had verified the suspicions she had felt in Ilium. It indicated the attitude she and James felt it safe to adopt. Mary intended to brook no criticism of Emily and Andrew, especially when it implied criticism of her. Any rebellion had to be stopped *now*.

She started toward Fourth Avenue to go in search of Emily, wondering what she could do if she could not find her. Luckily she spied Emily swinging along, hat in hand, in her direction.

"Ma! What's happened?"

"We are going home, Emily. I shall tell you on the way."

Mary told her in brisk, hard tones of how they had been ignored, how James and Laura had returned, then raced away without really speaking to her. She did not tell Emily of Laura's remark or the construction she had placed on it.

Emily's fingers clenched inside her white gloves. One more night that she would not see Andrew—not really see him!

It was Emily who felt discouraged, disappointed, tired, and hot when they reached the flat again. As she tore off her clothes to get into a cooling tub, her face broke into a wild expression of grief, fear, and anguish. She tightened her hands over her ears, her fingers digging into her skull as though to shut out the cry that she wished she could let out in the privacy of her bathroom. She loved her mother as she was supposed to. Even better, she liked her mother, and was glad to have her with her. Yet, if her mother did not go, if she could not see Andrew—!

She turned off the warm water and tested what was in the tub with her finger. She turned on the cold to temper it further. Bending and turning she saw herself in the mirror over the basin and a part of herself in the smaller mirror set above the white tub. Her face grew calm and thoughtful as she looked at herself critically, seeing the white, firm flesh of her young body, the curves of her upright breasts and the round softness of her shoulders. She smoothed away the red wrinkles which tight stays had left about her waist and ran her hand down one firm thigh to the knee. Her skin almost tingled at the touch of her own hand. Her face broke into a soft smile.

Emily had dried herself and slipped into a dressing gown when she heard a strange voice, a woman's high, quick voice that was yet familiar, in the other room and her mother's voice responding coldly. Then she knew who it was. It was Laura.

Laura, thinner looking than ever, brown hair plastered to her forehead with perspiration, her whole face suffused with a scarlet flush, was pleading desperately.

"But, Mother, James was in a great state when we came home and found you gone! He had patients waiting, but he had me go right down to the dressmaker's to look for you. I ran all the way and could scarcely talk when I got there. She told me Emily had been—"

"Of course I did not go the dressmaker's," said Mary triumphantly, as though she had scored an important point.

"Then when the maid told me you had gone home sick, hurt, and angry—"

"It is quite true!" said Mary. "I was never treated so in all my life."

Laura, getting redder and hotter with each step was pacing tensely up and down the living room while Mary sat cool and majestic in the low lady's chair.

"I don't blame you in the least!" she cried. "I should have done the same thing under the circumstances. But won't you please—"

"You might," said Mary thoughtfully, "have excused yourself in any way you could. You might have said, 'Mother, we shall be back in a half-hour.' It would not have taken a moment, and I should have understood perfectly."

Emily, hesitating in the hall outside the bathroom, decided not to go in. Her mother was establishing her position and enjoying herself hugely. Even Laura was enjoying the struggle and her self-abasement. Women!

"Mother," argued Laura, standing in mid-floor with one arm outstretched in oratorical gesture, "you know I think too much of you to treat you any way but kindly! Neither James nor I ever meant to hurt you in the least! Do you think I would have rushed over here in this heat—"

Incongruously and awkwardly the tears started down the tight, thin cheeks.

"There! There!" said Mary comfortingly. She got up and put her arm around the bony figure.

Laura broke into real sobs now, her shoulders heaving, their bony edges showing under her thin summer dress. She suffered herself to be led to a chair where Mary stayed patting her and murmuring soothing words.

Mary felt exultant. She had broken her daughter-in-law's attempt at defiance. There had been no need for open statement. Laura and James knew well enough what it really was that had angered her.

Laura, from being upset and her rush through the city's heat, was almost hysterical. That, thought Mary sincerely, was a shame. She saw it all now as James's fault. He should have come himself.

"James couldn't come," sobbed Laura, as though she had read Mary's thoughts. "He is having a consultation with Dr. Carter. They are afraid that little boy is going to die."

"Oh, the poor little fellow!" Mary cried. "I'm so sorry. Isn't there anything that can be done?"

"James has tried everything, but he only seems to get worse. That's where we had been and where we had to go back. Our poor horse! We almost drove her to death. And he's such a sweet little boy, just nine!"

"He may be all right," said Mary sagely. "Children can be very sick at that age and all right the next day. The poor little chap!"

"Hello, Laura," said Emily casually as she came in. "Inconsiderate of him to get sick today though, wasn't it?" But she spoke the last so low neither of the other two grasped her words.

"Emily, I'm so sorry—"

"Forget it," advised Emily evenly. "I may go mad one of these days, but it won't be because I don't see my charming brother and his equally charming wife. It's going to rain and cool off. We'll all feel better."

"Rain!" Laura jumped up and ran to the window. "Then I must get back. I'll—"

"You'll stay to tea and get some rest. You look as though you could do with both."

"Miz Emily!" Ellen was beckoning from the hall. Emily went toward her, and they walked together down the hall toward the kitchen.

"Y'all was in the tub," Ellen explained, "so I couldn' tell you. Mr. Gray he come by and say he won' be heah tonight. He say tomorra night shuah!"

Emily began to laugh. All her annoyance, all her tragic poses for nothing! She laughed louder while Ellen, not understanding but sympathetic, smiled at her and then began to laugh too. Miz Emily was lots of fun sometimes.

The storm began. The rain exploded from the heavens, pelting bulletlike on the roofs and bouncing as it struck the steaming pavements. The lightning zigzagged lividly, lighting the flat with ghastly light as they all ran to close the windows. The thunder rattled and crashed, growled away, roared back and sprang again. Mary hurried to put away the silver and the steel knives. Ellen hid in a clothes closet, Laura, the sea captain's daughter, glared at the storm as though it had come purposely to interfere with her return to Brooklyn.

Emily stood at an open window at the back of the flat and exulted in the storm. The Japanese silk wrapper open so that it exposed the cleft between her breasts, she stood tall and straight like a young Brünnhilde and wanted to sing and shout and vie with the fury of the storm. Her clenched right hand was pressed hard against the palm of her left. Lips drawn back in a dazzling smile, eyes wide and fiercely alive, her face showed all the mad, compelling, unreasoning joy and thirst she could not show when others were about. "Andrew!" she whispered. "Andrew!"

"Emily! Come away from that window, Emily. You'll catch your death of cold. Laura's going to stay." Mary had come in behind her.

The power and the splendor of the storm continued unrestrained.

"Andrew!" Emily whispered to the fury once again. Then she composed her face and turned. "All right, Ma," she said. "That's good."

"I'm glad I did what I did!" hissed Mary. "James has needed a lesson for a long time. It's not poor Laura's fault."

Chapter 24

"ANDREW, ANDREW, ANDREW!" Emily whispered again. They stood in the center of the floor with their arms about each other.

She had been singing and playing for him after their dinner. Her mother had gone to pay her visit to James and Laura. They had just heard Ellen go out. She was delighted to be spending the night with a cousin.

Their eyes were only inches apart. Emily's great blue eyes were filled with tears of happiness. Gray's were grave and tender. He smiled gently.

"I'm glad, too," he said quietly.

"Oh, Andrew!" cried the girl again. It was all she could think of to say.

They moved together to the settee, and she buried her head hard against his shoulder. Gently Gray stroked her hair. They stayed that way a moment, achieving calm from the pressure of their bodies against each other. Then the girl raised her head. She threw her arms about him and kissed him again and again. The touch of her eyelashes against his cheek sent a shock of desire through the man, but he did not move. He felt the girl's tears wet on his face.

"But I never cry!" she said, vexed with herself. "I never cry!"

"It was too long."

Emily laughed unsteadily and drew back to look into his face. "You're so handsome and good and kind, Andrew! So wonderful!"

Gray laughed.

"And you are very beautiful," he said.

"But only," she said wonderingly, "for you. This morning when ⌐ looked in the mirror I was dull and ordinary. Tonight when I knew you were coming, I was beautiful. I know I was. I am beautiful now. I can feel it."

"How does it feel?" he asked teasingly.

"You should know. You're beautiful too!"

They laughed and their laughter brought them even closer together. If Emily had been only beautiful, he thought, none of this would have happened. This wonderful or terrible thing would not have been. It was the girl's clear, intuitive intelligence, her blue, fearless eyes, her unashamed abandon, her helplessness before love, that moved and thrilled him just as her beauty aroused, and her youth touched his imagination and his compassion.

"I must seem very old to you, Emily." He forced himself to say it. She kissed the words away reproachfully.

"People who are alive at the same time in the world are all the same age," she explained sagely. "I've never thought of age that way, perhaps because Father is much older than Ma. I don't know. We are both here now. It's like that."

"It's not quite that simple," he began, marveling. "It's—"

"Don't argue, Andrew. I *know*. I know for both of us. I know what is right and good. I know what *is*. You could never hurt me. You could hurt me only by taking away what you are. I'd not want to live then."

"You *have* been thinking, haven't you?" he asked lightly.

But Emily was serious.

"Promise me you'll never die," she said tensely.

"I promise to be immortal."

"No, don't joke."

"I promise that I'll never die. Perhaps we never shall. We can't know that."

"I can know. I do know. The Bible says we shall live forever. I never knew what it meant. I do now."

Her intensity frightened Gray. He tightened his arm about her, felt her soft and yielding, expectant. Passion fired his body and his spirit, and a melting tenderness touched his heart. He felt as though he had suddenly come alive after endless sterile years. He marveled that men lived without love and did not know.

It was quiet in the room with only the hissing of the mantle in the gas lamp, with its rose-colored glass shade, turned low on the piano. The city had cooled after the storm of the day before. It lay heat-exhausted and silent outside the windows where the white curtains were stirring gently. The sound of a ship's whistle drifted in from the distant harbor. It sounded twice and was answered twice by lower notes from a tug or another ship.

Emily had moved. She lay still in his arms, looking up into his face. Suddenly Gray found himself pouring out his soul to the girl, marveling as he spoke at his own lucidity. He spoke convictions he did not know he had. He saw life whole, as though some fusion of her youth and wisdom and the experience and hurt which had come to him through the years, as they come to any man, had crystallized into a perfect sphericity.

"I think," he said, "too many things have always been a little too easy for me. I did not have to struggle to appear clever. I did not have to strain to write passably or to paint a little. Once I understood something, I did not want to bother repeating it. Somehow I have 'made money,' as the phrase goes, though I never really wanted to. I think because everyone around me was striving for it I wanted to compete and prove that I could do it too, though I refused to devote my life to the pursuit. Perhaps there was not sufficient stimulation. Perhaps I've wanted too many things."

Then his thoughts shifted, and it was he who spoke with wonder.

"I did not see you for the first time that day the peddler's horse wandered down a street in Brooklyn. It was as though you were someone or something I had lost long ago and without which there was no meaning in anything. I think I have always been reaching and searching for you. When I saw you, it was as though I had been in abeyance, my real life held back somewhere, unexpended."

Emily was touching his lips, his hands, his face, again and again, as though counting rhythmically, as though the touch of her hand moved with the beat of her heart.

"Don't stop," she whispered. "I want to hear your voice. It doesn't matter what you say. I love your voice, your hands, your face ...

> *I love thee to the depth and breadth and height*
> *My soul can reach when feeling out of sight*
> *For the ends of Being and Ideal Grace—*

Emily finished the sonnet as Gray looked down into her transfigured face. "I think," she said softly, "it is the most beautiful poem there is."

"It is beautiful," said Gray.

He thought of other sonnets. For an instant the words of one he loved hovered about his lips, but he did not speak.

"What were you thinking of? What were you going to say?" asked Emily curiously.

He shook his head lightly.

"What was it, Andrew?"

"Only that I love you."

"I want to know everything you think, everything you know, everything you are."

Gray looked down into the girl's waiting eyes. He bent and kissed her.

Emily did not respond.

"Andrew," she said, "tell me about her."

"No, Emily."

"Is she pretty?"

"Not as you are."

"Do you love her?"

"Not in the same way. You see, Emily—"

"No, don't tell me!"

He stroked her forehead and her hair. Emily trembled once, then lay still.

"There'll always be that, Emily."

She did not answer for a moment. When she did speak, the whisper was so low that it was just audible. Emily's eyes were closed.

"Andrew—you'll not leave me tonight."

"No." His voice was as low and quiet.

"You'll never leave me—not really."

"No."

Then, incredibly, the girl was asleep, a smile on her face. It was as if she were safe at home, at peace, after exhausting struggle. Gray's heart ached, then seemed almost physically to break under the weight of the pain and joy it held.

Chapter 25

HAVING PAVED the way and set the pattern, announced her principles and won a victory, Mary was having a fine time in Brooklyn. Laura, she noted with approval, could not be more attentive.

James she had hardly spoken to. In fact, she had hardly seen him. When he was at home, he was busy with patients. The rest of the time he was at the hospital or making calls. At dinner on the night of her arrival she had asked about the child who had had convulsions, and James had admitted that he was better, though both he and Dr. Carter had been afraid he would not live.

"I knew the boy would get well," said Mary firmly, by way of letting James know that she had not accepted his excuse. She had no intention, as she told Laura, of forgiving James immediately.

When she knew James was about, she kept out of his way. She was helping Laura make a new shirtwaist, sewing the hems while Laura, who was an able seamstress, did the buttonholes. Then they started to re-make one of hers, Mary slyly taking advantage of Laura to do work she could not do herself. James and Laura laughed about it in private.

Not until she had been in Brooklyn several days did Mary confront James. Then, to make the lesson very clear, she called on him in his office to ask his professional advice.

Gravely, James took her pulse and temperature. He looked down her throat and had her say "ah." Then he wrote out a prescription for a mild sedative.

"The tired feeling and the headaches," he said, "come from running around too much in the hot weather. What you need is rest."

"I see," said Mary formally. It was about time James paid her some attention.

"Usually," said James, tentatively biting at his thumb, "I recommend to patients that they go to the seashore or the mountains. In your case I feel that you would got most benefit from a good long stay in South Ilium, New York. There is a house on a hill there with a fine view of the Hudson. The air is clear—"

"Do you mean I should go home?" demanded Mary, her face alarmed. "If I'm not welcome here—"

"You are consulting me as your physician, Mrs. Stapely," said James. "Of course, if you do not wish to take my advice, I cannot force you to do so."

"I shall stay right here!" declared his mother. "Sick or well, I shall stay as long as I like."

James bowed.

Then it was too much for both of them. They burst into laughter.

"Well," said Laura from the doorway, "it was about time you two came to your senses."

"We're going for a drive to Fort Hamilton," said James, "and we're going right now. Get your bonnet, Mother. You may come along too, if you feel you have to, Laura."

Laura turned red, and her lips tightened.

"You mean you don't really want me to come?"

James shrugged. "We can put up with it, I suppose."

Mary, at mention of a ride, had hurried for her bonnet, gloves, and purse.

"If you and your mother," said Laura, biting off each word, "think for one moment—" Tears of vexation glinted in her eyes.

James reached across and tweaked one small ear where it showed beneath the roll of Laura's brown hair. Then he stood back and looked at her critically.

"Just adjusting it," he explained. "You had it on crooked."

Laura sprang at him and began pounding his heavy shoulders with small, determined fists. "You beast!" she cried. "You beast!"

James winced and ducked. "Make her stop, Ma!" he called. "Try to act like a lady," he advised his wife.

"If I'd married a gentleman, I might be able to!"

The next morning there was a note for Mary from Andrew Gray. He had some business to attend to near Coney Island, he wrote, before he sailed for England on the S.S. *City of New York*. Emily was going with him, and they would be delighted if she would go with them to Coney Island. Perhaps Dr. and Mrs. Stapely would join them for dinner at night. They would meet her at the Fulton Street ferry and then take the Coney Island boat from the Battery.

The big German restaurant on the Coney boardwalk was crowded that night, as it was almost every night during the summer season. A German band blared in one corner, and at one table a group of diners sang, banging their beer steins on the table top in time to the music. Respectably dressed men and women, sometimes whole families, sat quietly eating at other tables. A few flashily dressed men and rouged women were raucously noisy.

James and Laura had been a little late, but they had joined them immediately in the outing spirit. Laura was gaily dressed, and even James had put on a tweed suit in place of his habitual dark professional garb. Gray ordered wine for them all, whiskey for James and himself.

The wine warmed her, but Emily was cold with fear as she looked at Andrew Gray. In two days he would sail, and she might not see him again for weeks or even a month.

The German waiters, big-bellied men in enveloping white aprons, hurried among the tables bearing huge and heavily loaded trays. Some of the rouged women wore dog collars of imitation pearls and threw roguish glances at their escorts who looked like gamblers or race horse touts. Some of them were. Emily despised the women, then felt sorry for them, then forgot them as she looked again at Andrew.

Jesting easily with her mother and Laura, he flashed her a reassuring smile and turned to say something to James. Emily smiled back recklessly, and her fear vanished. James noticed her, and a slight frown came between his eyes. Let him frown! Let any of them think what they liked!

"Andrew!" she called. "Andrew! Do you think I might have another glass of wine?" She did not want the wine. She just wanted to speak his name.

Gray only smiled and raised his finger to the waiter who seemed to be watching.

Mary smiled too.

Andrew was James's friend as well as Emily's, she thought. He had been James's best man, and had lent him some of the money to build the new house. It was right and proper that Andrew should serve as Emily's escort. She watched closely. There was no tension. James was expansive. Laura was relaxed. They were not withholding judgment. Even Thomas, though he might frown at their extravagance, could find fault with none of this. Mary felt warm and comfortable with her two children and those they loved and who loved them about her.

Emily's eyes were still fixed on Andrew Gray's face.

Andrew, stay! she willed desperately. *Don't go to England! Don't go anywhere! Please, Andrew!*

Chapter 26

THE NEXT DAY James left the house as soon after morning office hours as he could. He had a slight headache from the whiskey he had drunk the night before. Worse than his headache was the depression he had been trying to evade for days. Without discernible cause, or cause which he could isolate, he fell into such moods, and they struck more frequently.

He supposed, as he drove slowly down the street in Brooklyn toward Third Avenue, it was a little of everything. Business everywhere was falling off. There'd be another panic soon. Men were being laid off at the dry docks and all along the Narrows water front. He could see the masts of lumber schooners and coastal tramps sticking up ahead of him at the end of the street. They looked dirty and abandoned.

He had no calls to make right away. He was not even on a street where he had business. He let the mare have her head. She slowed at a corner, as though asking directions. For no reason, James tugged slightly on the right rein, and they turned the corner.

Always having to keep up a front, for Laura, for his mother, for damn fool patients, for someone or another. He wasn't interested right now in keeping up a front, or in doing anything or being anything. He was jaded and bored. Probably his mother was too. It would account for her restlessness. Laura was never bored. She was active every minute, planning, scheming, determined on this or that end. Her furious activity in church affairs sprang from no religious impulse. It was just another opportunity to plan and carry out some strategy probably no one was aware of but herself.

Why in hell he had married he would never know! Laura was all right. She was no worse than other women. She was better than most, and certainly he saw enough women, all of them ailing or breeding, ailing or breeding, ailing or breeding. They were always eating too. Every time he went into a house, the woman was eating or had just eaten or was about to eat something.

He'd be delivering babies, pouring iodine on kids' scraped knees, and sliding pills down one great red throat into one great burbling belly-ache for the rest of his life.

The night before at Coney had been the first night off he could remember in months. He'd enjoyed it. Gray was a man of the world, good to talk to. What was between Andrew and Emily was, after all, no business of his. He was *not* his sister's keeper. He did not even want to be his own.

Besides, he was not in a position to quarrel with rich and worldly Andrew Gray who had been his best man, who held the first mortgage on his home, and who had already given him useful investment tips. They might pull the wool over his mother's eyes, but—well, Andrew was generous. Lucky for all of them, thought James cynically, that he had taken a shine to Emily.

Of course, someone had called while they were out last night; and, of course, the stupid maid had not got it straight. Who had called, he didn't know. He didn't care.

"Look where you're driving!" a carter called out angrily as he jerked his wagon to safety.

James did not look at him.

He was making a firm, even a spectacular, success of his practice. Yet he was dissatisfied. Perhaps he was getting what he deserved. He did not know why.

In South Ilium being a doctor had seemed the most important thing in the world. Just to be a doctor was the end-all, the well-nigh impossible culmination of his own and his father's desire and efforts. He knew differently now. It wasn't enough to be the hard-working general practitioner for some middle-class neighborhood.

Laura would never understand that. Neither would his father. A doctor was some mysterious, wonderful thing in their eyes. It did not matter whether Laura understood or not, but his father was growing older. You did not try to explain, and you did not disappoint a man like that. He would not know what he meant if he said he was sometimes fumbling, clumsy, and afraid. His father must be lonely with his mother still away. He had worshipped her all his life in his own way. James wondered why. Men were dupes at best.

Yet there were days when James exulted, though he could remember none now. A fracture nicely set, nicely mended, was a fine thing. A child's fever receding when it had been touch and go for days was also a fine thing. They made it worth the continuing round of measles, mumps, German measles, ailing women, and men with gonorrhea or the pip. He drove into his work then. Children were the best to work with—firm flesh, sound bones, clean blood. It was the difference between working with a piece of young oak or a piece of soft and crumbling poplar which frayed and splintered the minute you took a tool to it. James, too, was a carpenter's son.

A job well finished called for a drink. He felt exhilarated and needed it to steady him. A drink was the cure, too, when there had been too many night calls in a row, and the fatigue had sunk in until it was a foul taste in his mouth.

Without noticing it, he had driven out past the settled parts of South Brooklyn into the country, the region of sandy vacant lots choked with weeds, no sidewalks, broken glass and broken bricks beyond Bay Ridge Avenue. You seemed to hit such places any way you went except toward downtown Brooklyn. There was a wooded hill sloping down to the rural Shore Road between him and the Bay now. James pulled up and looked at it for a few minutes. It looked peaceful and cool, under a fair sky with lazily moving clouds, with the sun lighting it but not burning down though it was nearly noon. Beyond he could see an expanse of blue water and, from where he sat in the buggy, none of the ugliness of the water front. There were still stretches of open beach along there, he knew, not yet fouled with shipping.

He tugged out his heavy gold watch and looked at it. It was getting on. From another pocket he fished the prescription pad—they were supplied in quantity by a pharmaceutical house—on which he had jotted down his calls. He pulled himself up straight and took a deep breath of the clear air. His headache had worn itself away. He sat there another moment, then reluctantly turned the horse about and drove back to face his life.

The mare, seeming inspirited too, trotted briskly for a few blocks without his urging, then lapsed into a steady walk. It was fifteen minutes before James drew up at one house in a row of indistinguishable frame houses and tethered the mare. He had taken up his bag

and started up the wooden steps of the stoop before he saw the white crepe on the door. He was startled. The boy had been getting well. Then he saw that the red scarlet fever sign was gone from the window. He hesitated before pulling the bell, but the door opened as he stood there. A heavy woman, spotless, white face drawn but impressive stood there. They were Swedes. The woman fat with a fair, scrubbed face, could speak little English.

She looked at James. "He iss dead," she said.

"Dead?" James repeated. But the boy had been getting well! He had seemed well past the danger point. What had happened?

The husband stood now behind his wife. He too, was big and fair. He worked at something around the water front. He looked at James.

"Ve hired you to make him vell," he said stonily to James. "Now last night he is dead. The undertaker come. He is not here."

"Why didn't you call me?" asked James. "Did you let him get up? What happened?"

"Ve call you last night. You was not dere."

They both stood looking at him with no emotion showing in their faces, but he knew their hatred. Then the woman stepped back, and the man closed the door, leaving James standing there. For a second he considered pushing open the door and following. He would have to sign a death certificate. The boy had been recovering. He had been a friendly-faced towheaded kid, thin and weak, but getting restless as the disease and fever retreated.

It didn't matter. He was dead. He could make out the death certificate later and bring it back. They might not have called him the night before, and he had been there in the morning. People lied. Still, they blamed the doctor. They would hate him always—as though the power of life and death were his! He had lost patients before, many of them. Sometimes he had pulled them through when they were a lot closer to death than this boy had seemed. Sometimes they slipped away like this when all seemed well, as though they changed their minds about wanting to live. He felt defeated, crushed.

He dreaded telling Laura she could close out this account. Laura would want to know why. She'd want a practical reason and ask whether he had done this or administered that, or whether the boy had had a fever on his last visit. But everything was *not* practical. There were mysterious currents in life. Sometimes you were one with them, and it made you sure and strong. Other times you could not reach through, through the baffling and puzzling mazes of sensation and emotion to whatever it was that eluded and mocked, and then you lost.

He wanted to go to sleep and forget it. The kid had had clear blue eyes, not alight like Emily's or Will's, but simple and honest. He'd needed his hair cut after the weeks in bed, one lank lock dangling over his thin forehead into his eyes. The woman had cut it across in a bang, giving the boy a naked, defenceless look. Well, he was dead. There were a lot of things he'd not have to bother with. It was stupid to be sensitive, to have too much imagination ... yet you couldn't go to sleep and forget it all. You had to keep going or you were beaten yourself.

James stopped in a saloon and had two whiskeys. Then he went to a florist's next door and sent some flowers to the boy's home. He did not send a card. James knew nothing about flowers and, as he was willing to announce any time, cared less. But what else could he do? He went back to the saloon and had another drink before starting home.

Laura and his mother were finishing their lunch in the cool dining room and the maid was eating hers in the kitchen. They were eating sliced peaches and drinking some ginger beer Laura had bottled.

"You're just in time, James," called Laura. "Sit down. I'll get you something right away."

"Not hungry, thanks," said James. He sat on a black leather-covered sofa and looked at them.

"Lovely peaches," smiled Mary, spooning another luscious wedge into her mouth. "You always liked them."

James shook his head.

"Decided to go to South Ilium tomorrow," he said, "and see Pa."

Laura laughed. "You know you can't, James, though it would be nice. You have the Olsen confinement coming up and you can't let McCafferty's arm go—and the Linsen boy."

The Linsen boy! "I'm going by boat. Haven't been on the river in years. I can get the *Pilgrim* from Desbrosses Street at nine. I want a day or two away, and I've an idea Pa may be lonely."

It was the wrong thing to say. He had not meant to say it. Mary bridled instantly, putting her spoon down into her plate with a sharp clink.

"Your father is perfectly all right," she said sharply. "Your Aunt Maria and Aunt Julia are perfectly capable of looking after him. I had a letter from him this morning."

"James," said Laura quietly, "you know very well you can't let your practice go like that without any notice. You've worked too hard to build it up to take any chances. Now have some lunch."

"I'm not going away forever, and I'm not going to Timbuktoo!" roared James. "Perhaps I should. Dr. Whiteside can take care of them all till I get back."

The two women looked at each other with a meaning glance which enraged him further.

"Then you won't mind," asked Laura sweetly, "if Mother and I take the horse and carriage to Greenwood Cemetery this afternoon? We planned to. I want to get some sparrowgrass and another plant or two for the parlor basket at the greenhouse there."

"Take the horse and carriage to—go where you like," James answered her.

"I think, Laura," said his mother, "that you and I had better leave until James has found his manners again. Evidently he got up on the wrong side of the bed this morning."

Chapter 27

"WHEN *is* Ma coming home?" demanded Will fretfully.

He and his father were working alone with one helper, putting up a board rail fence about the pretty park which took in the crest of Ilium's chief hill and the wooded land below it. Work had not picked up. Instead of twenty or thirty men, Thomas now had only ten on his payroll, and he himself had again taken to doing some of the carpentering.

"Hand me that two-by-four," Thomas countered. "No, not that one—*that* one."

Will, his mouth full of nails, poked it across to him. It was a perfect summer afternoon, brilliant and still. Men were at work. Children, who played about the park in the spring and autumn were down at the river or at home. Only an occasional carriage with a parasoled lady in light summer gown and wide-brimmed hat, or a silk-hatted banker or industrialist, or a delivery cart passed along the shaded avenue of magnificent homes near which they were working.

This was a job Thomas had been glad to get, more as a mark of esteem for his workmanship than for the profit in it. That was one reason he had elected to work at it himself. He had waited weeks to get just the seasoned cedar posts, slotted to receive the finished rails, that he had ordered. He stood back and squinted to make sure they were following the guide cords they had nailed to temporary posts and to be certain the post he worked on stood plumb before he drove home the twenty-penny nails.

Will was tapping deftly at a joint that needed just a nudge of a sixteenth of an inch to be perfect.

Thomas, his powerful forearm glistening in the sun, swung his hammer from the elbow expertly and the new board was in place. Once again Will admired his father's skill. He could do finer cabinet work, but he was still no match for the old man at solid construction.

The helper was far ahead of them down the line, grunting posts into the holes already dug by two laborers and laying out the right number of crosspieces. A nursemaid and two small children, one holding each of her hands, walked across a distant lawn behind a sprawling barberry hedge. A cast-iron deer stood in the center of the lawn, a fierce iron dog at the entrance to the carriage drive. The nursemaid was homely and middle-aged. Will had seen her before. He was not interested. Too bad, though, he thought idly, that if the kids wanted to watch them she wouldn't let them.

Thomas saw where he was looking.

"Come, boy," he said sharply. "We'll never be done that way. And, if I were you, I'd watch myself with that girl of Jackson's."

In his surprise, Will spat out his whole mouthful of nails and bent to pick them up.

"Oh, Edith's all right," he said casually.

"They're all alike," said Thomas bitterly.

"Who are?" asked Will, going on with his work and mechanically handing another of the crossbeams over to his father.

His father had seemed mild and content lately, playing his cello softly to himself after he had finished working in the garden in the evening, or chatting pleasantly with Aunt Julia. He seemed to like her, though they were so unlike, and spoke more with her actually than with Aunt Maria who was his own sister. He would do little things to help Julia, wait for Maria to do things for him. Will blamed James's visit for the change in his father's mood. They had argued about something, he did not know what, and his father had been in ill humor ever since James left after a stay of three or four days.

"Women," said Thomas bitterly. "They're all alike. Some ways they're like children and have to be treated as children. But they get what they want. They keep at it."

Will was astounded. He had never heard his father speak like this. He went on with his work, put a board in place but did not hammer it, for he wanted to hear what else his father might say.

"Don't think so much of yourself because you could knock over

Jackson's girl perhaps. I never saw a woman yet I couldn't get if I'd wanted."

To cover his own embarrassment, Will drove in three nails in rapid succession, then tested the crosspiece with a tug.

"Squeezing themselves all out of shape, poking out their—fronts and pushing out their behinds!" Thomas corrected himself deliberately. "Their arses. Inviting a man on, then pretending to be frightened if a man looks at them. 'Twas the same in London when I was young. The dresses change. The women in them don't." He spoke harshly as though he were spewing out rancor that had been dammed up inside of him.

Will laughed tentatively.

"When — they — have — what — they — want — of a man," said Thomas, giving a savage blow of his hammer with each word, "then they're through and off to something else."

Will knew what it was now. Thomas felt hurt and neglected. He had no one else to whom he could talk. His father had hoped to say something to James, then James, probably, had wanted to talk only of his own affairs, and that was why he had got angry. He had never expected to see his father angry with James.

"Oh, I guess, Ma," he said as easily as he could, "will—"

"Who said anything about your mother?" demanded Thomas, though he would not look at Will. "Your mother is no ordinary woman. If she were, I'd never have married her." He stopped with hammer in mid-air. He sounded genuinely surprised. "I don't suppose it ever occurred to you that I could have married anyone I chose, and that your mother when she was young might easily have married another."

"Never thought about it," said Will unhappily.

Thomas went sharply back to work, lost in his own thoughts. Of course, the boy had never thought of that. He had never wondered about his own parents. His mother and father had been his mother and father to him. Even now he could not think of them except as husband and wife in the lodge where he had been born, and with his brothers and sisters. He tried to picture his father as he might have been when he was a young man before he had married. He could not. That would have been in the last years of the eighteenth century. His imagination would not do it.

"So watch yourself with that girl of Jackson's," he concluded lamely.

But Will had followed his work along. He was fitting in and nailing up the bottom rail while his father did the top one. Thomas hurried after him, slapping one piece hurriedly into place. He could come back later and check it. Somehow he did not want Will to get away from him.

"Your mother is looking after Emily, you know," he said quickly. "She found her in bed when she went over from James's, and she and the servant kept her there a couple of days. It was the heat, your mother thinks, and she's a bit better. They're getting about now. The letter this morning said they'd been for a drive to Riverside, and another day they had their tea at Highbridge. One night they went to Eldorado. Your mother says it is a fine place. You go in a boat, then up in an elevator for hundreds of feet, and the grounds are all lighted up with electric lights and different colored dangles over arches. They had supper and saw the performance. Do you know what it is?"

"No," said Will. "It sounds fine."

"Perhaps it's like the Crystal Palace," mused Thomas, discarding an imperfect rail and reaching for another. "You should see the Crystal Palace. There's nothing in New York to match London. Not but what I suppose New York is all right in its way," he added in fairness. Suddenly Thomas felt proud that he had a wife and daughters who knew their way about New York.

"Of course your mother will have to visit a few days with Agnes before she returns," he added, looking quickly at Will.

"Oh, Agnes!" said Will, a shrug in his voice.

Thomas smiled at Will's back, as his son kneeled to get at a difficult joint. So Will did not know, or if he did know, could not understand what it would mean to have the first child of another generation in the family, even though its name would not be Stapely. Thomas felt vindicated somehow, as though he had won a point. Then he remembered harsh and coarse things he had said before his son, such things as he had not said or thought for many years, and was ashamed.

"Watch what you're doing, boy!" he ordered brusquely, and stepped across to give the rail Will had been adjusting two hard raps with a heavy mallet he had picked up in place of his hammer. "This fence has got to stand a year or two. Do you want the first wind to take it down?"

Will leaped angrily to his feet. He had been doing all right.

"If you think you can do any better—" he started to say. Then he saw his father's shamed face and smiled. "All right, Pa," he said.

The helper had started back toward them. He was a chunky boy of sixteen or eighteen with a stupid, pimply face.

"You can knock off now and go back to the shop, Harry," Thomas told him. "Light the lanterns first so some fool doesn't fall into one of the holes tonight. It's near quitting time."

"Is it?" asked Will, genuinely surprised. He looked at his watch, held by a leather thong to the breast pocket of his overalls.

"You wouldn't, I suppose," asked Thomas humbly, "be going to St. Mark's with me tonight?"

Will shook his head.

"I'm going riding with Jim Garver."

About to enter his senior year at Yale, Jim was home for his last college vacation. Several times he and Will had taken a pair of the Garvers' saddle horses out for evening exercise. Each time they had raced down a country road, and each time, no matter which horse he sat, Will had won. He loved it.

"But I will go with you, Pa," he added virtuously. "I'll go next week."

"That I've heard before," said Thomas grimly.

Chapter 28

MARY HAD BEEN GONE so long that the return to Ilium seemed to her like another adventure. She got off the train bright-eyed and alert. Emily, pale but smiling, followed her. Thomas met them. He was unsmiling. His kiss was cold reproof as he took their bags, arranged at the express office to have their heavier luggage carted to the hill, and herded them aboard a streetcar.

Mary looked delightedly about her.

"It's so good to get home!" she enthused. "Everything looks so familiar and so nice."

"Ilium's not changed much," said Thomas dryly.

Emily smiled covertly, but Mary had seen people she knew in the car and was bowing to them. A woman smiled widely, and a man tipped his hat. Mrs. Roller was excited. She could hardly wait until she got home to tell the neighbors that Mrs. Stapely was home again and about time!

Thomas glowered at her, as if he suspected her intentions, and Mrs. Roller looked guiltily away. Her husband fidgeted. He thought Thomas was looking at him, and he wondered how he had incurred Tom Stapely's displeasure. He did not want that any more than did anyone else in South Ilium. The set look on Thomas' face caused him to urge his wife off the car two stops before their street, much to her shrill annoyance.

"Agnes is very well," Mary told Thomas, "and sent her love. James and Laura were both down with the heat, but they are better now. James has bought a whole new set of harness. I went to New York with him and helped him pick it out. Laura is *so* clever. She can do anything."

"So James says," observed Thomas unpleasantly.

Again, Emily caught the note of irony in her father's voice and wished she could warn her mother, but Mary prattled on, at the same time retaining her ladylike demeanor for the rest of the passengers.

"Agnes and I went shopping for a hood and bonnet for the baby, and Emily has brought a comfortable which she is going to work. Is Julia better? I've thought of her so often. There were not as many chances to write as I'd hoped, but I knew you would tell her the news. Did you know that Emily will have six music scholars to begin right after the first of September? What with her own lessons she will be very busy. That's why I insisted she come home for a rest now."

She was the finest looking lady in the car, in the whole of Ilium. Thomas was proud of her. He was happy that she was back. The house on the hill would be itself again, but Thomas' anger had been building up too long. Mary had written in this and that letter that she was not feeling well. Apparently she was in the best of health and spirits. She had enjoyed herself away from him—probably scarcely thought of him.

"I hope you will enjoy your visit home," he said.

Mary, who had decided, as soon as she saw his face, to ignore his evident annoyance, changed pace swiftly without disturbing the demurely smiling face she showed the car.

"Well, this is a very cold reception, I must say!"

Thomas did not answer. He was frightened now at what he had said.

"You know very well that I have been only too anxious to get home but was forced to stay in New York by Emily's illness and then by—other things."

Thomas continued to sulk, though he did not mean to. He had gone too far. He did not know how to mend matters.

Emily tried to help. "When is St. Mark's excursion, Pa?" she said. "I know it's not been yet, and I want to go if I'm still here."

It was the wrong thing to say. Thomas could safely speak sharply to his daughter.

"Do you think of nothing but your own pleasure?" he asked grimly.

"Well, I never!" gasped Mary, certain the shaft had been directed at her.

They were at the foot of the hill. Thomas pulled the signal cord sharply, and the driver halted his horses. The remaining passengers watched enviously as they got off. Tom Stapely must still be doing well for his wife and daughter to be in New York most of the time and to wear clothes like that.

They walked silently up the hill, Thomas angrily checking his quick strides so as not to outdistance Mary, who was walking with difficulty to show that she was tired and not at all well.

"It was the funniest thing you ever saw, Will," Emily told him as soon as she could see him alone. "Here was Ma hardly able to drag herself along"—she imitated their mother, slipping a resigned expression across the vitality of her face and masking her eyes with a lack-lustre vacuity—"and here was Pa so angry"—Emily clenched her white teeth—"he could have choked. I ain't had so much fun sence the hawgs et mah little sister!"

"What? What did you say?"

"Oh, it's something Andrew says."

"But I thought you were supposed to be sick!"

"I was sick enough," said Emily grimly, "but it wasn't what Ma thought. I put Andrew on the *City of New York* and then just stood there and watched the tugs push her out into the river. Then I went home and bawled my eyes out. I went to bed and I didn't give a damn if I never got up. That's what it was."

"Oh."

"Oh!" mimicked Emily. "Yes, I know, and I know everything anyone can say—everyone except you—but that's the way it is, and I can't help it."

"But where's his wife?"

Emily made another face.

"Home, I suppose. She's always there or in a sanitarium some-where. Andrew won't talk about her. She's supposed to be very ill. How can any woman be ill with Andrew there?" she demanded, as though the structure of logic had been strained.

Will looked troubled. Then his face cleared.

"St. Mark's excursion next week, Em. Jim Garver's home and he's going with us. He's coming over tonight. You'll like him!"

Emily grimaced, unseen by Will. She was no more interested in Jim Garver than she was in any other man, young, old, black, white, rich man, beggar man, or thief, except Andrew.

"The iron works had their excursion last week. They had the big

Argonaut herself. Half South Ilium went. I almost went myself." Will began to laugh.

"You should have seen it when the stove factory had theirs! They rolled barrels of beer on board in the mornings. When they came back, a gang of them rolled Big Mike Connors down the gangplank. They claimed all the beer was in him. They were all drunk, and Big Mike was too drunk to care!"

Will smiled happily as he remembered the splash when Mike Connors rolled into the water of the dock. It was only a few feet deep there and filled with garbage off the canal and river boats. Gasping and choking, Big Mike had clambered up all the banana skins and mud and waved to the cheering crowd.

Emily laughed too.

"And come here!" Will ordered. He led Emily to the old shop where they had once hid from James's wrath.

What he had to show her was a wall cabinet, twenty inches long and eighteen high, which he had almost finished. The door was of diamond-shaped panes of leaded glass, as were the sides. The inside of the back was an oblong of beveled plate-glass mirror, and the one shelf was of heavy glass.

"It's solid mahogany," said Will proudly. "I've still the beadwork to put on. Then I'll get August to help me stain and rub it down and polish it."

"It *is* nice," agreed Emily, rubbing the smooth wood. "What are you going to do with it?"

"Give it to you to match the rosewood sideboard Mr. Gray got you," said Will offhandedly.

Emily hugged his shoulders hard in a spontaneous embrace.

"Oh, Will! James is so busy and has let himself get so damned married, though he doesn't know it himself, and Agnes is so damned silly about her 'delicate condition,' though I suppose I shouldn't make fun of her. Ma's having the time of her life. And I'm going mad!"

"When does Mr. Gray come home?"

"I don't know! I don't know! He was only going to be gone six weeks, but he's been ill at his brother's house in London, and he's still there. Oh, it's horrible, Will! But I won't get sick again. I won't! It wears you out." Emily frowned.

Will kept watching her face. Andrew Gray had no right to make Emily unhappy. He'd change that! His own spirits had risen from the moment she appeared. He felt sure of himself again, as he used to feel when he and Emily raced about South Ilium.

They were still in the shop when Jim Garver appeared early that long summer evening.

After introducing them gaily, Will turned away to rub fussily at what the sunlight slanting in from the west made appear a rough spot in the smoothly sanded wood of the cabinet.

Jim Garver, quiet as always in dress and manner, seemed suddenly awkward and diffident. It was to put him at his ease that Emily spoke. "You are Will's best friend."

Jim looked at her. "No, you are," he said. He looked quickly away as if he felt that he had been staring. He looked at her again. "And you are very beautiful," he said. He flushed and was silent.

"Thank you," said Emily surprised. She looked at him curiously.

Jim flushed more deeply. "I didn't mean to sound impertinent."

"You didn't. You sounded very nice."

"Jim knows all about you, Em," said Will without looking up. He had got a fresh piece of emery paper and was rubbing lightly at the offending spot. He stepped back to look for other flaws in his work.

"All?" asked Emily lightly.

"I think it would take a very long time to know all about you," said Jim quietly. "I came really to tell Will that I shan't be able to go on the St. Mark's excursion after all."

"He'll be disappointed," said Emily. Will had gone to the littered bench to rummage for something.

"No more than I. Perhaps—may I come to see you sometimes?"

"I'm not often here."

"But when you are?" Jim's gray eyes were intent.

"If you like."

Will came back, wiping his hands on a handful of cotton waste. He tossed it toward a cluttered corner of the shop. He laughed, not at them or at what they had been saying, or at anything in particular, but because he was happy.

"Let's go for a walk somewhere," he urged, "before Pa wants me to do something, or Ma does or Aunt Maria or Aunt Julia or Carlo or somebody!"

It was not so gay and golden inside the house on the hill. Thomas was in a quandary. He had shown his resentment and now could not pretend that he had not or gracefully relent. His pride demanded that he maintain his position, though he was not sure what it was. Mary was determined to teach him a lesson by paying no attention to him. Julia was frightened. Her voice, always weak and strangely girlish, startled her by breaking into unexpected squeaks. Maria, her brother's self-appointed protector, was baleful-eyed, grim-lipped, and silent. Yet they were all trying to act as though nothing was the matter.

Mary had presents for them all, Irish linen handkerchiefs for Thomas, a white lawn collar of the latest pattern for Julia's best dress, a pair of grey silk gloves for Maria. Thomas spoke his thanks gruffly and went into the other room. The women exclaimed prettily over the gifts.

Then everything went flat. Mary seethed with righteous indignation. To be treated so in her own home! Thomas felt bitterly that they had all connived to put him in the wrong. Maria congratulated herself that for once Mrs. Mary Stapely was getting just what she deserved. Julia, shrinking into her sensitiveness, wished that she were home in England.

"He has been cross ever since James was here!" she managed to whisper to Mary in the kitchen.

"Because he is cross with James is no reason for his being cross with everybody!" snapped Mary. She went to the back door and looked into the yard. "My goodness!" she exclaimed in vexed tones. "My garden has not been weeded since I left! Look at my roses! And the lily bed is simply choked."

"I certainly have had no time to weed the garden!" snapped Maria. "What with getting the meals and doing the mending and washing and keeping the house clean I've had more than enough to do."

"But I've tried to help, Maria," said Julia piteously. "You know I've not been well, but I've tried—"

"H'mph!" sniffed Maria.

Mary turned on her.

"I'm sure," she said coldly, "that Julia has done more than her fair share. After all, she was not brought up to be a servant."

"A servant!" cried Maria. "I may not have been born and brought up in a big house and able to lord it over everyone, but—"

"That will be enough, Maria," said Thomas sharply as he came into the kitchen.

"I might have known that if I were not here to attend to things myself," said Mary, "everything would be neglected."

"Why, Mary," said Julia, surprised. "Maria and I swept and dusted all day yesterday getting ready for you. I'm sure everything is spotless."

The truth was that the house was in better order than it would have been had Mary been home. She had noticed it as soon as she entered, and seen it as a rebuke cunningly planned by Maria.

"I hardly expected my own sister to side against me," she said coolly.

"Oh, Mary, I'm not siding against you at all. I don't see how you can say that," said Julia with unexpected spirit.

Maria looked triumphantly at Thomas.

"We'll have no more of this," he said sternly to them all.

No one paid any attention.

"I, for one," said Maria, "was afraid to touch your precious garden, and I'm sure Julia felt the same way."

"I'd have done it if I'd thought of it," Julia said apologetically.

Ostentatiously, Mary moved the tea caddy from where it stood on the shelf to a position six inches away. She changed the position of the fresh tea cloths hanging neatly on a rack behind the door.

"Of course, Will had no time for weeding," said Maria spitefully. "He's far too busy with his girls and his picnics and anything else he can find to keep him away from home. Arthur has not been on a picnic this summer."

"Nor has Arthur earned his keep all summer," said Thomas. "Now let there be an end to this! I'll weed the garden tomorrow."

"I shall do it myself the first thing in the morning," said Mary. "I had hoped to rest after my journey, but I see that can't be."

Thomas, badgered and exasperated, started to speak, thought better of it, and walked heavily out of the room.

Maria capitulated, dangerously.

"We shall have to call on Cousin Harriet very soon. She has been very ill. The doctors almost gave her up. The heat was too much for her. I should never forgive myself if she died and I had not called. Blanche has been so brave and uncomplaining through it all."

Grateful for the truce, Mary hurried to agree.

"We must all go. I made up my mind in New York that it was one of the first things I should do when I got home. I can work in my garden in the morning and we'll go in the afternoon."

As it happened, no one worked in the garden the next day, for it rained steadily. The weeds stayed until frost killed them along with the last purple asters. But the rain did not interfere with their promised visit to Blanche and Cousin Harriet.

Before three o'clock the three women started down the hill, wearing dark cloaks, holding tight to their umbrellas and clutching their skirts firmly to keep them from dragging in the mud.

Blanche greeted them effusively, making a great fuss over Julia, and making solicitous inquiry of Mary for the health of all the family in New York. She shook her head meaningfully and whispered dark forebodings before she let them tiptoe from the parlor into the room where Cousin Harriet lay propped up in a huge oak bed. She was very white and thin. A thousand wrinkles showed in the old face, and the flesh hung in folds at her scrawny neck. She had been asleep. She opened her eyes and surveyed them vacantly. Then her eyes focussed.

"Don't tiptoe around," she said.

"It's Maria and Julia, Mother!" cried Blanche gaily. "And Mary is with them."

"I thought she was in New York again, or still there," said Cousin Harriet, looking slowly at Mary.

"I just came home last night," said Mary softly, "and came right over to see you."

"How many children does Agnes have?" asked Cousin Harriet frowning.

"Why, none, Cousin Harriet, though—"

"That's enough," said the old lady firmly. "Too many children around are a nuisance."

Maria and Blanche looked pityingly at each other.

Suddenly the old woman laughed. "I know what you said," she announced. "It was a joke. Blanche never knows a joke. She's too good to joke. Tell Willy to come and see me. He's the only one of you has much sense. You're too thin," she told Julia. "Men won't look at you unless you get some flesh on your bones."

Julia colored.

"I thought you were ill," said Mary reproachfully. "You're as well as I am. And I'm very glad."

Cousin Harriet looked at her unblinkingly.

"I'm sick enough," she said after a moment. "I'm old, and I don't like it."

"But she's so much better," trilled Blanche, hurrying across the room and expertly patting the pillow, set upright on the bolster behind the old woman. "She's so much better, aren't you, Mother?" She hovered efficiently.

"Go get the tea ready," her mother ordered.

"It is ready," said Blanche, smiling at the others.

"Then go boil it or strain it or do something. Take Maria with you. You always have your heads together anyway. I don't know what you find to talk about so much!" She watched them go out of the room, saw Maria's pursed lips as she smiled too sweetly at Mary.

"Look here, young lady," Cousin Harriet said distinctly, as soon as she was sure the others were gone, "you're not behaving yourself properly."

Taken aback, Mary looked her surprise.

"Now don't try that innocent look on me," said Cousin Harriet. "You're neglecting Thomas, and I know you are."

"Why, Thomas is all right!" said Mary, her face flushed.

"He's not all right. Take a look at him. You're neglecting him, and he feels it. And Thomas is a good man. I've known him since he was a boy—known the both of you since you were children."

There was no way Mary could talk back to Cousin Harriet. She looked at Julia, who embarrassed, looked hastily away.

"Now, now, Cousin Harriet," said Mary soothingly. "Just you lie still. Close your eyes and see if you can't rest a little."

"Nonsense!" said Cousin Harriet. "It's no use your trying to soft-soap me. It just looks to me as if you don't care anything about Thomas at all, as long as you can gad about New York. Thomas is a fine man."

"Don't you think I know that?" asked Mary stiffly.

The old woman looked at her reflectively.

"I don't think you're acting as though you know it," she said.

Both Mary and Julia were very red of face. Mary strove for composure.

"You're being unfair, Cousin Harriet," she said.

Cousin Harriet closed her old eyes firmly. "I'm not listening," she said, tightening her lips.

Mary and Julia stood there a moment.

"She's asleep," whispered Mary as Maria and Blanche came quietly back. Maria's eyes were glittering.

"But I'll have my tea just the same," said Cousin Harriet without opening her eyes.

Chapter 29

THE HOUSEHOLD was up at dawn the morning of the excursion. Thomas, who had shaved so closely that his face was pink, was roaring about in a fine stew. He could not find something. Will did not know what it was. As senior warden and virtual commander of the whole expedition in the continued absence of the rector, Thomas had heavy responsibilities and scores of last-minute details to attend to.

Mary and Maria were busily putting up more lunch than any of them could possibly eat, storing sandwiches and hard-boiled eggs in half a dozen shoe boxes carefully saved for the occasion. Julia was trying her best to get all their dresses laid out and ready. Will was scrambling into his new clothes to go to North Ilium for Edith. Her mother and father were coming too. Emily was out in the sunshine of the back yard vigorously brushing her hair. The sun was already pouring down on the fields. It promised to be a glorious day.

Three special cars were going to take them all from St. Mark's corner. More were going in wagons filled with straw, lent the church by the iron works. Others would get to the dock by whatever means they could. A whole block of South Avenue was in a magnificent uproar, with scrubbed and polished children racing in and out among harried adults dressed in their Sunday best. Girls were ostentatiously laughing with each other and ignoring two groups of young men who were studiously pretending complete unawareness of their existence.

Mothers tried to fasten fallen hair ribbons on small girls and get their husbands to find small boys and make them pull up their stockings. Conscientious Sunday-school teachers were striving desperately to line up their classes while black-coated dignitaries like Thomas worked hard to get some kind of order into the confusion. Straw-hatted car drivers, who had been doing this sort of thing all summer, grinned as they watched, and their horses champed lazily on the last of the oats in their feed bags.

The drivers began to clang the bells of their cars and families scrambled to get aboard. Well-wishers from other churches which had already had their excursions were waving and shouting them on, and the good-natured Irish called out their greetings or sent little Michael scurrying after a St. Mark's neighbor with an extra bag of candies for the young ones or a freshly baked cake for a surprise. Weeks and months of expectation were being materialized. They all knew that the white barge was waiting at the dock in Ilium, and the Hudson was running blue with gold-flecked waves, and the swings and base-ball diamond and beach and lemonade and popcorn stands were waiting two hours up the river at Sandy Point.

Somehow everybody got aboard the cars or the wagons. Thomas stood beside the driver of the first, impressive in his black suit and fresh linen, but his face alight like any of the children's. He did not know where Mary and Maria and Julia were, but he knew they were somewhere aboard, and he had not seen Will at all, but he thanked God for the beautiful day and silently asked His blessing on the whole parish. St. Mark's owned South Ilium that morning as the children in one car sang lustily and those in the others stuck their heads out of the open windows of their cars and screamed and shouted their happiness.

At the dock order was somehow obtained, and they sang *Praise God from whom all blessings flow,* and then Thomas, with hand upraised, prayed for their safe return. Will kept his eyes open to look down at Edith whose head was bowed, her dark hair gleaming in the sun. His bright tan shoes were already dusty. Surreptitiously he rubbed the toe of one against the other trouser leg.

A deckhand each side of the gangplank herded them in, grabbing intoxicated children who would have stepped off into the water in their excitement, and steering them in. Thomas, the captain, came aboard last. The gangplank was drawn up, the ropes were cast off. The barge drifted slowly to midstream as children hooted and howled in a transport of ecstasy. The engines caught, the paddle wheels churned, the steam whistle tooted noisily, and they headed upstream, the morning breezes whipping against their faces, and the good sun shining as it had never shone before.

Will played ball that morning with energy and fervor. Edith was looking on, and Edith was not the only girl he was trying to impress. Nor was Will the only boy arch Edith wanted to have see her watching and gracefully lounging with her companions.

When the game was over, Will's side having won by a single run, they were in a fine lather of sweat. Amid great laughter as to where they were going and what they were going to do, the boys trooped off around a bend out of sight, found a likely cove, stripped, and splashed into the water, dog-paddling and ducking each other, skipping stones, and racing until they had hardly enough strength left to put their clothes back on over half-dried bodies. They raced back just as the lunches had been set out on the long picnic tables and ate ravenously.

Will found Emily with Edith, and to all intents they were getting along fine. Somehow he felt relieved. His aunts were spreading out their cloth and setting out the plates of sandwiches and cakes, the pickles, the fruits, the boiled eggs. His mother, he could see, was off talking to some friends.

"Two prettiest girls in the place!" he said stoutly.

"Try getting your breath first, Will," Emily laughed. "You've used up enough energy already for a dozen excursions."

"Haven't begun yet!" he boasted.

Emily, who had been sitting with her skirts spread out around her on the grass, stood up to help Mary, who had returned and begun to serve the lunch. Thomas came back leading two other vestrymen, properly sober-faced before Mr. and Mrs. Stapely. One of their wives was fat and beaming; the other, thin and peering near-sightedly.

"What did you mean you haven't begun yet?" asked Edith softly.

"Oh, lots of things," said Will, who had not meant anything at all. His pulse began to beat fast. "Why?"

Edith fluttered her eyelids expertly.

"Oh, nothing," she said significantly. "Thank you," she said to Emily, who handed her a filled plate.

"Here, eat yourself sick," said Emily, handing a plate heaped twice as high to Will.

She was among her own family and among people she had known all her life and most of whom she liked. Yet she felt so lonely she could hardly bear it. She knew them, but they did not know her. Even her mother did not know her; only Will understood her a little perhaps. Where was Andrew, she wondered, right then, right that minute? Was he thinking of her? She could not visualize his surroundings, hard as she tried. She could not share his thoughts and feelings any more than she could openly share his life. She could never openly share his life. That was one of the things she had realized after he had left and she went through the first awful days alone.

"What, Pa?" she asked.

"Are you enjoying yourself, Emily?" her father asked. He was smiling at her almost tenderly. The others were looking at her and smiling.

"I said 'a penny for your thoughts,' " said Mary, "but you didn't hear me."

Emily smiled at them all and began talking quickly to the near-sighted woman who was sitting next to her on one of the green benches. The woman began telling at length of her sister's daughter who was in New York—such a lovely girl—learning to be a type-writer. She, too, was a piano player.

Emily smiled at the woman until her face ached, then sought excuse to wander off to join some girls she knew. Later, after the one-legged race and the egg-and-spoon race, and the married men's race, and the fat man's race, she lay back on the soft grass and looked through the high branches of interlacing oak trees into the blue depths of the sky. The shouts of those at play in the swings or playing catch in the field came distantly and musically. Even the voices of her father and mother seated nearby were an indistinct and pleasant murmur.

They were talking in low tones. It was impossible for rancor to survive the happiness about them and the beauty of the setting, the sweet mildness of the late summer day.

"I missed you, m'girl," said Thomas almost shyly.

"And I missed you, Thomas. You know I'd not willingly be apart from you." Mary smiled at him, and Thomas saw the girl he had courted so many years before.

"I know, Mary," he said.

"We'll just forget the last few days. We've all been very silly."

"Yes," said Thomas. Then he added suddenly. "I wish we could go home."

Mary laughed. "The boat won't be going for hours."

"No, no," said Thomas slowly. "I meant *home*—to the Forest of Dean."

A dozen of them, girls and older boys and young men, were playing catch with a large soft rubber ball. It came their way, and both Will and Edith scrambled for it. They missed and fell laughing in a heap in the deep grass, both reaching for the ball which someone else snatched and tossed back.

Edith clung merrily to Will, and he tried to break her hold by reaching out to tickle her. She clung tighter, and Will crushed the girl against him in a sudden fierce shock that struck and almost overpowered him. Edith's hair brushed across his neck and face. He closed his eyes, and the sun struck blood red through his eyelids. Dazed, he pushed her from him and sprang to his feet.

Edith laughed, brushed out her skirts, and raced off calling, "Throw it to me! Throw it to me!"

The violence of his own desire did not frighten Will as much as the girl's response. He could do as he liked with Edith! He knew now what, with mingled fascination and dread, he had been almost certain of before. He wanted her; but ignorance, inexperience, fear embarrassed him and he wanted to escape.

He avoided Edith for the rest of the afternoon, and on the way home on the boat stayed close to Emily. Boys, enfevered from the day's excitement, were chasing each other around the deck. Small children, tired and sated with food, slept in their mothers' arms. Groups of men and women chatted idly, some singing softly. Old men and women dozed, smiling vaguely or drooling in their sleep.

Once when Will and Emily passed by in the gathering dusk, Edith's eyes laughed out at him from where she leaned against the rail surrounded by boys. Will flushed hotly. His new shoes pinched, and his shoulders were fiery with the sunburn he had got swimming. He was not to see her soon again. Edith and her family moved away from Ilium.

Will and Emily climbed to the upper deck and stood in the prow of the boat, a streamer pennant whipping in the breeze over their heads. The setting sun threw a rainbow against the darkening water ahead of them, and the hills and church spires of the city, still miles away, lay in a soft blue haze edged with the brilliant last light of day.

"It's lovely!" breathed Emily. "Lovely!" She felt she had no right to enjoy such beauty without Andrew with her to share it.

Chapter 30

AGNES HAD BEEN the center of attention for weeks that autumn. Stapely intimates in South Ilium knew all about it and friends had inquired of Mary and Thomas even at old Mr. Wheeler's funeral. Soon after that, Will had been sent down to the express office with a package containing the embroidered baby blanket Mary had made, the pretty nightgown for Agnes which Julia had sewn, and the crocheted baby cap and bootees from Maria.

Mary had come down to Mott Haven weeks before the expected birth to look after her daughter. She found Agnes blooming and beatified. She told Mary, in almost the same words the visiting Baptist minister had used, of her blessedness and glory as a woman chosen of God to bring one of His angels to earth.

Soon firmly ensconsed as a member of the household, Mary comforted the swollen Agnes and helped practically by visiting and talking with patients who waited their turn to see Dr. Richards. Agnes' greatest worry was not her own condition but that, unless suitably entertained, some patient might escape while, unfit for public view, she had to sit helpless in the basement. It was why she had asked her mother to come so early.

So grateful was Agnes for her mother's crucial help and for her own sanctified role that in a moment of fear and tears she had her mother try on the handsome opera cloak Allan had given her, and told her as they hugged one another that if she died she wanted Mary to have it. The rest of her clothes she wanted to go to the deserving poor, and her prayer book to her father.

Now Agnes was invisible somewhere upstairs, about to produce the new being. Of them all, she alone was in a position of power. She could add to the sum total of humanity. Through her one of the heavenly host was about to assume human form for a few short years. The "little stranger" as she called it, "the baby" as her mother called it, "the child" as Emily called it, would be the first Stapely of the new generation. Thomas, in South Ilium, hoped it would be a boy. Allan hoped for a girl. He gave no reason for his odd choice, for Allan seldom gave reasons for anything. Instead, he disappeared to market and brought more dainties which he thought might appeal to his wife and guests.

Agnes, her homely face transfigured, faced her ordeal with joy and Christian resignation. Just as Emily liked to be told of her resemblance to Lillian Russell, Agnes liked to be compared to Queen Victoria, her ideal as Christian woman, loyal helpmeet, empress, and mother. She hoped she would bear her trial with the goodness and fortitude shown for more than fifty-five years by her idol.

Mary and Emily took practical advantage of the situation.

Aided by Ellen, whom Emily brought up with her from 19th Street, they donned aprons, wrapped tea cloths about their heads, and went furiously to work. They mopped and scrubbed, swept, and dusted. They all liked Allan and intended to see that for once he could come home to a clean, sweet-smelling house. They had themselves endured more than they could stand of Agnes' housekeeping, but been helpless as long as she was about.

Allan, grateful but unable through loyalty to his wife to comment, joined them in the early afternoon in a great hunt for roaches. They routed eighty-three of them from under the kitchen sink and behind the icebox, slaying them with brooms and wadded newspapers, and sprinkling a yellow sulphur powder in dirty, damp corners.

"Lend the powder here!" cried Emily, who was on her hands and knees, her face smeared with dust and her apron a ruin of dirt and grease. Squinting and wrinkling her nose, she shook powder liberally about the trap and drains in the darkness under the sink. She filled cracks and crevices in the floor. She pointed to a mouse hole. "This must be where the roaches march in from next door!" she decided, and even Allan was forced to laugh at Agnes' oft-repeated fiction.

He swatted another roach that was scurrying for cover.

"Eighty-four," he counted, then swooped for another big one. "Eighty-five!"

Mary was swiping down the ceiling with a cloth tied over the head of her broom. The grease came off in streaks. She looked her disgust. Her shoulders ached, and she was getting short of breath. She had to stop. She leaned on her broom like one of Thomas' navvies leaning on his shovel.

Emily's clout of newspapers descended again, again, again.

"We'll quit at an even hundred!" she called to Allan. "O-oh!" she made a face and clambered painfully to her feet. "You are going to have to treat me for housemaid's knee, Allan, when we get through this. Agnes all right?"

The attending doctor, a ridiculously tall and solemn-visaged friend of Allan's, had been in again and just gone.

Allan nodded soberly. If he was nervous, only the slight flush on his rather heavy face showed it.

"I'm going upstairs again," Mary announced. "Poor Agnes!" she added softly.

Will strolled self-consciously into the kitchen. Ellen had let him in upstairs. He was dressed in his best suit and carried a bowler hat. Staying at Emily's apartment, he had spent most of the morning dressing, and his entrance created a sensation. Emily nodded approval. Observant Will had learned quickly.

"Rich but not gaudy!" she commented. "Now take them off and get a broom."

"Think another think, Emily," he told her. "I'm on holiday, remember. I'm going to the rest of the Columbus celebration. You should see the crowds downtown!"

Immediately Mary wished she could go too, knew regretfully that she could not.

"Do you think you should," she asked, "with Agnes upstairs as she is?"

"What difference can that make?" asked Will surprised. South Ilium was always full of babies.

He looked uneasily at Allan. The idea that any man should want Agnes and that this should be the result was a little hard to believe. He felt awed and embarrassed.

"Hello, Allan," he said. "Well—uh—good luck."

"Uh—thanks," said Allan. "I'll get you something to eat."

"No thanks, I'm off," Will refused. " 'Bye, everybody. 'Bye!"

"Have a good time!" Emily called after him. "Allan, there's another! Get him quick! Oh, he's getting away! Good! Mother, give me your broom."

But Mary had gone upstairs again. She kept running up and down. A moustached and efficient practical nurse was with Agnes, but Mary did not trust her. Allan had gone into the dining room and was looking through the barred windows into the deserted street. Everyone seemed to have gone downtown to the celebration.

Emily made a face and, to ease her knees, sat on the floor. She couldn't get dirtier than she was. She sat there a moment.

Mary came hurrying back, and Emily raised her eyebrows in question.

Mary shook her head. "Not yet."

"Just like Agnes to keep everyone on edge! Call Ellen, and we'll get at the upstairs parlor."

Stubbornly, Agnes refused to ease the situation. By nine o'clock that night her child was still unborn. Mary and Allan had been upstairs and down innumerable times. The impossibly long and thin doctor had faded in and out again. Allan was beginning to look gray.

Mary was thriving on the tense expectancy. Emily's knees were raw and she felt bent and twisted out of shape by the reckless scrubbing and cleaning. She was sleepy.

The three of them sat silently about the dining room table in the basement front room.

"Is anything wrong?" asked Emily, suddenly fearful.

"Now, now, Emily!" her mother chided. "Of course nothing is wrong." She smiled understandingly at Allan.

"Then why doesn't it come?" demanded Emily.

Allan smiled ruefully, his face a dull red now from trying to repress him emotions, his eyes troubled.

"Is it always like this?" insisted Emily.

"Sometimes," he said. He looked at his watch again and moved his feet.

"Now, Allan," Mary told her doctor son-in-law firmly, "there is nothing to be uneasy about. Agnes is a very healthy girl, and she should have no trouble at all. Poor, poor girl!"

"It might not be till morning," admitted Allan. "Dr. Collins was not sure."

"Not till morning!" exclaimed Emily. "I'm never going to have any babies if it is all this bother."

"Emily! You must not say things like that."

"Allan's a doctor," laughed Emily. She reached a sudden decision. "I can't stand any more of this. If it's not likely to be till tomorrow, I'm going home. I'll leave Ellen here, and you can send for me if you need me. Otherwise I'll come back the first thing in the morning."

"You can't go alone this time of night."

"Oh, I want to be in at the—" Emily stopped herself in time. She had started to say "at the death." It would hardly sound right. "I'll be all right," she said. "The streets will still be full of people. The parade probably isn't over yet."

"I'll go part way with her," said Allan quickly. He seemed glad of the diversion.

"Well, I never!" exclaimed Mary indignantly.

The Columbus parade was over, at least had moved far uptown, but the littered streets, as Emily had foreseen, were still jammed with people milling about, laughing, talking, shouting, blowing tin horns. Four hundred years since Columbus discovered America. You couldn't say that every day. People did not want to go home. Good old New York! Good old Columbus!

A little nervous after Allan had left her despite her protestations, Emily hurried up West 19th Street, holding her skirts gathered in her right hand so that she could move quickly along. She let herself into her flat and felt relieved as she closed the door behind her. There was no light, which meant that Will was still out. She wished now she had gone with him.

She found a match in the kitchen and lighted the gas jet in her bedroom. The gas caught with its usual mild explosion and the yellow-tipped blue flame threw flickering light and shadow about the pretty room. Emily lifted her arm and began to unhook her dress at the side. Then she remembered that Will would be in and pulling a wrapper on over the half unfastened dress, began to pull the pins out of her hair. When she was tired, its weight always began to feel insupportable. She shook her hair loose, picked up a silver-backed brush from the set that had been a birthday present from the family, and began to brush vigorously. She was just finishing plaiting it in two long braids, when there was a sharp knock at the door. Probably Will. Emily wound the braids about her head and tied them quickly.

The impatient knock was repeated before she could hurry up the hall.

"That you, Will?" she asked cautiously.

"It's me, you idiot," a thick voice answered.

Emily felt alarmed. Then she thought it might be someone mistaking her door for another.

"Em, open the door!" This time she recognized the voice and, startled, yanked back the bolt and turned the door handle.

"James!"

" 'Bout time you let me in," he said coldly. "Been looking for the place for half an hour." Then he looked at her and grinned wryly. "How are you, Em?"

"James, what are you doing here?" Emily closed the door behind them and James walked, a little unsteadily, ahead of her into the front room. She hurried to light a lamp.

"Don't sound so delighted to see me," James cautioned her. He tipped his silk hat back on his forehead and sat down in a big chair, stretching his legs out before him. His boots were dusty.

"I've just come in," Emily explained. "Agnes is having her baby."

James shoved his hands into his trousers' pockets and laughed.

"Just what the world needs," he said, nodding profoundly, "another Agnes."

Emily laughed.

"Whatever happened between you and Agnes?"

James considered, thrusting out his lower lip in a way that made his pointed beard stick out too. He looked unseeingly at Emily.

"I just don't like stupid people," he said finally. "World's full of 'em too. Columbus discovered America, so four hundred years later a million lunatics go crazy on the streets."

"Oh, you went to the parade! Will's out somewhere."

"Watched it awhile," James admitted. "Stood over by the reservoir on 42nd and Fifth. Big stand there full of schoolgirls singing silly songs. Went over to the river and looked at the *Santa Maria* and the other two. Stopped in and had a couple of drinks."

"Or three," said Emily.

"Or four," said James equably. "Got anything around, Em? I could use another." He sighed, and his big shoulders drooped. "Tired," he said.

Emily hesitated, then decided. "Andrew has some whiskey here. I'll get it."

"Fine." James closed his eyes as Emily started for the kitchen. He did not open them until she thrust a small glass into his hand.

James looked at it, sniffed it, and nodded approvingly. "RX," he said. "Dr. Stapely. *Spiritus frumenti.* One quart before meals." He drained the glass, shuddered, held it out again, and Emily refilled it.

James looked at her shrewdly.

"How about you?" he asked.

Emily smiled, and shook her head. "No, thanks."

James shrugged and sipped at the small glass. He sighed appreciatively and stretched. "Walked miles," he said. His eyes were clouding.

"Have you eaten anything?"

James did not answer for a moment. When he did, it was as though he had recalled something spoken some time before.

"No," he decided. "Not interested in eating." He waved his glass, reached across for the decanter which Emily had set down, and refilled it again.

"Laura know where you are?" she asked suddenly.

James looked at her slyly and shook his head. "No," he said triumphantly.

Emily was watching him curiously, her face relaxed in a little smile. "What's wrong, James?"

"Wrong?" asked James thoughtfully. His eyes moved back into focus. He finished his glass, spoke vehemently. "Not a thing. Just tired, bored, sick of—sick of everything. Sick of patients, sick of toeing the mark, sick of myself. Told Laura I was going to make a call—ha!"

"You're making one," said Emily kindly. "I'll play patient. You'd better lie down. I'll clear the things off this sofa."

"Shtay here," said James stubbornly.

"No, lie down," urged Emily. She stood up and walked toward him. "You'll feel better."

James leaned coyly back in his chair. "Shtay here," he repeated. "Won' lie down."

"Come, James," said Emily sharply. "You need a good rest."

James looked at her owlishly, then his eyes wandered foolishly about the room. He stared at a Dresden figurine on the mantel and began to frown. He put his right hand to his face and began to bite thoughtfully at his thumbnail. Then he looked back at Emily.

"Agnesh' baby here yet?" he demanded.

"Not yet, James," said Emily good-humoredly. Poor James! So sometimes it was all too much for him too!

"H'mph," said James. "Tell it to wait outside. Haven't time now." Will burst in.

"You should have been along, Em, it was something!" he cried. "Band after band! A dozen regiments in full dress! Floats, millions of school kids. Torchlights, fireworks—"

"S'sh!" Emily put her fingers to her lips and indicated James in his chair.

James saluted him gravely and bowed without speaking.

Will looked at him, his eyes wide. "Is Agnes—" he began fearfully. "Agnes isn't—"

"Agnes is all right. James is all right too, aren't you, James?" said Emily. "Help me get him to lie down," she said quietly to Will.

Suddenly Will understood the unbelievable.

"Why, James!" he said. "Congratulations!" Grinning he stepped across and shook James's hand.

James nodded wisely as limply he let Will pump his arm.

"Knew your father," he explained courteously to Will. "Fine gentleman. Fine man."

"That's right," said Will, "now just give me your hand—"

James promptly tucked his right hand under his left arm.

Emily and Will looked at each other, trying not to laugh. "We'll just have to let him stay there," whispered Emily. "He'll be asleep in a minute."

"But what happened to him?" asked Will curiously. He stared at his brother who looked back mildly, giving no sign that he either heard or understood.

Emily too looked at James, and a sudden affection sprang up in her. "Nothing, or everything perhaps. Perhaps he tried to do too much too soon. And he does work hard, too hard sometimes."

James was listening anxiously now, humbly waiting their decision.

It was the way, though he did not know it, he had seen people look at him as he left a sick room.

"You'd better telephone Laura from the drug store down the street," Emily directed Will. "Tell her James is staying all night."

"I'll say he was called over because of Agnes," said Will quickly.

"Good idea."

"Want my hat," said James.

"No, Will is just going out a minute. He'll be back."

"Want my hat!" insisted James.

Will hesitated, but Emily waved him on.

James was struggling to his feet. With a great effort he lurched across to where his hat lay on a table and after two attempts picked it up. He looked reproachfully at Emily, who stood wondering what she could do if James tried to leave. She thought of running to the window and calling to Will before he got too far away. She had heard him going down the stairs but not yet heard the front door open.

Very carefully, James took four steps to the sofa. He made it without mishap and sat down. Watching Emily gravely, he placed his hat upside down on the floor. He bent and began to fumble with the laces of his black boots. Understanding, Emily dropped to her knees and helped him to get them off.

"That's the boy!" she encouraged him.

Together they tugged off his boots, James grunting cooperatively. He wiggled his toes inside his white socks. Straightening up, he inserted a finger inside the front of his collar and popped it open. He tugged off his white cuffs.

"The world," he told Emily distinctly, "is full of damned fools and wives who know it all."

Then he bent and very carefully fitted his boots into his hat.

"But, James—"

He waved her away and surveyed his handiwork critically. Satisfied, he lay back and went immediately to sleep.

Emily watched him with a curious smile about her lips. She had forgotten her own fatigue. The Great James! A wave of compassion went through her. She managed to unbutton his waistcoat though his broad chest was heaving up and down with his heavy breathing. She got a spare blanket from the chest in the other bedroom and covered him.

"Laura was wild," Will reported a few minutes later, "and all for coming right over, but I stalled her off. She'd been trying to locate him all evening. Good thing I can lie convincingly." He looked at James. "What will we do with him?"

Emily shrugged. "Let him sleep."

James's lips puffed in and out as he breathed. His beard stuck out at an angle toward the ceiling.

"Why, he looks like Pa!" said Will. "Imagine Pa soused!"

They both laughed. "I ought to go back to Mott Haven," said Emily looking troubled, "but I'm tired. Every bone aches. Ma and I cleaned up that filthy house. It needed it."

Will colored slightly. His collar was wilted and his shoes were dusty, but he still looked fresh and vital.

"Then Agnes—" he began. "The baby?"

"Allan thinks tomorrow now."

"But—?" Will frowned and looked his question.

Emily shrugged. "That's all I know. Women are supposed to know all about these things somehow, but I don't, and I couldn't very well show my ignorance."

Will laughed.

"We can go up first thing in the morning. I have two pupils in the afternoon, so Agnes had better get it over with before then. I'm going to bed now. Think he'll fall off that sofa?"

They looked at James again.

"Take a charge of dynamite to move him," said Will. He indicated the hat and boots. "Wonder where he got that idea?"

Suddenly the sight of James's boots sticking out of his tall hat seemed to both of them the funniest thing they had ever seen, and they began to laugh unrestrainedly.

"Probably leaves them that way every night in case he is called out!" Emily decided.

"Like a fireman sliding into his clothes!" agreed Will.

James stirred and opened one bloodshot eye, but the eyelid fell over it again as if of its own volition and the breath began to whistle through his lips on a different note.

"Leaky valve," diagnosed Will. He tugged at his tie and wandered off down the hall. " 'Night."

He woke early the next morning with the feeling of something pleasurable imminent. Then he remembered, and in rumpled pajamas with his bright hair tousled, hurried in to see James.

James was just sitting up and gazing dazedly about him. The blanket was snarled about his waist and hung like a bedraggled skirt over his rumpled gray trousers. His collar had sprung wide open and stuck out like wings each side of his neck. He had opened his mouth to air his thick tongue which he was working about. He closed it and wiped his bearded lips and chin with his hand as he saw Will. He scowled at him without speaking.

"How's it feel to be human?" asked Will eagerly. "You're making awfully hard work of it though. Pleasant dreams?"

James was massaging his face with his hands now. He stopped and looked at Will through his fingers.

"Let him alone, Will," said Emily, appearing in bright red slippers and a flowered robe over her nightgown. "Here, drink this James." She stopped stirring the cup of coffee she held and handed it to him.

James took it and sipped from the teaspoon.

"Doctor," said Will, simpering, "I wake up mornings with a terrible headache. I can't think what's wrong with me. I—"

James looked up at him. "Shut up," he suggested meekly. He spooned in more coffee and grunted his satisfaction. "Ah!" he said gratefully. He breathed deeply and threw back his head, grunting luxuriously. "Ah!" Suddenly he looked alarmed. "Laura?"

"I don't think she's awake yet, is she, Em?" asked Will. "Wait, I'll see." He made as if to head for another room.

"My God!" breathed James. "You little fools didn't—"

"It's all right, James," Emily assured him. "Laura's not here. Now finish your coffee and get a move on, both of you. I've got to get up to Agnes'. I'll get you some breakfast when you're dressed, though there's not much in the house."

A half-hour later, washed, his hair and beard combed and glistening with water, his clothes brushed out by their combined efforts, James was expansive and happy as they ate a sketchy breakfast.

"Slept like a log," he said proudly. "Haven't had such a sleep in years." He rubbed his chest and stomach with immense satisfaction. "Nice place you have here, Em. What are you doing down here anyway, Will?"

Will laughed. "He's feeling better," he told Emily. "What am I doing here? Keeping sober, if you must know. Do you always stuff your boots into your hat?"

"I put 'em on when I go out," said James. He bit down into a crisp piece of toast loaded with marmalade. "Patients don't like you to come in barefoot."

"You'll not have any patients if they see you like that," warned Emily sternly.

"They won't," James agreed. "Suppose I better call Laura," he added, but he made no move. He was content and comfortable. He looked benignly at Will and Emily. Maybe he'd lie down again, sleep while he could.

"Why don't you come up to Agnes' with us?" asked Will.

James grimaced and shook his head. "See babies enough."

"But this is Agnes' baby."

"Same as all the rest."

"What are you going to tell Laura if you don't?" asked Will.

"Oh," said James thoughtfully. "M-mm."

Agnes showed an unexpected sense of the dramatic. Emily, James, and Will had only just reached the Mott Haven house and joined their mother and Ellen who were waiting tensely at the foot of the stairs on the first floor, when Allan came heavily down the stairs, his flushed face beaming. Halfway down the flight he stopped so that his footsteps would not drown his happy announcement. They could hear Dr. Collins and the practical nurse moving about upstairs. There was no sound now from Agnes.

"Mother and daughter," recited Allan, "are both doing well."

Ellen's excited squeal was the first sound made. She clapped her hand to her mouth and scuttled down to the basement.

"My!" breathed Mary relaxing. "My!"

"Congratulations, doctor," said James, extending his hand as Allan reached the hall level.

"Thank you, doctor," answered Allan gravely. "Good of you to come. Will you go up?"

"No, no," James shook his head, formally declining the professional courtesy.

"I knew you'd come, James," said his mother with dignity befitting the occasion.

"Of course," said James clearing his throat. "Laura sent her best wishes." He did not look at Will or Emily.

"A girl," Will whispered to Emily. "Pa'll be mad."

Chapter 31

SMILING GENTLY, Andrew Gray spoke as though reciting words he had memorized. "I got better. I raced through what I had to do. I managed to get return passage on an earlier sailing. I'm here."

Emily seemed unable to believe that he was there. A tremor passed through her, and her shoulders twitched convulsively.

Gray kept talking as he held her protectively close.

"In mid-ocean I decided perhaps I'd better just stay where I was. I'm too American ever to be thoroughly English again, yet in London I felt so at home that America seemed unreal. But you are here, so I had to come all the way back."

"Oh, Andrew! Andrew! Andrew!"

"And then it would not have been fair to Ventnor and Apex or to the *Tribune* or to my publishers—or to me."

"You must never go away again! Never, never, never!"

"If I have to, I'll come back."

"You must never be sick again! To have you ill three thousand miles away—"

"I'll never be ill again," Gray promised gravely.

"I've sung and played until my throat was sandpaper and I thought my fingers would drop off. I've gone to picnics and slaughtered cockroaches. I did everything I could to keep from thinking. Nothing worked. Nothing ever will work."

"Slaughtered roaches?"

"I did! And Agnes has had her baby. Mother's still there. I should have been up again, but I did not want to go alone. Unless you are with me, I don't want to go anywhere or do anything. Andrew, you *are* here? You *are* well?"

Gray stroked the girl's hair and her cheek. He touched her lips to still them and kissed her eyes.

"I'm alive again now I'm with you," he whispered.

"We'll surprise Mother. She'll be happy too. But not yet! I want to keep you just for myself!"

Mary was more angry than happy just then. When the decision had been reached she did not know, but she suspected that it was a plot formed and executed by Agnes and Allan one night after she had gone to bed. The baby was to be called Rhoda after Allan's mother, though its middle name would be Mary.

Agnes hugged the baby happily as she told Mary, and the baby yowled its displeasure.

"Now, Agnes," said Mary angrily, "you will have to learn to be less clumsy."

Agnes looked sulky, then remembered that she was a Christian.

"I don't know what we'd do without you, Mother," she said in a high, sweet voice.

Mollified, Mary jerked her head to acknowledge that the recognition was due and decided that she loved the baby no matter what its name was. She felt to see that it was dry, took it from Agnes and fondled it to show the baby that she bore it no ill will for the stupidity of its parents.

"It's long past time I was getting home," she said decisively to Agnes.

"Oh, Ma!" cried Agnes, alarmed. "You can't go yet. You know how we need you!"

"Your father needs me, too," Mary reminded her. "I've been away weeks as it is."

"But—my condition!" Agnes reminded her tearfully. "I know it's been a long time, but I'm still so weak!"

"Perhaps," said Mary thoughtfully, "I can remain until tomorrow. I can send for Emily to put me on the train."

"Tomorrow! But, Ma, you can't. See," said Agnes cunningly, "how Rhoda loves you. Rhoda loves Grandma, don't you Rhoda? See her smile for you? You're the only one she smiles for that way. She won't smile for Allan or me like that."

"So I've noticed," said Mary complacently. "Well, we'll see."

She did not really see how she could go home for weeks more yet, and she wrote and told Thomas so. There was still, she explained, more than enough for her to do keeping the house and looking after the doctor's patients while Agnes attended to the baby. She was still very busy.

Mary had also been very happy managing her daughter's household.

She had received the callers who came to congratulate Agnes and the doctor, entertained the Baptist minister who prayed with Agnes, and poured tea as mistress of the house for ladies from the church who came to worship the baby.

Then there had been the first day they dressed the baby in the tiny blue and white shoes Julia had crocheted and the little brown flannel shirt and jacket embroidered with pink roses. There had been alarms when the baby cried, screaming with puny anger. Mary had been sure it had a stomach-ache and wondered whether Agnes had a sufficient supply of nurse.

Just as Allan, his face white and his brow furrowed, had been contemplating paregoric or a consultation with his colleagues, the baby had gurgled, smiled, and gone to sleep. The grave young doctor, eyes shining, had changed it, gathered up the corners of the fresh diaper and pinned them with the gold safety pin he had bought himself, and disappeared downstairs and into his office.

Allan did not know how to express his gratitude to life for having given him a daughter. Under the guise of professional care, he would take her from Agnes into another room and gaze at her, scrutinizing his child with wonder and joy. All he could do to tell his joy was to bring in more food for them all and more flowers for Agnes almost every time he left the house.

The day had come when it seemed safe for Agnes to venture downstairs, and Allan had been jubilant. A triumphal banquet was indicated, but a series of three confinement cases, then a run of insurance examinations forced postponement of his plan for several weeks. Allan made up for the delay by more elaborate preparations. He bought a goose, oranges, nuts, figs. He rendered down the bird himself, carefully pouring the grease into pint bottles so that Mary could take some of it home against the colds they would all have that winter. He basted the goose and cooked the vegetables, running up and down stairs between patients, and Mary made a roly-poly with suet pastry, filling it with black raspberry jam and boiling a hot sauce to be poured over it.

Her hair precisely arranged, a cameo at her throat, Mary presided over the table graced by Agnes' best silver and china. They gleamed on the fine damask cloth under the colored gas chandelier which hung low over the table.

Ellen went up to stay with the baby after they had managed to get Agnes downstairs, and toward the end of their feast, Allan went for his daughter. Swaddled in a pink blanket, its thin fair hair combed by Ellen into a tiny curl over its forehead, the baby surveyed the scene with bright eyes, then gave a toothless old woman's smile. Ellen stood with a broad grin on her young black face. Like the rest of them, she was stuffed with goose and pudding.

With unusual playfulness, Allan offered the baby a sliver of meat from the breast of the goose, bringing a horrified cry from Agnes and a light laugh from Mary, who sat upright with her long-fingered hands clasped in her silken lap.

"Look at 'at chile smile!" cried Ellen. "She the *cutes'* baby!"

The upstairs doorbell rang.

"Oh, dear," said Agnes, "I must—"

"You sit still," ordered her mother. "You are not *that* well yet." She rose swiftly, and before Allan could hand the baby to one of the others, walked firmly to the stairs.

There were two doors at the stoop entrance to the first floor of the Mott Haven house. The upper half of the inner door was of curtained glass looking into a small, marbled-tiled vestibule. All but the oak frame of the door to the stoop landing and the street was of heavy plate glass cut with the legend: *Allan Richards, M.D.* Mary could see who was there before the second door was opened.

Emily wore her beaver cape and the hat she had had made to

match it. She carried her splendid beaver muff. She was dusted with the fine early snow which had been drifting about since darkness. It sparkled on her head and shoulders and on her muff in the light from the hall lamp. Behind her, hat in hand, his left arm encircling a lightly wrapped gift of flowers, Andrew Gray stood smiling quietly.

"Ma!" cried Emily, throwing her arms about Mary as soon as they were inside, Gray carefully closing the door behind them. "Oh, Mother!" Her voice nearly broke.

They were none of them given to expressions of emotion. There were no mother and daughter confidences between Mary and Emily. The girl's unthinking gesture and cry were a measure of the depths which had been stirred in her by Gray's return and of the pain she had endured while he was away.

"There, there!" said Mary awkwardly. She moved slightly so that Emily would not disturb her dress or her hair.

"I'm very glad to see you again," she said to Gray. "We have all missed you."

"Thank you," he answered gravely. "I'm very glad to be back. I've missed all of you."

Mary and Gray smiled at each other as Emily, radiant, lifted the flowers Gray carried and separated two bouquets.

"These are for you, Mother. They're the new green and white carnations. Aren't they lovely? The roses are for Agnes. Where is she? Is she up yet?" Emily darted off.

"And you have entirely recovered?" Mary asked Gray. His face seemed thinner, and his eyes would have looked tired had they not been lighted with pleasure. He would look better soon, she decided.

"Fine," he said. "You look well—and as you always look."

"Thank you," said Mary prettily. She buried her nose in the flowers. "These are beautiful."

Gray bowed slightly. "Thank you for taking care of Emily," he said.

Mary smiled.

"We must go down to the others. They thought it was a patient, you know."

Gray shook hands with them all when they reached the basement dining room, even with the baby whom he regarded with humorous gravity.

Agnes beamed with joy and pride. "My flowers are just lovely," she said.

"But hardly a match for this little nosegay," said Gray gallantly. Agnes' face softened to even greater happiness as she looked again at her baby. "The Lord was good to spare us both," she said sincerely.

Emily took the roses and her mother's carnations to put them into vases at the kitchen sink. She was talking rapidly to Allan out there.

A few moments later, Allan, back from the kitchen, was flourishing his carving knife over the carcass of the goose. "You came just in time," he said, carving skillfully.

"Oh, but we've dined," refused Gray, holding up his hand.

"At Sherry's!" cried Emily, returning with a sparkling cut glass vase of flowers in each hand. "Mother, you should have seen the gowns and the jewels!"

"Sherry's!" repeated Agnes. She raised her eyes mildly. "Don't they serve liquor?"

"Of course!" laughed Emily. "All kinds, and they looked so pretty in the glasses, like rubies and amethysts and diamonds! We drank champagne to celebrate Andrew's return, didn't we, Andrew?"

"No goose?" said Allan, disappointed. "But surely you'll have some dessert and tea!"

Gray was about to shake his head again when Emily forestalled him.

"Oh, Allan, could we have just a little roly-poly, do you think? And some hot tea? It's so cold out." She hurried out to the kitchen again to help him.

"I could drink another cup," Mary called after her, "and it would be good for Agnes too."

"All right, Ma!" Emily called back gaily.

Agnes looked after her suspiciously. Superbly gowned, Emily was the authentic beauty in the grand manner yet all soft and glowing that night. The hard brilliance that sometimes edged her beauty had melted into an unguarded joyousness.

"Allan!" Agnes called sharply into the other room. "Emily knows where the tea things are. Perhaps you had better take the baby back upstairs, Ellen!"

"Yes'm," said Ellen doubtfully. She had been looking happily at Andrew Gray.

Allan stepped back into the dining room looking puzzled and unhappy.

"Rhoda's all right," he said, looking at his daughter. "She should be able to stay a little longer. And you feel well enough, don't you?" he asked Agnes solicitously.

"Of course, she does," said Mary sharply, "and the baby is doing very well right here." There was a subtle note of warning in her voice as she looked at Agnes. "Emily, hurry with the tea!"

One could hardly blame any woman, Mary thought, for not wishing to leave her husband alone with Emily, but Agnes should have more sense.

"All right," said Agnes uncertainly. "We mustn't be selfish with little Rhoda, must we, mummy's darling little girl, mummy's darling, mmm—" She buried her face against the infant, smothering her words in kisses and the melting affection of her heart.

Emily and Allan marched in from the kitchen, Allan with napkins draped over his arm, and both of them bearing trays. Allan served the warmed pudding with a flourish, while Emily feeling of the steaming teapot before beginning to pour, said, "You got no better tea in London, Andrew, I'm sure of that. Allan put in a spoonful for each cup and *three* for the pot, then steeped it just— how many minutes, Allan, by your doctor's watch? Did you ever see his watch, Andrew? It has a hand that tells you how often a patient's heart beats, and why it doesn't, and when it stops. You push a little lever, and it starts again!"

"The heart?" laughed Gray. "That's very convenient. Perhaps I should get a watch like that."

"You don't need it!" Emily laughed to him alone. She turned quickly to Agnes. "Rhoda looks like you," she assured her. "It has your eyes and hair. But there's something about her looks like you, too, Allan. I think it has your nose, or will have, when she gets one —and your chin."

She did not offer to take the baby. She was too beautifully gowned to handle a small and messy animal.

"It looks like Pa," said Agnes seriously. "The very first time Dr. Collins held her up, I knew she looked like Pa. I just hope Rhoda grows up to be as good as Pa is."

"She will if you can make her, won't she, Agnes?" asked Emily with a tartness belied by a dazzling smile. She handed a cup to Andrew. "Just as you like it," she said.

"As I like it," he repeated, looking at her.

He leaned over and offered his finger for the infant to grasp. The baby curled her tiny fingers about his straight forefinger. It was what he wanted.

Gray drew a gold sovereign from the right hand pocket of the waistcoat which fitted so trimly about his slenderness and offered it to the child. Agnes gasped. Tentatively the baby clutched at it, while Gray held his other hand cupped to catch the coin if she let it drop. For a second the baby seemed to grasp the coin. Watching intently, they all breathed exclamations of surprise and pleasure.

Gray handed the coin to Agnes. "It's a new one," he said, "so it has the year of her birth on it."

"Oh, thank you!"

Allan's good face was wreathed in a proud smile. "She can wear it on a chain when she grows up," he said.

Agnes was fingering the gold coin. She forgot her child for an instant.

"Did your father leave much?" she asked curiously.

"Agnes!" Emily murmured.

"More than I thought," answered Gray directly.

"Time for Rhoda to go beddy-bye!" cooed Agnes. "Ellen, will you take her up, please. I'll be there shortly." She kissed her baby lingeringly.

Mary kissed it perfunctorily, too busy talking of England to Gray. Emily pecked at it, disliking the taste, and wondering if the child would grow up to be like its mother.

"It's been so well behaved all this time," Gray said politely to Agnes.

"Rhoda is a *good* baby as well as sweet and lovely," said Agnes.

"Andrew, we must be going shortly," Emily warned, impatience in her tone.

"But not till we have finished," said Mary quickly. "Tell me, did you get out to Kew before the summer was over? Once—"

An hour later Emily and Andrew Gray left for the El train downtown. The snow had stopped with only small patches of it, blown by the wind, caught in gutters and crevices in the streets, but it had grown colder. Emily hunched deep into her furs, and Gray, the collar of his heavy ulster turned up, held one hand to his hat as they turned the corner. Emily's gloved hand was snuggled tightly under his left arm.

"You were so nice to them all, Andrew," she said gratefully.

"I like them," he said almost honestly. "Certainly I like your mother and your brothers—I like them all."

"And me?"

He tightened his arm against her hand.

Agnes spoke in the darkness after she and Allan had gone to bed. She knew that Allan was still awake. She had started several times to speak but had been unable to get up her courage to the point where it matched her anxiety, curiosity, fear, and titillated imagination.

"Allan," she asked in a scared voice, "do you think that Emily is living in sin?"

Allan had been afraid of the question or one like it. He lay still, pretending he had not heard. As though she knew he was feigning, Agnes repeated her question more firmly. "Is my sister living in sin?" There was a thrill in her words from which Allan recoiled.

"I don't know," he mumbled. He thought Emily beautiful, and he responded guiltily to her beauty and freshness, to her grace and laughter. It was pleasant to be near her, to admire without wishing consciously to touch. "Everybody is not the same," he dared.

It was as if he had admitted the truth of Agnes' worst suspicions.

"In the same house with our Rhoda!" she hissed angrily in the darkness. "I shall throw those roses away the first thing in the morning."

"That would be silly," said Allan boldly.

"I knew you would defend her," said Agnes bitterly. "While I have been up here helpless in bed! Emily is a wicked woman."

Allan felt sick. He moved away from his wife, trying to make no sound. Agnes had begun to cry. Anger rose with his nausea. He could not stay there. It did not occur to him to resent on his own behalf the injustice of Agnes' remark.

"I think I left the front door open," he said, and slid out of bed. He did not hunt for his slippers but felt blindly for the door. The floor was cold to his bare feet. Agnes was sobbing comfortably. He wondered if she were forcing the tears. He knew she could cry at will.

For a second he considered turning on the light to confront her. All women, he tried to remember, were sometimes ridiculous. They could not help it. But he kept on going, feeling for the banister, trying to walk in the center of the stair treads, where the carpeting was, so as not to make any noise.

"Is that you, Allan?" called Mary as he passed her room on the next floor down. Her door was open.

"Yes, Mrs. Stapely," he whispered. The dark house was cold. He, was cold in his flannelette nightshirt.

"Is Agnes all right? Is the baby ill?" called Mary in an alarmed whisper.

"They are all right. I forgot to close the door," he lied.

"Oh," said Mary. With a touch of self-pity in her voice, she added, "I can't sleep. Perhaps I should have taken my liver pills."

He did not answer but kept on creeping down the stairs. From the next landing he could see the coals in the new parlor stove glowing behind the isinglass in the elaborately decorated cast-iron door.

Allan made for the stove and stood with his back to it warming himself. His heavy feet and thick, stubby calves showed vaguely white in the room which was black save for the light from the coals. It fell on the skirts of his nightshirt, bringing out the pink and blue stripes.

He stood there for moments until his back was warm, then turned and held his hands over the stove. Agnes had got overtired and overexcited by the company and the talk. He should have sent her back to bed earlier. Agnes was not to blame. He was.

Yet Allan could not quite convince himself. Noiselessly, he drew up a chair and huddled in it close to the stove. He dropped his face into his hands, pressing the ends of thick, short fingers into his forehead.

Then he thought of his beautiful daughter, and his heart was glad, and he loved Agnes for having given her to him. He sat there a little while to be alone with his happiness.

The second step from the bottom, and then the fifth, creaked slightly as Allan went up the stairs again. He had known they would.

"Is that you, Allan?" called Mary again.

"Yes, Mrs. Stapely."

It was strange that older women seemed to wake at will. Older men did, too, but the women had to let you know they were awake and watchful. His mother had been the same.

"Good-night, Allan," whispered Mary from the darkness of her room.

"Good-night," Allan answered.

"We had such a good time, didn't we?"

"Yes, we did," said Allan. "Good-night."

"Good-night, Allan."

Chapter 32

THOMAS WAS confused.

Out in Chicago the great World's Fair and Columbian Exposition was displaying to the world the wonder and wealth of the United States. The country's almost incredible accomplishments were glori-

236

fied in Greek temples and stupendous exhibits. The markets of electricity and invention dazzled millions of visitors.

Side by side stood the old and the new. Replicas of the *Santa Maria*, the *Nina*, and the *Pinta* floated on Lake Michigan like toy sailboats while great lake steamers sped by. Ridiculous early railroad coaches looked their absurdity in contrast to the modern Pullman cars arrayed next to them.

Thomas read the accounts of the fair with awe. He appreciated all the marvels, but there were phenomena less marvelous than frightening closer at hand. It was a year of panic in the United States.

Banks were crashing; railroads slowing to a walk. Even the old and conservative bank in Ilium, where he had done business for years, tottered under the onslaught of an unexpected run. Rumor had got about that it held thousands of shares of Erie, and Erie had gone into receivership. So had the mighty Union Pacific. So had too many other roads and corporations. Unemployment was widespread. Shops and factories were closed. Groups of surly men hung about corners on South Avenue cursing, drinking, and spitting tobacco juice too near the shoes of anyone who looked prosperous.

Thomas despised them. There was plenty of work to be done. He shared the popular disapproval of the trusts and monopolies, yet he admired the accomplishments of the men who had organized and operated them. Such men got things done. It amazed him when one trust was smashed, and a larger one took its place. Little trusts were merely swallowed up in larger trusts, huge combines disappeared into huger combines.

Strike followed strike and Thomas was aroused to fury. He had all the hatred for organized labor possessed by the workingman who has risen by his own efforts into the employer class. What he and other men like him had accomplished, they had accomplished without the aid of unions. He saw unions as the refuge of the weak, the lazy, the incompetent, and the criminally rebellious. When Cleveland sent troops to quell battling strikers, he grimly approved and said so.

Thomas sympathized inwardly with the disgruntled radical who fired a shot through Delmonico's window at people who were dining too well while others starved. It was an honest, violent action, and he liked violent action. Yet he was glad when Coxey's rabble army of twenty thousand failed in its ridiculous march on Washington and was ignominiously disbanded and put to rout by a handful of police.

They were troubled, bitter times, and Thomas knew only two answers—work and God. There was little work to be had. The building business, like every other business about Ilium, had fallen off. Thomas, who had lived through other panics, knew that it would come back. Food, clothing, shelter, and the greatest of these was shelter. A man needed little to wear. He could always grow or buy or steal enough food to survive, but without a place to sleep in and live in he was an animal. Thomas turned to prayer and to his strong man's love of God.

What disturbed Thomas as suffering, drew Andrew Gray as spectacle. He looked at it thoughtfully, with a touch of foreboding, and with respect for the forces which he saw in inevitable conflict. He watched moves and countermoves, relishing the skills he saw displayed by giants, sympathizing with the growing desire of smaller men to share in their own destinies and in the rewards of their effort.

It was as though the forces which had been pointed toward physical accomplishment had suddenly been arrested and turned loose without direction. The energy which had been channeled into opening the West, into building railroads and forging steel, seemed out of control and raging. The speed of living had been increased by mechanical invention. The masses of men had not yet learned to keep pace. They felt outdone. Somehow they had been victimized, and they were resentful.

The Sherman Act, dutifully passed, was being dutifully ignored or skillfully turned. Gray appreciated intelligent guile. The tariff was going up and up by law. According to another law, seemingly an immutable law recognized by church, state, and society as a whole, the rich were getting richer, and the poor were getting poorer.

The yellow press was helping out by parading the passions and possessions of the *nouveaux riches*. It had the lower classes drooling with pleasure and seething with indignation at those who lighted their cigars with hundred-dollar bills or attended fancy-dress balls on horseback in a magnificent hotel transformed into a stable for the very profitable occasion.

Ultimate meanings might not be resolved for years, if ever, but the ferment, the gesticulating belligerence and the seething struggle were signs of a vitality so deep it could not be killed by any passing panic. Uncivilized men punched each other's heads in their favorite saloons over the gold or silver questions, or the comparative merits of Gentleman Jim Corbett and John L., or the comparative charms of Lily Langtry and Estelle Wintergreen. Civilized men tried to ruin each other financially, and often did. Dog ate dog and throve on the diet.

Sometimes, Gray felt and said in his articles, he thought they didn't really mean it. The rich rode happily up and down the avenues in their broughams or victorias. The rest of the world went happily clanging and banging off for a trolley-car picnic. Yellow press cartoonists had them shaking their fists at each other. Instead, the trolley riders shouted, waved, and jeered good-naturedly, and the ladies and gentlemen bowed, smiled, and sometimes waved back. The Few rode horseback about the reservoir in Central Park on Sunday mornings. The Many scorched or coasted along the Boulevard of upper Broadway on their bicycles. The factories could not turn out "safeties" enough to satisfy the demand.

Andrew Gray was no social idealist. Like Thomas, he had nothing against the enthusiasm of the man who had fired his gun through Delmonico's window. He was just glad Emily and he had not been there that night.

In the end it all mattered little, panics, politics, and all the rest. Compared to man's larger life of mind and emotion and art, they mattered not at all. Gray could be cynical about the one because he was serious about the other.

James lived in the same world as his father and Andrew Gray.

"A fine panic," he decided, one night when he and Gray were dining together in New York. "Making everybody sick, good and sick. I made thirty calls yesterday. Was up half the night. Be lucky if I can collect for ten of 'em. Will steel go up or down? What about Second Avenue bonds?"

Chapter 33

"Guess what, Ma!" cried Emily. She and Andrew Gray had come up to Mott Haven to take her mother to her flat. Ellen, who had been back at Emily's a week, had come that morning for her box and her traveling bag.

Mary had been dressed and waiting for an hour.

"You have another pupil?" she suggested.

"I've got *two* more, but that's not the important thing. The big thing—you tell her, Andrew!"

"Emily is to be soprano soloist at the Fifth Avenue Church," said Gray quietly.

"At the Fifth Avenue—the big church—where Dr. Rollins preaches?"

"The Fifth Avenue itself!" affirmed Emily. "I got a letter this morning. I'm to be one of their highest paid singers, one of the highest paid in the city, Mr. Fielding told me. He's the organist and choirmaster, and he's a composer too. Where's Agnes? I want to tell her!" She darted up the stairs.

Mary looked at Andrew Gray in amazement, her eyes questioning.

"I had nothing to do with it," he lied, "nor did Risviglio. Someone Emily met when she was filling in there last year suggested her. They already knew her voice. Tuesday she sang for Cecil Fielding and some others. They had already discarded a dozen other applicants. It's one of the city's wealthiest churches, of course—Manhattan real estate which they've owned for a century—and noted for its music."

"The Fifth Avenue Church!" whispered Mary, hardly able to believe it. "Thomas will be beside himself with delight."

"He should be," Gray told her. "Not many singers as young as Emily would have stood a chance."

Emily came tripping down the stairs again, her face still alight.

"What's the matter with Agnes?" she demanded. "She'd hardly speak to me. When I told her about my new post, she looked almost angry, as though she should have got it instead of me." Emily laughed.

"She's just tired, I imagine," said Mary quickly. "The baby is quite a care. And I know she's a little unhappy that I am leaving," she could not help adding. She hoped that Agnes really appreciated all she had done.

"She'll be down in a minute to say good-bye," said Emily, almost dancing about the small front parlor. She moved an ugly vase on the marble mantel an inch to the right, then moved it back with a *moue* when she saw she had left a ring of dust. She laughed up at Andrew.

"I should hope so," said Mary. She went to the foot of the stairs. "Agnes!" she called, trying not to let her impatience sound in her voice.

The unseen Agnes trilled a few notes on an ascending scale. The habit which annoyed Emily amused Gray.

Agnes came rustling down the stairs in a sober, high-necked, tight-bosomed afternoon dress with bulging sleeves, tapering to her thick wrists, and the suggestion of a bustle. It was a pattern she had chosen with care as both stylish and modest. It was suitable for the young matron, her dressmaker had assured her.

To Emily's amazement, she greeted Andrew Gray with veritable coyness, her voice affected as though she trilled her words in tune with the scale she had sung. She kissed her mother effusively, ignored Emily.

"I could not have got along without you, Ma!" she cried. "I know you feel you must go, but we'll miss you terribly. I don't know what I can tell Rhoda when she wakes and finds you gone. She'll be heart-broken, the little dear, and be looking everywhere for Grandma."

Mary looked pleased and complacent.

"There's cold meat already sliced in the ice chest for Allan's sup-per," she said, "and be sure you don't give the baby her bottle too warm. Test it on the back of your hand, and if it feels the slightest bit hot, you must let it cool."

"Yes, Ma," said Agnes obediently, "and I'll write Pa tonight that you have gone to Emily's."

"Don't tell him about my new singing job," said Emily quickly. "I want to tell him myself."

"I don't intend to mention *that*," said Agnes meaningfully.

"What do you mean by that?" asked Emily quickly, her face hardening.

Agnes looked innocent surprise. "Why, what could I mean?" she asked, her brown eyes wide. To Emily they looked malignant, to Gray obtuse and rather stupid.

"Your father, I know," he said, "is always glad to hear from you."

Then he was sorry he had been stupid enough to interfere, for Agnes turned to him.

"I didn't know you knew my father that well," she said sweetly.

"Kiss the baby for me," said Emily, before Andrew could speak again. She felt too happy to feel anger against her sister, "and give my love to Allan."

"Allan is very busy," said Agnes. "Here, Ma, let me help you with your cloak. It looks so nice. Have you your pills in your bag in case you feel ill in the night? Allan says they are the very best thing he knows."

"They are doing me good, I'm sure," said Mary. "I slept very well last night. Come, Emily."

Agnes watched them go down the brownstone stoop, Gray taking her mother's arm, Emily waltzing down the steps as though she were singing to herself. On the sidewalk they turned to look back, and Agnes pushed aside the long lace curtains at the parlor window to wave to them. Sweetly she blew her mother a kiss. Then her face darkened as she watched them out of sight up the street.

It was she, not Emily, who should be soprano soloist in a great church. It was she whose voice should have been trained, and they all knew it. The injustice of it aroused an anger in her that almost frightened her. Her face burned as though she had a fever. She felt of her cheek. One could stand just so much for just so long. She had meant what she said about writing her father. She would do it now before the baby woke or Allan came home.

The baby was awake and beginning to whimper when she went upstairs. Agnes ignored it and went to her bedroom for the lap desk her father had made for her out of choice walnut years before. It held all his letters and other objects she treasured.

The baby was really crying now. Either it was wet or it was hungry. It was always one or the other. She had no intention of soiling her new dress, and all her aprons were downstairs. The baby's cries grew louder.

Agnes went to the open door of the room.

"Be still!" she shouted, her face suffused with rage. "Be still, be still, be still!" The baby stared at her frightened and was silent for a half-minute. Then it began to cry again.

Agnes stared uncertainly at the infant in its crib, then she gathered up her desk and stepped out of the room, closing the door behind her so that she would not hear the noise of the child's crying.

She was proud of her Spencerian penmanship. At school she had lovingly practiced the perfect formation of her letters and the fine shaded signature. She wrote carefully.

Tuesday

Dear Pa:

While darling Rhoda is asleep in her little crib, I thought I would snatch the time to write to you. As you know, the Lord was good to me, and now I trust he will help me be a good Mother and to bring up our little girl in the Christian way. Ma has gone to Emily's and then she is going to spend a few days with James and Laura. James has not seen fit to come see the baby since that first day, but I know that like my Husband he is very busy. Still, though our ways lie apart it seems strange he does not wish to see his little Neice.

Pa I think you should come pay us a Visit as soon as you can. It is part of my happiness that Rhoda looks like you and I think you will think so too and Allan will be glad to see you. Mr. Gray came with Emily when they came for Ma and she has news for you too, but she told me very sharply that I was not to tell you, I would not like to see her get in trouble but I think that certain Things are not Right and I think you should see about them as in the Past. I would talk this over with our Minister but I would rather you would come. I have been out several times and twice to Church. Please write and say you are coming. Rhoda sends you a kiss.

Your Loving Daughter
Agnes

Chapter 34

ELLEN, resplendent in a new maid's uniform of black with starched white collar, cuffs, and apron, greeted Mary delightedly as she took her cloak and bonnet.

"We'ah so glad to see you, Miz Stapely!" she cried. "Ain't we, Miz Emily! An' Miz Emily she jes so *busy!*"

"Thank you, Ellen," said Mary primly. "And I'm very glad to get out. It's been very confining at my elder daughter's."

"It must have been," said Gray sympathetically.

"Your room's all ready, Ma," Emily told her. "We have it all ready for you."

There were fresh cut flowers on the dresser which was covered with a new embroidered scarf. A rich new coverlet was spread tightly over the walnut bed. There was a chair which Mary had not seen before. Pleased and flattered, she tried not to show her astonishment at all the changes she had noted with one quick glance about Emily's flat.

The old pieces of furniture, brought down first from South Ilium to Brooklyn, were gone, and expensive new pieces stood in their place. There were new rugs and pictures in the living room. Fine china gleamed behind the leaded glass panes of a mahogany cabinet.

"Do you like it, Ma?" demanded Emily excitedly. "We've been getting ready for you for days. What a scramble! But it was fun, wasn't it, Andrew?"

"You gave us a fine excuse," Gray told Mary.

"And look at these!" cried Emily. "Aren't they beautiful?"

She stood by two quiet water colors in slender gilt frames. One was a garden scene pleasantly composed in delicate colors. The drawing in the foreground was finely detailed. The background was a bolder treatment of blue sky and scudding white clouds. The second painting showed a shaft of sunlight slanted across a grove of evergreens and a still lake.

"Very pretty!" Mary murmured.

"Andrew painted them!"

"They're not very good," said Gray honestly. "I did them in England when I was beginning to get well but was still very sorry for myself."

"They *are* good!" contradicted Emily fiercely.

Mary and Andrew Gray smiled at each other as the girl turned to Ellen, who had just appeared in the doorway.

"All right, Ellen. Thank you," Emily said. "We're having dinner early so as not to be late," she told her mother.

"Not to be late?"

"For the theatre. Didn't Andrew tell you?"

"It's something we've wanted to see," Gray explained. "It's—"

"No! Let me be surprised," begged Mary, as they went into the dining room. "And new silver!"

"We really couldn't have the soprano soloist of the Fifth Avenue Church eating with her fingers, could we, Ellen?" asked Gray.

Ellen looked startled. "Eatin' with her—? Oh, no, Mist' Gray. No, suh, we couldn'." She shrilled laughter and disappeared into the kitchen.

Mary picked up one of the heavy knives, its handle encrusted with a pattern of twisting grapevine. "My!" she breathed wonderingly. "Oh, thank you," she said to Gray as he held her chair for her.

They went to Daly's at Broadway and Thirtieth Street to see *The Hunchback,* and Mary lived every moment of the drama, delighting, too, in the brilliant medieval costumes against the sober background of the plot. Instead of going to one of the restaurants for something to eat afterward, they returned to the flat for fruitcake and port.

Surfeited with pleasure and happiness, Mary went to her room as Emily was saying good-night to Andrew Gray. She was so tired it was an effort to get undressed. She could hear the murmur of the others' voices as she got into the sweet-smelling bed. Before Emily returned, she was asleep.

Emily, aglow from Gray's good-night kiss, feeling so alive she thought she need never sleep again, smiled in at her mother as quietly she turned down the hall light. She waited an instant before turning it fully out so that it would not give off its usual explosive 'plop,' then tiptoed to her own room.

Smiling into her mirror, she took down her hair. Dreamily she

244

undressed and slipped into her nightgown. She put out her own light, thinking she would just lie and watch the stars through her window. In the darkness she tried to picture herself singing before the crowded Fifth Avenue Church.

She heard the rustle of surprise go through the congregation, the stir of silent applause. She listened to their admiring congratulations as she left the church after the service. She ached with joy as she remembered Andrew's surprise and pleasure when she had told him. The wonder and richness and beauty of life overcame her. It was like a glorious song, like such full, deep, wild, and beautiful music as no one had ever heard.

A few days later she went for her first rehearsal, a private rehearsal with the organist and choirmaster before her first rehearsal with the full choir.

The congregation of the Fifth Avenue Church was made up of some of the oldest of old New York families and some of the richest. Its famous minister, the Reverend Samuel Rogers Rollins was no Beecher, Abbott, or Moody. His quality was goodness. Two carefully chosen younger ministers took care of most of the parish duties.

Cecil Fielding, a blue-eyed, aging musical fanatic, was undisputed dean of New York church organists.

He smoothed back his shock of white hair and turned away from the console. Aching and tired, Emily put down her music and sat gratefully in the chair he indicated near his organ bench. They were high above the empty, shadowed church in the organ loft. Before them soared the gilded false pipes of the organ whose splendid tones were still trembling about the corners under the galleries and about the dark rafters buttressing the vaulted roof.

Fielding looked intently at Emily.

"You have tone, volume, and poise," he decided, showing his teeth in an unconscious grimace which was part of his concentrated gaze rather than a smile. "You need greater control. That will develop. You must practice, practice, practice!"

"But no more today!" laughed Emily unsteadily.

She had sung scales and designated notes again and again and again while Fielding listened, his head bent low over the organ's keys. She had sung the soprano parts of a dozen arrangements, then verses of a half-dozen familiar hymns.

"No more today," he agreed, closing his console. "You did very well. *We* did very well. Your surplice will be ready by Sunday?"

"Mrs. McGowan has it almost finished now."

Fielding had swung around and was staring at the rose window. The winter sunlight streamed through purple and green and crimson, diffusing color through a beam of light in which danced a myriad particles of golden dust.

"Good! You'll meet the other three Friday night. I shan't have you sing alone the first week or two. Then we'll start you with something familiar."

"I'm so happy about it!" breathed Emily.

"Are you?" Fielding asked with a little smile. He looked at her reflectively. Andrew Gray, and he had known him for years, seldom made mistakes in judgment. "So am I," he said suddenly.

The contralto, Emily found when she met the others of the quartet on Friday, was short and fat with a comely, comfortable face and a rich, effortless voice. She had been beautifully trained, but she sang because she loved to sing, just as she loved to laugh and to eat. The bass was a magnificent animal, a viking figure of heroic proportions with a viking voice. The tenor was thin and slight with a nervous, irritable face and a narrow, balding head fringed with mixed brown and gray hair. His golden sweet voice was no indication of his character, for he was embittered and unhappy.

"Why, you're beautiful!" the contralto said to Emily without affectation.

"Thank you," said Emily, blushing in spite of herself.

She was so much younger than the others, so much less experienced, that she wanted to seem gracious yet coldly controlled, but her wonder and excitement would not be stilled. The first Sunday morning, heart beating fast as she donned her surplice in the choir's robing room, she wanted to turn and run in panic fear. By the time she stood with the others facing the great congregation spread far below them and waited Cecil Fielding's signal, she feared she was not fearful enough. The signal came and, with the others, she released the full splendor of her voice in the first anthem.

The quartet stood directly before the organist, the auxiliary choir fanning out on either side of them in double banks of white-surpliced figures. The dumpy little contralto had to stand on a step so as to appear of comparable height with the others of the quartet, but Emily was as tall as the tenor, though far shorter than the heroic bass.

Her joy soared with the music. She knew that her golden head and fair features were shown off well by the white lawn and black satin of the quartet's vestments. Underneath she felt the richness of her blue gown and of the sapphire brooch Andrew had given her to mark the great occasion.

She felt as though he were with her, though she knew he was not in the church. Often on weekends he was with his wife if she were at home or near enough for him to visit her. From a convalescent home in the Catskills she had returned to the house in Murray Hill. Now, with her nurse, she was on her way to Virginia for the remainder of the winter. Andrew had gone with them and was not to return until the next day.

Emily bowed her head in gratitude as intoxicating as her joy and her love, as Samuel Rollins, his own white head bowed far below her, began a simple and familiar prayer.

Chapter 35

IN SOUTH ILIUM, Thomas Stapely floundered miserably. Agnes' letter with its mysterious innuendoes had troubled him for days. What was Emily's news? It sounded threatening. Was the trouble Agnes talked about what he feared? Could Mary have been wrong?

There was no one he could talk to about it. If Mary were at home, she would know what it was best for him to do, but she seemed never to be at home any more. First she had been with Agnes for weeks and weeks. Then she had visited with Emily. Now she was at James's.

Thomas had showed the letter to no one, though both Maria and Julia knew that he had received it, and the news in family letters was usually common property in the household on the hill. The letter burned in the inside pocket of his coat.

If he went, he would miss church and Sunday school. He would have to get John Withers to take his place as leader of the Sunday school and one of the others to lead his Bible class. That he was jealously reluctant to do. His annoyance with Emily mounted, and his suspicions grew darker. He wished again that Mary were home where she belonged.

"I think I shall go to New York to see Agnes' baby," he told Maria finally. "Will can look after things at work."

Julia looked troubled. "But Mary is coming home Saturday."

Maria's eyes lighted. "And Thomas will not be here when she arrives. It will serve her right."

"That will do, Maria," said Thomas sternly. "I shall go in the morning."

Once he was on the train, dressed in his best, the St. George's cross presented to him by the vestry, gleaming on the heavy gold watch chain across his dark waistcoat, his heavy overcoat warm and snug, Thomas felt relieved. He was not going for pleasure, he assured himself, but to satisfy himself that his family was all right. He even enjoyed the swift motion of the train as it sped along the banks of the Hudson.

The scenery was winter dark and bleak, with snow on the high hills and in cuts and crevices along the way, and blocks of ice in the upper Hudson which was not yet frozen across. He brightened to the signs of life in the towns they passed through and to the coming and going in his warm car as passengers got off at Hudson and Poughkeepsie, and way stops between them. He ate the mutton sandwiches Maria had cut and wrapped for him and the thin piece of fruitcake. He dozed off after Tarrytown, awaking as the train pulled over the Harlem bridge into the 125th Street station. He could have got off there, but it was easier, he remembered, to go on to Grand Central Station and then take the Third Avenue Elevated back to the lower Bronx. The bustle and stir of the vast station with trains steaming in from everywhere under the long sheds and departing for distant points to the north and west stimulated him further, and he was glad he had come.

His reception at Mott Haven assured him that he was welcome. Agnes kissed him with tears in her eyes. Allan, his broad face lighted, hurried quietly out to buy a roast of beef and some small winter squash he was sure his father-in-law had never tasted. He roasted the beef and baked the squash himself, between attending to patients, while Thomas and Agnes went up to see the baby.

Thomas looked at the infant as, during his life, he had looked at four infants of his own. He felt abashed and reverent and impatient. He marveled again at the mystery of life and God's goodness. The appealing helplessness of the very young baby touched his heart at the same time that he was annoyed with it for taking unfair advantage of him by being so tiny and dependent.

Agnes lifted Rhoda and hugged her and smothered her with kisses, holding her up for him to look into her eyes and to love. She showed him happily that the baby's eyes were like his and that the little head was shaped as his was. She had been glad to have Allan and her mother and Emily about at Rhoda's birth, but this was her father. It seemed that she had not realized her baby until she could show her to him.

Distrust and envy of Emily vanished. In her happiness she could not remember the sharp and bitter feelings she had felt. Not till later that night, after she had got used to his presence, could she remember the malign urgency which had prompted her. Then, lips pursed and eyes glittering, she told him. Allan was out on a call. There were no patients, for evening office hours were over, but they sat upstairs lest some emergency bring a patient tugging at the door bell.

"Your mother has found nought wrong," said Thomas, his brow furrowed, "and she has been staying there."

"H'mph!" said Agnes daringly.

Agnes would never have ventured such a tone, thought Thomas, unless she knew more than she could say. His imagination raced, burning pictures into his mind.

"I have seen them together *here in this house*," said Agnes bitterly. "A woman—a married woman—could not be mistaken about such things."

It was the wrong thing to say. Thomas was sick of the self-righteous certainty of women and their hysterical judgments. Maria and Julia, even Mary sometimes—

"Anyone can be mistaken," he said coldly.

Agnes shifted quickly.

"Oh, I hope I am!" she cried eagerly. "I would give anything to know that I am wrong and that my sister is not disgracing her father and her family. Still, you know how she was when she was young. Had it not been for you, there is no telling what Emily might have done."

Thomas nodded gravely. Agnes was right. Yet he could hardly say so, even to Agnes.

"Judge not," he reminded her, "that we be not judged."

"Oh, I know," said Agnes contritely, her eyes misting over, "and I have tried so hard!"

"There, there!" said Thomas, patting her hand with his great, work-scarred hand. "There, there!"

Agnes dabbed at her eyes, but she managed a clear look at her father's face.

"It is not so much for myself that I mind," she said, "though I do try to lead a Christian life as a mother and as the wife of one who goes about healing the sick. It's that—" she stopped.

"What, girl? What?" demanded Thomas, after a few seconds. He could never bear to be kept in ignorance once his curiosity had been piqued, and Agnes knew it.

"It's her singing in the Fifth Avenue Church!" blurted out Agnes vindictively, her dull eyes flashing. "If what I think is true, it is a mockery of true religion and of Christ himself."

"You must not say such things," said Thomas sternly.

"Heaven knows I do not want to say them," said Agnes, beginning to cry again. "O, Pa, I'm so glad you have come. I've been so troubled."

"There, there!" said Thomas again. He, too, was glad that he had come. He could see now that he had been badly needed. "We'll see," he said, his face hardening. "We'll see about things."

Agnes lifted her head.

"Is that you, Allan?" she called sweetly. "We are up here, Allan!"

Allan came heavily up the stairs from the basement. His face was ruddy, and he was rubbing his hands together. He was so much surprised by his father-in-law's sudden presence that all he could think of saying was:

"It's getting colder again, very cold. Er—is it cold in Ilium, Mr. Stapely?"

The next day Thomas still hesitated. He was too comfortable in the Mott Haven house with Agnes and Allan, both trying to show how pleased they were to have him, each anticipating his every wish. Relaxed, as he seldom was, he shrank from possible unpleasantness. Andrew Gray was a gentleman and a communicant of St. Martin's. Yet Thomas knew that even such men could be tempted. Emily was a woman grown, poised, and assured. Could he order her about as he had done when she was a mere girl? Perhaps James—but he could not talk about it to James. If anything were wrong, it was his duty to right it. He prayed for wisdom. Should he storm the flat on West 19th Street and try to catch them in their wickedness?

His anger rose at thought of that wickedness. It was not for this that he had left the Forest and fought and labored in South Ilium. No ungrateful, strong-willed, rebellious child of his would flaunt her upbringing. He could fight and worst the devil now as he had before. His blood coursed strongly through him as he girded again for battle.

Sunday evening, he and Agnes went to the Fifth Avenue Church.

Awed by the size and splendor of the church but determined not to show it, Thomas took his seat with Agnes in a pew halfway to the front, to which a grave usher quietly led them. Agnes, in her best finery, settled herself primly by his side. Knowing that in this church he must not kneel, Thomas bowed his head for a moment, then covertly looked about him. The church was filling with the kind of people he had seen arriving in their own carriages or walking quietly down Fifth Avenue. Frock-coated, dignified men led their families to their pews. There was the rustle of silks and of whispered greetings.

Thomas did not see the organist enter, but suddenly the prelude began, soft and singing. Then the notes of the organ rose steadily into the simple statement of the melody. It was solemn but singing music of muted stateliness and grace. It spoke of sorrow and ease and peace, and it entered into Thomas, reaching the man through his real love of music. He knew its beauty and perfection and, as he listened, he was lost to all else about him until Samuel Rollins raised his hand and said, "Let us pray."

The choir rose for the opening anthem, and Thomas saw Emily for the first time.

"There, Pa! There she is," hissed Agnes.

Thomas twisted in irritation. As though he could not see! Even at that distance and high above him in the choir loft he could recognize Emily's features. Her golden head shone. Her features were cold and perfectly composed as her voice rose in harmony with the others. And the music was still beautiful, still perfect. Thomas thrilled to it as pride in Emily hammered at his heart.

Agnes sniffed.

"We used to sing that when I was in the paid choir in the big Presbyterian church in Ilium," she reminded him in another sharp whisper.

"Be quiet!" said Thomas.

Could Emily see them, he wondered? He did not think she could. She had given no sign. She could not, of course, even if she did see them. Suddenly, Thomas wanted her to see them. He wanted her to know that he was there. He stared intently at her as though he would hypnotize her into seeing him. The anthem finished, the choir closed its music and stepped down out of sight.

Samuel Rollins preached on the Good Samaritan. The aging minister adjured to nothing. He told his story as a story he knew that his parishioners knew and loved, then seated himself in quiet faith that they too understood.

It was then that Emily rose alone. Panic gripped Thomas as he saw her standing tall and slender in the great church. He wanted somehow to help her face the filled church. He was afraid she would falter, that her voice would fail her from nervousness. He almost rose from his seat.

Emily stood quietly, awaiting the introductory notes from the organ. They began, and Thomas saw the organist nod his head sharply. Emily's lips parted and she began to sing:

Abide with me. Fast falls the eventide.
The darkness deepens; Lord, with me abide.
When other helpers fail and comforts flee,
Help of the helpless, oh, abide with me.

The words of the familiar and beautiful English hymn, which was one of Thomas' favorites, came clear and true, the notes filling the church with their golden sound. The harshness which sometimes betrayed the power of Emily's voice was lost in the great church. Perhaps it was not there. She sang easily, with no trace of nervousness, the fluid notes pouring from her lips, the words distinct, no mannerism or affectation of the singer imposing on the sense or sound of the hymn. People about them murmured appreciatively as Emily sang her last note and stood for an instant silent. The new soprano would do!

Thomas had forgotten the determination with which he had come. The anger and distrust were melted from his heart. There were tears of sentiment and relief in his eyes.

"Emily sang very nicely," said Agnes miserably. She knew she had lost.

Thomas nodded, unable to speak.

After the benediction they lingered, not quite knowing what to do.

"I'll ask one of the ministers to have someone tell Emily we are here," said Agnes.

"Just wait, m'girl," said Thomas. "Emily has probably seen us."

"But she couldn't from there! I'll—"

A man was making his way toward them from the back of the church. It was Andrew Gray, controlled as ever, but smiling his pleasure. He held out his hand, and Thomas, smiling but his face stern and his chin lifted to hide his pride, shook it warmly.

"This is a real pleasure," said Gray sincerely. "I did not know you were coming. In fact, Emily does not know I am here. I hardly expected to be. Wasn't she splendid?"

"She was," said Thomas firmly.

Gray hesitated. "Then you are waiting for her here?"

"She doesn't know we are here," said Agnes pettishly. "I've been telling father—"

"You're surprising her! She will be delighted. I'll find her." Gray started off, but Emily was already coming up the aisle toward them wearing her coat and hat. Her face was eager. She seemed just to touch Gray's hand in passing as she hurried to her father.

"I saw you just as I stood up to sing!" she exulted. "I know it is your favorite, and I'd been thinking of you. I'm so glad, so glad!"

She put her gloved hands about his strong left arm, squeezing it hard, and Thomas stood bracing himself against his emotions. "Did Ma get home all right? When did you come? We'll all go right over to my place for tea."

"I told Agnes you had seen us," said Thomas triumphantly as Andrew shepherded them to the door.

Emily, breaking away from the young minister who stopped them at the door, hurried to catch up with Agnes, who trailed behind Thomas and Andrew.

"I think Pa is getting very old," said Agnes bitterly. "He's not himself."

"Why, I think he looks fine!" said Emily surprised. "Mind your skirts on that step. I almost broke my neck on it the other day."

Chapter 36

HER EYES ALERT, her fine features composed into a little smile, her dress carefully arranged, as it always was, Mary got off the train in Ilium on her return from New York and looked expectantly for Thomas. Though her energy was undiminished, she was satisfied for a time and glad to be home.

She knew just how Thomas would look. He would be dressed in his best, as he always was when he came to meet her, and freshly shaved. His face would be softened, his smile glad but shy. He would not kiss her or touch her in so public a place as the busy station, but she would know that he was pleased and that she alone could make him happy. People would turn and look at the strong handsome figure, and women envy her. It would be as it used to be when he met her at the station in Beechenford, when she had been down to London, or at Paddington when she was traveling the other way.

It was dark when Mary arrived. The long train shed and the station were brightly lighted. The engine of a train filling for Schenectady, Amsterdam, and the west, was hissing quietly on another track. An engineer in striped overalls and cap was poking a long and shiny oil can here and there about his locomotive's wheels and undercarriage. The fire blazed fiercely as the fireman knocked open the iron door of the boiler with his shovel and began to shovel in fresh coal from the tender.

Still she did not see Thomas. The station was crowded, and it had been a long train. Probably he was still watching at the gate or further down the platform. In a moment or two he would discover his mistake and come hurrying toward her. An announcer was calling that the train through the Hoosac Tunnel for North Adams, Greenfield, Worcester, and Boston was leaving on Track No. 7 at the other side of the station. The engine of her own train was puffing and snorting like a horse winded after a long run. Trunks, crates, and packages were being unloaded from its baggage car and trundled off in hand trucks. She wondered whether her own box, which Emily and Andrew had checked at the station, was among them and whether it would be broken.

The crowd on the platform was thinning. Passengers who had disembarked with her had hurried away, carrying their bags and other belongings. Mary stood there beside her own bag and began to feel puzzled. Thomas was never late. Then she heard someone call gaily and saw Will running up the platform, dodging in and out among the other people and the mounds of baggage.

"Hi, Ma!" he called again, as he came nearer, a wide smile on his face. He scooped up her bag. "Have a good trip?"

"Willy! Where's your father?"

"In New York!" laughed Will. "Surprised?"

"In *New York!*" repeated Mary, drawing herself up. "What's he doing there?"

"Painting the town red," said Will, delighted with the idea. "Gambling and going to dance halls and Barnum's. Come on, we'll miss the next car."

"Don't be silly," admonished his mother. "Nothing has happened?" she asked alarmed.

"No, honest. He went down yesterday, all of a sudden. It was too late to let you know. We thought you were at James's, and then—"

"Well!" said Mary, her lips tightening as she moved, tall and straight, after Will. "Well!"

She did not speak again until after they had boarded the South Avenue car. She was affronted and angry. That Thomas should go off to New York without so much as a 'by your leave' after refusing to come when the baby was born or all the time she was there, was unforgivable. It was humiliating.

"You look fine, Ma," said Will enthusiastically. "And I'm glad you're home. Gosh, has it been dull around there."

She did not have to pretend before Will. It would be a different matter with Maria and Julia. Evidently it was high time she had come home.

"But what made your father go off like that?" she demanded.

"Oh, I suppose he just wanted to," was all Will could offer. He felt surprised. Why shouldn't his father go to New York if he wanted to? Everyone else did. He tried to be tactful. "I guess he was lonely without you—though we got along all right."

"I've no doubt," said Mary coldly. She had not, she thought vehemently, been in New York for her own pleasure, but to help Agnes, as any mother would. Her indignation increased as the car jolted along. She realized now that she was tired and hungry. She would have to have a cup of tea as soon as they reached the house.

"We all missed you a lot," said Will uneasily.

"This looks like it, indeed," said Mary.

"How's Em? Did you hear her sing at the Fifth Avenue church? I knew she'd get along. Did you see Edna May in *The Belle of New York?* That's what I want to see when I go down again."

"How long does your father intend to be gone?" asked Mary, as though she spoke of some distant acquaintance.

Will shrugged. "I don't know. He had a letter from Agnes, but he didn't say what was in it. Probably she wanted him to see the baby."

He was amazed at the change in his mother when she reached the house. She greeted Maria and Julia with what, for her, was effusiveness, exclaimed that she was so happy to be home, saying she had wanted to come for weeks, and expressed her delight that Thomas had gone to New York.

Julia listened eagerly. Maria looked confused and chagrined. Without stopping to change her traveling attire, Mary sat down to tea and went into minute description of Agnes' baby to which the others listened with intent, excited expressions.

When Thomas came home three days later, Mary was still in the midst of furious housecleaning, cooking, and mending. Looking younger and refreshed, a spring in his step, relishing the fact that he had surprised her, he came into the house in the evening just as she was mixing the bread dough.

"Well, Mary!" he said, smiling broadly.

"Thomas! You surprised me," said Mary looking up and lifting flour covered hands. "Now be careful!" She turned her head for his kiss, holding her hands over the bread pan, then went on with her work.

Thomas, impatient to tell of his adventures, stood to one side as she went on mixing the dough, rolling it, kneading it.

He coughed. "All of them sent their love," he said, "and Mr. Gray sent his regards."

"Oh, you saw him too," said Mary perfunctorily. "Thomas, you are in my way."

Apologetically he stepped aside.

"Agnes misses you," he said. "She is very busy. It's a fine baby."

"I should think she would miss me," said Mary. "Certainly I was busy all the time I was there."

Somehow Thomas found he was in her way again and was forced once more to step aside.

He seemed continually to have to step aside for the next three or four days, for when Mary was not baking she was dusting or sweeping. He seemed to get no chance to talk with her, and all the lustre went out of him. Mary was polite and cheerful, but too busy to listen. All her news, she said, she had written in her letters. There was nothing to add.

Then there were all the Christmas preparations to get under way. She, Maria, and Julia had to cut up the mincemeat and put it into the big stone crocks, chopping, slicing, cutting the glistening white suet, drying lemon peel and shaving citron; making the rich plum puddings to set in the cold on the wide shelf in the summer kitchen. Thomas and Will could hardly get into the house through the crowded kitchen.

In the evenings she had calls to make to let people know she was at home again, and others came in to get the news of New York and of James, Agnes and the new baby, and Emily. Mary had time enough to laugh and chat with them, thought Thomas aggrievedly.

He grew bitter with Will, who found it wisest to stay out of the house as much as he could, and harsh with the few men working for him. The unfairness of it all angered him. He had been away a few days, while Mary had been in New York for many weeks. Still, he had to acknowledge, she did not know what had been in Agnes' letter, and he could not tell her. That circumstance gave Thomas enough of a feeling of martyrdom to prevent his exploding from frustration and annoyance.

Though the work was still slow, Thomas had vestry meetings at St. Mark's, Christmas music to practice with the choir, Sunday-school lessons to prepare, and the Christmas entertainment to engineer. Will, who had been adding to his repertoire, was to give *Casey at the Bat*, despite the season. Thomas had demurred, but the rest of the committee had decided it would do no harm. Whatever Willy did, said John Withers, was good. He chuckled as he remembered Will's Irish imitation.

Something, too, had gone wrong with the bellows of the organ.

Repair of the instrument he was so proud of, gave Thomas several pleasurable evenings of work. He would trust no one else to touch the organ. The rector twice came over from the parsonage to watch him, exclaiming over Thomas' work with what to him was a maze of pedals, levers, wires, and pipes.

Mary waited for an evening when she knew Thomas was to be home and Maria out caring for old Mrs. Jarvis who had *la grippe*. Julia, who had been complaining of a sick headache, she urged to bed after late tea.

"Will," she said, "I want you to stay at home this evening. Your father and I intend to have a talk, and I want you to be there. It concerns you."

"Me?" asked Will, alarmed though his face did not show it. "All right, Ma, though I was going—"

"You can go some other night," said his mother firmly.

Will wondered if she or his father had found out that he was spending much of his time at Flannagans with Mike, Mamie, and a few others. Edith and her family were in Glens Falls now. He had been anguished at first, then relieved. Mamie Flannagan, even if she was Irish and a Catholic, was prettier and more fun. He had never touched her. It was unlikely she would let him, though he burned to find out.

Thomas was busy at his accounts, adding columns of figures and jabbing the results down in big figures with the stub of a flat carpenter's pencil when Mary, followed by Will, came into the living room.

"Are you busy, Thomas?" asked Mary pleasantly. She sat down in one of the upholstered chairs, as though she intended to stay. Will stood uncertainly.

Thomas grunted, finished a column, put down his pencil, and took off his glasses.

"We must be getting out some bills," he said doubtfully. "There is not much money coming in these days and some people have been owing us a long time."

"I'll help you with them tomorrow night," Mary promised. "I've been wanting to talk with you for some days, Thomas," she went on brightly, "but you've been so busy ever since I came home."

"*I've* been busy!" said Thomas, astounded.

Will, watching his mother's calm but intent face, her overly watchful eyes, as she sat with her hands neatly clasped in her lap, wondered uneasily what was coming. He moved nervously where he stood.

Thomas turned on him. "Be still, boy," he ordered. "You'd best run along. Your mother and I have things to talk over."

Gladly, Will started to go, but Mary stopped him.

"I want Will to hear this," she said.

Thomas frowned and stared at his wife. The anger he had repressed for many days made his voice louder.

"Speak up, Mary," he said. "What is it?"

"The children miss us very much," said Mary complacently.

Was that all? Thomas felt relieved. He cleared his throat.

"I suppose they do," he said gruffly. "We missed our parents when we went away from home."

"That was different," said Mary, though she did not explain why. "The children miss us and they need us."

Thomas nodded in agreement.

"I've been in New York as much as I could," said Mary virtuously, "more than I've wanted to be—though some people may think differently." She had fully made up her mind. If Thomas was going to act the way he had in going to New York, she did not intend to spare him.

"I've just been there myself," Thomas defended himself.

"And I'm very glad you went," said Mary significantly. "You were able to see for yourself what I am talking about."

Will did not yet know what she was talking about, and he could see that his father did not either.

"They are getting along very well," said Thomas proudly. "Little did we think a few years ago that our Emily would be singing in the Fifth Avenue Church or that James would be a doctor. The Lord has been good to our family, Mary."

"I'm sure he has," said Mary briskly, as though she would be the last not to give the Lord his due, "but that is not quite what I am talking about."

"What are you talking about then?" asked Thomas, frankly puzzled.

Mary took a deep breath.

"Emily is very much alone most of the time," she said, "and it is not good for her. She is lonely. Mr. Gray is a very good friend, but he cannot be with her all the time. Some weeks, I know, he can only call once or twice all week. Of course, she has Ellen there, but that is hardly the same as having her own people about her. She is exhausted some days after she has given three or four piano lessons and done her own practicing. I felt very sorry for her."

"Everyone gets tired at his work," said Thomas bluntly, "and I never wanted her to live alone in New York."

"But she has to, of course," said Mary. "Then there are James and Agnes. Agnes could not have got along without me these past weeks, and James certainly needs help."

"James needs help!" repeated Thomas, amazed.

Mary took a deep breath. Her face remained still, but her color heightened. She felt she had done her best to break it gently.

"Thomas, I have been thinking it over for some time. I think we should move to New York or Brooklyn."

Thomas looked at her as though he could not believe what he had heard. His lips parted, but he said nothing.

"Ma!" exclaimed Will.

Mary looked at him, smiled, and nodded sharply.

"You mean," said Thomas slowly, "leave this house? Leave South Ilium? Leave my work?"

"It is time," said Mary gently, "that we realized our responsibilities to our children."

Thomas' face and neck swelled with rage. Slowly he doubled up his great fist. He smashed it down on the table next to him with a crash which almost split the hard walnut. His pencil sprang up and clattered to the floor, and objects on the mantel rattled.

Mary did not move. Thomas looked at her for seconds, his teeth bared, his fist still clenched as though he might even strike her. Suddenly he leaped up, knocking his chair back, almost knocking over Will as he strode to the door. Then he turned and faced them.

"I built this house," he roared. "I built half of South Ilium. With God's help I built our life here."

"I think I helped a little too," said Mary with maddening quietness.

"Our life has been here," said Thomas, biting off each word. "Our children grew up here. Our church is here."

"Our children are not here now."

"I could get a job in Brooklyn," said Will eagerly. "There's lots of building there. James knows people. I could—"

"That will do, Will," said his mother.

Thomas looked at them both, the anger blazing from his eyes.

"So you have been plotting it out," he said, "plotting against me. I—"

"Will knew nothing about this," said Mary. "When you calm down, Thomas, you will realize the truth of what I am saying. I think our work here is done. We should move nearer the children."

But her voice had lost its certainty. She had known that Thomas would be angry. She had wished to anger him, but perhaps she had gone too far.

"When I worked in London as a lad," said Thomas, "I knew always that the Forest of Dean was there and in the Forest was the lodge with my mother and father. I knew that my home was where it had always been. I could not have stood it otherwise."

"And I was there too," said Mary softly.

"You were there too," he said more quietly. "We shall stay here. James and Agnes and Emily know that we are here. They have chosen their lives, and they are living them well. We will not interfere."

"Interfere!" cried Mary, stung. "It is the last thing in my mind. I do not call it interference when I go to them." Will was aghast to see tears in his mother's eyes. "And I know what I am talking about, Thomas. How could you know what is going on from seeing them for a day or two? Agnes," she said, deliberately choosing to say what would hurt and stir him most, "does not take proper care of Allan or her house. Emily and I had to clean it from top to bottom, wearing ourselves out, and I spent two solid days mending Allan's socks and shirts. They have been shamefully neglected."

Thomas did not answer.

Mary waited before she spoke again, watching Thomas' face which showed nothing.

"And James," she added, coolly, "is drinking."

Will started. How had his mother found out about that night?

Thomas looked at his wife almost with contempt.

"That I do not believe," he said.

"I smelled liquor on his breath when I was in Brooklyn, and Laura told me. She did not wish to tell me."

"She lied," said Thomas. "Or if James is drinking, she drove him to it. A woman *can* drive a man to drink."

It was Mary who sprang up this time, but she was beaten, and she knew it.

"Well!" she gasped. "Well!"

Will's imagination had been leaping ahead, and he wanted to help his mother.

"I could room and board with James," he said. "There's not much work here right now. I could save you that much, Pa."

Mary turned on him. "Don't bother your father now, Will," she said. "Can't you see that he is upset?"

Will's eyes widened at the unfairness of her attack.

"I will not be tricked," said Thomas, looking at Mary, "by women's talk. Or by the talk of a young fool." He looked at Will. His voice was trembling, and his hands shook. Then his voice steadied. "I came here from the Forest. I will leave here when I die. Rather than leave this house I would tear it rafter from rafter, board from board. I would smash the sills with an ax and burn the ground."

It was of no use pressing the point further then, thought Mary practically. Perhaps she had not really meant it in the first place. An involuntary smile touched her lips. It was unlikely, she knew triumphantly, that Thomas would be off without telling her and fail to meet her the next time she came home. She had taught him a deserved lesson.

"We'll talk no more about it now," she said firmly. "This has been our home for a long time, Thomas, and, we've been happy in it. Still—"

Thomas looked at her as though trying to quiet himself and collect his thoughts. He saw his pencil on the carpet and looked ashamed as he bent to pick it up.

"I'll go on with my figuring," he said hoarsely.

He sat there with his pencil poised staring at the figures. He heard Will go out. Mary, he knew, was still sitting there. As long as she remained, he pretended to be busy with his work, adding and totaling results of several columns of his addition, making marks on the paper. Even when he heard her stir, he did not turn around. After she left the room, he sat looking blindly at the lined yellow pad with his meaningless figures on it.

His rage had left him feeling weak and numb with disbelief. So they thought, did they, that he was old and done? The ingratitude of Mary's attack, the disloyalty that it bespoke, stunned him most. It was as though all that he had accomplished with years of unremitting labor, and most of it for her, was now held at nought. He had tried to give her everything that he thought a woman would want, striven to make up to her for what she might have lost through marrying him and leaving England. She had let him think that he had succeeded, and he had walked like a fool with his head high in his pride in her and in their life. Humbly, he had never thought that Mary was as he or the other English of South Ilium. He had never acted as though she were. Now for the noise and crowds in New York, the big shops, and a few plays she would discard all that he had wrested for her from life and give it not a thought.

She was only a woman and could not understand everything—but the dull bitterness weighed like lead in Thomas' chest. He felt broken in, spirit. Was it his fault that there was a panic, and that business was bad? Emily with her fine clothes and Gray with his fine manners! It was they had done this to Mary and to him. James with his horse and carriage!

He wished he could strip the green bag from his cello and seek solace in playing. But he had heard Mary go upstairs and get into her bed. He could not disturb her.

Thomas dropped his head into his arms and hid in the darkness. He could not think. Pictures crossed before his eyes—of himself as a small boy learning his letters in the Forest school, of his father, broad-shouldered and strong, an honest servant of the King as he guarded the oaks and beeches in their stands, profane and godless at times, deeply religious at others. He saw himself learning his trade in Beechenford and Wakeney, working away from dawn until dark at the apprentice tasks assigned him; then as a journeyman carpenter in London, doing more than his day's work, building a great city. He remembered their voyage from Liverpool, with James and Agnes—small children then. There had been a great storm, then days of quiet sailing over calm, dark green seas stretching to the horizon and beyond it, America—and they knew not what.

Thomas got up and stumbled through the doorway, through the kitchen, and out, hatless and coatless, into the black and frigid night. Unthinkingly, he started down the hill. He met no one, and soon he was facing St. Mark's which stood black in shadow and silent as the night. He wished he could go in. He had a key to the side door, but the key was at home. Thomas climbed the steps and put his hands against the strong front doors of seasoned oak which he had made and hung so finely that they had never stuck or warped. They were almost a symbol of how he had lived and all that he had done, and that now Mary declared worthless.

He could not recover from the blow. For a moment he stood there senselessly pushing against the fast locked doors of St. Mark's. Could he have got in he would have prayed—for strength and understanding, for companionship in his lonely misery. He hunched his shoulders against the cold and leaned back for shelter from the wind. His teeth had begun to chatter. Helplessly, he turned and went down the steps and made his way home.

He was warming himself at the kitchen fire, where a kettle simmered and a pot of cracked wheat had been put to warm and soak overnight for breakfast, when Will came home. He looked up but did not speak as Will hesitated, then went to the door of his bedroom off the kitchen.

" 'Night, Pa," he said.

"Good night, Will," said Thomas.

But Will continued to stand there.

"I wouldn't really want to leave Ilium and here," he said. "I thought about it while I was out."

"It's all right," said Thomas dully.

"Aren't you going to bed?"

Thomas did not answer, and Will, wanting to comfort him, was helpless. He went on into his room. He did not know whether his father went to bed that night or not, though he tried to stay awake to listen.

The next day Thomas had a bad cough. His eyes were bloodshot and his nose was red and running. He looked ill and old. He drank his tea but would eat no breakfast. He did not offer to go to work.

"Thomas, you should be in bed," Mary said in mid-morning after watching him worriedly. When she saw that he was not going to object, she urged him on. "We'll get you into bed, and then I'll get something for that cold." He went meekly.

Partly in alarm, partly as penance, Mary got her coat and hurried down the hill. She went straight to the grocer's.

"I want a small bottle of whiskey," she said clearly to Mr. McCall. "Mr. Stapely has a cold and I think that might check it."

"We don't sell it, Mrs. Stapely," said the grocer sympathetically, "but if you'll stay here a minute, I'll run across to McGuire's and get you some."

"No, thank you, I'll get it," said Mary quickly, and he looked at her in astonishment.

Heavy, red-faced, black-haired McGuire looked up in astonishment as Mary entered his saloon. He was polishing glasses behind his bar. A lone workman leaned against it drinking beer. Nervously, but firmly, Mary told him what she wanted.

"Sure, sure, Mrs. Stapely," he said. "It's a pint, you'll be needin'. Best thing in the world fer a cold." He pulled a bottle hurriedly from under the bar, wiped at it with his cloth, wrapped it neatly in a piece of newspaper, and took Mary's money.

"By God," he said, looking admiringly after her, "I never thought I'd see her in this place. There's a woman for you. Knows what she wants and gets it. The old man's no slouch in his way, but she's got fire in her. Got style too. Ever see that blonde daughter a' theirs? She's down in New York now. Used to go hellin' around here with young Will."

"Yeah," said the drinker disinterestedly. He pushed at his schooner. "Gimme another."

Mary made a stiff hot toddy for Thomas and sat by his bed as he sipped it, making sure that he drank it to the last drop. "There now," she said. "Now try to get some sleep."

Thomas looked at her but did not attempt to answer. His throat was sore, and he felt choked.

By afternoon he was flushed with fever but lay in a dead sleep. He was breathing deeply but regularly. Mary, her conscience tormenting her, was worried. Thomas had had colds before. They lasted a few days, and he was all right again. But this time it looked worse.

Thomas awoke in late afternoon his fever gone and feeling better but indignant with his cold. Mary hovered solicitously.

"You stay right in bed," she ordered, "and I'll bring your tea up to you. I think I'd better send for Dr. Samuels."

"That would be a waste of good money," said Thomas huskily. "I need no doctor, and I'm getting up."

"You'll do nothing of the sort," said Mary warmly.

"I've work to do at the church," said Thomas gruffly. "Thank you for getting the whiskey. It did me good."

He felt weak and unsteady as he got into his clothes, but stronger when he was dressed to face the world again, a world which had suddenly become insecure and threatening. It was a measure of the depth of his perturbation that he had decided to talk with the rector.

Thomas Stapely did not seek the advice of other men. They sought his. Even now he could not fully acknowledge his purpose. He went to the rectory that evening ostensibly about a part of the cellar wall which was giving way. A leaking gutter had allowed the rain to weaken the heavy masonry foundation which was of large native stone placed in position probably by oxen, for a man could not lift many of them, nor two men.

There was a light only in the rector's study when Thomas, heavily overcoated and a thick muffler about his throat, knocked at the door. The rector himself answered. As usual, he had a book in his hand, a forefinger inserted to mark his place. He was older, thinner, and there were new lines in his face, but his eyes were still young, interested, and compassionate.

"Mr. Stapely!" he said. "Come in, come in."

"Thought we might have a look at that wall," explained Thomas, hoarse from his cold, "and see just what's to be done, though probably it can't be fully mended till spring."

"Of course. Let me have your coat. You've a cold," he said. "A bad one, by the sound of it." He looked at Thomas' red eyes, swollen nose, and white face.

"It will soon be gone," said Thomas.

"My wife is in bed. She's not well either," explained the rector. "I'll get a lantern."

In the low, dirt-floored and dark cellar, the rector held the smoking lantern high while Thomas expertly inspected the damage. The sills and underpinning, he saw with relief, were sound. He had feared they would be rotted. Some of the big stones had tipped and slid out of the wall to the floor in a heap of boulders. The air, cold and damp, poured in out of the night.

"It will have to be shored up for now," he decided, turning to the rector, whose face was in the light but whose body was in the black shadow which held most of the cellar. "I'll send a couple of men down in a day or two. In the spring this side of the house will have to be jacked up and the wall rebuilt with mortar and stones. We may be able to lever some of these back into place."

He looked around another moment or two, then turned, and followed the rector up the steps. At the landing they wiped their feet carefully before going into the kitchen.

"That's fine, that's fine," said the rector absently. "Now come into my room. I've a good fire there. It's warm, and we can talk for a while."

"I should be off," said Thomas, "but I'll be glad to stay for a bit."

They faced each other in the same pleasant, book-filled room where the rector and Will had talked years before, and Thomas blew his nose vigorously.

"I've some port," said the rector. "It would do you good."

"No," said Thomas. He'd had liquor enough that day.

"Yes," smiled the rector.

He left Thomas a moment and returned with a dark bottle and two small glasses. He filled one and handed it to Thomas, then filled another for himself. Before sitting down opposite Thomas, he threw another log and some kindling chips on the fire. The chips caught and blazed. Thomas noted approvingly that the wood in the box near the fireplace was good elm, beech, and apple, probably from Arthur Dawson's lot and brought by Dawson to the rector. He looked awkwardly at the ruby red of the port in his glass, which seemed too delicate and fragile for his big hand. He wondered how to begin.

The rector saw and wondered at the uncertainty and fear in his parishioner's eyes.

"We can't have you ill, you know," he said sincerely. "St. Mark's would be in a bad way."

"It would get along, I have no doubt," said Thomas grimly. "Mrs. Stapely thinks so."

The rector smiled and raised his eyebrows inquiringly. He got up to adjust the wick in his green-shaded student lamp and stood near it for a moment.

"I often think it could get along very well without me," he admitted.

Thomas did not answer. He put down the glass of port which he had not touched. "If—if that rainspout had been attended to in time," he said, "the wall would never have given."

"I suppose you're right," said the rector. "The proverbial ounce of prevention." He watched Thomas quietly.

There was no easy way. There never was an easy way. Trying, and failing, to control his voice, Thomas blurted out his story.

The rector listened. That, he thought, was some excuse for his life.

He could listen. He listened to the man rather than to his words. Tom Stapely had been hurt, deeply hurt, and his wounds were still raw. He was bewildered, as a man is when he finds that what he loves and values is not held as dear by others and that understanding he had assumed had never been there. Thomas Stapely was not formidable and forbidding now. He was lost and terror-stricken, scratched by brambles and branches. Worse, he was lost in what he had thought was a familiar place.

The rector hesitated. Except the great and abiding truths, there was so little one could ever be sure of. Thomas Stapely's faith in God had not been shaken. It was worse. Suddenly his faith in himself had been struck an unsettling blow.

The rector sipped his wine. It was warming and good.

"I know," he said finally. "A man loves his place. Englishmen, especially, I think. We grow to love the one place that we think of as ours, its shape and landmarks, its people, the sky over it, everything about it. And the longer we live there, the dearer it becomes. It seems to take on the life we have lived in it, our thoughts and actions, and our hopes—even our disappointments and defeats."

"Yes," said Thomas, surprised and grateful. "That's it."

He felt ashamed now. He wished that he could unsay all that he had said. He wished he could leave, but he did not know how to go. Besides the warmth and comfort of the square room with its books and mellowness made him loath to leave. He had worked on that room himself. Will had worked on it.

"And Mrs. Stapely," said the rector thoughtfully, "is an unusual woman."

"Her family is gentry," said Thomas proudly. "She was brought up to better things than I knew. Still, I have tried."

"And it is natural," said the childless rector, "for a woman to worry about her children, no matter what their age."

"That I know too," said Thomas. He sneezed and shuddered.

"They come first, you see," said the rector, feeling his way and doubting the truth of what he spoke even as he said it. "It is not that Mrs. Stapely does not appreciate you and her home and all you have done; but they are her children, and their welfare is uppermost in her mind."

Thomas regarded him stolidly. A little embarrassed by his expression, the rector went on more honestly, tempering his words with a gentle smile. "Besides, to the young in spirit—and Mrs. Stapely will always be young—there is the attraction of what is novel and colorful, a curiosity, and the need for change. Each of us has his temperament, and some demand more action and stimulation than others."

Suddenly Thomas felt disloyal to Mary, and annoyed with the rector for seeing and saying what he thought now he had always known.

"Mary has always done her Christian duty," he said a little more loudly than he had been speaking.

The rector raised his hand quickly. "I did not mean that at all," he said.

"I know," said Thomas loudly.

"You've not touched your wine. Won't you try it?"

"Thank you, thank you!" Thomas picked up his glass and sipped at it. He put it down quickly as another sneeze came treacherously upon him. He hid his face behind a large white handkerchief and sneezed violently twice again. He blew his nose once more and wiped his eyes. "Excuse me," he said abashed.

"To be truthful," the rector laughed, "I was doing the same thing myself yesterday. I hope your cold leaves you as soon. Do you know that ten years ago I planned to return to England? In a way, I suppose, I still do. My wife," he said, confiding to the other so as to lessen the difference between them, "has never been happy here. We have been home on visits, as you know, and I love my part of England as you love yours, but, like you, I have come to love South Ilium. I found I could not make myself leave it. Like you, my work has been here."

"You could not leave St. Mark's," said Thomas quickly.

"You are as important to St. Mark's as I."

"No!" said Thomas.

But it was a false denial, and the rector's words were sweet. The touch of healing reached his soul, and the rector saw it. He was moved as he had not been earlier.

The rector was glad. They could talk now not as priest and layman but as two men who had known each other for a long time.

"It's natural enough that Will should want to strike out for himself as James has done—as you did—and I did. And the ways of one generation are always different from those of the last."

"The ways of God," said Thomas sternly, "are eternal."

The rector nodded thoughtfully.

"But the ways of man change, and new ways are not always bad ways."

Thomas went home late that night.

Mary knew now that she had gone too far. Yet, in an odd way, she had not lost. She had discovered, what she had almost forgotten, that the world was firm under Thomas' feet, hence under her own.

As for Thomas, the rector had eased his pain, but he was not yet whole.

His face contorted and white with the strain, he looked desperately into Mary's eyes that night.

"Is—is our Emily—?" He could not finish. His own eyes begged her to deny what he feared. "Tell me truly."

Mary's face was composed but touched with pity. So much nonsense was talked about the truth. No one knew exactly what it was. Why was it always better to hurt?

Her voice was firm.

"You have just been there. You saw for yourself. I have seen nothing, Thomas, as I have said, which I consider amiss."

Thomas' face relaxed. His eyes softened with gratefulness and trust. The searing flame of uncertainty in his brain flickered and almost went out. The pain dulled.

"I love thee, Mary," he said.

It was Will who won.

"When I was your age," said Thomas suddenly one day when he and Will were at work together, "I was in London making my way. You've served your time. I can't hold you. You may go to New York if you wish." He tried to disguise his reluctance. Besides, Will was a good carpenter.

But Will heard it and knew his own unwillingness.

"I said I'd stay," he said, and sent home a nail with three sharp strokes of his hammer. Then he looked up excitedly. "Why couldn't I do this, Pa? I'll work for you when you need me here. I can get a job down there other times and come home when you need me again."

Thomas, who had been measuring a wall, folded his rule and replaced it in his hip pocket. He was pleased that Will did not wish to leave him for good, and he wished that he could show it. He tried.

"Perhaps we can work out something like that," he said brusquely.

Chapter 37

IT WAS SPRING, with the snow gone and the crocuses beginning to poke out of the ground along the south side of the house on the hill and the forsythia branches showing tightly curled buds, before Will could put the new plan into effect. There had been many preparations and letters back and forth before he left Ilium. James had the promise of a job for him at full journeyman's wages with a contracting carpenter who was one of his patients, and he was to pay Laura four dollars a week for his room and board.

Will's anticipations were high. Since Christmas he had been feeling and acting a new importance, yet when it came time to leave there was a queasy feeling in his stomach and his self-confidence, never strong, had almost completely evaporated. He had never worked except for his father, except as the "boss's son," and thus recipient of small privileges he could not assume elsewhere. He would miss August's friendly advice, his father's sure direction, the sense of accomplishment at seeing about him work that he had done. Only fear of ridicule kept him from backing down.

The next moment he was all anticipation again. New York would mean not only strange work in Brooklyn, which he had known only as a casual visitor, but also the theatre, the race tracks, seeing Emily, riding about with James, joking with Laura.

In a queer sense, he felt that he was abandoning his father, and he felt sorry. That it was absurd for him to feel sorry for the man he had long considered a ruthless tyrant did not occur to Will, whose feelings had been made acute by his impending departure. When, stumblingly, he tried to say something to Thomas, Thomas only remarked dryly that he'd manage to get along—if the bad times didn't land them all in the poorhouse. Mary had been twice more to New York and Brooklyn. He knew it would not be long before he would see her there again. It would not be long, in fact, before he was at home again. He'd have to be there for the St. Mark's excursion. The likelihood was that he would be back at work in South Ilium by midsummer or at least by autumn, though privately he was determined not to come back to South Ilium until the fall race meetings on Long Island were over.

He had had better luck lately, and had fifty dollars in his pocket that no one at home knew he had. Every time he dreamed of a winner, it came in. The trouble was that he could not regulate his dreams and had to select his choices on less dependable grounds when he failed to see the winners in his sleep. He pondered seriously on that mystery.

In New York, he took the El at 14th Street, then changed to a train which would take him over Brooklyn Bridge. By this time all his forebodings were over, and he was filled with eager expectancy.

"Hurry, Will," urged Laura meeting him at the door, kissing him, and shoving him along. "Liver and bacon. Smell it? Ice cream. James has been gnawing at his beard for the last ten minutes, but I made him wait. Wash your face and hands—and use the washcloth, not the towel. Cornelia!" she called to the servant. "Dr. Stapely's brother has come. We'll be ready in a minute."

James was sitting at his office desk with a white napkin around his chin and his knife and fork poised in his hands to emphasize the point.

"What did you do, walk all the way?" he derided Will. "Hurry up or we won't be able to get in a game before office hours, and I have a call afterward, and you'll go to bed. I promised Walters to deliver you sound and able to work in the morning."

Will was elated, and they were all in fine fettle at dinner. James beat him two games out of three, the last game after office hours, but that, Will claimed, was only because he could not keep his mind on the game.

"You'll have plenty of chances to get even," scoffed James. "Not that you will. So Pa was mad when Ma wanted to move down here."

"Mad! You should have seen him!"

James laughed. "I suggested something like that last summer, and it made him furious then."

"Oh, is that what happened!"

Before eight o'clock the next morning James delivered Will to David Walters, who proved to be a sour and suspicious, graying Scot.

He looked at Will dubiously. "But you're a mere child and a pretty boy too," he said. "I'd not have been so hasty perhaps if I'd known."

"I'm twenty-one," said Will hotly, though he would not be for some months. "And maybe I am prettier than some people."

Walters looked at him suspiciously from under shaggy eyebrows.

"If you're a good worker," he said, "you can stay as long as you like, or as long as I have work. If you're not, doctor's brother or no doctor's brother, you'll go."

Will, busy climbing into his overalls and made clumsy by his anger, did not answer. Walters looked at the tools in Will's open box and nodded approvingly, though Will could not see him. The tools were clean and sharp, a good sign.

Walters held the contract under a large-scale builder for the floors, windows, doors, and interior trim in a row of a dozen new houses further out than James's. He went there with Will in a surface car, showed him what to do, and went off to another job. Painters were at work outside the house and a plasterer was finishing a room upstairs. They paid no attention to Will except when one of the painters came to ask for a match and looked at him curiously. Will gave him the match, and, according to the ritual he had learned in Ilium, turned his back and went on with his work. The painter, educated in a similar school, understood and after watching Will silently for a minute, spat, and went away.

Will worked swiftly and with satisfaction. The feel of his tools in his hand steadied him. He ate his lunch sitting on a rough floor with his back to the nearest wall. Used to the lunch put up by his mother or one of his aunts, the sandwiches made by Laura's maid tasted strange but good. The cake was baker's cake which he did not like. He smoked a cigarette and sat there for a while. He could hear the voices of the painters outside, but not what they were saying. The plasterer had finished his work and gone. Will smoked another cigarette and waited for his lunch time to be up before starting work again. He was anxious to be at it, but he knew the painters outside would hear him, and it was not good form to start again until a minute or two after the whistle had blown.

Walters came back about half-past three and looked at what Will had done. He tested the firmness of a door jamb and ran his fingers over a window joint.

"Union?" he asked Will suddenly.

"No," said Will, alarmed. He had never thought of that.

"Good! I've no truck with the union. Loafers and wood butchers, most of them."

Will breathed more easily. "My father feels that way. So do I."

Walters grunted and looked about the room. "Do it fast. Slap it up. It's all time contracts. It has to pass building inspection, but it doesn't have to be good." He kicked a board contemptuously. "Half green. They get these places up and sell 'em before they're half done. Fools move into 'em. Serves 'em right."

Will resolved that he'd work both fast and well. He had no intention of dong sloppy work for anyone. Walters saw it in the set of Will's back and smiled. For a doctor's brother, the new man seemed well enough.

James won all three checker games that night. This time Will said it was because he was tired.

"Tired!" snarled James. "Wait till you put in the kinds of days and nights I do before you go around complaining of being tired!"

"If they re not sick when he sees them, he makes them sick," Will told Laura. "He makes me sick."

Meanwhile, in Manhattan, Emily was trying on an elaborate gown made for a very special occasion.

It took some judicious padding at the bust and hips, accomplished with giggling Ellen's help, before Emily felt she did justice to the new turquoise silk. At last she was properly formed to round out its magnificent lines. Chin lifted boldly, she paraded back and forth before the pier glass, practicing a majestic entrance followed by a sweeping progress across the room. She turned swiftly with a full swirl of lace-edged petticoats, pirouetted, and showed all her teeth in burlesque of a mincing smile.

Ellen collapsed on the edge of the bed and howled with shrill laughter.

Emily, shoulder lifted, stared down at her with annihilating disdain.

"Don' do it no moah!" begged Ellen happily. "Ah can' stand it!"

"We'll dress you up, too!" decided Emily inspired. She ran to the closet and began hauling down hangers. "Here, put this on," she ordered, flinging a pink, ruffled dress at Ellen. "And this! And this!"

"No, no, Miz Emily! Y'all stop!"

They struggled as Emily pulled and tugged the protesting young Negress into the finery, then took her arm, forced her into step, and sang a popular waltz melody as they paraded the room in chorus-line fashion.

"Fine! Fine! You're doing fine!" cried Emily, as Ellen found the wondrous reflection of herself in the glass and the tune irresistible. She began to preen delightedly and to step with a light natural grace.

In another moment they both fell laughing on the bed.

"Oh, Ellen, what would I do without you? You have to be dragon, friend, and playmate to me. All the rest of the time you listen to me practice or to those pupils of mine yowling and thumping the piano! How do you stand it?"

"Ah, loves it!"

"Don't ever leave me, Ellen," said Emily with tense seriousness. She clutched the black girl.

"Ah nevah will!" cried Ellen fiercely. "Ah ain' nevah goin' leave you, Miz Emily! An' you goin' be the pretties' lady at the whole ball!"

Will heard all about it when he came two nights later, dressed in his best, to see Emily. She was playing and singing softly as he climbed the stairs. Andrew Gray, a book in his finely shaped hand, sat listening quietly in a deep chair near a gas lamp in which the bright mantle hissed gently. Ellen let Will in, and he stood listening until Emily had finished. Gray smiled a quick welcome and nodded silently.

"Bravo!" he applauded when Emily turned.

"Will!" she cried. "Will! We were waiting, but I didn't hear you come in after all. Why didn't you tell me?" she asked Gray reproachfully as she jumped up to hug and kiss him. "What do you think, Will! I'm going to sing at the Press Club Fair. I was just trying several numbers to see which Andrew liked best. Isn't it splendid!"

Gray stood to shake Will's hand.

"We'll go everywhere and see everything, Will! Now Andrew can neglect me as much as he wants to! And you're going to the Fair with us. It's all arranged."

"I thought the Fair was in Chicago?"

"That," Gray explained, "is just a small affair. This is to be at the new Grand Central Palace on Lexington. It's bigger even than Madison Square Garden. And instead of Caruso and Patti we'll have Mam'selle Emilie de Stapelie!"

"Let him tease all he wants, Will. It's going to be wonderful. Band concerts, booths, thousands and thousands of people!"

Will, a little diffident before the older man with his aristocrat's face and immaculate dress, his quiet manners and humorous eyes, found a chair while Emily was talking. He smiled and nodded wisely.

"It sounds exciting," he said. But he could not maintain his pose. "But I don't know what you're talking about."

It was a remark Gray approved.

"I seldom know what people are talking about," he assured Will. "The Press Club is out to raise funds for a new building and to keep destitute and forlorn newspapermen from begging on the streets. As I expect to be decrepit and forlorn soon, I'm in favor of it."

Emily made a face at him.

"I've been active in the Club, and we all have to contribute. I'm doing my part by getting Emily to sing for nothing."

"Everybody is serving for nothing," said Emily, "even Mrs. Frank Leslie—she is stunning—and Ella Wheeler Wilcox."

Will knew that name. " 'Laugh,' " he quoted, " 'and the world laughs with you. Weep, and you weep alone.' "

To his surprise Gray laughed. "That's the one," he said. "Horrible, isn't she?"

Will laughed too, though he was puzzled. He liked the verse.

The Press Club Fair was bigger than any church bazaar Will had ever seen. The Palace, brilliantly lighted and shining in its newness, was the largest hall he could imagine. The crowds, the flowers, the music blaring from the magnificently uniformed 69th Regiment band, the splendid gowns of the women, the dignitaries in their formal dress intoxicated him.

Emily in her new gown, a diamond glittering at her throat, seemed to him the finest looking woman there. He swelled with pride as they made their way down the crowded aisles. Each newspaper had its own display. In one booth a new Hoe press was printing, folding, and tossing off copies of the *Journal of the Fair* at a tremendous speed.

Andrew Gray seemed to know everyone and everyone knew him. Will was surprised that many seemed to know Emily.

The Club president hurried up to thank Emily for coming to sing. Madame Van Caterna had sung the night before and Madame Fursch-Madi was to sing the next night, but he was certain neither of these famous ladies could hold a candle to Emily.

Emily laughed and curtsied prettily.

Murat Halstead came along as they were talking to Major Mc-Elrath, whose father had been Horace Greeley's partner. Halstead, a Southerner, bowed low over Emily's hand. Gray pointed out the president of *Judge*. He joked with an older newsman named Joe Howard, Jr., whom he seemed to know well. A young man in evening dress which was too large for him and a lock of lank hair which had escaped his pomade dangling over his high forehead, rushed up tell Gray that Chauncey Depew, an honorary member, had come across in great style with a letter urging their cause. He ticked off the names of others who had sent messages of congratulation—F. Hopkinson Smith, Joel Chandler Harris, Thomas Bailey Aldrich, Colonel Bob Ingersoll—.

Two grandly dressed women swooped down, talking and gesticulating. They were members, it seemed, of the music committee. Their glances flashed over Emily and Andrew Gray, then met in a meaning look which Will noticed but did not attempt to interpret.

The women carried Emily off, promising with great play of archness to return her later. Emily looked around helplessly, then made a comical wry face at Will and Andrew Gray as she disappeared into the crowd.

Gray looked nervously after her. He turned and pointed out several political notables to Will.

"Inevitably there is a certain amount of blackmail in affairs like this," he observed ironically.

"Blackmail?"

"They are afraid to stay away. They might hurt our feelings, and they never know when they will need newspaper support. Or they are up to something—they usually are—they are afraid the papers will find out about."

It was after ten o'clock when the Park Theatre orchestra struck up with a flourish. They played two numbers while Will and Gray stood uneasily waiting. The director held up his hand for silence, and Emily appeared under the brilliant lights on the platform.

She stood smiling and waiting for her cue as the orchestra played the opening bars of her first song. Discarding her first daring impulse to essay Lillian Russell's *Twickenham Ferry*, she sang *Drink to Me*

Only with Thine Eyes with lyric simplicity, and there was polite applause. The applause mounted in volume as she gave the *Battle Hymn of the Republic*.

Moved almost to tears by the sound and fury of the song, by the whole crowded scene, and the knowledge that it was Emily being applauded by the packed throng of well-dressed men and women, Will could hardly keep from shouting. He wanted to join in as she swung into the popular *After the Ball Is Over*.

When she had finished, the orchestra leader came forward to bow with Emily. He took her hand and held it high in his own before they backed gracefully away.

The applause now was insistent from all over the floor. There was a hurried, laughing conference between Emily and the musicians. The leader nodded and turned smiling with baton lifted again.

Prettily, coyly, bashfully, Emily began to sing *Over the Garden Wall*.

Will was astounded and delighted. Emily sang as though she were still in the kitchen in the house on the hill. This time her audience was wholly captivated. Long after Emily had run off the platform they continued to clap and call for an encore, but Emily did not reappear.

When she did rejoin them, Will was astounded again. Instead of being flushed with triumph, she was almost white, though spots of color showed angrily at her cheekbones. The smile she flashed to them as Andrew Gray hurried forward to her was artificial and fixed.

"You were wonderful, Em!" enthused Will. "Why, what's the matter?"

"Not," said Emily between her teeth, "a thing—not one damned little thing! She laughed delightfully for the benefit of any on-lookers. Then she looked at Gray and her face softened. "I'm being silly. I'm sorry," she said softly. "It was just those women and one remark I was not supposed to hear—or perhaps I was."

Gray's gentle, controlled expression had not changed. He touched her arm lightly, reassuringly.

"Will and I are very proud of you," he said. "And now," he said more loudly, "it's time for refreshments. Will and I have been waiting for you."

It was all gayety and lightness and sparkle after that. Emily glowed with happiness, and Will tried not to show his excitement.

He wondered how he could have stood South Ilium for so many years. The place where his father had triumphed over life was nothing to him now. He breathed the air of New York, and the raw, damp air of South Brooklyn, and found them both stimulating and delicious. His spirits sang to the sights and sounds about him.

Gray did not return to the flat with them, but handed Emily into a carriage, giving Will the money to pay the driver. It was an open hack, and the stars were bright high over them after they turned off the brightly lighted avenue. It was after midnight, and the streets were silent except for the clip-clop, clip-clop of their horse's hooves.

Sleepily Will dreamed back to Emily's singing of *Over the Garden Wall*. It was just the way she'd sung it as a girl, and that seemed half a lifetime ago.

"Em," he said happily, "you've everything you wanted, then. It's great!"

Emily looked at him.

"I'm not sure, Will," she said slowly, her voice like his low, so that the driver could not hear. "I'm not sure whether I have everything—or nothing. I've thought about it until the top of my head tries to break loose. Do you know what I'm talking about?"

"I—a little, I think."

"But I won't have less!" said Emily fiercely. "I'd rather have Andrew than ten ordinary men locked safe in the house at night and the key under the mat."

"You couldn't have ten. Not in New York State anyway."

But Emily would not be diverted.

"I'm not a fool, Will. I know what I'm doing. I knew three years ago. I was never the sweet young thing with her head full of the usual nonsense. You know why Andrew could not come home with us. He had to go to—his wife."

"I see."

"And if it isn't that, he has to be in Albany, or he just can't have me go to this or to that place with him. Sometimes I know where he is but I can't see him. It's hell."

Will listened to the sound of their horse's hooves and did not answer. He did not know what to say.

"This is my life, and it is the way I want it. Not Pa or James or Agnes or any holier-than-thou sisters of our pure and spotless press or the devil himself is going to change it. No, nor God. He wouldn't —not if He is what he pretends to be."

"I don't know much about him," said Will awkwardly.

BOOK 3

THIS MY PLACE

1897-1900

I might have been a hawk's scream, harsh and slow,
The plaint that's in the whippoorwill's still cry,
Six turning flakes of this down-drifting snow
Or neat track of a fox gone stealthy by
The hill field's rim. I might have been the rain,
March rain and cold or April rain and sweet;
Or scent of hay in June or faster stain
Across the light of speed to make it fleet.
Why on this earth? As well I might have been
Far darkness in the winds of starry space;
But I am quick and man, all these have seen.
I am them all and love for this my place.
My love is mine while planets, atoms, dance
And tremble 'round the cynic laws of chance.

Chapter 38

EMILY GREETED Andrew Gray at the door of her flat one afternoon more than three years later.

"You may enter," she said loftily.

She wore a dark shawl over a black dress, and a frilled, white house cap on her head. She had blown out her cheeks and pursed her lips. She held herself small and fat. With great dignity she preceded Gray into the front room, sat herself down with folded hands, and faced him.

"You may be seated," she said.

"Thank you," said Gray gravely.

Ellen stood holding both hands over her mouth to keep from laughing. Her eyes, whites showing wide, seemed about to pop. Emily regarded her coldly.

"That will do, Ellen," she said firmly. Her eyes were very bright, her cheeks were flushed, her spirits were a little too high.

It was too much for Ellen.

"She, Queen Victoria!" the black girl burst out in a delightful screech. "She been Queen Victoria all afternoon!"

"Oh," said Gray. He stood again.

"Mr. Gladstone, we believe," said Emily.

"Oh, no, your Majesty. I am—"

"Mr. Gladstone, we are certain. As we remember, we have detested you for years, though we have tried to be polite about it. What brings you again to Windsor, Mr. Gladstone?"

"Your Majesty is mistaken," said Gray earnestly. A slight furrow creased his forehead as he noticed the unstopped and only partly filled decanter of whiskey on the piano and the emptied glass.

"Her Majesty is never mistaken, Mr. Gladstone. You have refused to recognize her Great Grief *or* that, though She is *unwell,* She has worked consistently for the *Good* of Her people. You have tried to weaken the very grounds of *Her Sovereignty* by Ridiculous *Reforms,* causing wars with Russia and—and—we think it was Arabia—stirring up our *Dear Subjects* in Ireland and failing us in Sympathy and *Understanding.*"

Gray, his forehead cleared, fell to one knee, raising head and hand in supplication. Emily regarded him unmoved.

"Oh, my!" cried Ellen happily. "Oh, my! Oh, my!"

"Lady Ellen," said Emily finally, "you may show Mr. Gladstone to the gate. Perhaps our Cousin of Prussia or our Dear Leopold in Belgium or the Black Hand in Sicily will get him."

Ellen was dumbfounded. "You knows ah cain' do that, Miz Emily! This ain' Mr. Gladstone a'tall. It' Mist' Gray!"

Ignoring them both, Emily limped haughtily to the piano, adjusted her shawl, patted her cap, cleared her throat and began to play and sing in a cracked voice which was shrill and off-key.

For I'm called Little Buttercup, dear Little Buttercup—

"Bravo, your Majesty! Bravo!"

Emily turned slowly on the piano bench and looked at them shortsightedly. Surprise and displeasure clouded her face. She pointed accusingly at Ellen.

"You are not Ellen at all. You are the Prince of Wales. Have you been gambling again and running about with wicked women? Have you been drinking and smoking cigars?" She picked up the decanter and waved it at the maid.

"Me, ah ain' done nuthin' a'tall!" cried Ellen, eyes widening in alarm. "Hones' ah ain't." She grew indignant. "Y'all knows very well, Miz Emily, ah ain' done nuthin' wrong, not no time!"

She looked more alarmed as she saw the whiskey in Emily's hand. She had meant to put it away, as she had had to on several other occasions, before Andrew Gray's arrival—not that Miz Emily had drunk too much this time.

"We are not amused," said Emily, dismissing her. "You have *Disgraced* our *Family!* Begone!"

"You are the Sovereign, Ma'am," lisped Gray softly as poor Ellen left, "not only of my person, but also of my heart. My chivalry, my devotion are yours as they have always been, my kindest of mistresses."

"Dizzy!" cried Emily joyfully. "Dizzy! Have you another India for me?" But she drew back in sorrow and picked up a photograph of her father which stood on the piano. "Albert!" she breathed. "Albert!" She looked mistily at Andrew Gray, at the same time managing to look miserably red-nosed and wrinkled.

"Then, your Majesty," said Gray regretfully, "will hardly be interested in celebrating her Jubilee at the theatre and at supper afterward. It's too bad, for I already have the tickets."

"Oh, wouldn't she!" cried Emily. "Here, you be Queen Victoria while I get ready for tea." She draped her shawl about Gray, crammed her cap on his head, kissed him, tweaked his nose lightly, and disappeared. She returned and stood in the doorway, eyes laughing. "If Father and Will can be in England for the Jubilee, we can have one of our own just as good right here! I don't want to be Queen Victoria anyway. I'd rather be me. And you're better than any old Dizzy Disraeli Beaconsfield!"

Gray laughed after her, dragged off the shawl, which he decided must be Ellen's, and took off the frilled white cap, mechanically smoothing his hair which was entirely gray now but still thick and strong looking.

He looked for a moment at the whiskey decanter. Was Emily, after all, to blame, or was he, that sometimes she took that way of assuaging her loneliness? It was nothing, but—

He untied the string and took the wrapping paper off a small book which he had brought with him. It was richly bound in dark red morroco, with the title and the name of the author finely lettered in gold leaf on the backbone. The paper was fine, the type was a clear, modest face. Gray inspected it critically. The copy was one of a dozen especially bound and printed on paper different from that used in the regular edition.

He kept the book hidden as Emily and Ellen returned, the servant bearing the tray laden with the tea. He waited then until Emily had poured out his cup, then her own. They always made a ceremony of it, and Gray enjoyed watching her grace and deftness learned long ago from Mary.

He put down his Haviland cup and handed the book to her with a bow.

"With the compliments of the author," he said.

Emily looked at him, instead of at the book, her eyes widening in surprise. She pushed the tea things aside and reached for the book. For an instant she looked at it silently.

"Andrew, you never told me!"

"It's just a collection of things you've seen before. I wanted to surprise you. The illustrations are new though."

They were amusing pen and ink sketches decorating a page here and there. They were swift, sure, gay little comments.

Emily shook her head slowly.

"I think you're wonderful," she said finally.

"Oh, I thought we'd agreed on that long ago! Shall we put it here with the Shakespeare, where it really belongs, or over here with Fielding and Mark Twain?"

Emily looked at their bookshelves. There were sets of Balzac, Thackeray, Dickens, E. P. Roe and an ornately bound shelf of De Maupassant, more decorative than read. Andrew had kept her well supplied with books of every kind. They had read and discussed many of them as they appeared: *Sentimental Tommy, Hugh Wynne, Trilby*, whose vogue they had not escaped, the successive volumes of Kipling and of William Dean Howells, whom Gray admired more than Emily did, and the volumes, as they appeared, of H. C. Bunner, Frank Stockton, and their companion humorists of *Life* and *Puck*.

"We'll put it with the other Andrew Grays," said Emily decisively. Gray's three earlier books occupied their own place of honor between white jade bookends on a Chinese ebony table. "Tonight, though, I shall keep it under my pillow."

She was still running her fingers lovingly over the leather of the binding. "It feels so cool and smooth, and it smells so good!" She held it to her nose. "Oh, I love it!"

"Does y'all want anything moah fo' ah go?" asked Ellen, appearing in the doorway, her good humor recovered.

"Why, Ellen!" exclaimed Andrew Gray, "you look magnificent!"

Dressed in a pale green silk which Emily had given her and a hat with a wide, floppy brim and a sweeping ostrich plume, Ellen teetered uncertainly on high red heels. She wore white gloves to her elbows, and earnest corseting had made her small waist tiny. She was a comely young Negress with a fine skin.

"Let me fix your collar." Emily jumped up to adjust the imitation lace with which Ellen had embellished her dress. "There's that's better."

Ellen stood there another instant for their admiration. "Ah be back early," she promised, and turned with swirling skirts to skitter down the hall.

Emily looked after her. "Good-bye, Ellen. Have a good time! What I'd do without her," she told Gray, "I don't know. Ellen has more sense than I."

She still held his book. She had not put it down, even when she went to Ellen. She was afraid he would notice and tease her, but she could not let it go.

They were full, happy days for Emily. She practiced in the morning. Her voice and piano pupils took most of her afternoons. Friday evening choir practice was a pleasant event of the week. Sunday, with the choir singing at both morning and evening services and sometimes at special vespers given over mostly to music, was the climax of the week.

Conscious that she was admired for her beauty as well as for her voice, pleasantly aware that she was a favorite with Cecil Fielding, the clergy, and the congregation, Emily blossomed and expanded to the occasion. Winter and summer the Fifth Avenue Church parade thrilled her. She never saw it all, for the choir gathered early, but consciousness of her role as a performer only added to her pleasure.

Her mother, seeming to grow younger in spirit every year, was back and forth from South Ilium, sometimes landing unexpectedly for announced stays of a day or two which invariably were protracted into weeks. Emily's flat was headquarters too for other visits to James and Laura and to Agnes'. Though it sometimes meant hurried rearrangements of her plans and Andrew's, Emily was always glad to have her mother, whose presence meant reassurance, the comfort of sustaining background, the nearness of unspoken sympathy. Her father, noticeably older but hardly less forceful, seldom came to New York, and Emily felt it was just as well. Now he and Will were in England for the Jubilee.

She and Gray went to every important concert at Carnegie Hall. They saw as many of the new plays as they could. Sometimes when Gray could not get away, he sent tickets and she and Will went off for a laughing, happy evening—laughing and carefree for Will at least. Her own merriment was not always as easy.

Her days had to be more than full. Often Emily tried to arrange them so there could be no time for thought. Increasingly she had come to dread the days and nights and evenings when, except for Ellen, she was alone. Always there was a paining sense of incompleteness and deprivation, a gnawing fear, to keep smothered and to hide from.

She had not changed. She had chosen her way. She had no regrets. Her life with Andrew Gray had been and was perfection and beauty of which she could not have dreamed as a girl in South Ilium. She had embraced it knowingly, aware of the heartaches it would entail.

She and Andrew never spoke of his absences from her, absences sometimes of days or of weeks when she knew only too well where he was. They tried to ignore the minimum of incessant pretenses they had to make, the small subterfuges which were necessarily part of their lives. What they had was worth the pain they had to endure—only sometimes Emily could not endure it.

Their very deprivation kept desire and tenderness fiercely alive. Gray used flowers and jewels, and gifts of minor art treasures to say the things he could not say. She could never have enough of him, and she paid terribly sometimes for her love.

Despite his promise of years before, Gray had been seriously ill during the winter just passed. For weeks he had been in bed. He had written, when he was able, as often as he could; he telephoned, sent flowers. She could send none in return. She could not write. She could not know surely how he was.

Only Ellen knew of her raging about the flat, of her tossing sleepless night after night, trying to keep calm and sane as fever burned in her brain. Twice she had got wildly drunk. She had fallen finally into a kind of stupor, coming out of it to find Ellen desperately trying to take care of her. Like two conspirators, they had kept knowledge of all of it from Andrew Gray when, pale and thin, he had been able to come back to her.

At another time she had become obsessed with the idea that she had to bear Andrew a child. She loved him so that there had to be a helpless, smaller Andrew to love and care for, to grow to manhood, so that Andrew would never die. She had cried, pleading in the midst of dark and bitter nights. Her mind and body had been racked with pain that would not be stilled.

Yet pain is always stilled finally, if only in numbness. There were times when she and Andrew laughed, a little unsteadily, at their almost conjugal content. Emily said they were Darby and Joan in a world of Gibson girls and Gibson men, of signs in hundreds of electric lights beginning to appear on Broadway, of Trilby hats and shoes, of Pudd'nhead Wilson and his fingerprints, the new horseless carriages, and all the rest of a dazzling new age.

Her deep inner joy, the burning torment that struck sometimes when she least expected it, success with her music that had brought her engagement after engagement, had deepened Emily's beauty. Some of the girlish softness had left her face. Character, intelligence, and understanding had added depth and strength. She moved proudly erect, with chin uplifted, a radiance about her sometimes that attracted attention everywhere she and Gray went. Sometimes, hurt and afraid, there was an unbending haughtiness. She walked with a regal, icy splendor which cut Gray to the heart.

At church, at the theatre, at concerts, there were young men who cast admiring and longing glances. Several had dared tentative advances. One young musician, dark, intense, and gifted, had been insistent, determined, and tragic. Emily had been forced to scornful refusal which left him furious and raging but with his self-esteem intact.

One emotion shocked Emily to the depths of her being. In black hours she found herself wishing for the death of a helpless woman whom she had never seen. She fought against it, and the harder she fought the fiercer became the murderous wish in her mind and the sharper the pictures in her imagination. Once, in a dream, the woman spoke to her kindly and understandingly, commending Andrew to her care, thanking her for the peace and joy she had brought him. Emily awoke shudderingly, her body wet with cold sweat.

Chapter 39

IT WAS JUNE, and Emily and Andrew Gray were in a small village in Duchess County. This year again they had managed to steal away for almost a week to a place they loved. There was a white village church with a slim white steeple and a long carriage shed behind it, a crossroads store with long bamboo fishing poles leaning against its porch, a tiny post office in a white cottage, and an old inn with old maples and a wide, old lawn.

A maple-shaded road led from the village to a fresh, rolling country-side of meadows, farm land, and pasture. A wide creek, its shallow water clear and bright from spring rains, flowed straight under the bending willows on its gentle banks.

Later in the season when the sun was hot and the roads were dusty, there would be summer boarders at the little inn. Now, as in other years, they had the place to themselves. The faces of the landlord and his wife were warm and friendly. They ate golden johnny cake hot from the oven with country butter fresh from the spring house. While night mists rolled away before the new light, they gathered mushrooms in the dew-soaked fields of early morning. They came home at dusk from country drives to nights that promised even greater beauty than the sun-drenched day.

It was an idyl, and they knew it was an idyl. It was the present without past or future. They wished to linger and to savor, but every moment was precious. A sense of urgency hurried them on almost breathlessly.

" '. . . And the world well lost,' " smiled Gray.

A parasol over her shoulder, her summery skirts spread about her,

Emily sat on an outcropping of gray rock in a field well back from the road. Gray stood near her. She smiled back at him but did not answer. The only sounds were the calls of birds, the faint noises of insects, and the breeze through leaves and over grass.

There was no age, no youth, only this beauty. Gray lived again, but he had determined to make himself speak.

"It's pure poetry," he said. "Eternal in essence, perhaps, but so fugitive as life is lived."

"There is no prose ever," said Emily. Illogically she added, "And when there is, it is just as good."

Gray looked down over the fields. There were cows grazing on an upslope across the creek and beyond them a farmhouse with its red barns and outbuildings.

"I've had my life, Emily. Yours is still just beginning."

"Please don't, Andrew. I am no longer a child, and I have no life but yours."

"And I'm alive only in you, wherever I am." His voice tightened. "It's still not too late. You should marry, Emily. You should have everything there can be in a woman's life. My selfishness—"

Emily stopped him. It was not the first time he had spoken so. She laughed teasingly.

"Marry someone else? But, Andrew, what an immoral suggestion!" She grew serious. "Andrew," she said softly, "we mustn't spoil any of this. We can't!"

He bowed to her greater wisdom. What he had said seemed irrelevant here and had already lost its reality for him too. Emily knew best. Gratefulness welled again in his heart.

The happiness remained. It was with Emily after Gray had gone again and she was alone in New York. In a little more than two weeks she was going home to South Ilium for most of the summer. The Fifth Avenue Church choir had closed its season and would not appear again until after Labor Day. Her pupils, and she had twenty of them now, would be off to the country or the seashore.

Gray was to spend July in the Adirondacks near the sanitarium to which his wife had already gone. Will and her father were not expected to return from England until early August, but her mother was there and her Aunt Maria. Julia had long since returned to England.

The summer before she had remained in the flat except for brief holidays, and the heat had proved almost unbearable. This time the flat was to be closed, with Ellen sent to her parents and her innumerable brothers and sisters in South Carolina.

If she could not be with Andrew, Emily was glad to be going home.

She would sit in the shade at the back of the house or under the grape arbor and watch the sun and shadow play on the fields beyond the hill. She would let the breeze play in her hair, pick the wild-flowers, listen to the hum of insects.

South Ilium, sobered by the panic and the long hard times, had changed. It was quieter. Many had moved away to seek work elsewhere. Even some of the Irish families had gone. Girls she had known in school were married and had children. Some of them too had moved away to Albany or Amsterdam, or the little towns about. One girl had died of consumption, and a boy she had known had been killed at one of the steel furnaces. It seemed strange and terrible that some of her own contemporaries were dead. It seemed strange too that Cousin Harriet and other old people were no longer there.

She and Ellen went to packing with great industry, exhausting themselves, resting, laughing as they uncovered some silly bit of finery they had forgotten or a Kodak picture which reminded Emily of an occasion or person likewise forgotten. Ellen would have a great bundle of dresses and shirtwaists, hardly mended stockings, bits of ribbon, and other treasures to take home to impress her family, and Emily had bought her gifts to distribute among them.

One by one Emily was giving her pupils their final lessons. They were submissive or rebellious boys and girls who thumped and howled with energetic pleasure or, disdaining practice, detested their parents for revolting their souls with music lessons. One pretty girl in her teens, with a schoolgirl's crush on her teacher, showed real talent. Another, an unpleasant girl with dun hair, a runny nose, and dirty fingernails, played the piano with natural grace and a real love of music. Emily valued them both but was glad to be rid even of them for the summer.

When they were all gone and the packing was safely under way, she decided to perform a duty she had put off for so long that even undertaking it was embarrassing. She would call on Agnes before she left for South Ilium.

It was a beautiful warm and sunny day. Emily bathed luxuriously. She combed her hair, dressed it carefully, and put on a light dress which Ellen had freshly washed and ironed. She decided on her newest parasol, a light-colored muslin daintily picked out with a design in pink rosebuds, and carefully drew on her gloves. One visit to Agnes's untidy and dusty house would ruin the whole, but the day deserved her best. She called a gay good-bye to Ellen and went down the stairs to the bright and sunny street.

The neighborhood had become run down somewhat since she moved into the flat. Italians had moved in only a block away toward the river, and the Irish were pushing into her own street. The original families in the brownstone houses were moving uptown, and two of the brownstone and brick dwellings had been turned into rooming houses. Tenants moved in and out of the apartment house in which she had her flat, though perhaps half of the families had been there when she came.

She knew a few of the people by sight, several well enough to bow to. There was a clean-looking elderly gentleman who always said "Good morning" when she chanced to see him, no matter what the time of day, and a shy young housewife who smiled when they passed. Emily knew none of the others, except the bald-headed bookkeeper and his pale wife and small boy across the hall. The boy, a stolid-faced youngster of ten or eleven, sometimes ran errands for Ellen who handed him pennies, or now and again a nickel, with the air of a great lady rewarding a faithful retainer.

A woman had moved in upstairs on the other side of the building, however, whose profession was unmistakable. Emily had glimpsed her several times, but more often heard her male visitors climbing or descending the stairs late at night or in the early morning hours. Women like that, she had thought charitably, had to live somewhere. She wondered whether Andrew had noticed.

The woman herself was standing at the street entrance as Emily stepped out of the door. Evidently she had come out to enjoy the sun, for she wore no hat. It was not a business appointment.

They met face to face, and the woman smiled cheerfully and good-naturedly. Somewhere in her thirties, she was not a bad looking woman, though too vividly dressed and wearing make-up even at that time of the day.

"How are you, dearie?" she said, shrugging herself more comfortably into her clothes. "Steppin' out?"

Emily smiled pleasantly and stopped to open her parasol.

"Nice one," the woman offered, looking at it critically, taking in all of Emily's costume.

"Thank you," said Emily, tightening her lips a little in spite of herself. She had thought the other was going to reach out and touch the new parasol. Involuntarily she had drawn it back.

Her neighbor laughed.

"Oh, come off it," she suggested. "We're in the same business, ain't we? Wholesale, retail—what's the difference?"

Emily stepped back and stared at her unbelievingly. Her face went red, then deathly white.

The other looked surprised, then extended her hands in a humorous gesture of helplessness.

"I didn't mean nothin', so help me!"

Emily pushed back through the door and fled up the stairs. Ellen, who had been watching at the window to see her start up the sidewalk, heard her coming, thought she had forgotten something, and held open the door.

Emily rushed past her and into her own room. She flung her parasol at the wall, ripped off her gloves, the buttons popping to the floor as the threads gave, and tore off her hat.

She opened the door she had closed behind her. "I changed my mind, Ellen," she managed. "I shan't go to my sister's this afternoon."

She flung herself face down across the bed.

Chapter 40

THREE THOUSAND MILES away, Will marveled at his own innocence. He had thought New York the center of the world. London was the world's center, and the London of the Diamond Jubilee Year transcended everything he had ever known or imagined.

London, sprawling for miles in every direction, was the capital of the most powerful nation of the earth. England's empire was the greatest the world had ever seen. She was the owner of half the globe. Britannia ruled the waves of all the oceans and all the seas, and the sun never set on her estates.

Will and Thomas had come down from Ross-on-Wye two days before and taken lodgings in Russell Square near the British Museum. They had written ahead for them weeks before that and felt fortunate to get them in the already teeming city into which thousands more were pouring every hour. They had gone right to their rooms from Paddington, Thomas proudly directing the driver of their fourwheeler, as though he had been there just the day before. They had hardly been in their rooms since.

Back in South Ilium, Thomas had got more and more excited as, for months ahead, letters and newspapers sent from home had told them all of preparations for the Jubilee. Deep in him, so deep that he did not know it was there, was the conviction that America and his life in it were, after all, only imitations. Reality lay across the

Atlantic, in England, in Gloucestershire, in that part of Gloucestershire which lies, wooded, hilly, and English-green, between the Severn and the Wye.

Uneasiness became desire, desire grew into decision. He had to go home. Even Mary's astounding confession that she did not really care to return with him to England now that her parents were dead and her home was gone, had not deterred. It had led instead to realization that he wanted to take Will with him.

The decision to take Will welled from something equally deep in the man. It was the need to show England to his son and so show him the deepest truth he knew. It would make Will part of him by making them both part of what he loved with as helpless a passion as he loved his God and his work. It might somehow make up to Will for what had happened between them so long ago by making him understand so much larger a truth. Thomas did not consciously know these things; he felt them with a force rooted in his being.

This day in London the tremendous crowds had been gathering in the streets since early morning, a great, good-humored mass of cockneys and countrymen, colonials, proper Londoners, and people from all over the globe. The best vantage points for the procession had been obliterated by packed humanity for hours. Bobbies kept them in order. Hawkers shouted their wares. Everybody had been warned against pickpockets who were out in force for an opportunity which would not be duplicated in their lifetime. Cripples, beggars, ratty-looking little men and tough old hags, silk-hatted gentlemen and exclaiming women were crushed together all along the line of march.

There were cheers every time a uniformed man trotted by on horseback or someone in the crowd identified an empire figure or a distinguished foreigner being driven through the almost impassable traffic. The queen was said already to be at Buckingham, having been brought down from Windsor. She was to go from there in her state carriage to services at St. Paul's, then over London Bridge through the streets of the East End.

The newspapers had all printed descriptions of the line of march and listed the dignitaries who would be seen. There was hardly a hotel in the West End without its colonial minister or foreign prince, though the crowned heads of Europe who had been on hand for the Golden Jubilee ten years before were not coming. This was a British Empire celebration. There were a few visiting members of Europe's royal houses, like Franz Ferdinand of Austria, but England had no need of strangers. It was England's own who had gathered in London to celebrate the sixtieth year of the reign of Queen Victoria. She had ruled longer than any English sovereign. She ruled over more land and more people than her predecessors had dreamed of.

"We'll see the queen herself," Thomas kept saying, as though he could not believe it. It seemd to Will he had been saying it for days.

There were louder cheers and a great roar from the direction of Buckingham.

"Is that her coming?" asked Thomas anxiously. People were straining to see.

But it was just another troop of gorgeously uniformed cavalry cantering toward the palace.

"I'm getting hungry," said Will.

Thomas only laughed at him.

His father had amazed Will ever since they had reached England. He was a different man. Today he was like a boy. In the Forest he had been relaxed and deeply happy. He had treated Will almost as an equal. Will, who was seeing sides of his father he had never suspected, was touched with wonder.

Bobbies standing little more than an arm's length apart along the kerbs were pushing back the crowds. Mounted police, their shining horses stepping daintily, cantered along the edges, people dodging back from the hooves. Will pressed and stood on tiptoe to see. The roar toward the palace was increasing in volume. The martial strains of military music grew louder, the sounds of men marching, the squealing of bagpipes, the rumble of gun carriages. The shouts arose to delirious screams, hats were tossed in air. Union Jacks waved everywhere as the vanguard of the great procession came into sight.

The flesh on Will's forearms rose and his heart pounded. Tears of excitement streamed to his eyes. Thomas gasped as the display of Britain's might was paraded through the famous streets of London. English and Irish regiments in full dress uniforms swung by, detachments of Sikhs from India, kilted Scots with the pipe majors skirling airs of wild and eerie savagery. There were white men, black men from Africa, yellow men from Hong Kong. Mounted Riflemen from Victoria and New South Wales. West Indian, Canadian, and South African troops, the swords of their white-gloved officers flashing in the sun, rode stiffly by to the music of their bands. Turbaned Indians, Imperial Service Troops sent by the native princes of India, dazzled with the brilliance of their costumes.

But it was when the Guards and the Household Cavalry pranced into view that the crowds where Thomas and Will stood cheered and shouted until the roar was deafening. The magnificent state carriage was almost surrounded by horsemen in bemedalled and beribboned skin-tight scarlet tunics and cockaded helmets, with chin straps hiding most of their faces. Will had to thrust his face between the shoulder of a tall man in musty smelling tweeds and his perfume-doused fat companion to see. A crazy swirl of other figures danced before them, but for a moment, as the carriage slowly passed, he was able to see the little old lady for whom that day the world was standing still and the stars had stopped in their courses.

He saw the woman in the black dress and bonnet with white flowers and dipping aigrette as the great Queen Victoria whom all his life he had been taught, *ad nauseam,* to respect and admire. She was the symbol of England and home and empire, and Will was thrilled. Yet he saw, to his astonishment, that she was a comfortably fat and pursy little old lady, shortsighted and rheumatic just like dozens of similar old ladies in South Ilium and some of his older relatives and friends of his father he had just seen in the villages of the Forest. It was when he saw this that Will, who had been silent amid the clamor, understood, and he raised his voice and shouted his acclaim with all the millions on the London streets. He was moved and stirred as he had not expected to be.

When he looked at his father, he saw that Thomas was rigid and pale. His eyes were fixed and glowing. Will looked back to the procession. More troops—and more and more—men from Cyprus, from Borneo, from New Zealand. Suddenly Will felt sorry for the United States. The Ilium Battalions paraded every Fourth of July, the blue-clad Union veterans of the Civil War, Ilium's Own, Freeman's Zouaves who dressed like Turks, and the Boys' Brigade; one volley from a single detachment of these fearfully bearded Sikhs or these Indians with their cruelly curving knives, or a charge by one of these superbly mounted cavalry detachments, and the whole of Ilium's proud military might would be wiped out. England could lick the world!

Happy as Will had never seen him happy before, Thomas started the next day to show Will the things in London he most loved. Eagerly he led Will through St. Paul's, where he had attended services as a young workman in London, walked him beside the Serpentine in Hyde Park, where he had strolled on lonely Sunday afternoons, marveled with him at the crown jewels in the Tower of London, and showed him the Crystal Place as proudly as though he had built it himself. As proudly he showed Will houses and shops far out on Oxford Street which he actually had helped to erect. And one night they saw *The Pirates*. Thomas loved the music.

Proud, too, of still knowing his way about, Thomas was like a landowner showing a stranger about his estate. They got lost only once or twice, and then, as Thomas explained, it was only because landmarks had disappeared and stupid men had done stupid things to what had been better before. It was not until he had finally tired himself out and was content to rest for a day or two in their lodgings that Will could adventure for himself, mingling with the crowds in Picadilly and along the Strand, hunting inexpensive gifts to take home in the little shops in alleys and by-streets about Charing Cross, walking purposefully, as if he were just another smartly dressed young Londoner, across London Bridge, and wandering along the Embankment, watching the shipping on the Thames, listening to the booming of Big Ben.

Dutifully he went through Westminster Abbey, for Thomas had said there might not be time for them to go together, and he went quickly in and out of the British Museum. Madame Tussaud's was better. Thomas recovered quickly, and they spent several more days in sight-seeing before, loaded with the presents they had bought, they went back to the Forest, approaching it this time by way of Gloucester and out along the broad Severn.

Will was reluctant to leave London, but not disconsolate. All England, the fact that it was really there as he had heard about it since he could remember and that he was now in it, was wonderful. It was all wonderful, the neat, hedge-bordered fields they passed, the odd little train itself, the towns and villages that were so different from those in the Hudson Valley between Ilium and New York. It was all a miracle, but Will felt strangely more at home in England than he did when he was actually at home. Being in England was like holding a perfectly balanced hammer in his hand.

The greatest miracle remained his father. Thomas looked on with seeming approval as Will flirted pleasantly with a pretty twenty-year old cousin who lived with her parents, relatives of some kind, in an ancient cottage in Beechenford. He seemed proud of Will as he introduced his son to sober men and women he had known when they were all young. Thomas held his own head high as one who had ventured abroad and had a right to return to his own place well dressed and assured, with a handsome and personable young son; and there were those in the Forest, Will saw, who looked on Thomas humbly and showed diffidence in their pleasure at seeing him. Near the gray stone Forest lodge where Thomas had been born, a woodman touched his hat as they walked a path through the great oaks, and Thomas' eyes flashed.

Incredibly, he even gave Will money so that he and the pretty cousin could journey into Cheltenham for the races. The pound, two shillings and sixpence Will won that afternoon were as nothing to the heady pleasure of being knowledgeable about racing, race tracks, and horses to his pretty companion, of knowing that she saw him as a blond-headed adventurer from another world. Will's infectious gayety dissolved what was left of the girl's demure reserve and first shyness. Her mother frowned slightly at their flushed faces and unsteady laughter when they returned, but Thomas, deep in reminiscences with her woodman father, seemed not to notice.

"I'm coming back," Will told the girl tensely when he and Thomas had to leave for Liverpool and their ship home.

"That's as may be," she said, but her eyes were bright, and her lower lip trembled a little.

The next day, Thomas and Will stood in the stern of the ship watching the blue line of England fade below the horizon into a gathering haze shot with the sunlight of late afternoon. Will was about to speak, but something in his father's face kept him silent. After a moment he turned and went quietly away, leaving Thomas staring across the graying blue water.

Thomas sat wrapped in heavy blankets in his deck chair or lay in their cabin for most of the return voyage. Tired, lost, seemingly in his own thoughts, satiated, saddened perhaps that he had seen England for what might be the last time, he rebuffed the overtures of fellow passengers with an unfriendly coldness and paid little attention to Will. Will, anxious to wring the last drop of pleasure and experience from it all, quickly knew his way about the ship and made himself popular with fellow passengers and crew members alike.

One night in mid-Atlantic there was a heavy storm. The officers were casual or jocular about it at dinner in the saloon of the small one-cabin ship, which carried only about fifty passengers, but Will had noticed crewmen swiftly clearing the decks that afternoon, lashing down what could not be removed. As the force of the storm increased during the evening, passengers were requested to remain in their cabins.

Thomas sat quietly reading as the ship thudded into one giant wave, then broke free until the next struck. Time and again the whole ship shuddered. One of their suitcases broke loose and slithered across the cabin floor to crash against the wall. Outside the noise and fury of the storm rose even higher. Will stood it as long as he could, then thrust on his coat and forced open their door against the wind. He got the door closed behind him and held tightly to the metal bar fastened across it as he struggled for a foothold on the slippery, pitching deck.

For seconds he could see nothing and the wind seemed to ram his breath back down his throat. The ship wallowed and pitched, creaking in every joint. The propellers ground and spun screaming out of the water, their whine cutting through the roar of the wind. Hanging to the door, Will regained his breath and let himself tip and right, tip and right, with the roll of the ship. He could see a little now, and in a moment he was exultant.

All the world of darkness and crashing storm, the straining ship, the blackness and the vastness were his and his alone. He rejoiced in the fury, and he was afraid. He thrilled even to the deliciousness of his fear. The ship tilted, and a star flashed high above the storm. A wave crashed over the rail. It smashed against the white superstructure of the ship, then flowed away across the patch of deck glistening gray in the dim light from a porthole, washing into the scuppers before the next wave crashed into them.

The ocean was wide. The world was wide. The night was deep, and the power of the storm was sure. Will felt suddenly stronger than the storm itself, strong and unafraid. He shouted defiance into the roar of the wind and water. The rain and icy spray had plastered his trousers to his legs, and his hair was a cold wetness splashing down over his face. He had never felt so alive. He stood there moments abandoning himself to the force of the storm and the wild response that leaped from deep within him. Then holding carefully to the door, he exerted all his strength to force it open and thrust himself inside again.

Thomas now was lying in the lower bunk with his eyes closed and on his face a look of careful indifference to the storm.

"Asleep, Pa?"

Thomas opened his eyes. "What? What, boy? What?" The last word came as a shout as the outside noise abated for an instant.

Will stood in the center of the swaying floor peeling off his sodden clothes. Thomas watched him.

Abashed, Will forgot what he had been about to say. Whatever it was, it would have sounded silly now. Certainly it was not what he was surprised to hear himself saying, the words coming in a rush.

"Thanks, Pa! Thanks for everything!"

Thomas did not answer, but when Will turned away, ostensibly to struggle with one of his soaked shoes while he tried to balance himself, a smile touched his lips. "Yes," he said. Then more slowly he said it again. "Yes." The sound was almost a sigh. Pain and happiness, regret, longing, an unsure wonder, all were in it. That was enough of that. "Who is that girl you've been racing all about the ship with?" he asked sharply.

Will felt more comfortable.

"Who? Oh, her! Her name's Louise Morrison, I think. It's just—
I mean—"

Will tried to relive it all for Emily who was on the hill in South
Ilium when he and Thomas came home again. He also promised himself to tell Aunt Maria that she looked exactly like Queen Victoria.

"God, Em," he told Emily and Jim Garver, whom he was surprised to find with her, the night that he and Thomas returned, "you
never saw anything like it, and London's got New York beat six
ways from the middle. The Forest of Dean is all right, but London's
the place. I could have stayed there forever. I think Pa'd like to have
stayed in Trewsted or Beechenford and never come back."

Emily laughed. "And leave Mother?"

Jim Garver smiled.

"I don't think he ever thought of her. He was different in England,
Em. Perhaps he was the way he was when he was young. I think he
thought he *was* young! We talked to men older than he, and they
acted as if he were just a young fellow. He laughed a lot."

"Laughed!" exclaimed Emily bitterly. "He didn't hit any children
with a rake handle or yank anybody out of school and put them to
work just because he happened to be in a vile humor?"

Will looked surprised. "That was years ago, Em. You don't still
think of that, do you?"

"Not often, but I do sometimes. I can never quite forget."

Jim Garver, his face showing nothing, got up to go. "I'll be back
soon to hear all about your trip, Will. Good night, Emily." He left
rather abruptly.

"Say, what's the matter with you and Jim, Em? Anything wrong?"
Emily shrugged.

"Nothing that I know of. Will, let's go somewhere, do something!"

"Right!"

The panic was over. The long bad times seemed to be finished.
Ilium's mills and factories were going full blast once more. New
families were moving in. Thomas, busier than ever, had more men
working for him than he had ever had. An upstart carpenter, an
Irishman, had started in competition, but he was getting nowhere.
Thomas Stapely had the skill and the reputation. Repair jobs and
contracts for new tenements and cottages went to him almost auto-
matically. There was plenty for Will to do.

He decided to stay in Ilium the rest of the summer, perhaps the
autumn too. He'd miss the fall race meetings, but he'd been in New
York for the best of the plays. He could always get work with Dave

Walter in Brooklyn or in Manhattan. For Will the system balanced perfectly. He was in South Ilium when he wished or in New York. Now he had another scheme. He wanted to go back to England.

The sombre grays and browns, the massiveness of London satisfied. He felt part of it. He merged into England as though his father had never left it. England steadied and supported him. He felt older and graver and wiser there.

Wandering through London, he had wished to know more of English history and thoughtlessly said so one day to his father. Thomas, realizing that Will meant he wished he had had more schooling, looked uncomfortable, then angry. He strode off through Regent's Park, and Will felt sorry he had spoken without thinking.

He wanted to assure his father that it was all right. He was happy being a carpenter. In England he was not a carpenter at all. In London he was as good as any other young man about town. In the Forest he had been glad to name his trade with any man, and his father had boasted that his son was getting ready to take his place. Will had said nothing to that.

He was proud of his new scheme. He would work in Ilium or in New York, it did not matter which. He'd save his money and, when he had enough, try to triple it or better at the races. If he won, he'd be off to England again!

Will remained at home not only all summer, but also most of the winter. Not until some time the next spring was he able to speak of his new scheme to Andrew Gray, who smiled assent.

"If that's what you want to do, do it. Only be sure you win at the tracks."

"Can't be sure," laughed Will. "Where would be the fun if I were?"

Gray looked at him. Will's face was delicate, almost too delicate for a man, and it was never still. It was as vivid as his blond coloring. The clean line of Will's jaw was fragile. The chin was finely cut. The lips were full and sensual but clearly outlined. Will's blue eyes lighted easily with thought or laughter. It was a gay, imaginative, appealing, defenceless face, and Will looked so much like Emily that Gray would have loved him no matter what he was like.

"I'd be too timid to risk it myself," he said, and Emily laughed.

"I mean it," Gray insisted. "Well, perhaps—!" He did not finish but looked fondly at Emily who sat looking happily at them both. She loved to see Andrew and Will together. "Don't you ever want to do anything else?" he asked Will curiously.

"You mean not be a carpenter? Work in an office or something like that?" Will looked so horrified and contemptuous that the others laughed.

He flushed. "Maybe I'll do my own building some day," he said vaguely, "or be a construction boss for one of the big contractors. I've already been foreman carpenter," he said proudly, "on a number of jobs in Brooklyn. I got fired from one, though, because I'm not in the union. There's plenty of time."

"There's forever," Gray assured him seriously. "I've always felt that you and Emily are eternal. There's something wrong with the scheme of things if you are not."

Emily touched his hand. "Eternity," she reminded him, "is a sense of things. It's not a matter of years. Will is an infant and you are a mere child compared to the way I feel sometimes."

"You should see some marvelous years," Gray told them seriously. "The next century will be even more wonderful than this has been, and you will see a good half of it."

"I guess it will be much the same as now," said Will. He felt uncomfortable. He always did when an older man referred to the fact that he would be alive long after the speaker was dead. It made it sound as though he took unfair advantage.

"Saturday night," said Emily, "if you two don't mind coming back to this century for a minute, we are all going to see Julia Marlowe in *As You Like It*. Andrew brought the tickets tonight."

"But that's Shakespeare, isn't it?" Will looked doubtful.

Emily laughed. "It won't hurt you."

"Well, just this once. But did you see Anna Held? I went last week." Will rolled his eyes and sang falsetto, *I just can't make my eyes behave.*

Andrew made a pained face and Emily put her hands over her ears. Will laughed at them both. His high spirits were infectious, and they all responded to Will.

The lives of the rest of them had fallen into patterns over the years.

Agnes was firmly established, placidly aware of her dual sanctity in the sacred role of wife and the even more sacred role of mother. Yet she was both happy and worried. She redoubled her efforts to hold Allan's patients, battening Rhoda and their moulting canary in the basement dining room so they could not by any chance annoy the lame and ill who were their bread, butter, and cake. A boy bouncing a ball on their brownstone steps as he passed on his way to or from school sent her into a paroxysm of rage.

Will laughed at her. "Let 'em alone, Agnes!"

"Oh, dear, and he looked like such a nice boy, too! Do you think I upset him? Yet, if a patient—"

Will was the only one who could tease Agnes. She was no longer on speaking terms with James and Laura, and she made it clear that she received Emily and Andrew Gray only as a Christian duty—but she despatched her child to other parts of the house when, once or twice a year they came, lest Rhoda be contaminated.

Rhoda was a pale, gentle child whom Will liked. Pig-tailed, short-skirted, she was in school now and showing herself very bright at her studies.

Will liked to tease her by singing:

> Rhoda, Rhoda, had a pagoda,
> Serving tea, and ices and soda!

Rhoda did not like the song and signified her displeasure by pounding Will on the chest and screaming, "Pa, make him stop! You stop it, you!"

She did not dare scream when Agnes was about, but she had faith in her father.

"*Rhoda, Rhoda had a pagoda*—oo! Ouch!" Will cringed from the cruel blows, and Rhoda, fearful she had hurt him, looked worried. Tears came into the brown eyes, but she looked quickly relieved. "My father can fix it," she said proudly. "He can make you all right."

"Even your father," Will laughed to Allan, who was happily watching his daugher, "couldn't make me perfect."

"He can too, he can too, he can too!" Rhoda pummelled Will gleefully again.

Life might be serious for Agnes, and beautiful and sometimes bitterly real for Emily and Andrew Gray, but for Will it was something else again.

Freed from the bondage of his boyhood, Will skimmed the surface of his days, catching at the speed and light like a delighted child. He laughed at his brothers and sisters, hammered happily away at one job after another, eager only for the night's pleasures and to be in England again. He had no responsibilities. He wanted none. He was ready to help any of them, to play checkers with James or re-decorate a room, to be with Emily as much as he could, but not to risk his elation.

James had life by the throat now, and he intended to keep it under control. He and Laura were of one mind there. They meant to enforce their will, to dictate their terms, and there were times when life seemed to quail before their combined attack. When James showed signs of relenting, Laura's purpose hardened in proportion, and she drove him on.

Will laughed at them. "You and old Bones," he told Laura, "ought to take a deep breath and say 'ah.' You're trying to win every race on the card, even when no one is running against you."

"Why don't you go to bed some night before one o'clock?" Laura retorted. "You can hardly keep your eyes open this morning."

"I'm mortifying the flesh."

"You're the limit," said Laura, "and I love you—though I can't think why."

Perhaps a year later, after Will had been twice back and forth to South Ilium to work with Thomas on a row of three new tenements—one of the biggest jobs Thomas had contracted for in several years —James and Laura both went at him. There was something suspicious about their combined attack. James's manner was so off-hand that Will knew Laura must have put him up to it. Emily and Andrew were there, and they were all at dinner.

"Aren't you ever going to settle down?" James demanded. "It's about time you made up your mind to something."

"Consider the lilies of the field," Will advised him. "They toil not, neither do they spin. Yet—"

"They won't last long either," said James grimly.

"Last week," said Will, "I made twenty-five dollars with my little saw and hammer. Saturday I won eighty at Long Island City. What's the matter with that?"

"How much did you lose the week before?"

"Oh, well, if you're going to look at it that way!" grinned Will.

Laura, who had been waiting her chance, broke in.

"Will, you ought to get married. That's what we all think."

James winked broadly, and Will understood. Captain Gravet was coming in from what he had announced again was to be his last voyage, and Janet would be with him. So they were at that again!

"Marry!" cried Will, alarmed. "Marry! I'm too young to get married. Besides, I never did anybody any harm! Why should I have to get married?"

"Stop it, Will!" cried Emily. "No one's going to hurt you. We won't let anyone marry him, will we, Andrew?"

"Thanks, Em!" said Will gratefully. He flicked out his tongue spitefully at Laura.

"I give up!" Laura sighed.

If Will was compensating for the drudgery and drabness of his hard-working boyhood, he did not know it. Had he known it, he would not have cared.

Chapter 41

EMILY STOOD tall and poised. She held her music high and her head erect as she waited direction from Cecil Fielding, whose body swayed back and forth as his sure hands moved across the console with its tiered manuals of white keys, and his feet sought the pedal notes which added swelling sound to the music filling the Fifth Avenue Church. She drew in and held her breath until, eyes on hers, Fielding, threw back his head, then brought it sharply forward.

Emily's voice rose with the full chorus in accompaniment. It was the *Stabat Mater*.

> *When Thou comest to the judgment, Lord, remember*
> *Thy servants!*
> *None can deliver us.*
> *Save, and bring us to Thy kingdom ...*

As always, the Fifth Avenue Church was filled with men in frock coats or dark suits with stiff, white linen; women in magnificent hats and rustling silks and satins. Luxuriant flowers stood on the altar. Light streamed through the rich greens, reds, purples, gold, and varied blues of the great stained glass windows. The clergy in their black silk robes and rich velvet hoods sat on the thickly carpeted platform below the choir loft. The music of voice and organ sang and soared through the church.

Emily, breathless, stood there exultant as her part was done, and others took up the music. It was contralto and chorus now, then the tenor alone. She listened critically, watching Fielding. They were nearing the end. At the signal, she raised her voice with all the others in the final harmony.

This was *her* life, not Andrew's or Will's or her father's or her mother's or anyone else's. Of all the lives she lived as daughter, sister, companion, teacher, this was her real life. If Andrew Gray was the center of one of her lives, this was the center of another and perhaps even deeper life.

All the confusion cleared when she sang. Clarity came out of obscured and troubled depths. Conflicting emotions and the sharp, stinging ends of thoughts solved themselves. Jangling discords crystallized in pure sound. Emily knew the sweetness of creation and of the disappearance of self. She knew a sense of oneness with the perfection attained by artists who had lived and dreamed this music before she or Will or Andrew or even her father had been born.

Sometimes, intoxicated by the beauty of sound, she felt she was close to God and that He understood. When at Christmas she sang, *Come unto Him, all ye that labor and are heavy laden, and He shall give you rest,* she sang from her heart because of the glory of the music, the beauty of the words, and because she knew pain—and sometimes peace.

This Sunday it was a Bach *Magnificat.*

> *Et exultavit, spiritus meus in Deo salutari meo*
> *Quia respexit, humilitatem, ancillae suae; ecce enim ex hoc*
> *beatem me dicent.*

She stopped as the chorus began with the *Omnes generationes* and then the bass solo broke in: *Quia fecit mihi magna.*

Emily chatted happily with the comfortable little contralto as they took off their surplices and hung them in the choir room. The bass and tenor had long since left the choir, and others had taken their places. The contralto's hair was gray now, but her smooth, round face was unlined. She and Emily were old friends.

"I've no idea what the Latin words mean," the contralto confessed as she adjusted her hat before the mirror. "I could ask my youngest boy, but I'm ashamed."

"I don't know either, but I love it just the same!"

"I know you love it. That's the way you sing it," said the other affectionately. "Come and see me this week. You're always going to, but you never do. I'll make Mr. Gray bring you. It's a year since we've seen each other except at church."

Emily stopped drawing on her long gloves to tick the items off on her fingers.

"Tomorrow, six students. I'll be dead. Tuesday afternoon I'm singing at old Mr. Taylor's funeral. I'll be deader. Wednesday, more students, and Andrew and I are going to the theatre. Wednesday night, a wedding. I've sung more brides into domestic bliss than I care to remember. So have you. It's a good thing we've no consciences. Thursday, my own lessons in the morning. Friday, Andrew and I— you see. Now I must hurry home. Mother is waiting. She's never quite well enough or never gets up in time somehow to get to church. She explains about it all the rest of the day!"

The contralto, who had several times met Mary, laughed. "All right," she conceded, "but next week—"

Emily waved to her and hurried out. The conversation had delayed her. The church was almost empty. A small group of church dignitaries and their wives stood talking to Samuel Rollins at the door. The beloved minister of the Fifth Avenue Church, an aged man now, was even more gentle of voice and saintly of visage. He took long holidays now, but the congregation would not hear of his retirement. They knew it was not his real wish.

The Reverend Richard Slater was just bidding good-bye to a man and two women. There were no others. Slater turned, and his pale, aesthetic face broke into a glad smile, his dark eyes lighting, as he saw Emily approaching. There had been a real change in the young man's fortunes. Samuel Rollins's chief assistant had suddenly accepted a call to Hartford two years before, and Slater—whose expectations had been to serve only a few years as the third and least important member of the Fifth Avenue Church's ministerial staff and then, like his predecessors, move on—had succeeded to the more important post. He had matured swiftly. Richard Slater now had the respect of the important men of the church as well as the admiration of the younger people.

It was rumored that when Samuel Rollins died or was forced by his increasing infirmities to give up active participation, the coveted pulpit of the Fifth Avenue Church might go to Richard Slater. It had been apparent for some time that he could marry any of several wealthy young women of the parish. The wisest intimated that he would marry Margaret Simmons, whose corporation lawyer father was an important member of the Fifth Avenue Church's board. For Slater the marriage would be virtual insurance of the pulpit. Margaret was an attractive and pretty girl. Feminine members of the lay section of the full choir were certain that it would be a match. Emily, though she could not say so, was not so certain.

Richard Slater advanced toward Emily, his face lighting.

"I was afraid I had missed you."

Emily knew that she should have slipped out the side door. An impulse of curiosity and daring had made her risk coming this way.

"Didn't you know I was here?" she teased.

"Of course, I knew you were here! Didn't I hear you. You sing more beautifully all the time."

"Thank you," said Emily primly. She offered her hand. "Good-bye," she said.

He held her hand in his own long-fingered, thin, rather feminine hand.

"Oh, please don't race off." Those who had been talking with Samuel Rollins had left, and the old man had gone back into the clergy's robing room. There was just a sexton busy about the front of the church. The young minister looked intently into Emily's face. His eyes were a clear, amber brown, and brightly intent. "I do want to talk to you," he said quickly.

Emily looked at him.

"Richard," she said quietly. "We've been over this before. You know it's no good. I don't want you to upset yourself again—or me."

"Let me come to see you," he pleaded. "I promise to be good. There's something I want to tell you. Please!"

"Why—all right," said Emily, hesitating. Smiling, she drew away her hand.

"This evening after service?"

"Oh, no! Let's see. Could you come for tea Friday afternoon?"

"Tonight," he insisted eagerly. "It's important, Emily. Please!"

Her mother would be gone to James's. Andrew never came Sunday evenings. Ellen would be out. Perhaps that was as well.

She nodded. "But don't wait to go home with me. I'll be at home when you come."

Emily could not help feeling a certain thrill of pleasure as she left the church. Half the women of the congregation made fools of themselves over Richard Slater. Many of the rest would do so if they had a chance. His sensitive, appealing face, the dark, emotional eyes, the earnestness and quiet conviction with which he spoke when he preached on occasion, gave added allure to his position as a clergyman. The minister, any minister, supposedly apart from other men, dedicated, an enemy of the hungers of the flesh, was always a challenge to women. She had seen girls look after Richard Slater with sentimental yearning and older women look at him with naked eyes. Yet it was she he wanted.

She had known it from the first. She had made no slightest move in his direction, avoided rather than sought after him. It was probably that, as much as anything, which had attracted him. She realized this as soon as she saw that he was attracted, and tried then to be more friendly. Her emotional life was full. She had no wish for other men. She had many times rebuffed the attempts of others to get near her. Yet the knowledge that Richard Slater's eyes followed her while he was talking to other women, that when she sang he was there to listen and appreciate, that he found her comely and desirable was pleasant. For a long time they had known an electrical awareness of each other before anything was spoken. Emily had found it not unpleasant.

Slater's open declaration of love and passionate insistence that she marry him, coming soon after his accession to John Thompson's position as assistant at the church, had startled and horrified her. She felt frightened and remorseful. The unexpected intensity of the man's emotions and the fierceness of his demands had shocked her into a fear she could conceal only by an icy control which the man could scarcely credit. Slater's insistence, his tormented mind and body, finally his tears of anger and frustration had ended in a wild fury of hurt pride and unsatisfied hunger.

For months she had had to watch over him, trying to guide him back to control and peace of mind, hiding always the fact that there had been any passage between them. She had tried as best she knew to help and strengthen him. She had thought, and vaguely resented, that she had succeeded, and that Richard Slater had safely put her out of his mind, turning his emotions toward Margaret Simmons or some other woman. His violence and weakness had appalled and fascinated Emily.

He had seemed quiet and strong enough that morning. Perhaps he really had recovered and had news he wished to tell her. She wondered what it was, but somehow she dreaded seeing him.

"I slipped away as quickly as I could," Richard Slater told her that evening. He looked eagerly about the room. "It's a long time since I was here."

"There were almost as many at church tonight as there were this morning," said Emily, looking away from him, hastily. Perversely, she had made herself as beautiful as she could. "It was a fine congregation," she added.

The young minister leaned forward in his chair, his face excited, his fine lips parted.

"I've been offered the pastorate of a big church in Boston, one of the Boylston Street churches!"

"You have!"

"It seems that a committee visited the Fifth Avenue Church several weeks ago when I was preaching. They had already looked up my record. They want a young man this time. Last week they voted on it, and I received the call just two days ago."

"Why, that's wonderful!"

"It's a wealthy church with a large congregation, a better pastorate than three years ago I could have hoped for in my entire career." The pale, nervous face shone with excitement. His ambition was undisguised.

"I'm so glad," said Emily sincerely. "It's a fine opportunity, and it's wonderful that you have this chance."

"Shall I take it?"

"Oh, I can't decide that!"

"But you can. If I accept, will you go with me?"

Emily could not pretend to herself that she was surprised. Her imagination, racing ahead as she watched his face, had told her.

"Richard," she said quietly. "We've been all over that."

Sitting carefully still where he was, almost across the room from her, he shook his head.

"No," he said, "we haven't. Look, I'm calm now. You know I am. I know what I feel, and I know what I want. I love you, Emily. Will you marry me, and we'll go to Boston together? It would mean a new life for both of us. I would have a position of which you could be proud. And," he added humbly, "it would be an opportunity to do some of the things as a minister that I've wanted to do." The slight trembling of his voice told how hard he was striving for control.

"You mustn't talk like that, Richard," said Emily softly. "You know you must not."

"I've dreamed of this, Emily. I've dreamed of you. I can't help it! Together we could accomplish so much. We could be *so* much. I *know* what I am talking of. I don't want to sound sanctimonious, but I would have more strength for the Lord's work. For two years, I've been less than myself because I've not had you."

"Please don't, Richard!"

In novels the heroine was always so graceful and kind, so healing and sure. Unerringly she said and did the right thing to comfort her unhappy lover and send him on his way. But heroines were seldom in her position.

"But have you considered," she tried to say, "that perhaps you should not leave the Fifth Avenue Church? Perhaps your real work is here."

"I want neither Boston nor the Fifth Avenue without you," he said shrilly. "You know that."

Emily stood up, her face pale. She wanted to cross the room to comfort him, but she knew better.

"Richard, this is foolishness. Any woman would be pleased and flattered, but I—"

Slater jumped to his feet and darted across to her. He pressed his hands hard against her shoulders, as though to keep himself from crushing her in a convulsive embrace.

"Come with me, Emily. You must!"

Emily stood perfectly still, though the touch of his hands, the knowledge of his strong young body burned through her.

306

"Sit down, Richard, or we can't talk at all." Her tone was sharp, as though she spoke to a boy.

He wavered for seconds, then dropped his hands, but did not move away. Emily dropped back into her own chair.

"I couldn't be a minister's wife anywhere," she said, trying to laugh. "I'm not cut out for it. Imagine me chucking babies under the chin, entertaining the Ladies' Aid, bewitching unpleasant deacons, setting an example for the Sweet Young Things in the Sunday school!"

Slater's back was to her. He stood examining the jade and ivory ornaments in the curio cabinet. He turned, his face tormented and distorted.

"You mean you won't leave Mr. Gray."

The direct attack struck Emily like a blow. It took her breath away. It left her speechless for seconds.

"How dare you!" she managed, and the words sounded theatrical and ridiculous to her as she spoke them.

Slater looked frightened but reckless.

"You're not married to him."

"Please leave, Richard!"

"You're not married to him, and I love you. I have a right that he hasn't." He was staring into her face from where he stood. He was almost in tears again.

"You are talking like a child," she said cruelly. "Do you imagine you are the first person who has ever suffered—an inescapable fascination, a heart-eating love, a soul-devouring infatuation—whatever you want to call it? Perhaps it's a hammering lust."

Richard Slater misunderstood. Perhaps she had meant him to.

"But Andrew Gray has *had* his life!" he cried piteously.

"And now you want yours, is that it?"

"Is that so ridiculous?" he demanded hotly.

"There is no pat little system of balanced fairness," explained Emily wearily. "Because one man—or one woman—has this or that is no reason why another can have it too. I found that out long ago."

Without warning he had her in his arms and was kissing her passionately. It was as much a desperate attempt to convince her with his dry, burning lips and the force of his body as it was to ease his own passion.

Emily struggled, then submitted. Her dress had come loose at the shoulder. His hand was hot on her flesh, but she did not respond to his kisses, and she stood trembling but silent and tried to appear impassive. Spent and frightened, he desisted.

Then Slater, hope in his dark eyes, made a terrible mistake.

"I don't care what you have done or what you have been!" he cried.

Emily froze. She stared at him incredulously.

"You miserable, smug little fool!" she said contemptuously.

"You can't drive me away! If you won't marry me I'll not go to Boston, and I'll not stay at the Church. I'll give up the ministry altogether!"

Emily had no pity now. Her lip curled.

"God could scarcely survive that."

She adjusted her dress as the man sat again in his chair and after one desperate, pleading look into her eyes buried his face in his hands.

Emily turned and walked unsteadily from the room. Her heart was beating wildly. Her head whirled. A few minutes later she heard him stirring about the room. Once he called to her, hesitantly. A little later she heard him leave. She hurried to the front room window in time to see him start up the dark sidewalk. He moved quickly and steadily. She felt with relief that he would be all right. Like a child, he could recover quickly from a tantrum. She pressed a hand against her throbbing temple.

Two weeks later the Rev. Richard Slater's call to the Boston Church, a call he felt it his Christian duty to accept, was announced from the Fifth Avenue Church's pulpit. Emily did not lift her eyes from her music.

Chapter 42

SHORTLY AFTER the beginning of the loudly heralded New Century, Andrew Gray watched the world about him with troubled eyes.

The slow-paced, gentle, and friendly world of the 1890's was gone. In its place was Roosevelt ... the blowing up of the *Maine* ... Dewey, hero of Manila ... the villain Aguinaldo ... silver-tongued Bryan ... the brave Boers. This was a violent and explosive world, its energy out of control and raging.

In his own smaller world of life insurance there were threatening noises too. Equitable and Prudential were moving restlessly. Mutual, Equitable, and the New York Life had assets of almost a billion dollars. If Apex and Metropolitan were added, the total was well over a billion. It was an incredible sum. It meant power, and it meant danger.

Gray was on his way to Emily's. It was late afternoon. He felt tired and looked forward to tea. Emily, dressed and awaiting him, would have it ready. He still loved to watch her pour tea. She did it with the grace and sureness with which she did everything.

Morning and evening Pulitzer's *World* incited to riot, or seemed to. Young Hearst had come out of the West and was challenging the acknowledged master of sensational journalism with even more sensational journalism. It amused Gray that Hearst had had the audacity to hire space in the gold-domed World Building itself, but the Hearst papers sickened the newspaperman in him. The *American* and the *Journal* had done more than any other force to stampede the country into unnecessary war with Spain. Crime, scandal, and vice were emblazoned on their pages.

Pulitzer and Hearst in their battle for circulation did not seem to care what they destroyed or what they wrought. Yet essentials had changed little.

The rich still got richer, and the poor got poorer. It seemed a law as immutable as any in physics. One expected to have beggars knock daily at the back door, and if one was a Christian, one took them into the kitchen and fed them. It was safer than giving them money which, in all likelihood, they would spend at the nearest saloon.

Good men accepted their lot without complaint, and Thomas Stapely was not the only man who looked on the machinations of the labor unions with suspicion and disapproval. There were gentlemen and ladies, and there were the common people. Men and women knew to which category they belonged, and there was little serious complaint. A man took his fun where he could find it. The family entrance of the corner saloon had its pleasures; high-class wickedness was a preserve of the newly rich. Their orgies of display and extravagance were condemned by the righteous, but not without envy.

If the Bradley-Martin Ball was denounced from lower-class pulpits and by the sensational press, most of those who heard or read wished only that they could get a ticket of admission. If they could not, the next best thing was to read in the papers about fabulous banquets where guests lighted their cigars with hundred dollar bills and theatre queens burst almost nude from the slowly opening petals of huge artificial flowers.

Trust busting was almost as much fun. Few seriously expected to see the trusts broken, the rings smashed, and "the interests" defeated. No one knew exactly what they were anyway. It was just fun for *World* and *Journal* readers to see the big, fat men bullied and badgered in the cartoons.

And cowboy-hunter Teddy Roosevelt with his flashing eyeglasses and rows of shining teeth, charging up San Juan Hill shouting "Bully!" and "Be Prepared!" was as good any day as Weber and Fields or Montgomery and Stone.

Everybody imitated Teddy, and Will with the best of them, rushing about pounding the table with his fist, brandishing a Big Stick, and having a wonderful time. If anyone could dispatch the Standard Oil, Mark Hanna, the German Kaiser, the Bryan Democrats, the bums, the sissies, the Erie Railroad, the patent medicine crooks, the Turks, the Russians, and the Japs, it was good old Teddy!

Yet, with it all, the race was still to the swift and the Devil took the hindmost. He was sometimes so busy taking them in that he had to hire a staff of willing assistants. Most of them were Democrats.

Gray reached Emily's flat, but it was Ellen who answered the door —a wildly disturbed Ellen.

"Ah don' know what else ah can do!" she cried. "Ain' nuthin' lak this evah happen befoah!"

Gray stood very still in the living room.

"She been upset," Ellen explained piteously. "Ah don' know what happen'! Ah guess she jes' can' stan' it!"

"I'm afraid that's it, Ellen," said Gray quietly. "She just couldn't stand it."

They looked down at Emily who sat in the middle of the floor regarding them wisely. She was beautifully dressed. Her hair had been brushed until it shone with extra brilliance. She wore some of the finest of her diamonds. The smell of brandy permeated the room where a glass had been upset on the rug.

"We'll have to get her up somehow," Gray said easily to Ellen.

Emily's head fell forward. In an effort to get it upright, she tipped it too far back. "Comf'table where I am," she told them politely. "Ver' comf'table."

"I think you would be better in one of the chairs," said Gray persuasively. "Perhaps you'd like to lie down a little while."

Emily looked surprised. "Night time?" she asked. "Night time?"

"Miz Emily, you gotta git up!" urged Ellen desperately. "Yo can' jest sit theah!"

Emily listened brightly. She leaned back until she almost toppled over, but she righted herself and smiled up at them.

At a signal from Gray, Ellen put her hand under one of Emily's arms, while he took the other.

Emily jerked back convulsively and began to laugh wildly.

"Tickles!" she screamed. "Stop ticklin'!" As Gray stepped toward her again, she recoiled quickly, folding her arms tightly, and laughing helplessly.

"Emily, you *must* get up," whispered Andrew Gray, bending low over her. "You'll catch cold. You'll ruin your gown."

Emily whispered something back to him without opening her eyes. Gray looked questioningly at Ellen, who shook her head doubtfully.

"We didn't hear you, Emily. If you'll just try to get up! We'll help you." There were fine beads of perspiration on Gray's forehead.

"I said, 'You come down here'," hissed Emily in a stage whisper. "Both of you come down. Ver' nice." She patted the intricately patterned Caucasian with its mellowed and fading colors and sighed happily.

After she had fallen asleep, they carried her to the bed. Emily did not waken as Ellen tugged off her shoes and began to unfasten her dress.

Gray went into the bathroom to wash his hands and rinse his strained face in cold water. He combed and brushed his hair and adjusted his coat and collar. For an instant he stared unseeingly at himself in the mirror. Then he went back into the living room and sat down.

He picked up the nearest book and tried to read. He put it down to adjust a small table screen of jade quartz in an ebony frame. He picked up his book again, then saw that the screen was still not just where he wished it. Once more he tried to read.

"Ah bring you some suppah, Mist' Gray," said Ellen somewhat later.

"Don't bother, Ellen, thank you."

But when Ellen brought him tea and lemon, some thin soup, some thin bread and butter, and some cut fruit on a black lacquered tray, he found he was glad to have it.

"She still asleep," the girl offered. "She' be so sorry latah!"

"I know, Ellen. Thank you for taking such good care of her."

Gray was still sitting there when Will came. He had known that Will was expected.

"Emily's asleep," he said carefully. "She'll be with us later. Shall we try some chess?"

Will looked puzzled. "Em's not sick?" he demanded.

"Just a little upset." Gray kept his voice steady with difficulty.

Slowly Gray set up the ivory chessmen on the board. He had taught Will to play. They played silently and badly for three-quarters of an hour. Neither could keep his mind on the game. They listened for sounds from other parts of the flat. A half-hour later they heard them. Ellen was talking, and there were indistinct answers.

"Seemingly," said Gray painfully, "we always hurt those we love."

"Why?" asked Will coldly. He looked straight at Gray.

Gray looked back at him. "We haven't the power to hurt anyone else."

They gave up pretense of chess.

"How is your scheme coming?" asked Gray suddenly. "Will you be going back to London this year?"

"Afraid it will be the same story as last year. The horses have not cooperated very well."

"A trip abroad might do Emily good. It would get her away from things for a time—and from me."

"Yes," said Will. It was true, he thought.

"Could you go with her if she went? I mean, of course, at my expense."

Will's eyes opened in astonishment.

"I imagine I could—that is, I'm sure I could. Of course—"

"Let's not say anything to Emily right away," Gray cautioned. "We'll surprise her one of these days. I'll make all the arrangements. You'll be doing me a favor, you know."

"Doing *you* a favor!" Will's imagination raced.

Emily came in, walking steadily, but she looked pale and squinted a little from the light. She put her hand to her forehead.

"Hello, Will," she said. "So you beat me to it! How are they all in Brooklyn?"

"Have a good rest, Emily?" asked Gray. "Will and I have been having a fine game. You'll have to be quiet if you want to stay, won't she, Will?"

Andrew's patience and understanding! Will's loyalty! Their pretense was almost worse than recrimination would have been.

"I'll never learn this game, Em," said Will in discouraged tones. "It's too much for me."

"Any game is hard," said Emily. "I can't seem to learn even the simple one of living."

Chapter 43

EMILY WAS DESPERATE and resolved on desperate measures. A week later she went to see James. She had never dared before.

"I'm drinking again," she told him bluntly, "and I can't seem to stop. What can I do about it?"

James got up and closed the door of his office. Laura was out, but he did not know where the servant girl was or who else might come in.

"Why ask me?" he demanded, coming back and sitting down in the swivel chair at his desk.

"Not," said Emily sharply, "because I expected sympathy or understanding. But you're a doctor, and I do think you'll keep your mouth shut. Believe me, I'd not have come if I knew anywhere else to go."

James looked at her thoughtfully, biting gingerly at the sides of his thumbnail. "H'mm," he said finally.

Emily got up impatiently.

"H'mm," she mimicked. "I can say 'h'mm' just as well as you can. A lot of good it does. A lot of good anything does. Sometimes I wish to heaven I'd never left South Ilium."

"Pa decided that," said James brutally.

"Yes, Pa decided everything," said Emily savagely. "Except a few decisions you made and he resented. Suppose you make another. You're the cherished elder son."

"No use fighting with me," said James equably. "I'm not making you drink."

"No, I suppose not," said Emily wearily. She moved away from the window through which she had been staring into the street, and took her seat again. "But, James, you've got to help me." She threw out her hands. "Somebody's got to. I can't do it myself. I've proved that. You're the only one I thought might be able to suggest something—anything. It's got so that Andrew—"

"Andrew," repeated James carelessly. He shrugged.

"What do you mean by that?" demanded Emily stiffly.

"Nothing. Nothing at all."

"You're not going to come over all of a sudden moral, are you?" asked Emily very nearly with a sneer.

James shook his head. "Don't believe in 'em," he said simply.

"If you must know," said Emily apologetically, "I've not had a drink in a week, and I'm ready to jump out of my skin."

"Nobody's ever done that yet, not in my medical experience. Trouble is, you haven't enough to do."

"Not enough to do! What are you talking about. Between singing at the church, choir practice, weddings, funerals, my pupils—"

"Oh, singing!" grunted James disgustedly.

"You don't think that's work?"

"Well, then, you've got to keep your mind occupied."

"Don't be a fool, James. I know all those things. I know all the poppycock and drivel there is. If that's all I needed, do you think I'd have come here?"

"You hurt my feelings," said James.

"To hell with your feelings," said Emily sweetly.

James bowed. "That's what everybody seems to think," he said angrily. "Laura and Ma and you and everybody else. I'm not supposed to have any feelings, I suppose. Just because I'm a doctor, I'm supposed to keep going and going and going. To hell with your feelings." He mocked her accents.

"Oh, James, I didn't mean that exactly," said Emily contritely. "I know things aren't a picnic for you either. I'm not blind, or altogether selfish either, I hope."

The condition of Emily's nerves was apparent.

James moved briskly. "I could give you a sedative," he decided.

"I knew you would know of something," said Emily gratefully.

"But I'm not going to."

Emily's face darkened angrily. "I *had* hoped—" she began.

"It would only be worse than the other in the end."

"Then what *can* I do."

"Practice moderation."

" 'Practice moderation!' " Emily laughed scornfully. "Is that what you do?"

James laughed with her, his eyes lighting reminiscently.

"I've got so damned drunk practicing moderation you wouldn't believe it."

"I believe it," said Emily. "I've seen you!"

James shook his head. "You've seen me a little under the weather, that's all. You've never seen me really drunk."

"Why do *you* drink?" Emily shot at him.

"Why? Because I like to," replied James, surprised. "There's one point in there somewhere when everything's just fine. That's the time to stop."

"You always do, I suppose."

"Sometimes I forget." James frowned. "It's difficult to measure exactly. I always know when I start that I don't really need the last three drinks, but by the time I've had the first few I don't remember."

Emily was biting her lip.

"I may as well go back to New York," she said. "As usual, you're no help."

"No," said James. "I know what I'm talking about. You have to do this yourself, Em. It's rough, but that's the way it is. I know what I'm talking about, and I'm not just talking as a doctor. Drink will never get the best of me. I can stop any time I want to. So could you."

Emily laughed bitterly.

James looked annoyed.

"Well, you asked me, and that's the answer. I can't do anything about the things that are at the bottom of all this. You can't—or don't want to. So it's *got* to be a question of will."

"I haven't any," said Emily shortly. She had been wasting her time. She might have known.

"You have as much as I have."

Emily shook her head. "I'd like to think so. I'm just not as tough and thick-skinned or as determined as you."

James let the insults go, but not the challenge. "All right," he said, and reached for his black bag and hat. "Come on, I'll show you. Horse is outside."

"Where?"

"We'll get one drink, and that's all. You need it. One won't hurt me either. We'll have one drink, and then we'll go about our business. I'll show you it *can* be done."

They pulled up at the side of a Third Avenue saloon a few blocks away. It was late afternoon. The streets were comparatively empty.

"But I can't go in there!" said Emily helplessly. "You must be out of your mind."

James led the way toward the family entrance. "It's all right," he said firmly. He was out to prove his point. "They know me."

It was cool and clean in the back room which smelled of beer, but not unpleasantly. The tables were scrubbed and free of rings and stains, and the chairs were comfortable. James left Emily in one of them and walked through to the bar to order their drinks. She sank back gratefully and closed her eyes. Perhaps James knew what he was talking about. At least it was comforting to be able to talk to someone about it.

James returned with two double whiskies. He placed them carefully on the table and sat down.

"I'm sorry, Em," he said. "Honestly, I am. I could give you some harmless thing to quiet you for a few hours, but it wouldn't do any good. *I know.*"

For an instant he looked a little like Will.

Emily's face softened too.

"I suppose I'm the only one in the world who knows what you're really like. I'm sure Laura doesn't. You're so damned sensitive underneath, you can't stand seeing your patients suffer. That's why you kill yourself with work, and go to pieces sometimes."

James flushed angrily. "By God—!" He stopped fingering the glass of untouched whiskey and began to gnaw at his thumbnail.

Emily smiled gently.

"Forget it, James," she said. "I suppose you're right."

James sat looking at her.

"You'll do, Em," he said grudgingly. A touch of pride and defiance came into his voice. "They grew tough kids in Ilium. Well, drink up!" He drained his glass.

Two hours later Laura was trying everywhere to find James. She telephoned the drug store and two hospitals. No, no one had seen the doctor. Two patients were waiting. Another had telephoned for him to come. By the time Will came home from work she was frantic. One of the office patients had got tired of waiting and left, but two more had come. Meanwhile the telephone kept ringing.

"I don't know where in the world he can have gone! He wasn't here when I came home. Usually he tells the maid, but she didn't see him leave. You don't suppose—" Her eyes widened.

"I'll look," promised Will. "Here take my lunch pail. I'll go right now."

James, if that was where he was, could be in any one of several bars along Third Avenue. Will hurried down Fifty-fifth Street. He drew a blank in the first saloon he tried, but found James's horse, weight clipped to his bit, waiting patiently alongside the second. Will pushed through the swinging doors. There were a score of men getting a drink at the bar on their way home from work. The bartender saw Will in the mirror and turned.

He gestured with his thumb at the back room.

"Will!" cried Emily with enthusiasm. "C'mon in. What'll you have? C'mon in."

James viewed his brother expansively.

"Em 'n I been talkin' over ol' times," he explained. "Good ol' Em! Good ol' Ilium!" He wept quietly.

"Where's your bag, Bones?" asked Will, smiling. "We've got to get you home. Come along, Em."

"Anythin' you say," said Emily agreeably. She picked up her hat from the table and surveyed it distastefully. "Shall I sing now?" she asked Will.

"No, not now, Em," he said quickly. "We'll just go home."

"Oh," said James, a great light dawning. "So Laura's drunk again. What'd I tell you?" he asked Emily significantly.

"Better help him, Em," said Will cunningly. He picked up James's bag.

One of the barkeepers had come in. "I tried to stop 'em, Will," he said earnestly, "and I kept people outa here, but I couldn't do much with 'em."

"It's all right, Mike. Help me get them out the side here."

James and Emily went peaceably, Emily humming softly to herself and James comporting himself with great dignity. The barkeeper held the horse's head while Will helped the two into the buggy. James made the step on the third try. Emily, showing too much stocking, leaped in and almost out the other side. Will steadied her. Several people, including some pleased urchins, had gathered. Will clucked to the horse, wondering what they would do when he got them home.

"See," said James to Emily. " 's what I told you. Matter of will power."

"Good ol' James," said Emily patting him. "Good ol' James."

Laura was standing in the vestibule at the top of the stoop as Will drove up. Practical Laura had been used to men all her life. She set her standards and made her demands, and usually she got what she wanted. When she ran afoul of difficulties, she took them in her stride.

"Up here," she hissed to Will. "Bring them in this way. Help James, and I'll take Emily's arm. I think we can get them in without the people downstairs noticing."

Between them, Laura and Will managed to get the two upstairs, though Emily still insisted she wanted to sing and James was rumbling explanations of some kind. Laura let Emily sag to a sofa in the front room while they pushed and steered James into the back where he collapsed happily on one of the beds. He rubbed his beard enjoyably and closed his eyes.

Efficiently, Laura adjusted a towel barber-fashion about his collar and over the stiff front of his shirt. She hurried out and came back with a basin of cold water and a washcloth.

"Hold him still and swab him with this," she instructed Will. "I'll go down and get some hot tea."

Laura pushed her head into the waiting room downstairs as she hurried through to the kitchen. "Doctor will be with you in a minute," she told two women and a middle-aged man with a face like a prune. "An emergency." That, at any rate, was no lie!

Luckily, there were no serious cases. The man and one woman were chronic invalids, and there didn't seem much wrong with the other woman.

Emily had got up and strayed into the back room. Will called to her.

"Here, you can help me, Em. He won't lie still. Just squeeze the wet rag over his face. I'll hold his arms."

Emily was eager to help. "Water's good for people," she explained, splashing James's face and beard generously. James was gasping and spluttering now. Emily held the wash cloth two feet above his face and aimed at his eyes and then his mouth. When he twisted his face sideways, she got a tablespoonful down his collar.

"Shall I sing now?" she asked Will.

"No, just keep on soaking his head!"

"Dammit!" gasped James, as Laura flew back. "Get these wild Indians off me!"

"Will you drink this if I do?"

"Yes, yes, but make 'em stop!" James swallowed some of the steaming tea. "Ugh!" He swallowed again, spat, and held his head together with his hands as Will released his hold and drew Emily back. Wincing and choking, James sipped at the tea while Laura stood threateningly before him. He did not look up. He shuddered and managed to get down more of the tea.

"Who's down there?" he asked, looking sourly at Emily.

"Mr. Haskins, Miss Wyening, and some woman I don't know.

"Get me my shoes," said James gruffly to Will. He had them on. Will and Laura burst out laughing.

"Give him his shoes," urged Emily sympathetically. "He has to have his shoes. You're mean, the two of you!"

Laura was adjusting James's necktie and brushing his hair. She sniffed him. "Oh, well, get on down there. They've been waiting I don't know how long."

Laura was propelling James toward the stairs. She carried his bag. She turned to Will.

"What a family!"

Emily brightened.

"Sing now?" she asked helpfully.

Will grinned, but he was too busy to answer Laura.

"No, don't sing, please don't sing, Em. You can sing after dinner." Will looked at her. Poor old girl! "London soon," he promised her under his breath.

Chapter 44

IN SOUTH ILIUM, Thomas Stapely's Bible class had been studying Old Testament history, following the battle tactics of the warlike kings of Judah and Israel, the scandals of their courts, and the visions of their prophets, but this morning he was talking differently, and his class listened as children listen to a story.

There were men as old as Thomas in his Bible class as well as much younger men. The older men were honest, work-scarred, English or Welsh-born workmen of the mills and factories of South Ilium or the trades. The younger men were serious, with scrubbed and shiny faces, teamsters, steel workers, carpenters, and apprentice tradesmen. All were in dark heavy suits, tight, stiff collars to which they were unaccustomed during the week, and tight, creaking shoes which smelled of fresh blacking.

Thomas was telling them again of the great Charles Spurgeon whom he had heard many times at the Zoological Gardens of a Sunday when he had been a young carpenter working in London.

He told them how Spurgeon had been convinced of sin in his childhood and how, though he had struggled for salvation, he had found no hope or comfort. He had been certain that God would never save him, and his heart was broken. For six months he prayed, thinking that God would surely answer his prayers, but they seemed to go unanswered. At last he resolved that he would visit every place of worship in the town where he lived.

Some of the oldest men, with lined faces and vague eyes and hands that trembled slightly, nodded in agreement. They could have told the story as well as Thomas, but they loved to hear it again. Thomas went on, deep feeling in his strong voice.

Tom Stapely, too, was old. In his mid-seventies, his hair was white, and there were furrows in his handsome face that now had a touch of the noble and spiritual about it. His eyes had softened, but they were still clear. His huge, heavy-veined, calloused hands were steady.

He held his well-worn copy of Spurgeon's life, but he hardly had need to read from it, so well did he know the story.

Near them a young woman Sunday-school teacher was trying to keep her class of six small boys quiet. One was surreptitiously kicking another. His face was dazzling with innocence when she looked helplessly in his direction. "Tommy," she whispered in desperation, "do you want me to have to tell Mr. Stapely?" The boy's eyes went swiftly toward Thomas, and he stopped kicking his friend.

Close by, their chairs grouped in an intimate circle about their teacher, a class of young girls were being models of ladylike deportment for the benefit of a group of boys of their own age. In their own corner across the parish hall these were grappling with the vision of St. Paul under the direction of a confused young man who made harness on weekdays. The ears of one boy were bright red as he looked rigidly away from the girls.

Spurgeon had gone to many churches and many chapels, Thomas told his intent listeners, but nowhere had he heard the gospel fully preached, nor found how a sinner could make his peace with God. He had felt, he said, like the dog under the table, not allowed to eat of the children's food.

Then one Sunday it snowed so hard that he could not go to the church he had made up his mind to go to. He went down a little, out-of-the-way side street and there he found a chapel of the Primitive Methodists. Spurgeon went in, even though he had been brought up a Congregationalist. They were plain people, of whom it was said they sang so loud that they made people's heads ache. Thomas smiled, and several of the younger men seeing him smile, smiled too.

At first there did not seem to be any preacher. But then a thin, young man came into the pulpit and read the text. The text, said Thomas, intoning the familiar words, was, "Look unto Me, and be ye saved, all the ends of the earth."

"Then this young preacher," said Thomas in an awed voice, "looked down on this unhappy stranger and said, 'Young man, you are in trouble. You will never get out of it unless you look to Christ.' "

Here Thomas opened his book carefully to the passage he had underlined with his carpenter's pencil years before, and began to read slowly and impressively.

And then, lifting his hands, he cried out as only, I think, a Primitive Methodist could do, "Look, look, look! It is only look," said he. I saw at once the way of salvation. O, how did I leap for joy at that moment, I know not what else he said: I did not take much notice of it—I was so possessed with that one thought. Like as when the brazen serpent was lifted up, they only looked and were healed. I had been waiting to do fifty things, but when I heard this word *look*, what a charming word it seemed to me. O, I looked until I could almost have looked my eyes away, and in heaven I will look on still in my joy unutterable.

Thomas looked up at his Bible class, and his own eyes were filled with tears.

Agnes thumped her fat, towheaded baby down on the dust-covered rug on the dining room floor in the basement of the Mott Haven house and twitched herself more comfortably in her slatternly house-dress. Somewhere in the pile of dusty papers and packages, opened then flung together again, which littered the sideboard, she knew there was a box of writing paper. She began to dig for it.

The heavy baby had started to crawl rapidly. He bumped his head on one thick leg of the oak dining table and, standing still on all fours, let out a yowl.

"Be still, Richard! Be still or Mama spank!"

The baby yowled more loudly.

Moving more quickly, Agnes rolled a newspaper into a club and batted the child's hind end which stuck in the air. She got in a half dozen lusty blows before the infant removed her target by sitting down.

"That's a good boy," said Agnes sweetly, for the child, amazed, had stopped crying. "Here!" She kicked him half a dozen child's blocks which lay on the floor on the top of a cardboard box, and went on with her search.

Dirty laundry was piled on one dining-room chair. Clean but unironed laundry was piled on another. Agnes found the box she had wanted. She tugged it free, causing other cardboard boxes and papers to slide to the floor, where she let them lie. Blowing the dust off, she opened the box, and found the writing paper. It was faded but of good quality. She intended to let them see that she knew what was proper.

She began another search for the bottle of ink she knew was somewhere in the dining room and a pen which would work. The ink she finally found on one of the crowded shelves in the china cupboard. There were several pens with it, but two had broken and rusted nibs. She tested the others on the box which held the writing paper. One worked satisfactorily.

She stooped and patted the baby's head fondly. He looked up and smiled. He was trying to place one block atop another, but this engineering feat was too much for him. The child began to pound one block against another.

"Stop it, Richard," said Agnes. "Naughty-naughty!"

Mistaking her admonition for approval, the baby cooed, and using both hands, pounded with his block against the one on the floor. Vexed at having to stoop again, for it made her corsets cut into her bulges, Agnes slapped his hands sharply and the baby began to howl. Agnes let him howl.

She sat down in a rocker and began to write, wrinkling her forehead in concentration. She pushed back hair which had escaped and hung stringily down over her face. The result was a spreading blot on the writing paper which she had already soiled with a dirty thumb print. Agnes brushed it to the floor and took another sheet.

The baby had crawled to her feet and was tugging at the hem of her skirt. Agnes crossed her fat legs and let him try to swing on her foot. Laughing happily, the baby, clutched her black, high laced shoe and tried to swing with its movement. "Itchy, kitchy, coo!" Agnes trilled, kicking him up and down. Tiring of the game, Agnes pushed him away and went back to her writing. She wrote steadily for several minutes, then read what she had written, changing the spelling of several words, crossing out a sentence and writing another over it. Then she set herself to make a perfect copy. She had no intention of letting them have anything they could find fault with. She took pains with her beautiful penmanship.

"May 23rd," she wrote, and then copying exactly, put down the rest of it.

> My dear brother and sister:
> I have wanted to write you ever since the arrival of your little daughter in order to congratulate you. Rhoda has just gone to Ocean Grove with her Auntie Henrietta for a couple of weeks, so now I have a little time to myself in which to write. You will take so much comfort with her and your beautiful home will be doubly dear to you now that you have one of your Very Own to enjoy it with you—if the Lord spares her. I think you will find that your happiness flows from a different source now you will be watching all her pretty little ways. I speak from experience.

Agnes' fingers were getting cramped and she was tired from holding her breath lest she make another blot or misspell a word in copying and have to start over. Richard had gone back to his blocks now and was gnawing comfortably on one. Agnes watched him for a moment. She decided it would not hurt his teeth, and anyway it was keeping him quiet. Probably the paint would make him sick. If it did, Allan could take care of him.

> Richard walks and talks a little (she lied) and now sits at my feet making a house with building blocks I got him. He is proud because he is doing it for Mama. And so our hearts go out to the children in spite of ourselves. They are first, last and always in our minds, trying to bring them up properly. I hope your little girl will be a real comfort to you.

It was hardly likely she would be, not with the kind of parents the new baby had! Certainly James and Laura could not expect to have a gentle and obedient child like her Rhoda who was now eight years old. Rhoda had Christian parents. Agnes gloated over what was the chief point of her letter. She felt she had expressed herself humbly and charitably. If they made a mistake and thought they could walk all over her just because of it, they'd learn differently. She wrote even more carefully:

> I have wanted to write you ever since I have been living a Christian life to say that I sincerely regret treating you so meanly and if I have wronged you in any way to ask your forgiveness, no matter what provocation I had in so doing.

Agnes was proud of the last sentence. They'd know what she meant, all right! Her eyes wandered and saw the baby.

"Richard!" Richard sat comfortably on the floor. Next to him, rapidly melting into the carpet, was a small puddle. "Richard!"

Agnes lifted him by one arm and one ear and slapped him angrily. The infant screamed in surprise and pain. Agnes dumped him, covered the puddle with a double thickness of newspaper and, trembling with anger, picked up her pen again and plunged it so hard into the ink that some splashed on her dress. As it was already soiled with marks from cooking and washing, this mishap did not worry her.

> I ought not to have used you so. It was not only not Christlike but unwomanly besides. So I ask you to overlook it. While our paths lay apart there is no reason why we should go through the world with such a spirit towards each other. I should not like you to suppose that I became a church member with all that old hateful bitterness towards you though I still feel the fault was not wholly mine. I am glad to tell you that the Lord has given me a mind to do His Will. It is a good thing to serve the Lord. Try it. You will never be sorry if you do. It pays. May He bless you both is the prayer of your sister
>
> Agnes Richards

Agnes signed her name with careful shading of the capitals, selected and neatly addressed the envelope, and sealed it. She put it on the sideboard. Allan would have stamps, and he could mail it when he went out on his rounds that evening.

Agnes picked up her baby and hugged him. She was glad that this innocent little soul did not yet know that he had an aunt and uncle like James and Laura—and another aunt, his mother's own sister, who was little better than a woman of—of— Agnes could not bring herself even to think such words. She hugged her child protectively.

"Does um love his Mummy?" she cooed. "Does Mummy's little Richardkins love his Mummykins?" She felt his diapers. They had pretty well dried out. No need to change him yet.

Will, pressed hard against the rail by the crowd behind him, his eyes squinted against the bright sun, tried to follow the six horses bunched closely as they rounded the outside turn across the infield and headed for the judge's stand. Five were close together. The sixth, a slender bay which he had watched in the paddock only about twenty minutes before, was trailing by a good three lengths. The sun caught the jockey's flailing whip. Too late! He could never make it up.

People jammed against Will were shouting and screaming hysterically, Come on, you Golden Clip! Come on, Ticker Tape! Sir Porphyry's got it! Sir Porphyry!

Will, who had bet on the sixth horse, was silent. He was smiling, but he had bitten almost through his half-smoked cigar. He'd lost five in a row. Unless he could pick a winner in the last two races, he would have to eat bread and water for lunch all the next week and walk to work. Luckily he had put enough for carfare home in an inside pocket, or that would be gone too. One more bet.

He did not wait for the winner to be posted and the weighing in, but turned and squirmed his way past the club enclosure where the splendidly dressed men and gayly gowned women sat at their ease on the lawn. He worked his way through the crowd around the back of the towering grandstand, to the paddock again. Horses for the next race were standing there quietly or being walked around the tanbark by their grooms. The starter's post pony stood hitched to a post quietly swishing his tail at the flies. Will patted his rump as he passed.

"I think I should have bet on you, boy," he told the brown and white pony.

"Haw! Haw!" roared a track hanger-on uproariously. "That's a good one, that is." He measured Will with an experienced eye.

A gentle-faced lean man in racing checks sidled toward Will. He nodded at the horses in the paddock.

"Some beautiful looking beasts there, aren't there?" he suggested. "Beautiful horseflesh. They all look like winners. They always do."

"They all do," Will agreed, frowning.

The gentle-faced stranger lowered his soft voice and looked sharply about him.

"The stables know more about it than that," he said. "Perhaps a little information—"

Will, who had been scrutinizing the horses, looked up at him, grinned, and walked away.

The touts were out in force today. His trouble was that he had not been dreaming lately. How was he to know which horse would win unless he dreamed it? The accuracy of his dreams awed him, only he could not dream on demand. Why in England, where the horses ran from right to left, he had even dreamed them running backward and got three winners in a row at Epsom! Cash Sloane, Tod's brother and his Brooklyn bookie, had given him several tips on the ship going across, but his dreams had been more useful. Cash, in a little trouble on the American tracks, had done well in England that year, and Will had run into him at more than one track.

Soon he and Emily would be in England, and he could try his luck again at Newmarket and Cheltenham!

Will picked a long-legged, deep-chested gelding with a narrow head and ears high and went in search of a bookie. He exchanged his last five dollars for a slip of paper and wandered about the lawn waiting for the race to begin. He was alone, he had lost consistently, but he was happy. The sunlight, the crowds, the smells of the stables, and the pounding of the horses' hooves, the dust that rose as they ran, though the track was sprinkled after each race, the taste of the fresh cigar he had lighted, the colors of the jockeys' silks—these soothed and satisfied his whole being.

A half-hour later he tore up the slip of paper. Out of funds, he might as well go home. He did not. He stood watching intently at the rail near the judges' stand as the winner of the last race galloped home. Nostrils flaring, sides heaving, the horse was halfway around the track again before his rider could slow him to a walk.

On an impulse, Will decided to go into Manhattan instead of home to South Brooklyn. If Emily were there, she would be alone. Andrew Gray, he knew, was in Albany.

When he got there, before knocking at the door of Emily's flat, Will turned up the collar of his coat and pulled his pockets inside out. When Emily came in answer to his knock, he stood there with his hand out and a contrite, wistful expression on his mobile face.

Emily looked at him, then, without a word, closed the door and went back into her rooms. In a moment she was back with a slice of bread and a cup of water. "Here, my poor man," she said.

Will took them gratefully, and Emily shut the door again. Holding the bread between his teeth so as to give him a free hand, he knocked for her to come back.

"No butter," he explained, when Emily returned.

"It's all you deserve!"

"If," said Will with sweet reasonableness, "people only got what they deserve—"

Emily looked at him reflectively. "Come in," she said grudgingly.

Will's face lighted. "God bless you, lady," he said humbly.

"I thought," said Emily, when they were inside, "you were going to save every cent to spend in England. You were going to be so careful, no one would know it was you. We'll be going in three weeks, and I'll bet you've less money now than you had a month ago!"

"I have six dollars home and Ma owes me two," said Will virtuously. "Besides, I was only trying to triple what I had. Every time I try to accomplish something, I get blamed for it. It isn't right trying to stifle a young man's ambitions." His tone was piteous.

"You and your ambitions!" laughed Emily. She walked across to her desk and took a long brown envelope out of its top drawer. "I've a good mind not to show you this at all."

"I'm not interested," said Will.

"In that case—" Emily made feint of putting the envelope back again.

"What is it?" begged Will.

"You're not interested," said Emily firmly, closing the drawer tightly after replacing the envelope.

Will sulked, chewing dolefully on his unbuttered bread and sipping delicately at the cup of water.

"Oh, well!" Emily capitulated. She retrieved the envelop and tossed it on his lap.

It was the tickets and stateroom assignments for their passage back and forth across the Atlantic and drafts for substantial sums on banks in London and Edinburgh.

"Phew! Pa and I spent nearly three months there on less than this, including our passage!"

"Neither you nor Pa," Emily pointed out, "were young women of fashion traveling abroad with a courier-companion."

"I was a young gentleman of fashion, and I'm going to be again. I'm having my top hat shined right now. God, Em, what a time we'll have! Just water and sky and air for days and days. It's wonderful! Then Liverpool, London, Cheltenham, the Forest of Dean, the Lake Country, the little fields with their hedges, the way the people talk. You'll be dropping your aitches in no time. Wait till the Fifth Avenue hears you when you come back." Will began to sing. *'Oly, 'oly, 'oly, Merciful and Mighty!*

"Neither of you," said Emily fiercely, "was being exiled for being drunk and disorderly, a weak and disgusting creature who had better be got out of sight for a while!"

Will looked at her sharply.

"Andrew just thinks a change would do you good, and he's right. Things are different over there. They'll seem different to you, better —there, and after we get back. Have you started packing yet? You'll need a heavy coat. It gets cold at night on shipboard. And you'll want walking shoes. No, you can get them better in London. I have half my things in my steamer trunk already."

"Do you think I want to leave Andrew for all that time? Do you think I want to leave him at all—ever?"

"You know he'd go with us—go with you, I mean—if he could," said Will miserably.

Emily had got up from her chair and was striding about the room. She stopped again before her desk, opened a different drawer, turned, and handed Will a ten-dollar bill.

"I don't need it, Em," he said, flushing and drawing back.

"Probably you haven't any money at all, and you've got to have car fare at least till you get paid again." Emily thrust the note at him and ran her hand roughly through his hair.

Awkwardly, Will looked at the money in his hand.

"And don't worry about me," said Emily slowly, "in England or anywhere else. I'll be—muted *diapason,* talk *andante cantabile,* walk *pianissimo* if I have to. I'll be as sober as the metronome there."

"James," exclaimed Mary, who was in Brooklyn, in surprised and almost offended tones, "you're getting gray!"

James bit his lip in annoyance. It was true. There were signs of gray at his temples and a few gray hairs in his beard. Lots of men started to turn gray long before his age.

"With three women around," said James, "wife, mother, and daughter, I'm not surprised. I'm just surprised it hasn't turned white."

"If it will make you feel any better," said Mary sharply, "I shan't be here too much longer."

James knew that she meant she would be going back to South Ilium, but the opportunity was too good to miss.

"We all have to die some time," he shrugged.

"James! That is not at all what I meant. And is that any way to talk to your mother?"

James looked at her thoughtfully. The idea that there should be a special speech for mothers intrigued him. The idea that having a child made a woman ever after a being apart had always disgusted him. It was sentimental nonsense. They had children because they followed their natural inclinations. Then they wanted credit for it. Women always wanted credit for everything. Thank God, there was none of this motherhood nonsense about Laura.

"Oh," he said.

Mary decided not to be offended. She was having too good a time at James's. She and Laura had been somewhere almost every afternoon that week, leaving the maid to look after the baby while they were out. When they were home, she and Laura fussed over the baby to their hearts' content.

Laura had ideas about babies. One of them was that they should be scoured like a ship's deck, fed what was good for them and only what was good for them, and spend their time looking as much like the Gravet side of the family as possible. She complained humorously but angrily every time James said it looked like his father. So James kept thinking up more Stapelys whom the baby resembled—most of them imaginary Stapelys living in imagined parts of England.

"I think you should apologize," said Mary firmly.

"Apologize?" James thought it over. "Yes, probably I should," he agreed. He smiled sweetly. He did not have more than six gray hairs, eight at the most, in his hair and beard. He had been able to count ten when he shaved that morning, and damned near cut his throat while he was looking for them. His private opinion was that they would make him look more distinguished than ever. "Remind me to apologize sometime tomorrow," he told his mother. "I'll be busy all day today."

"A quart of that nice fresh peach ice cream at dinner will do just as well," said Mary. "And tell the man to pack it tightly this time. Laura is very fond of it."

"Laura! You ate—"

"I did nothing of the kind."

James heard a door open and footsteps coming toward them. He raised his voice. "Child is the spitting image of old Aunt Belinda in Great Byestead," he said loudly. "The spitting image."

"James, I've asked you not to say that," said Laura tensely. "The child is not the 'spitting image' of anyone. It's a very nasty phrase.

Martha will be learning to talk soon enough, and I don't want her picking up any of your horrid language. Besides, she doesn't spit!"

"Doesn't spit!" snorted James. "Go look at her pillow. Been drooling all over it!"

"She has *not*," said Laura vehemently, but she could tell nothing from James's face. There was always the possibility he might be telling the truth. The idea of a child of hers drooling on its pillow horrified her. She turned and went to make sure that it was not true. Mary hurried after her.

"Ah!" sighed James luxuriously and triumphantly. He thumped his chest and rubbed it complacently. "Ah!"

Chapter 45

THE HOUSE which Thomas had just finished in Ilium had been troublesome from the beginning. It was a larger house than he usually built, and in Ilium itself rather than in South Ilium. Thomas, who did not know that several large contractors in the city had already refused the job, was surprised when he was approached by John Flowers, a comparative newcomer to Ilium. Flowers, a thin, fox-faced man in his early fifties, had insisted on a time contract and exact specifications.

The time set had been short, but Thomas had felt he could be finished in time. He had not counted on cold weather which delayed the plastering, late deliveries of material, and a shortage of skilled help just when he needed it. He had ended by doing a large part of the work himself, working at night with August. He had even had to substitute more expensive trim for that specified because he could not obtain deliveries.

It was a job in which Thomas had taken small pleasure. He had been in a fever of anxiety for two weeks lest he fail to make the contracted date, and by terms of the agreement be subject to a substantial fine. He stood to make small profit by the transaction as it was. The painters and paper hangers, urged on to the point of rebellion, had finally finished and the house was ready to the day. He would be relieved to get it off his hands.

He arranged to meet Flowers, who was some kind of an insurance man with an office in a shabby brick building downtown near the river, at the new house to turn over the key. It was a ceremony which Thomas usually enjoyed. This time he wanted only to be rid of the symbol of ownership.

It was a large house on an old street of large houses with a wide piazza and elaborate scrollwork about the eaves, upon which the insurance man had insisted. Thomas went over it from top to bottom. The cellar was tight. He could see no light in the attic through any joint of the roof. The rooms in between, smelling of freshly cut boards, paint, and paste drying behind the wall paper, were all in good order.

Thomas had brought August with him to check on last-minute details.

"It seems all right," he said to him.

"Yah," agreed August, who had been tightening the screws about a window. "I suppose so, but I don't like dis place. T'ings was all the time wrong."

The sunlight poured in brightly, lighting most of the painted pine floor in a downstairs room. They heard brisk steps on the piazza. Flowers came in smiling and rubbing his hands.

"We're all ready for you, Mr. Flowers," said Thomas heartily. "I'll show you about." August did not look up.

"Fine! Fine!" responded the other, his eyes darting about. "Everything seems in good order?" He made it a question.

"You should know. Been here enough," retorted August angrily.

Flowers smiled at him and followed Thomas.

"I see. I see. I see," he assented as Thomas, treading heavily, pointed out details. "I don't care much for the paper in this room, however."

"You pick it out yourself," said August, who had followed them.

"Oh! So I did! So I did!" said the man genially. Then he spoke more sharply. "I thought there were to be three windows in here."

"The plans called for two," said Thomas shortly. He was used to having people appreciate the soundness of his building, not insinuate that he had tried to cheat them. "The specifications called for pine doors, too, but I put in ash. I was able to buy some at a good price, and, of course, they are much better."

"I see. I see," repeated the man. "Shall we go upstairs?"

August, staying where he was, scowled after them. It was ten minutes before they came downstairs again.

"The plumbing is in order, and the city will turn on the water when you tell them to," said Thomas. His dislike for the man had increased.

He would be glad to see the last of him. He dragged the key from the side pocket of his coat. "This is your key, Mr. Flowers. I shall send you my final bill tonight. Payment will be due before the end of the month."

Flowers made no move to accept the key which Thomas held out. He rubbed his chin.

"Pine doors were called for," he said.

"You've ash," said Thomas, looking puzzled.

"But I stipulated pine." Flowers smiled thinly.

Thomas's voice rose. "The doors are all fitted and hung. You can't expect me to change them now."

"You get more than you pay for and you still complain!" exclaimed August. "Vat you vant us to do?"

"I know you can't change the doors and still make delivery of the house on time," said Flowers triumphantly. "So you are liable to the stated fine. I shall deduct it from the purchase price."

"I'll change no doors at all!" roared Thomas, reddening.

"Then I refuse the house."

August stood dumbfounded. In all his years of work for Thomas Stapely he had never heard anything like this before.

"Refuse the house!" echoed Thomas.

Flowers nodded thoughtfully. "Yes, that's it." He licked his thin lips.

"But you can't do that!"

"I don't want to be unfair about this," said Flowers, "but I know the law. Still, because I don't want to take undue advantage and I know you must have notes outstanding on the house, suppose I take over your notes in payment for the house. Of course, I could sue for contract violation."

Thomas was pale now. He had out all the notes he could stand, not only on this house but on other work. He had counted on the money from Flowers to pay off other obligations.

"Get out!" he shouted. "Get out!"

Flowers lost his complacency. He drew back.

"Of my own house?" he tried to ask tauntingly.

"It's still my house!" roared Thomas. "It's not yours yet. Get out!"

"You've evidently made your decision, Mr. Stapely," said Flowers from the safety of the open door. "I have made mine. You'll hear from me—or from my lawyers."

The threat frightened Thomas. City ordinance and restrictions regulating building he knew by heart. Over the years he had forgotten most of what he knew of contract law. In all his proud career no one

331

had ever before questioned his honesty or intentions or accused him of not fulfilling a written or spoken agreement.

He flung the shiny new house key after the retreating figure. It struck the black coat on Flowers' narrow back and fell tinkling to the piazza floor.

Thomas sat down suddenly on the third step of the stairs and put his head in his hands. He was trembling and his heart was thumping. His head ached violently, and objects were vague and misted before his eyes.

August looked at him and began to curse, unbelieving.

Thomas lifted his head wearily.

"Don't blaspheme, August," he said weakly, and dropped his head again.

"I get you some vater," said August, alarmed. "You set right dere." He scurried out to return with a dripping dipperful of icy water from a nearby spring which the workmen had used. "Dot no-good fellow," he fumed. "Dot—!"

Thomas drank with difficulty. He touched his wet fingers to his forehead. He began to feel a little better. He tested his legs guiltily before he attempted to rise. When he was sure he could, he rose with a great show of energy.

"Come now! We've wasted enough time here," he said to August. Then he sat down again and stared blankly out of the open door through which Flowers had left.

"You goin' home, and I goin' vit you," said August decisively. "Don' try to be big vool!"

He felt better by the time they reached the house on the hill, but deeply disturbed. Anxiety alternated with a cold rage. Neither Mary, who had returned from Brooklyn only a few days before, nor Maria was at home. He sat down heavily in the kitchen.

"Ve fix dat guy und ve fix him goot!" promised August, who knew no more than Thomas what to do.

"Thank ye, August. Thank ye," said Thomas dismissing him. He was ashamed of his weakness. "I'll be down at the shop later."

August understood, but he was worried.

"You stay here," he warned, and left.

Thomas looked bleakly about the empty house. Mary was probably calling on her friends, telling them about Laura's baby—and it had to be a girl, after all that time. She was always out now, even when she was at home. Maria would be shopping. Emily and Will were in England. Of much use Will was to him with his pleasure-seeking ways. James was far away. Thomas felt bitterly that he was old, unwanted, and alone.

Flowers! The scheming little jacknapes! He could break him across his knee. He should have thrown him bodily from the house. But the banks would be demanding payment on his notes any day now, and he had not the ready cash to meet them. He could sell some of the Fourth Street property, but not quickly enough. He would have to sell at a loss, for values were down, and he did not wish to sell at all. The houses provided a steady income which he could not afford to lose. His head began to swirl as he tried to think. He would have to see a lawyer, but he feared and distrusted lawyers. They were the Pharisees and Sadducees. He lay down on the couch in the living room and fell into a sleep that was more stupor than sleep.

He awoke stupidly when Mary returned late from her calling. Sight of her animated and happy in her calling clothes annoyed him.

"Thomas, you home already! I'm so tired I don't think I could take another step. Maria and I went into Ilium this morning, and we called at the Simpsons before I went on to Mrs. Gordy's. Her son Harold is home for his holidays, and they were very pleased to see me. I must have James look at my knee the very next time I am in Brooklyn. It has bothered me terribly today. They all thought Martha is such a pretty name for Laura's baby, though Mrs. Gordy said if she has a grandchild she wants it called Alexandra after the Prince of Wales's wife. They wanted me to stay to tea." Mary bustled about removing her bonnet and putting on a fresh apron.

Thomas stared at her stupidly and put his hand to his aching head again. His heart was pounding once more. There was a weight in his chest. He felt frightened, and a black rage was freezing its way into his whole being. Fury choked him as he remembered.

He did not answer Mary. The day was past, he thought resentfully, when he could expect to share his troubles with Mary. It was all James and Laura with her now, or Will or Emily. They thought he did not know about Emily! Agnes might have understood, but she too was far away. He got up stiffly and ate his meal in silence.

"Maria has stayed to tea at Blanche's," Mary explained. "Of course they wanted me to stay, too, but I knew you would be alone. They were having cold roast. Agnes wrote this morning. She is coming up again next week if she can get away. Now that she has the two children it isn't easy for her as it was. She thinks she will have to get more help. Did you give Mr. Flowers his key?"

Thomas was not listening. The anger and hatred boiled in him so that he could not think. He muttered an excuse as soon as he had eaten and went to the old shop in the yard. He seldom went there now, but in a corner he found what he sought. It was a large, double-bitted timber ax to which he had sharpened and fitted a new ash handle one rainy morning. He moved steadily and purposefully now, though the pain battered at the inside of his skull. Grasping the ax, he strode through the yard and down the hill.

It was a long walk to the new house, but Thomas knew every short cut. He kept away from South Avenue as he strode unseeingly toward his goal. He was almost exhausted when he got there. Climbing the new steps on which the gray paint still glistened, made his legs ache sharply. He thrust open the door, which he was almost sorry to find unlocked, and pushed inside.

He had the heavy ax ready before he reached it. He brought it crashing down against the first of the ash doors he came to. The upper panel split and splintered into kindling, and the ax chewed deep into the horizontal cross piece. Thomas wrested it free with a mighty effort, drew it back over his shoulder, and smashed the blade through another part of the door. His face was distorted with frenzy as he hacked at the door until it was a ruin of jagged slivers and chewed wood. He turned wildly to look for another door, found it, and demolished his enemy.

It was August, who, unable to remember what they had finally done with the key Thomas had thrown at Flowers, and worried about the empty new house, found Thomas lying senseless on the floor of the dining room. The ax lay eight feet from him where it had bounced, leaving sharp gashes in the floor. He ran for help. Someone got a rig from a nearby livery stable, and this time a horse had to climb to the top of the hill. Three men carried Thomas inside while August, out of breath and fearful, hurried off to get old Dr. Samuels.

"But what happened?" cried Mary. "He was here at tea, and he was quite all right. What happened?"

They had got Thomas into bed, and he lay there very white with his eyes closed. Dr. Samuels, an even older man, bent and rheumatic, sat feeling for Thomas's pulse.

"He's had a shock, Mrs. Stapely. Will you get me some more warm water and towels. I'll stay a while."

"Will he—?"

"It's too early to say. He has a remarkably strong constitution though. We'll see."

Mary, her face showing surprise rather than grief, moved quickly and practically away to get what the doctor had asked for.

Maria looked terror-stricken. Her fat, wrinkled face was all awry, and her eyes were wide and red-rimmed. Her shoulders shook as she turned on Mary.

"My poor, dear brother!" she moaned again. "My poor, dear

334

brother! It's a judgment on you, Mary Powitt, for the way you've neglected him. It's God's judgment on your wickedness."

"It's nothing of the kind," said Mary shortly. "It's what happens when a man seventy-four years old refuses to take care of himself. Stop wringing your hands and get a telegram off to James to come right away. You might send one to Agnes, too. No, don't. Just tell James to get here as fast as he can."

"I'm the one," said Maria brokenly, "who has looked after him these last years. I'll be the one who is left. You'll be all right. Oh, yes, you and your fine sons and daughters."

"Will you go and send off that telegram or just let Thomas lie there?" asked Mary quietly, as she poured hot water into a basin, and pulled clean towels from a filled drawer.

James, after having hurriedly turned his practice over to his friend, Dr. Whiteside, was there the next noon. He hardly bothered to speak to Maria or his mother. He and Dr. Samuels went together into the sick room where Thomas lay still apparently unconscious, though twice he had opened his eyes. The second time there had been what looked like a gleam of intelligence in them before they fluttered closed.

It was some time before James came downstairs. When he and the older doctor came down, his manner was very professional.

"It's a good thing you got Dr. Samuels here as quickly as you did," he said.

"He's tough," said Dr. Samuels, trying to hide his pleasure. "You know how tough he is. Well, he's in good hands now."

"He's in your hands, doctor," said James quickly. "I'll be here to help as needed."

The old man's eyes lighted, though he said nothing.

"He may die," said James to his mother and aunt, "or he may be partially paralyzed. Or he may recover completely." He looked to Dr. Samuels, who nodded assent.

Maria, who had got control of herself, managed to look more like Queen Victoria than ever. Mary watched her son anxiously.

"What happened anyway?" James demanded.

They told him what they could, but it was from August they got the full story.

"I'm glad you here, James," he said earnestly. "I guess he go crazy mad. Dot Flowers. I could hit him vit my mallet."

"So that's it," mused James. "I knew that violent temper of his would end in apoplexy one of these days," he added virtuously. "I think we may be able to pull him through this time, but it's about time he learned to control himself."

"Like you, maybe," said the privileged August ironically.

James glowered at him.

"Who else knows?"

"I don' tell nobody. Today I go hang new doors. Vot happens about dot house now?"

"I'll take care of Mr. Flowers," said James darkly, and August felt better.

That afternoon Thomas moved his hand, and later he was able to swallow the clear soup Mary fed him from a spoon. He still did not speak, and his body was still. He watched those about him silently and impassively.

A few days later he was writhing with intense pain which seemed centered in his legs. Dr. Samuels and James were relieved and dared tell Mary and Maria that probably Thomas would fully recover. The pain was a good sign of returning life.

"Clot trying to get reabsorbed," James explained.

James spent hours with his father. In another week Thomas was moving uncertainly about the yard, looking old, frightened, and bewildered. James sat with him on a bench in the sun, and they talked.

Mary was tender, practical, and efficient with the sick man. Maria was subdued and self-effacing. With Mary and James both there, she felt pushed out of the position of importance she had enjoyed with Mary away so much. She gained some support with the arrival of Agnes who, grief-stricken and distressed, rushed untidily but earnestly to her father's defense, smothering him with attention and solicitude which Thomas, weak and still frightened, accepted gratefully.

Unwittingly, Agnes played into her mother's hands.

"It just shows," Mary told her two oldest children, "what I have been saying all along. Your father and I have got older than you realize. Your father should be near you, James, so that you can look after him when he is ill and needs you. And, of course, Agnes, he has always depended on you."

Innocently, Maria urged the cause on by her whispering complaints to Agnes.

"Perhaps this will make some people realize," she said darkly. "All of you owe everything to Thomas, yet some people have neglected him shamefully."

Once his father seemed safely on the road to recovery, James began to enjoy himself. He showed no impatience to be home. He wandered contentedly about the garden and walked down the hill to revisit old haunts. He walked to jobs that Thomas had under way and talked with the men he knew. He took the streetcar into Ilium by himself and came back after almost an afternoon of just looking about. He talked with Thomas about the decay of the Erie Canal and the condition of Ilium's industries. Ilium seemed no longer to be growing. He thought it had come to a standstill. Thomas disagreed, but had not the strength to argue. As his health improved, his worry returned. His affairs were at a crisis. His broad forehead grew fretted again. James listened but said little.

The next afternoon James went downtown again by himself, carrying his black doctor's bag as though he were going on a call. He did not expect to need it, but the worn bag was his weapon when he went abroad. He felt unprotected without it. He had reconnoitred the afternoon before and knew his way. He found John Flowers fussily shuffling papers at his roll-topped desk in a shabby two-room office. As it was a hot day, the door was open, and James walked in.

"I'm Doctor Stapely," he said fiercely. "Thomas Stapely's son."

Flowers, who knew of Thomas' collapse, looked at him with amusement.

"*I'm* not sick," he said smugly.

"You're going to be," said James.

"I don't like your tone."

"It will do for what I have to say. I came in to tell you that you are a thief, a scoundrel, and a shyster," said James deliberately.

Flowers jumped up from his desk, his narrow face livid.

"That's slander! I'll have the law on you."

"You tricked an old man into a fraudulent contract, taking advantage of his honesty. If anyone is going to suffer from the law, you are."

"That contract is perfectly legal," sneered Flowers, taking a folded paper from a pigeonhole of his desk and waving it at James, "and will stand up in any court. I intend to enforce it."

"And I intend," said James taking a step forward, "to break your dirty little neck."

Flowers was no coward, but James's eyes were blazing. His outthrust beard gave him a piratical fierceness. James was broad-shouldered and powerful. Flowers backed away.

"You're not going to frighten me," he blustered. "I know my rights in this, and I'm going to have them. Tom Stapely has lorded it over people around here long enough. I've heard things. This time he'll pay through the nose!"

"The nose, eh!" The idea seemed to please him. James fastened his eyes on Flower's prominent nose and flexed his fingers. He made a sudden move. Flowers, paling, jumped back further, almost falling.

James picked up the contract from the desk where Flowers had dropped it and tore it across. He tore it across again while he watched the other, then stuffed the pieces into his pocket.

"You have no contract," he said, "and you'll have no house, not at any price."

"Now you've done it!" screamed Flowers. "That's deliberate destruction of property. I'll have you arrested. I'll—"

James lunged at the man, then, contemptuously, did not touch him. Assault, he knew, was a charge that could be made to stick. As a doctor, he could not afford it.

"I could pick you up by the scruff of the neck and shake you like a rat," he told Flowers from a distance of six inches. "I will yet, if there is any further trouble from you. Go near my father again and I'll cut your heart out—with a dull knife I carry in my bag for dealing with people like you. I'll make out the death certificate for mange and distemper."

"I offered to buy the house! Ask your father if I didn't! It's costing me money in rent every day I don't have it."

"You'll not get it now at any price. I'm buying it myself. I might sell it to you in a year or two—at a profit."

"You'll hear from my lawyer, and it won't be just about the house now!"

"If I do," promised James, "you'll hear from me."

He went out elated. Just how many laws he had broken and what he was liable for he had no idea. The fellow, he supposed, could cause all kinds of a ruckus now, but he didn't think so. Flowers was too frightened. James bit off the end of a cigar, spat out the piece, gripped his bag as though it were the man's throat, and strode off.

Everybody in South Ilium knew Thomas was ill. Women came with broth and jelly. The rector stopped by every day. The story of his smashing the ash doors had gone the rounds, picking up action and color as it went, and men called admiringly to ask after him after work. It was understood that Thomas had wreaked his fury on the doors only because he could not find Flowers when he went after him with the ax, and Thomas was a hero.

There was life in the old boy yet, men decided gleefully. He might go preaching around like an old hypocrite, others said, but there was nothing mealymouthed about Tom Stapely when he got stirred up. Even the South Avenue boys in between stealing, assignations, and routine carousing were keeping a sharp lookout for John Flowers. If he dared show his ugly head in South Ilium, they threatened, they'd break it into very small pieces for him.

James had told no one of his errand. He intended to tell Thomas as soon as he could to set his father's mind at ease. He got no immediate chance, for he found them all outside on the lawn in the back. Thomas sat tensely in the chair which had been put out there for him. Mary, Maria, and Agnes were all around him, Mary and Maria sitting on straight-backed wooden chairs brought from the kitchen, Agnes standing posed as her father's daughter behind Thomas' chair. All of the women had changed into afternoon dresses, and Agnes seemed to have given more thought than usual to her appearance. Her hair was fearsomely curled, but it had faded enough so that it no longer concealed the switch she wore. It was darker and more vivid brown than her own hair.

"James will tell you," said Mary with dignity, as he approached. "I know that he agrees with me."

"About what?" asked James. He noted with surprise and indignation that his father regarded him unpleasantly.

"This has been proof enough," said Mary, "that your father should be near his children. It is time he realized that he is no longer capable of all he could do when he was a younger man. His health must come first now."

She no longer had any intention, if she had ever had, of wasting her remaining good years on this hilltop in a small, drab city, watching Thomas grow older and more feeble and feeling old age overtake her.

"We can discuss that later," said James shortly. He was surprised and angered. His mother had promised days before not to bring up the subject until he agreed. "How are you, Pa?" he asked frowning.

"I'll be well enough," said Thomas, with more force and spirit than he had yet shown, "if people would stop scheming behind my back—and if you and George Samuels would let me get back to my work."

"In a week or so perhaps," said James. "That is, if you behave yourself and don't get all excited about nothing."

Agnes found it easier to maintain a Christian attitude toward her brother in letters than to his face. They had hardly spoken directly to each other since her arrival. She was certain, anyway, that Allan could better take care of her father than James.

"That's no way to talk to Pa!" she said indignantly.

"Indeed it is not!" Maria backed her up.

James ignored them. He looked warningly at Mary, but without effect.

"I've thought it all out," said Mary firmly. "Thomas, you can sell your equipment and—and good will. We will have the rent from the houses. We could rent Mr. Gray's house in Brooklyn where James used to be. There are tenants there now, but I don't think there'd be any trouble about that—"

"No trouble at all," said James ironically. "The house is Emily's. Andrew put it in her name years ago."

Maria gasped, and Agnes sniffed. Thomas looked up from under his heavy white eyebrows. His jaw set as he listened.

"Then, if you feel you must work," Mary continued calmly, "James says you can make more money building houses in Brooklyn than here."

"You've said all that before," said Thomas bitterly, "and James has had his say. I didn't think while I lay helpless abed you were at it again." Tears of weakness sprang to his eyes.

"Pa would be better inside now," ordered James desperately.

Mary paid no attention.

"We could sell this house, and get a good price," she said, looking at it thoughtfully. "And—"

Sell the house! The full enormity of their betrayal struck Thomas then. He drove his fist bruisingly into his thigh. He opened his mouth, drawing back his lips in a grimace of pain and anger. He closed it again without speaking.

"Sell this house!" cried Agnes sentimentally. "The old homestead!"

"Never you mind, m'girl," said Thomas quietly. He patted her fat-fingered hand where it lay on his shoulder. "We'll not sell this house I made." But he spoke without conviction. He looked frightened. His eyes went to James for help.

James, despite himself, was looking at the house with an appraising eye.

"Then what will become of Arthur and me?" cried Maria, her face wrinkling. She seemed on the verge of tears.

"I've no idea," said Mary thoughtfully.

Agnes saw where James was looking.

"If the house is sold," she said quickly. "I'd expect my fair share. Allan and I have two children to think about."

Thomas jerked his shoulder free of her hand.

"I'm not dead yet," he told them all, "though I soon will be, if you all have your way. My work is here, and here I stay. Don't think I'd run away now." There was scorn and contempt in his shaken tones.

"Oh," said James triumphantly. "You needn't worry about that Flowers fool any longer. I took care of that." He tugged the torn pieces of the contract from his pocket, and fitted two top pieces together before he handed them to Thomas so that his father could see what it was.

Thomas stared at them. His face changed color. He started to speak, but choked. He had to clear his throat twice. His face was cut with pain as he stormed at his eldest son.

"So you think I'm no longer capable of taking care of my own affairs! I was doing a man's work and looking out for your mother, aye and for Agnes, too, years before you were born. I'll look after myself still, spite of the pack of ye!"

James was taken aback. Pleased with himself, he had not expected this.

"I tried," he said stiffly, "to do the best I could."

The women, not understanding, were staring at him. The bearded James looked like an abashed small boy.

Mary sniffed audibly and daintily twitched a small white handkerchief from her sleeve. She touched her dry eyes.

"You might think of the rest of us sometimes, Thomas," she said with apparent difficulty in a low voice, "instead of just yourself."

"I like that, indeed!" cried Maria. "As though my brother had ever thought of himself. If he had—"

Thomas had been staring at the pieces of his contract with Flowers. Suddenly he looked bravely at James.

"Thank ye," he said humbly.

Embarrassed, James looked up at the small bird which had hopped about the lawn, then fluttered to rest on the lowest large branch of the swamp maple where it seemed to listen to the whole conversation.

"I don't think you'll ever hear from him again," he said. "We'll talk about the new house later. I have some ideas about that, too, if you want to hear them."

Badgered, Thomas looked at them all.

"If Will and Emily were here," he shouted furiously, "they'd listen to no such nonsense as this! They have some sense and decency about them. They'd soon see the right of this and put an end to it!"

James and Agnes looked at each other for the first time. Their eyes met in an incredulous stare. Will and Emily, indeed!

Mary, though she was careful not to let her feelings show, was elated. Thomas was grasping at straws. Her eventual triumph was certain.

"Come, Thomas," she said solicitously. "You've been here in the sun long enough. We'll get you back to your bed for a rest before tea. James, I'm surprised you'd let him overdo this way!"

Chapter 46

"WELL, I'M DAMNED!" exclaimed Will, as he raced through the letter from James which Emily had handed to him. "Poor old chap! Do you suppose we ought to go back?"

They were in Emily's room in a hotel in Glasgow, and three letters had just come. They had been forwarded from their Aunt Julia's in Gloucestershire, so that they had news of Thomas' recovery at the same time they learned of his collapse.

"'Poor old chap'!" mimicked Emily. "I knew he'd lose his senses if anyone ever actually crossed him." She was reading hurriedly through one of the other letters in which Mary explained that she had not written immediately as they were too far away to get home and it was useless to spoil their pleasure. "Here, listen to this. It's in a P.S. 'We may be moving to Brooklyn soon. We will talk it over when you return and we have our plans made.'"

"Move to Brooklyn!"

"Ma's been at it long enough, but I never thought she'd make it."

Emily threw the letter down on the bed and moved restlessly across the somberly furnished temperance hotel room. She looked out at the rain which had been falling steadily all day.

"Pa'd never be happy away from South Ilium," said Will, frowning. "You know that. I don't think they should move. I wonder if he really is all right."

"We can't go back today," said Emily shortly. "Most of our things are at Aunt Julia's anyway. We'd have to go back there first. Besides —well, I have other things to do."

They had been abroad two months and, for Will, the trip had been perfect. They had stayed almost two weeks in the same Bloomsbury hotel in London where Thomas and he had stayed a few years before. They had spent a week in the Forest, and visited with Aunt Julia. They had traveled through the Lake District. They had seen cities and market towns. Will had been twice again to Epsom. Everywhere they went Emily had attracted attention and admiration.

They had sat at the captain's table on the voyage out, and Emily had starred in the ship's concert two nights before they landed at Liverpool, Will thrilling to people's knowledge that the beautiful and talented woman was his sister. Once on the street in London and once at a hotel Emily had been mistaken again for Lillian Russell, one man and woman refusing to believe she was not the famous American beauty.

Emily had blossomed in England, seeming happier and freer than at home. Will was certain that she had neither taken a drink nor wished for one. Revelling in his role as courier and seasoned traveler, he had tried to show her everything he knew and to uncover places he had not been before, but he had been careful to steer clear of restaurants and hotels where liquor was served. He was convinced that Emily had not discovered his strategem.

"I suppose it's all right," Will said. "James said it was a shock and he could have another. They usually do. Maybe Pa would be better off if he were near James and Allan, but South Ilium's home. They can't really move."

Emily swung around and laughed shortly.

"You show more concern for Pa than he ever showed for you! Damn the rain!"

"That's why we're going to the music hall tonight," said Will eagerly. "Trained horses, comic turns, acrobats, and all the rest. I asked downstairs, and they said it's good."

"All right! All right, but I warn you! I've made out a long list of the things I won't see in Glasgow. I don't want to see the column to John Knox or the grave of Sheridan Knowles, whoever he was. I saw all the shipyards on the Clyde from the train. And I *won't* go to the cathedral."

"It's not as good as Gloucester or Edinburgh," Will admitted.

"Spend half my time in churches in New York, so I'm not going to another cathedral if Thomas Aquinas built it with his own saintly hands." Emily began to laugh again, a trifle unsteadily.

Will looked at her.

"Crossing the Atlantic," gibed Emily, "to see some trained horses!"

Her face had relaxed, and Will felt easier. He laughed too. The trip *was* doing her good.

"You can get out now," Emily suggested dryly. "I'm going to dress for dinner."

"Right you are! I've an errand to do anyway."

"What?"

"You'll see!"

Perhaps, Will thought, there had been no letter from Andrew Gray. Emily wrote almost every day, and Gray's letters were the first thing she looked for everywhere they went. If they were delayed, she was upset. He hoped one would come soon. He could not bear seeing Emily hurt.

Most of the time, he felt, they had been as happy as two children. He had met another girl on shipboard, and Eleanor Wartham would be on the same ship returning. She stirred him, and he intended looking her up in New York, but there was no one like Emily. No girl he met on shipboard, or at home, or in England had Emily's beauty or her manner or her wit.

Will hurried downstairs and across the small lobby. He had decided that at each place he would surprise Emily with some little gift she could keep as a memento, even if it were only some tiny object to go into the crowded curio cabinet which he had made for her.

On busy Argyle Street, where umbrellas were bobbing and men had the collars of their mackintoshes turned up, he had passed a small bookshop, its shelves crowded with shiny new books and old calf-bound volumes of Beattie and Hume. He hurried there now. A book would be just the thing to get in Glasgow.

A little old man, wizened and grizzled, was in charge of the shop. He seemed to regard Will as an intruder and put down with a show of reluctance the old book he had been reading.

Will looked over the packed shelves and laden tables with a feeling of helplessness. He did not want a big book either. They had enough to pack and carry. The old man, his finger marking his place, watched him impatiently.

Finally he told the old man what he wanted.

"I'd like something suitable for a gift for a lady," Will said. "A young lady."

"You'll not find it among the mathematics then," said the bookseller grimly. "Is it a Scots book you want? Scott, Burns, Stevenson—or that Barrie, if you're like all the rest of them."

"I'm not sure," hesitated Will. "Let me see—"

"Come now! Is it a novel you want, or a book of poems, or whatever?"

"Poems would be all right, I think," said Will, jumping at the idea. "Some nice poetry would be just fine. *'The Assyrian came down like a wolf on the fold, And his cohorts were gleaming in purple and gold.'*"

"Byron," said the old man distastefully, "and bad Byron too!"

Inspired and pleased with himself, Will struck a pose.

> *Breathes there a man with soul so dead,*
> *Who never to himself hath said,*
> *This is my own, my native land!*
> *Whose heart has ne'er within him burned*
> *As home his footsteps he hath turned—*

"Scott," said the old man. "That's better." His hatred of Will seemed to lessen. "Here now's a nice bit of a book."

He handed Will a dainty little volume of Elizabethan poetry bound in tooled calf, its leaves edged with gold. It almost disappeared in Will's square, calloused hand. A slender strand of bright red silk was bound between the pages as a bookmark. Will liked it instantly. The book fell open to Spenser's *What guile is this, that those her golden tresses—*. The lines pleased him. They sounded as delicate as the book looked. He saw verses of Shakespeare and the names of other poets he did not know.

"Fine," he said. "I'll take it."

"That'll be three shillings," said the old man. Two shillings was the price, but Will was an American. Then he noted Will's work-hardened hands as he took the book to wrap it. "Two and nine," he corrected himself conscientiously.

Back in his room, Will dressed carefully, inserting his studs in a fresh evening shirt. He smoothed out his fair moustache before the blistered mirror.

He found Emily almost ready, and she had compensated for the dreariness of the day by the richness of her costume.

"Phew!" Will commented.

"Like it?" smiled Emily. "Andrew always does."

The hotel's modest dining room was bright and pleasant. Some of the guests were obviously commercial travelers and others were Americans, but many of the diners looked respectable Glasgow. Will was pleasantly aware that people looked up as they followed the waiter to their small table, but Emily, sailing graciously ahead, seemed not to notice. He slipped the book to the side of Emily's place, and she discovered it almost as soon as she was seated.

She picked it up gently and felt the cover. She opened it and ran her long fingers over the smooth pages, and turned to the title page opposite which Will had written, *For Emily, with love. Will. 12 August 1900*, before she spoke.

"It's lovely, Will, and they're some of my favorites." She turned the small pages, looking for something. She found it. She read quietly.

> *Dull sublunary lovers' love,*
> *Whose soul is sense, cannot admit*
> *Absence; for that it doth remove*
> *Those things which elemented it.*

Emily looked away from the book and across the room as she continued softly,

But we, by a love so far refined
  That ourselves know not what it is,
Inter-assured of the mind,
  Care less, eyes, lips, and hands to miss.

"Who wrote that?" asked Will curiously. "It sounds good—I think."

"Donne. It is good. You're good too, Will."

Will looked surprised.

"That's what I've been trying to make people understand for the last twenty-eight years."

"You're kind and good, though you don't even know it. You do more for Ma and Pa than any of the rest of us. You're really worried about Pa, aren't you?"

"Well—"

"And have to spend your time playing nursemaid to a sister who can't be trusted to stay sober."

"Stop it, Em!" Will was embarrassed. "I'm having the time of my life, and you know it."

The waiter came then to take their order. Emily waited until he had gone before she spoke again.

"If the family does move to Brooklyn—though I don't think they will—what will you do?"

"Why go with them, of course!"

"You could carry on the business in Ilium."

Will frowned. "I don't know. Ilium's not growing any more. I was talking to Jim Garver. I think he's still sweet on you, by the way. He's practicing law there now, though mostly just legal work for his father's company. He thinks Ilium will go downhill from now on. Besides, I'll have to go with Pa and Ma."

"But you *don't* have to, Will. You can't always be the dutiful youngest child, though Pa will let you as long as you put up with it. Mother, too, for that matter. They all impose on you. They've had their lives. It's time you were thinking of your future."

"You sound like Bones and Laura—this beef's really good. What's the future got that today hasn't right here and now? The potatoes are watery. Besides, I could get a good job in Brooklyn, if I wanted. Higgins offered me a job as construction foreman on six houses he's putting up out Bay Ridge way."

"Then why didn't you take it? The beef *is* good."

"Roast beef of old Scotland," said Will. "Oh, I don't know. For one thing, I couldn't be here now. There's an old hag over there

346

watching you with all four eyes. Turn a somersault or something so she won't be disappointed."

"Later," said Emily. "Will, you should have taken that job. The next opportunity you get, take it, no matter whose plans it interferes with."

Tight vertical lines cut into Will's forehead above his nose.

"I wonder if Pa really *is* all right?"

"Forget Pa! We're off to Loch Lomond, the Lakes of Killarney, Paris, and the other side of the moon."

"I don't think our tickets are good that far!"

"Well, we'll get some more then. No, we'll borrow these trained horses of yours and go that way. Where are they? Bring on your horses!"

Chapter 47

ANDREW GRAY and Ellen were waiting at the North River pier when they landed back in New York. Emily and Will saw Gray from the deck before the gangplank was lowered and, amid all the waving and calling, were able to attract his attention. Gaily he waved the bouquet he was carrying and swept off his hat with an extravagant flourish. Ellen, all her white teeth showing as she emitted a glad cry they could not hear, waved frantically with a brilliant scarf.

They cried out and waved in return, bade hasty good-byes to fellow voyagers, and were among the first down the gangplank. They got through the customs easily. Will hurried to leave the checks for their heavier baggage with the express company and returned to find the other three exclaiming over each other.

He shook hands with Andrew Gray, pretended he would kiss Ellen, who dodged behind Gray, and grabbed up as many as he could of the smaller bags. Ellen tugged at two more.

"I've a hack waiting," said Gray. "You weren't ill at all!" he exclaimed to Emily. "You're a better sailor than I!" Happiness shone in his eyes.

"Andrew, it was all wonderful—but this is better. It's so *much* better! And I'm better. I *know* I am."

"I'm glad," said Gray quietly. "Emily, it's been so long without you."

Emily's face was transfigured. Will looked quickly away. He would never understand wholly, he thought.

"Shall I tell you all about it in one breath?" he asked, as they got into the cab, stowing the bags about their feet, "or take two? I've got just"—he counted—"one dollar and twenty-six cents left. Isn't that good economic planning? We could not have stayed abroad another twenty minutes." He was looking about, standing in the cab. He saw Eleanor Wartham and her parents, took off his hat and waved. "I'm to call next week," he explained gaily to Emily.

"Another shipboard conquest?" smiled Gray. "No, Ellen, not yet!" he said warningly.

"One of several," Will admitted modestly.

"What are you two up to?" demanded Emily, as the driver chirped to his horse.

"Ellen and I have a little surprise," Gray admitted while Ellen grinned widely.

"Meeting us and these," said Emily, sniffing her flowers, her eyes shining, "was all the surprise I needed."

"Jes' you wait, Miz Emily!" screamed Ellen. "Jez' you wait!"

"Is Ma down?" asked Emily. "Is that it?"

"Any more news of Pa?" asked Will anxiously.

"Only that he is much improved," Gray assured him quickly. "No, this is something else."

"Driver!" called Will. "You've missed the turn. It's West 19th Street we want."

"No, go on, cabby. We've a stop to make first, if you don't mind," Gray told Emily.

"Of course not. It's a beautiful day to drive anyway. New York is beautiful. Everything is beautiful!" Emily exulted.

"Certainly somebody is," said Gray.

They continued northward, turning east to take the 86th Street cut through Central Park. Emily wondered about their destination which Andrew Gray seemed to have forgotten. Will was talking away animatedly about their return voyage, the ridiculously self-important Chicagoan, the little old Irishwoman coming out to see her son in Pittsburgh, the posing stock-company juvenile who had tried to impress Emily, the hard-bitten cockney steward who had consistently snubbed those he suspected would tip him too little or too much. Ellen lolled back at her ease, preening herself in the carriage as they passed members of her race afoot.

They turned into the expensive reaches of newly developed upper

Park Avenue, and the driver drew up before a recently erected apartment building whose fresh brick and stone work shone in the sunlight.

"This is where I have to make a stop, if you'll excuse me," said Gray easily. "A friend of mine is moving in. The building has only just been finished. Perhaps you'd like to look about. It's rather attractive inside." His eyes sought Emily's.

Will looked uneasily at the splendid entrance. "Like the West End in London!"

"It's all right," Gray assured him. "Ellen!"

"Yas, suh, Mist' Gray!" Ellen pressed her hand over her mouth.

They followed Gray inside, the cab waiting, and across the marble-tiled foyer. A uniformed attendant and a girl at a telephone switchboard looked up and smiled.

The elevator operator, a slight Negro, seemed to need no instructions. He stopped his car at the fifth floor, and Gray drew a latchkey from his pocket. He opened the second of three doors in the square hall, and held it back for Emily to pass.

As soon as she was inside, Emily's incredible surmise was verified. She saw her own familiar rugs and furniture, even her own linen and silver on the table which had been set for lunch.

"No!" she gasped. "No!"

"This is the little surprise. Do you like it?"

"*Do* I like it!" Emily sat down on the nearest chair.

"Perhaps you and Ellen will bring in the bags and pay off the cab," Gray suggested, handing Will a bill, "then we'll inspect the place."

Emily was in his arms as soon as they were gone. She buried her head in his coat, murmuring, choking, clutching him tightly.

Gray, smiling over her head, waited a moment.

"The old neighborhood was getting a little shabby, and I knew there were some things about the flat you found distasteful. Your mother came down from Ilium to help arrange things when your furniture was moved."

"Oh, Andrew, it's lovely!" Emily moved about, entranced. She turned and faced him. "And you thought a change of scene might well go with a change in habits? Oh, Andrew!" she said brokenly and came back to kiss him and be held in his arms again.

"And this isn't all. Risviglio and I have had our heads together. Fielding is enthusiastic, too. They think you are ready for a concert series right here in New York. I thought so long ago. It's all arranged."

"No!" said Emily tensely.

Gray smiled indulgently.

"You don't mean *that,* but perhaps I said it all too quickly. We'll—"

"I do mean it, Andrew. I used to think—but that was long ago."

"You'll be more famous than you ever dreamed. Everyone will hear you. Your voice will be better than ever!"

"Andrew," said Emily fiercely, "you must love me more than ever now!"

"I can't do that!"

They moved apart as they heard Will and Ellen returning.

"I invested a little money in this building some time ago," Gray explained to them all. "I own eighty or a hundred bricks of it, I suppose. In fact, I own this apartment on a cooperative basis. I could not move in myself, and I could not very well let it lie idle, so we installed Ellen. Didn't we, Ellen?"

"I's what we did!" Ellen told Emily. "Y'all see the kitchin yet, n' the little po'ch? They's seven rooms, Miz Emily, an' great big closets! You come heah n' look! Now ah got t' git lunch. Ah got it all ready 'foah we lef', on'y the tea watah!"

Will was examining the construction, feeling the walls, inspecting the trim and the work about the windows in the bright rooms.

"You say Ma helped move?" he asked.

Gray nodded, "But she's so busy now with her own moving that I have not seen her in a week or more."

"She actually is moving?"

"So I understand. Into the old house in Brooklyn. Your house," he told Emily. "Mrs. Stapely asked me, and I said I thought you would agree."

"I must get to Ilium right away then," said Will quickly.

He did not actually go until late the next day.

When he arrived Will found the South Ilium house a shambles. Carpets had been rolled up. Pictures, taken down from the walls, stood on the floor against the walls. Beds had been taken apart, and mattresses were airing in the yard. Three barrels, two of them packed with china, the third half-filled and waiting to receive more, stood in the middle of the floor in the summer kitchen.

Alarmed as she saw Thomas regaining his strength and will, Mary had realized that she had to strike while the iron was hot, to move quickly or once more lose to Thomas.

"Your health is much more important to me, Thomas," she had told him several times, "than this house, much as I love it. We can't have you collapsing again."

"No," Thomas had answered bitterly.

Will found him morosely hammering a crate together in the half darkness of the cellar. The rock walls had not been whitewashed that year, and cobwebs hung in the gloom of the sand-bottomed vegetable storage room. Crocks for pickles and vinegar jars, dragged out of the corners, stood about the floor. Everything was going to Brooklyn. Will had passed his mother, on her way down to get things ready in the Brooklyn house which the previous tenants had already left, as his train sped up the Hudson from New York.

"I've always tried to give your mother everything she wanted," he said bitterly to Will. "If she wants to leave her home, I'll help her."

"But you'll have a good home in Brooklyn," said Will, not meaning it, "and we'll all be together." It made him feel ill and lost to think of leaving the house.

"We'll see," said Thomas darkly.

"But I thought you were supposed to be sick," said Will tactfully. "You're not sick at all."

"Of course not, boy!" snapped Thomas, pleased. "Never been sick a day in my life." He conveniently forgot the hard cold which habitually incapacitated him for days several times a year. "Never been better in my life. I'm not through yet, and don't any of you make the mistake of thinking it."

"You should have been with us, Pa," said Will, wondering whether he should offer to help. He still wore his good traveling clothes. "We had a wonderful time in Ireland and Scotland. Everyone in the Forest sent his regards to you. Uncle Edwin wants you to come back next year."

Thomas stopped hammering, and sat on the crate.

"I should never have left the Forest when you and I were there. I didn't want to."

"I know you didn't, Pa."

His father fell silent. Will could see now in a shaft of light from the hatchway that his face was thinner and more deeply lined. He had put on his eyeglasses, thinking evidently that no one was about, and forgotten to take them off when Will came in. Somehow this touched his son.

"Did you stay at The Oak in Ironford?" Thomas asked eagerly. "Has Walter Wainstead trimmed his hawthorne hedge? I'd give much for such a hedge. Did you hear the new rector at St. James's?"

"He was away," said Will. Emily had gone several times to the Forest church, but he had not bothered. "Almost all the mines are working full tilt again. The hedge looked fine. It was past blossoming though. Old Mrs. Herron is dead, but you knew that."

"She wasn't 'Old Mrs. Herron' when I first knew her," said Thomas sharply. "She was Lizzie Freeland, and a fine-looking, rare lively girl."

"And Em and I saw *The Mikado* at the Savoy in London. It was perfect! We saw *The Pirates* there. Remember?"

"Aye, and bright music it was! Here now, you can get off your finery—if you're not too good for it now—and give me a hand here."

Will grinned in the darkness. "Be with you in a minute!"

Thomas grumbled a reply he did not hear as he ran up the stairs and climbed into overalls in his room off the kitchen, which was still intact.

"But I won't sell this house!" Thomas announced loudly, as Will re-entered the cellar, hammer in hand. "Take down those shelves yonder, and mind you don't split them. We can put them up again in that fool Brooklyn house. I'll maybe rent it, but I won't sell it."

A bent and rusted nail squealed as Will clamped the claws of his hammer about it and pulled. It was good to have a hammer in his hand again.

"Attaboy, Pa!" he approved.

"What? What did you say?" demanded Thomas.

Will was loudly knocking loose the first of the shelving. He grinned again. Slang infuriated his father.

"Of course you won't sell. We might want to live here again before a year or two is up."

"That's it," said Thomas mollified. He crashed his own hammer down on the head of a nail in the crate. "Your mother's got so she doesn't know her own mind."

The trouble with his mother, thought Will, was that she knew her own mind only too well.

"And we'll still have a good house in Ilium," suggested Thomas a little timidly. "James bought the last house I built, and he got a good one."

"I heard about that. What do you want me to tackle next? I'm glad he took it—and I'm glad you showed that fellow Flowers the way you did."

Thomas was silent for a minute.

"James fancies himself the head of the family these days," he said grimly.

"James?" laughed Will. Poor old guy! If he'd ever sworn bitter revenge against his father, it had been a long time ago. He had no wish to hurt him now. "Not much he doesn't. He's too busy surrounded by a thousand belly aches, and Laura's up half the night collecting and counting the money. There's no head of this family anywhere around but you!"

"See you remember that," ordered Thomas clearly, his voice happy in the protecting dimness of the cellar. "Come now! Going to take all day with those bits o' shelves? I've a plan or two yet, m'boy," he boasted. "I'm not one to tell all my business to everybody until I'm ready."

Will wondered whether his father meant what he said or was merely trying to cover his shame and defeat. He learned a few nights later when his mother, exhausted but happy, had returned in triumph to announce that everything was nearly ready in Brooklyn.

Laura and her maid had helped her with the last minute cleaning. As soon as the furniture came from South Ilium—and she hoped they had crated the mahogany library table with the plush insert in the top so that it would not get scratched—they could get started with the settling. In two weeks' time they would be comfortable in their fine new home where they could see the children any time they wished, and both James and Allan would be near at hand in case of illness.

Mary, all inspired energy, looked brightly around the tea table. She had still more news, but she knew better than to break everything to Thomas at once.

Maria looked steadily into her plate.

Thomas cleared his throat.

"You and Will will have to go on down without me for a while," he said.

Mary raised her expressive eyebrows. Her gray hair, touched with white at the hairline above her clear forehead, was as precisely arranged as ever. Her shirt waist with its boned collar was stiffly ironed and fresh. She wore a small cameo at her throat. Her finely oval face was scarcely wrinkled, its expression self-possessed, young, very much alive. She wore her victory with kindness.

"I signed a contract with John Wetnam this afternoon for a new shed at the machine works," he announced. He cleared his throat again. "And I'm to build the new hall for the lodge. I turned down two smaller jobs."

He looked a little frightened. A few minutes' handiwork with a timber axe had done more to enhance his reputation than all his years of labor and it had done more to speed his recovery than James and Dr. Samuels and all their medicine. Thomas Stapely was in demand.

"Good for you, Pa!" cried Will amazed.

His mother silenced him with a glance.

"Now, Thomas," she said firmly, "you know you can't do that. You can turn the work over to August. I thought we'd agreed on that."

"Turn these jobs over to August! What are you talking of, m'girl?

August can do cabinet work, but do you think August could put up structures like these?" Thomas was honestly amazed. He smiled at Will, who would understand the difference well enough between the capabilities of a real builder and a craftsman, even a fine craftsman, like August.

"Pa's right," said Will briefly. He felt proud of the old man and happy for him.

Mary's face wrinkled for an instant in blank dismay.

"Our plans are all made, Thomas, and you know we can't change now. The furniture is nearly all packed. The house in Brooklyn is all ready."

"I know all that," said Thomas impatiently. He was a busy man with work to do. He'd had enough of the foibles of women. "I'm not standing in your way, but how do you suppose we are going to pay the expenses in Brooklyn or anywhere else unless I earn the means? Just you and Will go along with things. I'll be there when the new jobs are safely under way—of course, I may not be able to stay long at a time for a while."

Mary sipped her tea formally. She intended to show no upset before Maria.

"But this house will be rented," she demurred a moment later.

Thomas and Maria looked at each other.

"I'll stay with Maria in the cottage," he said. "We've talked it over. I shall build on a new room."

"So you've talked it over!" Mary's voice rose in spite of herself.

"Sure," said Will, trying quickly to help them both. "That would take care of it. I'll stay on a while, Pa, and help you with the room. On the east side, you mean. That should be fine. I'll—"

"Be quiet, Will," said Mary.

She had realized quickly that there was no real problem at all. Thomas might have been very difficult in Brooklyn at first. This way she could have things established the way she wanted them without any interference. By the time Thomas was ready to come, the order and routine of the new household would be firmly in hand.

She looked thoughtful and very considerate.

"You can hardly be as comfortable that way, Thomas, as in your own home."

"The furniture won't be here. That'll be about the only thing different from what it's been in a long time," said Maria boldly. "I think my brother can manage to get along without a few sticks of furniture." Her tone was bitter.

Mary smiled in superior fashion at Will and deigned reply. This time she needed his help.

"It will be only for a short time, of course," she said pleasantly. "I've no doubt your father can put up with it for a little while."

Treacherously, Will sided with his father.

"I think it's a good idea and will work out fine," he said firmly.

"More cake, Willy?" asked Aunt Maria happily. She offered him the plate and he took another generous slice of caraway-seed cake.

"Then," said Mary with spirit, "it's fortunate I've made the arrangements I have."

"What arrangements?" asked Thomas, frightened again.

"I can hardly be expected to take care of a large house now the way I did a few years ago," said Mary.

Maria lifted her heavy brows this time, and set her face for a sniff, though she made no sound.

"Agnes and Emily both agreed with me, so I thought it would be a kindness to write and ask poor Cousin Mottet's daughter, Ann, to come and live with us, and act as housekeeper. She has been alone since her mother died in July, and she's a very nice girl, I'm sure. She's about your age, Will, perhaps a little older."

"Well, I never!" ejaculated Maria.

"H'mph!" said Thomas.

"Fine," said Will carelessly. "I promised to go see Jim Garver. I'll be home early." He touched his father's shoulder approvingly as he went out. Good for him! He could hardly wait to tell Em about it.

"Besides the rector's unwell again," he heard his father saying stoutly as he went out. "I couldn't leave St. Mark's now." His voice rose more strongly. "Will Gladstone lived to be eighty-nine, and *he* didn't run away to Brooklyn. He stayed where he belonged and chopped wood—and he outlived his son!"

BOOK 4

ALL IN PLAY

1901-1906

But thin membrane divides power-controlled
From uncontrolled, from force sprung past restraint.
He saw a streetcar rear up from its tracks
(Straight lines cannot be trusted overlong),
Its headlight was the eye, its clanging gong
Was happy rage fire-belching from the throat
Of monstrous predatory animal.
With sweeping claw he saw it rip a street
To screaming mess of stone and shattered glass
Stained with the twitching bodies of torn men,
Then, sinking watchful backward to its place,
A bloody grin aslobber 'round its lips,
Make feint to pounce again upon the street,
Desist and, like life, do it all in play.

Chapter 48

"A victory dinner for Ma," laughed Emily, "and how like her to disappear in the middle of everything!"

Laura laughed, too. "But this isn't getting the work done. Come now!" she ordered.

Nothing less than a full-scale dinner party, they had all decided, could signalize the move to Brooklyn. Emily and Ellen had come over from New York. Laura had also brought her maid down, and they were sweeping and scouring the house which had first been occupied by James and Emily, all of them working like navvies. Even Agnes had come over from Mott Haven to help. Rhoda was at school so she had had to bring her blond infant. The boy, who was large for his age, had been put to play in the back yard while his mother tugged and hauled at arranging the furniture. She knew, she explained, just where her father would like things.

"Where do these things go?" demanded Ann Mottet, appearing in the dining-room doorway with her arms full of table and bed linen from another box she had just opened.

"Oh, dear, I don't know!" Emily, standing on a stepladder, was stacking china on shelves as Ellen unwrapped it from a sugar barrel and handed the pieces up to her. "Ask Laura. She's somewhere upstairs."

Ann had arrived with her bags and trunks, adding to the general confusion, just before Mary left. She was small and neatly shaped, with an abundance of chestnut-brown curly hair and bright gray eyes in a determined face. Her lips were thin and severe, and her small chin was firm. She had a slightly Roman nose. Her movements were quick, and her Canadian-accented English was sharp and clear. The girl, who was cheerful, energetic, outspoken, and watchful, had quickly taken charge of getting sketchy meals for them as they worked.

"That one doesn't miss much," commented Laura dryly.

"We must be charitable," said Agnes. She remembered Ann as a small child when, as all their friends and relatives had done, she had stopped with her parents in South Ilium on their way out from England. Emily and Will began to believe that they, too, vaguely remembered Ann. "She seems a nice girl," Agnes added, "and she'll be a great help to Ma."

"She can make more of a mess of things in five minutes than Ellen and I can straighten in a half-hour," offered Emily, "but she seems to have a sense of humor to balance the chip on her shoulder."

"We mustn't judge," said Agnes sweetly. "Richard! Richard! What have you got into now?" She galloped into the back yard to shake her offspring warningly.

"She'll loosen his teeth doing that," decided Laura, watching through the window.

"Might improve him. He looks lumpish," said Emily, and Laura laughed.

Ann was back by this time. "I put the linen in the closet of the back bedroom on the third floor." They all knew Will was up there papering. "What a mess Will has that room in! The way you all spoil that young man!" Ann began to rip more paper and china from the sugar barrel. She left the litter on the floor and grabbed a dozen books from a stack leaning against the wall.

"Spoil Will!" echoed Emily smiling.

"You certainly do!" said Ann gaily. She put the books on the nearest chair and began to dust the sideboard.

"No one could spoil Will," declared Laura. "We're all in love with him anyway."

"In love with him!" Ann dropped her duster. "Perhaps I'd better start getting lunch and do this later."

That evening she watched Will as, tongue between his teeth, he concentrated on hanging the bedroom paper straight. He leaned back on the ladder and scrutinized his work for wrinkles.

"Hand me that cutting edge, will you?" He asked Ann without turning.

Without hesitation, Ann handed him a putty knife.

"No, no!" said Will impatiently. He turned and pointed to the floor. "That thing."

"How could I be expected to know?" demanded Ann sharply. "At home we always had men come in to do these things."

"We can't afford to have 'men come in.'" Will mimicked her good-naturedly as he trimmed carefully at the overlap of a panel.

Ann watched him silently for a moment. "Why doesn't James or your father do some of the hard work? After all, it's to be your father's house."

"Oh, I don't mind," smiled Will. Ann, he thought, was rather a pretty girl. Sometimes she looked very attractive. He enjoyed having her as appreciative spectator.

"I don't see why you let them all impose on you as you do. After working all day, you run all their errands, look after Emily—"

"Impose on me!" exclaimed Will, surprised. The reference to Emily had angered him.

Ann murmured something he did not hear, and this time handed Will the wide wall brush just as he was reaching for it.

"Thanks! You're learning fast."

"I generally do," said Ann in a self-satisfied tone.

Agnes was appointed to warn their father and produce him at the dinner. She elected to convey the message in person as it would give her a chance to see what was being done about the house on the hill and hurried off to South Ilium. While Mary was paying a state visit to Emily's new Park Avenue apartment, where Emily was to keep her until they could spring the surprise dinner, Laura and Ann began a great baking of bread and pies and cakes and meats and puddings against the banquet. As soon as Mary had moved on to stay with Allan while Agnes was away, Emily and Ellen returned to do the more decorative part of the catering, bringing some of Emily's finest silver and Venetian glass. Even Andrew Gray was pressed into service as messenger and delivery boy.

The dining room would not be nearly big enough. The table was set in the upstairs parlor with the portieres drawn back to add the space of the sitting room. Thomas, beaming and pleased at such attention and affection from his children, came down from South Ilium and was smuggled into the house in the afternoon. When Mary arrived, accompanied by Agnes and Allan and their two children, all scrubbed, starched, and shining for the occasion, the others were already there, all of them—Emily and Andrew Gray, Will, James and Laura with their pretty baby nestled in a clothes-basket crib, and Ann tastefully dressed and very busy running in and out of the kitchen to superintend the activities of Ellen and Laura's maid who had been brought to serve and clear away.

Mary, as they had known she would, refused to be surprised. She removed her bonnet, smoothed her skirts, and accepted the festivities with grace and dignity almost as though she had planned it all. Emily and Laura were delighted.

Thomas, resplendent in his best dark suit, shining stiff shirtfront and a new silk tie which Agnes had brought him for a present, bowed his white head humbly at the head of his table to say the grace in deep Gloucestershire tones. Mary opposite him at the end of the long table listened sedately, her folded, blue-veined hands tight so they would not tremble. She sat very straight.

Then the talk and merriment burst out as Ellen and her helper began to bring in the roasts and the fowls, the steaming dishes of vegetables, the freshly baked bread, and all the rest of the feast.

"All of us together!" cried Mary happily. "You see, Thomas?"

"Aye, m'girl," Thomas agreed, as they watched his face. " 'Happy is the Eye,' " he toasted, almost shamefacedly.

"Oh, Father," cried Agnes sincerely, "we're all so glad to have you here with us. It is going to be wonderful having you and Ma so near. Now we can come and see you both as often as we can. Of course, I could not very well call in Brooklyn before when Ma has been here."

Agnes just could not forego the chance for a dig, thought Laura. James must answer that letter of Agnes'. Aloud she said to Mary and Thomas: "James will be a different man now."

"That's a relief!" approved Will.

"And your flowers are as lovely as always," Mary said to Andrew Gray as the dishes were being passed and Thomas went at the carving with a will. He flourished his knife as he looked up to see whose plate was next.

"Not all my friends have both a town house and a country home," Gray smiled.

The phrase made it suddenly clear to Thomas what had happened, and he thought it was no bad thing after all.

"Rare or well done?" he asked Laura heartily.

"A city place and a country home. That's what I planned," decided Mary.

Ann sat pointedly silent with lips compressed. So she was to be ignored and treated as a poor relation! She wore a set smile which indicated to anyone who would look that she was hurt but forgiving.

"And we're all so glad to have you, my dear," said Mary noticing quickly. "You're one of us already. I'm sure you are mostly responsible for this delightful dinner."

Ann softened and expanded instantly. She smiled and nodded brightly. Laura, her scant hair carefully done for the evening with the single diamonds she liked to wear glinting in the sharp, thin lobes of her ears, nodded and smiled back to her across the table, and Emily also smiled. Like all the rest of them, Ann might have her faults, but they wanted her to feel at home.

"And I'm so glad to be here," said Ann. "After mother's death and all the trouble at home—" she sighed, but threw off her grief. She looked directly at Andrew Gray, who sat quietly smiling between

Emily, beautifully gowned and bejeweled, and Laura. "I'm afraid I'm very stupid," she confessed, "but I don't really know who you are. Are you one of the family?"

Emily looked startled, then angry. Ann knew very well who Andrew was.

"He certainly is!" said Mary firmly.

"A friend of the family," said Gray easily. His hair was turning white at the temples, and he looked tired, but his wise, understanding eyes were clear, his handsome face composed as he answered Ann. "An aged and not overly bright retainer of some years standing," he further explained.

The others had not heard amid the clatter of dishes and the general talk. James and Allan were already deep in a professional discussion, James emphasizing points with stabs of his knife. He and Allan had not seen each other in some years.

"Put your knife down, James, before you pink somebody," hissed Laura. "Do your operating at the hospital, not at the dinner table."

"He's never happy at the dinner table unless he can throw a knife at someone," Will explained to Ann. "Once he almost pinned me to the wall. Better be careful when you have him here to eat."

"He can't be as dangerous as everyone says he is," said Ann flirtatiously. "Our doctor at home was like that. He'd bluster and scold, but he was really very kind and nice."

"Well, I'm not," said James looking at her with distaste. "Haven't time to coddle patients."

Agnes, unusually well dressed in a rustling brown silk, pearls which Allan had given her at her throat, her hair in frizzy curls, left the table a moment to attend to her children. They had been put at a separate small table in the sitting room where they were within sight and sound of all that was happening, and both were being very well behaved. They were busily eating, with ten-year-old Rhoda taking efficient care of her younger brother and stealing fascinated glances now and again at Laura's baby who lay gurgling in its clothesbasket.

Sight of the children gave Thomas added happiness as he listened to James, answered Andrew Gray's interested questions about conditions in Ilium, and looked proudly at his wife. They had been fruitful and multiplied. Their differences of character and opinion did not matter just then. Wantonly he basked in the loyalty and affection around him, and Mary looked at him fondly.

"*Rhoda, Rhoda, had a Pagoda,*" taunted Will between mouthfuls of cherry tart smothered in whip cream, when he looked up and caught the child's eyes. But Rhoda was older now. She merely smiled indulgently and went on with her woman's work of looking after her fat, blue-eyed brother who stared at Will solemnly.

All the people she loved, thought Emily, were here in this room: Will, her mother, Andrew. She felt choked with emotion. Laura, wondering whether she and James had not already been away from the house too long, got up to see that the baby was all right. She was fast asleep.

"I'll wake her for you, if you want," offered Will. He, too, was happy. For once everything was all right, and nobody was angry about anything. Even Agnes and James had spoken civilly. They would not dare say anything before his mother who sat receiving the homage of her loyal subjects as her queenly due.

Later Emily sang. She sang Gounod's *Ah! Je veux vivre* and *Come, Thou Lovely May,* for Andrew, then *Comin' Through the Rye* for her father. They all joined in, and even James seemed pleased. He refused to see Laura's warning glances that they should leave, and sat down at a corner table to play bezique with his mother.

James, Will, and Andrew Gray, looking always for Emily out of a corner of his eye, were talking of Teddy Roosevelt and his astounding behavior in the presidency to which he had so unexpectedly succeeded.

"Poor Tom Platt!" laughed Gray. "He was caught out that time."

Ann, Emily, and Laura were exclaiming over some dress silk which Mary had purchased in New York while staying with Allan. Ann looked up, as she heard the men talking.

"I was at the Pan-American in Buffalo the day President McKinley was shot!" she cried. "My, was there some excitement."

"But I thought it was some anarchist did it?" said Will puzzled.

"Oh, *I* didn't do it!" explained Ann. "Not that I wouldn't have if I'd wanted to."

"I'll bet!" murmured Emily between her teeth.

Will pretended to dodge in alarm behind his upraised arm. Startled by the sudden movement, Agnes's youngest began to whimper.

"Not you, silly!" Rhoda comforted her baby brother. "Not you!" She looked indignantly at Will and, comforted, Richard stopped crying.

Allan tousled the child's hair and touched the shining head of his small daughter. How he loved those children, thought Will! He wondered if he would ever have any children of his own and, if he did, how he would feel toward them.

Mary and James, a cigar between his teeth, were quarreling violently over their bezique. James insisted on playing fairly, and Mary, who always felt that a certain amount of cheating was her due and

364

who certainly would stand for no *lèse majesté* that night, insisted he "play like a gentleman."

A moment later she swept in a hand with an exultant, " 'Er am a booty, am't her, Sam!"

"I'll be over just as soon as I can," Will promised Emily and Andrew Gray as they left. "What with helping one parent build new quarters in South Ilium and another get started here, I've had no time after work. And I'm foreman carpenter for the Smith Construction Company now, you know," he added proudly.

"The big builders?" Gray asked.

"Office buildings and factories, mostly," said Will. "I'm working down at the Wellbank Building going up near Whitehall now. If I get along all right, I'll be put on still bigger jobs."

"I told you you could do it," said Emily. "Didn't I?"

"I have to do it," Will told her ruefully in a low voice, while their father and Andrew went on talking. "It takes a lot to support a string of race horses—other people's race horses at that!"

That evening wound up with everyone in good spirits. It was a truce with each other and with life and the world outside.

Thomas was so pleased that he stayed the remainder of the week, busying himself with building a small greenhouse over the back steps so that Mary would have a place for all her plants. He walked up one afternoon to see James and be checked over. When James pronounced him fit again, he scoffed at the idea that he had ever been otherwise. James, grinning, took this as confirmation of his verdict.

At the end of the week, Thomas had had enough. He brushed aside all urging that he stay. He had neglected his work long enough, and the probability was that everything was going wrong on every job he had on hand. Besides, he was needed at St. Mark's.

Thomas protested and apologized unnecessarily. Mary had already laid plans for shopping and visits which did not include him. She demurred enough so that Thomas would not feel he could go off just as he pleased and every time he pleased, and went on plotting excursions with Ann. Ann was no dull stay-at-home, but as anxious to be on the go as she was. She was like her mother, Mary said—a mind of her own and not a lazy bone in her body.

"We can leave Will's tea all ready," said Ann with determination, "and he can get the things out of the ice chest and off the stove when he comes in. I don't believe in catering to any man. We can do the Brooklyn stores today, and go over to Fourteenth Street on Wednesday."

The kitchen might look like a wreck after Ann had finished cooking a meal, with flour and sugar spilled across the stove and the floor, and open pots and pans strewn everywhere, but the meals were always tasty and satisfying.

Will, tolerant of everyone who did not interfere with his chief pre-occupations, found Ann quick-witted and lively. She was usually good-humored, if too ready to scratch. He laughed and joked with her, or ignored her. Ann relished his attention, though she affected scorn of it to Mary, and noted his indifference with sullen impatience. She would show Mr. Cocksure one of these days!

Chapter 49

MARY MET WILL at the basement door as he came home from work one night a few weeks later. She opened the door from the inside as he turned the handle.

Will kissed her firmly, at the same time warning, "Look out. I'm pretty wet. The rain's stopping, though."

"I've been waiting for you, Will," said Mary. She looked around and lowered her voice. "Will, I want you to be nicer to Ann."

"Nicer to Ann!" echoed Will, turning from hanging his hat on the hall rack. His face showed honest surprise. "Why, I haven't done anything to Ann!"

"She's gone upstairs," said Mary, "and she's hurt. She's very sensitive."

"Well, I'm sure I don't know what it's all about this time. It seems to me she's always in a stew about something."

"It's very convenient and pleasant for me to have Ann here," said Mary firmly, "and you know she had a very hard time of it when her mother died. We were very close in England when we were young. And with the kind of father she has—"

"All right, all right!" laughed Will impatiently. "Dinner ready?"

He had thought at first that Ann's father, too, was dead. Then it had developed that he was an old man living in the English section of Montreal and apparently drinking as hard as ever. An allowance from a rich brother in Manchester supported him. There had been some kind of a scandal in England. What it was Will did not know, or care.

"Will, you're not going out again tonight?"

"I certainly am! Do I have a clean shirt? Is my suit back from the tailor's?" Reassured on both points, he hurried through his dinner, a savory meat pie followed by deep-dish apple tart.

"Good!" he pronounced, shoving his plate away after a second helping of the tart. "Now I must shake a leg, I'd better shake both of them or I'll be late again."

Ann compressed her lips. She was in the littered kitchen stacking the dishes before washing them while Will was hastily blacking his shoes. He had no time to stop for a shine. Most of the paste had dried in the tin. It took a liberal application of spit to get enough liquid to blacken his daubing brush.

Ann watched him ironically.

"We were at Agnes' this afternoon, your mother and I."

"Good!" said Will. "Fine! How is my delightful and benighted sister?"

"They all hate me," said Ann complacently. She poured hissing hot water from the kettle into the dishpan. It sizzled and steamed as it struck the tin.

"Well," said Will reasonably. "You hardly go out of your way to make them like you."

"I've always said just exactly what I felt and just what I pleased. I don't intend to change now," said Ann. She tossed her curly brown head and narrowed her gray eyes.

Will was hunting one more speck of soft blacking. He shrugged.

"*You* like me all right, don't you?" she demanded.

"Why, yes, of course," said Will carelessly. He looked up at her.

"Then I don't care whether the others do or not!" Ann flounced back into the dining room, presumably for more dirty dishes.

She came back immediately, her hands empty.

"I suppose," she said unpleasantly, "you are going over to see that girl on Riverside Drive again tonight."

"I am!" smiled Will.

"Men are such fools!" snapped Ann bitterly.

It was another half-hour before Will was completely satisfied with his appearance. It was half-past eight when he reached his destination.

Will was in love with Eleanor Wartham. Dark-haired, dark-eyed, slender, graceful, Eleanor had seemed at first just another pretty girl ready for a shipboard flirtation. Now Will found it thrilling to be near her, distressing to be away from her. They had gone a half-dozen times to the theatre that winter and once to a concert at Carnegie Hall. Will had even taken Eleanor to call on Emily.

He had told no one, not even Emily, but he intended to marry

Eleanor. Never before had he wanted to marry. The idea frightened but fascinated. He was almost sure he meant it.

Eleanor was waiting for him.

"We've been such good friends, Will, that I wanted to tell you first. We had such fun on the ship and ever since. Bob Bennett and I are going to be married as soon as he gets out of Harvard Law in June."

Will could not answer. What his face must have shown he did not know, then or later. It showed something, for Eleanor spoke quickly, contrition, dismay, even pleading in her own face and in her voice.

"But surely, Will, you couldn't—I mean it was never that way, was it? You knew there was Bob and that my family expected some day— And you know and like so many girls! Please, Will!"

He laughed then. Gay, carefree, heart-free Will! That was the part they all expected him to play. He stopped trying to think and managed to speak.

"Bob Bennett is very lucky. Me marry! I wouldn't make much of a husband, would I? Perhaps you'll ask me to be a bridesmaid."

"In flowered organdie!" promised Eleanor, the troubled look leaving her face.

It was replaced by another look. She looked at Will as if she saw him for the first time. Her lips parted, and her eyes deepened with expectancy. She had hoped Will would kiss her. She held herself very still.

Will smiled vividly, looking his handsomest, but he did not move toward her. His color was high.

"I'm not supposed to stay now, am I? Isn't that the way it is?" He was afraid he might cry. His chest pained.

"What? What did you say, Will? Oh, I hadn't thought of that! Yes, I suppose so."

Will turned brightly to take his strangled emotions and starved body back to Brooklyn. He walked slowly down Riverside Drive. He walked for miles.

Will's girls! Will's love affairs! The family fiction, he thought derisively, that he was sought after and irresistible. The truth was he was afraid, as much afraid of his own inexperience as of women themselves.

He came alive when there were young and attractive women about. He could laugh and jest with pretty girls—then be left unsure, hungry, and alone. You could not, he thought bitterly, start life on a brick pile in South Ilium and know the graces and the mysteries. Once more, for black hours as he strode through the darkness, Will hated his father.

The El trains, when he finally turned east, were slow and infrequent at that time of night. It was very late when he reached home. Their street lay in silence and in darkness, the street lamps casting slender tents of light down to the sidewalks and the roads. A light, turned low, had been left for him in the upstairs hall. Will fumbled for his key, only to discover that he had evidently forgotten it when he changed his clothes. He did not wish to ring and disturb his mother. Then he heard movements inside the house. Ann opened the door.

She was in her nightgown over which she had thrown a flimsy wrap. She held it loosely together at her throat. Little of her body was hidden, for the light of the hall lamp was behind her. She did not look as though she had been asleep, for her hair was neither in curlers or disarranged. Will caught the scent of Florida water as she held the door open for him to pass.

Involuntarily he took a step toward her, then caught hold of himself and brushed past, near enough almost to feel the warmth of her breath and her body.

Ann let go her hold at the throat of her wrapper as she refastened the brass chain at the door. Will released the latch on the night lock.

"Well," said Ann acidly, "you look sober enough. Did you have a good time?" She did not step back. Will put out his hand toward her, then dropped it.

" 'Night," he mumbled.

Ann smiled after him.

"Sleep sound," she said, an edge of scorn in her voice, but one she could have denied if accused.

* * *

Chapter 50

THOMAS STAPELY did not want to die. He trusted God, but he was not sure he trusted Him that far. Thomas, who had known that the strength would go out of him if he left South Ilium, was at home and safe. He knew the God of Ilium and St. Mark's. He did not know the gods of teeming Manhattan and sprawling Brooklyn.

He had been frightened the year before, but he was getting over his fear, and his position was perfect. He could, when he wished, feel old and deserted. He could also feel relief that he had been freed of most of the earthly possessions for which he no longer cared, and that he had been left free and independent. White-haired, vigorous, still capable of wrath but more careful of using it, he lived comfortably with Maria in the cottage, driving hard at his work, where he was busier than ever, musing slowly as he sat in the evening, sometimes with his cello, often with his Bible and Sunday-school books, or sometimes just reminiscing with Maria.

Letters came frequently, but Mary and his family seemed far away. Their concerns did not seem real. The sky was over him and the earth beneath him. In between was the tiny cottage near the house he had built on the hill of South Ilium. He and Maria might have been living in their childhood home. Sometimes they felt as though they were.

It was reassuring to Thomas that he was with Maria as he had been a lifetime ago. She with their long-dead parents and their brothers, two of whom were also dead, had been part of the first reality Thomas had known. Sometimes, when he had not been to Brooklyn for long weeks or months, it seemed to him as though Mary and his family and all that had happened since he was a boy in the Forest of Dean were unreal and a dream.

Usually Maria and he talked little. There was little to say. They had known each other too long. Arthur was on a truck farm down near Hudson in Columbia County and finally, working in the soil, seemed to have found work which contented him. Cousin Blanche and Aunt Simpson and Harry came to see them. Others came, but many of their English intimates, like Cousin Harriet, were dead. There were some, of course, who showed Thomas a sympathy he did not need but accepted.

They had always known, they said to each other, that Mary Stapely was selfish and headstrong. Other family friends said that he was a stubborn old man who should have gone with his family, but they smiled on him and were proud of him and brought him gifts from their gardens and their baking. There were strangers in South Ilium who did not know the Stapelys at all, but they soon learned who Thomas was. He was a tough old man and down along South Avenue they were proud of him, too. Tom Stapely's straight back and steady eyes, his grim face and his strong voice, Tom Stapely driving his men at work and walking to St. Mark's, his Bible and prayer book under his arm, reflected credit on them all.

Thomas *was* St. Mark's, its lay head and virtually its priest. His old friend the rector, a mere fifty-seven, had suffered a severe heart attack. Thin and white, he had returned to his native Surrey to recover. He would be gone for months or a year. He might never return. St. Mark's, its congregation smaller now, could not afford a temporary incumbent. The mill and factory owners who had contributed generously in earlier years were dead or absent. Employers who had suffered during the bad times were chary of contributions to church or charity. Workmen had other diversions these days. They had had the Spanish American War. They had the trust-busting campaigns of Teddy Roosevelt and more saloons now to keep them occupied and tractable.

The rectors and curates of Episcopal parishes in downtown Ilium administered the sacrament on stated Sundays. They came to bury the dead, to confirm, and to marry. Thomas and the vestry, old men like him, ran the church and the church school of St. Mark's, and Thomas preached.

Thomas preached, and the men, and women, and children of St. Mark's parish listened. Behind Thomas, they felt, was the knowledge of God and the wisdom of a long and full life. Thomas preached, and as he stood in the aisle before the altar he felt the surging strength of martyrs and Christian heroes, of the long and bloody history of the church, of the fiery Spurgeon and stalwart Gladstone, of their gentle and quiet rector, of the loving labor he had expended on the organ and the building of the church and the parish house.

He was no longer the builder of South Ilium or the husband of tall, graceful Mary Powitt or the father of Dr. James Stapely and Miss Emily Stapely of the choir of the Fifth Avenue Church. He was God's man, cleansed and warmed and made strong by the spirit of his Lord, his heart made glad, his arm and sword invincible, his spirit proud and humble.

The force and conviction of the man, what seemed his nobility, though the older men and women knew his violence, his weaknesses, and his bitter mistakes, moved them as they raised their voices with his:

> Almighty and most merciful Father: We have erred and strayed from'Thy ways like lost sheep. We have followed too much the devices and desires of our own hearts. We have offended against Thy holy laws. We have left undone those things which we ought to have done; and we have done those things which we ought not to have done; and there is no health in us—

The house on the hill had been rented to a prosperous Welsh family who were parishioners of St. Mark's. John Morgan was a coppersmith in steady employment at the steel mills. Jane Morgan, delighted with so much finer a house than the frame tenement they had left, was a scrupulous housekeeper and a woman who kept her children scrubbed, starched, and diligent at their chores. She knew Thomas Stapely's jealousy of his house and saw to it that he could see nothing to find fault with.

Thomas could not pass through the gate and the yard to what was now his and Maria's home without a pang or a dull ache, but he was pleased to have so steady and reliable a man as John Morgan, who also sang in the St. Mark's choir, living in his house. John could appreciate the house.

Occasionally Thomas stopped for a word or two with John in the evening, and they talked of England and Wales, of conditions in the mills and South Ilium in general, or about the affairs of St. Mark's. One evening, hesitantly, John admitted to having a spot of trouble with the roof. He did not want to trouble Thomas he told him, but he didn't want him to think that he or any of his had been careless like if he should see the bit of stain on the bedroom ceiling. He had looked in the attic, and there seemed to be a drip about the chimney.

Thomas went for a lantern, and together they tried to see what they could in the darkness. Thomas' worst fears were confirmed. It was the flashing again. Thomas, busy with several big jobs, could have sent one of the men up to repair it. Had he been a younger man, that is what he would have done. As it was, the flashing flaunted a challenge he could not ignore. The next afternoon he dragged a light ladder from the woodshop and clambered heavily up to the roof, Maria, limping a little with rheumatism, following him and urging him to be careful. Thomas ignored her.

He had no sooner got into position to work on the roof and discover exactly what was wrong, when he discovered that he had forgotten to carry up his hammer. Annoyed, his climbed down again to get it. He pried up some of the loose and worn sheathing, then had to climb down again to go to the shop for new sheathing. Maria went inside, and Thomas pounded away happily on the roof. The sun was high, and it was warm. High as he was, he had a clear view of the silver-streaming river and the shipping. He saw loaded barges floating downstream and heavier craft streaming slowly up to the basin. A white excursion boat went past, and, resting a moment, he followed it with his eyes. Later he saw another and thought he recognized it as one he had sailed on many times. Getting stiffly to his feet, he moved cautiously down the shingles, slippery from weather-wear, to the edge of the sloping roof. He had to get a pot of tar and pitch boiling. He had found the trouble and, this time, he had got it mended.

Holding to the brace he had nailed to the roof, he backed to the edge and felt for the first rung of the ladder with his foot. He felt it, or thought that he did, and stepped down. He stepped into air and hurtled to the ground, a section of wooden drain pipe on which he had stepped giving way and falling with him.

Siding and a window flashed by Thomas. He struck the ground full force, with nothing to break his fall and no chance to twist himself into position. He landed jarringly on his feet, then fell backward, his back crashing into the ground. The world spun, and lights flashed and burst before his eyes, but he did not lose consciousness. Jane Morgan, who was home alone, and Maria reached him at the same moment, Maria crying out, Jane, powerfully made and younger, kneeling swiftly to bend over him.

Thomas, the breath knocked out of him, could not speak. He looked up into Jane Morgan's broad face with dazed, frightened eyes. He felt no pain, but he seemed unable to move. He tried to reach around to his back, but could not.

Maria, who had toppled rather than bent to the grass, was trying to hug his head in her arms and succeeding only in almost choking him. She was crying and moaning wildly. Finally Thomas fought free and found enough breath to gasp, "I fell."

"Just you lie still, Mr. Stapely. Never fear, we'll take care of you," said Jane soothingly. Her voice was deep and comforting.

The sky was high and a deep, deep blue above Thomas. His head fell back and he looked up into it.

"Oh, Thomas! Thomas! Dear Thomas!" groaned Maria.

Together the two women managed to drag the heavy old man into the cottage and lay him on his bed.

"Now just you be easy in your mind," Jane told Maria. "It's just the wind knocked out of him." She dabbed a bit of blood from Thomas's lower lip with the hem of her clean apron.

Thomas closed his eyes. His heart was thumping wildly. The sickening thud and the violent blow came back to him, and he felt faint. His hands were scratched and torn. One knee throbbed. It was all he could feel. He tried to slow his heart by pressing with his hands.

Maria was trying to give him a teaspoonful of whiskey. Her hand trembled so that it splashed over his face. Thomas did not flinch. The liquid cooled. He let it lie there, but Jane Morgan wiped it off, and took the teaspoon and pint bottle of whiskey from Maria.

"Perhaps you had better go for Dr. Samuels," she whispered. "I'll stay with him." She did not like the color of Thomas's face.

It was a long, sleepy, sunny afternoon. Even with the windows closed and all the blinds drawn, the house was hot. In the back yard grasshoppers leaped in the grass which was long and gone to seed at its straw tops. It was very quiet with only now and then a distant cry from some other street and the sound of an organ-grinder's playing blocks away. It was coolest in the basement, and there Will dozed on a leather-covered sofa in the dining room. It was an old sofa brought from Ilium. Once it had had a leather fringe along the bottom, but Carlo had chewed it off in his spare time.

It was Emily who woke him.

"Will! Will! Where are you, Will?"

The urgency in her voice brought him sharply to consciousness.

"It's Pa. He's hurt. They telephoned me."

The rest of the family came running.

"Best thing in the world for a man his age, scrambling around on a roof," complained old Dr. Samuels bitterly to James. "Helping us along after we pulled him through the last bout. But, as far as I can tell, there are no broken bones. Internal injuries?" He shrugged angrily. "He'd better stay in bed for a while—I think you'll agree. I don't like it. I don't like it at all." Dr. Samuels fumbled at the half-glasses he had put on over his spectacles, got them off, and fumbled them into a worn case he fished from his pocket.

James looked grave after examining his father. Samuels, he thought, was right. No broken bones. But he did not like the way his father's heart was acting. He had had a shock of a different kind this time.

"He's got to have rest," he told the others. "Can't tell right away. You can go up but not all at once—and don't stay long. I want him to get settled down."

Agnes, her face creased with worry and grief, rustled past him before he could finish. Mary patiently waited her turn.

When Will went up, he came down almost immediately.

"He wants you, too, Em." He took her hand, and they went up together. "If I'd been here, I could have fixed that damned flashing in ten minutes."

Thomas was very white. His tongue pushed out stiffly between bloodless lips twice before he seemed able to speak. He rolled his eyes toward them, and they moved to where he could see them clearly without turning his head. There was a stubble of white hair on the deeply cleft chin. It grew thinly on cheeks that seemed sunken as he lay there.

Will's eyes were filled with tears. Emily, her face set, looked almost curiously at their father.

"I—" said Thomas. "I—I—that time—the rake—"

"Yes, Pa," prompted Will softly.

Thomas did not look at him. His eyes watched Emily's pleadingly. "Didn't—didn't mean to hurt," he mumbled.

"The bruise healed," said Emily almost coldly.

Will flinched. "Em!" he whispered.

Emily did not look at him. She did not want Thomas to grieve, but she did not wish him to change. He was as he was, just as she was as she was. He should remain himself. She watched her father's face, frowning a little. Suddenly she could stand it no longer. She fell to her knees at the bedside, clutched his hand and pressed it hard against her cheek.

"It's all right, Pa," she crooned to him. "It didn't hurt. I deserved it, perhaps—or I have since. Go to sleep now, Pa. Close your eyes." She began to hum softly, then she breathed the words with caressing sweetness in light, true, pure sound:

> *Abide with me. Fast falls the eventide.*
> *The darkness deepens, Lord, with me abide—*

Thomas' eyes closed, and a tremulous, childlike smile touched his lips.

"Will," Emily whispered. "I think he's asleep." She started to draw back, but Will lingered.

The tears were streaming from his eyes again. As though he hardly heard, he touched his father's forehead, then he took Emily's hand and they tiptoed out.

"Em, I think you're the best woman in the world."

Mary and Maria were alone together in the tiny living room of the cottage.

"Agnes and James are to stay at Blanche's," Mary said. "Mrs. Morgan is putting up Will in his old room, and Emily can stay there too. They'll probably go back tomorrow. I shall stay here, and, of course, I'll stay on."

Maria did not answer.

"My place is by my husband's side now," said Mary.

"I'll take care of him," said Maria humbly. "I'll take care of him.

It's not like the last time. It was just a fall." Then, afraid: "Thomas is going to be all right, isn't he?" she begged.

"Of course, Maria," said Mary cheerfully. She patted Maria's hand. "Thomas has had falls before. If he would only be more careful! We'll all feel better after we've had some tea. You're always so good to all of us, Maria. Then we'll see that Thomas is comfortable for the night, and we'll all go to bed."

Maria wiped her eyes gratefully, and they went together into the kitchen.

Thomas died during the night.

Chapter 51

THE UNDERTAKER and his men, his father lying in the coffin in the tiny parlor of the cottage, the descent of friends and relatives, the grief and tears and condolences, the murmurs of sympathy of the women, the rumbles of the men, the cooking and eating, the ministers of the South Ilium churches, and the rector and curate of Calvary in Ilium who came to St. Mark's to conduct the funeral service for Thomas Stapely ... though he was an active part of it all, it was a whirl and a fever to Will. He felt detached. He saw and heard, but there seemed no meaning. He felt lost, unprotected, and alone.

Jim Garver, whose father had died two years before, came to see Will. He lived with his mother and their servants in the big house in Ilium, and was now in control of the mills. Though he was Will's age, he looked older. He had a quiet, competent, thoughtful face. He had always been quiet. He had given up law entirely to direct the enterprise he had inherited, and Will knew that he was doing a capable and successful job.

"My father would have been here," he told Will. "I thought I'd come in his place." He offered his hand.

Will took it. "Thanks, Jim," he said, but he did not wish to talk and his friend understood.

The Stapely women had to rush frantically to buy mourning clothes, black dresses, and veils. The cottage overflowed with gifts of food brought in by sympathetic neighbors, English, Welsh, and Irish alike. Maria, overwhelmed by her grief, seemed stunned. Mary was pale and quiet and held herself very erect.

Emily's face showed lines of fatigue though her piled blonde hair shone in contrast to her black gown. James looked annoyed. To him death was death. He wanted now to get back to his practice and said so. Agnes was bearing up bravely with a display of fortitude and Christian resignation which blended, as it should, with the desolation that sent her into fresh torrents of tears each time a new arrival tried to comfort her. Poor Agnes! Her worship of her father had been very real.

Will wandered off to the shop to talk with August. They did not mention Thomas. They understood each other. They knew they had known the man.

"Will," said Emily tensely, the night before the funeral. "Get me something to drink. I've got to have it."

Will got it for her.

The morning of the funeral he walked up the hill behind the house. There was nothing he could do. He was in people's way around the cottage, where the women were trying to dress. The place smelled of too many flowers, of talcum powder and Florida water and cologne. There was too much rustling of silk, satin, and starched linen.

The day was beautiful, with the sun shining golden on the cool fields. The dew-soaked grass gave off country fragrances as it dried. It was very silent. Will looked down on the house on the hill and on the cottage, over the fields and woods and the factory chimneys and the furnaces at the mills to the smooth-flowing river. It was all the same.

He had not now so much a sense of loss or of sorrow for his father, as a feeling of surprise. It was as though a basic principle had been removed, a fact of existence. He plodded through the high grass which swished against his legs and looked down and wondered. He had seen funerals before, of other old men and women the family and he had known, and he had been sorry. He did not feel now as he had done at those times. Perhaps, he thought, realization would come later, but he did not think so. Thomas' death would make little difference in their lives. A man's death mattered little to anyone, certainly not to the man himself. His father had believed that no man ever died, and perhaps he had been right.

Will knew suddenly and deeply in an instant of clarity, that his father would not die as long as he, Will, lived. A man is not dead when there are those who remember him.

Will sat in the crowded church as the funeral service went on. He sat with the family but the strange feeling of not belonging to them persisted. He did not feel close even to Emily, who looked calmer now and self-possessed. The Calvary rector's quiet voice went on in a eulogy he seemed to feel, for he had known Thomas Stapely well. There were little sounds in the hushed church which his father had loved so well, sounds of stifled sobs, of a man moving his feet, of the rustle of a woman's skirts, of a creaking in the wood. The smell of flowers was heavy. Will remembered with surprise that flowers had been important to his strong, defiant, God-driven father.

His father lay there now in his coffin before the altar. The rector was drawing to the end of his eulogy. The organ had begun to play softly. Will was fiercely glad that his father had triumphed. He had died where he had lived. He looked at his mother but he could not see her face through the heavy black veil. Maria, shriveled and small, sat hunched next to her. Others were leaving the church now. Soon they would have to go up to look for the last time on the face of Thomas Stapely. Will did not wish to go. Panic seized him, then he steadied. He would go forward with the others, but he would not look.

Mary moved slowly up the aisle, with Emily and Agnes, on either side of her to steady her. Will noticed the balled white handkerchiefs they held clenched in their tight fists. Everything else about them was black. James followed, looming protectively over Maria and Laura, who had come the day before, her thin face solemn with commiseration.

Will did not wish to look at his dead father. He wanted to see him as he had seen him in life. Then he forced himself to look and stared steadily into the dead man's face. Even in death, he saw, Thomas Stapely looked a man who had met life and faced it down. He seemed to Will still the symbol of his own inadequacy to cope with life.

The next day, pleading his job, Will escaped and went back to New York subdued and alone.

Agnes noted his absence later in the week and interrupted her grief long enough to ask a question.

"Are Ann and Will alone in the Brooklyn house again?"

"Will is not a complete fool," Emily answered shortly.

Will missed Jim Garver's second call. It was Emily his friend spoke with.

"I suppose you are soon going back to the city?" he asked.

Emily nodded.

"I wondered—I didn't know." Jim cleared his throat. "I thought perhaps Will would stay here and carry on your father's business. Of course, you haven't been able to plan yet."

"I don't think so," Emily told him.

"This is going to make a difference with all of you," said Jim flushing slightly. "I hope it won't cut all your connections with Ilium."

"Oh, no, there's the house, you know, and the tenements on Fourth Street. Ilium will always seem home."

"It's a good place," said Jim earnestly. "I was restless for a little while. I kept running up and down to New York, but I feel differently now. There's depth and quiet here. One can be one's self. That is—" he floundered and brushed back his hair, which lay neatly on his head.

"I know," said Emily. "I feel that way too sometimes, and I think Will does."

"He'll come back some day, I think," Jim looked away.

"He might."

"I—," said Jim. He stopped and looked guilty and confused. Then he spoke in a rush. "I know this isn't the time, but I used to rather hope that we might be married. If you, that is—"

"Why, Jim!"

"Of course, I never said anything. Your music and being in New York. Ilium isn't New York, and I know I'm not exactly—but do you think we could, that is—you might." Jim's face was strained, but his eyes were bright. He looked shyly but hopefully at Emily.

"Oh, Jim!"

"I'm sure you'd like it, Emily," Jim went on, eagerly. "I know mother would be pleased. There's the big house, but I could get another if you liked. We can travel when you like. I'll try to be what you'd like me to be."

Emily took his hand. She closed her eyes and was biting into her lower lip.

"Don't Jim," she said. "I've always liked you. I think you know that. But I can't marry you—or anybody. Don't say any more."

"I won't, if you say so, but I've thought about it a long time. You might change your mind some day. I'll be here. Perhaps you'll let me see you in New York soon. I want to very much, though I'll always do as you say."

"Oh, why," cried Emily desperately, "does everyone want to marry me? The world is full of pretty girls, women younger than I, sensible, respectable women!"

"But they aren't you, Emily," said Jim, smiling.

Chapter 52

JAMES BIT HARDER at the sides of his right thumbnail for a time after his father's death and looked morose. Sentiment, he had decided long before, was for fools. He had no time for it. Death, as any doctor knew, was as commonplace as life. He shrugged impatiently when kindly patients offered condolences, yet he was unusually silent. Privately he resolved that he would give up drinking. It was only a symptom anyway of dissatisfaction with life or inability to deal with it. Well, he could deal with it all right. If anyone thought he had stopped drinking because his father's death had frightened him or as some sort of superstitious gesture to his father's memory, well, the bigger fools they. Laura, watching covertly, was careful to disguise by a sufficient brusqueness, the added tenderness aroused in her.

A little of the grimness which had begun to show about Emily's full, curving lips disappeared. With her father dead, there was a lessening of constraint. She had to maintain only a decent show of pretense about her life before her mother. The grimness about her mouth did not wholly fade. Life had begun to etch it there, though lightly as yet, and the lines of experience seemed only to mature and enhance her beauty. Andrew noticed, as he noticed everything.

The shock drew them all closer together. They were more often at the old Brooklyn house. Grown men and women, they sought comfort in each other's presence, though they would not acknowledge it. Thomas had been so formidable a reality that they now felt shaken and unsure. They had to look after their mother now. They explained this to themselves as they gave way to the compulsion. Mary, who seemed to grow taller and thinner with the stateliness of widowhood, was not unpleasantly conscious of an added power and importance. She received sympathetic callers with restraint and dignity.

It was Agnes who was most vocal and visible in her grief. She refused the slightest relief of color to the mourning she intended to wear for a full year. She wore it on every trip to South Ilium where she went often now to check on their father's "estate" and to talk sharply to tenants who might be tempted to be late with their rent or allow their children to mar what was now partly her property. She made even more trips to South Brooklyn to check on Will who, as joint executor with Mary, might be careless in his division of the rents.

"You can have my share too, if you like!" Will offered contemptuously. "Isn't it enough the old man died?"

"A nice way to speak of our father, indeed! It's easy to see why he thought more of—of some of us. And why he should have appointed you executor along with Ma, I'll never understand. I—"

"That will do, Agnes," said her mother sharply. She glanced meaningly toward Ann. "And I'm sure Ann isn't interested in all this."

Ann, her bright eyes intent, refused the hint and remained in the room. She merely nodded wisely and cheerfully and went on with her sewing.

Her sewing irritated Will. Ann, who was haphazard about all of her housework, always managed to have a bit of sewing in her hands when the rest of them were doing nothing. The action was a rebuke. It said, self-righteously, that she had always to be busy. Will suspected it was the same piece of sewing every time, but he was not sure.

"You can fight it out with Ma," he said shortly to Agnes and left.

Agnes compressed her lips. She had more in mind than she had spoken yet, she thought triumphantly. She was still her father's daughter. She felt now that she was his defender among strangers who had never truly understood or appreciated him. She was her father's earthly representative, and she was going to enforce his will. They'd find out!

Will had known with his mind that some day his father would die. He had never actually believed it. It seemed to him now that he had never done anything except in accordance with his father's wishes or, timidly, in opposition to them.

Always his father had been there looming protectively or threateningly in the background. Power and authority resided in his father. Will's very pleasure-seeking had been premised on the actuality of his father as haven or menace behind him.

His father was no more. He could not talk with him or write to him. Thomas Stapely no longer walked and breathed or played his cello or preached at St. Mark's or roared orders at his workmen. Will's imagination could hardly encompass the fact. Vertical lines of helpless concentration appeared on his forehead. They sat oddly on his clear, still absurdly youthful face.

He had disappointed his father. He was not what his father had hoped. He had not settled down. He had set himself to no purpose. He had worked hard at this job and that, but he had enjoyed the work. Thomas would have felt that it was thus no credit to him. It was not his peccadilloes Will regretted, the horse racing, the theatres, his flirtations. Those were unimportant. There had been a curious tolerance about his father who could fly into a rage over some petty mistake but accept, even as he denounced, forthright masculine wickedness.

He was his father now. Will determined vaguely, to work harder, to accomplish he did not quite know what. From foreman carpenter he might some day advance to construction superintendent with full responsibility for the erection of an entire structure. Yet that was not quite what he meant.

Ann looked amused and superior.

"I don't know why you take it so hard," she said. "Of course, it's hard when someone dies. I should know, for no one will ever know what I went through all alone when my mother died."

Will did not answer her.

"I think it was brutal the way he made you go to work so early. They've all used you for a good thing all your life. It's time you took thought for your own life, instead of doing everything all the others want.

"You don't know anything about it," said Will, hating her.

Ann smiled and sniffed. "Perhaps not," she said with the expression of one who could say much more if she chose.

Mary's coming into the room stopped their talk. She looked quickly at them both, a slight frown passing across her forehead.

"Agnes hasn't come yet?" she asked. It was a Sunday evening and Agnes was expected. "Oh, dear, I'm so tired." A Mr. and Mrs. McCallum, who had lived in Ilium, had come to pay their respects to the widow that afternoon. Then James had been in and, surreptitiously, he and his mother had played two games of bezique though it was Sunday. "Isn't it time for tea yet?" she asked Ann.

"But we've just had—" began Ann. She thought better of it. "I'll start things right away."

Mary watched her go toward the kitchen. "Ann's such a comfort," she said. "Always so bright and willing."

" 'I'm not going to cater to any man,' " mocked Will in Ann's peremptory tones. " 'A man would have to stand on his head before I looked at him. My mother certainly never spoiled my father the way some people do some people.' " He sniffed. "I suppose Agnes will be complaining that the Forests are behind in their rent again. He wrote promising to pay as soon as he can. He's out of work."

"None of us realized, I'm afraid, how much your father took care of and how many worries he had," said Mary mechanically.

It had frightened Mary that the death of Thomas did not seem to touch her heart. It left her lonely and afraid. She felt dismayed, almost annoyed, but her emotions were not deeply stirred. She had to reach too far back into the past to remember the young man, strong bodied, with excited and flashing eyes, who had talked about America in the Forest of Dean so very long ago—the shy, uncertain lover and her own delicious tremors. Somewhere in the intervening years she had lost Thomas to God and the hard work he worshipped —or he had lost her. Defensively she remembered that she had been very busy with the children and their home. Thomas had not properly appreciated that there were other things in life besides his building and St. Mark's.

She would need a new and better black bonnet, this one, perhaps, with softer ruffling and a touch of lace. She could hardly be expected to wear the same severe crape all the time. Emily would go with her to pick it out. Mary knew the added duty to her which widowhood placed upon her children. It was her due, and she knew how to exact it without spoken demand or comment.

She, Ann, and Will were just finishing their Sunday tea of cold sliced mutton with mint sauce and some preserved fruit when Agnes arrived. Will, who disliked cold meat of any kind, wished Ann had made more of her deep-dish apple tart. Ann was a good cook of the same substantial English fare to which they were all accustomed.

Agnes, rustling in her Sunday silk, lifted her veil to kiss her mother.

"Sit down, Agnes," Mary urged, "and have some good hot tea. Ann brews it perfectly." She resisted the impulse to rub her cheek. Agnes' lips were always so wet.

"If it's no trouble," said Agnes politely.

"Of course, it's no trouble," said Ann cordially. She bustled about, filling the hot water pitcher from the kettle simmering in the kitchen.

"You are bearing up so well!" Agnes exclaimed to her mother. Her tone was of surprise and admiration, but Mary caught the underlying reproach.

"Your father would have expected it," she said.

Agnes had kept her hat on but pushed her veil up out of the way. Her eyes filled with tears.

"There, there!" said Mary uncertainly.

Agnes managed to sip her tea. "It's just right, dear," she said gratefully to Ann.

Will decided he would wander up to see what James and Laura

were doing. He lingered, too comfortable to start. Bones and Laura were always so damned busy. James had an electric coupé now which rode silently along on its hard rubber tires. Bearded James, manning its tiller, looked like a piratical canary in a glass cage. Several times he had taken their mother along on his calls. Mary enjoyed it. She enjoyed any vehicle which kept her in motion.

"Have another cup," Ann was urging Agnes. She lifted the pot invitingly, and filled Mary's cup without asking.

Agnes allowed herself to be persuaded, and Ann poured the remainder into her own cup.

Will, who had stretched himself out on the sofa outside the cone of light from the lamp, watched listlessly. How women could drink so much tea was always a mystery. And they drank it so hot it was a wonder the steam did not come out their ears and nostrils.

He watched Ann sharply to see whether it did or not. Ann had boldly flaring nostrils which would show it best. The idea of going to James's became more remote. The women were chatting intently. Sleepily, Will kept his eyes on Ann's face. It was animated whether she was listening or talking. Her pretty hair shone in the light.

Will almost dozed. It was a careful but perceptible change in Agnes' voice which roused him.

"Oh," she said lightly, "I hear that Emily has lost another pupil." She had taken off her hat. Her hair was flattened in places, ornately curled in others.

"Has she?" asked Ann. There was eagerness in her tone, and her eyes glistened.

The composure of Mary's face did not change. She sat very erect, her hair precisely parted in the middle with the three curls on each side of her oval head and a cameo brooch at the high collar of her black silk.

"I happened to meet Mrs. King at Wanamaker's. It was a friend of her niece's daughter who has gone to another music teacher. They are very well-to-do. Mrs. King told me all about it." Agnes emphasized the 'all' slightly. She sounded a little breathless.

Ann, Will could see, was watching Agnes intently and expectantly.

"Emily is an excellent teacher and works very hard," said Mary proudly. "I have listened to her working with her pupils, and parents have often told me they know how fortunate they are to get Emily."

"Oh, I meant nothing against Emily's ability as a teacher," said Agnes quickly.

"What did you mean then?" prompted Ann.

"I only know," protested Agnes hurriedly, "what Mrs. King told me."

Will broke in sharply. "Annoyed her little darling hasn't got into Grand Opera yet? Probably belongs in a side show instead."

The women ignored him.

"Yes, Agnes?" asked Mary coldly.

"Oh—nothing," said Agnes. She sounded frightened.

Ann could control herself no longer. "Is it because—because of Emily's life?" she demanded happily.

Will snorted. "Well, I'll be damned!"

Ann jerked back and glared at Will. "I have no intention," she cried, "of sitting here to be sworn at!"

"That will do, both of you!" ordered Mary. "Agnes, I wish to know what you have been hinting at."

"While Pa was alive," cried Agnes harshly, "I tried to keep still! I tried to blind myself to certain things, even when I felt it was my Christian duty to act!"

"I should think so!" cried Ann, her eyes blazing.

"Go on Agnes," said Mary looking steadily at her daughter. Her thin hand moved to her heart.

"Now that Pa is no longer here, *someone* must see that certain things are made to stop. It's a wonder Emily has not lost all her pupils long before this! It is a wonder any mother would so much as let her daughter—! The brazen effrontery of Emily and that— that Mr. Gray all these years!" Agnes' voice was shrill. Her heavy face was suffused and contorted.

"I knew," said Ann triumphantly, "that some day—"

No one paid any attention to her. Will, staggered and aghast, looked at his militant eldest sister.

"Pa was so good," screamed Agnes, "and they are so deceitful, that he never saw! But I saw. I tried to warn him. *I've* known all along!"

"Did it ever occur to you, Agnes?" said Mary, her voice trembling in spite of herself, "that your father was no fool. Perhaps he knew and understood things that, evidently, are far above your comprehension."

"Thank God," retorted Agnes dramatically, "my father never knew what *one* of his daughters is like! Why, when my dear little Rhoda was born and I lay helpless in bed, Emily even tried to win Allan away from me. He scorned her, but she is shameless—perfectly shameless!"

Will raged at his own helplessness. He could not think quickly enough. Agnes' maniacal outburst could not be stopped with reason. Anything he said might only incriminate Emily.

"Let's have an end to this!" he said loudly, trying to get masculine conviction and authority into his voice. After all, he was now master of this house.

"Be still, Willy," said his mother. She shifted ground easily and calmly. "I have spent a good deal of time at Emily's," she told Agnes, "and I have never seen the slightest thing amiss."

Ann looked as though she would sniff contemptuous disbelief but did not dare. Her face urged Agnes on.

Agnes could not stop. She had waited too long to count her words now.

"And that—that Mr. Gray. He has been received in this house and treated as a guest. He has even been in my house and Allan's when I was helpless to object. Him with his sick wife—at least she is supposed to be sick. I can bear it no longer! I will bear it no longer!"

"Perhaps, Agnes," said Mary patiently, "when you are a little older, you will be able to understand some things better."

Older, thought Will. She's damned near fifty now and she looks a hundred. He could not remember Agnes' exact age.

His sister's face went even more tragic.

"And singing all this time in the Fifth Avenue Church as though she had a pure woman's right to raise her voice in God's house. It's—it's blasphemy." She paused as though the word had frightened her. "I sang in a church choir long before Emily. It was *my* voice should have been trained!"

"So that's it!" exploded Will. "Nice Christian charity, I must say!"

"But she won't any longer!" cried Agnes, bursting into noisy sobs. "I'll put a stop to that. I'll go to the ministers. I'll go to the vestry. I'd go to Mr. Rollins himself, if he were still alive!"

She dropped her head into her arms thrown across the table and sobbed bitterly, snuffling and choking.

Ann stared fascinated. Will looked at her with hatred and contempt in his eyes which were dark with misery. That an outsider should have witnessed and palpably enjoyed this bucket-of-blood scene, which never should have been played, made it filthy as well as incredible.

Agnes' fat shoulders were heaving. The sweat stains showed on her tight-bodiced dress below the armpits. The noise of her sobbing was ugly in the narrow dining room, where the only other sound was the hissing of the gas mantle in the lamp.

A little unsteadily Mary got to her feet. Tall and straight, she moved stiffly around the table and awkwardly patted her daughter's head.

"There, there," she said quietly. "That's enough. Come, we'll go upstairs. Just you and I," she added for Ann's benefit.

Agnes did not lift her head, though she tried to check her sobs. Ann was watching her curiously, chagrin showing in her face.

Will could not be as calm as his mother.

"Sure, Agnes. Better go upstairs and look at the Bloomingdale ads. Maybe they have hair shirts especially for good Christian women."

Mary shook her head at him.

"Come, Agnes," she coaxed, patting the woman's shoulder. "Come now."

Agnes lumbered upright.

"Oh, Ma!" she choked brokenly, reaching for Mary.

"It's all right. It's all right," Mary comforted. "If it will make you feel any better, I'll go myself and spend a few days with Emily."

She had planned to go anyway.

Chapter 53

THE NEXT MORNING was dark with rain threatening. Will awoke to find the house damp and silent. It was a moment or two before he remembered the unpleasantness of the night before and wondered what would happen now. It was so dark that he had to light the gas in the bathroom, and the hot water was barely warm. He made his way quietly downstairs to the kitchen.

Dirty dishes filled the sink, and the kitchen table was still littered with Ann's preparations for yesterday's supper, but a place had been cleared for him at one corner. Two boiled eggs in hot water had been pushed to the back of the stove. There was fresh tea in the pot ready for him to pour hot water over, and he found toast warming in the oven.

So Ann had been up but, evidently, had gone back to bed. At least she was keeping out of sight. Punishing him, probably, for his part the night before. He looked to see and found that his dinner pail had been put ready. He fished the eggs out of the hot water with a tablespoon, put one in his egg cup and began to tap the shell. Damn Agnes anyway! He wished he could see Emily to warn her, but did not know what he could say.

Will finished his breakfast. He put on his coat and took up his dinner pail. Undecided, he listened for a moment at the foot of the stairs. There was still no sound. He shrugged and went out to wait for a Third Avenue trolley at the corner.

One came within a few minutes, crowded with workmen and laborers at that hour, and Will climbed aboard. The conductor was one he knew.

"Mornin', Will," he said. He lowered his voice. "Got anythin' good for today?"

"What? Oh, no," said Will shortly. "I've not been betting lately."

The conductor grinned and lurched along collecting his fares. Lots of 'em were bad-tempered in the morning, especially Mondays. Some of the men in the car were asleep. A couple of grimy Italians were spluttering away to each other at the end of the car, and two Irishmen were having the usual stupid political argument. They quieted down, and the car swayed and bumped toward 39th Street where Will was going to change to the ferry.

He felt depressed and dispirited. Life was not what it had been. The idea that he had ever crossed the ocean and dashed about London in evening dress without a care in his head seemed impossible. The dirtiness and dreariness about the ferry slip, the toughs hanging about the all-night saloons, the rough-looking customers in the crowd, the sour smell of horse dung and the garbage washing around in the ugly green water depressed Will further.

There was fog on the water, though it was not heavy. Dirty tramp steamers and battered tugs were sloshing through the bay water. The harbor was always busy. Fog horns sounded down in the Narrows, and one blasted off from a freighter inching out of a pier in Erie basin. Will could not make out the flag dangling limply at the stern, but he could see that it was neither the American ensign nor the Union Jack.

His spirits lifted a little as they neared Manhattan. He and his men were putting the finishing touches on a big block of flats, an apartment house, as these dwellings were beginning to be called. It was a big job. The structural work was all steel, stone, and brick, but there was plenty of wood in it. They laid acres of birch flooring, fitted miles of ash trim, hung hundreds of doors, and fitted carloads of windows. This was building on a scale his father had never dreamed of, and Will had gone at it with zest. He had more men under him than ever before, and good men.

Driving, hard-swearing Jack Holley had left him almost completely on his own. Holley had enough to do fighting the unions, screaming for material deliveries, placating avaricious building inspectors, and keeping the plasterers sober enough to get the walls finished. He had even taken Will off his own job for a time to supervise the painters and keep an eye on Tony, the huge and blustering Sicilian who produced the labor gangs and kept them in some kind of order.

Will exulted in the atmosphere of big construction, with steam hoists and machinery hissing and clanging away, architects with blueprints and engineers with transits running about. He felt himself a muscled, hard-driving construction man and liked the feeling. His father, he felt, would have understood and been proud of him.

He had responded to the big job, going at it with zest, savoring his authority, trying to use it sanely. It had cut him off a little from the men, thrown him in with swarthy, equable Jake White who was his own age and ambitious to become a contractor in his own right, Happy Moran with his lined, bitter face, who knew more about tile work than any man Will had ever seen, and Joe McCall, the fat and sly boss painter who carried a pack of well-thumbed pornographic pictures in one hip pocket and a bag of cigar shavings in the other.

Days went fast on the job with the Smith Construction Company. The company was out to make money and make it fast, but it built to last. Like every other big builder, it would shave on materials where it could, save time by greasing fat political palms, hire the cheapest labor and toughs enough to keep it in line, and charge the highest prices; but with men like Jack Holley on the job, it did good work.

If things could be a little more pleasant at home, life might not be half bad again.

He got home that night to find the house apparently empty. Puzzled, he let himself in at the basement door and looked about. He had hardly hung up his hat and coat and washed in the kitchen when Ann, whom he had not heard come in, was facing him and exclaiming in annoyance as she pulled the hatpins out of her hair.

"Oh, dear! I tried to get here to have your dinner ready when you got home, but the El was delayed down near the bridge. I got everything ready, though, before I left. I won't take ten minutes. Hand me my apron, will you—no, behind the door. Thank you."

Will looked at her in amazement. The girl was unpredictable! Ann could be as merry and friendly as a child; the next moment, still like a child, sullen and spiteful or spitting, flailing, and scratching. She acted now as though nothing untoward had happened the night before and she had not avoided him that morning.

"You're the limit," he admitted, smiling.

"Eh?" asked Ann, though it was obvious she had heard.

She smiled in response as she moved briskly about the littered kitchen, the apron drawn tightly about her street dress. She opened the oven door, peered inside, nodded with satisfaction, and slammed the door shut again. She snatched the tea caddy from the shelf and tipped a handful of tea into the pot. She hurried to the cupboard for a measure of flour, spilling a little as she carried it to the stove for mixing the gravy.

"I took your mother to Emily's this afternoon," she explained, as she moved back and forth into the dining room where she was setting the table. "My! Emily's flat is lovely! Now don't go away. Everything will be on the table in a few minutes."

"But I thought you didn't like Emily!"

Ann faced him, eyes wide with surprise and innocence.

"Why, whatever gave you that idea? Your mother said to tell you your clean shirts are in the middle drawer of your dresser and that your socks are all mended and in the little drawer at the top. I don't know why she hurried so with them this morning. I could have darned them just as well."

"Oh, thanks!"

Wrapping a teacloth about her hand, Ann drew the roast from the oven. It smelled delicious. Expertly, she transferred it to the meat dish warming on the shelf of the stove. She poured hot water from the steaming kettle into the gravy she had been stirring. Will watched with unwilling admiration. Ann could do things when she wished.

Somehow he felt awkard and embarrassed as they ate, though he and Ann had eaten together alone before this. Usually, though, his mother had just been at James's or Agnes' for the evening and was to return later. In contrast, Ann was relaxed and gracious. She seemed to be enjoying herself as she poured their tea and served their food. Will felt that he should be doing the serving, but he did not know how to offer. Ann had taken charge. It occurred to him that Ann showed to better advantage on her own. Perhaps she felt hampered and overshadowed when his mother was there. That might explain some of her resentment and quickness to take offense. He found pleasure in watching Ann's manifest happiness.

"Dinner is very good," he said self-consciously.

"Thank you, sir," said Ann prettily. She hesitated a moment, eating politely and delicately. "Are you planning to go out tonight?"

"Why," said Will. "I—"

"I only asked," said Ann quickly, "because I want you to do just as you want to do while your mother is away. I think you deserve a little freedom. And I just wanted to know whether I should put the chain on the upstairs door."

"Well, I might go up to old Bones's for a little while. Time I whipped him at a game of checkers."

"You usually do, don't you?" said Ann eagerly.

"Not always," Will confessed.

"You do when you want to, when you really put your mind to it," Ann insisted. She looked very pretty at that instant.

Evidently, thought Will, he had been mistaken about Ann all along. At least she was not always vindictive.

"I needn't hurry up there. I'll help you with the dishes," he offered.

"That's not necessary at all. You go along and enjoy yourself."

"I'll help first," said Will, pleased with the idea of the sacrifice. "Where's an apron?"

"An apron?" Ann laughed. "I don't like to see a man working in the kitchen." But even as she protested, she helped him into a checked gingham apron of his mother's and tied it deftly behind his waist. They made a game of it, a game Will found exciting. His forearms tingled.

He pirouetted mincingly. He looked down anxiously at the hem of his apron.

"Does it hang all right?"

Ann laughed gaily as she splashed water out of the tap into the dishpan and added steaming hot water from the stove.

Before they were half through the dishes—and there were some from that noon as well as their dinner dishes—with Ann washing and Will drying and polishing fastidiously, he regretted having said he was going up to see James. He was having a good time where he was.

For the first time Ann seemed to be paying serious attention to him, and he found her attention gratifying. Almost consciously, he began to show off, imitating the accents of the cockney steward on the ship back the last time, and the brogue of the comical hotel doorman in Belfast.

Ann seemed to be delighted. She asked questions about the part of England she had left as a child when her parents migrated to Canada. Somehow Will found himself talking seriously about his work. He boasted a little.

"That's that!" said Ann emphatically. "Actually I hate doing dishes." She swirled her dishcloth about the inside of the pan, poured its contents down the drain, rinsed it out, hung it on its hook in the red brickwork of the chimney near the black stovepipe to dry. It banged sharply against the wall. "Now you hurry off to James's. I hope you beat him."

"I don't have to go," Will protested. "They're not expecting me."

"You have a good time while your mother's away," said Ann, again with the implication that his mother held him at her beck and call. "She'll be back in a week or ten days. Never mind me. I don't mind being alone. I'm used to it." She spoke merrily, but the edge of complaint was clear in her voice.

Will hesitated.

"Why not come with me?"

"To Laura's without an invitation!" Sarcasm and bitterness flashed into Ann's face and eyes. "I know better, thank you."

"About last night," ventured Will uncomfortably. "I think Agnes was just upset or overtired or something."

"Oh, that," said Ann lightly. "I didn't pay any attention to that."

The star-filled sky was bright and clear as Will walked swiftly up the street and across Fourth Avenue where a few carriages passed, horses trotted easily, and one gasoline motorcar, its acetylene headlights flickering, chugged slowly along. An electric glided silently by, and for a moment Will thought it was James's.

Will felt a warmth and surprised happiness as he walked past the rows of houses where lights shone comfortably from behind drawn curtains. He imagined the pleasant family scenes within. Somehow his own house had seemed like that tonight. For a little while it had seemed like his house, his and Ann's.

He was soon at James's where Laura, who had heard the door open, greeted him conspiratorially in the hall. He could hear the whining voice of a patient and James's rumbled monosyllabic replies in the office at the front, though the door was closed.

"He's in a wonderful rage!" hissed Laura, "and having a magnificent time. How are you and Ann going to get along with your mother away?"

"Fine! Ann and I always get along."

"You be careful, Will," admonished Laura, looking at him hard.

"What do you mean?" protested Will, coloring.

"You know very well what I mean, young man! Don't try any of your innocence on me!"

Luckily, for Will, they heard the office door open, and then the front door close behind the patient. James strode down the hall looking stormy, but he was soon in high good humor.

They had just set up the checkerboard and made their opening moves when a New Woman appeared with her notebook in hand.

Laura had managed to drive her away several times during the day, but she was as determined as any other suffragette.

"Our Society," the New Woman explained earnestly, "is investigating the ethics of New York physicians. Especially,"—she blushed—"concerning childbirth."

James looked up at her. "Generally speaking," he said, staring hard at the intruder, "I'm against drowning female infants at birth."

"You—you what, doctor?" Yellow pencil poised, the New Woman looked as though James had pronounced words she could not spell.

"When he makes exceptions," offered Will helpfully, "he keeps poking them under with a long pole."

The New Woman looked at them in horror.

"Some of them thrash around quite a bit," said James reminiscently. He wiggled his hands in illustration, and the New Woman fled. "Your move," he said impatiently to Will. "Your move!"

They broke even after a series of hard-fought games, and Will hurried home through the dark streets.

He was relieved when he saw lights still on in the parlor and knew Ann was still up. He had been afraid as they played the last games James had insisted on that she would not be.

"You shouldn't have waited," he said quickly. "I'm sorry I stayed so long."

"I didn't mind," smiled Ann. "I've been reading." She indicated the book next to her on the walnut settee. "It isn't really late anyway."

"They were both asking for you," Will lied.

Ann listened quietly, her gray eyes looking steadily into Will's blue ones.

"I had to stay up," she said, when he had finished. "Emily sent you her love. I never told you."

"Oh!" laughed Will. "You'd have remembered in the morning."

"I didn't forget. It just seemed a little silly to say. I don't mean silly exactly—that she sent you her 'love,' I mean."

The word hung awkwardly in the air. It was seldom spoken in a Stapely household.

Ann had flushed slightly, and her eyes were bright.

Vexedly, Will felt himself blushing. Would he never be safe from his ridiculous blushing?

"I'm not a bit sleepy," said Ann suddenly. "Are you?"

"No, I'm not," said Will.

His heart began to beat faster.

Chapter 54

Andrew Gray went less often to the Press Club, to his *Insurance Tribune,* and even to his office; more often to Oriental Importers. He was, he thought wryly, like some wicked and tired old monk of the Middle Ages who needed respite before undertaking new rascalities. He claimed sanctuary—whether from his own misplaced cleverness, or from the mischief inherent in life itself, he was unsure.

The little worlds which made up his universe were not running smoothly in their courses. There was no music in their spheres. An explosiveness which would involve Apex as well as the other great companies threatened in life insurance. It could mean disaster and destruction of a whole phase of his life.

His life in Murray Hill had further darkened. For so many years had the frailty of his wife's body and the elusiveness of her spirit been accepted part of his days and nights, it seemed impossible that ugly and final annihilation might suddenly descend. Now the grave warnings of the doctors had awakened long-forgotten memories and the ghosts of old emotions, but the feeling of surprise persisted.

Thomas Stapely's death had helped by relaxing one of the cutting tensions in her life, but it had wrought no miracle for him and Emily. Her pain, like her joy, was too deeply seated. It was almost part of her identity. Sometimes knowledge of it almost broke Gray's heart, though he knew his heart was old and tough enough to endure what might smash a finer instrument.

The oriental shop, almost a museum in miniature, soothed. It was cool, shadowed, and restrained. The old arts of China calmed him. They lengthened his perspective, healed his senses, dispelled his perturbations. He was surrounded by work done for love of the doing. It had been done in age-old traditions by an ancient people so highly civilized that complicated forms and symbols had taken on a timeless and placeless simplicity.

He touched jade intricately carved or polished into perfect surfaces, porcelains perfect in line and color. He fingered the circular body of a small bottle hollowed out of delicately tinted amethyst quartz. The pale blue and faded apricot-gold of an old rug, fine and thin, was at his feet.

Gray lingered gratefully. There were many lovely things in the world, but he returned always to these. They were small and restrained enough, simple enough, for the imagination to encompass, for their subtlety and sophistication to be understood, for the eye to see, and the hand to feel. Jade seemed to him perfect because for centuries a wise people had understood its perfection.

Gray could hardly say which he detested and feared most, the cheap magazines, especially *McClure's* and *Everybody's,* with their strident exposures of everybody and everything, or the ridiculous and equally dangerous human situation which had led directly to the bitter fight, flaring more and more violently, for control of Equitable. Actually it was not James Hazen Hyde and the Equitable Life Assurance Society. It was not Teddy Roosevelt or Sam McClure and his stable of wild-eyed zealots. It was not even Hearst and Pulitzer. It was all of them and a kind of revolutionary, evangelical fervor which seemed to be sweeping over the entire populace.

The shocking wickedness of the Beef Trust, the patent medicine industry, all the railroads, all the governments of all the large cities, all business, and all politics were being screamed aloud by pap-mouthed nurslings so innocent they were aghast at every bit of fresh evidence about what the informed had known all their lives. The public slobbered, slavered, and screamed for more.

There were not enough Standard Oil companies, there was not enough shame in all the cities, there were not enough trusts and railroads to satisfy the voracious appetite for scandal which had been aroused. But there were the giant life insurance companies.

Part of it, of course, was the natural hatred of those who had failed for those who had succeeded; part of it was man's malicious love, unchanging through the centuries, for hurling idols from their pedestals; part of it was feverish human delight in extravagant destruction. The zeal of shortsighted reform fanatics motivated the frustrated; and hypocritical amazement overcame those waiting wolfishly for their chance to dive in with fangs bared to seize the prizes being torn from others.

The whole intricate but orderly world of business and finance as he knew it was under popular attack. He could not think it would be destroyed. Its denizens were the hard and wily survivors of ruthless wars and machinations far beyond the knowledge or imagination of fledgling journalists. The structure business had erected was too basic in American life to be destroyed, though it might be shaken and suffer incidental damage.

Silliest was the underlying assumption—if there were any real point except exploitation for the sake of gain—that some kind of idealistic goodness could be substituted in business and politics for practical effectiveness. The yellow press was so horrified and indignant, at the same time that it was raking in rich present and future rewards, that it turned Gray's stomach.

None of this made the situation less threatening for the life insurance companies. For hunters like these they were fair game. The giants of insurance had hands no cleaner and hearts no purer than the railroad, packing, and oil interests: the millions of policyholders' funds in their treasuries meant fast, quick, and easy profits for those who had access to the money; they meant control of banks and brokerages, interlocking directorates, outright ownership of spectacular ventures.

Already there had been prying and probing. There had been vague accusations in the *World*. All of the newspapers were watching young Hyde, not only because that incredible young man's indiscretions provided colorful copy; but also because he might lead them into the tricky mazes of another business-finance-politics garden which reform journalists had already announced was not a garden at all but a sinkhole of chicanery, fraud, injustice, corruption, and infamy.

Young Hyde, who had inherited control of Equitable when he was only twenty-three, was pictured to the public as using his wealth and power with all the circumspection of a greedy child let loose in a candy shop. As majority stockholder of a company with deposits of more than a billion dollars, and as director of scores of railroads and corporations, Hyde was flattered, courted, and urged on to indulge his wildest fancies.

"You wouldn't, I suppose, consider that it comes within your province to shoot some of these people?" Ventnor asked Andrew Gray. "They're going to bring down the house on us." Ventnor's gruff tone and scowl were darker than his words.

Gray shook his head. "Not a good idea. Actually, I can't help feeling a certain synpathy for young Hyde."

"Sympathy? Good God!"

"What's the latest word? Who's going to control Equitable?"

"I can't keep up. It looks like Harriman, but I can't think Morgan will let go that easily. It might even be Ryan. I've not seen the evening papers yet."

An ex-financier of Boston was explaining life insurance in hate-filled prose which made previous exposés seem dull. *Frenzied Finance* was running in *Everybody's*. Men implicated raged helplessly or turned sick as the monthly issues were swept off the newsstands. The reading public had forsaken Ned Buntline's blood-and-thunder novels for this stronger stuff. The yellow press showed foam on its lips.

The *World* was screaming now for investigation and exposure not only of Equitable, but also of all the other big New York companies. The state legislature at Albany was being forced, however reluctantly and in the face of pressure against it by all the insurance interests, to take official cognizance.

Hurried meetings of officers and directors of all the companies involved were called. In some quarters fear and alarm verged on panic. Others tried to plan soberly. A few intrenched figures, aware of their unassailable positions in insurance, finance, the state, and the church, spoke confidence and defiance.

There had been governmental investigation of life insurance before. Companies and their important men had survived. It was a pother and a nuisance, but there were not likely to be any serious consequences. Damn the Equitable people anyway!

The legislature appointed the New York State Legislative Investigation Committee. William W. Armstrong of Rochester was made its chairman.

"Well, there's nothing else for it," said Ventnor at an extraordinary session of Apex's officers. "Turn over all the records they want. Give them everything. Bury them in papers. We must make it a point to cooperate and"—he glanced at Andrew Gray—"to let everybody in the world know that Apex is cooperating fully with the insurance investigation."

He looked tired. Others looked harassed. One or two of the men were white. They knew too much. Andrew Gray, victimized once more by the feeling of detachment which so often came over him, isolating him but sharpening his vision, looked objectively at the group. He could reach no judgment.

When selection of Charles Evans Hughes as chief counsel for the Armstrong Committee was anounced, Ventnor was curious. He called Andrew Gray in.

"Know him?"

"No, and none of the Albany boys do."

"Try to find out who he is, will you."

"The boys at the *World* know him. In fact, they put him up for the job. He was counsel for that city gas investigation a year or two ago. Remember? I'll find out what else I can."

Chapter 55

MARY SAT QUIETLY and happily in the spacious living room of Emily's flat. She sat almost in state, pleasantly conscious of the elegance of her surroundings and of being dressed as she would wish. Ellen had helped her with her hair, a luxury she enjoyed. Emily had taken her bath and was still getting ready for Andrew Gray, who would soon be in for tea. He was to stay for dinner, and Will was coming too.

Mary felt at peace and a part of her beautiful setting. Andrew's courtly deference and Emily's unobtrusive consideration for her comfort soothed and supported her. Andrew was so gentle and entertaining. Emily seemed so happy and busy with her pupils, her rehearsals, and her singing.

She looked out of the window into the pale blue of the New York sky, for Emily's flat was high above the street, and thought gently of Thomas. How handsome he had been when he was young! Did he know where she was now? He would no longer, Mary was sure, misunderstand and disapprove of anything. He would be glad they were all happy.

Mary closed her eyes and, long-fingered, blue-veined hands folded about her fine lawn handkerchief, dozed off for a moment.

"Mother, you were asleep!" Emily accused.

"I was nothing of the kind!" said Mary indignantly.

"Of course you weren't," Andrew Gray assured her, his eyes mischievous.

Mary was startled, for she had not heard him come in. Instinctively she brushed her skirt smooth in her lap.

"It's so pleasant to see you both, both of you so beautiful, after a day downtown," said Gray. "Tea, yes, please, but no—nothing to eat," he told Emily. "I'm looking forward to my dinner."

"We'd not be having tea at all," Emily explained, "if it were not for Mother. There'd be the devil to pay if we skipped as much as one cup during the day. You've no idea how my tea bill has gone up since Mother's been here."

"It is serious, I know," said Gray soberly. "It's one sure way to the poorhouse."

"Well, I never!" gasped Mary, determined to give as good as she got. Firmly she set her cup and saucer down on the little marble-topped table next to her chair. "I'll not drink a drop of it."

"But, of course," said Gray, "it's even more serious to let good India-Ceylon cool and go to waste."

"Oh, much!" Emily agreed.

"Well, if that's the way you feel," said Mary with an arch and roguish look which delighted them both, "I'll make myself drink just a drop or two."

They chatted gaily after that, each thinking his own thoughts, Emily hoping and planning despite her resolve not to, Gray remembering at odd moments what he had tried to get done during a day of frantic activity in preparation for the impending life insurance investigation.

He looked up to see Emily regarding him thoughtfully and tenderly. He sent back an intimate, warm, and trusting smile which touched her heart. Everything that Andrew did, everything he was, would always touch her heart, especially when he was disturbed or hurt. He looked tired and strained. He had understood so much, forborne and suffered so much for her. He knew when agony was real and when happiness was. He knew everything.

They were still laughing and talking, subtly making Mary proud center of attention when Will, resplendent in his best, appeared. His face fell as he saw them.

"I'm too late? Dinner's over? I'm to be starved?"

"Another martyr!" cried Emily, running to him.

Will bent to kiss his mother, shook hands easily with Andrew Gray. He had scrubbed and changed at work and was in high spirits. His mother looked at him sharply, then proudly. Will had seemed so serious since Thomas' death. He seemed to feel his new responsibilities so keenly. It was good to see him more like himself again.

Their festive spirits kept up all through dinner. Will's white teeth gleamed as he laughed. His fair hair caught the light, and his blue eyes shone. He was conscious of his elation and of his appearance. He felt good looking and brilliant. He felt this about himself with pleasure but without conceit, almost as an appreciative onlooker.

"Will, what are you up to?" asked Emily later when they were alone for a few moments in the hall. "Win a fortune? A new girl? What's this one like?"

"Nothing! Cross my heart! I just feel kind of alive again."

"Ann taking good care of you?"

"Oh, all right." Will shrugged.

Emily lowered her voice tensely.

"Andrew's wife is very ill. I mean dangerously ill this time. They don't know whether she will pull through."

"Oh!"

"Will, I have so much. I've been so fortunate, so—it's been so wonderful sometimes that I've been scared. Still—"

"Stop it, Em! It's all right. Whatever way, it's all right."

"Don't let Andrew suspect I told you. You know what he's like about—about that part of his life."

"Why is it," Will asked Gray seriously, when they were alone in the living room after dinner, "that old Teddy is chasing around so after Big Business and the trusts? Is it just to get votes? I guess there really is something wrong though at Equitable, isn't there, if the papers have it right?"

"Something is usually wrong in the best of all possible worlds," Gray assured him, avoiding direct answer about Equitable. "Roosevelt? He's the poseur of all poseurs, of course, yet there may be more to it than that." Gray frowned to show Will that he took his question seriously. "Perhaps people's attitude is changing toward some things. Standards do change slowly under pressure."

Will looked questioning.

"Well," Gray explained, "competition in business, its extreme forms anyway, used to be considered natural and even laudable on the victor's part. Now it seems to be considered a crime."

"Isn't it 'the life of trade,' the spur to accomplishment, and all that?" asked Will wisely.

"The reformers seem to think it injures the incompetent—and all reformers are incompetent."

"You can't win," said Will reasonably, "unless somebody else loses."

Gray looked surprised.

"Learned that at Belmont and a couple of other tracks," explained Will. He was surprised and pleased that he had somehow impressed Andrew Gray. "I don't see anything wrong with that."

"Nor I," said Gray. "That's the trouble."

"The trouble? That's the fun of it. If it were a sure thing—"

"Nothing ever is. Nothing ever will be. Perhaps, as you say, everything any of us gets is always at the expense of another. Life has its own system of balancing the books."

Will shrugged. "As long as I get back to England again next year! I'm saving a little. As soon as I get enough, I'm going to invest it at the track. Maybe I can make this trip at the expense of a mudlark and a few platers."

Mary advanced decisively with her deck of cards. She gave them their choice. "Halma, cribbage, or bezique?"

Will laughed. "If any of us win this time, Ma won't speak to us for days."

"I'm a better player than any of you," said Mary simply. "Come, Willy, move the table and bring your chairs over."

Later, Emily urged Will to stay the night, but he pleaded the necessity of getting fresh work clothes and a metal tape he needed at home. All evening he had been aware of Ann alone in the Brooklyn house. He had felt both warmth and guilt.

It was well after midnight when he got back to Brooklyn. He was surprised that there was a light in the dining room. He let himself in through the basement door and found Ann seated at the table. She looked up as he entered. Her hair was disordered, and it was evident that she had been crying.

It was too late to back away. "Hello!" he said more loudly and cheerfully than he intended.

"Hello," said Ann quietly. "I'm sorry."

He would never know which way Ann would jump. Her quiet voice and simple dignity confounded him. He sat down.

"I'm glad to be home," he said sincerely, "though we had a good time."

"It was just a letter from my father. I know he drinks and all that, but he's really very nice, and he's old. I—I get a little lonely sometimes, I suppose."

Will's easily aroused compassion was stirred. Life had not been easy on Ann. She was lonely, too. He went over to her.

"Never mind," he said. "Things work out. At least, that's what they say." He touched her shoulder to comfort her.

Ann sprang up and faced him. "Oh, Will!" she cried, and burst into tears again. "Oh, Will!" She slipped into his arms.

It was another full week before Mary returned. As always, she extended her visit beyond its planned limits. Emily came with her. Will was not yet home from work, and Ann greeted them with unusual warmth. There was a new softness about her, a new lighted vitality which both women remarked. They looked at each other.

Mary praised the appearance of the house, told of the excitements of her visit with Emily, and thanked Ann for taking care of Will.

"Will's no trouble!" cried Ann. "We get along fine!"

The three women drank tea and visited for an hour or more. Mary had brought back new clothes which had to be tried on and inspected.

They decided that one skirt was not quite right. They would have to have the dressmaker look at it.

"You should have seen Will one night!" laughed Ann joyously. "He was helping me with the supper dishes, and he had on one of your aprons. He pretended it was a dress. He was really funny about it."

"Will helping with the dishes!" Emily murmured.

Mary decided to be outspoken. She was glad Emily was there to witness the warning.

"There would be no use your setting your cap for Will, Ann," she said gently. "Will can marry any girl he likes. Besides, he plans to return to England as soon as he can."

" 'Setting my cap'. The very idea!" Ann's sharp face flushed with anger, and her eyes widened with indignation. "As if I would set my cap for any man! What is there so wonderful about Will that you seem to think he is so sought after? I can't see—"

Mary, smiling as one who knows better, left the room.

"And don't try setting any traps for Will either," said Emily bluntly, when she was sure her mother was out of earshot. "Will can get all the women he wants."

Ann's anger seemed to subside as suddenly as it had risen.

"Need you be quite so coarse?" she asked sweetly. "I suppose you must."

"It seems best to be very plain with some people."

"We'll see," smiled Ann. "We'll see."

"What do you mean by that?" demanded Emily.

"Oh, nothing!" protested Ann, all innocence again. "Nothing at all!"

Emily opened her mouth to speak, thought better of it, pressed her lips coldly together, and looked hard at the other.

"Vixen!" she said under her breath. She could not help it.

Ann lifted her eyebrows demurely. Her gray eyes darted defiance. "Eh?" she inquired politely.

Chapter 56

Dr. Allan Richards walked quietly, almost furtively down the dark enclosed stairs from his office on the first floor to the basement of the Mott Haven house. Despite his caution the treads under the dust-laden stairs carpet creaked slightly under his weight. He had got heavier.

It was late afternoon or early evening, and his last office patient had just left. He did not think Agnes had heard the woman go, but he was not sure. Through the glass panel of the door at the bottom of the stairs he could see into the dining room and the short connecting hall which led from it to the kitchen. He stood there behind the door.

Rhoda, big-eyed and serious with braided pigtails of brown hair hanging down the back of her white middy blouse, sat at the dining table, where the light was already on, poring over a book. From its size and color Allan knew that it was her geography. Rhoda, who was twelve and in the upper grades of public school, loved all her school subjects, adored her teachers, but loved geography most of all. She could recite the names of all the capitals of Europe and of every state of the United States without hesitation. They made a game of it sometimes with Agnes joining in. Sometimes they went up to his office in the evening when the patients were gone and drew maps of South America with the Amazon running down through it or of Egypt and the Nile, and Rhoda colored them with crayons.

The white tablecloth, showing various stains and crumbs from the last meal, was still on the table where Rhoda read. Agnes seldom removed it between meals. The crowded dining room was littered, with half-emptied paper bags on part of the table, bundles of clothing on the chairs, a muddle of dishes on the high and dust-coated oak side-board. A molting canary slumped miserably on the perch in his dirty cage which hung from the ceiling near the windows where the shades were drawn. Smoke, dust, and lack of air were going to finish it off like its predecessors.

Something was burning on the stove, and smoke was drifting through into the dining room.

"*Will* you get out from under Mama's feet, Richard!"

Allan heard Richard's protest, the thump, and the boy's outcry. He turned and went back up the stairs as silently as he had descended.

He took his hat, brushed off a speck of dust before he put it on, and went quietly out the front door. He would eat, as he so often did, at a quiet hotel down in the Thirties.

"Set the table, Rhoda, then come help Mama in the kitchen," Agnes called.

"Yes, Mama." Obediently Rhoda closed her book and went to the sideboard drawer for the silver and their napkins.

"I'm hungry!" wailed Richard from the stool near the stone wash-tubs where he had been made to sit. He was a big and heavy child, though he would not be in school for another year. "I didn't do anything."

"Be still, Richard." Agnes was stirring something at the stove. She wrapped part of her apron around her hand to move a boiling pot. "Go upstairs and see if your father is in."

Richard sniffed. "I don't want any more old stew again."

"Think of all the poor little boys who don't have nice warm stew."

"They can have mine," said Richard generously.

"Be off and do as I told you." Agnes waved her big spoon threateningly. She frowned and brushed the gray hair back out of her eyes. Beads of perspiration stood out on her forehead, and her eyeglasses had got steamed. The beans she was warming from the day before had got burned. Emily, she remembered angrily, had Ellen to do her cooking, and Laura always had a girl.

"I've set the table, Mother," said Rhoda at her elbow, "and I put glasses of water at every place, but I couldn't find Richard's napkin."

"Papa's not home," reported Richard. "I looked and looked. I even looked under his desk and in the cupboard, but he wasn't there."

"Of course, he wasn't there!" laughed Rhoda, hugging him.

"I go under his desk sometimes," argued Richard, "and once I went in the cupboard."

"Why didn't you put your napkin back in the nice ring I bought you?" demanded Agnes. "Now you go show Rhoda where you put it."

A moment later Rhoda came running back into the kitchen.

"It's Uncle Will!" she cried happily. "Uncle Will's come." She ran back to be lifted up and hugged.

"Why, Will!" Agnes lifted her smudged and sweaty face for him to kiss, holding the dripping spoon away from her stained housedress. "You're just in time for supper. There's nothing special, but—"

"Glad to," said Will, rumpling Richard's hair as he put Rhoda down. His tone was jovial, but his face looked strained and worried.

"Get another plate and a knife and fork for your uncle," Agnes ordered Rhoda. She began to untie her apron.

"Phew!" said Will. "What have you been burning? Rubber?"

"Just some beans got a little scorched. I threw them away. The rest are all right, I'm sure. How's Mother? Is she home?"

"She's home, and she's fine. Allan here?"

"He was called out somewhere. He was here, I think—Richard, stop that! Now just sit down, all of you. Will, you sit here."

"What's the biggest river in the world?" Rhoda dared Will.

"The Hudson," he said promptly.

Rhoda shook her head.

"The Harlem then?"

"No!" cried Rhoda gleefully.

"Then," said Will firmly, "it's the Thames. I should have know in the first place."

"No, it isn't," called Rhoda from the kitchen from which she was returning carefully with the covered dish of mutton stew. "It's the Nile!"

"Oh, well, if you're going to count the ones with alligators and crocodiles and snakes in them!"

"When I get big," boasted Richard, "I'm going to have a snake that big." He stretched his arms out full length as Rhoda tucked the napkin into his collar and straightened it out over his blouse.

"If *you* get any bigger," said Will, "you'll burst."

"I will not," said Richard, staring at Will.

"Don't contradict your uncle," said Agnes mechanically.

Will laughed at her. It was Allan he really wanted to see. His nervousness returned. He tried to hide it, continuing his chaff with the children.

"Will," said Agnes sweetly, after they had finished supper and Richard had been put to bed, "I think I shall go up to South Ilium in a few days. Someone should check on the tenants and see to things, and I know you're busy at your work."

"Why don't you let things alone, Agnes," suggested Will shortly. "Go on up if you must, but try not to upset everyone up there. Your last visit to Brooklyn did no one any particular good after all the upset it caused."

"It was my duty to Pa," said Agnes stubbornly. Her eyes softened, though her face went stupid and obstinate. "I have done everything I could. If Ma won't see, she won't. There's nothing more I can do about it."

Will felt relieved. "That's good," he said.

"I wish Pa were here," said Agnes, almost in tears again. "There was no one like Pa."

"You're probably right there. I miss him, too," Will admitted.

Perhaps, he thought to himself, it was a good thing for him and for his father, too, that he wasn't alive. "Evidently Allan's been held up."

"I don't know," said Agnes listlessly. She had taken off her glasses and her eyes looked vague. Will felt almost sorry for her. No one could help what one was. It was about the only excuse he could manage for himself.

Rhoda had come back from somewhere and sat across from Will looking at him. She liked Will.

"Will you tell me some more about England, Uncle Will?" she asked politely.

"It's time you were getting ready for bed," said Agnes.

"But you always let me stay up until Papa comes home unless he's out *very* late."

"England?" said Will. "Oh, England's a fair and pleasant land, a—something—jewel set in a silver sea. It's all kings and soldiers and big oak trees in the Forest of Dean, and Dick Whittington and his cat—"

"Oh, I know that story!" cried Rhoda. " 'Turn back, Dick Whittington, Lord Mayor of London!' You tell it to me."

"But you know it! You should see the horses at Epsom. They run backwards."

"Run backward! How can they do that? They *can't* do that!"

"Yes, they do. They run the wrong way around the tracks."

"Well, that isn't running backwards."

"It's just as good," Will decided. "Stay out of the Tower of London though. They chop off your head in there."

"They didn't chop off yours!"

"Probably they should have," said Will thoughtfully. "They didn't have time that day," he explained to Rhoda. "They will next time I go back."

"Then I wouldn't go back," said Rhoda happily. "I wouldn't go anywhere just to get my head chopped off." She loved Will's fooling with her. Her father was much better than Uncle Will, but he never joked with her the way Uncle Will did.

"All right, then," Will said. "I won't go back. I'll probably never be able to now anyway."

"Why, Will, I thought you planned to go back next year," said Agnes.

Allan's entrance saved Will from answering. Allan was glad to see Will. Had he known Will was there, he would have returned sooner. They talked for a little while. Finally, Will looked at his watch, though a clock was ticking on the mantel near him. He had kept wishing Agnes would go away.

"I did want to see you a minute or two, Allan," he said in a strained voice, though he was trying to appear casual. Lines of worry had appeared in his forehead and the palms of his hands were moist.

"Why, Will, you're not sick?" asked Agnes alarmed.

"Oh, no," Will mumbled. "Just wanted to ask Allan—" He flushed vividly.

"Of course," said Allan, calmly, though his kind eyes had searched Will's face. "I have to see to one or two things in the office. Why don't we go up there?"

Agnes could hear their muffled voices overheard as she swabbed away at the supper dishes with a none-too-clean cloth in the kitchen sink. She wondered what they were talking about. Privately she resolved that she was going to order the Gibbons out unless they paid up their three months' back rent. Then she would have a good long talk with Aunt Maria in the cottage. A talk with Aunt Maria always did her good.

It was an hour before Allan and Will came downstairs again. Allan's face showed nothing. It seldom did. Will looked both sober and a little feverish or excited. He left soon afterward.

"What were Will and you talking about?" Agnes demanded after he had left.

"Oh, everything," said Allan vaguely. "About the job he's on now. Smith Construction has a huge new loft building, a big warehouse well under way down at Erie Basin. Will expects to be shifted there soon."

He'd have to face it and make the best of it somehow, Will thought, on his way home. He was too worn out by his emotions of the past week to think more now. If Allan was right, and he should know, it was all that was left to do. How to tell his mother, he did not know. At all costs he wanted to avoid any scene, any uproar.

What he did not take into account was Ann's temperament. She chose her own way to tell Mary.

"James is just a drunkard!" cried Ann, her eyes flashing, "and Emily, with all her airs and her fine clothes and her jewelry is nothing but a—a slut! Agnes is right. I don't see how she dares sing in a respectable church!"

Mary paled and drew back as though struck.

"You are not to say things like that, Ann! You know they are not true."

"Every word I said is true! And Agnes herself—huh!"

"If that is the way you feel about my family," said Mary stiffly, "I think you had better pack your things and leave."

"I won't leave! You can't make me leave!"

"Perhaps your friends at home were used to such talk. I am not."
Mary felt weak and ill.

"My friends are a lot better than any of you!" screamed Ann. "Do
you think they would stand for a woman's carrying on as Emily does?
And you—you've encouraged her all along. I have eyes in my head!"

"Pack your things this instant," ordered Mary, "and leave this
house!"

"So you think you can drag me down here and then discard me
just like that! I'll go to the minister! I'll go to the police! I'll tell
people what goes on in this family!"

"Stop it!" cried Mary feebly. Ann's strident voice pierced every
nerve. Her distorted face was like that of a malignant fury.

"So you think you can turn me out, do you? You think you can
get rid of me just like that! Ask Will if you can. Ask him! Just ask
him!"

"What do you mean, Ann?" cried Mary fearfully. "What do you
mean?"

Ann sneered triumphantly.

"Ask Will!" she shouted again. "Ask your precious son!"

Chapter 57

MARY STAPELY sat looking out of the window of her sitting room
into the gray South Brooklyn street. It was an evening early in
June and still light, though a fine spring rain had begun to fall.

Erect in her chair, a white lace handkerchief in the thin hand
which lay on the black serge of her skirt, Mary had never looked
more dignified. Her fine face, marked now by tiny wrinkles about
her eyes and brow, was composed, but her eyes were thoughtful. She
was aware of people who passed, hurrying through the rain, and of
the sycamore, its slender trunk protected by a wrought-iron railing,
bursting into leaf in the tree belt, but she did not consciously see
them.

Had anyone told her that she and Ann had been in conflict over
Will ever since Ann came to the house, Mary would have been surprised and indignant. She had been aware of no conflict, just as she

had never acknowledged any conflict of wills between herself and Thomas. As she saw it, events had taken their natural course. They had indicated finally that she had been right in wishing to leave South Ilium, and Thomas wrong.

She acknowledged no contest with Ann, yet, illogically, she now suffered a sharp sense of defeat. She had no intention of admitting to others or to herself that Ann had scored a frightening victory.

Mary knew unerringly that such would be the most dangerous course. Nothing really conclusive had happened. It was the reason she had summoned James and Laura and Emily and Andrew Gray. She had to move quickly and take command.

Her mind moved swiftly as she awaited their arrival. One reason she had been caught off guard was that it had never seriously occurred to her that Ann would dare challenge her authority or her wishes, spoken or unspoken. None of her own children would, she well knew. What remained was to face the situation firmly.

Later they would see what they would see. She could bide her time. Thoughts of which Mary had not thought herself capable rose darkly in her mind. Mary disliked treachery. She found opposition almost as hard to bear, and Ann had opposed them all.

That Ann had engineered and schemed to her own ends, Mary felt certain. Will would never deliberately have sought Ann, nor would he have considered rebelling against her as the real head of the family. Mary, with no announcement of retaining it, had never relinquished moral authority over her children, especially over Will who, despite his being nearly thirty-two, was so much the youngest of them all. Mary knew this, and all of her children knew it. They would appear this evening as she had asked, and they would do as she indicated.

James and Laura came first, James's electric bumping to a stop at the kerbing. They were dressed, Mary noted approvingly, not in their best but certainly not in their everyday clothes. Emily and Andrew, arm in arm under his silk umbrella with the ivory handle carved in the shape of a sleeping dog, came hurrying up from the Third Avenue Elevated a few minutes later.

"But what is it, Ma?" cried Emily. "You look so serious!" She shook raindrops from her skirt where it had trailed on the walk.

"I thought, of course that you wanted to play cards," grumbled James. He had two particularly worrisome cases on hand. People were a nuisance. He would have done better to be a veterinary. Dogs and horses at least couldn't complain of their symptoms.

Mary silenced them both with a glance.

It was more of an effort to speak than she had imagined it would be. Her heart fluttered, and involuntarily her hand went up to press it. James noticed her action uneasily. Laura looked removed. She was going to have a second child. She felt surprised. She had told no one yet, not even James. She looked at him. There was more gray in his hair and beard. He looked tired but strong. Andrew Gray, sitting quietly, looked at Emily. His wife had not died. Miraculously, she was to live once again, though she never really lived. Emily, looking at Andrew, wondered what he was really thinking about. How did he really feel at the very bottom of his heart? She decided she would never really know.

"Will and Ann," said Mary clearly, "are going to be married."

"No!" cried Laura unbelievingly. "Will and Ann!"

Emily looked grim. She kept her eyes on her mother's face.

"I wanted to tell you," said Mary, pale now, "before—before any-one else could. Ann is out this evening. It seemed a good opportunity."

"Will can't be fool enough," said Emily finally, "to go through with it."

"It's necessary," said Mary firmly. A slight color came into her cheeks.

James, unable to stand the silence which followed her remark, laughed unpleasantly.

"It's happened before in the history of the world," he said shortly. "The young fool!"

"It was not Will's fault," snapped Emily. "We could all see what that little vixen was up to."

"Of course it wasn't Will's fault," said Laura tensely. "I tried to warn him, but he hadn't a chance."

"What I wish you to do," said Mary, as though none of the others had spoken, "is to act as though there is nothing out of the ordinary. We are all going to welcome Ann for Will's sake."

Andrew Gray watched her with admiration.

"May I say," he murmured, "that I think you are being very wise."

"Andrew!" cried Emily reproachfully. "I'd like to tear her hair out by the roots! I may yet!"

Gray touched her arm reassuringly.

"But why did he have to! Will could have married anyone. That girl in England was crazy about him. So was that St. Louis girl on the boat. Even in Ilium—"

"They'll be married very soon," said Mary significantly. "I must tell Agnes. I shall do it in my own way." She spoke quietly but with almost a threat in her voice. The taste of victory was good again.

Laura got up and went to her.

"We'll do anything you say," she promised Mary. "James will behave. I give you my word."

"Where's Will?" growled James suddenly.

"Downstairs. I asked him not to come up."

James and Laura found Will in the dining room where he was ostentatiously reading the evening newspaper. He looked helplessly young and handsome with the lamp lighting one side of his face and his wavy blond hair.

Will looked up straight into their faces, though his color was high.

"Let's not have a lot of talk," he said boldly. "I'm a villain, a fool, anything you like. That won't change things—they are as they are, and they'll stay that way."

James looked surprised.

"Brave, aren't you?"

"But you don't love her, Will!" cried Laura, tears in her eyes.

"I don't know whether I do or not," said Will. "Does it make any difference?"

"Maybe something else can be done about it," muttered James. "I'll take the chance if Ann—"

"No!" said Will. "I know Ann wouldn't—anyway the idea makes me sick."

"No, I'm sure Ann wouldn't," said Laura bitterly. "Oh, Will, I don't know!"

"Neither do I." Will tried to grin. But what was the use? They all understood each other. "Just wish the happy couple well," he suggested.

Suddenly he felt disloyal. "Ann *is* all right. I understand her better than you do. You'll get to like her."

Impulsively, Laura kissed him and followed James out of the house. James had a patient to see.

Will shrank from seeing Emily and Andrew Gray. He walked out into the darkness and started slowly toward Fourth Avenue. He had been betrayed by his own weakness, by pity, by stupidity, loneliness, hunger. He was the fool who had learned nothing in all his years. He felt not guilt or remorse, but chagrin and dread—and, underneath, despite himself, a timid hopefulness.

He could hardly remember now the beginning excitement and awareness, the growing intimacy with Ann, the warmth flaming into desire. There had been too the intoxicating feeling that he was no longer just the son and brother but a man in his own right, a feeling of triumphant surprise and gratitude; and there had been a depression, sprung though he did not know it, of physical satisfaction without emotional fulfillment.

All Will knew now was panic. He was trapped and caught. Catastrophe collapsed around him, and there was no escape. He fought to control his fears. It was not that bad. It was not tragedy. Men married. What the women they married were like made no real difference in the end. He had heard others say that. He had heard James say it, but not as if he really believed it.

He kept seeing Ann's clear eyes. The expressions of her face and voice changed. They were playful, thoughtful, sullen, raging, or soft with feeling. Always her eyes were hard and watchful.

He had as good a right to marry as anyone! Ann was as good as any other woman and better than some. James and Laura, Agnes, even Emily, would have to understand that! But even as Will tried to convince himself and decided on a course of action dictated by necessity, he could not quite believe.

When he returned home he found that Mary had gone to bed early. Emily and Andrew were gone.

The house was silent with the lights on only in the dining room when Ann returned from a triumphant visit to a friend she had met at church.

Her face was soft and appealing. She looked so transfigured that Will marveled. Why was she not contrite or afraid or accusing? She was so happy and trusting that he was moved and ashamed as she held tightly to him.

"Oh, Will!" she breathed.

"Had a good visit?" he asked teasingly.

Surprisingly, elation and happiness returned. He felt on the threshold of a new and firmer life. He felt strong and defiant.

"I wanted to be home with you!"

Suddenly fierceness came into Ann's voice and her body tensed in his arms. "I know they've all been here. I know what they think. They're trying to separate us already. They'll always try, but they'll never get you away from me. Never!"

The dawning elation vanished. Will felt distaste and dread again. Awkwardly he patted Ann's shoulder. Ann had been hurrying. An odor of perspiration rose through the scent of her toilet water. His lips twisted slightly in distaste.

"Perhaps," he said tentatively, "Emily and Andrew would go with us Saturday."

"Do you think," cried Ann, drawing back from him, "that I would let two people who live as they do stand up for us at our marriage!"

Will could hardly believe he had heard rightly, but he wanted only to keep things peaceful.

"How about Agnes and Allan?"

"That would be very nice," said Ann primly. "Oh, Will, I'm sure we are going to be so happy!"

"Of course," said Will, trying to smile, though Ann could not see his face. "I wish, though, that Ma were not so unhappy about it."

"She'll come around," prophesied Ann evenly. "She'll have to. It will be our home now, and she'll be living with us, not the other way around. She'll realize soon enough."

Chapter 58

ANDREW GRAY had been present at every session of the Armstrong Committee's insurance investigation in the aldermanic chambers of New York's City Hall. They had begun early in September. It was now mid-October.

The giants of life insurance—rich, powerful men of strongly marked character and formidable reputations—had been marched across the stage and been made to answer for their deeds. Most of them were in or near their seventies. They had been for so long in positions of absolute authority, accustomed to deference and all the privileges of rank, that they could scarcely credit the indignities to which they were being subjected.

The gleeful public saw their bewilderment only as further proof of an awful and pervading guilt.

From the beginning it had been a holocaust, and the merciless destruction was still raging. The disclosures had been sickening and marvelously entertaining. The yellow press was hugging itself in an ecstasy of moral indignation—and skyrocketing circulation. There was no war. It was not an election year. The Armstrong investigation was a front page gift, good, week after week, for banner heads and boxed editorials on civic virtue and the abuse of public trust.

The insurance companies had wasted policyholders' money. That was irrefutable now. Officials of some of them had paid more attention to enriching themselves than to lowering premium rates or paying benefits. At the same time, the life insurance companies had performed signal public service. There was the record to show it, but no one paid any attention to that now. The shrillest organs of the press were trying, convicting, and sentencing each witness as though the investigation were a criminal trial. It was more like a court-martial even than a trial. The presumption was that every witness was guilty. All that remained was to determine the extent of his guilt.

His old friend C. J. Smith of Mutual had been right, Gray thought, when recklessly he had called the investigation, in print, an inquisition. Smith, always a fighter and fanatically loyal to the company whose interests he had served for many years, was risking everything in his defense of life insurance. He was fighting both in his own *Insurance Record* and in press despatches he was sending out everywhere.

Yet, Gray knew that Smith, like him, must have been sickened as well as surprised by some of the disclosures. No man in Smith's position or his own in any of the companies could know all that went on behind the scenes. It was probable that the company presidents and other high officials did not know it all, though they were being made to look like fools and knaves for not knowing.

He and Smith and everyone of any stature in Equitable, New York Life, Mutual, Metropolitan, and Apex, knew of the lobbying. It had been an accepted part of their jobs. It was part of the working routine of any large business subject at all to legislative control, and due as much or more to the venality of politicians and the corruptness of government as to company ambitions. It was a kind of semi-legal blackmail which only the naïve could find surprising.

Andrew Gray felt particularly bitter that afternoon. It was hot outside. The windows were open, and flies buzzed among the participants and spectators. Now and again an inquisitive English sparrow flew up from the grass of City Hall Plaza to flutter against the ivy on the window ledge near him.

The crowd was sweating and smelling. It was the same crowd day after day. Reporters at the press table were hurriedly scribbling notes. Many of them Gray knew. They were workmen doing their jobs competently. Many times during the investigation he had envied them. He knew the kind of copy he would have turned in. Some of the witnesses were pretentious old fools whom he, too, would have enjoyed pricking, but he would defend the stalwart old men and the sound structure they had built of life insurance. It was what he was doing issue after issue in the *Insurance Tribune,* and making no impression at all.

The seated witness that afternoon was the elderly and goateed chief actuary of one of the companies, and one of the most eminent men in his mysterious profession. On the stand several times before for long sessions, he had been frank, clear, and firm. He had strained to simplify the complicated problems of his craft. For all of this he had been described in the newspapers as an old fool, a wily evader, a simpleton. The insinuations made day after day were that he was also a thief, a scoundrel, a hypocrite, a conscienceless malefactor, and a defrauder of the poor.

Charles Evans Hughes was relentless. The red-headed, red-bearded, big-nosed, and big-toothed chief counsel of the Committee was being made the hero of the investigation. His brain sharpened by his good fortune and his dawning political ambition, the forty-three-year-old Hughes was doing ruthlessly the job he was paid to do. Gray admired the man's competence and the way he handled himself, and detested him.

All of the newspapers were ringing with praise of Hughes's fairness in his conduct of the examinations. He stuck to the facts. He eschewed irony. Because of the odor of sanctity and muscular rusticity about him, he had been dubbed the "Baptist Pope," and he was living up to the public conception of his immovable righteousness. He was being boomed for mayor, for governor, even for the Presidency.

Hughes's studied courtesy was almost an insult as he kept after the actuary, a man thirty years his senior. The older man, stiff in broadcloth, a high, starched collar, and a dark cravat, made attempts to oversimplify his explanations and trapped himself into apparent contradictions. Young reporters wrote gleefully at the press table.

The three state senators and five assemblymen on the Committee listened attentively. William Armstrong was toying with his gavel, flicking it noiselessly against his forefinger extended on the long polished table where the Committee sat. Several of the others looked hot and tired. To Gray's surprise, for he had known politicians enough, the men had been thoughtful and attentive during all the hearings. They were making a conscientious attempt to perform an arduous duty. Upstate representatives, most of them, they knew the value of a reputation for probity. All of them, Gray decided, would be re-elected.

In his anxiety to be clear, the actuary made another slip. It was simply an unfortunate choice of words. Gray saw Hughes's eyes light, though his face showed nothing. The Committee lifted their heads. Reporters grinned. Gray saw the next morning's headlines: *Actuary Admits Juggling Figures. Premium Rates Based on Fancy, According to John Monroe.*

Hughes gave Monroe every chance to correct his error, but the old man grew confused, and there was laughter in the room. Armstrong rapped for order. Flushed, Monroe looked away from the Committee and found Jerome staring at him reflectively. William

Travers Jerome, District Attorney of New York County, sat with arms folded and legs crossed. He was present to select those witnesses whom he might later indict for fraud, bribery, perjury, or any applicable charge.

The companies had been such fools! Such indiscreet and unbelievable fools! There had been blatant contempt for public opinion and the ordinary conventions of business behavior. Time and again, Gray recalled, he had tried to warn Ventnor and the others.

It was worse that responsible witnesses could not or would not account for large sums of money supposed to have been spent for legitimate expenses but actually used for bribery and lobbying. In many instances the men who could testify most accurately had fled the country or were "too ill" to appear. Some had completely disappeared.

Gray himself, with the aid of a few carefully selected agents, had handled the necessary Albany work for Apex. It would come out in time. There was no help for it.

Mutual's president, truculent old Richard McCurdy, had claimed to know nothing of such practices and been ridiculed for his stand. John McCall, president of New York Life, had proudly accepted full responsibility for everything his company did. He had been pilloried for his honesty and courage. The affairs of Equitable were in such a mess after the fight for control and the company's own investigation of its condition, that it had been wholly condemned. Metropolitan, Gray thought, was posing as too righteous and too surprised to be believable.

The strain was telling on everyone as the investigation went on day after day. Only Hughes remained cool and efficient in triumph. He was, Gray thought, sadistically calm. The man was enjoying himself.

Thus far Apex had got off fairly easily. Compared to the defiant McCall and the furious McCurdy, Ventnor had been a good witness. Despite indignation at the effrontery of the state and the public in questioning either his honesty or competence, Ventnor had answered questions freely where he could and referred Hughes to others in Apex who could give him details with which he was unfamiliar.

It was soon apparent that Apex, like the other companies, had been prodigal in payment of its highest officers. Certain general agents and suppliers had been favored and profited handsomely. It was also proved that Ventnor was rich, very rich, and dictatorial in both public and private life, but those well advertised facts the public already knew.

It was happily reminded. Ventnor was branded a thief and a

scoundrel. He oppressed the poor and betrayed widows and orphans. The yellow press screamed for his immediate deposition and incarceration, and the cartoonists added long series of digits to the dollar signs with which they had always decorated his waistcoat.

Ventnor shrugged and affected a thicker skin than he enjoyed. There were other Apex officers, particularly one weasel-faced accountant, shown to have been juggling figures for years, who might die of fright. A few might go to jail. It was more likely that one vice-president would explode with apoplexy.

Gray faced his own ordeal with trepidation. Yet he was eager to say bluntly and firmly what he thought. He would soon have his chance.

The advertising and publicity of all the insurance companies was under scrutiny. Most of his counterparts had already been on the stand. Stephen English of the *Insurance Times* and C. C. Hine of the *Monitor* had been questioned sharply and dismissed. Wily and clever old Joe Howard, Jr., veteran of a long and varied New York newspaper career who had worked for both Equitable and Mutual, had not helped. On the witness stand he had been amusing, alternately too respectful and subtly taunting. Cynically, he had virtually admitted to suspect practices, been evasive about others and almost derisive about the whole. All of the insurance writers and editors had been treated politely but with ill-concealed contempt, as though publicity was always dishonest and men who practiced it were slimy and unscrupulous.

This was made bitterly clear when C. J. Smith was called to the stand as Gray sat there. Only three or four years older than Gray, "C.J." was far older in New York journalism. That afternoon he looked older still. Forty years before he had been city editor of the *Sun* when it was owned by Moses Y. Beach, even before Dana took over. C.J. had known Greeley himself. Later he had founded a daily of his own which prospered for a few years before its disappearance. Then he had bought and edited a Sunday newspaper. He was a brilliant writer and a painstaking newspaperman of the old school.

He had turned to insurance journalism as a profitable field when he had depleted too much of his substance battling for workingmen's rights, for which he had been an early fighter, and other advanced causes and been very successful with the weekly which he started. He believed in the insurance doctrines he preached in the *Insurance Record* and had gladly accepted Mutual's offer of a position as head of its "literary department." C.J. was one of the powers of the insurance press as well as an outstanding figure at Mutual Life.

All of the older men at the press table knew him, though some of the younger ones knew him only by reputation. C.J. was sharp, facile, polished, deceptively unassuming. White-haired and impeccably attired, a figure of firm but gentle dignity, he took the stand. Despite himself, there was a touch of disdain in his manner. Eminently civilized, he disliked the whole noisy circus and resented what he saw as an intrusion on his privacy. He resented, too, what he saw as unwarranted interference with the actions of men whose accomplishments he respected. C.J.'s views accorded basically with Andrew Gray's.

Smith's manner at first was poised and graciously polite. Unfortunately his nervousness betrayed itself in his voice which had grown thin in recent years. It seemed to squeak with indignation as he answered simple questions as to his name, residence, and connection with the Mutual Life Insurance Company of New York. A few spectators laughed. Hughes frowned, and Armstrong gestured for silence.

C.J. was on the stand for two unhappy hours. Before he was released by the victorious Hughes he had been forced to admit that during the investigation he had paid large sums of Mutual money—as much as a dollar a line—to file company publicity releases through a telegraphic bureau as legitimate news despatches. Some of the despatches had come very close to ridiculing the Armstrong investigation. All of them had upheld the position of the life insurance companies. It was an outspoken enemy whom Hughes demolished that afternoon.

Andrew Gray rose in his seat to try to intercept C.J. as the witness was freed. C.J. saw him, but they were separated by the crowd. He nodded brightly, though his face was white, touched his hat, and hurried briskly away.

Gray's heart ached for his friend. There was not a more intelligent or, according to the code they understood, honorable newspaperman in New York. For his own reasons, C.J. had tried to protect his employers by letting himself be blamed and ridiculed for actions for which he could not have been wholly responsible. As the insurance writers who had preceded him on the stand had been—and as he might well be later—C.J. would be crucified in the evening and morning papers.

"Andrew, I could help," insisted Emily that night. "There must be some way I can help."

Gray smiled wryly.

"Only annihilation of all my newspaper and business past could help. The *World* and *Journal*, I imagine, will suggest decapitation. I'm told—Mr. Hughes is telling me—that C.J. and a few others and I were all wrong. I don't think we were. At least it did not seem stupid at the time. Stupidity is always the worst."

Chapter 59

EARLY IN NOVEMBER, Will, his face white and strained, looked down nervously at the child he had never intended. It looked raw and very naked in James's hands. He tried not to show his distaste.

"So that's what they look like, is it?" He strove to make his tone light and detached. All the weeks and months of misery for this! It seemed impossible.

"Usually," said James, without looking up. He turned the newborn infant over as though it were a pound bag of meal, inspecting it minutely. "Seems to have all its parts. Not too bad." He held it dangling.

It was red and wrinkled. To Will its skin seemed loose. It looked like an obscene miniature of an aged man. Will nearly shuddered.

"I see," he said desperately. He wished James would take the child away. "I—I didn't realize they were so small."

James looked up from under his thick eyebrows.

"Had enough, papa?" he inquired sardonically.

Will's fists clenched in anger.

"How's Ann?" he asked doggedly.

"Being Ann, she's making even more than the usual fuss, but she'll do."

To Will's relief, James turned and took the indecently new baby to do whatever was done with newborn infants.

"James!" he called after his brother. "James?" He gestured.

"Yes, you can go in. Don't stay."

Will knew he had to go in to see Ann. His mother was there. He straightened his shoulders.

A few moments later he started down the stairs. He felt no pride, no elation, only a sick depression. He tried to smile as he neared the bottom steps.

"A wonderful child, a marvelous child!" he threw flippantly at

Emily. "Be walking and talking in a day or two." He gave up. "Ugly little bastard!" He made a face.

"Not bastard, Will," corrected Emily. "Ann saw to that. Don't feel too badly." She saw Will look about. "Andrew's at court again or he would have come with me. I'm afraid things are going badly for him."

"I'm sorry about that," said Will mechanically.

"Why be sorry about anything? It isn't worth it. Well, I'll see what I can do to help before Agnes gets here and makes it impossible. Why don't you go to work? You'll feel better with something to do."

"Do you think I could? Do you think it would be all right?" asked Will, relieved.

"Of course. Oh, Andrew asked me to give you a message if things turned out that way." Emily's voice hardened a trifle. "He said to tell you any man should be proud to have a son."

"Andrew said that?"

"It does sound—oh, go on!"

Emily watched Will as he left the house. Will had always been so good to her, to them all. Now this! Bewildered innocence, that's what it was. Life was for the hardhearted, the selfish, the stinkers!

It was a cold, sullen morning, more like early winter than late autumn, yet Will found it good to get into the air. He could be at work before half the morning was over. It was good to get out of the overly warm house and into a world he could understand. He had had no sleep and was feverish. He felt numb and clumsy. The birth of the child was fact. The child was fact, but he felt no realization of it except as something inexorable—as Ann was inexorable. Life had slotted him neatly into place and nailed him there. His head ached dully.

Jack Holley was not in the construction shack when he reached the job. No one was in the pine-boarded box of a room where blueprints littered the crude shelf-desk and papers and tools cluttered Jack's own battered table. Will was glad no one was about. The potbellied cast-iron stove was red hot. Will yanked overalls and a heavy work coat off a nail and dragged them on over the clothes he wore.

Steam machinery hissed and clanged. Two hundred men were at work on the great warehouse, carpenters, painters, bricklayers. Shouting teamsters were backing their drays up to the loading platforms. Will saw a timekeeper scurrying in out of the cold. He knew the man, but he did not want to see him. He wanted to see none of them. He fumbled with the buttons of his coat. For once he did not want to pitch into the work. He did not wish to be where he was any more than he wished to be at home.

He jerked open the door of the shack and headed for the looming structure which a short time before had been only a great skeleton of steel, then an outsized box of concrete and brick. He started for the temporary stairs which had been thrown together on the lower floors. They gave out at the fourth floor.

The gray morning was viciously cold along the dark water front. The wet salt wind driving in from the bay pained as it struck. Will climbed a ladder from the top floor of the huge building, pulled himself through a hole in the roof, and met the full force of the wind as he stepped out on the expanse of tar and gravel surface.

A heavily clothed workman who had been jumping up and down and flailing his arms against his body for warmth hurried off when he saw it was a foreman.

Will, after one quick look, leaned into the wind and fought his way across to where eight or ten men were struggling to lower a large skylight into place. It swung from a block and fall secured over the extended arm of a heavy winch fastened into a stationary position.

The men strained to hold the huge skylight which the wind had caught as though it were a sail and threatened to fly across the Narrows high over the ugly green water and the busy shipping to the New Jersey shore. Obviously they were in trouble. Will hurried to lend his weight.

As with everything else on this job, there had been more than enough trouble already with this skylight. First, it had been built to the wrong dimensions and, after being hoisted to the roof had had to be lowered again and sent back for rebuilding. The second time it had swung against the side of the building as it was being hoisted to the roof, smashing a part of the heavy frame.

Will grasped a corner of the unwieldy structure just as one man, his hands numb and clumsy in the cold, let go and sprang back from the gaping hole in the roof.

"Steady!" roared Will to the others above the wind, as he lifted and thrust with all his strength. "Easy! Easy now!"

"Look out!" cried the man next to him. "She's going like a kite again! I can't—!" He let go, and a man across from them staggered and fell.

The weight increased crushingly and seemed to strike as the released skylight swung wild. Will was yanked off his feet. Somehow he could not let go.

"Will! Look out, Will!"

It was Jack Holley running hard across the roof, but Jack was too late.

For seconds he seemed to be holding his own. Then the monster dashed off again, struck crushingly, and Will, the breath battered out of him, felt himself hurled helplessly toward the opening. The gaping hole in the roof rushed up to meet him. It was a drop of twenty feet to the floor below. He could not even cry out.

Chapter 60

"STILL UNCONSCIOUS," said James quickly as he entered the hall. He shut the door hard behind him. "It's the morphine now. He came to for a few moments. We had to put him right under." He began to strip off his overcoat.

It was almost ten at night. Emily and their mother had been waiting tensely in his office. They had been waiting, it seemed to them, for hours since James returned to the hospital. Laura had just gone upstairs to see that Martha was safely asleep.

"But things don't happen this way!" cried Emily again. "They just don't happen."

"It happened all right," said James grimly.

"*Why* can't we go down?" insisted Mary. "I *intend* to go."

"You can't," said James sharply. "Will is going to be all right, but you can't help him now. I've been there almost all day. You'd not be allowed in anyway. Has Ann been told yet?"

"No. Agnes is with her, and Ellen's there."

"H'mph!"

"Why can't we go to Will?" demanded Mary again. "I'm his mother. I—"

"James, you *have* told us everything?" Emily's face and voice were fearful. "It's not worse than you've said. Will *is* going to be all right?"

"I've told you again and again," said James wearily, though he was trying to be patient. "He has a compound fracture of the left leg, a bad fracture, a mess. We can't be sure for a few days that blood poisoning won't set in. He fell on a pile of lumber and steel scrap and Lord knows what else—probably the only reason he's alive. It broke his fall."

"But why did it have to happen to Will? Hasn't enough happened to him already? And what's to be done about Ann and the baby?"

"I'll see to them," said Mary firmly. "We'll all do our best. We must all do our best for Will's sake. Will will soon be getting well, I *know*. He has hurt himself before, and he always gets well."

"Good for you, Ma!" approved James gratefully.

If they had seen that horribly lacerated leg, skin torn wide, blood, dirt, steel shavings stuck to the shattered white bone!

White-faced and drawn, Mary looked ready to drop. They had all been up since before daybreak.

"I'll see where Laura is," she decided unsteadily.

The other two watched her go.

"I've got the best surgeon on the staff on it," said James soberly, "but I don't know. Billings himself doesn't know."

"Know? Know what?"

"Whether we can save the leg."

Horror distorted Emily's face. "You mean that Will might—that you might have—!"

"It's an ugly break. Whole thigh was ripped open. He's lost a lot of blood. If septicemia sets in, it may be the only way to save his life."

"Oh, God!"

"Have you told Andrew?"

"I haven't talked with him. I don't know what to do. He has trouble enough of his own right now. Oh, why Will? Why Will of all the people in the world!"

The telephone rang. Emily held her breath as James answered.

"Stapely," he said gruffly into the mouthpiece, as he took down the receiver from the wall. He listened a few seconds, then shook his head at Emily. Her heart began to beat again.

Laura insisted on brewing tea before they left, and soon after James drove them home. He disappeared upstairs to look in on Ann and the child.

Agnes, her face stupid with fatigue and bewilderment, began to cry when she saw them, and Mary hastened to comfort her.

Emily felt she could not stand and talk to Agnes or anyone else. With what she tried to make a confident and reassuring smile, she slipped past them and up the narrow stairs to the top floor. There was no sound from Ann's room as she passed. They were all sleeping in makeshift quarters, and she had a cot in her mother's sitting room.

Emily had decided what she would do. She wished she could do it now, but there was nothing else for it. She began to undress in the dark by what light sifted through the lace curtains from a flickering street lamp. She lay down certain she could not sleep; but Mary found her asleep and breathing deeply when she limped exhausted up the stairs.

Awake early, Emily dressed hurriedly and silently so as not to wake her mother. The house was cold and damp, and her skin tightened against the coldness of her clothes as she pulled them on. Ellen stirred on the dining-room sofa as she crept past to the kitchen.

Her face sleep-creased, her kinky hair knotted with bits of rag, and her body lost in an old flannel bathrobe of Will's, Ellen struggled to put the kettle on.

"Get back to bed, you little fool!" Emily scolded. "You've probably been up most of the night again."

" 'At," said Ellen, paying no attention, "is jes' the cutes' li'l baby!" Then she remembered. "Po' Mist' Will!"

Emily had almost forgotten the baby. It had not looked cute to her.

"You can tell the others," she told Ellen as she sipped the scalding tea, "that I had to go back to New York this morning. Tell them I'll be back tonight if I can. Anything you want me to bring back?"

Ellen could think of nothing they needed.

She knew only the general direction, but a friendly policeman she found on the corner at Third Avenue was helpful, and a conductor told her where to change streetcars. The ride in the jolting trolley, in which for a time she was the only passenger, seemed interminable, then, after all, she made a mistake, changed to the wrong car, and had to retrace part of her journey. She rode through parts of Brooklyn she had never seen before. The huge, gray hospital when she got there, was larger and more forbidding than she had imagined.

Her heart ached anew when she thought of Will helpless and alone somewhere inside the great stone pile. There seemed little activity about as she climbed the wide steps to the pillared entrance. Repelled and shrinking inwardly, she would have turned back had she not been determined. Her heart beat fast as she tugged open a heavy door.

A woman in a nurse's uniform sat at a desk in the entrance going over some records. She looked up as Emily went inside. Knowing she would be refused admission, Emily looked quickly away and walked rapidly past the desk as though she knew exactly where she was going.

She found herself headed down a long, dim corridor, all in ugly chocolate brown with long rows of identical doors opening off both sides. A white-jacketed orderly walked far ahead of her down the hall. A nurse carrying a bedpan wrapped in a towel hurried out of one door, and another nurse hurried into a room carrying a breakfast tray. The smells of medicine and disease permeated walls and ceiling. Emily hurried on.

She was forced to step quickly to one side as a stretcher was wheeled out of a side corridor. On the stretcher was an old woman, unconscious. Blood seeped out of a corner of her mouth and hung down over her chin in a sickening black line. The procession moved in a cloud of ether fumes. Emily's hand went to her throat after they had passed.

She was in near panic now. She wanted to find Will, not combat this monster of a place. She dared not ask directions of anyone who looked official. It was a scrub woman on her hands and knees at a stair landing who came to her rescue.

"Can you tell me where the men's surgical wing is?" Emily asked sharply in a low voice.

The woman raised and turned her head, about which she wore a knotted cloth. Emily saw then that she was very young, probably a nurse in training.

"Why, it's right over us," she said in a pleasant voice. "Just go right up these steps."

"I'm looking for William Stapely," dared Emily, trusting the girl's face and the careless authority she put into her voice. "He came in yesterday."

The girl was looking at her admiringly.

"Is he the one that got run over?"

"No. He—"

"Oh, I know the one you mean." The girl got to her feet, looking pleased at a chance to leave her task. "I can show you." She straightened her skirts, then looked doubtful. "It's not visiting hours. Did you get a card at the desk?"

"I'm Dr. Stapely's assistant." Emily lied without hesitation. "I got turned around somehow."

"Oh!" The girl smiled in relief and led the way. From the top of the stairs she pointed. "That door there, the second one."

"Thank you."

The door was ajar. Emily pushed it fully open before she could lose her courage.

There were three beds in the square, bare room. A figure with almost its entire face bandaged and the bandage stained a dirty yellow lay motionless in the first bed she saw. A bald man who was lying on his side squinted at her from another bed. Then she saw Will.

His face was almost as white as the pillow on which his head lay. His fair moustache and the day's growth of beard on his face seemed dark by contrast. He was asleep, but sleep had caught him in a grimace of pain, drawing down the corners of his mouth and cutting a triangle of lines deep into his colorless face. He lay on his back, and the hospital sheets were mounded about the lower part of his body as though barrel hoops had been inserted beneath them.

"Will!" breathed Emily. "Will!"

He did not stir. The bald-headed man stared at her silently.

Emily's own face was as drawn as Will's. She imagined the horror beneath the mounded sheets. James had said they had not yet set the fracture. The wound had to be kept open until they were sure it was clean. He and Dr. Billings were going to re-examine it and reach a decision that morning. They might have to call in others for consultation.

Emily stood tense and tall in the center of the floor. There were sharp footsteps behind her.

"What are you doing here, Miss? Who let you in?"

A gray-haired, grim-faced nurse confronted her.

Emily looked at her.

"I—!" She put her gloved hand to her mouth, turned, and fled blindly. She almost ran into an orderly who was wheeling a stretcher into Will's room. Another nurse followed.

There was no need to hide now. Emily started rapidly in what she thought was the direction of the entrance. The hospital was growing busy. Doctors and nurses moved through the halls. Ambulatory patients in hospital gowns and a variety of robes shuffled along. Some looked at her curiously. From somewhere came a cry and then a groan. Attendants were hastily arranging a screen about one bed in a ward she passed. There were sickening smells. Emily thought she would be ill. She pushed desperately for the door and the air outside.

A white ambulance, horses galloping, gong clanging dashed in at a side entrance as she reached the top of the wide steps. Another broken creature being delivered to the charnel house! Emily breathed deeply.

Then she saw the lone figure struggling up the steps. The woman limped a little and moved slowly as though she were trying not to spill whatever it was she carried in a brown paper bag held awkwardly before her. Emily's eyes narrowed as she watched her.

"Hello!" she said in mock surprise when Agnes was near enough.

"I came with James and Dr. Billings," Agnes explained, breathing hard, "but they went in another way. James told me to come in here."

The pent fury in Emily burst. Andrew accused of things he had never done! Will trapped and broken!

"They won't let you see him," she said coldly. "He's not allowed visitors."

"I know. James said that he and Dr. Billings might operate—not operate, I don't know just what. They wouldn't tell me. Allan is on his way." Agnes spoke humbly, her face miserable.

"It's a judgment, isn't it, Agnes?" cried Emily bitterly. "God is punishing Will and me for our sins!"

Agnes flushed, but her voice was resolute.

"Will was so upset he didn't know what he was doing. He has never done a wicked thing, and I won't let you say so even if you are my sister! I've brought him some broth they can warm in the kitchen. Allan says hospital food isn't always—"

Agnes burst into tears. Emily, contrition and amazement struggling in her face, reached out for her.

"I'm going to send Ellen to New York for the old uniforms I wore when I lived with James," she said swiftly. "I still have some of them somewhere. I'm going to stay right here and take care of Will. James can arrange it somehow with the hospital to let me be a special nurse or an assistant or something. I can sleep at Mother's. You have Allan and the children to look after. It's about time I was of some use to someone!"

"But—Mr. Gray? Your pupils?"

"I can't help Andrew in what he is having to face right now. The pupils can go to someone else, preferably to the devil. It's Will matters now."

Like a schoolgirl, she had recoiled from the sight of physical suffering. As though she had not learned what suffering was! If anyone could fight life for Will, she could.

"Come Agnes, we'll find James. That broth will be just the thing for Will."

Chapter 61

GRAY WAS ABLE to see Ventnor before he left that morning for City Hall. He tried to be jocular and appear at ease.

The investigation had aroused Ventnor and nearly exhausted him. He was alternately bitter and defiant. Where Apex would stand in the end, what action its directors would decide to take or be forced to take, what measures the State of New York might force upon all of the insurance companies, no one knew. In a few weeks neither employer nor employee might be where they were now.

Gray was one of the few left whom Ventnor could trust. Others had their own axes to grind. Some feared dismissal. Others feared prosecution for actions divulged by the inquiry. Two were nervously ill and in sanatoria. Opportunists were waiting to jump when they could see how best to take advantage of the situation.

"I shall stay on the job if they let me," Ventnor told Gray. "I'll clean out a few people—you know those I mean—and scrub up a few dirty spots. Then, when it can be seen that I was not forced out, I shall resign."

"You may not want to when the time comes."

"A man doesn't like to be blamed for what he has prided himself upon."

Gray nodded. Then he shrugged.

"If you need a small scapegoat, if there are any more little Apex peccadilloes lying around loose you'd like me to confess to —"

"Better see Craig," said Ventnor heavily.

Apex had William J. Craig as its attorney at the investigation, just as Mutual had James M. Beck on hand and Metropolitan, Richard Lindabury. They afforded the witnesses what protection they could.

"Craig will brief you, but you shouldn't have much trouble."

"I've already talked with Craig. No, most of it is out now."

"Some things, Andrew," said Ventnor, "I'm sorry I ever got you into."

"I didn't object at the time. It doesn't matter now."

Gray slept little that night. He breakfasted on a sliced orange and tea, unable to eat even a piece of toast. He sat numbly through Border's examination, hearing scarcely a word of it. He had sympathized with the others as they awaited their turn, knowing imaginatively what they must be enduring. Probably it was not as bad as he had thought. One always overestimated the emotions of others.

Hughes finished with Border, a slight, stoop-shouldered accountant who peered ludicrously through thick-lensed pince-nez attached by a black ribbon to the satin lapel of his frock coat. Recess was declared until two o'clock.

Gray avoided everyone he knew, just as he had avoided Emily for days. He wished neither advice nor sympathy. He walked across crowded Chambers Street to the North River, down West Street to the Battery, stopping near Washington Market to swallow some raw oysters. He bought a cigar and lighted it in the wind as he stood near the Battery's sea wall looking out over the inner bay.

It was a bright, clear, early winter afternoon, not too cold. The water, a dirty gray at his feet, was green out toward Ellis and Governors islands, blue where the shores of Brooklyn and New Jersey tightened in to form the Narrows. He could make out the huge building which, he knew, Will was helping to build and wondered if he were at work there as he watched. A Hamburg-American liner was going out on the tide, tugs snorting at prow and stern. Snub-nosed, battered ferries chugged sturdily across to Jersey City and Richmond. The Statue of Liberty gleamed tall and gold in the sun. A dirty cargo ship flying a South American flag steamed toward the open ocean.

On the Battery peddlers hawked toy balloons and large, dusty pretzels skewered on sticks. Clerks snatching a breath of sea air before they hurried back to offices in Whitehall or up Broadway, passed and repassed. Old men and women bundled in their coats dozed peacefully on faded green benches, and a bluecoat with heavy shoes and a drooping, dull-brown moustache wandered by swinging his tasseled nightstick.

Daily Gray had formulated answers to hypothetical questions, answers ranging from simple statements of truth and necessary evasions to vehement denunciation of the whole investigation.

An old fear returned and brought the perspiration out on his forehead and on the palms of his hands. He wiped them hard with a fresh handkerchief.

Would his long love affair with Emily be brought out in order to discredit his character and testimony? The yellow press would make him out a lascivious old man with a drunken mistress. He had feared such a disclosure all along. Hughes and the Committee had scrupulously avoided such tactics. No attempts at character impeachment had been made all during the long investigation, and both counsel and Committee must have known of rich cause for new scandals had they cared to adopt such tactics. They had not done so so far, but they might.

He could not face that. It would kill his wife. It would kill Emily for it could mean the end of her career at the Fifth Avenue Church and as a singer and teacher. Such public disclosure would hurt everyone connected with him, even those who had long tacitly accepted a relationship they could not overtly approve. Emily and he had not discussed it, for they could not admit to what they did not acknowledge, but he knew that Emily shared his fear.

He walked steadily up Broadway with its unconcerned thousands pushing and crowding about him. An office boy shouted insults at a telegraph messenger. A motor dray rumbled past, smoking and seeming about to explode. Horses reared, and irate drivers shouted at the chauffeur. Other motorcars dashed by, though one was broken down at the kerb with, as always, a curious and derisive crowd about it. An electric coupé glided silently by with a bearded gentleman holding the tiller in gloved hands.

He felt very old, older than C. J. Smith, older even than old Joe Howard. Probably C. J. had felt much the same yet felt, like him, that he had little to lose. Their connection with life insurance had been incidental. It was not with them, as with Ventnor, old John McCall, McCurdy and the others, the central fact of existence.

The first shock came when it was announced that Charles Evans Hughes was not to be present that afternoon. The Committee sat in full force, as it had at every session. The reporters and photographers were all on hand, as many as for a first-class murder trial. The crowd, cynical and experienced now, but still avid, sat expectantly.

In what was described as Mr. Hughes's unavoidable absence that afternoon, the counsel for the Committee was neither James McKeen nor Matthew Fleming, who had taken part in various phases of the investigation, but still another member of the Committee's legal staff. Gray had assumed that he had assisted in preparation of the briefs, for he had seen the others consult with him on numerous occasions. He did not catch the lawyer's name when it was announced and was not certain of it until he read it in the newspapers later.

Gray moved forward mechanically as his name was called. His face was flushed, but he felt cold. He took his seat with what he hoped was an appearance of calm in the railed-in witness chair. The attorney rose, papers in hand, at the counsel's table.

He was an older man than Hughes with a thin, sharp nose in an otherwise pudgy face and with short pudgy fingers. Gray had noticed before that there was something of the toady in his manner and of the fanatic in his sharp eyes. The lawyer would have to follow the line of questioning which the chief counsel had laid down, but Gray saw immediately that the man intended to make the most of his brief appearance in the limelight. He glared at the witness, looked significantly at the Committee and at District Attorney Jerome sitting watchful in his raised chair. The clerk took down the simple facts of Gray's name, place of residence, and company affiliation.

"What is your occupation, Mr. Gray?"

Andrew Gray cleared his throat. He began to speak in a voice which he realized was too low. He raised it and was almost frightened by the sound. By an effort of will he steadied himself.

"I am a writer," he said finally.

"Of what?" The lawyer's tone was contemptuous. It angered Gray.

"Of books, advertisements, pamphlets, articles, brochures, a few stories. Shall I go on?"

"*Only* a writer?" The lawyer looked amused.

Was what he dreaded coming now? With Hughes present he would have been safe from such attack. With this stranger he could not know.

"I'm afraid," Gray managed icily, "I don't understand."

"I suggest that you have had other interests and occupations— or should I call them diversions?"

Numbly, Gray waited for the blow to fall. The lawyer's face blurred before his eyes. Sounds came as from a great distance. He strove to speak but could not. Then he heard the man's next words, his insinuating, triumphant tone.

"Is it not true that you were at one time owner and editor of a New York newspaper which supported William Marcy Tweed despite proved evidence of his criminal mismanagement of the government of this city?"

So great was his relief that Gray could hardly believe he had heard correctly. Suddenly he wanted to laugh. He could almost feel the blood seep back into his heart. Then he realized the import of the question and, his earlier fear forgotten, the unfairness of it angered him again. Yet he spoke calmly.

"It is true that I owned and edited a newspaper which nominally supported the party to which Mr. Tweed belonged. Those were days too—some time ago, I might point out—when newspapers were strongly partisan."

"But you continued to defend the so-called Tweed Ring after the evidence of larceny and general corruption were incontrovertible."

"Perhaps I did not think all of his attackers were wholly disinterested or that reformers generally are apt to offer more efficient or more honest government than their opponents."

It was the wrong answer, and as soon as he had spoken Gray knew it.

"You are against reform on principle?" suggested the lawyer quietly.

"I did not say that," was all that Gray could answer.

The lawyer smiled.

Gray, more at ease now that the worst of his fears had not materialized, at least to this point, and that the first passage was over, looked at the audience. He could recognize faces in what had first seemed only a blurred mass. Ventnor was watching him with an expressionless face. He was surprised to see C. J. Smith present, an inscrutable expression on his rather gentle face. Then he saw his office assistants. They looked worried. Their loyalty touched him.

"I take it," said the Committee's counsel offhandedly, "that you found the newspaper which you had at that time a profitable venture."

"I have not yet become a public charge!" snapped Gray.

Again it was the wrong answer. Sounds of amusement rose about him, and one man laughed aloud. The public impression and reiterated hope was that more than one witness would become an involuntary public charge as soon as Jerome decided who was to be indicted and tried.

Gray's questioner smiled in a self-satisfied way and made a point of refraining from comment.

"You are connected with the *Insurance Tribune?*"

"I am, sir."

"You are, in fact, its proprietor?"

"Yes."

"How long have you been the owner of the *Insurance Tribune?*"

"Eighteen—no, nineteen years."

Counsel's voice rose, and he spoke more rapidly.

"Is it not a fact that in this paper throughout the whole of this Committee's investigation you have consistently defended the life insurance companies and their officials despite evidence of extravagance, financial mismanagement, favoritism, attempts to bribe public officials, and general betrayal of the public trust?"

"I have tried," said Gray, clipping off each word, "to defend a socially useful institution against attempts to destroy it, and men of integrity against unfair insinuations, malicious slander by the sensational press, misinterpretation of actions taken in good faith, and public condemnation by the inexpert and uninformed."

He had scored this time, and he knew it. A gasp ran through the room. Armstrong, who had been watching the witness thoughtfully, looked genuinely surprised. The faces of other Committeemen had reddened.

The pursy lawyer was chagrined. He was evidently searching for words. He started to speak. One of the Committee interrupted harshly.

"I would like to ask the witness a question."

Counsel bowed.

"Mr. Hughes," said the Committee member sternly to Andrew Gray, "has commented several times on the extreme fairness which is being shown in this investigation. Comment generally has been favorable. Do you disagree?"

The man's face was honest. His pride had been hurt. He was one of the upstate legislators, and his indignation seemed genuine.

"I did not mean to imply that," said Gray quietly.

"Do you think this investigation was ordered because the life insurance companies have been perfect and the conduct of their officers above reproach?" The man's tone was angrier.

"Few things are perfect, and the conduct of few men is beyond reproach. Yet there is nothing which cannot be attacked and perhaps destroyed."

"What *did* you mean, then?"

"I believe that there were abuses in the conduct of life insurance which needed correction, and that this investigation has shown what some of them are."

The Committee member snorted while the lawyer smiled derisively. Gray ignored the lawyer and watched the legislator. It came over him suddenly and to his surprise that he rather liked the man. Obviously he was uneducated, but he seemed intelligent and honest.

The man seemed to sense Gray's approval, and his face showed a curiosity.

"Go on," he said.

"You wish further expression of what is merely my opinion?"

"Go on!" The man gestured impatiently.

"I believe, then," said Gray firmly, "that the basic causes which resulted in this investigation lie deeper than anything which has been brought forward here. There has been, as you know, widespread clamor against the so-called 'trusts.' There, again, there has been undoubted cause for legitimate complaint, but these complaints have been fomented by writers in the popular magazines and in the sensational press into an indiscriminate hatred of all that is big and successful in business. These men, in my estimation, have shown even less regard for public good and more for private gain than the men and institutions they accuse."

The Committee member looked puzzled. The lawyer shuffled his papers impatiently. Armstrong wished that Hughes was present to deal with a difficult and time-consuming witness.

Gray raised his eyebrows to his interrogator who nodded, his alert eyes fixed on Gray's face. With an odd sense that this had become a private conversation between them, Gray continued.

"It is envious human nature, I suppose, to try to destroy what men of stature have accomplished. There is human delight in destruction and in humbling the pretentious. Putting the intelligent and effective on trial by the ineffective and subjecting them to public ridicule is one way of accomplishing it. I have always disliked seeing producers pilloried by those who have never produced and never could produce anything of value to anyone."

"So you think these big insurance men"— the legislator stumbled as though he had wanted to say "scoundrels"—"should be allowed to do as they like?" he asked hotly.

"No."

The man was satisfied. He nodded to Armstrong.

"If we may get back to the facts," suggested counsel sarcastically. "Have you also found the *Insurance Tribune* a profitable undertaking?"

"Reasonably profitable," said Gray pleasantly. The point of real danger was well past. He had said what he wanted to say, placed his protest on record. He felt strong and confident.

"You have accepted and published advertising from the Apex Life Insurance Company by which you are also retained as a publicity writer?"

"Yes."

"You have also run reading notices—disguised advertising actually —favorable to that company?"

"Some that were favorable, some not so favorable. I have done the same thing for other companies selling life insurance."

"And been paid for publishing them?"

"In some instances."

"And sold Apex and these other companies quantities of reprints for distribution as advertising?" The lawyer was unsmiling, but his satisfaction was evident.

"Yes."

"How many would you sell, on the average?"

"You have the records."

The lawyer read triumphantly from his notes. "Ten thousand, twenty thousand, forty thousand on occasion," he told the Committee. "How does such practice conform with your announced conception of business ethics?" he asked Gray.

"It conforms with established usage on the part of the companies and the trade press generally."

"Would it surprise you that these established practices may soon be changed?"

"No," said Gray honestly.

Abruptly his questioner shifted grounds.

"Do you know or have you met 'Judge' Andrew Hamilton?"

"I have met him."

"Where?"

"In New York."

"Never in Albany?"

"Occasionally in Albany," Gray was forced to admit.

"Do you also know, or have you known, Andrew C. Fields of Mutual?"

"Yes."

"Did you ever visit the so-called 'House of Mirth,' the house which it has been established was maintained in Albany by one of the insurance companies as a lobbying headquarters?"

"Never."

"Was that not because Apex maintained in Albany a separate establishment of its own?"

"No."

"Is it not the truth that you were actually in charge of this house for the Apex Life Insurance Company?"

"No such place existed."

"How much did Apex contribute to the activities of Mr. Hamilton and Mr. Fields—both of whom, unfortunately, are abroad for their health."

The cue was sure-fire. Laughter rang through the room. Looking annoyed at repetition of the worn joke, Armstrong rapped for order.

"Nothing."

"You are certain of that."

"To the best of my knowledge—nothing."

"Wasn't that," inquired Gray's tormentor gently, "because you yourself were the Albany agent for Apex, the counterpart of Mr. Hamilton and Mr. Fields."

"I have been stationed in New York City during all of my connection with the Apex Life Insurance Company."

"And you have never been in Albany . . ." The lawyer paused.

"Many times." It could easily be proved that he had been.

". . . Attempting to influence legislation, disbursing funds where they might prove most useful to your company?"

Further evasion would be useless.

"The assumed naïveté concerning lobbying in all its forms, as practiced for many years by interested groups of all kinds, which has obtained throughout these proceedings, has seemed to me incredible and hypocritical!" Gray burst out.

"May I remind you, Mr. Gray," said the lawyer happily, "that there is such a thing as contempt of this Committee?"

Gray bowed.

"It is a fact, then, that your work for Apex has been the same as that of Andrew Hamilton and Andrew C. Fields for the companies they represented?"

"I am in charge of newspaper, magazine, and pamphlet adver-tising for the Apex Life Insurance Company—in charge of all of its publicity."

"The Committee knows that. But have you not also acted as Apex's agent in other ways to promote the welfare of the institution of life insurance, which you claim so to revere, and the interests of Apex in particular?" The lawyer's tone was mocking.

Gray did not respond.

"We find here under date of February 10, 1897," said the lawyer, consulting his notes again, "records of an expenditure by Apex of $20,000 for 'general advertising.' How was that money expended?"

"I assume for newspaper or magazine space, or for pamphlet publication."

The lawyer read off similar records for dates over a period of years, some of them for smaller, some for larger amounts. "All of this money," he asked unpleasantly, "was spent for legitimate advertising?"

"I assume that it was."

"How does it happen then that inclusion of these amounts brings the total of Apex's advertising expenditures to a much higher total than amounts given in the company's statements?"

"I neither keep nor audit the company's accounts."

"But you have disbursed Apex's funds—policyholders' money—on occasion?"

"I have sometimes spent company money as seemed advisable. I was empowered to do so."

"You mean you disbursed it as you were instructed by your superiors?"

It might do Ventnor no good, but assertion to the contrary would help no one. He himself, Gray realized, was beyond help now.

"No!"

"You were wholly responsible for such lobbying use of company funds?"

"I was wholly responsible for disbursements made for all of the company's advertising and publicity."

The lawyer was nettled.

"Perhaps," he suggested desperately, "because your experience and association with members of the Tweed Ring, and other corrupt fig-ures in public life, made your talents in that direction well known and useful to the executives of the Apex Life Insurance Company."

Armstrong broke in quickly.

"Perhaps we should stick to the facts, Mr. Counsel!"

The pursy lawyer flushed vividly. There had been no precedent for such public rebuke in all the previous hearings.

"Your contention is that you were a principal rather than a mere agent in Apex' attempts to influence insurance legislation pending before committee or up for consideration and vote by the legislature of the State of New York?"

"I admit to practices long recognized and used not only in Albany, but also in other state capitals," said Gray boldly.

"You hold that what you claim is a customary procedure justifies such actions?"

"I know of no other way in which actions and beliefs become socially sanctioned."

"The law thinks differently," threatened the lawyer, still smarting under Armstrong's rebuke.

More names, dates, and sums were brought forward. Gray answered questions mechanically. He felt very tired. The points had been made. The lawyer had made his. He had made his own. Whether or not he was being proved a criminal he was not sure. He did not feel he had been proved a fool.

The lawyer indicated finally that he had finished. His smugness had returned. He sat down solidly, satisfied with his achievement. Gray looked toward the Committee to see whether hc had been dismissed. Armstrong was about to speak when the same Committee member who had interrupted before broke in again.

"You still believe the things you said before—that this investigation is doing more harm than good? You think life insurance is really pretty sound and that some of these insurance presidents and their help are doing all right?"

"I don't think," said Gray, "that press exaggerations, or even legislative action which may follow on the findings of this Committee, will cure all the evils of the world or even of life insurance."

The man was not without humor of his own. He ignored the chairman's obvious wish to terminate the session, Jerome's frown, and the pursy lawyer's stare.

"You don't think that the elected representative: of the people, the politicians, are smarter and more honest than everybody else?"

"Until now," smiled Gray, "that has not been my experience."

The man grinned back and looked as though he would like to say 'or mine either.' He sat down, and Armstrong announced a recess until the next morning.

The crowd was already leaving. Their backs were toward Gray as stiffly he climbed down from the platform. A few men faced him. One was Ventnor. Other Apex men thrust out their hands as he neared, and Gray, smiling wryly, shook hands with each of them. One reporter hesitated, then turned and hurried after his fellows.

Ventnor looked embarrassed. "Andrew, I—well, thanks."

Gray shook his head slightly, smiling affectionately.

C. J. Smith was waiting unobtrusively near the door.

"You came to see my performance, Andrew," he said, "so I thought I should reciprocate. Fun, isn't it? I think you performed better than I."

"No," said Gray, as they walked together down the steps of City Hall and into the park.

" 'The punishment of men who have accomplished by men who have never done anything and never can.' I agree. You put it better than I could have done."

"It's what I meant."

"Moral indignation and self-righteousness," said Smith musingly. "I could never abide them. They're the unforgivable sin. I've found them nauseating and cruel always. Cruelty and stupidity usually go hand in hand."

Already they were just two more men in an incurious passing throng. Gray looked comically disappointed. The effort was almost too much. He felt exhausted. "Is this the way all matinee idols are treated?"

"Disappointing, isn't it," said Smith soberly. "Look!"

A stalwart, red-bearded man hurried past into City Hall. It was Charles Evans Hughes returning from wherever he had been.

C. J. raised his hat to the broad back. *Morituri te salutamus!* he murmured. "Let's have dinner somewhere tomorrow night—not at the Press Club. By that time the papers will have had their chance at you. We can compare press notices."

"Fine!"

Gray turned blindly away as Smith left. He was glad to be alone. For moments he walked slowly and unseeingly across the Plaza. Then he quickened his step and hurried toward the Third Avenue Elevated, stopping first to buy a small bouquet of late flowers from an old woman who sat on a campstool surrounded by her wares.

They had escaped! What he had most feared had not happened. He could not tell her so, but Emily would know when she saw him. What one most feared seldom happened. Perhaps there was decency in the confusion of things after all. Perhaps beauty, unawares, had its own safeguards. A kind of elation seized him. For the first time in months he felt really free.

The Negro doorman at Emily's apartment house smiled broadly. "Ah ring Miz Stapely you heah."

"No, I'll surprise her," said Gray.

Jimmy, the elevator boy, sniffed at his flowers.

"Nice posies," he offered. "That's what my maw calls 'em."

Gray pressed the mother-of-pearl button at Emily's door. He almost swayed with fatigue as he stood there, but a smile lighted his face. For seconds there was silence. He pressed the button again.

There were hurried footsteps then, but they were not Emily's. It was Ellen who opened the door. She looked flustered and confused. Several white dresses were draped over her arm.

"Oh, Mist' Gray! Ah thought maybe 'twas Miz Emily."

"She's not at home then?" Gray tried to hide his disappointment, but he could not hide it from himself.

"She been in Brooklyn all night. Ah come back this mawnin' git some things. Ah—"

"Perhaps she'll be back shortly."

"She say to tell you she be back this evenin' foah a little while. Then she—"

Gray hardly heard her. He felt lost and abandoned. He had been so sure as he rode uptown that Emily would be home. It seemed to him now that he had just been trying to hold on to his strength until he could reach her side.

He gestured awkwardly with the flowers. The hand which held them began to shake slightly.

Ellen noticed. She shifted the dresses in her arm to take them. "Y'all come in an' sit down while ah git some tea or some whiskey."

Gray shook his head and swallowed. He could not bear to stay there alone.

"Thank you, Ellen. I'll return."

"Ah put 'em in watah right away," Ellen promised. "Miz Emily be back. She—" But Gray had gone.

He went home. He did not know where else to go. The stern-looking nurse came to meet him as soon as he had let himself into the darkened hall.

"Mrs. Gray is finally asleep," she said accusingly. "The doctor had to give her an extra sedative. You'll be quiet, won't you."

Gray nodded, not trusting himself to speak. He climbed the thickly carpeted stairs, his legs aching at every step.

For a moment he looked out of the window of his study at the familiar street, the roofs of other houses, the three black lines of wire which slanted at a sharp angle across the strip of sky. To his surprise, a small bird, which should have known enough to leave for the south weeks before, was perched on the middle wire. The bird seemed to look back at him. Either it had forgotten the date or was staying on in Manhattan for reasons of its own. Probably the thoughts and actions of birds were as senselessly complicated as those of men.

Slowly Gray turned. He began to take off his clothes. He ran a full tub of warm water in the adjoining bathroom, bathed, and dressed carefully in fresh underclothes, socks, shirt, and a different suit. He adjusted his single pearl pin carefully in a dark-blue cravat of rich and heavy silk. He took a different hat, brushed it, went down the stairs, and out of the house which had been his home yet not his home for so many years.

He tried not to think, not even to think of where he could go. He could go to the *Tribune*. There was always work to do there. It was haven as well as familiar enterprise. No, he could not go even there. They would have to write and set the story of the day's developments at the Armstrong investigation without his help or interference this time. He could go to Oriental Importers where jade, ivory, and silk had so often soothed, but he had no wish to go there.

Almost an hour later, Gray found himself seated alone on a bench on the Hudson near Grant's Tomb. Some said the tomb was a hideous monstrosity. Others exclaimed over its grandeur and impressive beauty. Grant, the hero—Grant the dupe of the corruptionists of an earlier day!

It was between five and six o'clock. The nurses and their perambulators, the romping children, the fat women who walked their unpleasant little dogs along Riverside Drive had all gone home. It was getting dark. Gray looked across to the blue-shadowed Palisades. A tug was pulling a string of barges up the middle of the wide Hudson. A ferry, its lights twinkling, was making its way slowly back from Fort Lee to its 129th Street slip.

Honesty was not enough, nor cleverness, nor tenderness, passion, pity, intellect, conviction, selfishness, nor sacrifice. He was not naïve. He had never thought they were. But he had half hoped . . . for what he did not know, only that it was not for this. A man had to hope, for cynicism was admitting the failure of himself or of life without attempting to live.

A small dog trotted up and looked at him from three feet away. It was a dusty fox terrier with one running eye and one inquiring eye and a stump for a tail. It trotted away again, expressing nothing. A small boy, following the dog, repeated the performance in every detail save the flick of a tail as he left.

Never before had Andrew Gray felt so tired or quite so alone. He had bought three of the evening papers as he left the subway, but not yet looked at them. He was not afraid, but tired. He opened one with some difficulty against the wind and read the account of his appearance as though it spoke of someone strange and removed.

APEX' PHILOSOPHIC MESSENGER,

read the subhead under

MORE DISCLOSURES AT THE INSURANCE INVESTIGATION.

The account began:

> Andrew Gray, self-styled advertising and publicity man for Apex Life, described with cynical effrontery the ethics of corrupting legislators, terming them accepted practice in business circles. Stunned by the witness's bold assertion that the Armstrong Investigation is doing more harm than good, the Committee and its Assistant Counsel were forced to listen to a diatribe which for pure depravity matched anything encountered thus far in any session of the Investigation. It speaks much for the patience and forbearance with which this Investigation is being conducted...

In another of the papers Gray found himself

> An emissary of the Insurance Interests, glib and skilled in corruption, who brazenly defended the insurance malefactors as he had once defended Boss Tweed. In both cases, obviously, his motives were the same; profit first, last, and always.

The tone of this story modified, however, as it went on, as though the writer was not too sure of his grounds. It referred to Gray later as a well-known writer and newspaperman of established reputation whose connection with insurance was only one of many interests.

The most conservative of the three evening newspapers reported his testimony in full, with little comment. Gray discovered why. He had been made subject of the lead editorial.

> An unusual session of the Armstrong Investigation was marked this afternoon by the first absence of Mr. Hughes and the presence of a thoughtful witness, some of whose remarks are worthy of serious consideration. Taken with the seriousness which they deserve, they might well have a salutary effect on the further conduct of the Investigation and whatever legislative action is taken later.
>
> Mr. Gray dealt not only with factual details, courageously admitting full responsibility for acts which, if habitual, are difficult

to condone, but also with concepts, political and social, underlying an investigation such as this. Some of his ideas seem old-fashioned, as when he intimated that the public does not have the moral right to ask the officers of a public trust for an accounting of their actions and practices.

Other thoughts which Mr. Gray expressed are distinctly modern and pertinent. Hysteria and frenzy do not create the proper atmosphere for judicial procedure and calm decisions, and we must admit that certain sections of the press have been guilty of creating most of this hysteria. The accomplishments of the officers of the life insurance companies should be recognized and acknowledged as fully as their shortcomings. It should, in the end, be recognized that the conduct of life insurance, as of any other business, is safer in the hands of trained experts than in those of untrained and inexperienced legislators, no matter how zealous they may be in the performance of their duties, and idealistic in their beliefs.

Gray felt better, miraculously better! All that he had dared say had not fallen on deaf ears. There was the Committeeman who had seemed to agree with him, in part at least, and there was this editorial writer. Gray thought he knew who it was, for he had seen the man at the press table that afternoon. It was a man whose judgment he respected.

It was getting darker and colder. Gray stood up. He folded the first two newspapers and stuffed them neatly between the slats of the bench seat. The third, after a second's hesitation, he put into the side pocket of his overcoat. He looked about him. A carriage with its top up rolled quietly by, its rubber-treaded tires noiseless on the dark macadam and asphalt of the Drive. Two four-wheelers creaked by in the opposite direction. Several motors, driven by leather-capped and begoggled chauffeurs had passed while he sat there.

The lights of the Claremont shone invitingly from the windows of the old hostelry set back on its deep and darkening lawn. Gray realized that he had scarcely eaten all day, eaten little for several days. It was still early, but he was hungry. He thought of rare roast beef, wine, black coffee, a cigar. Erect and his step vigorous, he walked across a deserted cement path between winter-browned stretches of grass. One of the carriages he had seen was stopping at the Claremont, and the coachman was helping his fares dismount.

It was nearly nine o'clock when Gray returned to Emily's. Ellen admitted him again. She looked subdued, made as if to speak, thought better of it, and simply took his coat and hat and silently disappeared.

Gray found Emily seated in a tapestry-covered chair near the curio cabinet.

Her face, half in shadow, was perfectly still. Her hair was simply, almost severely dressed. She wore a plain gown which was one of his favorites—and her eyes were deep with suffering.

She did not move as Gray went straight to her and placed his hands on her shoulders.

"Andrew!" she breathed, putting up her hands to cover his. "Andrew!"

"I know, Emily," he said in a voice almost as low.

"Ellen told me you had come—and I wasn't here! I saw a newspaper. I had been waiting, Andrew. I—" She stood to hold him.

"I know," he said again. "But it didn't happen. I mean—there was nothing—"

"You're all right?" She touched his face.

"Yes, Emily."

She released him and sat abruptly.

"It—it's Will, too, Andrew. There was an accident. He's been hurt—terribly hurt! I was in Brooklyn. I must go right back!"

Chapter 62

"IT'S NO USE," said James bitterly. He had just come in from the hospital for the third time that day. "It's no use. No good, no good, no good. Billings will have to amputate. He doesn't want to, but he'll have to."

It had been too ghastly a wound, too splintered a break. Despite all their efforts, infection had set in. The dreaded gangrene had followed. They had fought frantically to keep Will alive, and more than once it had seemed impossible. James and Emily had seen him racked with unendurable pain, fighting in delirium, a stricken animal battling for survival. They had seen him drugged and exhausted, his pulse barely perceptible. There had been nights when none of them could be sure there would be a morning for Will.

"Stop biting your thumb, James," said Laura.

James ripped his thumb angrily from between his teeth.

"Things seemed to be going better for a while yesterday. Now he's so full of poison again, it's a wonder he doesn't burn up. He wouldn't be alive at all if he hadn't been such a healthy young ass."

"Will may still be all right," tried Laura. "He—"

"Try not to be such a damned fool! If we don't amputate, he'll continue to suffer, and then he'll be dead. Billings has *got* to operate tomorrow. I couldn't reach him from the hospital, but I will tonight. I'll have Knight there too. If Billings won't do it, I'll do it myself."

"There were patients waiting for you most of the afternoon. Mrs. Green called. Her boy is worse. I had to tell her, finally, to send for Dr. Summers. James, I know it's Will and all that, but you can't keep letting everything else go. Why, you could lose your practice!"

"I can get another practice, but where's Will going to get another leg?" James glared at his wife, hatred in his eyes. "I'm going down to tell Mother."

"I was only trying to calm you! I'll go with you."

James relented.

"Should have cut it off a month ago," he said grimly, as they went along. "Been a clean job. Could have saved more of the leg."

"You couldn't have known."

"Stump'll be too short. Not enough healthy flesh to lap over the bone."

They found Mary and Ann about to have a late supper. Both had been at the hospital most of the afternoon, where Emily was in attendance. Will had not known them. Their faces were strained and tight. They wore house aprons over street clothes. Mary's was starched and spotless. Ann's was clean but rumpled, and there was a dark brown stain on one cuff. It was evident she had been doing the hasty cooking.

Once she had recovered from the childbirth and the first shock of Will's accident, Ann had surprised them all by her courage and competence. She had taken hold of household affairs with practical effectiveness. Yet she was essentially unchanged. Her quick eyes saw everything, and her darting tongue was only leashed.

As though he wanted to get it over with before he lost his own courage, James told them what he had come to say. Laura watched anxiously.

Mary's fine-featured face went very white and still. The skin drawn over the fragile structure of her face seemed almost translucent. She sat erect before the untouched food.

For a moment she did not speak.

"I see," she said desolately, her lips tightening as she looked straight ahead. Then she added gently, "We all trust your judgment,

James." She did not lift her eyes, half-hooded by their blue-veined lids.

Ann was a different matter. She stood in the doorway between the dining room and the kitchen with the tea kettle in her hand, steam hissing from its spout. She turned, banged the kettle down hard on the black stone sink, and returned.

"But he'll be a cripple! Will a cripple! What will become of him? How can a man with one leg take care of his family? Oh, poor Will!"

"Now, now, Ann," comforted Mary. "You've been so good and so strong all through this that you must not give up now. It's hard on all of us, you know."

"I know, I know, I know, but you're not married to him! You're not his wife! Oh, Will! How can you do this to him?"

"You can have him with one leg or you can have him dead," said James brutally.

"If you and the others had taken care of him properly," blazed Ann, "he'd be well now and home! What did you *do* to him? What *did* you do?"

"I'm off to find Billings," said James abruptly.

"I'll stay a little while," Laura whispered.

"Perhaps, Ann," said Mary clearly, her voice stronger so that James heard before he left, "you should think over what I have suggested several times. It might be better for all of us if you and Will separated now. It *will* be hard for you tied to a cripple." She forced out the last hated word bitterly.

"Will is *mine!* You'll never get him away from me, no matter how hard you try—never!" Ann danced in the doorway in a paroxysm of rage, grief, and self-pity. "I'll go down to him tonight and take the baby with me. Other people will realize. They'll not put me out!"

"There, there," soothed Laura, hurrying across to Ann and putting her arms around her. She nodded sharp dismissal to James who stood, red-faced, near the door. "You're just very, very tired, and no wonder, and this isn't doing Will or any of us any good. Come now, let's have our supper."

The amputation was performed almost too late. It was dark before James came home the next night.

"Billings did a neat job, and I think—anyway, Will knew nothing about it." James looked ruinously tired as he sat on the edge of the couch in the dining room tugging at his shoelaces.

"I stayed all day with your mother and Ann. Ann quieted down after last night, poor girl. They were good—but it was awful!"

James dragged his legs up and stretched out full length on the couch. He stared at the ceiling unblinkingly. Then he closed his eyes.

"Then Will will come back to consciousness and realize that—" Laura could not go on.

James did not answer.

None of them except James was allowed to see Will for unreal days of torturing suspense. Even Emily who had worked with the nurses and as a nurse in caring for him before the operation was kept away. For untold days Will lay doped or in a stupor. Then he writhed in agony as sedatives wore off, for the poisons were still being drained from his ravaged and mutilated body.

There was a whole winter, gray and salt-cold along the vicious Brooklyn water front, of which Will knew little. His own world, when he grew conscious of it again, was far removed from any he had known or suspected before the accident.

It was the smells of phenol and formaldehyde, ether, iodoform, food, sweat, gangrenous exudations, flowers, and his mother's dress or Emily's starched white uniform as she bent over his bed. It was the feel of the coarse hospital sheets and gowns, the cold iron of his bed, the bedpans, and the basins. It was the screams, moans, and strangled whispers that cut through the nights, the footsteps of the nurses, Emily's hand moving before his face, the growl of James's voice. It was the sight of blood and pus-stained dressings. It was the horror of waking each time to realization of where and what he was and of desperately trying to crawl back into the warm oblivion of sleep.

Once when he came to consciousness in the cold, gray daylight of early morning, Emily was there, as he had known somehow that she was always there. Back deep in the swaying and throbbing darkness, he had planned what he was going to say.

He drew on all his strength to speak, and Emily, her face creased with fatigue but her eyes lighted to see him conscious, bent close to listen.

Will tried to grin, though his face was tight and his lips were cracked and parched.

"Don't look like that, Em," he jibed. "Whose leg did they cut off, anyway?"

Then Emily's face blurred and faded as he slumped back into the darkness again.

As the strength began to seep back tentatively into Will's wasted body and sharpness to stab back into his mind, he steeled himself to see them, fearful of what their faces would say. Only James and one nurse, for Emily had been home in an exhausted sleep, knew of the night when he had cursed them for not letting him die, then burst into helpless sobbing. He begged them to let none of the others come, to let no one see him. He was a helpless, useless cripple. They had not been able to quiet him.

He was calmer when Mary came, and he saw her clearly for the first time. Dignity and composure were in her face as always. Her bright eyes were tired but did not admit rebuff. She tried to act as though Will had caught another bad cold, but she had plenty of goose grease and camphor stored away in the pantry of the house on the hill, and honey and licorice for his cough.

Will shrank from her only once.

"Ann will bring the baby tomorrow. She wanted to bring him today, but I persuaded her not to. The baby is fine."

"No, please don't let her! Please, don't, Ma!" Will's voice rose shrill with alarm. His face wrinkled as though he were about to cry again.

"Ann has been very unselfish in letting me come all these times while she has stayed with the baby, though she wanted to come herself. She takes wonderful care of him."

"Yes, but not yet," insisted Will. "Not yet!"

Nightmare and delusion, weakness and false strength, hope, gratitude, and horrible fear. He wondered how he could have lived so long and learned so little. Other men had been boys, and then they had grown up. He had never grown up. Too suddenly he had had to learn everything: pain, fear, hope, life, and nearly death. Perhaps he could begin now. Perhaps his fall had wiped out the formless past.

When Ann came again, he knew that it had not.

In some way which the others could not understand and he could not understand himself, Ann loved him. He was necessary to Ann, and, as she had so often told him, she had no one and nothing else. He had taken or accepted, he did not know which. He was bound. Ann's might be a selfish love, but it was as binding on him as though he loved her. He was not sure that he did not.

Ann laughed and cried. Her vital face was suffused with conflicting emotions. There was joy at his recovery, pain at his hurt, pride in her possession, courage for the future, panic fear, and calculation in her eyes.

"We'll have our own place somewhere," she planned, "where the others can't bother us. I'll do everything I can."

"Some day perhaps," said Will doubtfully.

"And if you every try to leave me," Ann threatened merrily, her eyes moist but her mouth hard, "I'll take a room right across the street where you will see me every day and the baby, too."

"Perhaps there won't be a room there!"

"I'll find one."

"I'll get a job," Will promised fiercely, "some kind of a job. We'll make out somehow once I can get out of here. We'll be all right."

"You'll have to go now, I'm afraid, Mrs. Stapely," said Will's nurse coming in.

"You'd better, Ann," said Emily, who had come in with the girl. She pressed Ann's arm gently.

The nurse was a pretty, dark-haired girl. Except for Emily, she was in some ways the person he knew best now in all the world. Even James admitted that Eunice Sperry was one of the finest nurses he had seen. Laura had told Mary she was sure Will and Eunice were in love. Mary had understood and even tried to plan.

Ann looked at the girl.

"You're the famous Miss Sperry, I suppose. We seem to have just missed each other so often." She made the statement an accusation.

"I'm Eunice Sperry," said the girl softly. "We've seen each other before, though somehow it was usually one of the other nurses when you came." She smiled. "Isn't our patient getting along famously?" Her eyes sought Emily's. They did not like the tense, excited look on Will's face.

"My husband," said Ann distinctly, "will soon be home where I can look after him properly."

Will flushed miserably as they all went out and twitched to get his stump into more comfortable position. His lips twisted and tightened back over his teeth as he remembered what it had looked like the last time the dressings were changed. He had wanted to get away from it, to disown it. It was no real part of him, could never be.

He came to learn that his stump, as though it had a life of its own, insisted on trying to pretend it was a whole leg. It tried to take steps he could not make, the nerves leaping forward of their own volition. The sensation sickened him. His stump refused to know that it was a mutilated abortion, and Will hated it as a separate entity.

Agnes brought Rhoda, and the tall schoolgirl stared at Will with great, dark, sympathetic eyes. She cried when Agnes said finally that they had to go home. Next time, she said, she would come with her father. Then they could stay as long as they liked, because he was a doctor.

One day Laura left Martha with him while she went into the corridor in search of James. Martha was now a pretty blonde and blue-eyed little girl, beautifully dressed, her delicately colored face alight with Laura's intelligence, though it was shaped like the Stapelys'.

As soon as her mother was out of the room, the child slipped from the chair in which she had been sitting carefully so as not to disarrange her dress and came over to Will's bed.

"What did they do with it, Uncle Will?" she whispered quickly.

"Do? Do with what?"

The child looked down at his bed.

"You know," she breathed hurriedly, looking at the door for fear of Laura's return. "With—it!"

"Oh, why I don't know!"

"Did they bury it?"

Martha scuttled back to her chair as James and Laura came in. James looked critically at his brother.

"H'mph," he observed, evidently satisfied by what he saw. "You're going to owe me quite a bill for all this."

He looked acutely embarrassed when Will answered seriously.

"I know, Bones," he said humbly. "I know you don't mean money —I never have any anyway—but you pulled me through, didn't you? I've heard Billings and Knight talk, and you should hear Eunice."

"Damndest nonsense I ever heard!" said James. "Perhaps I owe you a little for some things. I—forget it!"

Laura drew her breath in sharply. The hurt to Will had crystallized all the force and anger in James. He had fought off death for Will, and he'd fight for life for him. There was a new purposefulness and decisiveness in James's words and actions.

"And I'm going to get that stump into shape so you can wear an artificial leg, no matter what anyone says. I've got an idea for a contraption to draw the flesh into place. By God—!"

"Don't swear before Martha," said Laura mechanically.

"Oh, I know lots of words," Martha assured them from where she sat with her small, white-stockinged legs dangling over the edge of the chair. " 'Damn,' 'scaredy-cat,' 'hell,' 'by God'—"

Laura, red-faced, grasped her quickly, and Martha let out a surprised squeal.

Will's dreams were the worst. He dreamed of racing like a deer along South Avenue in Ilium, twisting and dodging up the steep hillsides, and in and out of the stinking alleys behind the saloons. He dreamed of climbing trees, throwing a leg over a limb and pulling himself up with no more effort than it takes a bird to fly. He dreamed of running across the fields and hills behind the house in South Ilium, looking backward and letting out string fast to get his kite to dart surely to the sun. He saw himself stumbling over a stone

or a woodchuck's hole and hardly pausing before he sped sure-footedly on.

He could never get the kite fully into the air. It knifed down just when it seemed about to soar. It dragged on last year's tall, brown grass, caught in the juniper clumps or the alder brush, and tore itself on fence posts.

Waking always brought back stabbing reality.

"What *can* a half-man do?" he demanded bitterly of Eunice. "Get some pencils and a tin cup and lay his cap on the sidewalk with the rest of the beggars? I wonder if anybody has that spot at Fulton and DeKalb? Lot of people go past there."

"You mustn't talk that way, Will! And you mustn't let your mother or the doctor—or Mrs. Stapely—hear you either. *Please* don't say things like that!"

"There are so many things I must not do, aren't there?" But Will was ashamed. "I can't help it sometimes."

"I know you can't," said the girl softly. "Besides," she said inconsequentially, "there's the little baby—your son."

"I asked Ann not to bring him here," said Will harshly. "She wanted to. I don't want to see it—him."

"Perhaps that's best," said the girl sagely. "I must do things, but I'll be back." She went out quickly.

Will was asleep the next time Andrew Gray came.

It was an occasion. Emily, who had not been in her flat in almost two months and who had worn scarcely any dress but her nurse's uniforms, had gone to New York to return with him. She felt rested and refreshed in her own clothes, and she meant her appearance with Gray to show Will how much he had advanced.

Gray looked down at Will and was ashamed. Here was the cleansing reality. His own petty discomforts were as nothing.

Ventnor was through. He had not been able to resign as he had planned. He was broken, smashed, dazed, and he would never come back. Young Hyde was safe in France. Others were there. The Mc-Curdys were out of Mutual. Poor old John McCall of New York Life, who just the year before had been lecturing proudly on insurance at Yale, had been thrown into the discard like a soiled rag. Scores of lesser men, some of them dupes, a few of them accomplished rascals, most of them neither one nor the other, had been tossed into the streets. Charles Evans Hughes, riding the wave of righteousness triumphant and the swells of popular applause, was on his way to the governorship of New York.

Gray himself had no more connection with Apex. Jerome showed no signs of prosecuting him, as he might well have done. As usual,

Gray realized, he had escaped. Yet he could not pretend, even to himself, that he had not been shaken.

Today the easy courtesy and the humor of his manner seemed to have a forced jauntiness behind them. He watched Emily as she tiptoed across the room and whispered to Eunice Sperry. It was always Will. Emily did not know it, but Will always came first.

Gray, who found work on his *Tribune* savorless, who found that he could not write as he wished and that even the jades at the Fifth Avenue shop did not appease, felt a pang of jealousy. More than ever he had needed Emily, but she had not been there. She had been with Will. He understood now some of what she had suffered alone when she needed him.

The next time they were able to return together, they found Will sitting in a chair for the first time. It was a wheel chair which had been set near the window in the late winter sun. Will wore a dark robe which hid the emaciation of his shoulders, neck, and chest, and the lower part of his body was swathed in a tartan robe which he and Emily had brought back from Scotland.

Emily, who had been there in the morning, then raced home to bathe and change and wait for Andrew felt almost too happy as she looked at Will. She had worked to the point of exhaustion and beyond. She had watched over him asleep and awake. Life had demanded all of her through Will, all that she had had to choke back for so long. She had been there through it all. She had seen the worst ugliness of illness and the aftermath of terrible surgery, conquered her repugnance, and helped heal the ugliness away. She had found she could meet the worst and face it down. She had been strong, and she marveled at it. She could help Andrew in his hurt now, as she had helped Will and would always help.

"Doesn't he look different today!" cried Eunice proudly, as she ushered them in.

Emily assumed a critical expression.

"Thinks he's a lot, doesn't he?" she gibed in childhood accents.

"N'yah!" retorted Will unpleasantly.

"Just because Pa fell off a roof, you didn't have to be a copy-cat."

"It was a bigger roof," boasted Will, "and I fell further."

"Progress," approved Andrew Gray. "And, as I've recently learned, you can't stop 'progress.' "

"I wish something had stopped me," said Will ruefully.

"You're fools, the two of you!" cried Emily, tears in her eyes. "My two good fools!"

"At least," Gray told Will, "yours was a decent tragedy. I've been slapped like a naughty boy and told to stand in the corner."

Will's eyes brightened. "Wasn't Jack Horner in the corner when he pulled out all the plums?" he demanded.

"By George, you're right! I'd not thought of that. Emily, will you bake me a good-sized pie?"

"I can't, and you know it, but Ellen might."

Will sat there after they had gone. He was very tired. He wished he could get back into the bed, but he could not do it alone. He would have to wait until Eunice returned. The humiliation tasted bitter in his mouth. He would always have to wait until someone came to help.

Eunice had returned, and he was safely in his bed when Mary came in quietly a little later. Too tired to speak just then, he smiled at her.

Mary took her chair and smiled back. She looked less tired than she had looked a few weeks before. Her eyes were courageous and clear. Her presence comforted. Will felt secure. No one could hurt him while his mother was there, and sight of her sent him asleep thinking of home—not of the Brooklyn house, but of *home*.

The house which Thomas had built on the hill always smelled of wood smoke and faintly of coal gas, of camphor, starch, Brussels carpet, kerosene, and furniture polish. Often there were the delicious smells of roasting meat or of new bread baking in a slow oven. Sometimes there was the damp smell of kneaded dough left to set overnight in a pan on one of the kitchen chairs. At other times there was the smell of wet clothes soaking in the tub and the sharp smell of strong washing soap, or of wet wool when coats were hung in the warm back entry to dry after someone had come in out of the rain. Sometimes his mother or Aunt Maria had scattered bits of cinnamon bark and allspice over the front of the hot stove after it had been blackened, and the incenselike smell of them as they burned was a sharp delight. There was the smell of Carlo's coat or the tangy fragrance when his mother dashed drops of Florida water on her handkerchief after she was dressed for church or a visit. The scent reached Will now and mingled with those other remembered smells that were the smells of warmth and home.

Often in a week-long spell of spring or autumn rain, when everything you touched was wet or damp, and the rain shone on the bright, new grass or on the fallen oak and maple leaves, the whole of South Ilium smelled to Will like the wet wool of his cap and stockings. In summer, when the sun poured richly warm on their hill and all the windows and doors were open, the smells of the warmed earth, of grass and flowers and tangled vines, were wafted through the house by the soft river wind. Then you could smell the curling split-oak shingles on the roof and the softening tar in the joints of the rain gutters around the chimney.

Always, too, for this was a carpenter's house, there was the pungent scent of fresh pine sawdust and of bright, hardwood shavings as they curled from his father's plane. Usually something was being painted. Acrid, clean smells of turpentine and other oils and of clayey pigments mingled with the other smells, like those of melting wax and steam as the weekly ironing was done.

Mary saw that Will was asleep. There was even the hint of a smile about his relaxed mouth. She put down the book she had brought and had been trying to read, though she had forgotten her spectacles. It was almost dark outside. James would soon be in to take her home. She closed her eyes, and what she saw was her father's great house in Gloucestershire.

The old part had been built so long ago, before the wars in Cromwell's time—she thought it was Cromwell. She saw the wide, sunny lawns on which she and Julia had played. They had used to catch the white and yellow butterflies which dodged about in spring, and they'd played hide-and-seek in the coolness of the well house where the cold, spring water ran in under thick masonry walls and out the little sluiceway into the brook.

There had been another great wall all along the outer edge of the lawns with roses climbing over it and the fruit vines trained there by old Joseph Winslow, the gardener. He had used to tip his hat, first wiping his hands on his smock, when her father came riding by.

Mary tried, but she could not remember her mother's face, just her tall, slender figure in a light summer dress, and her light laugh, and the soft fragrance of her hands as she touched their faces and their hair after calling them from play before sending them to Anna to be cleaned and dressed for tea—.

"Fine lazy pair!" said James gruffly. "Haven't you two anything to do but sleep all day?"

"I just closed my eyes for a moment," said Mary with great dignity.

She felt guilty. Only old people dozed off thinking of their childhood, and she was *not* old. There was enough to think about in the present and to plan for the future. She shook herself impatiently.

Chapter 63

JACK HOLLEY, his wide shoulders looking wider than ever in his blue serge suit and his strong outdoor face red from a quick after-work shave, had come with Ann this time. He had been coming every few days since he first swore his way past the doctors and nurses to see what the hell they thought they were doing to his man.

"There'll be a job for you, by God!" he told Will again. "All right, you can't go climbing ladders yet, but there's plenty for a good construction man to do on a job, and you're going to do it. The company got you into this. They've got to do something about it. I made Dickson promise."

"Expect me to be a damned timekeeper," asked Will, exasperated, "or a bookkeeper, or something like that?"

"What's the matter with that?" demanded Jack belligerently. "Somebody's got to keep track of things or they'll steal you blind. Learn to do drafting then. You can handle a blueprint now as good as I can."

"Ever notice," asked Will, "the train callers and sweepers around a railroad station. Most of them lost a leg or an arm or a head or something when they were brakemen or whatnot. The railroads give them some little job to keep them off the Bowery."

"Go ahead, you damned fool! Be sorry for yourself! All right, then. Get out of building. Go sit behind a desk somewhere and buy and sell stuff. That's the way to make money. All you do on a building job is work your heart out and die broke."

Jack glared disgust, but he had a point to make.

"Doc tells me you'll be out of here in a week or so. Once you're on your pins again—"

"My pin," corrected Will.

"All right!" roared Jack, "your pin!"

Ann could keep silent no longer.

"At least, Will," she said indignantly, "I think you might be serious about this. Mr. Holley is just trying to help. We must decide something."

Holley swore under his breath but not so far under his breath that he could not be heard.

"I sent you up on that stinking roof, didn't I? Besides, I've had

454

a hell of a time ever since you lay down on me. Everything's been going wrong on that job. I've needed you every damned day. Dickson seems to think I can do everything all by myself. Well, I can't, by God!"

Will watched Holley's red face, and he brightened in spite of himself. It was decent of Jack anyway.

"You see!" cried Ann happily.

Will smiled at her.

"We'll see," he promised. "There's plenty of time. I may just retire and be a millionaire. Say, I'm getting so I can navigate on these crutches like a house afire. Here, hand them to me. Watch this!"

The truth was that as the time neared for him to leave the hospital he was more and more afraid. He shrank from meeting the outside world again, the crowds, the curious stares, the knowledge of his pitiful inadequacy. Spring had come on. The horses would be running in the sun, and he could not even walk.

Others were planning for him too. In the cellar of his house James was sawing and nailing away clumsily at the contraption of wood and pulleys he had thought up to stretch and force Will's stump into shape. He had already—telling no one—been to the shop of the best maker of artificial legs he knew and told them what he wanted, ordering the best device anyone had been able to concoct.

Mary sat holding Will's child and thoughtfully watching Ann do up the supper dishes. It was her fault for ever having brought Ann into the household. Eunice Sperry was the kind of girl Will should have married. Her eyes narrowed slightly as she planned.

In the softly lighted, richly furnished flat in Manhattan Jim Garver, who had several times come down from Ilium to see Will, sat watching Emily. Emily had begun to spend part of her time in New York again, though she had not really moved back and would not until Will was home. It was evening, and she and Jim had talked for some time.

Jim hesitated now. It might sound presumptuous, and he did not want to sound presumptuous. Somehow he had to say all he felt.

"I know all you have done for Will. Will knows, too."

"Done for Will! It's what Will has always done for me, for all of us! Even by this horrible thing! James has outdone himself. He is a better doctor than he ever was. Agnes has been wonderful. I mean it. We've even come to appreciate qualities in Ann which we couldn't see before."

She stopped herself and laughed wryly, though there was still wonder in her eyes.

"Oh, we've not really changed. The archangels needn't fear the competition. But it was Will gave us the chance, and Will who paid for it. He said once that no one ever wins unless someone else loses."

"My father offered Will a job in the factory years ago," said Jim, almost hurriedly. "The offer is still good. I could use Will. Any factory would be glad to have a man like Will in charge of maintenance and construction. It would be perfect, Emily, all around."

"Oh, Jim!"

Emily wore a simple gown of light blue silk which she liked. Her hair, which Ellen had brushed and brushed to rest her, shone in the light which put soft shadows in the beauty of her face. The man ached to touch her.

He flushed slightly.

"It almost sounds like bribery, doesn't it?"

"No, it doesn't. It just sounds like you, Jim," said Emily fondly.

She watched his kind and thoughtful face. Only the intentness of Jim's eyes showed the force of the emotion he so carefully controlled. There was steadfastness and strength in Jim Garver, an utter dependability. Generations of wealth and responsibility showed in his bearing and quiet manner. Life with him would be simple and understandable. And for Will return to Ilium, even with Ann and the child, might be the best possible solution.

"I've always thought," said Jim, his eyes drinking in every detail of Emily's face, "that some day you would all come back to Ilium, and I've wanted you to come to me."

"There is never any going back for anyone, certainly not for me."

"I didn't say it very well perhaps. I meant—"

"It's not fair, Jim, to let you go on. There's so much you don't know and could never understand—about me, I mean."

"I know all I need to know," he pleaded. "The rest you can tell me or not tell me, if it would be better that way. I—please, Emily." His controlled expression gave way slightly. "You know I love you. You've always liked me. It's not impossible."

Emily shook her head, but the thoughts raced through her mind. It would be sensible to say 'yes' to Jim. It would be easy, for he was decent and good. Her position would be secure. Her marriage to Jim might mean everything to Will, security, another chance. Even their mother might be glad to return to Ilium now.

"Your place is beautiful, Emily," said Jim, looking about. "Like you."

Emily followed his glance. Everything she saw meant Andrew and a part of her life with Andrew, a world of beauty and emotion no

456

one else could ever understand. All the ecstasy, the pain, the lone-liness, the transport.

"Jim, don't plan on anything which—isn't likely to materialize." She started a tentative, helpless gesture, trying with her smile to take the hurt out of her words.

Jim sprang up, his eyes lighting, his face wholly unguarded.

"You're not sure, Emily. You were thinking. I know you were! It *would* be good for Will, though heaven knows the job is there for him whether you take on—this other job—or not. Believe me, Emily, you'd be happy. I *know* you would. So much has changed. Mr. Gray can't always—well, he's no longer young, Emily. He's had a bad blow, and I'm sorry for I like him. There's been so much pain and confusion for you. I understand, honestly, I do. I want to make up for it."

He spoke rapidly. Emily was moved, as she was surprised, by his eloquence.

"You must be selfish about it, Emily," he urged, "You've a full life to live yet. Live it with me. I'm being selfish. I want my life too."

"Almost," said Emily, "thou persuadest me!" It was a fool thing to say. She knew it as she said it. She did not know what else to say. "Perhaps, Jim—perhaps not now, but—"

"Oh, Emily!" Jim moved toward her, his hands starting out.

They both started as the telephone rang harshly in the hall.

"Let it ring, Emily!"

"No, it might be—"

She moved swiftly from her chair. The sound had broken a spell. Jim Garver's hands moved nervously as he paced the room's soft-piled rug.

"Yes?" he heard Emily say in the hall. Then her voice changed. It softened and went low. The thrill of deep, sure happiness was in it like music. "Andrew! I didn't recognize your voice. Imagine! I've been away so long. Oh, he seemed better than ever when I left. If we can keep his spirits up. And then, Andrew, I'll be home again. Home!"

What else she said did not matter to the man listening. He had heard it in Emily's voice. He saw it in the peace in her face when she returned.

It seemed as though he were compelled to complete the movement interrupted by the ringing of the telephone. His hands went out again to fall lightly on her shoulders. Feel of the silk and the soft flesh beneath sent a shock through all his being.

Emily did not move but looked smiling into his face.

He raised his hand to touch her hair gently.

"Will you tell Will I'll see him again next week. Perhaps you'll be there, too. I hope so. Good-night, Emily."

When Jim Garver returned a week later, it was Ann he went to see first. His emotions were mixed. Uppermost was his deep desire to help Will. He had also to prove to himself that in this at least his motive was unselfish.

"I've thought about this for a long time," he told her slowly. "I want to know how you feel before I suggest it to Will. When he is able, I'd like him to return to Ilium as construction and maintenance superintendent for me. I think he would like it, and I think you would be happy in Ilium. I know I would be fortunate to get Will."

Ann, who held her baby in her lap, smiled unpleasantly.

"Imagine anyone's consulting me or worrying about my feelings!" Yet she could not completely hide the sudden dawning of hope, and the man saw it.

"Next to Will you would be the one most concerned."

"Another way of getting around Emily? You're as crazy about her as everybody else." Ann's tone was bitter.

"My interest is in Will," said Jim coloring, "and in you because of him."

"I see," said Ann as if amused.

The child was asleep. She stroked its head gently. Her hand trembled slightly.

"About Emily," said Jim doggedly, and there was surprise as well as an almost pleading note in his voice, for he had not intended such words, "you should be able to understand my feelings better perhaps than anyone else."

"I'm married to Will," said Ann fiercely. "I'm his wife. That's different."

"I suppose it is," said Jim quietly. He looked at the sleeping infant. "It looks like you, Ann," he said kindly.

"He does *not* look like me! He looks like Will! He looks like Will!" cried Ann. "He *has* to look like Will!"

Jim Garver had had to fight down his distaste at coming to talk to Ann. He had made himself come out of a sense of fairness and a sense that if Ann felt less neglected she might somehow be better for Will. He felt sympathy now, almost a fellow feeling.

Ann broke completely from behind her aggressiveness.

"Will's *mine,* and the baby. He's mine to take care of, too. If I did not have to fight them always, I know that I—" The tears started down her tight cheeks.

"In Ilium you would have Will to yourself."

Ann could not stop.

"I'm not the way they all think I am. Probably you think so too. They're the ones that make me have to fight and seem—" The tears came faster, though she remembered to sit very still so as not to wake the baby.

Jim spoke gently but more quickly.

"I have a little house in a different part of Ilium that I know you and Will would like. It would be a good place, I think, to bring up your son. And Ilium is home for Will. He'd be himself again soon in spite of this rotten thing that has happened."

Ann had stopped crying. Her hard eyes narrowed as she looked through and beyond Jim Garver. What difference did it make to her whether or not he was in love with Emily? Much good it would do him anyway!

"We'll see," she agreed finally. But she had already decided. She and Will and the baby were going to Ilium. She would make Will go whether he wished to or not! "And thank you," she added, as if remembering to be polite. She changed again. "Oh, thank you, thank you, thank you!" she breathed.

That night at the hospital they talked to Will. Jim spoke almost shyly; Ann, with a new eagerness and hopefulness.

Will seemed confused at first. He shrank from decision, recoiled even from facing it as part of all that he had still to face. The tears came to his eyes.

"I know you want to help, Jim, but I can't let anybody, not even you, take me on out of pity or kindness." His voice was grim.

Jim smiled.

"I'm not soft-headed when it comes to business, and don't think I am. You should know better. You knew my father."

"I don't even know what I'll be good for, how much I'll be able to do or how well I can do it."

"I'll risk that part of it."

"I'd like to work for you, Jim, of course, but—" Will looked at Ann.

"Will, it would mean a start for us! We would be by ourselves. We could have our own place, our own things! It would mean everything!"

Ann's eyes were bright. Her voice was insistent. Jim Garver, watching his friend's face, saw Will try not to wince, and a stab of coldness cut through to him. Perhaps it was worse for Will than he thought.

"It can't be for some time, Jim, you know that." Will gestured. "This has to heal. I have to learn to manipulate a damned wooden leg. All the rest of it."

"There's no hurry."

"Oh, Will, Will, Will!" cried Ann happily.

Bitterness and hurt pride forgotten, her eyes were alive with hope. The fierce life in her shone unguarded in her face. Perversely, Ann would always show people her worst side, hide or deny the best in her. Only Will knew the urgency of her need to love and be loved, as she knew the fire and strength it could arouse in him. Fulfilled and at peace, the force of her nature integrated and strong, there was nothing that she could not do for him, for them both.

Watching Will, Jim Garver knew that he had been right, as right, at least, as any man can be about another. Will would feel secure in Ilium where he belonged. Ann would have a chance. With Will in Ilium, he might not feel so lost himself. Surely, Emily would come sometimes, and some day she might come to stay.

Will spoke again, looking at Ann.

"We'll go. But we'll go to South Ilium, to the house on the hill. It has to be there."

EPILOGUE

Epilogue

MARY GREETED Emily conspiratorially in the upstairs front hall of the Brooklyn house.

"S-sh!" she ordered. "Ann is at the hospital, but the baby is asleep. Come into the parlor quickly."

"Jim Garver called again last night. He—"

"Later! Now, listen to me. Will is to be released from the hospital Wednesday."

"I thought it was to be Thursday!"

"It was, and Ann still thinks it is to be Thursday. It's Wednesday, and James says about noon. I've arranged everything, and I want you to be there at noon sharp. James will take us all in his new car. It will be very comfortable for Will, much better than an ambulance." Mary's eyes danced with excitement. "We are not coming straight home!"

"What?"

"What would Will like most?" Mary demanded. "What would be the best possible thing for him the first day?"

"I thought it was all planned for James to take him right to their house at first so that he and Laura can look after him for a month or so while the leg is being fitted. Perhaps Ann should go to the hospital alone with James. That would be right, wouldn't it?"

Mary shook her head impatiently.

"Ann still thinks he's to be released on Thursday. We'll surprise her by bringing Will here late Wednesday afternoon. First we're going to the races."

"The races!"

"That's what Will wants. I know it is! I've heard him in his sleep and when he was delirious."

"Mother! It *mustn't* rain!"

"It won't rain, you'll see. It *can't* rain!"

They stood at the rail, almost at the first turn, a safe distance from the grandstand and the crowd for fear that Will, unsteady on his crutches, might be caught in the surging throng and knocked down. The bugle had blown for the first race. The horses were at the post.

It was a glorious spring day. The grass of the landscaped infield was a vivid spring green. The freshly trimmed steeplechase hedges gleamed in the sunlight. A pair of white ducks with bright yellow bills wandered sedately from one small pond in the center of the field to another.

Mary's bearing was almost regal. The white hair, so precisely arranged, just showed beneath the furled and flowered edge of a new bonnet. Her chin was tilted slightly above the lace collar which was high and tight about her throat. Her clear eyes looked eagerly down the track past the club house and grandstand to the starting post where the handlers were struggling with the nervous horses.

"They're almost ready!" she reported. "Oh, that big black fellow's acting up again! Isn't he a beauty?"

Emily, dressed in a light, spring frock, a wide-brimmed sailor hat, white gloves to her elbows, an impudent-looking parasol slanted across her shoulder, leaned forward against the rail. She pretended that she, too, was straining to see. Her face was lighted and happy. The woman was more beautiful than the girl had ever been.

The soft spring wind blew through Will's hair, and the blue eyes in his pain-wasted face shone with excitement. He was looking not down the track but across the infield, and his expression was almost of disbelief.

It was beautiful, beautiful! It was more beautiful than he had remembered, more beautiful almost than he could stand!

The scene became unreal as he looked. In a few short months he would be in South Ilium again, this time with Ann and the child. The thought no longer dismayed but somehow calmed. He felt curious, even expectant. He wondered about his life. Was his real life over or was it just beginning? He did not know. Would he ever know, really? Does anyone ever know?

Suddenly the roar of the crowd rose. It could not drown the blood-quickening pounding of hooves as the field of eleven horses flashed down the straightaway. Beautiful horses and straining, brilliantly clad riders seemed to be bearing right down on them.

Horses running in the sun!

"They're off!" cried Will a little late. Putting all his weight on one crutch, he rapped the rail smartly with the other. "They're off!" His voice broke.

"Come on, black boy!" urged Mary. "Come on, boy!"

Emily wanted to reach out and grasp Will, but she was afraid of throwing him off balance, of somehow hurting him.

Will turned, his blue eyes flashing, his face all wonder. "Look at them go, Em! Look at them!" He swung to the track again. "Watch Black Knight! Come on, Black Knight!"

The tears started down Emily's cheeks. She forgot her fears and clutched Will's arms, her strong pianist's fingers biting deep into the thinness to make sure he was there.

"Run, Black Knight!" she cried. "Run, boy!"

Still holding Will's arm, she turned a little, her eyes narrowing, to look for Andrew. Her eyes widened and lighted. Her face softened. A quiet smile about his lips, he was walking toward them across the grass.